BLOOD SO
DEADLY
DIVINE
a novel by
J.M. GROSVALET

Ebook ISBN: 979-8-9892880-0-7

Paperback ISBN: 979-8-9892880-1-4

First Edition: November, 2024

Cover Design by Ellen Ferreira

Edited by Earley Editing, LLC

For those who've battled their own shadows and kept going—
This is for you. May you find strength in every step, no matter how dark
the path.

For the soul of this tale—Jessica.

In your whimsy, I found worlds. In your memory, they bloom eternal.
This story is for you, my starlit sister.
Till we meet again in the faerie's glen.

AUTHOR'S NOTE

Dear Reader,

Before you dive into *Blood So Deadly Divine*, I want to take a moment to address some themes and scenes that may be difficult for certain readers. This story is dark and layered with intense emotions, and while I believe in the resilience and strength of my characters, I understand that some of these elements may be triggering for you.

The journey through these pages includes depictions of violence, death, dark magic, trauma, emotional and physical abuse, mental health struggles, torture, imprisonment, graphic blood magic, ritualistic practices, and non-consensual drug use.

I want you to know that it's okay to step back or take breaks if any of these topics feel overwhelming. Your well-being comes first, and while this story explores the darkness, it also holds moments of strength, healing, and light.

Throughout the book, you'll encounter phrases in Irish accompanied by numbered references. These correspond to endnotes in the back of the book, where you'll find their translations. To ensure authenticity and respect for the language, I worked closely with a Gaeilgeoir, who guided me through every detail. While you're welcome to flip back and forth as you read, I recommend immersing yourself in the story first and exploring the translations later for a fuller experience.

Thank you for choosing to embark on this journey with me. I hope Elara and the others' resilience inspires you, but please be gentle with yourself as you read.

With all my love and respect,
J.M. Grosvalet

TO UNCHARTED NORTHERN WILDS
THE GREAT REALM OF
LATHERIA
MAPPED
IN THE PRESENT AGE
CAPITAL CITIES
NOTABLE SETTLEMENTS
MINOR SETTLEMENTS
ARWN'S VOID
THE LOCHE FIOR
BRAVELL
THE MOORLANDS

VREDIA
GREYMOUNT CASTLE
ELDHAM
THE NORTHERN RIDGE
BLACKSTONE MANOR
ULRITH
ARINTHEL
THE WHISPERING WILDS
AEWORA
THE HARTLIN FOREST
ANSYL CITY
THE VERDARA SANCT
THE JADE SEA

PROLOGUE

A thunderclap woke me from the long slumber. Piercing through eons of silent meditation, a reverberating clash that rippled through my being.

The earth shook, but not in a manner accustomed to the slow, grinding shifts of continents, nor akin to the habitual kisses of storm upon soil.

No, this was an anomaly, a rude awakening, fracturing the stillness that had cradled me in a serene embrace for time immemorial. It was as though a star, unbound and searing, had plummeted into my embrace. Carrying the taste of fresh rain upon the parched ground—an untouched river coursing through age-old valleys.

An insatiable curiosity unfurled within me, and I stretched beyond myself—reaching, tasting. For I harbored an unyielding greed, a hunger untouched by time, a craving to engulf this fresh, pulsating essence, to experience the novelties of existence through this new, vibrant lens.

Yet, when I finally uncovered this anomaly, a horrifying discovery made me withdraw.

It was a moon child—radiating a fading glow of Starfire—that had found herself ensnared, her essence fettered in a tangle of darkness; a predatory force that had leached upon me, gnawing and corrupting, forcing me into languid numbness.

The darkness draped around her delicate form, striving to restrain the wild surge of life within, to silence the vibrant song in her veins. It was an entity both known and feared, a marauder feeding upon the pristine light, a ravager of harmony.

With an agonizing slowness that resonated in the depths of my being, I beheld the extinguishment of her spirit, the fading of that divine Starfire from her sight.

An internal scream of despair echoed within me, a mournful reverberation at the witnessing of such loss. Every molecule of my vast form quaked with grief as I saw her final breath released.

CHAPTER I

Beneath a storm-crowned sky, a veil of mist swirled across the moor, thrumming in rhythm with the sacred cadence of the Druids' hymn.

It echoed in the thunder—in the wind.

The Druids sang, and the storm sang with them, a symphony of power that swelled with every haunting note.

The pull was magnetic, almost seductive. An otherworldly voice weaving itself around Elara's will like a silken thread. One that tugged at her very being, compelling her forward, deeper into the heart of the tempest.

The rain beat against her mercilessly, tearing at her with icy claws, leaving her skin stinging and red. Her thin chemise clung to her like a sheath of ice, and her raven curls, usually lively and defiant, now lay lifeless against her pale, rain-drenched face.

Of all days, it had to be today; she cursed inwardly, fighting against the lure of the spell that aimed to keep her docile, even within her own mind. Each droplet that ran down her frozen form felt like another betrayal from the fates.

She *hated* this moor. Hated how the Druids—how the High Priest—venerated it, when all she sensed, all she tasted in the air, was the bitter tang of death.

The lines of Druids looked upon her slow march with desperate hope as if she were their beacon of deliverance.

Their gazes, their faith, it was all a *lie.*

They saw salvation in her. But all she could see was the doom she heralded.

Her stomach churned, the weight of an already damned world pressing into her shoulders. This moor, *this sacred ground,* was not a sanctuary but an elegy to a dying realm.

Cloaked in deep emerald and onyx, the Druid's robes billowed in the storm, the shimmering threads reflecting the moon's silver kiss. Their gazes, hidden beneath hooded cowls, raked over her like cold fingers brushing against her skin. Each step she took seemed to amplify their song—their eyes flashing brighter, glowing with an unnatural fire, as their lips moved faster in a song that tasted ancient.

Elara suppressed a shiver.

They called themselves the men of the earth—the whisperers to the skies, keepers of the ancient order. But, what they asked of her ... it was *monstrous.*

A sharp cough jolted Elara out of her thoughts. Her head snapped toward the sound, a thread of tension pulling her gaze to meet almond-shaped eyes—Avis.

Relief fluttered through her. In this dark realm, Avis was a patch of sunlight—a rare touch of kindness. She might be the only one Elara thought of as an ally, if not quite a friend.

Avis drew her hood back, revealing clear eyes, untouched by the haze of ether that marked the other acolytes. Underneath her golden-brown skin, a faint paleness hinted at unease, and a question formed in Elara's narrowed eyes.

With a subtle flick of her head, Avis gestured down the procession line. Elara's stomach plummeted, her heart hammering a warning in her chest.

Gods, not again.

Her gaze followed Avis's hint, landing on the all too familiar figure of Branwen, clutching those accursed ogham staves. He glared back at her, his lank black hair hanging like a dark curtain around a face pale as bone.

Elara dragged her gaze back to Avis, a flicker of shared wariness mirrored in the Druid's sympathetic grimace. With a hard swallow that did nothing to rid her of the lump lodged firmly in her throat, she tried to force down the panic. Her steps faltered, the Druids' chants echoing in her ears like a physical force, prodding at her heels. Each note seemed to amplify Branwen's pull, his malevolence a tangible force, a black hole drawing her closer.

She braced herself, every instinct screaming to turn and flee, but her traitorous feet carried her on.

The moment she stood in front of him, his scrying lashed out. The savage intrusion pierced her mental barriers, her vision momentarily blurring. She gritted her teeth.

There was nothing gentle in this force, no guidance or foresight, only violent demand.

The staves clattered to her feet, rolling in the muck as the incantation spilled from his lips; an ancient language she could only guess at. But she had no interest in deciphering his divination.

Though the ether of the Druids tugged insistently at her, urging her forward, Elara had danced with this power before. She had learned the cadence of its pull and the subtle ways to defy it—if only for a moment.

Her jaw tightened as her eyes, glinting with challenge, locked onto Branwen's.

His pupils dilated, just a fraction, perhaps expecting her to falter. But instead of merely stepping as the spell beckoned, she deliberately planted her foot atop one of his staves, grinding it into the mud and finding the sensation of the cold muck squelching through her toes oddly satisfying.

His eyes widened, nearly swallowing his face, his knuckles whitening from the urge to strike her. And she was certain any other would've felt the wrath of his hand. Yet she stood tall, her chin lifted, meeting his blazing eyes without a flicker of fear. Basking in the one shield her position granted her—immunity.

Elara didn't bother with a backward glance as she strode forward, her foot landing squarely on one of his precious tools and grinding it deeper into the muck. If he wanted to unsettle her, he'd have to try harder than that.

"Think you're above us all, do you, *Hallowed*?" The venom in his rasp made her pause. "Tonight, you'll learn your place."

A fleeting glance revealed him clinging to his muddy staves, a grotesque smile carved into his face. A prickle of revulsion crawled up her spine.

What a gods-damned creep.

Pushing aside the uneasy feeling, she mustered a flicker of disdain, rolling her eyes at the twigs he so cherished. Whatever cryptic nonsense his sticks foretold meant nothing to her. It was as irrelevant as the man himself. His staves could whisper all the doom they pleased; Elara didn't give a damn.

Today, of all days, she refused to put up with Branwen's divination. Not when it was Summons Day. The whole ordeal was a charade—pomp and ceremony draped in the pretense of sanctity, but anyone with half a brain could see it for what it really was. She certainly did.

It was just another power play, a reminder that she was nothing more than a tool in this cursed realm—a figurehead to be controlled, a marionette in their hands.

As she moved down the final length of the procession, she couldn't help but peer back at the hardened faces watching her. The people she encountered daily, who she prayed with, shared meals with—they too bore the same unblinking stare. They watched her, but their eyes didn't see her.

They saw the vessel.

A small voice, one Elara tried to suppress whenever it dared to surface, tiptoed into her consciousness.

What if Branwen spoke the truth?

What if, by some cruel twist of fate, his spell *actually* held water this time?

"You have upset my apprentice, Elara."

The High Priest Edgar's voice, smooth as polished stone, rang out as she completed her journey down the path, stopping before him just as the Druids' chant faded into the storm.

Edgar stood rigid, his silhouette stark against the tempest. A raven perched on his shoulder, then took flight at his whisper. The downpour only sharpened his regal bearing as his gaze returned to her.

That irritating, all-too-familiar twinge tugged at her chest, and for a split second—just a breath—her confidence faltered.

Of course, he would rush to Branwen's defense.

The thought was so pathetically predictable she almost laughed.

"Well, perhaps he should consider a less sensitive line of work," Elara said, fluttering her eyelashes in mock innocence.

A petty jab, but she couldn't help the satisfaction it brought.

Edgar's reaction was as swift as it was predictable. His expression tightened, the flicker of irritation clear in his piercing gaze.

A twisted sense of pleasure pricked at her. Ruffling Edgar's composed feathers, even slightly, felt gratifying. Beneath the stern priest was a man who could be ruffled; a man who wasn't as unshakable as he pretended.

It was by Edgar, within the province of Aewora, that she had been kept hidden away from the rest of the world. Only emerging when summoned by the Lord Sovereign—*Osin*, who ruled over the realm of Latheria.

Edgar was her jailor, her guardian, and her only connection to the world outside of the southern region.

In Latheria, power was ostensibly shared between the Lord Sovereign and the High Council—Edgar included—a blend of highborn Druids and secular lords. However, the real control often seemed to lie with those who mastered ether, and with the Druids who whispered in their ears. Her journey today was a direct result of such political maneuvers.

In three days' time, Osin would hold the Convergence Ceremony— a spectacle where his followers, after years lost in training, would stand before the masses and attempt to bind their blood with her own. Such a ritual, they believed, would tether their souls to an element, awakening the concealed ether that surged like a hidden river through her veins.

This ether, a dormant force within Elara, stirred only when invoked and sanctified with prayers—when transformed from a mere whisper in her blood to a roar in theirs.

Her blood was a gift, they said. An offering, they preached. But all Elara saw was a curse, a cruel joke of the Fates who wove her destiny with threads of pain and sacrifice.

Her gift, her *curse*, had become her existence—something she could never outrun.

For she was the Hallowed. Her blood the final reservoir of pure ether within the realm. It was a power that was not hers to wield, but hers to give. A gift she paid for with every beat of her heart, every drop of her blood. And it was all for them. For the High Priest, for Osin, for the realm that needed ether, and for the gods that had abandoned her.

"Recite your prayers, Elara," Edgar commanded. "May the Mothers bestow blessings upon your travels, and may the discerning eyes of Osin deem you worthy."

Her temples pounded, but she forced her gaze down, a careful show of submission, and drew in a breath.

"Rhiannon, in death and balance, guide my path," she whispered, her voice barely audible over the roar of the elements. "Epona, life's nurturer, enrich my spirit. Aine, sun and moon, instill courage and wisdom."

Her words were like fragile tendrils in the storm, reaching out for the divine beings that had gifted her to a world that had forsaken her.

"Divine Trinity, hear my plea; walk with me."

In the vast expanse of the cosmos, where gods were as numerous as stars, three divine sisters stood apart from the rest, forging the mortal realm of Latheria. Rhiannon governed the mysteries of death, ensuring the balance of the afterlife. Her counterpart, Epona, breathed life into every crevice of the world, nurturing growth and ushering in every new beginning. Between them stood Aine, the goddess of both sun and moon, who governed the cycles of time, painting the skies with daylight's brilliance and night's tender luminescence.

While many gods have their domains, it was these three who sculpted the very essence of the mortal realms, their legacy echoing through every sunrise and sunset, in every birth and final breath. And Elara hated all three of them.

Edgar reached for her. The jasper stone set in his iron ring reverberated, charged with the ether set to transport them directly into Osin's throne room where the blood rite awaited.

A knot coiled in her stomach, and Elara bit back the urge to grimace as she slid her hand into his. She gritted her teeth, bracing herself as they prepared to leave the line of Druids. But then—a soft, barely-there whisper threaded through the air.

It brushed past the towering oaks behind her, a quiet, mournful sigh that seemed to carry on the breeze. It stirred the fabric of her chemise, a fleeting touch, but enough to make her breath hitch.

Edgar's impatient tug barely registered; her feet rooted to the spot, every nerve straining to discern whether the haunting melody was real or just a figment of her fraying sanity.

Yet, there it was—the song of the earth.

A chill prickled at the back of her neck.

It was a song of yesteryears, sung in hushed undertones, woven through the threads of time. It echoed through the tempest overhead, threaded its way into the storm's heart, and nestled within the turbulence. The ground pulsed beneath her, a gentle heartbeat that resonated up through the soles of her feet and wrapped around her bones.

Elara's breath caught as something primal stirred within her; a presence that felt as ancient as the oaks and as savage as the storm.

She held onto it, gripping it tight like a warrior grasping a shield.

"Elara!" Edgar's voice cut through the air. His dark eyes pierced hers as the pounding in her chest morphed into a defiant drum, the rhythm countering the mounting pressure that thrummed through the land.

She quickly scanned the surrounding faces.

But it was as if she stood alone in a world gone deaf and blind.

Huh.

Edgar's fingers dug into her arm, setting her teeth on edge.

The crystal in his ring flared, sending out a discharge of energy that crackled in the air as he tore open a rift before them.

Elara took a deep breath as she stepped into the Void, and for a fraction of a heartbeat—she existed everywhere and nowhere.

CHAPTER 2

Endless night unfurled around Elara, a darkness so absolute it devoured every thought, every fear, every dream she had ever clung to. This was a quiet that transcended mere absence of sound; it was an emptiness that negated existence itself. She found herself unable to tell where her own flesh ended and where the vast expanse of the Void began.

They had become one, indiscernible from each other.

Within this realm, time shed its significance. Her thoughts echoing back at her were the only proof she still existed in this nothingness. That, and Edgar's harsh grip as they moved through the Void's thrashing currents.

A sliver of light appeared in the distance, sending her heart into a frenzied beat.

Edgar yanked her forward, and Elara braced herself, every muscle locking tight as the sensation slammed into her.

It was a tearing, a shattering, and then a violent reassembling.

But just as abruptly as it had started, it ceased.

The harsh winds calmed, the shrill noise faded into the backdrop, and as she opened her eyes, blinking against the lingering brightness, she found herself standing in Mordenhall—Lord Osin's sovereign court.

The cavernous room, clad in polished onyx, stretched endlessly before her. Walls twisted into bizarre, organic patterns that mirrored bones grown over centuries, reflecting her sodden image back at her. Every detail in the room, from the claw-like chandeliers wrought from blackened iron to the sharp and predatory design of the furniture, spoke of a place not meant for comfort or ease, but a place of power.

"Do what they say and keep a civil tongue," Edgar drawled, his voice dripping with the familiar, chilly condescension that never failed to leave a throbbing ache behind her eyes.

Her gaze rolled upward. "Your concern is overwhelming, truly."

Elara's fingers twitched, a restless, involuntary movement. But then Edgar paused, and she saw an uncharacteristic flicker in the depths of his cold eyes.

His jaw ticked, hesitating as he chewed over words. "Hallowed," he muttered, taking a deep breath. His pale face tensed, drawing his already pronounced cheekbones even sharper. "There are whispers afloat. The Lord Sovereign's temperament is rather... fragile as of late, even for him. I'd advise utmost discretion on your part. Now is not the time to play the rebel."

Her heart clenched. Every summons to *Arinthel*, the capital, was a game of roulette where every spin had the potential to seal her fate. Every journey back left her less—less bright, less strong, less herself.

And all the while, Edgar watched.

He did nothing. *Said nothing.* Reducing her agony to a mere routine, an itinerary to be followed meticulously with an almost clinical detachment. It was like salt being rubbed into a corroded wound. A constant reminder of her worth. She felt like a utility, a resource. Less than human, and entirely alone.

With one last pointed look at her, he turned and stepped through the rift, his cloak billowing behind him as the Void swallowed him whole.

A cold sweat broke out on the back of her neck. Edgar typically stayed longer than a few moments, didn't he? Damn it all. If he was this nervous then perhaps she did need to watch her step closely tonight.

A throat cleared behind her, pulling her attention away from the fading glow of the rift. Elara turned on her heel to find one of Lord Osin's many attendants, a figure adorned in garments worthy of a lavish festivity rather than the grim duties of the day. Yet in this court, even servitude was a spectacle of grandeur; a direct result of Osin's relentless pursuit of beauty and order that extended even to the staff.

"Hallowed." Fenlin dipped his head, his soft brown hair falling over his brow. "Under these circumstances, 'nice to see you' seems a bit out of place, doesn't it?"

She smirked. ""When have our meetings ever been conventional?"

Among the countless faces in this cursed kingdom, Fenlin's was her favorite. They had met seven years ago in the Verdaran archives—she was fourteen, he seventeen, but their age difference had never stopped him from treating her with kindness, nor had her title ever intimidated him. She could always count on him to *"accidentally"* leave out forbidden scrolls and books for her to find, treasures she'd devour in secret, her heart pounding with the thrill of it.

But it wasn't just the books. It was the way he'd sit beside her long after the scribes had left for the day, telling her stories about the eastern mountains he called home. Stories about wild storms that could split ancient trees in half, about meadows that bloomed with flowers so vibrant they looked like they'd been painted by the gods themselves.

Once he'd found her crying in the far corner of the archives, her face buried in her hands after yet another brutal summons to Ulrith. He hadn't asked questions. He'd just slid a handkerchief onto the desk beside her, its edges embroidered with tiny, clumsy flowers she knew he'd sewn himself, and said quietly, *"The first book I leave out for you tomorrow will be something happy."*

And it was. A ridiculous tale about a fox who outwitted a king, full of mischief and cleverness. She'd laughed so hard she forgot, just for a moment, the reality of her life.

Though his time in Verdara had been brief, his kindness lingered, following her whenever she was summoned to Ulrith. She'd missed him, but knowing he was in the eastern kingdom had always been a small comfort—a sliver of warmth in a court where cruelty was currency.

His eyes flickered, softening as they traveled over her body. "What in the realms have they draped you in? You look like you've been swimming in a monsoon."

She arched a brow. "I got caught in a southern storm. But it's not as if I can simply ask Osin to delay the rite because of a little rain."

"Fair point," he conceded, his smile laced with a trace of irony. As his hand unfurled, warmth emanated from his palm—a warmth that was far from comforting. It carried with it the scent of something unnatural, a malodorous reek of charred flesh and sulfur.

Elara shivered as wisps of heat snaked across her skin, drawing the moisture from her sodden dress until, thread by thread, she stood completely dry.

A flush of relief rose to her skin, despite the lingering scent of Fenlin's ether. She wasn't warm, but at least the unpleasant dampness was gone.

Despite their roles in this dark place, Fenlin, like other staff, was granted a touch of ether—a rare privilege in their world. The modest sunstone embedded in his iron ring might've been minute, but it held power. Enough, at least, to serve the needs of his station.

Elara thanked him and forced a grin, a hollow attempt at levity. "What do you think? Do I look ready to be carved up for the greater good?" She gave a little mocking twirl, her chemise dancing around her ankles.

Twisting horror into humor was a tactic as familiar to Elara as breathing. It was a game she'd mastered long ago, walking the razor-thin line between laughter and despair, as if a well-placed joke could keep the weight of her world from closing in on her.

But Fenlin wasn't laughing. The humor in his eyes faded, replaced by a deep concern that brought out the faint lines beside his eyes.

"You may be confined within this life, Elara, but don't think for a second that I don't notice." He took a step closer, his gaze searching hers. "Even in this place, you grow a bit each day."

A knot tightened in her throat, and a rush of something raw and tender swelled in her chest. He had never called her by her name before. To the people of Ulrith, she was a title, a symbol, and never just *Elara*. The rebellious thrill of hearing her name echo within these halls set her heart racing. It felt liberating, like a barefooted step on forbidden ground. And for a heartbeat, she felt lost, searching for the right words to mirror his kindness. Before she could grasp them, the grand iron doors groaned in protest, announcing another arrival.

The subtle scuff of leather against stone immediately sent her stomach spiraling.

Godfrey, Osin's personal Druid, entered with hesitant steps, the tray he carried quivering in his unsteady hands, each vial threatening to tip.

His dark hair, pulled into a neat topknot, projected an austerity that masked the timid soul she knew hid beneath. His green eyes met Elara's from across the room. The fleeting connection lasted only a beat before he looked away and set the tray down on the ceremonial table, his knuckles white around the edge of the polished wood. A lone droplet of sweat journeyed down his temple, and Elara's eyes narrowed.

This wasn't his first rite, so why was he acting like a green apprentice?

They had never spoken, but there was something in those weary eyes that hinted at a shared understanding. Was it sympathy, or perhaps pity? Did he, too, take part in this sacrilegious rite out of forced duty? Even if he harbored such sentiments, he'd never voice them.

Osin strictly forbade them from speaking, and Godfrey was nothing if not obedient.

"Lord Osin will arrive shortly," Fenlin murmured, the subtle furrowing of his brow betraying his unease. "It is best you take your position below the dais." With a slight bow, he gestured for her to follow, guiding her through the vast space that sprawled before them.

Massive obsidian pillars flanked their path. Monoliths of an older era, their glossy surfaces reflected the torchlight, painting an illusion of warmth.

Her heart pounded, pulsing in time with the echo of their footsteps in the silence. The anticipation in Fen's every step spoke louder than any words could. The minute she reached the base of the dais, Elara sank to her knees, the chill of the floor seeping through her dress.

Lord Osin didn't demand her subjugation verbally, but he didn't need to. Her very presence in his kingdom was command enough. And like a puppet on invisible strings, she obeyed, keeping her head low, and awaiting his arrival like the good little captive she was.

Elara's gaze followed Fenlin as he took his position beside the immense banquet that groaned under the weight of golden platters, boasting delicacies from the far reaches of the realm. The array was dazzling: crystal decanters filled to the brim with amber spirits, ruby wines, and golden meads all gleamed under the candlelight, standing proud at the feast's vanguard.

The subtle shift in Fenlin's demeanor didn't escape her. She saw a brief tightening around his eyes that matched the almost imperceptible set of his jaw. This was more than just a feast; it was a blatant display of extravagance and a vivid reminder of the chasm that separated the elite of Arinthel from the masses.

"*Ah*, the fragrance of fear."

Elara's heart catapulted into her throat.

Osin's honeyed voice echoed before he even appeared. The very shadows in the room seemed to intensify, reaching out tendrils of darkness that kneeled in worship. He sauntered through the gathering miasma, moving fluidly into the dim light.

Elara couldn't help but notice his attire, tailored to every contour of his form. His jet-black velvet coat clung to him, accentuated with intricate embroidery of deep crimson and gold. While his clothing screamed of unparalleled luxury, a haunting weight in the air surrounded him. A dangerous allure signaled he was more than just a ruler. He was a force of malevolence made into flesh.

"Do proceed," he commanded with a flick of his wrist toward Godfrey, who hesitated momentarily before frantically sifting through his tinctures.

Elara averted her eyes, but it was futile. Osin was already closing the distance between them; every footstep echoing like the toll of a war drum. He stopped in front of her and lifted her chin, forcing her to meet his gaze.

Piercing blue eyes met her own, taunting her, feeling even colder than his immaculately groomed, icy blond hair. He was a canvas of hard angles, every inch of him carved with imposing authority. Yet, it was his smile that felt the most treacherous—a wide, malicious, mocking curve.

"You've been well, I trust?" he purred with a smugness that made her skin crawl. "I can only imagine how dull life must be in the intervals between our little meetings."

Elara clenched her teeth so hard her jaw popped, and Osin's self-satisfied grin deepened, his thumb pinching her chin before the swish of his robes echoed in the chamber as he moved to claim his throne.

She drew a deep breath, trying to steady herself. But the moment Osin settled onto the throne, the room's massive doors groaned open.

In synchronized steps, rows of soldiers advanced, their impassive faces mirroring the frigid cruelty of their leader. Each wore armor that bore no insignia, no sign of individuality. It was merely a mass of power and force flowing in to flank the dais. They were The Legion, Osin's elite guard.

Her eyes flicked downward, settling on her hands clasped tightly before her. The amassed gazes around her suddenly felt like tangible pressures, small points of force pinching at her flesh. These were the very soldiers responsible for the scars that marred the region.

For the past ten years, conflict ravaged the realm. Aewora, Bravell, and Ulrith—once proud and distinct territories—were now subsumed into a single oppressive dictatorship. Only the Northern Kingdom of Vredia, isolated and stalwart, stood defiant. It was the last bastion of resistance, an enduring flame of hope against the all-consuming shadow. Yet even Vredia had proven no match against the wicked sorceries wielded from the east. For years, the realm had heard nothing from the north, as if a silencing spell had blanketed their lands.

And maybe... maybe Vredia was no more. Maybe the silent kingdom had become nothing more than a whispered story to quell the despair clinging to the bones of the world. Maybe there was truly nothing left to hope for.

Elara's chest tightened, and with conscious effort, she drew in a tremulous breath. But then Godfrey materialized before her, and every errant thought leeched from her mind.

His eyes locked onto hers as he released his ether with an unsettling elegance, his quartz ring gleaming with the effort. A stench slowly filled her nostrils, like a corpse in the late stages of decomposition; so potent she could almost taste it on her tongue.

Godfrey's ether waltzed through the air, writhing and coiling around her, gnawing at her flesh, spawning angry red abrasions that blossomed like flowers on her skin. Suddenly, the power surged—unforgiving and fierce—slicing through layers of scar tissue until blood spilled from her wrist in rivulets, splashing onto the onyx floor.

Elara's vision blurred, but she forced herself to watch, taking a twisted solace in the methodical, reverent way Godfrey extracted the sacraments from her blood before sealing it within glass vials. Her offering flickered like captive stars within the tiny bottles—as beautiful as it was horrifying.

She closed her eyes then, thinking back to the teachings of the Druids, to the whispered mantras that urged her to transcend the pain. Despite how she felt about their people she had accepted their help and learned to endure this torment through the mastery of *ritualized control* —a skill that had become as vital to her survival as the air she breathed.

With every drop of her blood spilled, she focused on the intricacies of her own mental discipline. The tightening of her jaw and the clenching of her fists were not signs of submission, but declarations of her willpower. It was her fortress against the torment, the place she discovered her true power. And in this strange, quiet space, she found something precious. A sliver of control and a shred of dignity in a world that sought to strip her of both.

Her breath steadied as she walked the familiar paths of her routine. The pebbles she arranged in her room—homage to the earth. The measured breaths at dawn—reminder of the air she once breathed freely. The moments of solace in the flame of a candle's dance.

The crimson pool at her feet marked her as a lamb to slaughter. But in her mind, untouchable, she drifted far away, bound only to her own thoughts. So she stayed by the candlelight, her fingers hovering close to the flame, daring it to burn her. It never did.

A crash reverberated through the chamber as the throne room's massive iron doors flung open once again, but this time with a force that rattled the walls.

Elara's heart leapt into her throat as her eyes snapped toward the sudden disturbance—a shadowy figure cut starkly against the ambient glow of the corridor.

Curse it to the Void.

At least Branwen wasn't around to witness his prophecy hitting the mark.

It had been years since she last laid eyes on him, and a small part of her had dared to believe that perhaps he had met his fate in the arms of Rhiannon, the Goddess of Death. But as he swaggered into the room, a god in his own right, every shred of that wishful thinking shattered.

Her gaze trailed him as he strode across the hall, an inexplicable tug at her core drawn to his every movement. His battle-hardened leathers clung tightly to his powerful frame, punctuated by the dull glint of a glaive strapped to his back. It was the mask she found most captivating —a wicked sculpture of black stone crowned with twisted horns. But it wasn't just a mask. It was a symbol of his elevated position within the Legion, marking him as their most fearsome and unwavering warrior.

A hunter of unparalleled skill and unyielding devotion.

In every hushed corner and shadowed alley of the realm, people whispered his title, each syllable dripping with dread. *'The Hunter.'*

A name forged from a legacy steeped in fear. One that carved crimson paths across the provinces, seeking and mercilessly snuffing out the last strongholds of those devoted to the old ways. The Script Keepers of *Tirr*—the rebels.

Back in Aewora, the Druids whispered of the cruel genius of Osin's reign. How he'd systematically strangled the old world's voice, forcing everyone to speak only his tongue. The vivid accounts of public squares filled with roaring fires consuming manuscripts penned in the *Tirrish* script had haunted her. With the help of the Hunter and the Legion, the essence of a culture had burned to ash.

With chilling stillness, the Hunter surveyed the room from behind his obsidian mask. His dark eyes settled on Elara, a cold, calculating gaze making her feel like nothing more than an insect waiting to be crushed beneath his boot.

She kept her gaze steady, her eyes locked on his even as the air grew heavy around her. He had this effect on her every time they occupied the same space. His stare was intense, almost invasive, like he could peel back her skin and see everything she was trying to hide. But years ago, she had made a vow to herself. She'd never let him see it—the way her nerves sparked under his gaze, the way his presence seemed to unravel her from the inside out.

These monsters from the east—they could *smell* fear, breathe it in, feast on it off the very air. And he, much like his master, seemed to have developed a particular craving for hers.

The thick scar across her throat throbbed under the Hunter's gaze as he settled in next to his master.

Elara fought the urge to touch it, to soothe the mark that wasn't the result of any sacred ritual but rather of violence. His eyes dropped to it as if he *knew* it was bothering her, as if he could read their shared damnation etched across her skin.

Her eyes snapped shut, a stabbing pain throbbing at her temples as the memory she fought to contain began to seep through her defenses.

"Minva sölk harn."

She sucked in a ragged breath, clinging to the mental path she had painstakingly constructed. But one by one, the bricks crumbled, giving way to the heterochromatic gaze that haunted her dreams.

Shit. She pressed her eyelids tighter, as if sheer will could barricade the past. But this memory defied every attempt at control; no mastery, no ritual had ever been enough to contain it once unleashed.

In a single breath, she was transported back—back to being twelve, naive, and sheltered in the capital, back to the night Thane, the Hunter's older brother, had quietly slipped into her room after her lady's maid had tucked her in.

His presence had been confusing but not immediately alarming. Elara had recognized him from court—always alongside his younger brother, his striking features made more unusual by his mismatched eyes and the posture of a man bound to a place he clearly despised.

Elara's interactions with the both of them had been nothing more than brief, awkward exchanges—stiff and formal, staged during the times Osin paraded her around to burnish his own image of sanctity. She hadn't really minded; those court gatherings had been her rare chances to watch other children, the noble offspring who were always so proper, if not a bit mischievous.

The Hunter had always stood out to her among them. Even at the young age of thirteen, every move he made seemed calculated, every facial expression meticulously controlled. He had a sharp, almost prickly demeanor, a coldness that suggested distance and a touch of superiority.

Never once did she think he had noticed her, so absorbed did he seem in maintaining his composed, untouchable façade. That was, until the night his brother crept into her room.

All she vividly recalled was the shock that gripped her as the cold edge of Thane's blade traced her throat, the surreal warmth of blood streaming down her neck, and the strange pang of guilt for the brand-new chemise, now ruined, and how her lady's maid would fret.

She didn't even scream—didn't get the chance to—before the room erupted into chaos. There was a shout, the crash of something breaking, and then—the dark, wide eyes of the Hunter fixed above her, swirling with a depth of emotion she had never seen in him before.

His trembling hands had gripped her neck, stanching the blood flow, while his words spilled out feverishly like a sacred chant. *"Minva sölk harn. Minva sölk harn. Minva sölk harn,"* he had hissed, his words moving over her skin like fire, burning into her memory until at last, a healer had arrived to take over.

The Hunter had saved her that day, and even now, she couldn't fathom why.

"Minva sölk harn," he had murmured, a litany against the panic. Those ancient words had flowed from him as naturally as breath. She hadn't understood them then, but the earnest tremor in his voice and the image of his ashen, stricken face were something she would never forget.

Thane's betrayal had cost his family everything. From what Elara had pieced together, the boy was cast out to the bleak fringes of the realm, his family name shorn of its titles. And for the Hunter's unwavering loyalty, he was spared—taken from his family by Osin and made into his personal ward, entrusting the Hunter with responsibilities and shaping his identity to align with his own strategic goals.

Once, he had a name, one that Elara could almost remember, but now it lingered just out of reach. Now, he was only known as the Hunter, his name lost to the life he'd been forced to abandon.

And Elara knew he hated her for it—hated himself even more. She could sense it—the heavy, charged air of it—every time they occupied the same space.

"Rise."

Elara flinched at Osin's abrupt command, her gaze snapping up to find Godfrey arranging tray after tray brimming with vials of her blood. *Gods.* She had been so caught up in the Hunter's sudden arrival, so completely consumed by the shock of seeing him again, that she hadn't realized the ritual had ended.

She struggled to her feet, her legs shaking as a dizzying wave swept over her, blurring the edges of her vision.

She had given far too much this time.

Her temples pounded as Godfrey tended to her wounds. The vile touch of his ether crawled up her damp palms, and she fought to keep from recoiling as it twisted around her wrists and stitched her skin back together. But even with his treatment, her scars would never leave. Wounds inflicted by ethereal means always left traces, whether borne on the surface or etched deep within, and Elara carried too many to count.

Once Godfrey completed his task, he gingerly picked up the tray, his hands trembling noticeably as he navigated toward the distant end of the room. With great care, he set it down at the ceremonial table before joining Fenlin in a silent vigil.

Elara rolled her shoulders, trying to shake off some of the tension, and took a deep breath, bracing herself for the onslaught of venomous words Osin seemed to relish. It was always the same with him—petty jabs meant to wound, a dismissive wave, and then she'd be free of this cursed room for another three months.

She watched him as he rose from his throne, a lazy yet calculated movement, and closed the gap between them.

"You wear your suffering so elegantly, Hallowed. It's almost a pity the rest of the realm doesn't get to witness it as I do." Osin's thumbs traced her newly sealed wounds in an intimate mockery of comfort, and she flinched, sucking in a breath through clenched teeth.

Osin tilted his head slightly, a tender smile pulling at his lips. "Such a delicate thing, yet so full of fire," he whispered affectionately. "You know, it's always the ones who fight the hardest who break the most spectacularly in the end. I *do* hope you won't disappoint me."

Heat scorched her neck, a wild storm of anger and shame building inside her. She shook with the effort to hold it back.

A satisfied smile curled on his lips as he gave her wrists one last squeeze before letting go.

"You're dismissed."

But as she reached the far end of the hall, her eyes searching desperately for the familiar rift that had brought her here, a soft tsk cut through the silence, freezing her mid-step.

Elara's heart skipped, a knot of dread forming in her stomach as she slowly turned back. It felt like the temperature dropped several degrees; the air growing dense with the threat of violence.

Shadows bled from Osin's fingertips.

"But not until your little *friend* returns what doesn't belong to him."

CHAPTER 3

Fenlin's gaze, wild with panic, caught Elara's in a fleeting moment—a silent, desperate scream of warning. But just as quickly as their eyes met, he spun on his heel and ran.

Elara's heart did more than skip—it ceased altogether, as if time itself had fractured. She had no time to process, to understand, as within the space of those shattered seconds, Osin flew.

He was twilight incarnate, a blur against the fading light, moving with unnatural speed. She'd known, of course, about his dominion over the shadows, the way the night seemed to curl affectionately around his fingertips, gathering in the hollows of rooms he frequented. Never had she imagined he could *become* that very darkness.

Elara's hands shook as she watched Fenlin flee, Osin's shadows snapping at his heels like ravenous hounds. She couldn't move, paralyzed by helplessness.

Like a bolt of lightning slicing through the darkness, Godfrey threw himself in Osin's path.

Sweat glistened on the Druid's flushed face, trailing down his temples. His gaze never wavered from his masters. Godfrey, the man who had always adhered to the rules, who had never sought to stand out, now positioned himself against the Lord Sovereign in a move that

Elara could only interpret as a desperate bid to grant Fenlin a few precious moments.

As his hands danced, a crescendo of crackling energy ignited. The air fractured, splitting apart with a resounding snap, and a shimmering barrier materialized before Godfrey. It hummed with an otherworldly resonance, cascading ripples through the chamber like waves upon a still pond.

But as the shield formed, the ambient light began to waver. It seemed to be drawn to Osin, gravitating toward him like iron filings to a magnet.

Elara's breath came in ragged gasps.

Move, move, move.

But her legs might as well have been pillars of stone for all the good they did her. Everything felt distant, surreal, as if she floated outside her own body watching a nightmare unfold in slow motion. It wasn't until Osin's laugh—a chilling, honeyed sound that slithered around the room —that she snapped out of it.

"Fen!" Her voice cracked, raw with terror, as she forced her body into motion.

But Osin's shadows were quicker, more ruthless.

They surged like a dark wave, smashing through Godfrey's barrier with brutal ease. With predatory speed, they seized the Druid, then whipped around to snag Fenlin by the ankle. In one swift motion, he was yanked across the cold stone floor, his body coming to a harsh stop next to Godfrey.

Elara's body screamed in protest, her movements sluggish and unco-ordinated as she raced toward them, but then—like hitting an invisible wall—she stopped cold in her tracks.

"Time to go, Hallowed." His gruff voice fanned out between them, prickling the hairs on the back of her neck. His hand clamped around her arm with an iron grip, anchoring her to the spot.

Elara didn't have to glance back to identify its owner; she'd know the voice of the Hunter anywhere. But right now, the threat felt secondary. Thought gave way to sheer instinct as she wrenched her arm free and sank her teeth deep into the tender flesh of his wrist.

The muffled yelp that escaped him—so out of place from the stoic warrior he was—might have made her laugh if the situation weren't so dire. His grip faltered, and he stumbled back, cursing under his breath.

She didn't wait. She ran.

Her heart pounded like a war drum, each beat a hammer against her ribs, propelling her forward in a surge of panic.

Faster, her mind screamed, urging her trembling legs as she dashed through the rows of towering pillars toward the two men. She didn't know how she could help once she got there, but doing nothing was not an option.

Her bare feet slapped against the cold marble, echoing sharply in the vast chamber as Osin wielded his shadows with a cruel flick, hurling Fenlin into the air like a plaything caught in a web.

"My lord, if mercy exists in your heart, let it fall on him—"

But Godfrey's plea broke off abruptly, his voice choked out as dark tendrils tightened around his throat.

Osin's cold, mocking laughter echoed through the chamber as Fenlin's limbs contorted. The sound of bones snapping and flesh tearing filled the air, a gruesome symphony of agony that sent waves of acid rising up Elara's throat.

An agonized scream tore from Fenlin's lips, a sound so piercing it sent a lance through her heart, spurring her feet to move even faster. She spun, lunging toward the buffet, and snatched the nearest weapon—a glass decanter.

Elara flung it toward Osin's head, wine trailing behind it like a comet's tail. But just as it neared its target, an unnatural gust summoned by a Legionnaire swerved it off course.

Around the room, the Legion moved as one. They were a tide of lethal power, each step and gesture coordinated to form a protective barrier around their lord.

Before Elara could catch her breath, much less concoct any semblance of a plan, rough hands grabbed her, shoving her toward the grand buffet with bruising force.

She slammed into the table, the impact forcing a hiss from her throat. Dishes shattered, wood splintered, all thundering in her ears. Before she could catch herself, she hit the floor with a brutal thud, pain flaring up her side, ripping a deep, guttural groan from her throat.

Gods. She couldn't see.

Once, twice—she blinked, but it made no difference. Her heart raced, panic gnawing at its edges as she tried to rise, to clear the blood streaming from a gash on her forehead. Her hands, trembling, fumbled in darkness until they found fabric, whimpering as she pressed it firmly against her head.

Fenlin.

Elara lifted her head, eyes darting through the shadows—

Her blood turned to ice.

She blinked, heart hammering, as Osin's power tightened around Fenlin's neck, spiraling down his body.

Then—slowly—guided by nothing but Osin's will, a vial slipped from Fenlin's inner pocket.

It hovered in the air between them.

The glint of her blood, catching the dim light.

"Such boldness, Fenlin." Osin's voice dripped with venom. "I almost admire it. *Almost.*"

Fenlin was shaking, not with fear, but with a rage so intense Elara could almost feel its heat. Their eyes locked in a silent exchange, a blaze that leaped across the space between them, before he turned his fierce gaze back to Osin.

"You might sit on that throne, feasting while the rest of us starve, *Lord* Osin," he rasped, blood flecking his lips. "But remember, empty bellies breed brave hearts. *The realm remembers.*"

A hush blanketed the scene.

Then, in the blink of an eye, Osin's shadow struck. A sickening snap echoed through the room.

Fenlin's neck.

Elara's vision tunneled. A roar filled her ears. Her chest heaved, gasping for air, lungs burning like she was drowning on dry land. Desperate, she scrambled forward, fingers clawing at the floor as she dragged herself closer. Closer to Fenlin. To the stillness.

Glass bit into her palms, her knees. Every inch felt like a mile, grief and shock making her limbs heavy. But before she could touch him—a rough hand yanked her up.

A vise-like grip that swung her over a broad, armored shoulder.

She thrashed, fists pounding uselessly against the solid back of her captor, legs kicking wildly, desperate to break free. Her gaze locked on Fen, refusing to let go, silently begging for any sign of life.

But there was nothing. Only the cruel shadow cast over his face, the unnatural angle of his neck, and the way his fingers curled inward.

Hot, bitter tears mixed with the blood dripping from her temple as she struggled. Her vision blurred, but she forced herself to look at Osin. To see the twisted satisfaction in the cruel curl of his lips.

Her scream ripped through the silence, while his arched brow mocked her from across the room and seared into her memory. Another scar to carve into her already broken heart.

Then, as if the ground itself rebelled, her captor tore open the fabric of the world beneath them and leapt into the gaping maw of a swirling rift.

A SOFT BREEZE, redolent of blooming oíche blossoms, whipped against Elara as they burst free from the rift, drying the tears and blood that had painted tracks down her cheeks. The gentle zephyr belied the savage grip encircling her waist, her body swaying with each purposeful stride of the man who carried her.

Her vision pitched between smears of darkness and fleeting glimpses of the pale moonlight. Each forceful step he took sent jolts through her, a cruel rhythm as he stalked his way down the mossy path that led to her prison.

A creeping coldness started at her fingertips and slowly spread inward, as if her blood were crystallizing into ice. The world grew distant, and sounds became muffled, like she was submerged beneath dark, still waters.

Why? her mind whispered faintly.

Why did he do it?

What could Fenlin possibly want with my blood?

Osin's routine exploitation, she understood—it was to maintain his twisted order. But Fenlin and Godfrey? It didn't make sense. They had access to her—more than most. So why the need for such recklessness?

Her thoughts buzzed dully, like distant gnats, and her limbs felt heavy and unresponsive, as if they weren't her own.

"Put me down," she whispered.

But he didn't stop. With each step he took, her body jostled against his armor, the cold metal biting into the soft flesh of her stomach.

"Put me down."

Her voice wavered. She tried to draw a steadying breath, but the motion, the pressing cold, and the restraints felt like hands around her throat.

Closing her eyes didn't help; memories of Fenlin's last moments flooded in, suffocating her like she was being dragged under a tide.

"Let go of me!" she choked out, desperate for the ground, for stability, for the overwhelming wave of terror to subside.

Finally, he stopped.

The silence between them stretched, marked only by their synchronized ragged breathing. Then, with a begrudging exhale, he gently lowered her to the ground.

The moment Elara's feet touched the earth, her legs crumpled beneath her like wilted stems, eliciting a sharp curse from her captor as she hit the ground hard.

Her head spun wildly, her stomach churning, and before she could draw another breath, she was retching violently. Each heave tore through her, her insides twisting in agony until the waves of nausea finally began to ebb. She wiped her dirt-caked hand across her mouth, gasping for air.

Cocooned within Verdara's stone walls, she was privy only to the petty squabbles among guards and the whispered disputes between Druids. But this... this visceral brutality—especially against Fenlin—was a horror nothing could have prepared her for. A strangled sob broke through her clenched teeth.

"We shouldn't linger." The frigid, familiar voice cut through the heavy haze of her grief.

Elara's gaze shot up, meeting the eyes behind that dark, horned mask, gleaming like the gaze of a wolf catching light. The corners of her mouth twitched downward, her eyes hardening as a sour taste lingered on her tongue. In all the chaos, she hadn't realized it was the Hunter who had grabbed her.

"I need a moment," she bit out, pushing aside the curls that clung to her sweat-dampened face, her skin smeared with a grimy mix of blood and dirt.

The sound of strained leather groaned as his fingers curled into a fist. "We don't have that luxury."

Heat flared in her chest. "What's the rush to return to your master? Eager to share in his latest triumph?"

The tightness around his eyes, barely visible within the slits of his mask, betrayed his irritation. "Your friend committed treason." He reached out, flexing his fingers as if expecting her to comply and take his hand.

She slapped it away. "Don't touch me."

"It's my job to return you in one piece."

"Oh, how *fucking* noble of you."

Elara took a deep, steadying breath, hating that the bastard was right. She needed to be back in Verdara before Edgar and his dramatics took center stage. His ever-watchful ravens likely already had a play-by-play of the night's events. Speaking to animals was one of his gifts, but the way he exploited it felt invasive. It wouldn't be long, she mused bitterly, before his armored guards came swarming out of the woods.

Elara pushed herself upright. The last thing she expected from the Hunter was a truthful answer, yet the question escaped her lips before she could rein it in. "Why did they do it?" Her eyes bore into his with a steeliness that dared him to lie.

Every line of his muscular form went rigid, his stony gaze locking onto hers with an intensity that felt like a blade's edge. She recognized the novelty of their exchange. It was the first conversation they'd ever shared, and from the slight shift in his stance, it seemed the realization was dawning on him too.

The weight of his stare threatened to pull her gaze away, but then, to her immense surprise, he gave her an honest reply. "People act recklessly when there's nowhere left to turn."

Elara scoured his gaze, probing for a flicker of sarcasm, a hint of contempt, but there was none. His eyes were unwavering, fixed on hers, and that intensity—it knotted her stomach. He saw their pain, understood it, perhaps, but his heart remained unmoved. His indifference scalded her frayed nerves like a brand to bare flesh.

When she finally found her voice, it was laced with a boldness she barely recognized.

"Then perhaps stop *barricading* every damned exit."

A cruel light danced in his eyes. "You wouldn't last a day without those barricades."

It would be a smart move to retreat, to show some semblance of fear. But the weight of the evening had rendered her numb to anything but the searing anger that ignited when he opened his stupid mouth.

Elara took a dangerous step closer, raising her chin. "Is that what you tell yourself at night? That you and your lord are protecting me from the dangers of this world?" She bared her teeth. "*You* are the danger. A beast who preys on his own. Tell me, how many lives have you destroyed in the name of duty?"

A gust of wind whipped her dark hair across her face, but her eyes never left his.

There was a slight shift in his posture—a minute tilt of his head, as if he was zeroing in on every syllable she uttered. It was a scrutiny she hadn't anticipated; a predatory attention that made her pulse quicken.

He let out a low, mocking laugh. "You seem rather fixated on my morals, Hallowed. Should I be flattered?" He stepped closer, his voice dropping to a murmur. "If you're looking for guilt, you're asking the wrong man. I've lost track of the blood I've spilled, and I sleep *just* fine." His eyes roved over her, and Elara suddenly became hyper-aware of her disheveled state. Bloodstains from the rite marked her chemise, and a rip along her stomach exposed a patch of flesh. It must have torn when one of his comrades had thrown her into the banquet. She quickly raised her hands to cover herself, but he caught her wrist, stopping her.

His other hand hovered just above the jagged tear at her side, and a gentle warmth radiated from his palm, washing over the small cut she hadn't even realized was there, and knitting the flesh together.

Elara gasped as the air swirled with ether, unlike any she'd ever encountered. His carried the scent of wood smoke mixed with the sweet sharpness of tree sap. It was fire, she realized with a quickening heart, but not the type that burned and blistered. This fire mended, healed—how was such a thing even possible?

Under his near touch, she felt frozen, immobilized even though his hands never actually met her skin. He shifted his focus to the gash on her forehead, and inexplicably, she allowed it. She couldn't fathom why. This one stung, drawing a wince from her, but the pain gradually subsided, replaced by a tender warmth she hadn't known fire could possess.

The Hunter's gaze dropped to the fluttering pulse at her throat. "You speak as if you know the weight of command. Every soul I've claimed was a sacrifice that needed making, so spare me your righteous anger. It's as misplaced as your accusations." His dark eyes lifted to meet hers again, a wicked glint sparking in their depths. "If you truly think me such a monster, you should be more careful—you wouldn't want to make yourself too tempting a target."

The darkness in his voice sent a shiver down her spine. He would indeed relish in the hunt.

Bastard.

She wanted to hurt him, to make him feel even a fraction of the pain he'd inflicted on others. The boy who had once saved her, who had stood against his brother's cruelty, was no more. Osin had seen to that, had stripped him of that humanity.

But curse it all to the damn Void—provoking him was the fastest way to get herself killed. Her heart pounded so hard it felt like her ribs were bruising. Her eyes darted back and forth, searching his gaze.

Maybe he *would* kill her if she pushed him, if she punctured his ego deep enough. Maybe he'd even do it here, in the dirt, lay her down next to her own sick—finish what his brother had started all those years ago. And maybe she wouldn't even care. It would spare her from this life, from this endless torment, and it would ruin the Lord Sovereign in the process. Have him do what she was too much of a coward to do herself.

She opened her mouth, not even sure what she was going to say, when a shout of her name pierced the air. And like magnets repelled by an unseen force, Elara and the Hunter shot apart.

The ground began to shudder under the pounding of hooves and Verdaran guards surged from the tree line. At their forefront was Dario, the captain of the guard, his body rigid, every muscle coiled. His gaze flickered sharply between her and the masked hunter as he dismounted with a grace that belied the stiffness of his posture. The dust his boots kicked up had barely settled before he was by her side, his honey-brown eyes searching hers.

"By the gods, El." His voice wavered between anger and frantic worry. The familiar grit of his calloused hands slid down her arms, affirming in their quiet way that she was indeed there, present and real. He drew her close, and she buried her face in the crook of his neck, the comforting scent of juniper and worn leather surrounding her.

He drew back slightly, and stray strands of his sun-kissed hair tumbled forward in a disheveled crown. "What happened?" he whispered, his voice so comforting and soft it nearly undid her. Tears threatened to spill, the burning sensation hard to suppress. The horrors of the evening felt impossible to put into words. The events still bore a dream-like quality. Speaking them aloud would shatter that illusion, binding her to a reality she wasn't prepared to face.

"Tonight was revealing, in more ways than one," the Hunter drawled, his gaze briefly catching on the tear in her dress. "The Lord Sovereign was far from pleased."

Elara's brows pinched together in a scowl—but the Hunter's focus had already moved past her, drawn to the guards who were now dismounting briskly. Moonlight danced on their armor, casting a soft, silvery-blue glow that made the metal shimmer subtly in the night. Crafted from layers of supple leather and reinforced with interwoven ringlets of burnished bronze, the armor allowed for the fluid movement needed for the agile and intricate combat styles the Verdaran guard were renowned for. On the chest plate of each soldier was the sigil of the Druid Sect. It was an ancient symbol composed of three interlocked spirals, representing life, death, and rebirth. The spirals moved in harmony, embodying the eternal rhythm of life that the Druids held sacred.

The guard lined up solidly behind Dario, their gazes lingering on the Hunter with a silent reverence in the slight tilt of their heads.

As the Hunter's voice, cold and devoid of any feeling, recounted Fenlin's death, a fresh wave of acid surged up Elara's throat, fueling a savage desire to rake her nails across his face. To leave scars as jagged as her own.

"Osin sure knows how to keep things interesting, doesn't he?" Lorien quipped, drawing laughter from the others.

Lorien, always quick with a jest and a smirk to match, was one of those guards Elara found insufferably arrogant. With a haughty demeanor and a flexible moral compass, he was the sort she would rather not cross paths with. His voice grated against Elara's raw nerves, her nails unconsciously digging crescent moons into her flesh.

Beside her, Dario stiffened protectively ever so slightly. "We should get you back." His voice was steady, though his eyes, locked onto the Hunter's, betrayed a challenge.

The Hunter's gaze flicked to Elara, his eyes looking empty, *dead*. The fire she had stoked in him earlier was gone. He inclined his head. "For the realm and the ruler," he declared.

The guards responded in practiced unison, their deep voices echoing through the clearing. "By Osin's command!"

Elara clenched her jaw as the chant rang out, each word striking her like a slap. No, she wouldn't utter those words. She hadn't before and she wouldn't begin now, not even with Osin's Hunter standing before her.

His gaze locked onto hers, the coldness in his eyes making her chest tighten. The guards around them fell silent, and each passing second felt like a countdown. Perhaps he would strike her down here, before all these eyes, a brutal message to any who dared defy. But the strike never came.

With a swift motion, he summoned a rift, and vanished into its depths, its maw snapping behind him.

Dario exhaled sharply, the tension in his shoulders visibly melting away. "Your stubbornness might be the death of me, you know that?" Before she could register his movement, he had enfolded her in an embrace—a gesture so raw, especially under the watchful eyes of the guards. But Dario had always been a storm of emotions, consequences be damned. "We'll get through this—but Elara." He pulled back slightly, locking his gaze onto hers. "Don't bait the wolves, especially *that* one."

CHAPTER 4

Elara's shoulders relaxed, her breath steadying as the gloom of the Hartling Forest gave way to the open road. The distant silhouette of Ansyl City beckoned, painting the vista in hues of moonlight against the expansive night.

Tucked against Dario as they rode, Elara was acutely aware of the steady beat of his pulse where his wrist, guiding the reins, grazed her hand. His arms cradled her, not with the greed of a collector, but with the reverence of a guardian, and she felt, for a moment, like a treasure he would go to the ends of the world to protect. But she was no stranger to the cruel irony that men often imprisoned what they held dear. That love, unchecked, could be its own kind of cage. After all, aren't treasures, even drenched in the light of adoration, still confined to the hands that claim them?

Each hoofbeat seemed to echo the whispered sentiment. She was being returned—*claimed*—once more by a place that had never felt like home.

Dario's fingers clenched around Elara's waist as their horse vaulted a fallen tree, the sudden movement causing his armor to shift just enough to reveal a glimpse of the ink etched into his wrist—the totem of his kingdom and city.

She remembered the first time she saw the tattoo, about a month after they had met. Curiosity had gotten the better of her then, as it always seemed to do. "Your tattoo," she had started, hesitant yet hopelessly intrigued, "it's unlike any totem I know."

Under Osin's stringent rule, each citizen was mandated to have their kingdom and city affiliations tattooed in a prominent place, such as the upper part of the wrist or forearm. This served as a broad identifier of the citizen's nationality. The specific combination of the national symbol and the city details allowed officials to quickly identify a citizen's origins, as well as potential political leanings or allegiances.

The citizens of Ulrith bore sunbursts on their skin, each totem a glowing symbol of ether and the power central to their eastern kingdom. To the west, Bravell's people displayed open books emblazoned with flames, fiery symbols of their quest for enlightenment and the intellectual rebellion that had led to their downfall. Further south, in the kingdom of Aewora, people wore totems depicting a tree entwined with a scroll, merging the devout and Druidic fibers of their culture.

But in the north, in the kingdom of Vredia, the skin of the people remained unmarked, untouched by Osin's edicts. This absence became a mark of defiance. To be unmarked was perilous—equivalent to declaring oneself an enemy of the state. Those found without a totem were swiftly condemned. No trials, no juries—just the cold, abrupt finality of the gallows.

But Dario's totem was different—he had the familiar markings of someone born to the west, but instead of having his city's unique emblem incorporated into the country's symbol, he had a different marking underneath—a complex pattern of interlocking circles and arcs.

He had hesitated before responding, his eyes scanning her face for the right measure of trust. Finally, with a gentle touch, he traced the lines of his totem. "This," he had said softly, "is a map of the stars under which I was born."

That was all he had offered, and she didn't press him for more.

A chill swept down from the Torvern mountains, cutting through the air and biting at Elara's skin. Her teeth chattered uncontrollably, her torn and bloodied chemise offering little protection against the chill.

"Do you need my cloak?" Dario offered, pulling her closer to him.

Elara shook her head, disgust rolling in her gut. Edgar *loved* seeing her like this—like some sacrificial lamb fresh off the altar. He made a point of parading her battered, broken state in front of everyone. It wasn't just for show, either. It was all part of his plan, his sick, twisted way of binding them all closer to him. Of making her suffering look noble, necessary, something to be admired. As if her pain somehow validated his authority, cemented their loyalty not just to her, but to him, and Osin's entire damned regime.

Even if she wanted Dario's cloak, she couldn't take it without enduring a tirade from Edgar later. And besides, they were nearly there.

Ahead, the Verdara Sanct dominated the horizon, its formidable sun-bleached battlements and spires standing as a silent guardian over the city that sprawled below. They tore past tall timbered houses with whitewashed walls, weaving their way up the cobblestone streets where the structures grew grander: large townhouses boasting ornate stonework, balustrades adorned with carved motifs, balconies with intricate wrought iron railings, and lofty pillars that framed grand entranceways.

The once bustling market square lay dormant, their stalls shuttered up. Only the occasional sounds of drunken revelry drifted out from taverns, a merry interlude in the hushed cityscape.

As they neared the gatehouse, the measured trot guided them beneath the imposing shadow of the towering portcullis. The High Priests' sentinels stood there, their stances rigid with discipline, and their sharp eyes fixed solely on her.

Her protectors, Edgar often claimed.

But the way their gazes tracked her, like hawks eyeing their quarry, left no room for misinterpretation. They were there not as her shield, but as her shackles. The lie had become so apparent she wondered how she'd ever believed otherwise.

Beyond them, the barrier loomed. It was Osin's own creation; an ethereal ward that moved and shimmered like gossamer in the moonlight.

Each step closer brought a surge of energy, the barrier responding, recognizing the soul it was bound to protect—to *imprison*. It was supposed to be a bulwark between her and those who would see her as nothing more than a prize to be claimed or a treasure to be stolen.

Edgar had told her as much anyway, his warnings ringing in her mind as they approached.

The acrid bite of the barrier stung her nostrils, making her recoil. The grand portcullis cast a shadow over her as they crossed the threshold, its iron bars looming like the fangs of a great beast. The ward glinted in the pale light, vibrating subtly.

The guards cast wary glances her way as they crossed into the bailey. Their silent judgments pierced her skin, quietly acknowledging the turmoil she had endured. Their eyes darted away when met with hers, avoiding any further acknowledgment of her presence, as if she were an inconvenient truth they preferred not to confront. But she was used to it. After years of enduring their indifference, she had become an island.

It was a cold familiarity she wore like armor.

They nodded curtly to Dario, acknowledging his authority despite his age, as the clang of metal sliced through the brisk night air, blending with the sounds of a few castle workers still toiling under the dim torches.

Dario's role as captain had earned him respect among the ranks, his authority unquestioned despite being twenty-one. It was a sobering reminder of how differently their lives had been shaped. Like many from the west, his past was marked by hardship. His province, Bravell, had a history both proud and painful. It was the first and only region to defy Osin at the start of the war. The kingdom's rebellion ended in ruin—Umzar, Bravell's capital, obliterated. The destruction became a warning to all, a lesson written in the scars of its people and the haunted look in Dario's eyes whenever the past whispered too loud.

As they moved toward the hitching post, laborers scurried like busy ants, their movements punctuated by the occasional whinny of a horse and the soft, rhythmic clopping of hooves against the night's stillness.

"Need some company to the citadel?" Dario asked, dismounting, and extending a hand to her. "I've got some time before my morning duties. If there's anything you need..." His voice trailed, the offer hanging in the air. He knew it was pointless. Even if she wanted his company, the Druids wouldn't let him get anywhere near her.

Elara glanced from his outstretched hand back to the looming citadel, a fortress of memories. Some cherished, and others she'd give anything to forget. "It's a stone's throw away, Dario. I think I can manage it." She allowed him to help her down, but the instant her feet touched solid ground, she stepped back, eager to create space between herself and the waves of pity she sensed radiating from him.

He studied her face intently. "You look... pale."

She arched a brow. "Paler than my usual ghostly shade, you mean?"

He didn't laugh. Didn't even crack a smile, and that—more than anything—told her just how much of a mess she must look. Dario never failed to smile. It was one of the things she cherished most about him. She sighed, her limbs feeling like lead and her soul hollowed out like an empty shell. She must look as bad as she felt. Maybe worse. And if that pitiful stare of his was any indication, she couldn't really blame him.

Gods, she could sleep for a week. No—a month. Just curl up somewhere soft and let the darkness take her under. Let everything else fade away. But she knew what awaited her the moment she returned to the citadel. The Druids, ever meticulous, ever indifferent, would descend with their cleansing rituals. Concoctions of oils, litany of prayers—none of it would help.

"You would tell me if you weren't alright, wouldn't you?"

Elara shrugged. "I'm always alright."

As if she had a choice.

It didn't matter that every time she returned, another part of her soul seemed to shrivel and die. There was no escaping it, no outrunning her fate. All she could do was pretend it wasn't real, live her life in the space between the summons as fully as she could. Because one day, she knew, they would call her, and she would never return.

He studied her for a lingering moment, skepticism faintly shadowing his nod. He gently captured a lock of her hair between his fingers, absentmindedly playing with it. "You look like you need a stiff drink, not the drivel from those moss-munching nut jobs."

Elara's eyes narrowed, her voice dropping to a whisper. "Don't. His ravens could be listening."

Dario's lips pressed into a thin line, his jaw muscles tensing. He handed his mount over to a waiting stable hand, issuing sharp commands to the guards with an authority that seemed to flow from him effortlessly. They nodded in response, but his attention was already back on Elara.

"I'm escorting you. Don't argue."

She sighed but didn't resist.

They passed through the bailey, entering the courtyard where the garden still thrived, defiantly lush under the moonlight despite the chilly nights leading up to the autumn equinox. Silence blanketed their journey to the citadel, heavy with all the things Dario didn't ask and Elara couldn't say.

Her gaze caught his jaw tightening once more, his eyes flicking to meet hers before darting away. Every line of his face strained with effort to hold back his questions.

Dario had always been able to read people—better than anyone she knew. Now, as his eyes settled on her, Elara could feel him absorbing the weight of her pain without a single word, without pressing for answers she wasn't ready to give. His silence was a gift, one she hadn't realized she needed until that moment, and she was grateful for it. Grateful for him.

She reached out, hesitating as her fingertips brushed his rough hand, causing him to stumble slightly. A flicker of surprise crossed his face before it quickly vanished, his hand gripping hers in a silent reassurance as they moved toward the citadel's grand oak doors.

A heavy pause settled within Elara as they walked up the stone steps. She wished she could stay there, holding Dario's hand a bit longer, but the Druids had other plans for her.

Elara took a deep breath and disentangled her fingers from his, preparing to confront whatever lay beyond those doors. But a sudden, firm grasp on her wrist halted her.

"I'll be right here come dawn," he promised, his eyes fervently blazing in the dim light.

A faint smile tugged at her lips. "The Druids will bar your entry before you even attempt to knock."

"Let them try. I've never met a door I couldn't break through."

"Dario," she whispered, her voice a fragile thread weighted with unspoken emotions.

It had been three months since the last time she'd been summoned to Ulrith, and when she returned that night, something inside her had snapped. She had slipped into his barracks under the cover of darkness, her heart racing with a determination she couldn't quite explain. Every visit to that wretched place felt like a countdown, like the world was closing in on her, and time was running out. The fear of leaving this world untouched, unloved—it gnawed at her, hollowing her out until she could no longer ignore it.

But Dario had always seen her differently. From the very beginning, he'd been one of the few who didn't treat her like a spectacle, like some untouchable, unreachable symbol.

He offered her something few others ever had: respect.

When he looked at her, he saw *her*—the raw, flawed woman beneath it all. His gaze never lingered too long, never pried, but there was something in it, something that made her feel *seen*, understood in a way that stripped her down to the bare truth of her humanity. The others gawked, whispered, tried to decipher her like she was some celestial puzzle, but Dario... he just *looked*. Saw her for who she was, not what she represented. There was something else in those glances as well, in the way his eyes softened every time they met hers. Affection. She'd felt it, too, ever since they'd met over a year ago.

So, that night, three months ago, Elara had finally crossed the line she'd been dancing on. She kissed him—recklessly—and when he kissed her back, gods, the intensity shattered her. The way he held her, as if she were something fragile, something precious, made it feel like he wanted to drown in her just as much as she wanted to lose herself in him.

They'd stayed like that, tangled together until the early morning light seeped through the cracks in the walls, but she had known even then that it couldn't last. It had been a brief rebellion, a moment of selfishness, of letting herself feel something more than fear and pain. But it was dangerous. It was a line they shouldn't have crossed.

Because letting it happen again... letting it consume them both would only end in ruin.

Osin's gaze followed her everywhere—cold, possessive, calculating. If he ever discovered what had passed between her and Dario, there would be no hesitation, no mercy. Dario's fate would be sealed in iron and blood. So she had distanced herself, pulled away, and Dario, in that quiet, steadfast way of his, had respected it.

But something had shifted between them since then—something unspoken but impossible to ignore. His eyes lingered just a second too long, his fingers brushed against hers when there was no need. It was subtle, so subtle that anyone else might have missed it entirely. But not her.

His watchfulness transcended his responsibilities. And somewhere within, a fragment of her took a guilty pleasure in his lingering attention.

Drawn by the ghosts of that stolen evening, or maybe just the cover the night provided, Elara found herself closing the distance between them. Rising on her tiptoes, she let her lips brush against his in a fleeting kiss. It was barely anything, a whisper of a touch, but it was enough to set her heart racing.

Tonight had broken something inside her, left her aching in a way she couldn't put into words. And selfishly, she needed this. Needed a moment of warmth, in a life that felt perpetually cold... even if guilt would eat at her come dawn.

CHAPTER 5

"We are but vessels for the earth's energy," Avis's voice floated to Elara as softly as the falling night. The full moon cast her delicate features in a soft, silver glow, her hair—a river of night—blending with the evening breeze.

Despite Avis's soothing tone, a chill wrapped around Elara, making her skin prickle. Moonlight cast a silvery path ahead, cutting through the darkness and leading them toward the Cillareen River.

In the heart of the meadow, where the starlight kissed the river's crest, the spirit of the river awoke. It was a venerable presence that had dwelled within these waters long before the Druids or the kingdoms. Ethereal and fluid, it moved with a grace that belied its age, its form coiling and uncoiling in a silent dance like a ghostly serpent.

To witness the spirit of the river was to see the soul of the Cillareen itself—timeless and serene, guarding its sacred waters. It could appear as a whisper of mist over the river or a sudden surge in the current, reminding those who came near they were in the presence of something far greater than themselves—something eternal.

In Latheria, ancient spirits of the elements dwelled in hidden corners, and the southern Druidic Sect counted themselves fortunate enough to live near one such spirit. These ancients bore no names; they transcended such human trivialities. They *were* the essence of the world itself. The river's flow, the mountain's rise, the wind's caress, the fire's dance.

Some ancients were hostile, others as mild as a summer breeze. However, this spirit's demeanor varied greatly. To most it might seem friendly, but with Elara, it revealed a completely different side—unpredictable and temperamental. Something about her presence seemed to unleash its true nature.

Around Elara, Elmweavers, Greenhearts, and a Soothsayer or two clustered, the air thrumming with their gentle incantations, their words floating on the breeze and playing with the loose strands of her hair.

"Close your eyes," Avis whispered gently, "and let the river's touch wander through you. Last time, it gave such lovely gifts. Imagine what wonders await you tonight."

Gifts. Elara almost laughed. Calling what the spirit revealed to her as "gifts" was being overly generous. Every time she gave it her breath, it reciprocated with "visions."

They were more like erratic flashes, disjointed and bizarre, pieced together like a fever dream. Yet, the Soothsayers never seemed discouraged. They obsessively dissected each fragment, trying to make sense of the chaos. They treated every vision, no matter how scrambled, as a puzzle to be solved, despite Elara's warnings that the spirit was just playing its games.

But their faith was blind. Hers was not.

A shiver ran down Elara's spine as the cool night air brushed against her skin. She closed her eyes. *Fen.*

Her breath caught as tears quietly trailed down her face. She didn't bother wiping them away. What was the point? New tears would only chase the old.

She tried to find calm, to escape to that quiet place in her mind, but each time she tried to step forward onto the path, the ground beneath would give way, fragmenting into pieces until there was nothing left to hold her.

This cleansing ritual called to something old and buried within her, a flicker of the child she once was—hopeful, open, *wounded*.

As a child, Elara had carried a deep ache in her chest, a yearning to connect with the earth. With the Mothers. Especially Aine, who had brought her to this place, who had gazed at her with eyes full of hope before abandoning her to a monster. *Why?* That question haunted her every breath. She needed to understand. So, she had sought the goddesses with a raw, bleeding fervor. But time and time again, that fervor was met with nothing but silence. And as the years piled up like layers of armor, Elara had let the tender parts of her heart harden, forming a bulwark against the quiet scorn of the gods.

The gods, if they ever returned, would find no purchase in the fortress she had become.

Unfortunately, this resolve didn't exempt her from the recurring cleansings.

Elara's breaths were shaky, her heart a wild drumbeat of fear and anticipation as gentle hands guided her into the river, the docile current tugging at her ceremonial robe. The water's chill was a slap of deep winter frost, drawing sharp gasps from her with every step.

The Druids peeled away Elara's robe, leaving her bare beneath the sky. But she didn't flinch, didn't lower her gaze. She kept her chin high, her shoulders square, though the chill kissed her skin. Here, in this circle, there was no shame in nudity—it was something else entirely. A declaration. A surrender. The Druids saw no sin in the human body; to them, it was sacred. Each curve and hollow, every scar, a mark of life crafted by the Mothers. It wasn't weakness or vulnerability, but truth. Raw and unvarnished. And in this, the only honesty that mattered.

The Cillareen River brushed against her breasts, sending a shiver across her shoulders. But she steadied her mind and her heart, for she knew what was to come.

"Have faith in the waters; their healing touch has mended many before you," Caelum, a Soothsayer, murmured against the backdrop of the flowing river. He drizzled a blend of sacred oils over her, the liquid gold running down her form.

His deep emerald eyes didn't meet hers as he worked, his touch almost reverent, but there was a detachment to it. Like most of the Druids, he hid behind a veneer of indifference, a practiced neutrality that made it easy to forget there was anything personal in their ministrations. To him, she wasn't Elara—she was just another body, another soul seeking healing. Not a person with thoughts and fears and desires, but a part of the endless cycle they served.

With a subtle nod, Caelum turned away, disappearing into the crowd of Druids.

As the oils seeped into her skin, Elara could almost feel the edges of her consciousness blur, the barriers between her soul and the river thinning.

"I'll be right here," Avis murmured, reaching out to interlock their fingers.

The touch was easy, comforting.

Elara returned the Druid's squeeze with a tight smile as something bitter buried deep within her reared again, whispering words she tried to shut out.

Unlovable, abandoned, used, alone.

The words chanted in her mind, even as Avis stayed at her side. Elara took comfort in her steady presence, and outwardly, she was thankful for the companionship. But in those deep, still hours of the night, when the world slept and her thoughts roamed freely, a fragile hope would sometimes take root. A ridiculous, pathetic hope—that maybe, someone out there believed she was worth the fight.

Tears pricked at her eyes, and she blinked them back fiercely. She forced herself to match her breathing to the rhythm of the river, each inhale a battle to steady the storm raging inside her. *Just get through it,* she told herself.

Steeling herself with one last look at the moon, Elara exhaled and let go, slipping beneath the surface. The cold hit her like a blade slicing through her skin, straight to the bone. Her chest seized in protest, the icy grip of the water squeezing her lungs. She balled her fists, pushing back the instinct to flee even as her heartbeat roared in her ears, drowning out the soft murmur of the river.

Before her, the water stretched out like a void, dark and endless. Long strands of kelp twisted around her legs, ghostly fingers trailing across her skin like sirens beckoning.

Above, the moonlight filtered through the water in trembling, fractured beams, casting eerie patterns across the sand below. Elara's breath, *her offering,* burned in her chest, held tight as her eyes darted from one shifting pool of light to another, searching, straining, for any sign, any ripple, that might betray the presence of the spirit.

She didn't have to wait long.

There, amidst the swaying dance of kelp, it revealed itself—a current alive like a serpent of the deep, wild and writhing as it surged toward her.

Elara's heart leapt into her throat, her pulse hammering with a mix of primal fear and awe. She exhaled, and the river eagerly snatched the bubbles of her breath, swallowing them before they could even dream of reaching the surface. She could almost sense its glee, a dark, hungry joy in seizing whatever it could from her.

The spirit twined around her, a swirling vortex that nipped at her eyes and tugged fiercely at her hair. Its kelp snaked around her ankles and up her legs like chains, dragging her to its watery bed.

They tightened.

"Surrender," whispered the spirit, its voice a slippery hiss.

Everyone seemed to want a piece of her, even the river.

Morbid curiosity flickered within Elara. She had never given herself over to it completely. And, curse it to the Void, if there ever was a time for the spirit to take advantage, it was now.

Ever since the Hunter slung her over his shoulder and rifted her away, the truth she'd been fleeing from clawed at her.

Viscerally. Relentless.

The reasons behind Fenlin's actions, his decision to steal her blood —it didn't matter. At her very core, she believed it was her fault, her *sin*.

Fenlin had needed her. But he never reached out, never asked for help with whatever he was wrestling with. The walls she'd constructed around herself—walls meant to protect her from others, to keep everyone at a safe distance—had done their job too well. Each brick laid in fear and self-preservation had isolated him. Kept him from trusting her.

Elara bit down hard on the inside of her cheek, the coppery taste of blood filling her mouth.

If the river craved her breath, then let it have its fill.

Maybe that had been the Druids' plan all along—to bring her here when she was so frayed just to see what the spirit would do with her—or to her.

Maybe it wouldn't give her back at all.

Before she could second-guess herself, Elara exhaled, surrendering to the river. Its vines tightened, claiming victory, as the spirit's murky fingers slid down her throat, flooding her lungs.

~

HER CONSCIOUSNESS BLOOMED INTO BEING, senses awakening to the taste of rain—crisp and slightly acidic, with a subtle hint of the earth it had touched as it slipped past her lips and onto her tongue. She opened her eyes to a world lit softly by the dawn, cradled by a breeze whispering through a forest and the rhythm of raindrops pattering on her skin.

"Awake, sweet one," a serene voice murmured. Elara's eyes fluttered open to the sight of her creator—the Goddess Aine, standing above her like a figure carved from sunlight. Her voice was a melody that seemed to weave the very passage of time into its tones—the ebb and flow of the sun and moon, the silent whisper of the ages slipping by. "Awake and fulfill your purpose. Heal and restore. Give and consecrate."

Each word fell like seeds into fertile soil, taking root deep within the furrows of Elara's heart. Wide-eyed, she took in her surroundings, a soul birthed into a world of quiet wonder.

The goddess lifted her from the dew-kissed earth, infusing life and knowledge into her with every exhale. She was a flower blooming in fast-forward, petals unfurling in the morning sun, drinking in the goddess's breath and growing from it. There was no toddler's babble for her, no faltering first steps; she was made whole and complete in an instant, her spirit blossoming with the full, rich awareness of her destiny.

Give. Give. Give.

Elara blinked, her vision sharpening. The Goddess was radiant, almost painfully so, with a cascade of red hair that spilled over freckled shoulders, tumbling nearly to her feet like a torrent of flames.

Blood. It was the first word, the first real thought that pierced through the fog of Elara's mind as her eyes traced the crimson spirals. She didn't know why she had made the comparison, reaching back to the essence of who she was and who she was meant to become—lines painted in deep, rich red.

A young man stood next to the goddess. He was a lordling, Aine said, Osin by name. His hair was slicked back like the feathers of a crow, and he had icy blue eyes that didn't just look at you but seemed to pierce right through.

The wind played with Aine's words, lifting them to swirl around her before snatching them away again. "He is your guardian, and you, his guiding light."

But the way Osin's eyes devoured Elara felt far from safe. Doubt whispered through her thoughts, a shadow curling around her heart, but against the weight of divine will, what could she do but nod?

Aine smiled as she guided Elara forward, her hand—a delicate, almost fragile thing—finding its way into Osin's imposing grip.

"In the light of the Hallowed, you shall rise to sovereignty, guiding my children, and ushering in an age of greatness."

Yet, as Osin's fingers closed around hers, a chill slithered up Elara's arm. His fingers, elegantly long, felt like they were leeching the very life from her veins.

The two continued to speak, but Elara felt only half-present, suspended between realms. It was as though her soul had been cleaved in two; one part trying desperately to reconnect with her body, while the other lingered, untethered, unable to fully integrate back into her physical form that stood below. It was a paradox that left her grappling for a sense of reality that seemed just out of reach, scattered by winds she could neither see nor control.

Elara didn't notice Aine's departure until the goddess was already gone. It wasn't until the abyss had swallowed her whole that she realized she'd been falling all along. And the true path of her life only became clear when she lie bleeding on the cold floor of Osin's throne room, her eyes finding his in that moment of raw, brutal clarity.

The dread that had hissed through her veins at their first touch wasn't just her imagination—it had been a warning, a sharp, clear song resonating from a part of her that had known danger even before her mind could grasp it. It was a harbinger of how mercilessly humans could wield their malice, a foretelling that cruelty might be all that remained.

CHAPTER 6

A midday breeze swept across Elara's bare arms, a fleeting relief from the heat. She'd pushed her sleeves up, welcoming the warmth of the sun as she worked beside Avis, gathering herbs from the Sanct's gardens. Autumn would soon come barreling in, stealing the heat, but for now, the sun was hers, and she planned to soak up every last bit.

She swiped her curls away from her neck, frustrated with herself for forgetting to bring a tie. Her hair was a mess, sticking to her damp skin where the sweat had collected, making her neck unbearably itchy. Tugging it back with a huff, she silently cursed the distraction. It was small, insignificant really, but enough to pull her out of the focus she'd desperately been clinging to.

With a sigh, she refocused as she moved quietly through the underbrush, gathering the last of the season's offerings—berries, mushrooms, red clover, wild fennel—all nestled in patches that would soon wither under the first frost. The work was steady, predictable, and Elara tried to lose herself in it.

Out here, away from the Astromancers' endless demands to chart yet another map of the stars and the Soothsayers' cryptic musings, the world felt calmer. The quiet let her thoughts settle in a way only research or a good book could. There was no pressure, no constant hum of expectation—just the earth beneath her hands and the fleeting peace it offered.

Elara could feel Avis's eyes on her, that quiet, unspoken concern that had become constant over the past year. She knew what it meant—Avis was worried. She had been since the night before. But Elara wasn't ready to deal with it. She didn't need her friend's pity or the reassurances that would inevitably follow.

What could be done about it anyway?

After months of silent concern, it had started to wear on her. It wasn't that Elara didn't want to be cared for—she did. Part of her wished Avis's worry could somehow fill the emptiness inside her. But it didn't. It was a reminder of a wound that wouldn't heal, a thorn lodged too deep to pull out. And Elara was tired of pretending it didn't hurt.

So, she did what she always did—ignored it. She squeezed her eyes shut, trying to block out the world, but the taste of the river lingered on her tongue—a bitter, brackish mix of silt and decay.

The river spirit—it had revealed her very first memory.

Elara had buried that day long ago, the first flicker of her existence, deep within her mind, hidden in a place so distant that even her darkest thoughts rarely wandered there. It was a fragile piece of her past, one she'd avoided for years. But now, the river had dredged it all back to the surface.

She could still feel it—the wonder and awe, mixed with a hint of something darker, a sense of destiny that seemed to pull at her even then. The spirit didn't just show her the memory; it immersed her in it. But to what end? She had allowed herself to hope, perhaps foolishly, that by yielding to the spirit it might impart something profound, something transformative. That maybe it would have even whisked her back to the Otherworld, dissolving her into a mix of stardust—or whatever cursed substance she was made of.

But there was no revelation, no understanding, only a bitter taste in her mouth.

"What did you see?" Caelum had demanded, his voice edged even as she sputtered and coughed, expelling water from her lungs.

Avis had been the only one immune to the spirit's influence. With a single stern look, she silenced Caelum, and moved to Elara's side, steadying her as she coughed out the remaining water. Meanwhile, the others had turned to the moon, eyes lifted in silent reverence, murmuring their thanks to the Mothers for their endless blessings. Elara sat among them shivering, and by the time they decided she was ready to leave, dawn was painting the sky in shades of pink.

She'd barely gotten a few hours of sleep before Randall, the cook, shook her awake, and she dragged herself to breakfast duties, groggy and irritable. After that came her usual rounds with the Greenhearts. The healers always had her restocking supplies—bundling fresh herbs, sorting dried ones, refilling tinctures and salves. Sometimes she ground ingredients into powders, labeled vials, or ensured the healing poultices were ready. Linens needed washing, bandages had to be folded, shelves reorganized. Always something to keep her hands busy. She was just getting into the rhythm of things when Avis pulled her away, reminding her they needed to forage before the sun climbed too high in the sky.

Elara opened her eyes, pointedly ignoring the Druid, and focused on the task before her. She sifted through the underbrush, fingers brushing through the cool, damp soil as she plucked a few sprigs of fennel. Its bold, earthy scent mingled with the sweet, honeyed fragrance of red clover blooming in nearby patches. Her basket was heavy now, brimming with herbs and berries. She slipped a plump one into her mouth, its skin bursting as sweet-tart juice coated her tongue.

The Sanct gardens were vast, stretching like a sea of green and gold behind the towering citadel. Rolling hills dipped and rose, framed by the stone walls of the Sanct but still enclosed within the protective barrier. Light shimmered off the surface of the veil—a delicate, translucent layer of ether that rippled like silk with every breath of wind.

A rustling nearby drew Elara's gaze up to Avis, who now stood beside her, the burnished copper folds of her robes shifting softly in the breeze. "I think we've done enough for one day."

Elara straightened, brushing the dirt from her hands. Foraging was only part of their routine—the rest would be spent inside, surrounded by stacks of parchment and paints. Avis had been diligently adding to the Sanct's archives for months now, her journals filled with detailed, hand-painted illustrations of the plants they gathered. Every leaf, petal, and root was captured with painstaking care, the colors mixed just right to reflect the vibrant greens and soft purples they'd found in the fields.

Elara's job was simple enough—filling in the details, listing each plant's properties, its uses in salves, teas, remedies, and how it adapted to the changing seasons. But she didn't mind. There was a certain satisfaction in the quiet work, a sense of purpose in knowing they were building something that would last.

She followed Avis, the soft rustle of their baskets the only sound as they wandered through the gardens. With each step, the air shifted—the fragrance of earth and herbs gradually fading into something colder. The damp, stony scent of the courtyard crept in, and the peace of the gardens, that fragile calm, began to slip away.

Then it came—the jarring clang of steel on steel, cutting through the air. Elara sighed, feeling the tension creep back into her shoulders.

The courtyard buzzed with energy. Sparring rings were marked out in the dirt, thick ropes tied to iron posts anchoring the borders. Inside them, men and women faced off, the sharp clash of swords cutting through the air with every strike, the metallic rhythm echoing around them. Elara's gaze swept over the scene, tracing the sweeping arcs of the blades, until settling on Dario. There was something almost hypnotic about the way he moved, his sword an extension of his will, each parry and thrust delivered with a grace that made it easy to forget just how lethal he could be.

Had he actually tried to break in this morning, like he'd threatened? The thought of him squaring off against the Druids just for a chance to see her almost made her smile. *Almost.*

He was panting, flushed and breathless, his cheeks glistening with sweat as his eyes locked onto hers across the field. He stilled, eyes flicking over her quickly before settling back on her face. And then that slow, lopsided smile spread across his lips, the kind that made her heart stumble. She hadn't even noticed she was smiling too until she felt the ache in her cheeks.

Her chest tightened. Gods, *why* had she let herself kiss him? Foolish, reckless—*selfish.*

The image of his gaze, that soft, almost fragile look he'd given her when she'd pulled away, lingered, haunting her. When she'd broken the kiss, his eyes had flickered with something raw, a hope he'd tried to hide but couldn't quite suppress. As if that was the moment he'd been waiting for—her, finally stepping over that line, finally saying she was ready.

And she hated herself for it. For being the one to put that unguarded joy in his eyes, for giving him something she couldn't take back, even when she knew she could never give him what he wanted.

Elara had once dared to imagine a different life—a quiet cottage filled with books and trinkets, a corner of the world that was wholly her own—but it was only ever a fantasy. Her fate was bound to Osin and the Mothers, her path carved before she could choose it, leaving her as little more than a puppet to divine whims with no strings to sever. That flicker of hope had been nothing but selfish grief, a weakness born of losing Fen.

Never again, she resolved.

Dario was too precious to jeopardize.

Elara's eyes narrowed as Lorien sidled up beside Dario, his gaze finding hers. A cruel smirk spread across his freckled face.

"Well, well, if it isn't the Hallowed herself, deigning to grace us with her presence," he said, his red hair glowing like embers in the late afternoon sun. "Shouldn't you be busy kneeling at some altar, acting the pious maiden?"

Acting?

Elara's gaze snapped to Dario, finding his expression murderous.

No, he wouldn't have said anything. He understood all too well how dangerous it would be if it slipped out they had been together. Dangerous for them both.

Elara fixed the guard with a cold sneer. "Aren't you overdue at some brothel, Lorien? Or have you already contracted every disease they offer?"

It was bold, even for her, but at the moment, her patience for his antics was hanging by a thread.

The red of Lorien's hair seemed to bleed into his features, his knuckles turning white as he jabbed a finger toward her. "You bitc—"

A crow, black as the midnight sky, swooped down with a raucous caw, snapping its sharp beak at his pointing finger.

Lorien jerked back, his hand coming away stained red, vibrant against his pale skin. He spat a string of curses as the crow flew away. He ripped his sword from its sheath and hurled it in a blind arc, striking the wooden rack with a resounding thwack.

He didn't look back, didn't see his sword trembling in the rack like a spent arrow. Lorien turned on his heel—a storm of red—and stalked away.

Elara's heart raced. Edgar's ravens were silent collectors of secrets, their keen eyes always watching, gathering information to carry back to him. They never interfered. So why did this bird seem almost... protective of her? She stared, holding her breath, as the bird soared toward the clock tower, perching high above before turning to fix its piercing gaze on her.

A chill raced down her spine.

"That was unusual."

Elara blinked, almost forgetting Avis was beside her. "I thought the little things hated me."

Avis tilted her head, thoughtful. "Oh, they don't hate anyone. Ravens are clever, you know. They can solve puzzles, mimic voices. Maybe this one's picked up something new about you."

Elara started to glance back at the bird but found herself looking at Dario instead. He was watching the raven too, eyes narrowed, a flicker of concern—or was it fear?—crossing his face. She could almost see the gears turning. But then, a shout from one of his comrades pulled his attention away. He threw her a quick, unreadable look before disappearing back into the fray of training.

A quiet throat-clearing beside her made her flinch, her gaze snapping away from Dario's retreating figure.

Petr, one of her personal guards, had somehow slipped up beside her without her noticing. He stood there, hands clasped behind his back, his face impassive as ever. But she knew he'd been watching her this whole time.

"The High Priest requests your presence for dinner tonight."

Elara sighed, closing her eyes. *Of course he did.* He would want to talk about the capital, about everything that had gone wrong. Her hands tightened around the basket. She wasn't ready for that conversation—wasn't ready to relive it all again.

She lifted her gaze to find Avis watching her, brow furrowed.

"It's just dinner," Avis said softly.

"I know," she replied, lips pressing into a tight line.

"You've been through worse."

Elara exhaled a quiet laugh, nodding. "I have."

Without another word, Avis leaned in, kissing her cheek before taking the basket from her hands. "I'll meet you after. We can finish the book."

Elara nodded, but the heaviness in her chest remained.

Petr led her through the courtyard, passing through a wide stone archway and into the citadel's dim corridors. Torches burned along the walls, their glow barely cutting through the thick air, making the stone walls feel as if they were closing in. Each hall branched off into smaller passageways leading to the Druids' living quarters, simple doors spaced evenly along the stone walls, each marked with hand-carved symbols that represented the room's occupant. The air smelled faintly of herbs and smoke, the remnants of past rituals lingering in the stone itself.

Petr didn't say a word as he led her deeper, past rows of high, arched windows that overlooked the training yard below. Finally, they stopped at her door—a heavy oak slab with faint runes etched along its edges. He pushed it open, gave her a curt nod, and turned back toward the courtyard, leaving her in silence.

Soft evening light spilled through her room, her sheer curtains swaying gently in the breeze that carried hints of salt and jasmine. It brushed against the hanging bunch of dried flowers above her chipped dresser, a piece that somehow still held together after all these years.

Her room—if she could call it that—was small, but the pale walls and sparse furnishings tricked the eye, making it seem bigger than it was. Beyond the window, the Jade Sea murmured, its rhythmic waves lulling her toward a yawn, but a bath was already waiting, steam curling from the tub in delicate wisps.

Elara sighed, peeling off her sweaty dress, the fabric sticking uncomfortably to her skin. She slipped into the bath, grateful that the water wasn't scalding, just warm enough to soothe the ache in her muscles. She grabbed the bar of oatmeal and lavender soap, scrubbing at her skin until it felt raw. The scent rose with the steam, soothing in a way that did little to reach the ache sitting deep in her chest. She ducked her head under the water, working her fingers through her hair, pulling out the stray leaves that inevitably found their way into her curls whenever she foraged.

Stepping out of the tub, she barely bothered to dry off, pulling her linen robe over her wet skin. The fabric clung to her, but she couldn't bring herself to care. Exhaustion weighed on her, heavy and hollow. Water pooled at her feet.

She drifted to her dresser, reaching for her brush, fingers moving automatically as she started to untangle her hair. Her gaze fell to the small collection of pebbles she kept there. Each one held a unique tone, from the deep, soothing hum of a smooth river rock to the soft, light tinkle of a tiny quartz pebble.

Precious stones were more than just beautiful; they held deep significance and power. Every caster had a stone that connected them to their elemental prowess. Jasper for those who commanded the earth, sunstone ablaze for the fire wielders, quartz, light and airy, for those who danced with the winds, and amethyst, deep like the waters they controlled.

Bonding with an element wasn't just an honor; it was a trial by fire. The four stones—jasper, sunstone, quartz, and amethyst—were awarded only to those who endured the grueling process and emerged victorious. The regimen of rigorous training, fasting, and meditation purged both body and spirit. Only after this cleansing could one partake in the Convergence Ceremony, presided over annually by Osin in the heart of the capital. There, the worthy were given the choice to bond with a single element, forging a deep connection to either earth, fire, wind, or water through their chosen stone.

They would mingle a drop of their blood with a drop of Elara's, carefully placing the mixture on a stone set upon the altar. The ether in her blood acted as a bridge, linking the caster's life force with their chosen element. But the bond was far from guaranteed. The element had to choose the caster in return, an acceptance that was as unpredictable as the elements themselves.

Most Druids in the Sanct were bonded to an element, but Avis, among a scattered few, was not. She had failed the Convergence, but she didn't seem to mind. Some Druids believed that one only needed the sun to summon a bit of ether. And so, Avis would sing to the sun—and sometimes, she said, it would listen.

Elara had witnessed just one Convergence Ceremony in her lifetime —the inaugural one following her arrival to the realm. Osin had been the first to step forward, and everything about it had been a catastrophe. He hadn't prepared, no fasting, no training, which the Druids later realized were crucial for bonding properly with an element. When he mixed a drop of his blood with hers, carefully placing it on a stone at the altar, the ritual didn't connect him to an element as intended. Instead, it devoured his life force, dragging him into the Void. He had clawed his way back, but he was forever changed, bound to its shadows.

Since that day, no other aspirant who attempted to bond with ether —or any element—had been sucked into the Void like Osin had. No one could explain why it had happened to him; there were theories, of course, endless whispers and speculations. But what everyone knew for certain was that Osin stood unmatched as the most formidable caster of their age.

She traced the stones with her fingers, careful not to topple them, finding a strange sense of calm in their subtle lines and divots. These stones were devoid of ether, yet they were anything but empty. They sang to her, as all stones did—a soft, continuous melody.

Reluctantly, Elara withdrew her hand. She would never be permitted to attempt a Convergence; her role was to aid.

Heal and restore. Give and consecrate.

She pressed the heels of her palms into her eyes. Give and give and give until there was nothing left of her. *That* was her purpose.

The harsh cry of a raven drew her attention from the stones to the window. There, perched on the sill, was the same raven that had bitten Lorien.

"Tell your master I will join him shortly," she drawled.

The bird's reply was a more demanding squawk.

Elara sighed deeply. Even when promised moments of privacy in her room, she never truly had them. It was always something—the ravens, the guards, or—

A knock echoed from her door.

She sighed again. *Or Beatrice.*

CHAPTER 7

Beatrice was not one to bother with formalities like invitations.

The door groaned softly as she nudged it open, her head slipping through the gap.

"A fine afternoon, Hallowed," she crooned, her velvety voice dripping with ulterior motives. She glided into the room, the very picture of fragility with her slight, bent frame, but there was nothing frail about the sharpness in her gaze. "The Sanct is abuzz with whispers of last night's events at the capital. There is talk of traitors and plots against the Lord Sovereign." Her brow pinched, a perfect portrait of concern.

Elara kept herself tightly wound, every muscle, every expression carefully controlled. Any crack, even the tiniest slip, and Beatrice would pounce. In the dangerous dance of court politics, Beatrice was a master at twisting words and emotions into deadly weapons. With a mere look of irritation, she could spin a tale of treason by evening.

"Thank the Mother that your association with that *traitor* hasn't tarnished your own reputation." Beatrice's lips curled into a knowing smirk. "One shudders to think what the Lord Sovereign might do if he were to discover such... questionable connections."

A hot flush crept up Elara's neck, coloring her cheeks a bright, angry red.

So much for staying composed.

"If you're looking for a tale to satiate your thirst for drama, I suggest you look elsewhere," she snapped. "I have no intention of discussing the matter."

Beatrice's eyes glinted with feigned innocence. "My, my, someone's prickly today. I merely thought you'd want an ear. But very well."

Her gaze held Elara's for a moment longer, a hint of calculation flickering behind her eyes before Elara broke away and seated herself at the vanity. Beatrice sifted through the wardrobe, scrutinizing each gown. "These vibrant hues would be splendid if not for your ghostly pallor," she muttered dismissively. Each sharp word felt like a needle pricking at her patience, but Elara held her tongue.

Even as Beatrice chose the solemn gray dress from the back of the wardrobe and yanked Elara's hair into an elaborate updo, causing waves of pain to crash against her temples, Elara maintained an unwavering mask of calm. By the time she reached the refectory for dinner, the tension in her head had morphed to a full-blown migraine.

"You're late." Edgar's frigid voice sliced through the air.

The High Priest sat near the center of the refectory, beneath a massive tree whose roots burrowed through the floor and branches stretched up to the rafters.

Around the room, members of the Druidic Sect sat, their robes blending seamlessly with the autumnal hues of fallen leaves and moss-covered stones. Elara's eyes darted across the room from one group to the next: Scribes, Greenhearts, Elmweavers, Soothsayers, and Astromancers. Each cluster was deeply engaged, some poring over age-worn tomes, others softly speaking to young seedlings that sprouted eagerly around them.

They came from every corner of Latheria: Scribes on the storm-lashed cliffs of Valdor's Reach, keepers of history and lore; Elmweavers in the rain-soaked groves of Elderglen, herbalists who worked in harmony with root and leaf; Greenhearts in Bravell's fertile valleys, healers who drew life from soil; and in Ulrith, Soothsayers reading futures on Mistwatch's fog-bound cliffs, while Astromancers traced the heavens from Nightspire's starlit peaks. Each year, as apprenticeships ended, they gathered at the Verdara Sanct to serve the High Priest and await their fates, handed down like cards in a game they could never play. Perhaps that was why none sought her friendship, Elara thought bitterly; attachments meant nothing when everyone was destined to be scattered in the end.

Candles set in hollowed-out logs cast a warm, flickering glow over the feast of glistening meats and bowls brimming with bright fruits and vegetables. Elara's stomach twisted.

She shut her eyes, breath hitching as memories crashed over her. A Legionnaire's shove. A harsh collision with the table. Fenlin's eyes—wide, terrified.

She swayed, the room tilting under her.

"Are you well?" Edgar asked, his voice carrying a rare note of genuine concern.

"Fine," Elara managed to say, pressing a hand against her chest where her heart hammered wildly. She knew better than to reveal her true feelings to him; it would only lead to lectures, judgments, or worse, punishment. So, taking a deep breath that barely steadied her nerves, she moved to sit beside him, keeping her expression carefully neutral.

Before her, a massive eel was coiled and skewered from end to end, its mouth frozen open to reveal rows of sharp teeth. Its glassy eyes seemed to follow Elara's every move, twisting her stomach and completely erasing her appetite.

"Algernon mentioned you fared well during the purification," Edgar began, taking a sip from his chalice. "He's optimistic about your return to the archives by tomorrow."

Elara snorted. She knew Algernon didn't truly care about her well-being; he just wanted to avoid the tedious task of organizing the scrolls the acolytes had scattered throughout the archives. His laziness was legendary.

"How utterly generous of him. Perhaps if I prove myself worthy, he might even grant me the honor of sorting his socks by color."

The thrill of drawing one of Edgar's scowls was like collecting treasures, rare and delightful. But now, as his gaze fixed on her with that usual blend of annoyance and reluctant tolerance, she felt nothing. No spark of triumph, no secret thrill. Just an unsettling numbness spreading through her, quiet and deep.

And he saw it—the lack of fire in her eyes.

His gaze lingered on her face, probing, but after a moment, he seemed to give up on whatever he was searching for in her expression, his attention shifting to the Druid waiting to serve them.

Desmond, a stoic Astromancer on duty to serve the Sanct this evening, avoided her gaze as he heaped food onto her plate—enough to overwhelm even the heartiest of warriors. She must look truly awful if Edgar had quietly instructed him to bury her plate under a small mountain.

Elara shot a glare at the priest, but Edgar paid her no mind, already engrossed in his meal.

No matter, the wine was better company anyway. She knocked back her glass like it was water, not even pausing to taste it. Then, for a lark, she threw a casual glance over her shoulder.

"Desy, would you be a dear and refill my glass?" Elara asked, her tone dripping with sweetness.

"Elara," Edgar warned, his fork clattering onto his plate.

She knew the rules—one glass per dinner. And although Desmond was aware of this directive, it had never stopped her from testing the boundaries.

"I understand the events at the capital were... *taxing* for you," he began, his voice dipped in faux sympathy as he took another sip of wine.

"Taxing?"" Her eyebrows shot up. "Fenlin is *dead*!" Her voice boomed through the chamber like a thunderclap. Wide-eyed, the Druids all turned to look at her, their faces showing everything from surprise to mild concern.

A heavy silence fell over the room, only interrupted by the gentle clinking of utensils and the soft crackling of the fire in the central hearth.

Edgar's jaw clenched as he leaned in toward her. "The boy was a traitor and deserved a traitor's death," he hissed, the veins on his forehead standing out against his flushed skin.

A sharp pain gripped Elara's chest, radiating through her entire body. Every word sliced into her, each one twisting the knife a little deeper. Memories of Fen flooded back—laughing, challenging, vibrantly *alive*—hitting her with the force of a tidal wave. Her fingers curled tightly, nails pressing into the tablecloth.

"Leave us, Desmond," Edgar said gently, waving a dismissive hand. His gaze softened as he looked at her, a flicker of understanding replacing the earlier coldness. He gripped her hand, and despite herself, she felt comforted.

His touch had a bewildering effect on her—calming yet infuriating all at once, a contradiction she couldn't make sense of and deeply resented. Despite her resistance, she felt a strange vulnerability, one she couldn't fully explain. But under the weight of his gaze, she felt trapped. Stifled. Silenced, until every roar within her dimmed, leaving only the faintest piece of herself intact.

"You mustn't champion traitors, Elara. It paints a target on your back."

"I doubt there's a brush large enough to paint me the traitor," she murmured, picking at her plate.

Edgar raised a brow. "People talk. Whispers have already infiltrated the High Council. Rumors of your supposed assault on the Lord Sovereign are spreading like wildfire. Osin has chosen to dismiss it as the mere hysterics of a fragile woman. You should thank the gods he didn't cast you into the Pit."

At the mention of the prison, a chill prickled across her skin, and she fought the urge to wrap her arms around herself. She had never seen it, but the terrifying stories of that hellish place were infamous throughout the realm. Rumors circulated that once you were thrown into the Pit, you never came back.

Is Godfrey there now? Is he even still breathing?

"Why did he take it?" she blurted out.

Edgar blinked, clearly surprised. But it didn't make sense. Both Godfrey and Fenlin had already bonded with their elements—what other use could they have for her blood? "Is Lord Osin blessing the realm on Luminalia?"

The Festival of Reverence—another excuse for Osin to bleed her dry, a "ceremony" dressed as a blessing of the elements. Loyalists from across the realm flocked to the capital, praising his leadership and thanking the Mothers for their mercy. To them, Osin was the bridge between mortal and divine. She'd never seen it herself; she wasn't allowed to. All she knew were whispers of endless feasts and gilded masks, extravagant parties culminating in the solstice spectacle when the capital became a shrine to Osin.

Most believed his pleas had swayed the Mothers to spare the world, crediting him with their salvation. But Luminalia was more than deliverance—it marked a miracle: the day the Goddess Aine appeared for the first time in nearly two millennia, ending the Great Divide's long silence.

Elara had come with Aine, a divine gift to purify the world. She'd been eleven, not an infant, when the goddess presented her. Only years later did she realize how strange that was and pressed Edgar for answers. His answer had been unsettlingly simple: the goddess had created her as a young woman from the outset; she had never been a babe. A revelation that had disturbed her deeply.

During her first year in Latheria, Elara stayed in Arinthel under Osin's watchful eye. However, after Thane's attempt on her life, Osin deemed it necessary to shield her from the world. So, he sent her away, exiled her to the Verdara Sanct, deep within the southern province.

A decade passed, and to Elara, it seemed that the people of Latheria had allowed her to fade into the background of their history. They had forgotten—or perhaps chosen to ignore—that her arrival marked the return of ether.

But maybe... maybe Fenlin and Godfrey had seen through the spectacle, glimpsed the truth beneath the pageantry. What if they were trying to twist it, to make her blood a true offering to the Mothers?

It made sense; after all, most people wholeheartedly revered and believed in it.

"*Of course* he is," Edgar said, his voice taut.

Elara kept her gaze steady and stayed resolutely silent. She'd learned something useful over the years: if she waited him out, the silence would press in, prodding him to fill it, often with more than he intended. She almost smiled when he let out a weary sigh and settled back into his seat.

"You want to know *why* traitors turn against their own? Because they crave power. They plot and scheme, desperate to seize it for themselves, hoping to wield it against those of us who uphold the sacred plans of the Mothers. If the goddesses deemed them worthy, they would have been chosen. But they weren't. So, it falls to us to protect what's sacred. To protect *you*."

He gave her shoulder a single, reassuring squeeze before resuming his meal, and Elara couldn't help but feel dulled, like a blade that had lost its edge. Could the drive that fueled Fenlin and Godfrey be so simple, so painfully mundane, as mere lust for power? The thought of it scraped uncomfortably against her insides.

It was too neat, too convenient. There had to be more...

Her gaze trailed upward, locking onto Edgar as he sat across from her, a forkful of something unremarkable halfway to his mouth. There was a certain... artifice in his casual demeanor, a carefully constructed facade he wore as easily as his well-tailored clothes. It was a feeling that surged within her, a knowing without words. *He was masking something.*

His eyes flicked to hers, as if her sudden insight had summoned his gaze, and something stirred within her—subtle and undeniable. But when his hand closed over hers, a creeping numbness bled into her skin, crawling up her arm and flooding her veins. Her thoughts dulled, corners blunted, as if her mind were wading through heavy water. Blinking felt like dragging stone lids over her eyes, and the vibrant colors around her leeched into a wash of gray.

CHAPTER 8

A crisp breeze nipped at Elara's cheeks as she stepped beyond the citadel and into the garden. The sensation felt distant; her awareness cocooned in a fog that even the sharp bite of the coming winter could not pierce.

One hour—that was all the freedom Edgar granted her before she was expected to retire for the night. At least he had allowed her that much.

After dinner, he calmly informed her that the freedom she once took for granted would now be a luxury, doled out sparingly, and under strict conditions—for her safety, he claimed. Her deeds at the capitol, he had reminded her, were not without their repercussions.

As she wandered, she found herself measuring each breath, each heartbeat, each second slipping away like grains of sand in an hourglass. She sighed, trying to savor the gardens while she could, but everything around her seemed muted. *The flowers aren't singing today*, she thought, swaying with the breeze.

"Elara!"

Her name sliced through the quiet dusk, snapping her out of her thoughts. She turned, her heart skipping a beat at the sight of Avis.

"Come with me," Avis whispered, taking her hand and leading her down a rocky path, their shadows merging in the fading light. Everything around her seemed to blur, the lilac bushes speeding past as Avis guided her to a hidden glade. Here, the only sounds were the occasional chirp of a bird and the soft flicker of fireflies. In the center stood a weathered stone bench where Avis settled down, and Elara, with a trace of anxiety in her steps, sat beside her.

Warm hands cradled her face, and she closed her eyes, savoring the touch.

"That wicked man," Avis murmured, her voice a blend of anger and concern.

Then, Avis began to sing—a song Elara had never heard, in a language she didn't recognize. She furrowed her brow, trying to decipher the words, but the rhythm of Avis's song, its haunting melody, gradually pulled her deeper into the comfort of the Druid's hands.

Before she knew it, Elara couldn't even remember what had seemed so strange about the song in the first place.

"Here, chew on this."

The gentle command pulled her back. Her eyes blinked open to a small mushroom in her hand. Its cap was thick and densely layered, a cascade of soft, creamy white tendrils that gave it an almost fluffy appearance.

"What is it?"

"Lion's mane," Avis said, her voice steady as she carefully brought Elara's hand to her lips. "*Eat.*"

She popped the mushroom into her mouth. A rich, nutty flavor spread across her tongue, with a hint of fresh, rain-soaked earth. Slowly, the fog clouding her mind began to lift. Wide-eyed, she looked to Avis.

"She's back," Avis declared, twirling a strand of her hair around her finger.

"What—what happened to me?"

Avis offered a shrug that seemed to hold more weight than levity. "Knowing you, too much wine."

Elara's frown deepened. "No, it wasn't that," she murmured. Maybe it was a reaction to the eel...

"Well, you're all patched up now, thanks to that little mushroom," Avis said with a light sigh, her voice soft as she moved toward the ofche blossoms at the garden's edge. "I've talked your ear off about lion's mane mushrooms, haven't I? You'd think some of it would stick, but I guess not. Sometimes I wonder why I bother, but then, talking to you is a bit like talking to the moon—lovely, but not much for answers."

Elara watched as Avis massaged the oíche blossoms' delicate petals, each touch careful not to bruise. Avis was a passionate advocate for spreading these flowers, not only in the Sanct's gardens but throughout Hartling Forest. Known as nightflowers because they only bloomed under the full moon, their silver stamens, valuable in many potions and poultices, could only be harvested once a month. But Elmweavers like Avis knew the secret to making the petals open any time they wished.

She cupped the delicate pink blossom in her hands, her fingers brushing its petals with reverence. *"Druvakh."* The word didn't match the softness in Avis's tone or the tenderness with which she handled the flower, but it rippled with power—primal and ancient—weaving through the air like a song meant only for the blossom.

Elara rose from the bench and knelt beside the Druid, eyes fixed on the delicate petals trembling awake, catching faint glimmers of light along their silver stems. The moment Avis pulled her hands back, the oíche blossom's petals curled inward, almost shyly.

"That was beautiful," Elara murmured, a faint pang of jealousy twisting inside her.

Avis smiled, her eyes gleaming with quiet mischief. "Perhaps you'd like to try it."

Her heart skipped. "It's forbidden."

Avis's smile only widened. "And since when have you become a paragon of rule-following?"

Elara scoffed. "Well, given my impeccable track record, I'd hate to shock anyone with my sudden descent into lawlessness."

The Druid raised an eyebrow. "Yes, it would be a shame to ruin such a sterling reputation. But... think of the flowers. They might never recover."

She rolled her eyes. "Gods forbid I scandalize the floral community."

Avis's laughter rang out, her grin so infectious that Elara couldn't help but smile back. Being around Avis felt like stepping into a clearer, softer world. She didn't put on airs or pretend—Avis simply existed, purely and sincerely herself, and that honesty had a way of making everyone around her feel a little more real too. Elara often wondered if the Druid had any idea how much she depended on that simplicity.

"You're thinking very loudly, you know. I can practically hear your whinging."

Her mouth fell open in mock offense. "Can't a girl ponder in peace?" She was fairly certain Avis couldn't actually pluck thoughts from her mind...

Avis fiddled with her hair. "Should I raid Algernon's whiskey stash to keep them quiet, then? Seems to work wonders on you."

"That would be decidedly counterproductive."

Avis raised an eyebrow. "Oh, really? Because last time, you swore you'd rather drink bog water than endure a sober evening. I can't remember if that was before or after you tried to convince Dario and I that you spoke *fluent* squirrel."

She groaned, cheeks burning as she hid her face in her hands. "I swear, Edgar was right—you're a terrible influence."

The moment the priest's name left her lips, Avis quieted, and Elara snuck a peek at the Druid, finding her expression sour. None of the other Druids would dare show such open disapproval.

Elara's mouth quirked as she thought back to the last time they had filched a bottle of whiskey. Naturally, Edgar caught them—hardly a surprise, given they'd wrapped up the evening belting out ballads atop the bailey's roof. The ensuing punishment, harsh as it was, and the weeks they were barred from each other's company, somehow felt worth it.

A thoughtful expression shadowed Avis's face. "Just do it for me," she said, motioning to the flower again.

She sighed, the sound laced with all the dramatic resignation she could muster. She wasn't technically supposed to attempt casting ether —not that it made any difference. She'd tried once, back when she was naive enough to think it might actually work. Though, of course, it hadn't.

Avis, ever the optimist, took her sigh as consent and grabbed her hands, placing them over the flower. "Connect without touching," Avis instructed, as if it was the simplest thing in the world.

Summoning ether felt... unnatural. Wrong. But there was something in the way Avis looked at her, so steady and earnest, like she truly believed Elara could do this, that stirred something stubborn inside her. As Avis's voice rose again, chanting the ancient word, Elara took a breath and joined in.

Come on, little thing, she pleaded silently, a bit startled by just how much she wanted this to work. Out of the corner of her eye, Elara saw the flower in Avis's hand begin to bloom, its petals slowly unfurling as if lured by the first soft glow of starlight. But the flower under her own watch remained infuriatingly closed, refusing to so much as twitch. She'd told herself not to get her hopes up, but the sharp pang of disappointment cut deeper than she'd anticipated.

Avis's chant faded into the stillness, her flower folding in on itself as silence settled around them. But then—a faint golden flicker in the distance caught her eye, a tiny glimmer against the darkness.

Her mouth dropped open.

Silk sprites.

Dozens of them emerged from the forest, gliding toward them as dusk laid its golden blanket on the world. Her heart pounded in her chest as their radiant, whisper-thin forms danced like strands of satin spun from moonlight.

Avis's laughter rang out. She extended her hand, and Elara watched, perplexed, as the sprites twined their tiny forms around her fingers.

"How did you coax them from the wilds?" Elara breathed, wonder filling her voice. As though drawn by her intrigue, the sprites drifted toward her, a few weaving softly through her hair.

"*I* didn't lure them out."

Elara furrowed her brow, fingers brushing the sprite nestling just behind her ear—a soft, velvety whisper against her skin. She'd only seen sprites once before, as a child, and even then, she'd convinced herself they were just a figment of her overactive imagination. Sprites belonged to another age, back when Fae and humans roamed Latheria together, side by side.

Generations of stories said these wispy creatures were the chosen heralds of the Mothers. The old tales claimed that once, long ago, the Mothers didn't simply observe from some distant realm—they walked these very lands, their presence gracing every hill and grove, with sprites flitting in their wake.

While most dismissed such tales as mere fables, the Druids revered them as sacred truths. Every Druid child, given up by their earthly mothers, knew no warmth but that of the three goddesses they prayed to—their only Mothers, as they'd been taught from birth.

This unwavering devotion only strengthened their bond to the ancient stories. The silk sprites were like living remnants of those tales, silent witnesses to a time long past. No one quite knew if they stayed in the mortal realm of their own accord or if something bound them here against their will. The stories said they were drawn by intense emotions, flitting between the blurred edges of joy and sorrow, captivated by the tangled passions of mortal lives.

But still... what on earth could have drawn them here, now? Surely, her own heartache wasn't enough.

"I noticed you wearing the colors of mourning," Avis noted softly. "Fenlin was dear to you, but it might not be wise to grieve him so openly."

She blinked, following Avis's gaze down to the gray folds of her dress. *Oh.* She nearly laughed. Beatrice had dressed her in mourning garb.

That crafty little wretch.

Elara scowled, feeling equal parts grudging respect and irritation, and leaned back against the cool grass with a tired sigh. "It wasn't intentional. Beatrice was playing one of her games, and I walked straight into it. I didn't realize the old bat had it in her to be so devious."

Avis snorted. "Never underestimate her. She's far nastier than she looks." The surrounding air filled with quiet contemplation, only broken by the fluttering of sprites and the soft whisper of the wind. "How are you holding up?" Avis asked, her voice laced with understanding and a hint of already knowing the answer.

Elara's eyelids fluttered shut, memories pressing down heavily. "I need to understand, Avis. If you know something, please... don't keep it from me." Her eyes snapped open, and she tensed, anticipating mind games, manipulation—everything she had come to expect from others. But instead, Avis nodded, meeting her gaze squarely.

"I often come here to listen to the whispers of the stars and the tales of the moon," Avis murmured softly. "They speak loudest when the night is deep."

She extended her hand, offering a small stone. As Elara's fingers enclosed it, a surge of intense warmth shot through the stone, prompting her to jolt and toss it between her hands as if it were a glowing ember.

"This is…" Elara managed, her voice quivering from both the surprise and the temperature of the stone.

"A moonstone," Avis said, her eyes never leaving Elara's. "Though, not just any. This one likes to sing."

Careful to shield her skin with the fabric of her sleeve, Elara examined the small gem. It *was* a moonstone, its surface dancing with blues and purples, a luminescent entity echoing the celestial body it was named after. She had read quite a bit about them in *Celestial Alchemy: A Compendium of Astral Gemology.*

But moonstones were supposed to be cold.

"What did you do to it?"

A flicker of uncertainty passed through Avis's eyes. She looked away, the sprinkle of freckles on her nose scrunching. But as quickly as the doubt appeared, she seemed to push it aside, replacing it with a steely glint as she met Elara's gaze once more.

"There have been disturbances. The land, the sky, and even the stars whisper of unnatural forces at play. It's as if the very fabric of our realm is being twisted. Stretched thin…"

"Stretched thin?"

Avis's voice dropped to a murmur. "I've heard tales of shadows moving in the night, of stars blinking out of existence, only to return moments later, as if obscured by something unseen. It's as if the boundaries between worlds are weakening, and something is trying to break through."

A cold unease settled over Elara. Her gaze flickered to the sprites, their delicate dance painting golden whispers in the twilight.

"What does it all mean?"

Avis sighed heavily. "I don't know. But after hearing about Fenlin and Godfrey's mad attempt with your blood, I can't shake the feeling that he might've known something—seen something in Arinthel. Something that ties his desperation to this unrest."

Elara's fingers brushed over the moonstone as if it might provide some clarity. She struggled to find the link between the two, but then, she wasn't the one who could decipher the language of the stars.

Avis, perceptive as always, caught the subtle crease of Elara's brow and the faint twitch of her lips, lifting her own brow in silent challenge. "Life, as you well know, isn't always linear." A sardonic smile played on her lips. "Actions create echoes, and those echoes have been resonating louder. Many of us Druids sense it—those ripples."

A particular Druid carved its way into Elara's thoughts. "Branwen?" The name escaped her lips like a barbed whisper.

Avis smirked. "Exactly. Though trust him to muddle through in the most vexing way possible."

"I just..." Weariness settled into her bones. "Why didn't Fen and Godfrey just come to me? If they had asked for my help, I would have given it freely." The words spilled out, the ones that had been circling in her mind endlessly.

Avis captured Elara's hand, her fingers giving a reassuring squeeze. "They couldn't have asked you. In Ulrith, trust is a commodity more precious than gold. Even the bonds of blood are not sacrosanct; suspicions can turn brother against brother." She exhaled, a weary sigh blending with the cold air around them. "Your hands are clean. Fenlin chose his path. It was his doing, not yours."

Elara clung to Avis's hand, searching her face. "Any news of Godfrey?"

A flicker of pain crossed Avis's features. "They imprisoned him."

In the Pit was what she wasn't saying out loud. The only place Osin threw traitors and sympathizers.

"Then he's as good as dead," Elara whispered, her voice threading through the air like a wisp.

Avis stayed quiet, providing neither comfort nor contradiction. The silence that settled was thick and suffocating, making the sprites fluttering nearby seem even more fleeting, their delicate light flickering like the last whispers of a world slowly fading away.

CHAPTER 9

"Are you sorting, or just lost in fantasies up there?" Algernon's voice, warm and slightly amused, floated up to Elara as she perched atop the ladder, her hands delicately placing an ancient scroll back in its proper place among the towering shelves.

She rolled her eyes. "Only dreaming of a better filing system, *sir.*"

Dust motes danced in the shafts of golden sunlight that poured through the archive's lofty arched windows, itching Elara's nose. The room was bathed in a soft, buttery light.

She shifted her weight on the groaning ladder, taking in the labyrinth of towering bookshelves that surrounded her. "It really is a disaster up here," she muttered to herself, pushing aside a bulky chest with a determined grunt. She was making room for a new addition, *Herbal Alchemy: The Potency of Nature's Elixir.*

Algernon muttered something indecipherable, his attention firmly anchored back to the task of incessant scribbling, crafting the lines of his latest manuscript.

The air was heavy with the scent of parchment as she descended through the stacks that housed Latheria's illustrious history. She passed through the ages of Osin, the rise and fall of the empires, and the detailed accounts of those who lived through the war. She skimmed past the earliest historical accounts—the tales of the Mothers' intervention that led to the separation of the Fae and mortals.

Elara wrinkled her brow. "Are you sure you want it here?" It seemed like an odd spot for *Herbal Alchemy,* but then, Algernon's way of organizing books lacked any discernible pattern or logic.

He peered over his glasses from behind the mountains of parchment that littered his ancient desk. With a gentle nod, he said, "Ah, yes, kindly set it there, right next to *Ethnobotany of the Fae.* It should feel quite at home."

Elara's gaze swept back over the mess of scrolls and tomes strewn before her. Her eyes paused on titles that delved deep into the mysteries of the Fae: *Fauna of Dusk and Starlight: A Comprehensive Study, The Great Divide: Historical Analysis of the Cataclysm That Sundered Realms, Tír na nÓg: Scholarly Insights into the Fae Realm,* and *The Ether Exodus: Tracing the Fae's Theft and Humanity's Reclamation.*

Elara had pored over those volumes, absorbing them voraciously at one time. *The Ether Exodus* particularly held her interest. These texts explored the catastrophic period known as the Great Divide, when the Mothers split the realms apart to protect the distinct species from one another. According to these scholars, it was then that the Fae stripped all ether from the land. This act wasn't just theft; it was a devastation that marked the beginning of a slow decay across the world.

Initially, the changes were subtle shifts in weather patterns, but soon they escalated to widespread famine as the earth turned barren, the seas grew toxic, and even the gentlest creatures became savage, driven mad by hunger and despair.

Beside *The Ether Exodus* lay a thick, well-worn volume that Elara despised above all: *Osin's Sacred Journey: Beseeching the Goddesses for Ether.*

Unlike the scholarly works that surrounded it, this book dripped with religious zeal. It lacked citations, cross-references, or any semblance of rigorous research—it was purely the proclaimed word of one man, accepted as divine revelation. And yet, everyone revered it. They wept over its pages, and *gods,* she'd bet some probably clung to it in their sleep.

Elara despised it most because she was mentioned in it, reducing her to an object within its narrative. She was described as merely a vessel, a relic, glossed over as if she were *nothing*—a reflection, she realized bitterly, of how Osin truly viewed her. It shouldn't have come as a shock, but sometimes, she admitted, she could be naive.

"Has something special caught your fancy?" Algernon called out, adjusting his position to get a better look at her.

"Not at all, nothing up here catches my interest," Elara replied, pushing *Osin's Sacred Journey* to the back of the shelf, out of sight. She quickly arranged the rest of the *Herbal Alchemy* volumes where the old Druid had instructed, then turned back to face him.

"Is there anything else you need, or can I leave now?" Elara asked, impatience coloring her voice. Not that she had pressing plans—pathetically enough, her evening's highlight was to watch the equinox festival from the solitude of her tower. She couldn't help but crave the sight of the celebrations, the distant laughter, and the spicy scent of the harvest that seemed to ride the wind straight to her each year.

Algernon flashed a quick smile. "Actually, if you could take a look at these calculations before you go..."

Elara's eyes flicked to the stack of parchment he pointed to—star charts, half-finished graphs, and the unmistakable scrolls of divination scattered about his desk. She nearly sighed, biting it back as she glanced over the mess. "Fine," she said with a tight smile. "Whatever you need."

Elara climbed back down the ladder and looked over his work. Algernon was focused on graphing star patterns—he'd mentioned it in passing a few days ago—but his enthusiasm for astromantic theory often led to careless mistakes in the numbers. And that's where she came in. Elara had always been quick with math, quicker than most, and her reputation had spread through the sanct. From scribes to astromancers, they sought her out, handing over their half-done work, hoping for a second set of eyes.

She set the scrolls down on one of the reading tables, skimming the first set of numbers. It didn't take long for her to spot the error. He had miscalculated the angle of the star's declination in relation to the lunar cycle. A simple mistake, but one that would throw off the entire chart. Her mind worked quickly, automatically correcting the equations in her head. "You've offset the meridian by three degrees," she said, not bothering to hide the mild exasperation in her voice. "If you plot the stars based on this, you'll end up with an entirely different constellation."

Algernon blinked up at her. "Really? I could've sworn…"

Elara sighed. "If you'd double-check your base calculations, you wouldn't need me to fix these for you every other week."

But truthfully, she didn't mind. There was something calming about numbers. Equations never lied, never twisted themselves into the unpredictable mess that people did.

She glanced back at Algernon, who had already begun adjusting the graphs. She turned to leave, but his voice stopped her.

"Oh, one more thing." He flashed that charming smile again, the kind that made him seem a bit too innocent. "If you could sort out these scrolls before you go, I'd be most grateful."

Elara's eyes drifted to the mountain of parchment he had clearly pulled down in a fit of inspiration and promptly abandoned. She forced a smile. "Of course," she muttered, knowing she couldn't exactly say no. Her fingers flexed as she gathered the scrolls, already mapping out the fastest way to organize them in her head.

She climbed back up, scaling the towering shelves. Navigating the archives by ladder was the quickest way, and she hardly minded how mad she might appear, flying through the stacks like a bat out of hell.

With a thrust of her foot against the side of the sturdy shelf, Elara sent the rolling ladder hurtling down the row of towering bookcases. The screech of metal wheels echoed through the vast archives, as stray curls, escapees from her hastily made braid, danced wildly around her face. The sensation, that brief thrill of flight, stirred something deep within, and a small, irrepressible smirk curled her lips.

But the rush of wind against her face, that intoxicating rush, was abruptly soured by a familiar, cold sting of ether.

With barely any time to react, the ladder jerked to a sudden stop, sending a shock through her spine. Elara's fingers tightened around the rung, a desperate grip to keep from tumbling. But as her body jerked, the divination scrolls she was carrying slipped from her grasp. She help-lessly watched as Algernon's meticulously arranged work scattered, his efforts undone in a heartbeat.

Elara took a deep breath to calm the trembling in her hands, the twinge of anger simmering in her gray eyes. She didn't need to turn around to know who was responsible.

"Branwen," she hissed, spitting the name out like a curse. "Have your little predictions bored you *so* much that you've taken to playing god with my *life*?"

Branwen stepped out from behind the towering bookshelf, his smirk sharp and joyless. "Why would any god bother meddling in your affairs when you've turned self-destruction into an art form?"

Elara's jaw tensed, his words striking a raw nerve. Her hands clenched around the ladder's rungs, knuckles bleaching under the pressure, as she wrestled with the impulse to retaliate. Instead, she drew in a deep, steadying breath, and began her descent, each step down the ladder a swallowed comeback, until her feet finally met the solid ground below.

"What exactly is your issue with me?"

His contempt seemed too deep to be random. *Could it be envy?* His devotion to the Mothers bordered on the pathological, spending every day and night bound in ceaseless prayers, like a pendulum swinging to the same haunting rhythm. The more she considered it, the more suspicion crept in. It was a gamble, but she was never one to shy away from playing her hand when intuition called.

"Don't tell me you're jealous." She laughed as a cruel smile played on her lips. "Afraid the Mothers favor *me*, the wayward child, over their ever-devoted son?" There was a flicker in his eyes, a crack in his otherwise stoic facade. She couldn't help but push harder, the words flowing like a sharp, sweet poison. "Perhaps, like your own mother, they too find you lacking."

The fury that surged across his features provided all the confirmation she required. Yet, her fleeting triumph swiftly curdled as his face contorted into a snarl, pale with rage.

With a vicious flick, Branwen unleashed a tendril of ether toward her.

The sheer audacity of his attack stunned her into stillness, leaving her unable to dodge in time. Not that it would have made a difference—Branwen's bond was with the wind.

Around her, the air thickened, charged with repulsive threads that wrapped around her, constricting her lungs, turning each breath into a struggle. His ether smelled of rot, a sickly sweetness that slithered down her throat, leaving a poisonous trail in its wake.

Branwen's laughter, cold and mocking, echoed around her. With each step he took, she stepped back, a dance of predator and prey until she felt the spines of ancient books dig into her back.

"You think you're *so* fucking clever?" he sneered, leaning in close, the strands of his greasy black hair brushing against her face. "I know truths about you, secrets that would make your skin crawl. You are *nothing*. Less than nothing."

Tears stung Elara's eyes. The weight on her chest, the thick smog in her lungs—darkness began to nibble at the edges of her vision, the last strands of consciousness fraying when the world shifted beneath her in a jarring lurch.

They both crashed to the ground, and through tear-blurred eyes, Elara watched as thick vines surged, yanking Branwen from her side. With a violent snap, they flung him across the room into a bookcase. He hit it hard, the thud echoing through the silent archives. Books tumbled from their shelves, each hitting him with sharp, punishing thwacks, accumulating around him like a verdict rendered by the archives themselves.

But it wasn't archives.

"You imbecile," Algernon's voice rang out, carrying a weight of disappointment that seemed to chill the very air around them.

Elara blinked hard, trying to clear her vision. She could just make out the elder Druid. His usually tranquil eyes were fierce and directed squarely at Branwen. She looked around to see the once-organized section on the flora of the southern regions in a state of disarray. Books that Elara had seen cradled in Algernon's hands, cherished and revisited time and time again, lay scattered—their spines broken.

She steeled herself for the Arch Scribe's reaction to the devastation of his beloved collection, anticipating a tempest to echo his earlier intervention. Yet, when she glanced at him, he met her with an indifference that left her more unnerved than any outburst might have.

Just a single tome teetered precariously on the shelf above Branwen, wavering as if undecided about joining its fallen brethren. With a subtle flick of his wrist, Algernon summoned a gentle wisp of ether. Vines sprang from the sturdy bookshelf, delicately encircling the lone book. They nudged it gently, carefully orchestrating its descent until it landed with a definitive thud atop Branwen's head.

"There's a time to challenge and a time to refrain, young acolyte," Algernon said calmly, his eyes observing Branwen as he groaned, cradling himself. "True wisdom lies in discerning the difference."

Despite the lingering bitter taste of Branwen's ether in her mouth, a smirk crept onto Elara's lips.

Algernon turned his gaze to her, the intensity that had previously marked his expression giving way to a softer, gentler demeanor. "On your feet, child," he instructed, offering his hand.

A tingling sensation spread through her fingertips as she gripped his hand, and her face twisted involuntarily. Algernon's ether was distinctively pungent. While all ether carried a tainted aura, his was overwhelming, redolent of the earth in its final throes—a putrid blend of rotting leaves and mold, sickly and decayed.

He ushered her away, his voice cold and crisp as he flung a final instruction over his shoulder. "Attend to your mess. Once you have set things right, come find me. We shall then speak of your... penance."

With each step she took, the air around her seemed to lighten, the dense fog in her mind starting to clear as thoughts raced through her head. It struck her—Algernon had leapt into action to save her, abandoning his beloved books to disarray. Why would he risk them for her? He had never displayed such care for her welfare before. Why start now?

With measured steps, Algernon guided her deeper into the sprawling labyrinth of the archives. They soon reached a dimly lit alcove. An ornate desk sat bathed in the soft glow of enchanted lanterns nestled amid the towering bookshelves. Potted plants seemed to spring up from the piles of books, their leaves casting dappled shadows in the flickering light.

"Please, have a seat," Algernon offered softly, easing himself into his aged wooden rocking chair. But a cat was curled up on the cushioned chair intended for her. Its wonky eyes lazily glanced up at her, quietly asserting its territory, while its tail twitched with mild interest.

"Biscuit," Algernon called with a calm but authoritative tone, "would you kindly make some space for the Hallowed?"

Biscuit meowed, stretching out slowly before giving her a reproachful look and finally moving aside.

Algernon's lips quirked slightly as Elara settled into the orange-fur coated chair. He clasped his hands together thoughtfully before beginning. "Your efforts these past days have been most beneficial," he began, nodding toward the orderly stack of scrolls between them. "Thanks to your assistance, I've managed to advance my research significantly." He leaned back. "In another life, you would have made an excellent scribe."

There was a hint of warmth in his voice, a twinkle of kindness, but all Elara felt was a sharp pang of bitterness. Long ago, life's circumstances crushed those dreams, those "what ifs." Why pine for things that could never be?

She attempted to keep her face impassive, but Algernon's gaze was discerning, almost knowing. Her mind scrambled as she tried to fill the awkward silence with some semblance of a polite response, but he interrupted her thoughts, producing a delicate piece of paper from his robe. "A gift," he murmured, sliding it across the table.

Elara raised an eyebrow. "What's this?"

He leaned back, the ambient light catching the deep lines of his face. "Consider it the beginning of understanding your own tale."

She huffed a humorless laugh. "I know my story. Forged from the cosmos, blessed by the Mothers, destined to stand but forbidden to wield." The rehearsed verses flowed from her; words she had chanted, heard, and internalized countless times.

Algernon's chuckle cut through her recited lament.

"What?" she retorted, the sharpness unintentional. But he remained unperturbed, offering a kind smile, while the small piece of parchment sat innocuously between them.

She snatched it up, her annoyance flaring as she struggled to make sense of the hastily scribbled script. It was barely legible, requiring her to pore over it three times before its meaning finally sank in. Her eyes snapped up to Algernon, wide with surprise.

"You'll require a pair of Avis's robes," he announced, a twinkle of amusement in his gaze.

Elara sprang from her seat, the stool falling behind her. "Have you lost your mind?" Her voice was a hushed whisper, her eyes darting between him and the illicit message. The loops and scrawls became clearer every time her eyes passed over the words. *"If you still seek answers, they will find you when the sun and moon embrace. Forgive me, Godfrey."*

Elara's thoughts swirled. *Mabon*—the day the sun and moon stood shoulder to shoulder in the sky. *The harvest celebration.*

"How do I know this is real?" she whispered.

"It is," was his placid reply.

Her gaze pierced his. "Why would you help me?"

Algernon reclined in his seat, fingers thoughtfully combing through his gray beard. "Let's just say every tale has its twists, and I'm rather keen to see yours."

A shiver of apprehension crawled across Elara's skin, a silent warning she couldn't shake. It was unheard of, even reckless, to venture beyond the Sanct without her usual guard. Yet, here she was, tempted to place her trust in the old Druid against her better judgment. Fenlin's recent death and Avis's cryptic hints had left her with too many questions. And then there was Godfrey. Had he really sent a message from the Pit? Or had he escaped? She needed answers.

"I would be detected the moment I approached the barrier."

A sly grin graced his features. "Indeed, you would," he said, unfolding his hand to reveal a jasper ring. "But not while wearing *this*."

CHAPTER 10

If Elara ended up on the wrong side of this gamble, she'd have only herself to blame.

Her gaze swept over the line of workers before her, a slow-moving snake of weary bodies eager to find rest beyond the Sanct's heavy gates.

And there, at the very end, stood the barrier.

The ward throbbed with energy, a massive curtain stretching skyward, almost grazing the fledgling stars. As the sun dipped lower, rich purples, fiery oranges, and molten golds played across its expanse, turning the barrier into a vibrant, living mural.

Elara allowed herself precisely one hour of panic after she stormed out of the archives, Algernon's ring a cold weight in her clenched fist as she made her way to her room. She oscillated between caution and daring, measuring every risk against its potential reward, until she had caught her reflection in her small, cracked mirror.

The question that stared back at her had been simple. *What type of person am I?*

A dutiful puppet pretending at rebellion, or someone willing to risk it all for a taste of freedom? She wanted to believe she was more. That she wasn't just a captive bowing to the whims of her captors. But the truth was... she hadn't dared to break free. Not really. Not when it mattered. Because Osin's wards weren't the only thing trapping her. Fear, doubt—they held her just as tightly. Elara had stared at the ring in her hand, wondering if she could really claim to be a prisoner if she wasn't willing to take the risk.

She might not know exactly what awaited her, but she was certain of one thing: she had to make a choice. And if everything fell apart because of it? So be it.

What else was a prisoner supposed to do when handed a key? The real question wasn't whether she would succeed. It was whether she could live with herself if she didn't try.

The Autumnal Equinox—Mabon—was in full swing, and time was not on her side.

A cool breeze played through her unbound hair, mussing it into buoyant curls and carrying with it the spicy fragrance of the harvest. Her heart skipped a beat, and she tugged her hood lower over her face. The emerald and onyx robes she pilfered from the Druids' laundry were snug, but with some pulling and adjusting, she managed to smooth them over her gown. Algernon had suggested she borrow robes from Avis, but something inside her hesitated. Deep down, she felt it was safer to keep Avis out of the loop. The idea of dragging someone she cared about into her mess...

Elara's throat tightened. She was a walking storm—*a curse.*

Fenlin's death was proof of that.

"Excuse me, miss, could you look at this for me? Just while we wait?" The hesitant voice came from behind Elara.

Turning, she saw one of Edgar's scullery maids, a young woman with anxious eyes, gently supporting her wrist. The way she held it, with her fingers gingerly wrapped and a wince with each subtle movement, hinted strongly at a sprain.

Curse it to the Void. She was wearing Greenheart robes.

This woman thought she was a healer.

"I'm so sorry." Elara's voice wavered, and she cleared her throat. "I was given strict orders from the Arch Healer to... give my ether a break. I've overdone it today, and it isn't safe for me to overexert myself." Her heart pounded in her chest, the lie tasting bitter on her tongue. She remembered hearing a Druid mumble something similar months ago, but she had no idea if it was even true.

The woman's hopeful expression crumbled, her shoulders slumping in disappointment. She glanced down, her fingers twisting the edge of her shawl, but she didn't question Elara's words.

"But make sure to elevate it, wrap it tightly, and take some willow bark for the pain and inflammation," Elara advised, her voice steadying. "If you can, see a healer in town. Here." She reached into her pocket and pulled out a gold coin, the one she had brought just in case. "Take this."

The woman looked at her strangely, her brow creasing in confusion. Elara pushed the coin into her good hand, feeling the roughness of the woman's calloused fingers, and turned quickly before she could figure out who she was. Gods, if she got caught this quickly, she would never live down the shame. She was lucky Edgar's constant smothering had kept her identity somewhat vague, even here within the Sanct. And by some stroke of luck, his ravens were nowhere to be seen. Still, this brief respite hardly softened the sharp twist of dread knotted deep within her. She unwittingly nibbled at the skin around her nails and twirled her ring, trying to calm the nervous energy bubbling up inside her.

The ring felt like death on her skin. When she had slipped it onto her thumb after leaving the citadel, it seemed to wake to her touch, a living thing entangling its rot through her veins. How did anyone bear it? The moment she put it on, she wanted it off. But Algernon had insisted she wear it until she was well past the barrier. *My ring will cloak you, get you past the wards specifically set up to keep you in.*

Elara wasn't surprised to hear Osin had set up extra safeguards to monitor her movements, but it still made her stomach churn. She glanced at the ring again, its dark metal seeming to pulse with a life of its own. Grimacing, she buried her hand within her robe's pocket, her fingers brushing against Godfrey's note. Soon she would be far from here and could rip it off, but for now, she needed to focus.

The closer she nudged to the portcullis, the clearer the guards came into view. They would know her. She was certain of that. But maybe the ring would shield her as Algernon had promised. If she kept her hood up and her face down, maybe she could—

A booming, drunken laugh made her blood run cold. Lorien.

Of course, it would be him.

Lorien was already three sheets to the wind, a flask swinging loosely from his hand. His loud, raucous laugh echoed off the stone walls as he barked at something one of his comrades had said, slapping his thigh like a damn fool.

Maybe he wouldn't notice her. His eyes were already glazed over; he probably couldn't see a foot in front of him.

With each slow, steady step closer in the line, Elara's heart thrashed violently against her ribs. She kept her eyes firmly on her shoes, daring not even a fleeting glance upward. But then, from the corner of her eye, she spotted boots approaching—boots that unmistakably belonged to one of the guards.

She was so fucked.

"Look sharp, you lot, or I'll have you emptying your pockets faster than you can say 'thief,'" Lorien's words were thick with drink and he staggered slightly. "I wouldn't put it past any of them to sneak a silver cup or two under their rags."

The other guards cackled like idiots, obviously too drunk on equinox cheer to realize they were still on duty. It was the harvest, sure, but one would think they'd at least *pretend* to be sober until they staggered out of the Sanct. Elara could practically hear Edgar's head exploding from here. His idea of a slap on the wrist usually involved less wrist and more slap. Yet, oddly enough, these men seemed utterly unfazed by the prospect.

Lorien sauntered closer, his hand reaching out to toy with the tassel on a Soothsayer's robe in front of Elara. The woman stiffened visibly.

"So, any visions about tonight, love? Think you can predict our chances together?" Lorien snickered, a sneer tugging at his lips as the Soothsayer yanked the tassel from his grasp.

Undeterred, he sauntered up to Elara. "No matter, I suppose my odds with a pious seer are slim at best. But a greenie," he slurred, stepping close enough for Elara to feel his boozy breath. She lowered her chin, a bead of sweat trailing down her spine. "Everyone knows greenies are accommodating. Healers have such tender hands, after all."

Elara's heart leapt to her throat as Lorien reached out toward her. Her instincts screamed for her to run, to duck away and disappear.

Maybe he wouldn't notice it was her if she bolted; maybe she try again once he had left his post.

She spun on her heel, but Lorien was quicker, his grip firm on the back of her arm. "Where do you think you're going—"

"Ah, there you are."

Elara's breath hitched, her heart pounding as she looked up to find Dario before her, his expression stern. He glanced at her briefly, his concern palpable, before his eyes fixed sharply on Lorien.

"I was just coming to relieve you of your duty." Dario's voice was calm yet carried an undeniable authority.

Lorien grunted, his grip on Elara's arm tightening painfully. "Captain, I was just ensuring this greenie hadn't pocketed any forbidden herbs or potions."

"That is utterly unnecessary. Release the Greenheart, Lorien. Now."

Elara sensed the conflicting tension in Lorien's grasp. His hold tightened, then loosened, clearly struggling with obedience, before finally, begrudgingly, he let his hand fall away.

"Yes, Captain." Lorien's response was clipped, his frustration evident as he stormed off, slapping a comrade on the back before disappearing through the barrier and out of sight.

Elara's body trembled uncontrollably, sweat beading on her forehead. That had been close—too damn close.

"May I have a moment of your time, miss?" Dario asked, his gaze fixed ahead, not meeting her eyes. *Mother save her.*

Dario's hand was firm on her arm as he swiftly pulled her out of line. They moved quickly across the bailey, dodging between clusters of chatting guards and busy servants. Without a word, he steered her behind the ancient stone wall that marked the boundary between the noisy courtyard and the gardens, hidden from prying eyes.

"So, when was I supposed to find out you were making a run for it? After you'd vanished, or when Edgar inevitably caught up with you?"

"I don't see why you'd suddenly start caring now. You haven't bothered to see me in days."

She knew her words were petty. He had promised to check on her, a promise he hadn't kept, and it stung more than she wanted to admit.

Exhaustion etched into his features. "I tried to see you, El. But you were right, Edgar had the Sanct locked down tight. No one could get in or out except for Beatrice." Elara's brow furrowed. She knew Edgar was overly cautious, but this was extreme. "After that, he tasked me with overseeing the city's patrols." Dario's explanation was casual, but his eyes told a different story.

"What happened?"

"Nothing significant." He ran a hand through his hair. "But it's clear Edgar's preparing for some kind of threat. He heightened security measures, tripling surveillance on the festival to mitigate potential risks."

A knot of dread twisted in Elara's stomach. Could Edgar possibly know about her plans? No. If he did, he would have already stormed into her room and sealed her away indefinitely. This had to be about something else... "Has he given you any reason for his nerves?"

As Captain, Dario would typically be the first to know of any external threats. But he simply shook his head. "I believe it's more intuition than evidence driving his caution. His ravens have taken to perching in every corner of the city, and he's dispatched an additional flock to scour the Hartling Forest just to be safe."

That explained the absence of ravens in the courtyard.

Elara closed her eyes briefly, trying to calm her racing heart. This plan was doomed. With Edgar increasing patrols and all his ravens deployed, she'd be spotted in an instant.

Dario touched her arm, his eyes narrowing as if really seeing her for the first time since they'd started talking. His eyes lingered on her disguise, a smirk slowly forming on his lips. "What are you wearing? Don't tell me Avis is trying to indoctrinate you."

Despite herself, her lips twitched into a smile. "As if the *Hallowed* could ever join such ranks."

His eyebrows climbed higher, a spark of mischief lighting up his gaze. "What's this, then? Playing out one of your hidden fantasies? The virtuous Druid waiting at the gates, longing for a roguish knight to whisk her away?"

She smacked his arm with a quick flick of her wrist, drawing a theatrical wince from him. "You're insufferable," she scolded. "Of all times, you choose *now* to joke?"

But Dario's amusement faded quickly as he noticed her exposed hand, where Algernon's ring shimmered in the setting sun. His expression turned deadly serious; his eyes wide as they settled back on her. "Where did you get that?"

"Does it really matter?"

Dario's face paled. "Forget that you *stole* someone's ring and guards are likely out there right now looking for it—for *you*." She started to shake her head, but he cut her off, his tone growing more urgent. "This ring's power isn't enough to get past all the security measures. There are protocols, safeguards in place..." His voice trailed off, his expression contorting as if the words caused him physical pain. "By dawn, you'll be in chains, and *I'll* be the one forced to drag you back in them..."

He shook his head as if to rid himself of the haunting vision. But one of his statements stood out to her.

"How long would it take Edgar to notice my absence?"

He raked a hand down his face. "Maybe a few hours... at best."

Elara's voice softened to almost a whisper. "That could work."

Dario's mouth opened, perhaps to chide her again, but the crunch of footsteps nearby cut him off. Instantly his hand clasped hers, tugging her further behind the wall, to the very edge of the courtyard where the protective wards hummed softly. Pressing a finger to his lips, he drew her close, her body pressed against his. She could feel his heart pounding against her chest, a rapid thud echoing her own. As the footsteps gradually receded, Dario exhaled a heavy sigh of relief, dipping his head until his forehead rested gently against hers.

"Why do you want to leave?"

The question hung in the air, so naive it almost made her scream. Her disbelief must have been painted across her face because it took him only a moment to catch the absurdity of his question, and with a sheepish twist of his lips, he withdrew, shoving his hands into the safety of his pockets.

"All I need is a handful of hours."

His eyes sharpened. "For?"

A sigh caught in her throat. She felt torn between confiding in him and protecting him from the web of her plans. "There's someone I need to meet."

His expression morphed from confusion to outright betrayal,

leaving his mouth agape in shock—a sight so unexpected that she nearly laughed. "It's not what you're thinking."

"El, for the love of all that's sacred, speak plainly."

She sighed, struggling to find the right words. "This is my mess to handle. I don't want you getting tangled up in it. We're... well, I'd like to think we're friends..."

That word lingered in the air, weighted with everything they had left unsaid. What exactly were they to each other? Their relationship was a patchwork of stolen moments and charged looks. Could a handful of whispered conversations and one close night really mean they were friends? She wasn't sure. She wasn't even certain she knew what true friendship looked like. Is a friend someone who shields you from the harsh realities of life? Or is it someone who dives into the thick of it with you?

Out of everyone close to her, Dario and Avis were the two she might consider friends. But both had watched her suffer and did nothing. They never rebuked the Lord Sovereign's abuse or spoke against him. Sure, they checked on her, made sure she was okay, but they never really helped her or validated her feelings. Was that friendship? Maybe she didn't understand the term because she had no real experience. Maybe this was what friendship looked like. She knew they had their own lives to think of and protect, and she would never want them to jeopardize themselves. She just wished... she didn't know. For something more?

The shift in her emotions must have been clear on her face, for Dario closed the space between them. He tilted his head, attempting to meet her gaze. "Elara," he murmured, the word holding more weight than a mere name. "Let's get one thing straight. You and I? We're friends. In every sense of the word. Trust it. If you trust nothing else."

Warmth blossomed within her, radiating outward, seeking the icy shards that had encased her heart since Fenlin's death. She felt it begin to thaw the frozen fragments, drawing the pieces of her fractured self closer. A smile spread across her lips. They were friends. It wasn't about the grand gestures or daring rescues, but perhaps, in his own way, Dario's subtle acts of kindness were his method of extending a hand in the darkness, to let her know she wasn't alone.

"Good," she whispered, her grin mirroring his.

"Friends share..." His words were light and teasing, but the look in his eyes was not.

Elara paused, her gaze tracing the familiar contours of his face that had become dear to her—the curve of his full lips, the sharp line of his nose, and the warmth radiating from his honey-brown eyes, always so open, and kind. Like Avis, he warranted shielding from the shadows that perpetually trailed her. But he already knew about the ring...

Before she could think better of it, she found herself spilling the sequence of recent events: Fenlin's betrayal, Avis's caution, the cryptic note from Godfrey, and the unexpected aid from Algernon.

He listened raptly, his body becoming unnaturally still, especially when she brought up Algernon. "Algernon is not to be trusted. He has never been the altruistic type."

"I know that," Elara acknowledged. "But I *need* to pursue this. You can either stand with me or move aside, but either way, I'm going."

He sighed deeply. "This is utter madness."

"The real madness," she retorted, her voice cracking like a whip, "is what's being inflicted upon me. It's the madness of Fenlin, so desperate to take my blood that he risked *everything*!" Her voice wavered, but she willed calm into her veins. "I need to know why."

Dario froze, the tension draining away as his eyes melted into something soft—something achingly desperate. "You're going to get yourself killed, El. Or worse."

Her laugh echoed, hollow and lifeless. "What fate could be worse than walking through life as if I'm already dead?"

A weighted pause hung in the air as he seemed to absorb her words. His throat bobbed, the muscles in his neck tense, but his eyes never left hers. "A fate where you lose the chance to see how beautiful life can still be, even after pain."

She thought back to what he had told her. Losing his family, his village, his home. He had endured so much, his words laced with the weight of his experiences. And yet...

She gave him a small, sad smile. "If pain becomes the lens through which all beauty is seen, does it not taint everything?" Her words seemed to crush him in a way that made her wonder how she could have ever doubted his friendship. With a sigh, she reached for his hand.

"Seeing beauty in suffering is a luxury I cannot afford, especially when it doesn't erase the scars. Why should I trust it not to inflict more?"

"El—"

"Pain is the only truth I know, Dario," she stated firmly. "This isn't up for debate. I'm going, no matter how you feel about it."

For a heartbeat he remained silent, his gaze sweeping over her as if he were trying to decipher secrets hidden beneath layers of steel. But there were no secrets, no shadows lurking behind her resolve, and something in his eyes shifted as this truth settled between them.

He smiled, a flicker of amusement that didn't quite touch his eyes. "Guess I'm coming with you, then; someone needs to ensure you navigate this with a semblance of elegance."

CHAPTER II

"Stay close and keep your head down."

Elara gave a quick nod to Dario, her heart pounding as they slipped from behind the stone wall. The queue had vanished; only the deepening shadows remained as the sun dipped below the horizon, casting long, eerie shadows across the ground.

They approached the guards briskly, Dario taking the lead with a confident stride. "When's the next shift change?"

"Five minutes, Captain," one of the guards replied, his voice wobbling as he struggled to sound sober.

"You're relieved. I'll stand watch until the others take over," Dario responded dismissively, and a chorus of thanks and festive well wishes followed, with several guards mentioning they'd have a drink waiting for him at The Fish whenever he could join them.

After the last of the guards had drifted away, Elara raised an eyebrow at him. "The Fish?"

He flashed a mischievous wink. "It's a den of debauchery. We could always skip the plan and head there instead." Her expression flatlined, unamused, and he laughed. "Ready?" He gestured toward the shimmering ward.

A knot tightened in Elara's throat, but she managed a determined nod, fingers nervously twisting the ring on her finger. This had better work.

Dario squeezed her hand tightly, just once, as if to reassure them both, before letting go and walking through the barrier. The air around him came alive, crackling and spitting like it was angry at his intrusion. He moved through it, and then, with a blast that felt like it split the air, the barrier snapped closed behind him, leaving a ringing silence.

Elara's heart pounded in her ears. *Move dammit.*

But she stood frozen. Never in her life had she faced a situation with such potential for disaster. For too long, Edgar's commands had smothered her, extinguishing any hint of her own desires or choices under the pretense of protection. But it was a leash. One so delicately placed that she mistook it for safety.

How *easily* she'd slipped into those chains, convincing herself they were armor against the harshness of the world. Elara's nails pressed hard into her palms. *No more chains.*

She was done being someone else's to command.

The barrier's electric hum sent jolts through Elara as she breached its shimmering boundary. Static clung to her, raising goosebumps across her arms as the world around her transformed into a dizzying swirl of blurred colors, flickering lights, and shifting shadows. Elara bit down on her lip, stifling a gasp as Algernon's ring burned hot against her skin, the ether that lay within fighting hard to keep her under its veil.

She held her breath, her entire body tensing with anticipation as she took the final step and crossed the threshold to the other side. A sour taste clawed at the back of her throat, and she pressed a hand to her mouth, swallowing hard. She waited for the fallout, but no blood-curdling screams pursued her. No tendrils of ether snaked their way toward her. Nor did Edgar materialize, seeking retribution.

Instead, everything seemed to stop. The air grew heavy, and the sound of her own breathing echoed in her ears. Only the distant whinnying of horses from a nearby barn and the soft rustling of leaves drifting to the ground broke the silence. Her chest tightened. It felt like time itself had paused, a fragile calm, and Elara couldn't help but wonder if Fate had decided to spare her. If only for now.

She risked a glance at her hand. Algernon's ring sat innocuously, but the skin around her thumb was marked with a vivid, red burn, as if scorched by intense heat. She bit her lip to stifle a scream, carefully sliding the ring off her finger. A sigh of relief escaped her as she felt the pressure lift, though her thumb still throbbed intensely, the skin raw and blistered. She knew she should wait, but the pain was nearly unbearable. Perhaps just keeping the ring close would suffice.

Grimacing, she wrapped it in a cloth she had brought and tucked it away in her pocket alongside Godfrey's note.

"Lost your way, Druid?" Dario's grin was nothing short of roguish as he leaned down from his horse, extending a hand toward her. "You look like you could use a knight in slightly tarnished armor."

Elara rolled her eyes before hoisting herself up behind him, her arms wrapping tightly around his waist. The coarse fabric of Dario's tunic bit into her fingers as she gripped him, every muscle in her arms taut. He guided the steed with an ease that belied the tension in the air, the horse's steady rhythm kicking up a muted cloud of dust from the worn dirt path. Their pace was unhurried, as if they were on a leisurely evening ride and not the desperate flight it truly was.

But as the towering ramparts of the castle turned into nothing more than silhouettes against the horizon, Dario's control snapped.

With a fierce kick, he urged the horse into a wild sprint, the animal's strength sending chunks of earth flying behind them. The pounding of hooves became the soundtrack of their escape, melding perfectly with his lean into the wind, his body and the horse moving as a single entity.

Ahead, Ansyl City sparkled like a beacon in the night, its lights a promise of refuge. And with every beat of her heart, that promise seemed to grow brighter, drawing them ever closer.

The wind wove its fingers through her hair, setting free every loose strand. Elara inhaled the night's chill, letting it fill her with a rush of pure, unbridled joy, so alien yet utterly exhilarating. She could never run far enough to escape her duties, but maybe now, if she was careful enough, she could carve out a semblance of normalcy while still honoring the weight of her oaths. She wrapped her arms around Dario, holding onto him as if he were the only solid thing in a world spinning out of control. The speed at which they moved glued them together, his warmth bleeding into her, calming the wild beat of her heart.

Her voice came out softer than she intended, the raw truth in her words leaving her feeling bare, but she fought against the instinct to recoil. "Did I ever tell you," she found herself whispering, letting the night carry her words, "just how amazing I think you are?"

Dario flashed her a devious grin. "You could stand to mention it more."

Laughter burst from Elara, loud and unrestrained—a sound so unfamiliar it startled her. Her throat hitched, a sharp pang cutting through her chest, as though something inside had cracked open. She was used to the persistent presence of a muted sorrow, smothering any flicker of joy that dared surface. The idea of unfiltered happiness felt like a delicate ember, vulnerable to the faintest breeze and always on the verge of being snuffed out.

Dario looked over his shoulder and smiled. "It's good to hear you laugh, El."

The warmth in his words danced over her skin, stirring an unexpected chill that ran down her spine. A soft blush tinted her cheeks, and she nestled closer to him, hiding her face.

He laughed, jostling her. And right then, with every inhale of the cool night breeze and the sound of Dario's laughter mingling with the darkness, she understood that tonight was about more than just finding answers. She was staking a claim to herself, shouting back at the cosmos to remind it—and, more importantly, herself—that despite everything, she was still strong. That there was still a spark of joy within her that refused to be snuffed out.

Osin, Edgar, the High Council—they might control so much of her life, but they didn't have all of her—not yet. She couldn't control the pain inflicted upon her, but she could control her response to it. The pain was real; the loss was real, but so was the fire inside her. It might flicker and wane, but it wouldn't go out. Not as long as she had a say. And despite everything, she still had that—*a say*—a voice; a part of her that was unbroken.

And there, under the cover of night, she made a vow to herself: she would never let it be forgotten again.

CHAPTER 12

"You did *what*?" Dario's voice was a blend of disbelief and reprimand as he shot a sideways glance at her, his posture rigid against the saddle.

Elara's grip on him tightened. "I gave the woman a gold coin. She asked for healing, which I obviously couldn't provide. I felt bad—what else was I supposed to do?"

"You start by not handing out gold," Dario said, shaking his head. "You do realize a *single* gold piece could pay a healer's wages for half a year?"

"All the better then!"

His brow knitted together. "Yes, but you might as well have announced your presence with a fanfare." His voice softened slightly. "No Druid handles money, Elara. It's practically heresy."

Shit.

She sighed. "Well, I didn't know that, did I?"

"Clearly," Dario retorted, the corner of his mouth twitching.

"I don't regret what I did."

His response was a soft, warm smile that lingered a bit too long, causing her cheeks to burn even hotter. She cleared her throat and turned her gaze to the horizon, her heart thudding against his back. They were nearly there.

The city's gates, massive like the ancient dragons of legend, stood proudly against the backdrop of the shimmering Jade Sea. Their ramparts cast long shadows over the cobblestone path that led up to them, with the great doors swung wide open to welcome the ceaseless flow of life.

Beyond the gates, traders rolled carts heavy with spices and silks down to the docks, where ships bobbed gently on the sparkling waters. Merchants haggled loudly over their laden carts—apples, grains, and fresh catches of silver fish that glinted in the sun, all piled high and ready for bartering.

"Does the city always feel this alive?" Elara asked, her eyes wide with wonder.

Dario guided their horse with an expert hand through the open doors into the heart of the festivities, weaving through the crush of bodies. The mingled scents of sweat and cloves filled the air, as close as the press of people around them. Dancers swirled in vibrant costumes while musicians plucked at strings.

"No, the city becomes something else entirely during the equinox," he explained, his voice low as overhead lanterns cast shifting pools of light that highlighted the honeyed flecks in his eyes. "From this point forward, keep your hood drawn closely. Edgar's ravens are scattered everywhere; we'll need to tread cautiously."

Elara tugged her hood lower, shrouding her features until the fabric brushed against her lashes. All she could see was the broad expanse of Dario's back directly ahead. The narrow field of vision felt suffocating, almost claustrophobic. Tentatively, she eased the hood back just a fraction—enough to let in a sliver of the festival's vibrant lights and colors. Surely, a little glimpse wouldn't hurt.

"In what ways does the city change?"

Dario shifted uncomfortably in his seat, the leather saddle emitting a soft creak that seemed louder in the quiet of the alley. He seemed to gather his thoughts before he spoke again, his voice low and reflective. "On a night like this, people have a way of setting aside their differences to pay homage to the Mothers. But don't mistake this display of unity for true harmony. It's a night of forgetfulness, not forgiveness."

The ghostly echo of Fenlin's last words wove through Elara's thoughts. *"You might sit on that throne and feast while the rest of us starve, Lord Osin. But remember, empty bellies breed brave hearts. The realm remembers."*

Her flesh prickled as an involuntary shudder threaded its way down her spine.

Rebels. Edgar had painted them as minor nuisances, easy to snuff out. But maybe there were more Script Keepers out there than the priest had let on. Perhaps they weren't as scattered and powerless as she had been led to believe.

They wound their way into the city square, which teemed with masked merrymakers flushed with drink and heady delight. Their masks were beautiful. Some were shaped like fierce beasts, fangs bared in silent snarls, while others glinted with a lavish array of ribbons and gems under the lantern light.

They swirled around a massive bonfire, keeping time with the rhythmic plucking of lutes and the pulsating beat of drums. As they danced, their clothes caught the lantern light, setting them aglow. The earthy brown of fallen leaves, the fiery orange of a setting sun, the blooming yellow of ripening fruit pooled in the folds of their garments. They swirled and twirled, merging and breaking, a kaleidoscope of autumn captured within the confines of silk and satin.

Elara watched, fascinated, as children dashed through the streets, their laughter echoing around her. They waved sticks decorated with flowing ribbons, vibrant like spirits in the breeze. Their uncontained joy was palpable; some raced back to their parents' open arms, while others reveled in the night's freedom, climbing crates, and howling at the waxing moon. A pang of longing struck her, yet a smile still found its way to her lips as she wondered what life might have been like had she known the carefree days of a normal childhood—or any childhood at all.

She pushed the melancholic thought aside and took a deep breath, savoring the air rich with spices that seemed to warm her from within. Her senses were in overdrive—every smell, every sound, every sight amplified a thousandfold. It was almost too much, but there was a wild beauty in this unfettered flood of life. It wasn't a dream, though it felt like one.

It was real.

She was real.

And for the first time in her life, Elara felt a part of something greater, something immense and powerful.

"Why are they wearing masks?" she asked, her gaze lingering on the crowd.

"They are a tribute to Aine," came Dario's reply, pulling her focus back to him. He dismounted, his boots thudding softly against the packed earth, then secured his horse to the public hitching post before turning back to her. He offered his hand to support her waist as he helped her down. "They're an ancient tradition. The masks are an honor to Aine and a nod to the shifting of the seasons and the shifting of Aine herself."

It made sense, then. According to legend, Aine often took on different forms when visiting the mortal world, her most famous being a crimson mare. Elara's gaze drifted across the sea of masks, a sad smile tugging at her lips. Tonight, there would be no red mare grazing on the edges of the festivities. No soft, divine eyes watching them from the heavens. Only the vast, indifferent cosmos spinning on, deaf to the many tributes rising in her honor.

"Wait here," Dario murmured, his eyes holding a glint of mischief as he vanished into the crowd. Elara bit her lower lip, her gaze tracking him and landing on the stall awash in amber light. Through the thick crowd, she caught a glimpse of Dario's animated chat with the seller and the glint of gold passing between hands. A few moments later, he reappeared with two masks in hand and a victorious smirk playing on his lips.

He presented one to her, light glinting over its gem-studded surface —deep purples, vivid emeralds, pleated feathers fanning like wings.

"A bird?" Elara asked, eyeing the delicate work. Before she could touch it, Dario lifted it to her face and tied the black ribbons, his fingertips brushing her neck.

"A starling," he said with a quiet smile. "They move in great flocks, following the wind as one. From the outside it looks like chaos, yet there's beauty in their unity—always adapting, always surviving."

Her amusement softened as his gaze lingered.

"And when the light catches them, they're extraordinary," he added, voice low. "Complex, resilient, impossible to ignore. Like you."

The world seemed to hush. Elara could only stare, surprise melting into something warmer, unexpected. A slow smile curved her lips.

"I've never been compared to a bird before," she teased. "But coming from you, I think I like being a starling."

His smile widened, so open and genuine that Elara found herself looking away. She cleared her throat, a shiver of anticipation running through her, mingling with the excitement of the unknown and the cool caress of the evening breeze weaving through the lively square. When she looked back, she found Dario fastening his own mask—a rather obnoxiously large replica of a luna moth. Its long, curling antennae waved with his every movement, while the wings, bathed in a soft, pale green, nearly engulfed his face. He looked absolutely ridiculous.

A snort of laughter escaped her. "Really?"

"What?" He tried to feign innocence, but the chuckle in his voice betrayed him.

Elara, still trying to stifle her giggles, was about to slide off her mask when Dario's hand stopped her. His playful demeanor shifted.

"For our protection, leave it on. I'm sure our contact will be masked as well."

Elara's laughter fizzled out, choked by the sudden reminder of reality. The note in her pocket felt like a weight, pulling her back from the night's enchantment that had briefly let her forget. Unfolding the paper, her eyes scanned the words, grounding her. This wasn't a festival jaunt; it was a search for Godfrey.

Dario scanned the pulsing crowd, then shifted his gaze back to Elara. "What now?"

"I'm not certain," she confessed. "The message was rather cryptic."

Dario tilted his head, leaning closer. "May I?"

She nodded, handing him the crumpled note. Elara watched as Dario's eyes flicked rapidly across the paper. She could almost hear the words as he silently read them. *"If you still seek answers, they will find you when the sun and moon embrace."*

His brows rose, and a playful glint appeared in his eyes as they fixed on a point just above her head. A grin spread across his face, and he leaned in slightly, whispering with a mock air of conspiracy.

"Sometimes the Fates have a funny way of being painfully obvious, don't they?"

Elara turned, and her breath caught.

In the heart of the city stood a magnificent sculpture of the moon and sun entwined in an eternal orbit, hovering in the twilight. It looked like the work of master alchemists, blending the tangible and the ethereal. Light from the intricate metal designs bounced off nearby structures, and a soft glow hinted at the ether keeping them suspended. Gazing at it, she could almost feel the thrum of energy, like a pulse beneath her fingertips.

Elara sighed. "Let's hope Fate shows its kinder side tonight."

CHAPTER 13

Under the dance of sun and moon, Elara tapped her foot impatiently on the cobblestones, its rhythm drowned by the nearby minstrels' lilting song.

All around the square, laughter mingled with the swish of costumes as masked revelers danced, lost in the moment. Her gaze flicked across the crowd, seeking a familiar face, even as the wine Dario had given her to soothe her nerves sat beside her, untouched.

Where was he?

Godfrey had left the details frustratingly vague, and with each ticking second, Elara's window of opportunity shrank. Her anxiety mounted as she chewed on her lip, scanning the bustling square. She couldn't just stand here doing nothing; she needed to act, and quickly. If she couldn't go directly to Godfrey, maybe there was a way to make him come to her.

She yanked at the ribbons securing her mask.

"What are you doing?" Dario's hand snapped out.

"He won't recognize me with this on."

Dario tensed, his grip tightening on his drink.

"We're running out of time," she urged, glancing at the moon's position in the sky.

He exhaled slowly, the dim light catching the faint mist of his breath. "*Fine*, but if we're going to do this, we're going to do this right."

Without waiting for her reply, Dario headed to a bustling stall adorned with golden liquids in ornate bottles. After a brief exchange with the vendor, he exchanged some coins for two shimmering drinks. Returning, he handed one to her and removed his mask, his eyes twinkling. "To bold choices," he toasted, downing his drink in one gulp.

Elara lowered her mask, her attention drawn to the gleam of her drink, the fragrant notes of citrus and mint blending with the sharp bite of spirits in the air. She wrinkled her nose. Surely one drink wouldn't wreak the same havoc as the entire bottle of whiskey she'd shared with Avis...

"Wait! You have to finish your wine first."

She peered over the rim of her glass, one brow arched in bemusement. "And why's that?"

The corners of his eyes crinkled. "It's bad luck otherwise."

"That's absurd."

"I swear on it. Ask anyone. If you begin your next drink without finishing the last, you're doomed to reverse your dance steps all night."

"You're a liar, Dario Voland."

He tilted his head. "Merely a bit of local lore," he teased. "But if you find yourself tripping over your robes, don't say I didn't warn you."

She rolled her eyes, quickly downing her wine before chasing it with the citrus concoction.

Dario laughed and extended an arm. "Dance with me."

Her gray eyes widened in disbelief. "We're not here to dance, Dario."

"Indulge me," Dario suggested with a wry smile. "What better way to blend in than to lose ourselves in the crowd?" His gaze flicked to the towering buildings around them. "And if you're set on showing off that face, let's at least find a spot where we don't stick out like sore thumbs."

Fair point.

With a resigned sigh, Elara set her empty cup on a nearby table and took his arm. He deftly navigated them through the sea of gilded masks and whispering gowns, dodging dancers in sweeping costumes until they found an open spot.

The melody shifted, pulling at memories tucked away in the corners of Elara's mind—from her first year in the capital. She closed her eyes, letting the rhythm paint vivid images of the grand ballroom and the regal dances she had watched from the sidelines.

Céilí—the name of the dance rang in her mind. It was a social dance that revolved around patterns and pairs, with lines of couples executing a sequence of steps with their partners and those next to them. But she didn't know the steps.

Dario's lips twitched into a half-smile as he caught her eye. "Just stick with the beat—and me," he whispered, his breath lightly teasing the wisps of hair by her ear.

Warmth spread across Elara's cheeks, and her heart fluttered. Before she could second-guess herself, she tightened her grip on Dario's hand, letting him lead her into the dance's first step. Her first attempts were clumsy, resulting in apologetic winces as she stumbled over Dario's toes and jostled nearby dancers. But as the music swelled, something within her clicked. Gradually, her movements found harmony with his, their steps weaving together seamlessly like the ebb and flow of the ocean— cascading, retreating, and surging anew.

As the music crescendoed, the rest of the world seemed to fade away. But out of the corner of her eye, a figure appeared. He stood broad and imposing, cloaked in black, with a raven mask hiding his features. Elara's pulse spiked as he approached, and before she could react, he effortlessly severed her connection with Dario.

She stumbled over the cobblestones, but the stranger caught her hand, steadying her with a firm grip. He confidently pulled her back into the dance's rhythm as Dario vanished into the swirling crowd.

"Stay calm and dance," he murmured, his voice smooth as velvet. It hit her then—the raven mask wasn't just a disguise; it was a signal. She was dancing with her contact.

"You're not Godfrey."

Her head spun, a warm flush from the drinks coloring her cheeks as the stranger twirled her smoothly. When she faced him again, his dark eyes were narrowed.

"I'd be concerned if I were."

An icy shiver ran up her spine. "Is he alive?"

"For now." His voice was low, meant to be chilling, but his eyes betrayed some other emotion. Elara could see the heaviness in them, the strain they carried.

The stranger spun her again, and as she twirled, Elara caught sight of Dario watching her from the sidelines.

"Your friend?"

Elara's attention jerked back. "Yes."

There was a brief pause before the stranger spoke again. "Do you trust him?"

Her eyes darted back to Dario. His gaze was steady, piercing in a way that made it seem like he could read her thoughts. She knew, with just one nod, that he would cut through the crowd to her.

Her heart squeezed as she turned back to the stranger. "I trust him."

The stranger gave a slight nod. "Call your watchdog, then. We need a quieter place to talk."

ELARA DUCKED behind a stack of crates in a shadow-laced alley, glancing between Dario and the stranger, their eyes locked in a silent, wary standoff.

"How did Godfrey send word from the Pit?" she asked, drawing the stranger's attention. Another question pressed against her lips, heavier and even more dangerous: *And how did it end up in Algernon's hands?*

But she kept that one to herself.

"We have eyes and ears within the prison." The stranger's words were brief, clipped. Then, off came his raven mask, revealing a face that even in the muted light was striking. Deep-set, almond-shaped eyes with long, dark lashes, a strong jaw giving way to unexpectedly soft lips, and sleek, black hair that flowed past his shoulders.

"We?" Dario echoed.

The stranger nodded, and a surge of understanding washed over Elara like a cold wave. "You're a Script Keeper?" she breathed, disbelief lacing her tone, and Dario tensed beside her.

His eyes flashed. "Fen and Godfrey, too. They were some of the last Keepers we had in Osin's employ."

Elara wasted no time. "Why did they steal my blood?" Her directness didn't seem to faze him.

"They flouted orders." His jaw tensed. "Thought they could—" He cut himself off, looking over at Dario before shaking his head as if to dispel the memory. "It doesn't matter anymore."

Elara saw a flicker of something in his gaze—remorse, perhaps?

"What does Godfrey want with Elara?" Dario asked, practically buzzing with unease. He looked ready to bolt.

But the stranger didn't address him, didn't even look at him. He only had eyes for Elara. "He wants to save you."

Footsteps thundered down the alley as figures clad in raven masks appeared, their silent numbers swelling behind the stranger as if conjured by ether.

Dario's grip tightened on Elara, his body instinctively moving to shield hers, but a heartbeat too slow. A masked assailant emerged from the dim, his sword raised high. And with a ruthless swing, it came crashing down, its pommel connecting with a sickening crack against the back of Dario's head.

Elara screamed, reaching for him as he collapsed, but the stranger yanked her back against his chest. She thrashed in his grip as one of his men knelt beside Dario and forcefully rolled up his sleeve, revealing the totem beneath.

"You were right. He's got one."

What?

Elara's gaze darted from wrist to wrist, a tight knot of dread coiling in her throat with each glimpse of bare skin where a tattoo should have been. *Vredians.*

The stranger's grip tightened. "Cut it off."

Elara's breath caught in her throat as the man holding Dario swiftly pulled out a knife, but, instead of removing the totem, he sliced off the map of stars tattooed just below it.

Blood spurted from Dario's wrist, and Elara tore herself free from the stranger's loosened grip. "Get away from him!" she snarled, pressing one hand against the wound to stem the flow while the other frantically searched Dario's bandolier, fingers closing around the hilt of a dagger.

"He'll survive," the stranger said, his tone dismissive enough to make her see red. He gestured to one of the taller figures in a raven mask, then looked back down at her. "Save your concern. He was no true friend to you."

Rage ignited within Elara, her grip tightening on Dario's dagger. She was no fighter; her understanding of blades limited to the basic idea that the pointy end was meant for the enemy. And this man... he was most certainly her *enemy.*

Her heart thundered, a rush of heat flooding her veins as Elara lunged at the lanky figure advancing. Her attack was awkward, untrained, and he swiftly parried it with a casual flick of his forearm. The dagger slipped from her fingers, spinning perilously close to her leg before it clattered to the ground.

The stranger's face twisted into a scowl. "You'll likely end up stabbing yourself before you get a hit on anyone else if you can't even keep a grip on your weapon," he snapped, striding toward her. "Bryn," he barked out sharply. A figure stepped forward, tearing off their mask to reveal a woman with deep auburn hair and round brown eyes that glinted in the dim light.

"We can't rift," she said. "There are new wards set up. I—it must have just happened."

The stranger blew out a sharp breath. "He knows she's missing. We need to move—now."

Elara pulled against his hold. "I'm not going anywhere with you."

He met her gaze, his eyes deep and earnest under his lashes. "Look, I get it, Hallowed. You've got no reason to trust me. But believe this—I don't want to hurt you." He squared his shoulders, a determined stance that matched the resolve in his voice. "I'll do whatever it takes to get you out of here. Work with me, and we can make this easier on both of us."

Yeah, not happening.

Elara kicked out, aiming for his shin, and his sigh morphed into something like a growl. "Gideon!"

"Got it!" the tall one snapped as he moved swiftly behind Elara, his hands clamping onto her face. Before Elara could even flinch, a bitter tonic was forced down her throat, sending a shiver rippling through her body.

It started as a faint stirring—a barely noticeable tickle of unease at the crown of her head that snowballed into a wave of dizziness. The sensation spread through her body, turning her insides into a churning vortex. She took a shallow breath, her chest tightening as the lanterns overhead merged into a blur.

"Dario." The whisper barely escaped her lips.

"Sleep, Hallowed," the stranger's voice faded in and out. "Everything will make sense soon. You're safe." He repeated those words, a steady mantra as Elara's body went limp in his arms. She wanted to scream, to brand him a liar, to tell him she'd never felt so exposed, so utterly defenseless.

But the scream never came.

CHAPTER 14

The world swirled back into focus bit by bit, colors bleeding together like a watercolor left out in the rain. Elara squinted against the dull ache that pulsed at her temples. Trees—tall and gnarled—brushed past her vision, a blur of green and brown. She was in a forest, that much was clear, but beyond that? Her memory was a fog.

Elara tried to adjust, to get her bearings, but her limbs were leaden, uncooperative. It felt as though bands of iron clamped around her. She was moving—*no*, being moved—swayed gently from side to side in a rhythm that almost felt soothing.

Had they taken her? The Vredians?

Her chest heaved as she thrashed against the firm grip that bound her, the rough texture scraping her wrists raw.

"Easy does it, Hallowed."

The voice that interrupted her panic was calm and authoritative. Elara stilled. It was the stranger. She took a shaky breath and blinked rapidly, willing the world to stop spinning. As her vision cleared, she realized she was on a moving horse, her hands tied.

A cold sweat broke across her forehead. "You drugged me."

His arm constricted around her waist, muscles coiling tight. "I didn't want to."

"Go *fuck* yourself with a rusty sword." The words scraped out; her mouth felt stuffed with cotton, dry, and painfully arid, but the twitch of his body, the sudden rigidness, made it worth the effort—at least until he laughed.

"A divine creature with a filthy mouth? How charming."

Elara bristled, looking around for a knife to stab him with. Then, like a dam bursting, memories flooded in—sharp, piercing. *Dario.* His name carved a hollow in her chest, an ache that spread and squeezed until she thought her ribs might splinter under the pressure.

They had hurt him, abandoned him—

"Where is my friend?" Her voice was raw, the words barely audible as she struggled for breath.

"Your friend is safe," he said, voice smooth, infuriatingly calm. "We left him in a secure spot. His men will find him soon enough, patch him up. He'll have nothing worse than a nasty headache and a few scratches."

Her heartbeat pounded in her temples. *A few damn scratches?*

Elara stifled the urge to retch, half-tempted to let it spill—this lunatic deserved far worse than ruined pants.

But punishment was likely already on its way. He had dared to kidnap her, and no one crossed the Lord Sovereign without facing severe repercussions. Edgar, she knew, would already be unleashing fury across the realm to find her. And if word reached Osin... She shivered at the thought. The Legion would be relentless. These fools had no idea of the chaos they had invited to their doorstep.

The horse bucked, a sudden jolt snapping her head back onto the stranger's shoulder, her neck suddenly too weak to hold itself upright. Heavy-eyed, she lifted her gaze to meet his, his face hovering in her blurred vision. His eyes were deep and dark, fringed by lashes so thick they cast shadows upon his high cheekbones, and a scatter of freckles marched across his nose.

"Who are you?"

He shifted, his gaze sliding away. "Dominic."

"Planning to kill me, Dominic?"

Her reply slipped free before she could stop it, laced with a bitter chill of memory—*cold metal pressed against her throat.* Elara twisted her neck to face him squarely, searching his expression, defiant. His dark eyes met hers again, a sharp glint flickering within them.

"If I were, we wouldn't be talking."

She scoffed. "Well, isn't that a relief?"

Her vision was still blurry, coming and going, but she could make out his party moving alongside them. They'd taken off those raven masks, and now she could see their faces—rugged and seasoned, like they'd been through more than their fair share of hardships.

"How long have we been traveling?"

They were moving so slowly. They must have covered significant ground to feel this comfortable at such a leisurely pace...

"A day and a half."

Elara's stomach flipped. She glanced up at the trees once more, squinting, hoping to glimpse a raven. "Why are we traveling on horseback and not rifting?"

Dominic paused for a moment before responding. "How about a deal, Hallowed? You keep firing questions at me, and I get to throw a few back your way."

"Oh, so now you're a fan of fair play?"

His eyes sparkled with mischief. "I've got to keep you on your toes somehow."

Prick. "Fine."

He exhaled a laugh, his chest brushing up against her back. "We're not rifting because Osin has the Void under tight surveillance. He caught wind of your... liberation a lot faster than we expected."

"What do you mean he's surveilling the Void?"

The idea seemed absurd. The Void was just that—interstitial nothingness, a realm between realms that belonged to Rhiannon, the Goddess of Death. How could Osin, or anyone for that matter, keep watch over such a place?

Dominic arched a brow. "Osin's had control over the Void for the last ten years, ever since the war started." He spoke as if it was common knowledge she should have already possessed.

Goosebumps pricked her skin. "How?"

She felt him shrug behind her. "No one really knows for sure. The day Aine presented you to Osin, he declared himself god-chosen, seizing control of ether, and with it, the Void." His voice carried a bitter edge. "That's our best guess, anyway. Whoever controls ether controls the Void."

"But you can still use it?"

"Hold up, it's my turn now," Dominic said with a slight grin, loosening his grip just enough to see if she could keep herself steady on the horse. After a moment, he reached into his bag and pulled out a canteen and some food. "What's it gonna be first—something to eat or a drink?"

Elara froze. "Is that really your question?"

"Oh, come on, I'm not that cruel," he teased. "You must be starving, and I make it a rule to keep my companions well-fed."

"You mean your prisoner," Elara retorted, shaking her bound wrists for emphasis.

"Semantics," he quipped.

Elara's scowl deepened. "Drink," she finally grumbled, and he obliged, lifting the canteen to her lips.

"To answer your question, yes, we can still rift if we gear up with the right wards, but Osin's got us under constant watch now, so we're better off taking the scenic route. He's bound to keep an eye on the Void from here on. But our best casters are all over it. We'll figure out a way around it soon enough."

After Elara gave a nod to show she had finished drinking, he stored the canteen, and broke off a chunk of bread, holding it out to her. If she hadn't been so famished, she might have bitten his finger just for the cheek of feeding her like a bird. But hunger won over pride this time.

She bit into it, not bothering with niceties. "Where are you taking me?"

"North."

North? Elara's heart skipped a beat, then started pounding furiously. "Where north?" Ulrith lay to the north, but so did Vredia.

He paused, his face a mask of stone. "Just north."

Elara craned her neck to glare at him and he laughed—a low, rumbling sound. "I'll get more specific when I decide you're trustworthy."

"And I'm just supposed to trust *you*?"

Dominic's smile was all edges. "The irony of trust—it's always a gamble, isn't it?""

As he spoke, the clatter of hooves cut into their conversation. Elara recognized the newcomer immediately—the fire-haired girl from before. "We gotta pull over," Bryn declared, maneuvering alongside them. "These horses are dead on their feet, and if Gideon doesn't shut up soon, he's going to find himself with a knife in his leg."

Dominic arched an eyebrow, the smirk still lingering. "When did you get so bloodthirsty?"

She narrowed her eyes. "Around the time I realized it might be the only way to keep up with you lot. And anyway, it's not me you should be worried about." She nodded toward a barrel-chested man whose horse was nearly buckling under his weight. Elara felt a pang of pity for the poor animal. But Bryn was right; something about the man was off. His stares *were* like knife thrusts, all directed at Gideon.

Dominic exhaled deeply, a sound heavy with the weight of command. "We're stopping here! Water the horses, stretch your legs." The group's immediate flurry of activity followed, each member springing into motion.

Elara seized the moment, her eyes darting from face to face as she tallied the group—twelve in total. They were a diverse lot, a motley crew of men and women, and even a boy who couldn't have been over seventeen. Her gaze lingered on him, noting the way his eyes darted nervously, like a cornered animal.

"Yoni," Dominic shouted, aimed at a man with dark braids woven back from his face. "Scout ahead. Throw out a few *ceirín* ten leagues out, then double back."

"On it," Yoni replied, giving a lazy salute before he and Bryn coaxed their horses into a trot.

"What's a *ceirín*?" Elara asked after the pair was out of sight.

Dominic's gaze scanned the tree line as he spoke. "It's a kind of tracking device I came up with. It detects signals or spells recently cast in the area. Helps us know if anyone's creeping too close to camp." His voice held a hint of pride.

"Did you use alchemy to create this device?"

Dominic's eyes met hers, his grin broadening. "No, Hallowed, I used *Tirrish*."

A shiver of surprise ran through Elara. "But *Tirrish* is a dead language. It's said that only the Fae could harness its power."

"Only if you believe what Osin's scribes claim." Elara was about to argue, but Dominic cut her off. "Hold on—before you say anything, answer one of my questions first."

He slid off his horse.

Elara narrowed her eyes, still wary as he reached up to help her down. "Go on then." Her feet landed on the soft ground and a wave of unsteadiness hit her; the remnants of the sedative lingered in her system. She held onto the horse for support, pausing a moment to let the world stop spinning and her vision clear. When it finally did, Dominic's gaze was on her.

"Why did you leave the Sanct? What drove you to seek Godfrey?"

Elara felt a surge of incredulity at his question. "Fen died." The words were a struggle, her throat constricting around them. "Whatever he wanted with my blood—it wasn't for his own benefit. *I know Fen*. I just...I need to understand why."

Dominic's face stayed unreadable, yet his eyes moved sharply over hers, searching, digging for something. Whatever he was looking for, he must have found it convincing because a small, knowing smile eventually crept into his expression.

"There's a clear line drawn in this world," Dominic said, leaning in close as he gently untied the ropes around Elara's wrists. "The truth-seekers and the blind believers—the latter might as well be dead for all the good their ignorance does them. If you're sure you want to chase the truth, I'm here to throw you the rope. But remember, once you step through this door with me, there's no going back to pretending."

Elara studied him, really took him in. This man had hurt Dario, had drawn her out of the Sanct and kidnapped her. And yet, since then, he'd been open and ... nice. The thought made her stomach twist. *Nice?* She nearly rolled her eyes at herself. But then, there were answers she needed, truths dangling just out of reach that this man could provide. If playing along got her those, then maybe it was worth the compromise. Her resolve hardened; she straightened her shoulders, lifted her chin with a defiant tilt.

"I never cared much for pretending, anyway."

A wicked grin spread across his face. "That's what I like to hear."

CHAPTER 15

As the sun sank, spilling fiery orange across the horizon, the group finally ceased their endless bickering and decided to set up camp for the night.

A biting wind cut through the air, but Elara barely felt it, her attention captured entirely by the sight of her captors. She watched in wonder as they moved with practiced efficiency—tents rose from the ground like mushrooms after rain, and fires sparked to life, casting long shadows across the clearing, all while their voices wove the ancient *Tirrish* language into the crisp air.

The melody was haunting, touching something deep within Elara, a stir of emotions she couldn't quite name. She could have drowned in the sound, let it wash over her all night, but eventually, they stopped, the camp secured within wards that shimmered like spider silk yet promised the strength of steel.

So, Osin and his scribes had lied.

The truth shouldn't have surprised her, yet a shiver rippled through Elara all the same. *Tirrish* was not a dead language—it pulsed with a power that could still be harnessed, despite the Fae being banished to another realm. She had always been taught that the language's strength was inherently tied to the essence of the Fae themselves. But perhaps that wasn't the case...

The wards crackled, their energy buzzing over her skin and causing the fine hairs on her arms to stand on end. This sensation was novel, unfamiliar—not like the ether she knew. *Tirrish* vibrated with life, each thrum of energy making the ether she was accustomed to feel static, almost dormant by comparison.

Why did ether feel so wrong? She had never questioned it before— it simply was...

"You look like you could use a drink."

Elara's heart leapt like a startled hare when Dominic suddenly appeared beside her, that maddening smirk playing across his face. He offered her a cup—dark, dubious—and something deep inside her recoiled. She was prepared to listen, sure, but trust him? *Not a chance.*

"Offering me a drink is possibly the worst of your many bad ideas."

"Your loss." Dominic gave a nonchalant shrug before downing the contents of the cup in one smooth gulp. "Let's get you into some fresh, warm clothes. Feels like the cold's about to bite harder tonight."

He guided her through the maze of tents, their canvases flapping gently in the cool night breeze, until they reached one that stood slightly apart from the others.

"This one's for you," he said, holding back the flap for her. "Inside, you'll find a mix of clothes from a few of the girls in the group— nothing fancy, but they'll keep you warm."

Elara's smile was tight as Dominic's figure receded, his back a silhouette of strength and muscle outlined against the flickering campfire light, a cup raised to his lips in a final, hearty swig. She let out a heavy sigh and ducked into the tent.

Inside, the space was sparsely furnished but functional. A hanging lantern flickered, swaying gently in the evening breeze that slipped through the entrance. Beneath its light, a small cot was topped with a neatly rolled bedroll and a pile of clean clothes. These garments were just as plain and unassuming as everything else worn by these people: brown breeches paired with a green tunic, a black cloak, and boots.

Elara slipped into the pants, a sly smirk tugging at her mouth. She could almost hear Edgar's scandalized gasp—*not fitting for your station*—followed by a lecture on decency and image. She was finally ditching the gown for something she could actually run from her problems in—or toward them. Whichever. She tucked the ring and Godfrey's note into the pocket, yanked on the tunic, and went.

Outside of the tent she was immediately assaulted by the smell of dinner. Roasting meat and some kind of spicy, earthy herbs. It was like being lured by an invisible rope tied around her waist, pulling her toward the main fire. Around the flickering flames a clustered group came into view. Their voices were light their mugs clinking—a strange sight indeed. For a band hunted by the Druids and possibly even the Legion, they seemed unusually at ease.

Clearly, they placed great faith in the strength of their wards.

Her gaze swept over the assembly, catching on Dominic, Bryn, and Yoni, who were looking in her direction, their conversation pausing as they noted her approach. Something in their glances—a mix of calculation and curiosity—made her stomach tighten. Dominic raised his hand, beckoning.

"There she is—divinity herself." Yoni's voice was smooth and warm as he lifted his glass in a mock toast and took a deep swallow.

Elara rolled her eyes as she slid into the space next to Dominic, who promptly handed her a plate brimming with food. Pheasant dressed with butter and herbs, freshly baked bread, and wild mushrooms—it was a feast for the eyes, looking every bit as heavenly as it smelled.

"Thank you," she mumbled—more to the plate than to Dominic—as she dug in. The scrap of bread she'd stolen earlier hadn't touched the hunger, and with each mouthful she felt less like a fugitive, more human. By the time the plate was clean, she looked up and found all three of them watching her, their quiet focus intent as a predator's before the pounce. Her pulse skidded. She cleared her throat, slid the empty plate aside, and met their gazes, waiting.

"Everything you've been told about this realm—it's all a lie, starting with Osin himself." Dominic's expression was serious, his gaze intense. "Ten years ago, Osin was just another face in the crowd, a lowborn with mud on his boots. Then he takes this so-called pilgrimage, claims he's won the Mothers' favor, and suddenly, he's the Messiah of the masses." He scoffed, shaking his head with a rueful grin. "They say Aine appeared because of him, but that's a stretch. More likely, he stumbled on something powerful, something that could make a goddess take notice. And he's been riding that lie ever since."

Elara's throat tightened. "What did he find?"

Bryn shrugged. "Nobody knows. But whatever it was, he got what he wanted in return. He's untouchable."

Yoni leaned in closer. "Whatever boon he's been granted, it's as twisted and corrupt as the power he wields."

A bead of sweat trickled down Elara's back. The unease she always felt near ether had never been voiced by anyone else—until now. "You can smell it too? The wrongness of it?"

His eyes flashed. "Yes, Hallowed."

Whatever Osin had received, *she* was part of that deal—handed over to heal a dying realm, to restore the ether that had been drained when the Fae left. A chill ran through her. Could she be the corrupted power they hinted at? Elara looked down at her hands, as if they might hold the answers. It made sense, didn't it? Aine's so-called gift to the realm had sparked a new era of ether, one that was altered and strange. Why? Maybe that was why they had taken her—to peel back the layers, to unravel the mystery she unwittingly represented.

Her eyes lifted, hardening. "So what? Fenlin and Godfrey took my blood—you abducted me to figure out what I am?" A wave if bitterness filled her as the chilling realization took shape. They intended to use her as well. Just like the rest, eager to exploit whatever unique property Osin harnessed from her blood, *to turn it against him.*

With a heavy sigh, Dominic met her eyes. "I won't sugarcoat it—we have no clue what you are, and yeah, we're itching to figure that out. But trust me, we're not here to exploit you. Our goal is to cut Osin off, to stop him from using you like a tool. We want to end this cycle, Hallowed, not perpetuate it."

Bryn's expression softened. "We don't buy into what Osin has labeled you. But you're different, that much is clear." Her gaze flicked to Dominic, seeking some silent affirmation before returning to Elara.

"Change is on the horizon. We could really use someone like you on our side."

Elara's voice cracked as she spoke. "I don't understand what I can possibly offer. I have no power, no influence. The title *'Hallowed'*—it's a joke. Do you really believe anyone would rally behind me? Osin might parade it around for his stories, but the truth is no one knows me. People don't care about me. Not really."

Her confession tore open a wound she usually hid behind the title, bitterness spilling out before she could stop it. She bit her lip, steadying the tremor.

Dominic shook his head. "You're wrong about that. Your friend, what we removed from him—it was a suppressant, specifically designed to dampen something within you."

Elara froze, her muscles tensing as if ice had been poured down her spine. *A suppressant?* "I don't understand."

"It's an old spell," Yoni began, his voice steady, like he was explaining something he'd said many times before. "Designed to prevent ether from accumulating in someone's body. They call it power-binding. Think of it as shackling someone's powers, restraining them to their core." He paused, brushing a braid back, revealing a tattoo that snaked down his neck. "It's like a storm trapped within, always searching for a crack to burst through."

Dominic took over with a nod. "To control this, binders employ what are known as Echoing Seals—constructs that suppress the power, silencing it, and pushing it into a state of dormancy. Each seal echoes the effects of the Binding Sigil." He leaned forward, his eyes intense. "Binding isn't just a one-off; it's an ongoing struggle, a fierce contest of wills that demands both dominance and submission, testing the endurance of everyone involved." He paused, the rough timbre of his voice softening. "The seal we removed from your friend was one such construct. His proximity to you, even the slightest touch, would have suppressed your abilities further."

The world tilted, the ground beneath her seeming to give way. Pressure clenched in her chest, squeezing the air from her lungs. She shook her head. It couldn't be true. Dario wouldn't—

"But just removing it from him wasn't enough." Yoni's gaze hardened. "I can feel it—your bind. It's struggling, trying to break through the wards we've set up. There's... likely another seal on you, placed by someone else. The priest, most likely. Or one of the Druids."

Elara pushed herself to her feet, her movements shaky. "I don't believe you," she said firmly, even as her heart felt as though it was splintering into pieces. "Dario would *never* do that to me. He—he's my friend."

They were lying. They wanted to use her. Just like Osin. Feeding her the lines, the tales, whatever it would take to enlist her help. The totem on Dario—it was from his homeland. He'd told her the stories. He had been...

A numbness crept through her. Dario had been *catapulted* into a position of power right after joining the guard, despite his youth—an elevation everyone else had blindly accepted. The realization caused a dull ringing in her ears, a fracture spreading through her chest. He had been assigned specifically to her patrols, always there, always watching. Not just as a guard watches a charge but with a focus that had fooled her into feeling seen, understood. She had believed he cared, that he saw her as more than the Hallowed...

Had it had all been a lie?

Tears stung her eyes. Elara drew a sharp breath through clenched teeth, fighting for composure. Below her, Dominic, Bryn, and Yoni watched—pity plain in their eyes. Heat flushed her skin, and she pressed a cool hand to her cheek. Then Yoni's earlier words surfaced, stopping her short.

"You said the sigil prevents ether from accumulating in someone's body?"

He nodded.

"That doesn't make sense. Ether does not amass in the body. It's sourced from my blood and then set into rings." Her gaze darted around, landing on their hands for the first time, realizing with a start that none of them wore the iron rings typical of casters. Her eyes widened, heart pounding.

Dominic's gaze held hers with an weight that felt like it could shift the ground beneath them. The man who had first seemed so easygoing, almost reckless, had vanished. In his place stood someone darker, more serious. "It builds up in *us*. That's why we can cast just by speaking *Tirrish.*"

"How?" Elara's question was a whisper, barely audible.

"We're the remnants," Dominic said, his voice rough with a mix of pride and a hard-won resilience. "The ancestors of the half-breed Fae that got left behind after the Great Divide. And we believe, we *hope*, that you're the key to something bigger."

CHAPTER 16

On her trek back to her tent, Elara felt as if she were barely touching the ground, floating on a cloud of thoughts rather than stepping on the earth. Dominic had told her to sleep, to take the night to process their conversation and revisit it in the morning.

She rolled her eyes. As if the thoughts racing through her head would allow her *any* rest.

"We're the remnants."

A tremor rippled through her. Could she be a remnant too? She mulled over the possibility, like turning a key in a lock that refused to click. Dominic had admitted he didn't know what she was and even doubted Osin's claims about her identity. Yet, her own memories contradicted that doubt.

Who could she trust? What should she believe? It all felt so crushingly overwhelming.

The sting of Dario's betrayal twisted like a knife inside her, her heart clenching with a pain so intense she had to pause to catch her breath. Dominic had accused him of suppressing her powers, but the pieces didn't fit together neatly. Could it be that he thought he was protecting her? Or was she a fool to grant him any semblance of understanding? Everyone seemed to use her, each in their own way. Perhaps Dario was assigned to keep her subdued, climbing the ranks by keeping her under thumb. Maybe he told himself that suppressing her was for the greater good. He could imagine, couldn't he, that by gaining power, he might better aid the common folk? That he could rally the Druids to use their ether for those in need, offering the help he himself never received. And if suppressing one girl was the cost of that vision, perhaps, in his mind, it was a justified sacrifice.

Inside the tent, the dying light of twilight bled through the fabric, casting trembling shadows that stretched and recoiled across her cot. She collapsed onto it, pressing her face into the scratchy surface. It smelled of the wild—of pine, damp earth, and survival.

Before leaving the group to the last of the dwindling fire, Dominic had offered her a choice: *join them, and they would take her north.*

If not, well, he hadn't specified what would happen if she chose to leave, but he framed it as a choice. Yet, deep down, Elara knew it wasn't really one. What real options did she have? She would not go back to Verdara; how could she return to a place where those she trusted had deceived and exploited her? Running wasn't feasible either; Osin could find her anywhere. At least with Dominic and the others, she could hide within their wards. It seemed her only viable option was to leave with them.

But if what Yoni said was true, the Druids were tracking her, even now, through the seal placed upon her...

Elara tossed and turned on the narrow cot, the thin mattress barely cushioning the hard, creaking frame beneath her. Her mind kept circling back to Summon's Day. Osin had called it a noble, purifying act, claiming the sacraments in her blood brought balance back to the realm. But was any of it true? He had portrayed her power as a holy sacrifice, a gift she couldn't control. And yet, she might be capable of so much more...

Aine's voice drifted through her thoughts, her vision clouding with the image of the goddess, a wavering mirage that beckoned with outstretched hands. *"Awake and fulfill your purpose. Heal and restore. Give and consecrate."*

Elara recoiled, curling into herself, and burying her face in the musty scent of her sleeve. Reality felt like it was slipping away, like fine sand sifting through her fingers—grains of truth mixed with lies. *Why had Aine named her the Hallowed and treated her with such reverence? What was the real purpose behind it?*

If people could use *Tirrish*—if a language alone could conjure ether —what need was there for her? One didn't require a ritual to bond with a language. They wouldn't depend on her blood...

Sleep came to her fitfully, like a restless sea that ebbed and flowed, always pulling her back into the same haunting dream. A forest ablaze with flames reaching up into the dark sky, consuming the night while shadows danced under the moon's indifferent watch. Each time she woke, the dream stuck with her—the smell of smoke still in her nose, the sound of crackling fire in her ears. It must have been just before dawn when a shrill, desperate scream pierced her nightmare, jolting her awake.

Her tent flap was violently thrown open, and a sliver of pale, early light cut through to reveal Bryn on the threshold, her eyes wild. "They're here," she whispered as she clutched Elara's arm and yanked her to her feet.

As Bryn pulled her from the tent, Elara's gaze shot skyward, and she gasped. Above, thousands of ravens formed a swirling mass, their black wings nearly blotting out the morning light. Caws filled the air, and those beady eyes—countless and piercing—felt like arrows aimed straight at her. *Shit.*

The camp erupted—people spilling from tents, blurring as they sprinted for the horses. Elara barely registered the shouts before Bryn's grip tightened on her arm, hauling her through the crush. Horses whinnied, metal clashed, men shouted as armor was dragged into place.

She stumbled over a fallen pack, but Bryn kept her upright, kept her moving. Somewhere, a horse screamed—a high, keening sound that cut through the din.

"Bryn!" Dominic's voice boomed, already mounted, and maneuvering his steed. He charged toward them, halting so suddenly that his horse skidded, flanks heaving. His shirt was half-on, hastily pulled over his torso, and a sword was strapped to his back. "What's the latest from the *ceirin*?"

"They're just over a league out," she managed, her voice rough with exertion. "We have minutes."

Dominic swore a string of curses as Yoni rode up, his horse snorting, eager to charge. "Our wards are intact. It shouldn't have been possible for the High Priest to locate us."

Bryn began braiding her hair back. "What about her bind?"

Yoni shook his head. "The bind is still pressing against our wards but hasn't broken through." Looking down at her, his eyes were like dark pools. "The only explanation is that she carries something of theirs, one of their signatures."

"Signatures?" Elara asked, her heart pounding.

"A ring, girl," Bryn snapped.

Elara's blood ran cold. *A ring.* She had almost forgotten she even had it after everything that had happened. Yoni didn't need to ask; the look on her face said it all.

"Fuck!"

Dominic swung down from his horse in one fluid motion. "Give it to me."

Elara's hands trembled as she pulled Algernon's ring from her pocket and handed it over, the metal icy against her palm.

"No one thought to check her?" Yoni snapped, his eyes blazing.

"We don't have time to argue," Bryn said, wringing her hands.

Dominic threw it on the ground, stomping on it with a force that sent a crack through the air. The jasper stone shattered, releasing a wisp of smoke that curled into the air like a dying breath.

Mother above. What *was* that?

Dominic's entire body shook with barely contained fury as he turned away, barking orders that cut sharply through the frenzy. "Head west—fast and hard!" He turned to Yoni. "Take the Hallowed to the safe house. It's a straight shot through the southern pass, less cover but faster. I'll lead the flock west toward the old mill, then light a beacon on the western ridge once we've diverted them. Wait for that signal before you even think about leaving. Stay sharp, stay hidden, and keep her safe."

Yoni dipped his head, then turned to Elara. "Up." He boosted her into the saddle and vaulted up behind her. She gripped the worn leather as the horse surged into a gallop.

Everything became a blur—shadows and dawning light merging, the camp disappearing behind them. Yoni held her tightly, his arms forming a protective cage as he began to weave *Tirrish* around them, the ancient language tumbling from his lips like a sacred hymn. Each syllable spun out, shimmering gold, and enveloping them both in a gossamer cocoon.

Elara's muscles tensed reflexively, a cool sensation tracing her nerves as the spell tickled her skin. It felt as if they were being lifted, floating through the trees, their bodies as insubstantial as wisps of mist. She dared a glance upward, half expecting the dark watch of ravens against the pale sky, but there were none. Relief fluttered through her. Yoni's ether was hiding them.

She shut her eyes and drew a slow, steady breath. They'd claimed breaking Dario's seal would grant her access to ether, but she felt no different. She searched inward, reaching for that quiet place—and found only herself: the beat of her heart, the rise and fall of her chest, the hush of her own thoughts. Disappointment settled, cold and heavy. There was no time for it.

Yoni urged the horse faster, breaking through the dense woods into a wide, open clearing. "Yah!" he shouted, and the horse responded with a burst of speed, hooves pounding the earth, dirt flying up in a wild spray around them. Elara's hair whipped about her face, a tangled, wild mane of its own, and she felt a surge of exhilaration so fierce it could rival the storm of hooves below.

"How far are we from the safe house?"

"Thirty minutes to the closest one," Yoni said, his breath hot against her neck. "Once we reach the pass, we'll be out of—"

Yoni didn't finish. Through the scattered gaps between gnarled tree branches, an armada of Verdaran guards burst forth, with Dario at the helm. His eyes found Elara's across the distance, wild with a fear bordering on madness.

Elara's breath caught, a sharp twinge of pain clenching at her heart at the sight of him.

"This ring's power isn't enough to get past all the security measures,"

he had said. *"There are protocols, safeguards in place. By dawn, you'll be in chains, and I'll be the one forced to drag you back in them."*

Safeguards. Had he been talking about the Binding Sigil? Had he been admitting it right then, and she'd been too blind, too stupid to see it? The realization hit like a punch to the gut, and any last threads of doubt about Dario's betrayal vanished in an instant. A surge of rage flooded her veins. He had played her like a fool, just like everyone else in her life.

Elara's eye contact with Dario abruptly broke as Yoni violently pulled the reins to the right. Startled, the horse reared up on its hind legs, hooves slashing the air, before it crashed back down and charged back into the dense forest. Branches whipped cruelly at them, snapping against their faces and hands as they barreled through the underbrush.

"Keep your head down!" Yoni shouted just as an arrow whizzed past Elara's neck, thudding heavily into a tree trunk.

Elara ducked but risked a glance over Yoni's shoulder, her heart pounding. The light blue silver of the guard's armor flickered through the trees, catching the morning light, and shimmering like shards of ice. They were closer now, moving so fluidly they almost seemed like ghosts weaving through the forest. A curse escaped through her clenched teeth. They weren't going to make it.

Yoni shouted a spell, his voice slicing through the clamor, and a towering wall of earth erupted behind them, surging upward like a monstrous wave.

Elara's heart pounded in her chest as she watched the forest floor rise, the air filling with the sounds of cracking wood and the deep, guttural groan of the earth tearing itself apart. She gripped the reins tighter as the ground beneath her horse's hooves shuddered. And in mere moments, the wall of earth expanded and thickened, forming a formidable barrier, effectively cutting off the advancing guard.

Her breath steadied, though her hands still trembled as they gripped the saddle. *This* was the power of *Tirrish*? *This* was the ether the Keepers wield? It was incredible, almost impossible to comprehend.

Ahead, the earth rose, funneling into a narrow pass squeezed between two towering, jagged cliffs that seemed to touch the sky.

The southern pass.

The horse surged forward, muscles bunching beneath her as Elara leaned into the stride, urging them on. The world narrowed, edges blurring as the distance closed.

Then—heat and light exploded.

It was as if a vengeful star had torn through the forest and into their path, splitting trees and scorching the air around them.

Elara screamed as they were ripped from the saddle. She barely felt Yoni's grip as he twisted them midair, turning the fall into a controlled spiral and pulling her beneath him before they hit the ground.

The impact punched the breath from her lungs.

"Fuuuuuuck." The word was a long exhale. Gods. Air—*she needed air.* But Elara couldn't catch her breath. Her hands shook violently as they pressed against the scorched earth, the nearby fire licking at her skin as she rolled onto her side.

She froze, her heart slamming against her ribs as her gaze locked onto Yoni beside her. A gash split across his forehead, and blood was spilling out in a slow, steady stream. Too much, too fast.

"Yoni!"

Elara's voice cracked as she grabbed his shirt, her fingers trembling as she shook him, but his eyes stayed stubbornly closed. He must have hit something hard—a rock, maybe—knocked himself out. *Shit.* They needed to move, but their horse was long gone, bolted in fear, leaving them stranded in this burning hellscape. Could she carry him? Drag him through the pass on her own? Maybe she could—

A flicker in the flames caught her eye, cutting off her thoughts. She squinted against the glare as the fire shifted, parting as if an unseen hand had drawn back an infernal curtain.

The crackling blaze, the burning forest—everything else fell away, the world dimming at the edges.

The fire bowed.

There, standing in the heart of the flames, was the Hunter.

CHAPTER 17

Elara's heart stuttered to a halt, jolted back to life, and then stopped once more, all in the span of a second.

Their gazes locked. It wasn't the deep color of the Hunter's eyes, nor the fiery ring of amber that framed his irises that stole her breath—it was the cold, hard promise they held.

A beast lying in wait.

Before she could summon her scattered wits, he was striding toward her, each step exuding raw, untamed power.

The blood-orange fire played a treacherous game with the twisted horns of his mask. He was a tempest embodied in human form, moving as if the flames were a mirage that bent to his will.

Elara sprang to her feet, heart pounding like it might burst through her chest as she grabbed Yoni's lifeless body.

Wake up, dammit, wake up.

Elara clenched her teeth and hooked her arms under his, hauling him up despite the weight threatening to buckle her knees. She dragged him back inch by agonizing inch—but with every step, the Hunter closed in.

Her breath hitched, coming fast and ragged. There was no escape, no hidden path out of this nightmare.

She turned to face him, resolve hardening as words formed and fell away.

The air went icy. Shadows—darker than a moonless night—bled across the moss, advancing without sound. No rustle of leaves, no snap of twigs. Only silence, and the screaming dissonance in her mind.

Mother above.

A gasp tore from Elara as shadows shot forward, chaining her ankles and yanking her hard to the ground. Yoni crumpled beside her. She dragged him close on instinct, her heart hammering.

The shadows writhed, thickening, twisting into something almost human—and utterly wrong. A mockery of life.

Moonlight caught on elongated fangs, carving a cruel smile across its sallow skin.

Cold sweat slid down Elara's spine as it growled, the sound a low vibration in the still air. Its eyes were empty as they fixed on her, nostrils flaring as it scented the night. *"Tuatha,"* it hissed, the word dripping with malice.

"She's with me."

The Hunter's voice cut through the tension like a blade—calm, commanding—right behind her. Elara's heart leapt into her throat.

"Inform your master that what was lost has been reclaimed."

But the creatures gaze never left hers. *"Do uafás[1],"* it whispered, voice slithering around the words like poison, the corners of its mouth curling in a twisted smile, *"tá sé níos milse... cé chomh aisteach.[1]"*

The Hunter's presence closed in behind her, a subtle shift in the air that prickled her skin. The beast's attention wavered, its head tilting, elongated neck moving with serpentine fluidity. Its gaze lingered on the Hunter, eyes gleaming like broken glass. Then, with the smoothness of mist gliding over a cold lake, it melded back into the shadows, disappearing into the dense forest.

Elara's breath rushed out in a shaky exhale.

"Are you injured?"

The Hunter circled to her front, and she shivered, as if physically responding to his words. He must have mistaken her trembling for a confirmation, because after a beat, he descended to her level, his tall silhouette folding into a crouch.

He extended his hand, and she shrank back.

"I'm not going to hurt you."

It was less of a comfort and more of a command, leaving no room for a reply. His mask hid everything except the narrow slits of his eyes, but this close, Elara could see the crease of them—the dark lashes and even darker gaze fixed on her.

Beside her, Yoni groaned, pulling their attention. His eyelids fluttered, his arms lifting to cradle his head.

He's alive.

Relief surged through her.

"Hallowed," the Hunter said, reaching out again. As his arm extended toward her, she noticed something odd—*his hands were bare.*

In every encounter she could remember, he'd worn gloves. Now she found herself staring. His hands were unexpectedly refined—broad-palmed, long-fingered, the warm doe-brown of his skin marked by scars, scratches, and ground-in dirt. But it was the iron ring on his middle finger that caught her breath, set with crystals for all four elements.

Her eyes snapped to his.

Impossible. Every caster she knew was bound to a single element—if any at all. She'd seen aspirants struggle for years to master even one, failing again and again to form a bond. The idea of him, bound to all four, shattered every rule she had ever learned. How was that even possible?

"Elara!"

Her name cut through the air. Elara spun to see Dario bursting from the underbrush, eyes locked on her. He dismounted in one smooth motion, his usually sun-kissed skin pale in the dawn light.

His gaze flicked between her and the Hunter as he advanced, smoke curling around his ankles. When he stopped, his attention fixed on the Hunter, chin lifting. "Release Elara to me," he said, "and I'll ensure her safe return to the Sanct."

Slowly, the Hunter rose to his full height. "You've failed your duty, guard. The Lord Sovereign entrusted the High Priest and his men with *one* job—keep the Hallowed safe. And yet, here we are."

"My duty," Dario replied evenly, "is to Elara first and foremost. Mistakes were made, that's true, but I am here to correct them."

The Hunter snorted. "The Hallowed isn't some prize for you to restore your tarnished honor. Consider yourself fortunate that *I* claimed her before one of Osin's shades could. If they had, you'd be dealing with far worse than just a blow to your pride."

Shades? Was that what it was? The word spun through Elara's mind, dredging up half-remembered pages and sketches from the archives, bits and pieces of lore she'd studied long ago. But nothing matched...

Dario's face drained of color, a visible reaction that gave her a flicker of satisfaction as she stood. "I am not a possession to be handed over. I belong to no one." It wasn't entirely true, but she wanted it to be. She'd tasted freedom—just a flicker—but she wasn't ready to give it up. Elara fixed Dario with a fierce glare, then turned to the Hunter, her gaze cold and unyielding.

He studied her through the flickering firelight, and for a brief second, his usually stark, steel-black eyes softened, the hard edges blurring as if touched by a whisper of light. "Maybe so," he said, "but in this world, everyone is bound to someone, willingly or not."

A shiver rippled down Elara's spine, the faint ring of amber in his eyes flaring briefly, like the final spark of a dying ember. But just as quickly, it was gone. Snuffed out as Yoni lunged from below and drove a knife deep into the Hunter's heel.

CHAPTER 18

Fury blazed in the Hunter's eyes as he snarled.

Embers scattered across the forest floor flared to life, drawn to his rage, their orange glow licking at the shadows around him.

Yoni moved first—blurring aside as a searing orb tore from the Hunter's palm, scorching the earth where Yoni had lain seconds before.

"Elara, move!" Dario bellowed, yanking a dagger from his bandolier.

The acrid scent of smoke and burning pine choked the air, the flames coming off the Hunter licking dangerously close. Elara sprang back, but every direction she turned, the searing heat and roar of the fire blocked her way.

She gasped as her gaze locked onto Dario. He moved with deadly precision, launching dagger after dagger at the Hunter, showcasing years of rigorous training. The blades sliced through the air, swift and true, as he sprinted toward her. But the Hunter was faster.

With a flick of his wrist, fire erupted—a scorching barrier that swallowed the daggers mid-flight, spitting molten drops across the forest floor.

Elara's stomach knotted as Dario charged straight through the flames, weapon raised, fury carved into his face. Her heart clenched, torn between running to him and cursing his name.

Betrayer.

Defender.

Fool.

He'd lied to her—again and again—yet here he was, fighting as if she were his to save. Part of her wanted to believe there was a reason behind every broken promise. But even if he survived this, Osin would never forgive him. He was gambling everything for her—his life, his loyalty, his station—and she didn't know whether to scream at him, run, or collapse into his arms and weep over the ruin of it all.

Amid the fray, Yoni moved like a wraith. His dagger flashed cold in one hand while an unnatural glow pulsed in the other. His voice threaded through the noise, words older than the forest. The ground beneath the Hunter shifted, almost imperceptibly at first—a tremor he barely noticed. But then it came alive. The earth lurched and split open, hurling stones and leaves into a screaming spiral, a storm of dirt that howled as if the land had finally chosen sides—and it wasn't his.

Elara's heart pounded so fiercely she could feel it in her throat as she lunged for the nearest tree, fingers digging into the rough bark. The ground beneath them writhed, hungry and wild, pulling everything within reach toward its gaping maw. Trees groaned, boulders tilted, all drawn toward the chasm that that clawed at the Hunter's feet.

She couldn't move. Could barely breathe as the earth consumed him inch by inch, relentless, unstoppable. Until it wasn't.

A sound tore from him—half roar, half something primal and broken—and with a burst of power, his fist slammed into the earth.

A bone-deep shudder rippled out, a violent quake that cracked the ground, split the silence, and ripped the spell to shreds.

The Hunter rose with a snarl, raw power rippling through him as flames erupted in his hands, curling like living serpents eager to strike. A whip cracked through the air so fiercely Elara flinched. It was a sound that stole the breath from her lungs, the sharp tang of smoke filling her nose as he lashed the fiery arc toward Yoni.

She hit the ground instinctively, the blistering heat licking just over her head as Yoni twisted away, rolling. She barely had a moment to think before Dario blurred into motion, faster than she could track. His blade gleamed—a single, merciless arc—and plunged into the gap beneath the Hunter's arm where steel met flesh.

A harsh grunt of pain escaped him.

It was the sound of opportunity, and Elara did not hesitate.

Her heart thundered in her chest as she ran, each beat a frantic rhythm that drove her forward. Dario loomed to her left, Yoni closing in on her right, both like wolves circling their kill. But she didn't slow, didn't hesitate. Her body moved before her mind could catch up, veering swiftly toward Yoni.

There was no time for second-guessing, no space for a glance over her shoulder to gauge Dario's reaction. The choice was made the moment her feet left the ground.

Yoni's hand flashed to his belt, a blur of motion as he drew another weapon, his expression fierce and laser-focused. *"Faster, faster,"* his eyes seemed to scream.

But the Hunter was running too.

With a sweep of his hand, flames erupted, slithering across the earth like vipers. The fire spread, tendrils snaking outward until one found her, coiling around her ankle with a scorching grip that burned through her boot and into her skin.

Elara barely had time to scream before the whip ripped her off her feet, snapping her connection with Yoni. She flew, the world spinning, wind tearing at her face—then the ground slammed into her with a bone-rattling thud.

No, no, no.

Gasping, she clawed at the dirt, nails scraping as she tried to drag herself free. It was useless. The Hunter hauled her back, her body skidding over the scorched ground until she lay trembling and breathless at his feet.

Ash burned her throat, every breath brittle as she stared up at him. He was a shadow against the blaze, his black armor catching the firelight, every flicker painting him in molten gold. He didn't move. Didn't need to. He stood there like something dragged straight from the nightmares of old. A Seraph ripped from the Otherworld, cloaked in flame and shadow—a harbinger of death, here to collect his due.

Elara could hear Dario shouting—could see Yoni weaving spells into the air—but it all felt muffled, like she was underwater. The Hunter had sealed them in, a barrier crackling with power that felt eerily familiar.

Even through the mask, she felt the tension radiating off him. He reached up, grip steady, and yanked Dario's dagger free from his armor. A brief grimace slipped beneath the mask—a crack in his composure—before he tossed the blade aside and drew a slow breath.

"Hallowed," the Hunter murmured, his hand outstretched once more.

The word struck like a curse. Dread coiled low and cold in her gut, tightening until her breath stuttered. Her shoulders sagged as the truth settled—brutal and inescapable. There was no way out. He would deliver her to Osin, and the life she knew would end. Osin wouldn't kill her; she was too valuable for that.

And the thought of what he *would* do—of the pain he could inflict—

Death would be a mercy.

So, Elara snatched the dagger at his heel.

Blade flashing, she struck. A swift, harsh slice across his waiting, open palm.

He froze, eyes blinking in brief confusion, as if her boldness hadn't fully registered. Then his gaze dropped to the blood welling in his hand, dark red stark against bronze skin, and reality crashed back in.

With a snarl, he seized the knife by the blade, uncaring of the blood spilling from his grip, and hauled her up. "Stubborn, *impossible* woman," he growled, smearing blood across her skin.

Elara thrashed wildly, every kick and punch a plea for him to lose patience and end it. Better to die fighting than face whatever Osin had planned. In the struggle her hand brushed his ring.

Like flint striking steel, a spark caught.

Power tore through her, ripping down her veins in a violent surge. The world emptied to white noise, her ears ringing as everything blurred into nothing.

Elara clawed at her chest, her head tipping forward until her gaze landed on the Hunter. The first thing she saw was his eyes—wide with a horror that mirrored her own. Within them, a flicker of amber pulsed, alive, syncing with the wild hammer of her heart.

He'd collapsed opposite her, one hand pressed to his chest as if he could feel the pain tearing through her. The air between them crackled with the residue of their clash, each breath a labor, mirroring the others, as if they were both drawing from the same strained lung.

The Hunter drew in a rough breath, shedding the disorientation like a discarded cloak, and rose with the fluidity of a seasoned warrior.

This time, when he reached for her, there was no pause—no silent question. In the space of a breath, he seized her arm and hauled her upright, yanking her hard against his solid frame.

Elara dug her heels into the earth, muscles burning as she fought to hold her ground. It was useless. Resisting him was like bracing against a gale; her efforts vanished beneath his strength.

Beyond the shimmering barrier, Dario's face was flushed, eyes frantic as he watched helplessly. Yoni never stopped, spells slamming again and again into the invisible wall, desperation etched into every strike as sweat slicked his brow and his strength bled away.

Elara knew it then—deep in her bones. It was already over.

She should've taken that dagger to her own throat when she had the chance.

As the Hunter dragged her toward the rift, it felt as though she were being torn between two worlds. Behind her, the Void screamed, its icy winds clawing at her hair and clothes. Ahead, the forest beckoned with the promise of safety.

But she would never be safe. That was a fairy tale—a sweet lie she'd told herself. She'd been a fool to believe it could ever be real for someone like her.

A numbing detachment settled over her. Even through the haze, Dario's eyes never left hers, filled with a devastation she didn't know how to carry.

He will hang for this.

The thought echoed bleakly as the Hunter dragged her through the rift. Elara almost felt the warmth of Dario's hand as the barrier finally fell, just a hair's breadth from her own—

before she was gone.

CHAPTER 19

The silence was deafening, so thick that Elara could hear the pounding of her own heartbeat and the faint whisper of her clothes rustling as she trembled in the Hunter's grasp. Her eyes remained fixed to that spot on the wall, the place where the rift had just been, as if her gaze alone might summon it back into existence.

The Hunter's grip loosened, and her boots hit the floor with a solid thud. She faced him—the painfully familiar pillars and tapestries of Osin's court swirling into view.

This was the reckoning, wasn't it?

Elara had always feared the day she would step into this room and never step out. Yet she hadn't expected that her own actions, her own desperate bid for a sliver of control, would hasten that end. Her vision swam, the edges of the room dissolving into a haze until only the Hunter remained.

His posture was rigid, as if locked in an internal battle. He took a step forward, then stopped.

"Don't fall behind."

His hands curled into fists before he turned on his heel and walked away without a glance. His heavy stride echoed down the aisle, cloak snapping behind him like black waves in a choppy sea.

What exactly had happened back in the forest? She had barely touched his ring, and then... it felt like everything inside her had detonated—and from the shock in his eyes, he'd felt it too. Yet there he was, striding away as if their worlds hadn't just momentarily fused and fractured...

Elara willed her legs to carry her forward, each step sending a tremor through her as she walked down the familiar path, her gaze fixed ahead. But as they approached the dais, every fiber in her body tensed, instinctively ready to drop into the ceremonial kneel ingrained in her since childhood. However, to her surprise, the Hunter didn't stop. He veered right, leading her toward the iron doors—doors she hadn't passed through since being sent to Aewora.

Her feet stumbled as surprise flickered through her, mingled with a rush of curiosity that tempered her fear.

They stepped into the grand reception hall that connected the royal chambers. It was just as she remembered: opulent and imposing. Vaulted ceilings soared overhead, adorned with intricately carved beams and massive chandeliers dripping with crystals that cast shimmering light across the polished stone floor. Richly colored banners hung from the walls, each embroidered with Ulrith's totem, fluttering slightly as they passed.

Around them, staff whisked by, their eyes—trained to ignore—glossing over her. Yet, when it came to the Hunter, there was an unmistakable shift in their demeanor. They'd straighten a bit, their eyes widening with both respect and apprehension. Each person they passed instinctively gave way, bowing slightly in reverence. It was as though the Hunter commanded a stature akin to Osin himself.

Elara's jaw locked, a hard, tight clench that felt like it could crack her teeth. Watching Osin and the Hunter—the so-called heroes, lauded as saviors—made her want to scream. It felt as if the very notion of goodness had been eradicated from this world. Maybe there had never been much of it to begin with. Maybe the last flicker had died with Fenlin.

The Hunter stopped short, and she nearly collided with him, scrambling to catch her balance. He turned, eyes raking over her. Silence pressed in before he finally spoke.

"You're in no state to meet the Lord Sovereign."

Elara blinked. "What?"

"Your appearance. It's not...befitting. You'll need to change."

She glanced down at herself, noting the smudge of dirt on her cloak and the slight tear along its hem. Still perfectly presentable. Her gaze snapped back up to his. "You can't be serious."

His eyes sparkled with a hint of amusement before he turned and strode forward, silent once more.

Bastard. That was the first word that came to mind. The only one that seemed fitting. Did he really expect her to primp before being tortured? *Cruel, heartless bastard.* She glared at him, wishing her eyes could somehow morph into daggers and just...stab him.

He guided her down another corridor, then vanished around a corner. Reluctantly, Elara trailed after him, only to halt at the threshold of a bizarre chamber.

Dominating the space was a grand copper tub, massive enough to fit at least ten people. Her gaze swept the room: ornate mirrors framed with intricately carved wood, rows of shelves laden with crystal vials and jars filled with colorful salts and oils, lush towels stacked neatly on brass racks, and a vast array of clothing in rich, deep colors hanging from the walls. Beside the tub, a small fireplace was built into the wall, its soft glow casting a warm light over a collection of plush, inviting chairs.

The room was a strange mash-up of bath and wardrobe, like some disturbing grooming station where Osin morphed his guests into whatever twisted version he liked best. The whole setup was unsettling.

The Hunter cleared his throat and glanced toward the attendants, who promptly lowered their eyes. "She has an audience with the Lord Sovereign." He shifted his stance to face Elara's direction, though his eyes never met hers. "I'll be outside."

Elara lifted a brow, a trace of a sneer playing on her lips. "What, you're not here to handpick my lacy bits?" She waved dismissively at the piles of intimates arrayed on a table behind her.

The tension in the room grew as the women shifted uneasily, their eyes darting between her and the warrior, obviously shocked by her audacity. But truly, what was the point in playing docile? She was furious and itching for a fight before any chance of confrontation was stripped from her forever.

The Hunter didn't slam the door or raise his voice as she'd braced for. Instead, he cocked his head and stepped closer, closing the space until it felt impossibly small. He loomed over her, lashes casting shadows beneath the mask, dark eyes glinting.

Her breath hitched when he reached behind her and lifted a dark red slip of fabric, letting it dangle from his finger.

"Should I take this as a personal invitation?" he asked quietly.

Heat surged through Elara. She snarled, yanked the fabric from his fingers, and flung it into the fire. "*Pig.*"

Dark amusement flickered in his eyes. He turned to the attendants with a dismissive wave. "Make sure her dress is nothing short of spectacular. Perhaps add some extra lace? She seems to favor it."

He left without another glance. The door shut with a finality that made her teeth grind, the urge to rip it open and claw at his mocking eyes nearly overwhelming.

There was no time to indulge the fury.

The attendants descended, hands cold and efficient, stripping her without a thought for dignity. She stood bare and exposed, every inch of vulnerability laid open.

She folded her arms across her chest, shoulders curling inward, trying to make herself small beneath their stares. Always the outsider. Always the oddity. She was used to it—but under their scrutiny, it still cut like thorns. They were searching for something. A flicker of the divine.

Let them look. Let them dig and prod. All they'd find was flesh and bone—human, breakable, just like theirs.

One of them turned away to ready the tub, and Elara's eyes narrowed as a simple twist of the tap released a rush of steaming water. Warmth fogged the air almost instantly, the putrid tang of ether making her head swim. She'd heard rumors of such luxuries—hoarded by the upper crust while places starved of ether treated them like legend. In Verdara, Druids gathered around open flames, heating water in soot-blackened pots, every drop of ether counted and conserved. To waste it on a bath felt obscene.

And yet, as the heat seeped into the room, she understood the appeal.

The attendants eased her into the tub, hands gentle as steam curled around her. Fragrant soap—almond and honey—slicked her skin. One worked a fine comb through her hair, oiling it as she teased free leaves and knots.

Once clean, they lifted her out and wrapped her in plush linen, already murmuring over what she would wear, speaking as if she weren't there at all. They chose a gown the soft blue of a robin's egg. Pearls and crystals caught the low light as she moved, as though the night sky had been stitched into the fabric. The laces were drawn tight, the square neckline dipping lower than she'd ever dared, her skin prickling in the cool air.

Edgar may have imprisoned her—but he'd never paraded her like *this.*

With deft motions, the attendants summoned a gust of ether, lifting and shaping her hair until it settled into a regal coiffure threaded with pearls and crystals to match the gown.

Elara met her reflection and barely recognized herself—alive, color blooming in her cheeks and lips against the shadows in her sea-gray eyes. But no amount of skill could erase the scars circling her neck and wrists. Their attempts to hide them felt almost ironic. Those marks were a twisted point of pride for their master.

Finished, they guided her back into the corridor, dipped quick curtsies to the Hunter, and vanished like whispers.

Her gaze caught on his, and the hollow look there sent a shiver down her spine. Whatever sharp retort had been waiting on her tongue withered. The process she'd just endured left her feeling... diminished. There was a particular cruelty in dressing someone up for torture.

"Come."

He set off down the corridor at a relentless pace, too well matched to the pounding in her chest. They stopped before massive oak doors, their polished surface gleaming. For a beat, the Hunter stiffened, as if bracing himself, then raised his gloved hand.

Ether sparked. The doors swung open.

Beyond the doors lay a study of breathtaking grandeur. Mahogany walls rose to arched ceilings, crimson-stained windows bathing the room in a thick, velvet glow. Shelves of leather-bound books climbed to impossible heights.

At the center stood a dark oak desk, commanding the space like a throne. Osin sat behind it, his presence as imposing as the opulence around him.

The Hunter sank into a deep bow. "I've returned what was lost, my lord."

The air thinned as Osin's gaze locked onto hers. His sharp features were carved from ice, precise and unforgiving. Then came a soft crinkle —like parchment tightening in a grip—breaking the hush.

"Our vessel seems to have developed a spine during her little escapade."

The Hunter whirled around, his usual mask of disinterest momentarily slipping. Then it hit her, a cold realization twisting in her stomach —*she hadn't knelt.*

Her knees hit the floor hard, the impact lost beneath the thunder in her ears.

"Perhaps the Hallowed needs a reminder of her place here," the Hunter said, his voice a dangerous murmur.

Osin took a moment. His fingers tapped lightly on his desk, the sound echoing eerily through the grand chamber. "That won't be necessary," he ordered coolly. "Proceed with your account."

The Hunter stood, his voice clipped as he recounted the chase. His words painted a vivid picture of her—desperate, fleeting—detailing not just his hunt but her betrayal, her collusion with the rebels. "It was one of your units that caught up to her, halting her at the boundary before she could cross the western border."

Elara shivered at the memory. *One* of his units?

The silence was oppressive, a heavy curtain that Elara didn't dare disturb by looking up to gauge Osin's reaction. Time seemed to slow— first one beat, then another—before Osin finally stood. His cloak whispered around him as he circled his desk.

Elara exhaled slowly as his black, polished shoes halted before her, pressing lightly against the sweep of her gown.

"When, Hallowed, did the secure life I provided become so *tiresome* for you?" His words slid out smoothly, each syllable tinged with dangerous calm, and Elara fought the urge to shiver. "Look at me!"

Her head jerked up and a cruel smirk curled his lips, a stray lock of blonde hair tumbling into his eyes as he leaned forward. "Do you fancy yourself untouchable? That your life holds *such* value to me that you may disregard my authority with impunity?"

Elara had been in this position many times in her life—kneeling before the Lord Sovereign, close enough to feel the chill of the Void curling around his fingers. *But his eyes.* Never before had such venom flickered in those depths. She swallowed hard, her throat constricting as his thumb traced her lower lip.

"What shall I do with you now?" he mused. "Sending you back to the Druids is out of the question—not after they've proven themselves utterly incompetent. The High Priest, it seems, is incapable of handling even the simplest of tasks."

He paused, casting a thoughtful glance at the Hunter before returning his gaze to her. "Perhaps I should keep you here among my collection of treasures. Hang you like a tapestry to be drawn upon whenever the whim strikes." His thumb pressed harder, pulling at her lip ever so slightly before releasing her. "I could even arrange viewings, charge the devout a handsome fee to witness your beauty up close. And for those willing to pay a premium... more intimate interactions could be arranged." He smiled. "It could prove *quite* profitable."

Elara's gaze dropped to the floor. Shame coiled hot in her chest.

Without another word, Osin walked to his desk, the sound of a chair scraping against the stone floor jarring in the quiet room. "Sit," he commanded, positioning it right in front of her.

Elara pushed herself off the floor, her legs feeling weak as she sank into the seat.

"Now, tell me, pet," Osin drawled, leaning back against his desk, arms crossing over his chest. "How did a little thing like you manage to slip past my wards?"

Elara pressed her lips into a thin line, fists curling at her sides. She wouldn't speak. She'd sooner swallow her tongue than play the informant.

Osin chuckled, dark and sinister, raising the fine hairs at the back of her neck. "You realize, of course, that I could simply take what I want from you." His smirk twisted into something almost feral as his gaze flicked to the Hunter, a silent command passing between them, before returning to her. "I had hoped for a display of loyalty from you, but now I see that was expecting too much."

It took every ounce of her strength not to tremble when the Hunter appeared behind her, his presence overwhelming. His hands closed on her shoulders and yanked her from the chair with a force that stole her breath.

"Keep her still," Osin said, and the Hunter's calloused fingers clamped down, his armor biting into her back as he caged her in.

Tension radiated through Elara's frame, drawn out as Osin savored it like the slow pour of a dark, rich wine. A shadow crossed the blue of his eyes as he stepped closer. His hand dropped to the sheath at his side. When the dagger slid free, dread jolted through her.

The blade pulsed with golden light, sunlight forged into something lethal—an ancient relic humming with the weight of history.

"Now," he purred with cold delight, "what mischief have you wrought upon my faithful?"

Elara ground her teeth as the blade bit into her arm, a low groan tearing free while she locked her gaze on the wound. As the dagger pressed deeper, it wasn't just steel she felt—shadows bled out like smoke, twisting and coiling, slithering into the cut.

Then, the pain hit—searing, *brutal*—ripping a scream from her throat.

She struggled against the Hunter, but he didn't yield. A broken sound scraped up her throat, crushed behind clenched teeth, every breath a fight. Cold seeped into her veins—unbearable, invasive—but it wasn't only chill. It burned as it spread, a merciless frost sinking deep, stealing sensation nerve by nerve.

Elara trembled, her lips forming words she couldn't voice. When she finally dared to look down, *her skin...* it was tinged with blue. But the sight didn't stir anything in her. She couldn't even bring herself to care. All that filled her was emptiness, a hollow void. And it was a relief— such a sweet, bloody relief—to finally feel calm.

She stepped into the numbness, the last of her resistance gone.

"You're killing her," she vaguely heard the Hunter say, his voice a distant echo. She couldn't feel his hands on her anymore, couldn't feel much of anything except for the shadows. They drifted within her, searching, probing, until they gathered near her chest, lingering there as if they were peeling back the layers of her soul, one by one, examining each piece.

"Fascinating," Osin murmured, his gaze drifting over her with a detached curiosity before he pulled his shadows back. Slowly, she felt a touch of warmth. Hands on her face, calluses scratching her cheeks. "Ivan," Osin said, and behind her, she felt the Hunter tense, his hands quickly pulling away.

Ivan. Elara's mind whispered through the cold, latching onto the name. *Ivan. Ivan. His name is Ivan.* Her body slumped against his frame, tears rolling down her cheeks as a memory flickered to life like a candle in the dark.

"*Ivan,*" a girl's sneer echoed from the past, as they watched from the sidelines of the court. *"He tripped Lord Artan's daughter on purpose at the last gathering. Just hooked his foot around hers when no one was look-ing. Sent her sprawling into the mud."* She had snickered, eyes glinting with cruel amusement. *"Thinks he's too high and mighty, just because he's the king's shadow."*

Elara's heart skipped. How had she forgotten? She strained to recall the girl's name, but only fragments floated back to her—a wisp of her face, those tight strawberry blonde curls framing cruel green eyes...

The Hunter's low, rumbling voice brought her back to the present. "Yes, my lord." His words vibrated against her back.

"The vessel seems to have tampered with her bind. Not only that, but she's been significantly aided. It seems there are rebels in Verdara who have all but escorted her straight to the traitor prince himself."

Traitor prince?

Elara's heart skipped a beat. Her thoughts raced back to the group of rebels she'd been with. None of them had worn totems... Vredians, she had suspected, and now this only confirmed it. A prince? Could he mean Dominic?

Her mind spun, the pieces clicking together in a way that made her stomach lurch. Had Osin somehow read her mind? The thought was like ice in her veins. Acid scorched the back of her throat, her vision tilting as she swayed, fighting against the rising dread that she had unwittingly exposed—and put at risk—*everyone* who had helped her.

"The Hallowed must be rebound, and I want you to administer the new seal." Osin crossed to the bookshelf behind his desk and pulled out a worn, ancient tome, its spine barely held together by fraying threads and what seemed like a whisper of ether. "I'd rather not summon *her* unless absolutely necessary."

Osin extended the book to the Hunter, and Elara felt the tension coil in his body behind her. His voice was tight with caution when he finally spoke. "With all due respect, my lord, my talents are better suited to the northern border—"

"Are you denying me?"

"Never, my lord."

"Good," Osin said, his voice creeping through the room like frost on glass as the Hunter reluctantly took the book from his outstretched hand.

Osin turned—his full attention settling on her. Time thinned beneath his gaze, every inch of her exposed to it, measured and found wanting.

His words fell like a tomb sealing shut.

"Take her to the Pit."

CHAPTER 20

With every resounding step down the winding stone staircase, it felt as though a noose was tightening around Elara's neck. The frosty air of the Pit seeped into her bones—a chill that went beyond its deep-set location beneath the eastern stronghold or the damp stone walls weeping with frost. It felt as if Osin's malice had infused the very air, crystallizing around her and, freezing each breath in her throat.

If the biting cold hadn't already stripped her fingers and toes of feeling, the remnants of Osin's shadows would have finished the work. All warmth had drained from her, leaving only the sluggish crawl of darkness through her veins, tendrils tightening as they choked the last sparks of life from her body. Her legs trembled, threatening to buckle. The only thing keeping her from crumpling into a heap at the bottom of the staircase was the Hunter's unwavering grip, his hand like an iron band around her waist, holding her upright.

Ivan. Her mind whispered, the name swirling in her muddled thoughts. Such an ordinary name for a man whose reputation was anything but common.

Elara risked a glance at him, only to catch her own distorted reflection in the gleaming surface of his mask.

She quickly averted her eyes.

It was unsettling—the sudden return of a memory she hadn't known she'd lost. Hearing his name had snapped her back to a past that had somehow slipped away. What else had she forgotten? Ten years could blur many things, but this felt too important to have simply faded. Not just the Hunter's name, but the knowledge that she'd once had... a friend, or something close to it. As close as court life allowed. Elara held to that much. But the memory itself...

"He tripped Lord Artan's daughter on purpose at the last gathering. Just hooked his foot around hers when no one was looking. Sent her sprawling into the mud."

Elara's brow knit as a dull ache pulsed at her temples. Why did it feel like there was more—an unspoken undercurrent, a shared resentment between her and that girl? As though Lord Artan's daughter had wronged them both. The memory hovered just beyond reach.

The solid thud of the Hunter's boots on stone snapped her back as they reached the foot of the stairs. He released her waist and strode down the narrow hall, cutting through the torchlit shadows.

Elara blinked, the world blurring before it slid back into focus. She leaned into the cold stone, eyes closing as she forced herself to breathe.

A slow exhale from the Hunter drew her attention. He'd turned, already walking back toward her.

"Can you walk?"

She pushed off the wall. "I can walk."

His gaze swept her, unimpressed, seeing straight through the bravado to the pain beneath. If he *dared* to toss her over his shoulder again—

"Then keep up," he said, already turning away.

Prick.

But what had she expected? Because he'd helped her once—years ago, when they were children—didn't mean he cared now. Didn't mean he'd ever help her again.

Elara drew on what little strength remained, forcing her feet forward, one step at a time. She wouldn't stumble. Not here. Though she wondered why she still clung to scraps of pride. In the Pit, what use was dignity?

The narrow corridor widened with each reluctant step. Cells

yawned from the stone on either side, the air growing colder, heavier—saturated with the quiet despair trapped behind iron-latched doors.

Wards etched into the metal pulsed with dim ether, their low hum brushing her senses as she glanced inside. Most cells stood empty. A few held figures huddled against the far walls—silent remnants of what they'd been.

Traitors. Like her.

A bitter taste filled her mouth as she glared at the Hunter's back, silently willing him to burn beneath her stare. He was the reason she—and countless others—were trapped in this place. She couldn't help wondering what the world might look like without him in it. If Osin hadn't chosen him as his ward, would any of this have happened? Would they have fared better?

The corridor ended at a massive gate of stone and iron, its shadow swallowing what little light remained. It reminded her of the barrier Osin had raised around the Sanct—but where that one had been gossamer-thin, this was brocade: dense, tightly woven, and utterly unyielding.

The Hunter lifted a hand. Ether sparked, and the wards fizzled out one by one, their light bleeding into the air, leaving a whisper of power that prickled across her skin. When he seized the handle and hauled the door open, a rush of blinding light poured through.

She raised a hand to shield her eyes as the glare burned through her fingers. When her vision cleared, a vast cavern unfurled before her—thousands of floating orbs casting a rich, buttery light across the expanse.

It sprawled like the roots of an ancient tree, pathways branching into countless tunnels that webbed outward in every direction. Cells lined each path, hundreds of them, their sheer number staggering even from a distance. Between them stood guards—towering figures in black armor that ran to their wrists, swords hanging at their sides.

One of them rushed to attention. "My Lord. Four shades have been seized and await your questioning, though—" The guards' voice halted abruptly as he noticed Elara.

"That will be all, Theron," the Hunter said, his tone clipped.

"Report to the warden—tell him the Hallowed is secured and intended to stay here indefinitely."

A shudder coursed through Elara, pulling an unwelcome glance from the Hunter. "Ensure she is seen by a healer. She has a wound on her wrist that requires an anti-venom." His eyes roved over her once more. "And perhaps," he paused, considering, "a dose of Pyrewarmth to stabilize her body temperature."

The guard's expression flickered with confusion, his mouth opening, and then snapping shut.

The Hunter's gaze narrowed. "Is there a problem?"

"No... *no*, sir. No problem—"

"She may be in custody, but she's still the Hallowed and will be accorded the respect due her status."

The guard bowed, a quick dip of his head. "Of course."

The Hunter's hand clenched into a fist at his side. "Good. See to it."

With another quick bow, the guard turned away, leaving space for the Hunter's lingering gaze to settle on her once more. There was a weight in that look, something unreadable yet intensely focused, before he finally turned, and strode away.

As his footsteps faded, two guards closed in, iron grips clamping onto her arms and hauling her forward.

"I can walk on my own," she snapped, struggling against them.

The taller guard snorted, a cruel smirk curling his mouth. "Like we'd trust a mutt like you off its leash."

Elara set her jaw as they dragged her deeper into the cavern, down another stone corridor, stopping at a cell that stood apart from the rest. It was marginally larger—a bare rectangle with nothing but a cot shoved into one corner. The mattress was thin atop a rickety frame, its sheets crumpled and worn nearly to threads.

To the far right, iron bars ran from floor to ceiling. A single torch cast long shadows across the cell, and Elara squinted through the dim light, searching for any sign of life beyond them.

One guard shoved the door open, the hinges groaning in protest. As it swung inward, the wards flared, sparks of light skittering across the stone.

"Get in," he grunted, thrusting her forward.

She stumbled, wincing. "Was that really necessary?" Her legs were frighteningly numb, barely holding her upright.

"Aye, that it was, girlie."

The door began to scrape toward closing.

"Wait! I—I need to pee."

She didn't, of course. But if she could buy herself a moment outside the cell—one more look—she could carve the prison's layout deeper into her memory.

Maybe she'd even spot Godfrey, if he was still trapped here.

The tallest guard stepped fully into the cell, looming over her. "Who's stopping ya?" he challenged, brows lifting as he folded his arms.

Elara's mouth fell open, and he let out a rough chuckle, glancing pointedly between her legs as if he expected her to piss herself right there on the spot.

"Malak," one of the guards sneered, his lips curling. "Think Osin's little pet knows any tricks?" He gave a lewd tug at his pants, drawing howls of laughter from the others.

Elara bit the inside of her cheek, tasting blood.

The tall guard, *Malak*, ignored his comrade and leaned closer to her, his breath stinking of stale tobacco. "Listen up, girl. You try anything clever, speak to anyone else—I'll know. Step out of line, and you'll learn why even the rats keep their mouths shut around here."

With a final, menacing glare, he slammed the cell door shut. Laughter faded down the corridor, leaving the echo of his threat behind.

Elara clenched her teeth as tension rolled through her. She drew in a slow breath, forcing it deep, until the cell seemed to expand with her lungs.

This was her reality now—the price of one misstep, of reaching too far.

Exhaustion crashed over her. Her eyelids drooped, anger dulling to an ache as the world smeared at the edges. She needed to lie down before she lost consciousness.

Her legs shook as she turned for the cot. She didn't make it. The stone struck her side, cold and unforgiving.

Gods.

Her heartbeat thudded sluggishly in her ears as she lay there, cheek pressed to the floor. But just as her breath began to slow, a flicker at the edge of her vision snapped her back to life, her heart racing wildly.

Across the way, in the neighboring cell, someone stood watching her. His sheer size was enough to hold her attention—every muscle carved with definition, even beneath the layers of grime caked on his skin. Amber eyes, burning with a fierceness that seemed to outshine the torches, locked onto hers, unwavering. His hair, jet-black and matted with sweat, clung to his brow, framing a chest riddled with scars. But it wasn't the scars or his towering frame that held her breath—it was the pointed tips of his ears, barely visible through the wild tangle of hair. *Fae.*

Denial surged through her, louder than the roar of blood in her ears, rejecting the sight of him.

The books she'd read about the ethereal beings spoke of elegance, maybe even a hint of fragility, likening them to the woodland sprites, not the towering monolith before her now.

His eyes were like molten gold, deep and endless, drawing her in, offering an anchor as her vision blurred. She clung to his gaze—the only fixed point in her reeling senses. But the darkness was faster, pulling her deeper into its embrace.

CHAPTER 21

Elara's awareness crept back, slow and painful, the cold stone biting into her cheek with every breath. She groaned and lifted a hand toward her pounding head—only to feel a tug at her wrist.

With an effort that felt monumental, she turned her head, vision swimming as she followed the length of her arm stretched through the bars. A sick twist of fear coiled tight in her stomach.

She wasn't alone.

Strong fingers encircled her hand, snapping her attention upward. Her heart skipped, then raced. It was her cellmate—the Fae male. The proximity of him, so close, was overwhelming. Shadows from the flickering torchlight played across his face, deepening the sharp angles of his high cheekbones, chiseling his jaw into something that seemed too perfect to belong in this world.

She blinked rapidly, struggling to make sense of what was happening. His head dipped closer—so close that she could feel the warmth of his breath ghosting across her skin, his lips just barely brushing against her wrist.

A breath caught in her throat—a jolt of confusion and alarm rippling through her. She jerked her arm back, but his grip was tight, his cheeks hollowing as he drew in a deep breath at her open wound.

Then, with a harsh exhale, he spat a dark, viscous substance onto the ground.

A rush of cold clarity flooded through her—*he was sucking out the shadows.*

Elara was captivated, unable to look away as he continued, his lips brushing her skin with a disconcerting intimacy that sent a ripple of goosebumps across her skin. When he finally pulled back, his lips stained that vivid red against the pallor of his face, she could only stare. Words failed her, and her body refused to move. It was only when he spat out the last of Osin's shadows, that the world snapped into focus, a veil torn from her mind. Her heart raced, her limbs shook—but she was coming back.

Their eyes locked, and in the liquid fire of his gaze, Elara felt utterly exposed, as if he could peer straight into the core of her. *"Braithim do chroí ag bualadh arís,*[2]*"* he whispered. The exotic lilt of his words, the way his tongue wrapped around each syllable, sent an involuntary flutter of nerves coiling through her.

"You speak *Tírrish?*" The words slipped from her lips before she could stop them, and she winced at her own foolishness.

Of course, he can speak Tírrish. He is Fae.

"Do you speak Latherian?"

He said nothing. He only held her gaze with such intensity that she couldn't help but drink in the sight of him—every angular line and chiseled contour of his face. The bold sweep of his cheekbones, the firmness of his jaw, all cast in the flickering light from eyes that danced like fireflies through the cavern's gloom.

Devastating. That single word whispered through the chaos of her thoughts. The most breathtaking thing she had ever laid her eyes on.

Her gaze darted around, suddenly aware of her changed position—she was no longer in the spot she remembered but pushed up against the bars separating their cells. This close, she could see the imprints of his palms on the ground next to her, marks of his reach through the bars to help her. But then, he pulled back, retreating with the smooth caution of a cat retracting its claws.

"Bás mall dúinn ar fad scáth do rí. Coinnigh i do chuid fola rófhada é agus beidh géag in easnamh ort ... nó níos measa fós.[3]*"*

Elara shook her head. "I'm sorry. I don't understand." She placed her hand on her chest and gazed right into his eyes. "Thank you."

He cocked his head, studying her as if he were seeing her in a new light. His broad hand moved to his chest, mirroring her action. "Reynnar." The syllables were a mystery to her, yet she felt a strange comfort in their utterance.

There was a noticeable shift in his demeanor as he watched her, a gentleness creeping into his expression that suggested he recognized the gratitude on her face. The absurdity of the moment struck her then, a laugh bubbling up, ironic, and a bit self-deprecating. She had already disregarded Malak's stern instruction not to engage with the other prisoners.

So much for heeding warnings.

The Fae's amber eyes widened, a glint of intrigue lighting them up. A playful curve danced along his lips. But as quickly as the smile came, it vanished, replaced by a deep, contemplative look.

"Coinnigh greim daingean ar an tsolas sin. Tá sé de nós ag an áit seo an uile rud a sciobadh uait.[4]"

He gave a nod, a silent farewell before retreating from the iron bars and disappearing into the shadows of his cell. There was a sadness in the way he'd moved into the darkness, as if he'd resigned himself to it. His sunlit eyes and the depth of his gaze lingered on her mind, long into the night.

Elara jolted awake, the harsh clash of iron slicing through the dungeon's gloom. Her eyes flew open, wide, and searching, but no guard stood at her door.

"Tank yeh!"

The Fae in the neighboring cell spoke on a breath, urgency threading straight into her chest. He rattled the bars once more, pain flickering across his face as he let go. "Suas. Tank yeh."

Boots on stone—fast, closing—snapped Elara fully awake. Clarity and panic surged together as she understood the warning. Even as her pulse spiked, an absurd thought surfaced: *Thank you.* He'd taken the words for her name.

The urge to laugh caught and died as the footsteps drew nearer. She pushed to her feet and pressed her back to the cold stone, pulse skittering.

The Fae gave a single shake of his head and jabbed a finger at his own face. *"Eagla s'agatsa sin fórsa beatha s'acusan. Ná léirigh ach do chuid fraochtachta dóibh.*[6]*"*

His words spilled out, edged with warning, a feral light igniting in his eyes. Elongated canines flashed, a ripple of alarm skating her spine— but it wasn't fear that took hold. It was kinship. His stance wasn't a threat; it was a challenge, urging her to fight, to endure. She might not be the predator here, but she didn't have to be prey.

Elara's expression hardened, every line setting into resolve. Anger, she decided, was far better company than fear.

Boots clanked to a stop outside her cell. Her stomach tightened. Malak.

"Get up. You've been summoned."

A hard lump formed in her throat as the door swung wide. She rose, a shiver climbing up her legs not entirely from the chill.

Summoned.

"The Hallowed must be rebound, and I want you to administer the new seal."

Dread coiled in her stomach, a heavy, sinking weight.

"Move! We ain't got all bloody day."

Elara shot him a withering glare, chin tipped in defiance, even as pain throbbed through her wrist with each step. Blood dripped steadily behind her, marking her path from the cell.

The light—if it could be called that—offered no sense of time, but her body knew a night stolen of sleep. Silence pressed in as they moved down the tunnel. No one spoke. Not a breath out of place.

The Pit had its rules she was starting to realize. Speak, and you suffered. Elara wasn't sure who she hated more—the guards who enforced it, the prisoners who obeyed, or herself for falling into line so easily.

Her gaze swept from cell to cell, searching for another Fae. Yet every iron cage she passed stood empty.

At the top of the spiraling staircase, they emerged from the Pit into a vast atrium of stone columns and vaulted ceilings. Sunlight poured through narrow windows, fracturing across the polished floor. Servants hurried along the edges while soldiers lingered near the columns, voices low. Nobles in silk and steel drifted past in murmurs beneath the steady hum of movement.

Something was stirring—an assembly, perhaps?

Her fingers twitched as she caught her reflection in a nearby window —wrinkled dress, fresh bloodstains dark as bruises against the fabric. Her hair... she didn't need to look. She could feel the loose strands slipping from the ruined chignon. She stood out like a smear in a pristine painting, misplaced in all that order.

Malak didn't slow. He cut through the castle with single-minded purpose, straight for the throne room. The iron doors swung open, and Elara's thoughts screeched to a halt.

The High Council waited inside, stiff and regal, seated in a rigid line. Twelve chairs—eleven filled by the High Lords, the Sovereign's chosen enforcers spread across Latheria. Elara's throat tightened, her heart stuttering as their gazes locked onto her, tracking every step.

And at the center of it all sat Osin himself.

While the council sat cloaked in black, Osin burned like a flame among them. Deep red robes—the color of aged wine—marked him as the center of power. Where the others were severe, he was lavish: gold embroidery coiled in intricate spirals, dragons and phoenixes woven through the fabric. Symbols of power. Of rebirth. Of a rule forged in fire and blood.

As Elara stepped forward, their gazes bore down on her, heavy as a sentence already passed. Each look stripped her bare, cataloging every flaw. She felt it all—the bloodstains, the wrinkles, the loose strands of hair—magnified beneath their scrutiny, as though her very existence were on trial.

And maybe it was.

A cluster of Druids came into focus to the right, and Elara's stomach dropped at the sight of Edgar and Avis among them. Avis's expression was hollow, distant, as though she were looking straight through her. Confusion tangled with the ache tightening Elara's chest.

"Hallowed," Edgar said, voice tight as he inclined his head. He looked afraid, though he tried to hide it. She couldn't tell whether his fear was for her—or himself.

Osin clapped his hands, the sharp sound making her flinch. "Let's get started, shall we?"

His voice was smooth, almost pleasant, as he rose from the throne and descended the dais with infuriating ease. He stopped before Edgar, towering over him like a wolf sizing up a rabbit. "You have one minute—exactly one—to justify your grievous mishandling of my most prized possession before I decide whether you're worth the air you're breathing."

Edgar straightened, pale fingers trembling as they gripped his robes. "My Lord, the fault is mine entirely."

Elara's brow furrowed as Edgar continued, his tone polished with subservience. "I sought only to grant the Hallowed the honor of attending the equinox festivities this year. The city was secured—I ensured the most stringent lockdowns were in place. Yet somehow, the traitors managed to infiltrate. I assure you, my lord, I took every precaution, every measure to—"

Osin's shadow struck, quick as a whip. Edgar's neck twisted with a sickening crack.

Elara's knees buckled as the air slammed from her lungs. The world smeared at the edges, a hollow ringing filling her ears and swallowing the sound of Edgar's body hitting the floor.

"*Lies,*" Osin murmured, brushing an invisible speck of dust from his sleeve. "Lies, my pet, are such tiresome things."

He clicked his tongue softly, shaking his head. "A pity, really. I had hoped the High Priest would surprise me. But no matter." He stepped over Edgar's body to her, his voice lowering to an almost conspiratorial tone. "You understand, don't you? The world has little use for liars. And even less patience."

The faint twitch at the corner of Osin's eye was her only warning. Druids swarmed her, hands tearing at her hairpins and tugging at the ties of her dress. Rage shook her as she stared at Edgar—until fingers reached her bodice. She reacted on instinct, arms flying up to clutch it tight to her chest.

Osin returned to his throne without another glance.

"It's okay, Hallowed." Avis's voice was as cold and empty as her eyes. "You won't be summoning a spirit today, so you can keep your chemise on for the ritual."

In that fragile moment, Elara found her friend again—and somehow, it steadied her. She dipped her chin, swallowed the swell of emotion, and let them continue.

They stripped away her gown, leaving only the thin silk chemise clinging to her like a second skin, tracing the soft curve of her waist, the rise of her breasts, rosy beneath the pale fabric.

She shivered, drew a slow breath, and forced her nerves into something like control. Then the doors to the right of the dais groaned open. Footsteps followed—measured, deliberate. She didn't need to look. She could feel it.

Still, she lifted her gaze, drawn to the inevitable.

The Hunter strode in, flanked by two of Osin's Druids, the marks of recent battle clinging to him. His armor—usually immaculate—was scuffed and dented, grime streaking the skin beneath his mask. He favored one side as he walked, the limp unmistakable. He hadn't expected this summons any more than she had.

He stopped across the dais and faced her. Then, to Elara's astonishment, the Druids stepped in and began stripping away his armor.

Straps were unbuckled, metal lifted free and dropped to the stone in echoing thuds. Chest plate, pauldrons, gauntlets—piece by piece—until he stood in a plain white tunic, rumpled from the weight it had borne, and sturdy breeches.

When the Druids reached for the Hunter's mask, he stopped them with a look sharp enough to cut steel. They bowed low—nearly to the floor—and withdrew.

The room went still. His dark gaze found Elara's and held, unwavering, sending her pulse skittering. He didn't look away as he lifted a scarred, battle-worn hand and removed the mask in one smooth motion.

Elara's breath caught. Time seemed to stall.

He was striking. Dark curls spilled over rich brown skin, framing a face carved with harsh, masculine beauty. Sweat darkened his neck and brow, some strands clinging, others falling wild and untamed to his shoulders. His cheekbones looked carved from marble, with a brow that seemed perpetually furrowed, softened by his full, brooding lips.

This—this was the Hunter?

Elara's thoughts reeled as she tried to reconcile him with the boy she remembered—haughty, distant, always watching from the sidelines, like he didn't quite fit in. Hiding behind a mask even then. She'd assumed the years would have done their work. That the blood he'd spilled, the horrors he'd unleashed, would have twisted him into some kin d of monster.

A *beast*.

But unmasked, he was only a man. Flesh and blood and bone.

And somehow, that was so much worse.

Heat surged through her, rooting her in place as he closed the distance. Avis gave her a gentle shove, and Elara stumbled forward, unsteady, unsure of what was expected—of what they were meant to do.

The Hunter stopped inches from her, the space between them barely enough to breathe. His scent washed over her—smoke and something darker, rich with cedar and clove. His gaze swept her with unsettling focus, lingering on the wreck of her hair, the line of her neck, her parted lips, before dropping to her arm, where blood still seeped, stubborn and bright.

His jaw tightened. Something flickered in his eyes—gone before she could name it—and then he turned away.

Osin slammed his palm onto the table, the crack reverberating through the chamber.

"Ah! Tonight's entertainment," he announced to the High Council. "I cannot recall the last time these halls witnessed a binding ritual. Truly, it's a tradition we should indulge in more often."

He rose in one smooth motion, eyes gleaming with playful malice. "Elmweaver."

The word snapped like a lash. Avis rushed forward, bowing so low her forehead nearly brushed the floor.

"Yes, my lord."

"Proceed with the ritual. I understand you are intimately acquainted with its finer points, given your unique role as a seal bearer."

The world tilted beneath Elara's feet.

Avis was the second seal.

Her fingers dug into her thighs, nails biting deep, but the pain couldn't ground her—or stop the burn behind her eyes. A tear slipped free, then another, tracing down her cheeks before she realized she was crying.

"Yes, my lord."

It's not true. It can't be true. The words pounded through Elara as Osin demanded to see the seal. Avis lifted her hand and pulled the robe from her shoulder. The air seemed to vanish as the fabric fell away, revealing the mark Elara prayed wouldn't be there.

Her knees nearly gave out as the last threads of denial snapped. She tore her gaze aside, fixing on anything—*anything*—to keep from reacting, from crying, from giving Osin what he wanted. Her hands trembled as she clenched her chemise tight.

Osin inspected his nails as he spoke. "So you've performed the ritual before?"

"I have," Avis replied. "About a year ago, when I was first sent to Verdara."

Elara blinked, tears blurring her vision as she stared at Avis.

They had never performed any ritual together...

"Keep her awake this time," Osin cut in. "I want to see the moment it happens. When the light fades from her eyes."

Elara's stomach lurched, nausea surging so fast she barely held it back. *Keep her awake this time.*

Avis hesitated, uncertainty flickering across her face. "It will be... much harder to control her if she's awake, my lord."

"Are you saying it can't be done?"

"No, it can, it's just that—"

"Good. Proceed."

Elara went rigid as Avis rose, Yoni and Dominic's warnings crashing back all at once. An ancient spell. A battle of wills. Dominance and submission—each side pressing, testing, trying to break the other.

But what if she didn't break? What if she refused to submit?

"On your knees, if you would," Avis said.

Before Elara could process the command, the Hunter dropped to his knees without hesitation. Shock rippled through her at the sight of *him* kneeling before her. But when his gaze flicked up to hers, there was no defiance in his eyes. No submission, either. Only emptiness.

Avis's hand brushed her shoulder, light as a feather and just as searing. Elara flinched and shrugged it off before the weight could settle. She didn't look at Avis—didn't want to face the betrayal coiled there. Instead, she knelt opposite the Hunter, eyes fixed on the floor. She couldn't meet his gaze either, so she focused on his hands.

A ring gleamed in the dim light, four elemental stones marking a power she didn't possess—a power she would have to face.

Could she fight back—against him, against the seal?

He wielded the strength of all four elements. She had nothing but a broken bind she couldn't even feel. No hidden surge. No power waiting to answer—only silence.

The Druids began to circle them, each holding a vial of dark, grainy powder. Their chanting rose into a low hum, voices blending into an unsettling harmony that vibrated through Elara's bones, jolting her limbs.

It wasn't *Tirrish*. There was no gentle cadence, no whispered rise and fall. This language scraped—rough and guttural, the words grinding against her skin, almost painful to hear.

As they moved, the Druids tipped their vials, ash spilling in fine, glittering streams to form a perfect circle around Elara and the Hunter. It didn't settle at once—hovered briefly, then sank into the stone, leaving a faint, glowing boundary behind.

The circle constricted. The air thickened, pressing in as Elara's skin prickled with static, the hairs on her arms lifting.

Then the stone beneath them began to glow—first under the Hunter, then beneath her. Elara's breath caught as the light shifted and swirled, etching patterns across the floor. Constellations emerged. Two sets. One beneath him. One beneath her.

Elara shivered.

"This is a map of the stars under which I was born."

As the constellations formed, they began to twist and merge into a single pattern. Elara's heart sank. It was unmistakable—hauntingly similar to the mark Dario bore. Tears burned as she fought to hold them back. She'd known he'd lied, known he'd betrayed her, and still it hurt—some last, foolish hope clinging to the idea that there might have been an explanation.

"Hunter," Avis said, "this dagger has been blessed by the light of the blood moon. Obey your lord and use it to bind yourself to the Hallowed."

Nausea roiled through her, despair flooding close behind—and beneath it, a slow, gathering rage. Her gaze snapped to the Hunter as he reached for the blade. He had to stretch, arm straining, because Avis didn't cross the boundary—couldn't. Elara saw the hesitation at the circle's edge, as though something unseen barred her way.

The Hunter took the dagger—and to her surprise, didn't hesitate. He cut through his tunic, baring his chest, then carved a circle into his flesh with a steady hand, the blade slick with his blood. Elara couldn't look away as he reached for the boundary, mixing blood and ash along the blade's edge. He didn't flinch, though his jaw tightened as he pressed the ash-laden steel back into the wound, sealing the circle.

The moment felt unreal, dreamlike. The ritual wasn't something done by instinct—so how did he know exactly what to do?

Then it struck her.

The book.

Osin had pressed it into his hands earlier—the one he'd accepted with visible reluctance. He must have studied it, memorized every detail.

He was prepared for this.

She wasn't.

The Hunter slid the dagger into his belt, clearly unwilling to leave a weapon within her grasp again, then pressed his fingers into the wound, pulling them free slick with blood. When he held his hand out to her, her breath caught, anger blunting into paralyzing fear.

She didn't want this. Didn't want to be bound to him, to anyone, but especially not *him.* The very thought of it sent a cold, creeping dread curling through her.

"I'm not going to hurt you," his voice cut through her panic, firm enough to draw her gaze to his. When their eyes met, she froze. There—

flickering in their depths—was something she hadn't seen in years. Something she'd glimpsed only once before, back when they were children.

"Minva sölk harn."

"I'm not going to hurt you," he repeated, his tone gentle, as if soothing a frightened animal. The absurdity nearly made her laugh. He *was* hurting her—every second of this was tearing her apart.

His words unsettled her more than cruelty would have. Still, she didn't scream when he reached for her. Didn't claw at him as he used the blood on his finger to draw a matching circle over her heart.

His dark eyes held hers, unwavering, as though nothing—not the ritual, not the Druids' rising chant—could pull his focus from her. The air hummed, the sound vibrating up through the stone beneath her knees.

Elara watched, dazed, as the circle carved into his chest began to glow—soft at first, then brighter—until it flared against his skin. Light rippled, shadows leaping across his features as a constellation etched itself into his flesh, each line burning briefly before sinking deep, permanent.

Her gaze dropped to her own mark, expecting it to fade the same way. Instead, the light surged—hotter, blinding—searing into her skin. Shock tore through her as two more seals bloomed into being.

She froze, instinct screaming at her to move, to *do* something—but all she could do was stare. Her gaze flew to Avis, searching for an answer. When their eyes met, a cold emptiness caved in her chest.

Avis's face was drawn tight, her shoulder blazing as the mark glowed like molten iron.

Elara's gaze snapped to Osin, hunting for any sign he might be glowing too.

Because... *because* there was a *third* seal on her.

The realization punched the air from her lungs, breaths coming ragged. Fury roared up, hot and savage. She wanted to scream, to tear the castle down with her bare hands.

Fuck this.

With a harsh inhale, she slammed her eyes shut, blocking out the world. She retreated into that quiet corner, the one she'd always used to escape, to hide from the pain. But not this time. This time, she wasn't looking for peace—she was *hunting*.

Elara slipped through her mind like a shadow, every thought sharpening to a single, relentless focus. The roar of thoughts fell to nothing, even the erratic pounding of her own gods-damned heart dulled as she focused. At first, there was only stillness, an empty void stretching out. But then—there. Faint, barely more than a whisper, a pulse. One that was not her own.

Her eyes snapped open, a jolt shooting through her, but she stayed locked in, her mental grip on the pulse tightening with every bit of will she had left. She squeezed, digging in, determined to hold on, to crush it, pull it out by the *root*.

A gasp cut through the air beside her, and Elara caught a glimpse of the Hunter collapsing, felt a rush of blood pour from her nose. But she didn't let it distract her. She shut her eyes, pushing deeper into her mind. The sight only fueled her, her grip on his pulse tightening, squeezing with everything she had. She didn't know if she wanted to kill him—didn't even know what she was trying to do—but the rage pulsing through her veins was blinding, all-consuming.

She forced her eyes open, finding the Hunter crouched low, one hand braced against the floor, the other clutching his chest—just like in the Hartling Forest. Elara's fury honed to a lethal edge. She shut out the world—the frantic hum of the room, Osin's voice rising outside the boundary, barking orders to the Druids. It didn't matter. They couldn't touch her. The barrier held firm, trapping her and the Hunter inside.

She latched onto his pulse harder, *digging* in, and suddenly his head snapped up, his eyes locking onto hers. The ring of amber around his pupils blazed.

A warning.

Something inside him waking up—something powerful.

Her breath hitched just before it happened—a blinding flash, violent and unstoppable, burst from both of them, tearing through the space like a wildfire.

The boundary shattered as light flooded every inch of the throne room, chasing the shadows away with a brilliance so intense it felt like the sun had exploded.

The power tore through Elara, surging through every vein, setting her alight from the inside, unstoppable, untamable. Her skin burned with it, her muscles trembling.

The shockwave that followed hit like a battering ram, rattling the walls and sending cracks racing through the stone, knocking back anyone caught in its path.

Osin staggered, his face twisted in shock, hands thrown up in a desperate, useless attempt to shield himself from the light, the High Council's shouts echoing in the chaos.

And then, just as suddenly, the light vanished, leaving her hollow. Silence crashed down, crushing. Her hands shook, aftershocks rippling through her as she braced her palms against the cold stone, fighting for breath.

Something inside felt... off.

Wrong.

Nausea twisted her stomach, but the emptiness—the void the power had left behind—was worse.

"Did it work?" Osin's voice cut through the quiet, laced with a frantic edge. "Is she bound?"

Elara lifted her gaze, vision swimming as the room came into focus. The council lay scattered—some slumped in their chairs, others thrown clear, one even cowering behind the table. But Osin still stood. Barely. His face was ashen, disbelief hollowing his expression.

Avis struggled upright, hands trembling as she tried to speak—but the Hunter answered first.

"It worked," he said, tone flat as he rose, his movements almost too controlled.

But Elara could feel him—every frantic beat of his heart, every shallow, uneven breath he tried to steady, even the bead of sweat slowly tracing its path down his temple. She squeezed the pulse again, testing it, and saw it—the faintest twitch in his eyes.

Subtle, but enough to betray him.

A spark of satisfaction surged through Elara, quiet and clean, like a blade slipping between ribs.

He was *lying.*

CHAPTER 22

Why would the Hunter lie?

The question thundered through Elara's chest—louder than her heartbeat, louder even than Malak's heavy footsteps as he dragged her back to the cell.

Despite Osin's words, lies were the true currency in Ulrith. She knew that. They were traded like silver in the markets above, passed from tongue to tongue with a smile. But what had his lie cost? What price did his deceit demand? Power? Fear?

Elara bit her lip.

Perhaps he was stalling—buying himself a few precious seconds before Osin's fury came crashing down. The ritual had failed. That much was obvious. Any competent observer could see it.

But then... perhaps it hadn't failed in the way Osin believed.

Something about the bind unsettled him. Something he didn't want Osin to uncover. Elara knew he had no desire to be bound to her—no more than she wished to be bound to him—but men like the Hunter never acted without calculation. If he was lying, it wasn't for Osin's sake. And it certainly wasn't for hers.

Her stomach twisted, a sharp, sudden pang cutting through the thought. Hunger. When had she last eaten? A day—barely more? Fear and upheaval had pushed the need aside, buried it beneath more urgent concerns.

But now... now it made itself impossible to ignore.

As the hunger settled, something else followed. A spark. Small but stubborn.

Osin had wanted her broken. Had wanted to watch the light die in her eyes. Instead, she felt the opposite. A faint pulse thrummed beneath her skin. The ritual hadn't crushed her. Not the way he'd intended. Somehow, she'd held on, even without understanding how.

But with every step deeper into the Pit, her grip on the Hunter's seal began to loosen. Bit by bit. Like water slipping through her fingers. *Does distance weaken the connection?*

Her cell door waited open at the end of the tunnel, iron-bound wood groaning as they neared. Malak shoved her forward, fingers digging into her arm, rough and careless.

Then someone cleared their throat behind them.

Malak froze mid-step, his grip tightening before he let her go. Elara looked back to see a Druid striding toward them, emerald robes billowing with purpose. A Greenheart. The color alone marked her, but the tension in her face made it clear she hadn't stumbled on them. She'd been waiting.

"I have orders from the Hunter to tend to the Hallowed's wounds," she announced, voice firm. Her gaze flicked over Elara in a swift assessment before snapping back to Malak, daring him to object.

Elara blinked, startled. The cut on her wrist had slipped her mind entirely. After the ritual, she hadn't even registered the lack of pain. She glanced down now to see the wound had finally clotted.

The Greenheart handed Malak a neatly folded missive. He hesitated, eyed it as if it might bite, then unfolded it, parchment crackling as he read. His expression darkened, his lip curling in distaste.

With a grunt, Malak crumpled the paper in his fist. No explanation. No argument. Just that sour look. Then he turned on his heel, stomping off into the darkness.

Elara watched him leave, her brow knitting. When had the Hunter found time to send the order? And why, after everything, was he still watching out for her?

"Follow me," the Greenheart said. Her gaze lingered on Elara for a heartbeat before she bit her lip and turned away. Elara fell into step beside her as they took the far-right tunnel. The air grew colder. The passage was similar to the one leading to her cell—narrow, dimly lit, the stone walls damp with moisture.

The tunnel seemed to shrink around them, the ceiling lowering, the walls pressing closer until finally, at the very end, there was a door.

The Greenheart pushed it open, revealing yet another tunnel, but this one was different. It yawned wide, massive, the ceiling arching high above as it stretched endlessly into the dark.

Elara's gaze traveled upward, where cells stretched out in every direction, not just on the ground but rising level upon level, tier after tier, like some twisted library of the damned. Iron catwalks crisscrossed between them, suspended in the air, barely wide enough for a person to walk, their railings rusted and thin.

It wasn't the size of the place that hit her—it was the people. Elara's movements slowed, as if the world around her had blurred. Her mind numbed, unable to fully process what she was seeing.

The cells—they were filled. *Packed*. Figures huddled in the shadows, pressed against iron bars, their faces pale and sunken, skin stretched tight over bone.

Eyes, so many eyes, staring out—blank, hollow, lifeless.

The stench of rot and sweat clawed at her nose, thick and sour. Her mouth went dry, her stomach twisting violently. She tried to breathe, to swallow, but she felt like she was drowning in it—drowning in the sight, the smell, the sheer number of people trapped here.

No, not people—*Fae*. Hundreds, maybe even *thousands* of them crammed into cells like animals. Elara's heart stuttered, then kicked into a frantic rhythm, pounding so hard she could feel it in her throat.

How? How was this even possible?

She doubled over, pressing a hand to her mouth as if she could physically hold back the bile rising in her throat. The sheer scale of their suffering—it was overwhelming.

"Come," the Greenheart urged, now standing in front of her, but she shook her head, refusing to move. She leaned back against the wall, only to jerk forward when wards crackled against her skin, sending a sharp sting through her body.

Elara shuddered and met the Druid's gaze, throat tightening as she swallowed. "How are they here?" she rasped.

The Druid said nothing, not a flicker of emotion passing over her features. The silence felt intentional, like she was forcing Elara to draw her own conclusions, to see more than what was in front of her.

Her chest tightened as her hands curled into fists at her sides. "Why show me this? Why not just heal me in my cell?"

The Greenheart's eyes danced with something unreadable as she stepped closer, her voice dropping to a near whisper. "Because there's nothing anyone can do for them. But there is power in knowing, *in seeing*. To witness what's hidden is to carry the burden of truth, and truth, as you know, has a way of making itself known." Her gaze drifted down to Elara's chest, where the seals had revealed themselves just an hour ago, now concealed within her flesh once more.

"What hides in shadow does not remain so forever," she added, a faint smile touching her lips. "Light, in its own time, finds its way."

The Greenheart's hand was warm and steady, grounding Elara as she led her out of the chamber and through another door.

"The infirmary is just through here," she murmured, but Elara wasn't listening. The space they entered was nothing like the nightmare they had left behind. It felt ancient, as though it had existed long before the cavern walls were hollowed around it. As if the earth itself had cradled the place, protecting it—keeping it sacred.

The air was cool, heavy with damp stone and a faint, almost floral trace, like incense sunk into the walls. Her footsteps vanished into the vastness, but the low hum of power did not. It pressed against her skin, a subtle vibration.

Dominating the room were four monoliths, massive stones thrusting up from the ground as if they'd clawed their way out of the earth. They towered above the women, worn smooth in some places, rough and scarred in others. Elara couldn't tear her eyes away. They felt holy, untouched, like the gods had left their fingerprints here.

She stepped closer to the stones, and that strange prickling at her skin intensified. "What is that?" Elara whispered, almost afraid to disturb the air.

The Greenheart's steps faltered, just for a moment, before she forced herself to keep moving, her pace quickening as if to escape the question.

"We aren't to speak of the stones."

"Why?"

The healer shot her an exasperated look over her shoulder, but there was something else there too—*fear.*

~

"Do your best to keep the wound dry. Constant exposure to moisture will interfere with the scabbing process and delay healing," the Greenheart said briskly, moving from her cluttered worktable to where Elara sat on the edge of a low stone slab.

The infirmary was dimly lit by flickering candles set into the rough-hewn walls, their light skimming shelves lined with jars of herbs, dried roots, and ancient tomes. Earthy, medicinal scents hung close, prickling Elara's throat.

The Greenheart picked up a tub of salve and began rubbing it into Elara's cut. "Wounds tampered with by ethereal means—"

"I know," Elara interrupted, her voice flat. "They take time to heal and always scar."

The Druid paused, then dipped her chin in acknowledgment. "Of course you do. My apologies."

Elara winced as the woman worked the salve in, biting back a hiss. She fixed her attention anywhere else, her gaze lifting to the Greenheart's face.

She looked to be in her late thirties, faint threads of gray slipping from beneath her hood. Exhaustion lined her eyes, yet there was an enduring grace to her features, a quiet beauty worn thin but not erased. Her eyes caught Elara's attention most—deep, rich brown, steady despite the fatigue.

Elara's gaze drifted to the woman's totem. A familiar tree wrapped in a scroll. Aewora.

A southerner.

"What's your name?"

The healer had thrown her earlier, those cryptic words still echoing in her mind.

What hides in shadow does not remain so forever.

A hint, clearly. But at what?

The woman paused, fingers stilling at Elara's wrist, her mouth pressing into a thin line as she looked up. "Saria," she said at last.

A sharp knock broke their gaze. Saria set the salve aside and went to the door. The moment her back turned, Elara's trembling fingers darted out, snatching the jar and slipping it into her underthings at her hip

Sweat formed on Elara's palms. The odds of her having access to a healer again were slim, and in a place like this, any advantage, no matter how small, could make all the difference. Better to be prepared, just in case.

Saria cracked the door, murmuring, "Two minutes. That's all I can give you."

Elara's stomach tightened as she looked up. Avis stood in the doorway, expression composed as she nodded to Saria. But her eyes were fixed on Elara, pinning her in place.

Saria slipped out, the door closing with a soft click that rang too loud in the sudden quiet.

As Avis stepped closer, a faint trace of oíche blossoms reached Elara —delicate, sweet, painfully familiar. The scent struck deep, stirring a pang she wasn't ready to face. Her throat tightened. It was the smell of safety once. Of softness.

"El—"

"Don't," Elara snapped, shoving herself off the slab. Her heart thundered, but she kept her gaze cold. "I don't want your excuses. I know about Dario." The name scorched her throat. "Who is the third?"

"Edgar," Avis said, not missing a beat. She edged closer, eyes softening, brows knitting in a silent plea. "I won't pretend I will mourn him, but you have to see—we didn't have a choice." Her voice stayed gentle, as if that might blunt the impact, make the knife in Elara's back twist a little less.

Elara shut her eyes, but the memory struck anyway—Edgar's neck snapping, sudden and final. Her eyes flew open, nausea rolling through her. "I don't want to hear it," she said, reaching for anger and finding only exhaustion. "I'm done playing this game."

Avis shook her head. "If only it were that simple. The game doesn't end until you *start* playing it."

"What the hell does that even mean?"

"It means that pretending you're not involved won't save you. It means the rules were set long before you had a choice."

Elara wanted to scream, to rip the room apart, to let the fury inside her explode and consume everything in its path. But all she could do was stand there, seething. Avis's words were meaningless. More cryptic *bullshit*. She bit the inside of her cheek, tasting blood, her fists clenched so tightly her nails dug into her palms.

Avis stepped forward cautiously. "I did what I had to. Dario did too. Edgar forced us to place the seal on you. It was before we knew you—before we understood what it would mean. Edgar... he couldn't handle you anymore. He was getting older, and you, Elara, were getting stronger. Too strong for him to control."

"So you helped him cage me?" Elara's voice was ice, sharp enough to cut. "Every time you were near me, touched me..." The ghost of Dario's kiss pressed against her lips, the sensation lingering as if it had just happened. The pressure of his hands, the way he'd cupped her face with such tenderness.

"We did it to protect you," Avis said. "Edgar assured us that by tempering whatever power lies within you, we were safeguarding you from a greater danger." She paused, her hands tightening into fists at her sides. "We never sought to cause you pain."

Elara's chest tightened. Every memory, every touch, every word from them felt tainted now, twisted and poisoned. The ache inside her was unbearable, a raw, burning throb that made it feel like her ribs might crack under the pressure. She ground her teeth, forcing the words past the fury choking her. "Where is Dario?"

Her throat bobbed. "I haven't seen him since the day you left."

"He ran?"

Avis shook her head, her expression pained. "No. He didn't take anything with him. He went out to find you... and he never returned."

Elara turned on her heel, eyes squeezing shut. Was he dead? She shouldn't feel a damn thing—she didn't want to. But the thought of Dario lying somewhere lifeless and cold...

Gods, why did she *still* care?

She clenched her fists, wanting to slam her head against the wall, do anything to drown out the mess of emotions raging inside her. The anger, the hurt, the guilt—it was all too much.

"Elara, I don't have much time."

She pressed her palms to her eyes, breathed once, and turned—eyes narrowing on Avis.

"Stay quiet. Keep your head down. Don't cause trouble," Avis said, her gaze flicking toward the door, as if every second counted. "Algernon's trying to get you out, to get you back home."

Elara's lips curled in a bitter smile. "That place isn't my home."

"It is better than here," Avis said tightly, the strain breaking through before she paused, eyes closing briefly. When she spoke again, her tone was softer but no less intense. "You cannot imagine what Osin is capable of... the things he does to those who—"

The door creaked open, and Saria stepped in, two guards shadowing her.

"Thank you for assisting, Healer Hartwell," Saria said smoothly, her tone polite but firm. "I'll take it from here."

Avis dipped her head in a quick, controlled bow. "Of course," she said, her voice steady, betraying nothing. Without another word, she turned to leave. But as she reached the doorway, she hesitated, glancing back at Elara.

Something flickered in her eyes. Another warning, maybe. Sadness, definitely. Then Avis turned away, her footsteps fading down the corridor, leaving the room colder in her absence. The faint scent of flowers still lingered, the only trace that she had been there at all.

MOTHER SAVE HER, she was so bloody tired of being manhandled.

Elara shoved herself upright, jaw tight as she clutched the bundle of clothes Saria had practically thrown at her. *"Healer's orders."*

By the time they reached the cell, she was hauled inside like cargo.

The door slammed, iron grinding against stone as the wards flared, ether buzzing in the air like angry wasps.

She lifted her chin, eyes blazing as she memorized the guards' faces. One looked half-dead, sallow and pocked, like he'd crawled out of a sickbed. The other, jittery as a rodent, his eyes darting everywhere. She stored them away, adding them to the growing list of bastards who'd dared lay hands on her.

They didn't spare her a glance as they walked away, talking amongst themselves like she wasn't even there, their crude laughter looping down the tunnel.

Elara clutched the clothes tighter to her waist, pressing the bundle against the small jar of salve she'd hidden earlier. If Saria had noticed the awkward bulge beneath the fabric, she hadn't said a damn thing. And now, as Elara sat with her heart still racing from the thrill of having smuggled it away, she couldn't help but wonder if the healer might have simply given it to her, had she only thought to ask.

Pushing herself up from the floor, Elara placed the stack of clothes on the cot, her gaze darting around to ensure no one was watching. She grabbed the pants first, sliding them on in one smooth motion. They were soft, thicker than anything she'd worn in weeks—months, maybe. With a swift yank, she peeled off the thin chemise and reached for the tunic, followed by the chunky, knitted wool sweater that carried a faint scent of rosemary and mint.

The smell pulled her to a stop.

Such a small, simple thing, yet it steadied her for a brief moment. It brought to mind her room in the Sanct—the herbs she had hung by the window, and the gentle way the sun filtered through the curtains. And for just a second, she could almost feel it again. That sense of safety.

Elara closed her eyes. She knew the Sanct had never really been safe. Not truly. Not in the way she'd wanted to believe. It had all been a lie— a fragile illusion she'd clung to before the veil over her eyes had ripped apart.

Still, for a moment, it had felt like safety, and some part of her longed for that lie.

The socks came last. Wool again. Soft and warm, and she sat down on the cot, pulling them on one by one. She could have cried at the feel of them, how they instantly heated her cold, aching feet. But as she slipped on the second sock, something hard pressed against her toes, smooth like glass.

She stopped short, then tore the sock free and dug inside until her fingers closed around something small and solid. A vial.

Her breath hitched as she uncorked it, hands shaking. Inside was a tightly rolled scrap of parchment. She unwrapped it, nearly dropping the tiny pill that slipped free.

Her eyes scanned the words hastily scrawled on the note: *"Wait for the signal, they come in threes, then swallow this. Make sure you've got an audience when it kicks in. Don't hold back on the theatrics."*

A shiver traced her spine as she stared at the pill. And here she'd thought the day couldn't get worse. Elara let out a sharp breath, slid the note back into the vial with the pill, and shoved it into her pocket.

She was tugging the sock back on when a low, resonant growl sounded behind her, stopping her cold. Elara spun, locking eyes with the Fae. His gaze burned with a fierce focus as it swept over her, lingering long enough to make her skin prickle.

"Rinne tú go maith, Tank yeh.[7]*"*

A laugh burst from Elara despite everything she had just been through. She shook her head, a wry smile tugging at her lips as her hand pressed to her chest, feeling the wild dance of her heart beneath the skin. "Elara," she named herself.

His brows drew together, a question in his gaze. She extended her hand, pointing toward him. "Reynnar?" she asked. He nodded slowly, confirming her guess.

"Eilíara?"

His attempt to mimic her name raised goosebumps on her skin, a strange thrill coursing through her heart.

"Yes."

"Tá sé deas bualadh leat, a Eilíara.[8]"

His words were as incomprehensible as ever, yet the sentiment he expressed seemed to bridge the gap between their languages, and a strange, profound connection blossomed in that space.

"I'm glad to have met you, Reynnar."

His answering smile flashed white in the dim light, the sharp tips of his fangs glinting like hidden daggers. Warmth stirred in her chest—an unexpected ember against cold stone, iron bars, and the shadow of an uncertain future.

The vial pressed against her leg as Reynnar cast her one last look before vanishing into his cell. A spark of hope flared in Elara's chest.

In this wretched place, she was not alone.

CHAPTER 23

Time lost its edges—day bleeding into night, night dissolving back into day, until it all felt like one endless stretch of gray. Elara, alongside Reynnar, drifted through their days like ghosts occupying the same space.

Life had settled into a numbing routine, a continuous loop of mundane tasks punctuated only by the sporadic arrival of meals too scant to sate any hunger. The occasional appearance of the jailers, heralded by the metallic scrape of trays and the shuffling of the weary souls throughout the Pit, marked the only variance in the monotony that had become her reality.

Each captive was allotted two buckets: one for bodily relief and the other for washing, a situation that was as degrading as it was disgusting. The water they provided for bathing was always dirty and cold, and no matter how vigorously Elara scrubbed, each attempt to wash seemed only to embed the dirt further into her skin. When she redressed in the same grimy, sweat-soaked clothes, it felt as though she would never rid herself of the filth—or the shame.

And Elara did feel shame. So much of it. Shame for endangering the Keepers by bringing a ring into their midst, shame for her role in Edgar's death, shame for deluding herself into thinking she could be anything other than what she was. How stupid—how painfully naive—to believe her darkest days were behind her.

Her cell was a prison in every sense. Her hair clung to her scalp, clothes sticking to her skin with a dampness that never left. Raw patches had formed at her wrists and ankles from constant friction, and her fingers, swollen and blistered, bore the beginnings of sores. Every inch of her body felt like it was slowly decaying, making sleep impossible.

Her nights were spent twisting and turning, searching for even a sliver of comfort that never came. The weak torchlight would flicker against the walls, playing tricks on her, turning shadows into monsters that lurked just out of sight. But it wasn't just the walls trapping her—it was the crushing sameness of it all. Day after day, nothing changed, nothing shifted. The repetition was worse than the bars, worse than the stone. It was the slow death of everything she'd once been. An erosion of her spirit.

In those first days, she searched the prison for any sign of Godfrey, holding onto the faintest hope of catching a glimpse of him. She even tried to request another visit with Saria, praying it might give her a chance to see more of the Pit and map out its layout in her mind. But she'd been right—seeing a healer was a rare privilege down here, one even the sick and dying didn't receive. Every day, the air would reek of death, and bodies—*so many bodies*—were carried out of this wretched place. Almost always, they came from the tunnel where the Fae were held.

Each night, like clockwork, Elara's mind drifted back to the binding ritual. To the way the Hunter's seal had been hers to command, how she'd held it in her grasp, feeling his power throb beneath her control. It was intoxicating, that rush. But now, after hearing Avis's excuses, it left a sour taste in her mouth. She didn't know what to feel. Edgar had ordered them to control her? *Fine.* But they could've at least had the decency to tell her what they were doing. To explain it. Make her understand. Instead, they hid behind their lies, protecting themselves, and left her to piece it together, left her to rot in the dark.

After what felt like hours of twisting beneath the covers, Elara would finally give in, curling into herself, knees pulled tight to her chest. Sleep was elusive, always just out of reach, so she spent those endless nights chasing it through the only way she knew—ritualized control. Over and over, she walked that familiar mental path, searching for any trace of the seals, pushing herself until exhaustion finally dragged her under. But even in her dreams the memory of that *force*, that blinding light kept replaying on a loop. It had been pure instinct, an impulse that flared to life in the heat of the moment. And now, she didn't have the faintest idea how to call it back.

A fragile connection with Reynnar offered her a sliver of contact with the world outside her cage. It wasn't much, but it kept her tethered, kept her from drifting entirely into despair. Alongside this, she became an expert observer, gathering scraps of information like a squirrel hoarding nuts for winter. From fragmented whispers to the soft shuffling of bodies in the dark, she pieced together that this place was filled with Faeries.

So many of them.

She had always assumed the prison was filled with rebels, yet she seemed to be the only human captive here.

She thought back to that small group of Keepers she'd traveled with and the knot in her stomach twisted tighter. Had they survived? If her suspicions were right—if Osin had used that dagger, sent his shadows crawling inside her mind, picking apart her memories—then he'd seen them. He'd seen their faces, marked them all. The traitor prince, he'd called Dominic. Elara's heart clenched. She could only hope they'd made it out alive.

But hope felt thin, fragile—especially in a place like this.

Tortured screams echoed through the tunnels every night. On some occasions, the sound was so unbearable that Elara could only curl into herself, sobbing until exhaustion finally dragged her into a fitful sleep.

Reynnar, though—he never broke. Night after night, he stood at the front of his cell, motionless, as if he were carved from stone. His eyes never closed, his body never sagged with exhaustion. He stayed like that, silent, as if he could feel every scream, every cry, like a blade cutting into him. Elara couldn't fathom why they'd locked him away from the others, why his cell was placed in this nearly abandoned tunnel. But maybe that was the point—a twisted form of torture, making him listen to his people's suffering, knowing he couldn't reach them. Couldn't help.

Osin's audacity baffled her. Why risk the Mothers' fury?

What need did Latheria have for captive Fae?

And most concerning of all, *how* had he done it?

It shouldn't have been possible. The Mothers had decreed that neither race could cross into the other's realm. Yet, there they were, defying the very laws of their existence. And Elara was hellbent on figuring out how.

When Elara did find sleep, she would dream strange, unsettling dreams. They weren't nightmares, but they left her with the same feeling of being unmoored. Like the visions the river spirit used to give her—fleeting images, fragments of something just beyond her reach. She felt adrift, searching for something she couldn't name.

And then, always—him.

The Hunter.

Every single night.

Sometimes he appeared as a boy, standing in the court with eyes too knowing for someone so young. Other times, she saw him as the warrior, cutting his way through the forest, the crackling flames at his back as if they answered to him alone. But it was the other vision that haunted her most—the man on his knees, surrounded by ash, his hollow eyes fixed on her, empty and waiting.

Each time she woke, her heart thundered in her chest, her skin damp with sweat. The dreams left her shaken, so rattled that she'd stumble to the murky, foul water in her cell just to splash some sense back into herself. But it never helped.

In the mornings, when the first round of guards would dole out tooth-cracking bread alongside a questionable, fishy-smelling soup, Reynnar would quietly slide a portion of his food across the cold floor to her. He seemed to think she needed it more than he did. After a while, she stopped arguing and accepted it.

Their shared mornings became something of a sacred routine, a quiet communion in their imprisonment. His voice became her dawn, the exotic cadence of his native tongue weaving a spell of comfort around her frayed edges. The stories he told, indecipherable as they were, carried a beauty that didn't need translation, their rhythm a lullaby that coaxed her into a semblance of peace she hadn't known since being trapped.

In return, she would whisper stories of Aewora's towering mountains, how she'd spent hours in the Sanct, watching the sun bathe their golden peaks and dreaming of scaling them, just to capture the entirety of Latheria in one sweeping gaze. She spoke of her longing for the ocean, of the pull she felt toward the endless stretch of blue, imagining what it would be like to dive beneath the waves and taste the sweet freedom they promised.

Reynnar listened intently, his eyes never leaving hers, offering soft, empathetic hums, and quiet smiles that kept her grounded, kept her from slipping away into the dark. In a place where it would have been so easy to lose herself, his steady presence kept her tethered to something real. Something that still felt like hope.

By the fourth or fifth week in captivity—Elara couldn't be sure—she watched in horror as the guards dragged Reynnar from his cell. His brief struggle barely made a difference, a flicker of defiance snuffed out almost as quickly as it sparked. She had yelled at them to stop, rattled her bars like he had done for her on that first morning. But Elara quickly learned why the others stayed silent, why they didn't interfere.

For this was a place where voices died on bruised lips.

Malak had burst into her cell, cutting off her plea with a brutal backhand that whipped her head to the side, pain exploding in her jaw. Before she could even recover, his boot slammed into her ribs, knocking the air from her lungs and leaving her gasping, crumpled on the floor. He stormed out without a word, and in the throbbing silence that followed, a cold realization settled over her.

Osin hadn't just caged them—he'd somehow stripped the Fae of their power.

Reynnar's words should have been imbued with the strength of the ancients, but they were empty, hollow, drained of the ether that was rightfully his. But it couldn't just be him; it had to be all of them. Osin must have robbed every Fae of their birthright, reducing them to mere husks of themselves, powerless against their shackles.

When they tossed Reynnar back into his cell, broken and bruised,

Elara had to force herself not to look away, swallowing the sob that threatened to escape. His body was a map of suffering, slashed, and smeared in deep purples, blacks, and blues, each mark screaming of the torment he'd endured. She stood by the bars that separated them, gripping the cold iron as if it could somehow bridge the distance between them, watching helplessly as he fought to breath, his chest rising and falling in a jagged rhythm.

Time felt like it dragged on, the seconds heavy and painful, until finally, he stirred.

But when his gaze met hers, there was a trace of something shattered in his expression, a fracture deep within that hadn't been there before. And seeing him like that broke something inside her too.

Their eyes met, locked in a silent exchange of shared pain, until he dragged himself closer, inch by agonizing inch, to where she knelt.

All Elara could offer was the small comfort of running her fingers through his hair while applying salve to the wounds within her reach. A gesture that felt so pitifully inadequate for the magnitude of his suffering.

But when her hand touched him, his eyes fluttered shut, a pained smile tugging at his cracked lips, reopening the scab on his mouth. And in that moment, she knew. It hit her with a force she couldn't ignore—her purpose, her path, crystallized with a clarity so sharp it cut through everything else she had ever known.

It wasn't just about escaping her pain or finding freedom. It was about *them*—the Fae, Reynnar, all those crushed beneath Osin's power, just as she had been. For so long, she had fought in silence, trapped in her own suffering, numb to the world around her.

Their pain reflected her own, but Reynnar's presence stirred something deeper—something she'd never felt when fighting for herself. He reminded her that she wasn't in this battle alone anymore. She wasn't the only one clawing her way out of the darkness.

And that changed everything.

So, she would play Osin's game. She would learn, grow, and then turn the game on its head.

She'd make them pay.

Every single one of them.

CHAPTER 24

"I will not," Elara stated, lips pressed into a thin line as she fixed Reynnar with a determined stare. "*You* need to eat."

As if on cue, their breakfast arrived with a metallic clatter, the sparse meal tossed carelessly onto the floor of the cell. And just as predictably, Reynnar nudged his portion toward her.

He hadn't eaten the night before—not after they'd thrown him back into his cell. He'd spent the night sprawled near the bars, and she'd watched him the whole time, the steady rise and fall of his chest her only reassurance. By morning, a dark bruise bloomed across his jaw, swollen and angry.

It explained the untouched meal. But Elara wasn't about to let him miss another. She couldn't—when every bite might mean the difference between him surviving this or not.

"You need it to heal," she insisted, her voice threading through the chilly cell air as she pushed his portion of what looked like pig's feet and potato stew toward him. At least this meal was hearty. It would do him some good.

Reynnar studied her beneath the dim orb-light. He seemed to weigh every shift of her expression before the corner of his mouth twitched into a tentative smile, cracking the scab on his lip and drawing a bead of fresh blood.

"*Íosfaidh mé, mura mbeadh ann ach go mbíonn tú chomh gleoite sin nuair a bhíonn tú tiarnúil.*[9]"

She watched, barely breathing, as Reynnar finally took a bite. The tension in her shoulders eased, just a little. Only then did she lift her own spoon, though the knot in her throat made each swallow feel like stone.

She tracked his movements as he ate, relief settling in when he finished the last bite. He pushed the tray aside and stretched, muscles in his chest and stomach pulling taut—catching her gaze for a heartbeat too long. She looked away. She was used to seeing him shirtless by now, but that didn't mean she needed to ogle him. Even if sometimes it was hard not to.

When she looked back, Reynnar was smiling—that half-smile she'd come to love, the one that showed just the faintest tips of his fangs.

Elara gestured toward her teeth, curiosity getting the better of her. "Do you... what are those for?"

She had heard stories of the *gwyllgi*, the black hounds known to stalk travelers through the night, draining the life from both humans and beasts. She couldn't help but wonder if there was some truth to those tales when she looked at his fangs.

Reynnar mirrored her gesture, fingers brushing over one of his fangs, his eyes gleaming with something almost playful. "*Fiosrach fúthu seo? I gcomhrac, tá siad ceaptha greim a fháil san fheoil - díreach anseo.*[10]" He tapped his neck. "*An áit a tapúla a ritheann an fhuil. Gasta, éifeachtach - níos úsáidí ná lann i ndlúthchomhrac.*[10] *Ach is féidir iad a úsáid ar bhealaí eile freisin,*[10]" he added, his grin deepening. "*Ní le haghaidh troda ... nó ar a laghad, ní sa bhealach a shílfeá.*[10]"

Elara blinked. "That was a lot of words." She laughed, shaking her head as a small smile tugged at her lips, mirroring his. But then, a sudden flash caught her eye—an errant ball of light drifting into her cell.

In an instant, they were on their feet. *What—*

The orb hovered midair, softly glowing, one of the thousands that drifted through the Pit like aimless stars in the dark. But they never entered the cells. *Never.* The faint light flickered, casting strange shadows across the rough-hewn floor as it hovered just before her. A chill swept over her skin, her breath quickening.

"*Gabh siar, a Eilíara.*[11]"

She snapped out of her daze, instinctively stepping back from the orb before freezing mid-step. Her heart pounded louder in her ears as she turned back to it. Could this be the signal? After all this time? The thought sent a rush of ice through her veins. She had given up weeks ago. Had nearly crushed the pill beneath her heel more times than she could count. But something—some small, stubborn part of her—had kept her from doing it. Had kept her waiting.

The orb pulsed brighter—once, twice, three times—before darting out of her cell, vanishing as quickly as it had come.

The signal comes in threes. This was it.

Elara's hands shook as she glanced toward the center of the Pit, where the guards had started to gather, their armor clinking as they laughed, taking bets on which prisoner would break first today.

Her eye twitched.

The note had been clear—*make sure there's an audience when it kicks in.*

It was right before the shift change—her only window. She had maybe ten minutes, if that. Elara glanced at Reynnar, nerves coiling as she bit her lip. She wished she could warn him.

His gaze stayed locked on hers, steady, as if he already sensed what was coming. The familiar intensity burned there, and she echoed the gesture he'd made that first day—pointing to her face. A signal. One he'd understand.

Reynnar stilled. Something dark flickered in his eyes. Then his lips curved into a slow, wicked smile.

A thrill shot down her spine.

"*Not the prey.*" She whispered into the space between them.

Heart hammering, Elara edged to the side of the cell, careful to keep her distance from the wards. Her gaze drifted to the wall near the bars— to the loose stone she'd discovered during her first week. The vial was still there. Waiting.

Whoever had left the note—Saria, most likely, though Avis crossed her mind as well—expected her to trust a mystery pill? She almost scoffed. Trust was a luxury she no longer afforded. Not without proof.

Still, that didn't mean she couldn't play along. See where the game led.

On her terms.

Don't hold back on the theatrics.

Oh, she'd give them a show.

Elara raked her fingers through her hair, tugging free a few pins and pocketing the cool metal. Her hair spilled loose in messy waves over her shoulders. She untucked her tunic, rumpling the fabric, then reached for her cloak. Her hand lingered on the edge—her last scrap of warmth —before she tore it from her shoulder.

She winced as the ruined cloth fell away and set her shoulders, ignoring the cold seeping in.

Focus.

She cleared her throat, a smirk tugging at her lips, tipped her head back, and launched into a song—loud, and deliberately off-key.

"Oh, I knew a bloke from down the street, his breath was foul, his socks were sweet, he'd boast of women, wealth, and fame, but couldn't remember his own damn name."

Elara grabbed what remained of her breakfast and dumped it down the front of her tunic, smearing the greasy mess into the fabric. She slammed the plate against the stone—clang. Again. Harder. Then against the bars, rattling them as she made as much noise as possible.

She wanted them to think she'd snapped. That she was losing it. Her movements grew wilder, more erratic, as she kept singing.

"He'd swagger 'round like he owned the place, with an ale-stained shirt and dirt on his face, claimed he'd bedded a duchess or three, but when it came to it, he'd wilt like a tree."

"Shut your bloody noise, you daft woman. You sound like a dying goat."

Malak.

Elara didn't stop. She locked her eyes on him, widening them in exaggerated madness, and belted out the rest of the song at the top of her lungs, banging the tin plate against the stone with every word.

"So raise a pint to men like him, who can't tell their arse from a proper whim, for life's a mess, and so are we, at least we drink 'til we're piss'd for free!"

"She's cracked," another guard muttered, and soon enough, a small cluster of them gathered outside her cell. They stood there, arms crossed, weapons hanging lazily at their sides, as if they couldn't quite decide whether to laugh or be concerned. Elara didn't bother acknowledging them, though she caught a glimpse of Reynnar from the corner of her eye, watching silently. He probably thought she'd lost it too.

She started the song over, tugging at her clothes, rolling her eyes like a madwoman as her voice climbed higher with every line. But even through the act, something inside her twisted. A cutting pang, right in her gut.

Avis. That night. The one time they'd gotten well and truly pissed together. Sneaking Algernon's whiskey, laughing so hard they couldn't breathe, drunk on more than just the booze. It felt like a lifetime ago. The memory sparked, uninvited, and she snuffed it out, hard. Buried it deep where it couldn't touch her.

"Maybe we should call for Saria," one of the guards muttered under his breath. Elara caught the words and ramped up the performance, her voice rising into a full-blown wail.

Yes, she thought. *Call the healer. Call the bloody healer.*

"Can't. She's out for the day," Malak muttered, the words just loud enough to pierce through the racket of her own voice.

Shit. *Shit.*

Could it be that the note wasn't from Saria?

"I'll take it from here."

Her head jerked up, the voice cutting through her like ice down her spine. The Hunter stood at the entrance, fully armored, mask in place, exuding that terrifying, unshakable calm.

Oh, she was cursed. Well and truly *cursed*.

He barely bothered to look at the guards, just flicked his hand, lazy, like they were nothing. The men shot her one last confused look before scuffling off. All but Malak.

"No one goes in or outta that cell but me," he growled, chest puffing out like some overstuffed bird, the leather of his armor groaning with the strain.

The Hunter didn't so much as blink. "She's my charge. I'm here to reinforce her bind, and I will see her regularly. If you have an issue, take it up with the warden. My orders come from Osin, not *you*."

Malak's jaw clenched, the scar on his cheek pulling tight. Silence stretched before he gave a slow, grudging nod. The wards flickered, energy humming once before sputtering out, leaving the cell exposed.

The Hunter cocked his head. "I need privacy. To concentrate."

Malak opened his mouth to argue, then snapped it shut, nostrils flaring. He shot Elara one last venomous look before storming off, leaving her alone with the Hunter.

Elara's song died in her throat.

He was quiet for a beat, studying her. Then he shifted, crossing his arms and leaning against the doorframe as if the whole thing bored him.

"So," he said at last, voice smooth and low, "I'm guessing you didn't swallow the pill."

Elara's cheeks flushed. "That was from *you*?"

He dipped his chin, the faintest hint of amusement in his eyes. "Why?"

"I needed a way into your cell."

Her body went rigid, a sudden spike of tension coursing through her. Slowly, her hand slipped into her pocket, fingers wrapping around one of the sharp pins.

"What do you want?"

"It wasn't a lie," he drawled. "I do need to reassess your bind. But I'd prefer to do it quietly, without the Lord Sovereign breathing down my neck."

Elara bristled. So, she had been right. He needed to fix whatever mistake he'd made without his precious lord finding out. That's why he'd lied.

"Like hell you are."

She spat the words, watching the Hunter tense, poised to move. Before he could, a growl rolled through the cell—deep, ancient, echoing like war drums in a fog-choked forest.

Her muscles locked, breath snagging as she spun.

Her gaze collided with Reynnar's.

His posture was predatory, knuckles white from the force of his grip, and his eyes — they blazed with a rage so visceral that it felt as though the very stone beneath their feet might crack. It was an undiluted, primal show of protectiveness, leaving her heart racing, a cocktail of alarm and unexpected thankfulness.

His eyes narrowed at Reynnar, barely a flicker of emotion beneath the mask before he turned back to Elara. "Listen, Hallowed, I don't want this assignment any more than you want me here. But let's not make this more difficult than it needs to be—for either of us."

Elara let out a cold laugh, the sound cutting through the tense air. "Go ahead, try it. I dare you." The confidence startled even her, rising unbidden, dark and coiled beneath her skin. Maybe it was her hatred of anyone marked with a sunburst. Or Reynnar's presence so close she could almost feel him through the bars.

Or maybe it was the memory of the Hunter at her mercy—how he'd squirmed when she held his seal, how she'd savored it. There was no chance she'd surrender that power without a fight.

She didn't stop to think.

In one swift motion, Elara spat. The glob struck true, splattering across the glossy black of his chest plate. Satisfaction curled low in her gut as surprise flickered through his eyes—there, then gone before she could savor it.

He didn't rush. He wiped the spit away with a slow, deliberate sweep of his gloved hand. Then he lifted his head and met her gaze.

That was when she saw it—a spark of challenge smoldering just beneath the surface. A silent dare. A gauntlet thrown without a word. And *gods,* if it didn't make something in her stir, daring her to rise to it.

"Has anyone ever told you how impossible you are to deal with?"

Elara's fingers closed around the pin in her pocket, the edge biting into her skin. Her pulse raced, but she kept her face cool, meeting his gaze with a smile that was all teeth.

"Funny, you're the first to pay me such a compliment."

The air between them tightened, and she welcomed it, let it settle like a second skin. She wasn't backing down. A slow smirk curved her lips, daring him to take the bait.

When he did—when he stepped into her cell—she struck.

She clamped down, the seal pulsing in her chest, snaring the rhythm of his heart.

She cut it off.

A dark thrill surged as he staggered, cursing. Blood traced a thin line from her nose. Elara didn't hesitate. She slashed the pin toward his eye.

Even with his seal in her grip, he was faster. His hand snapped up, catching her wrist inches from his face.

Before she could react, the Hunter slammed her into the cold stone, the impact knocking the breath from her lungs.

"Stop *fucking* doing that," he growled, seizing her flailing arms with one hand, pinning them above her head.

Fury roared through Elara as she lashed out, jerking her knee upward, aiming for that one vulnerable spot that could bring even the strongest warrior to his knees. But his reflexes were infuriatingly fast. His thigh intercepted hers mid-strike, effortlessly deflecting the blow.

Reynnar roared from his side of the bars, but there was nothing he could do to help her.

Elara's breath hitched as the Hunter wedged his leg between hers, pinning her in place. Panic flared. She twisted and strained, every muscle screaming for escape—but the harder she fought, the tighter his grip became.

"Is this the famed Hunter's method? Overpowering women who can't fight back? What's next? Going to shackle me to your bed?"

His armor pressed deeper into her wrists as he leaned in, a smirk curling around his words. "If you have a thing for being tied up and held against your will, all you had to do was ask, *Hallowed.*"

Elara's eyes flared. She didn't flinch or shrink back like he likely expected. Instead, she leaned in, deliberately pressing herself against the solid wall of his body. For a heartbeat, she saw it—a flicker of surprise, a hitch in his stance.

Her own breathing stayed steady, controlled, hiding the wildfire in her veins. A slow, daring smile curved her lips as her voice dropped to a whisper, barely brushing the cold surface of his mask.

"Is this what you had in mind, *Hunter*?"

The air between them crackled, taut as a bowstring, their breaths tangled in the thick silence. Then, without warning, he let go.

The abrupt loss of his weight sent Elara stumbling, her legs giving way as she crumpled to the floor.

"You're a real piece of work, you know that?"

Even through the mask, his voice carried a rasp.

"And you're a real piece of shit, so I guess we're even," Elara snapped, though the fire behind her words had dimmed. Her head pounded, a dull ache, and her limbs felt like dead weight. With a weary sigh, she slumped against the wall, the world tilting slightly as she lifted her chin to meet his gaze. Her eyes remained sharp, but her strength was slipping fast.

The Hunter watched her for a long, measured moment, something close to wariness flickering in his gaze before he let out a dismissive snort. "What exactly did those Druids teach you down south? Casting without a conduit will kill you."

Casting. Is that was she was doing?

The Druids hadn't taught her a damn thing, but there was no way in hell she was about to tell him that.

The silence stretched again, and for a brief, foolish second, Elara dared to hope he might actually leave. But, of course, luck was never on her side.

He sank into a crouch in front of her, the gold in his eyes burning brighter the closer he got, though Elara wasn't sure if it was real or just the exhaustion warping her senses. She was so focused on that flicker, on the intensity of his gaze, that she didn't even notice how close he'd come —until his hand slid into her hair.

His fingers grazed her neck, the touch so soft, and unexpected it sent a jolt through her.

"What are you doing?"

The Hunter pulled back slightly, the dim light catching the sharp points of her hairpins now held between his fingers. "Planning to skewer someone else while you're down here?"

She scowled. "Depends on the day."

He shook his head, amusement flashing briefly in his eyes before he caught himself. The shift was so subtle, like watching a door close, shutting her out again. "I'm going to assess your bind, and you're not going to attack me this time."

Elara snorted, the sound tired and bitter as it echoed through the cramped space. She didn't move when the air shifted, when the faint hum of ether crackled and a wisp of power slipped from his palm, curling toward her like smoke.

"What will it do?" she whispered as his ether drifted lazily, curling in delicate loops before settling against her chest, right over the hidden seals.

He didn't answer. His focus locked in, so complete she could feel it even through the mask. Elara closed her eyes, reaching for the sensation —and then she felt it. A faint tickle. A thread of warmth slipping into her, subtle and strange. Different.

Her skin prickled as the feeling spread, sparks racing along her nerves as if something inside her were waking.

Then it was gone—yanked free as he cursed, low and vicious.

Elara barely managed to crack her eyes open, her body too drained to do more. But she saw him—his gloved fingers tapping lightly against the stone, his gaze distant, unfocused. And then, without a word, he rose to his feet, as if whatever decision he'd been turning over in his mind had been settled.

The Hunter bent and lifted her with effortlessly, cradling her in his arms. Elara wanted to protest, to push him away, but her limbs refused to answer. He set her on the cot, his touch unexpectedly careful.

"Sleep will help," he muttered, voice clipped, and turned to leave.

Just before the cell door clicked shut, he hesitated. His gaze flicked back to hers, meeting her bleary eyes. Elara braced herself for a biting remark, something cruel or condescending, but nothing came. No snide retort, no venom.

Only silence.

"What was the pill supposed to do?" Her voice came out rasped as she fought to stay awake.

The Hunter's eyes flashed. "It would've made you convulse, scream loud enough to shake the walls. The guards would've thought you were dying. They'd have dragged you out, right to me." He paused, and for a second, his voice shifted—just a fraction, a hint of something less controlled slipping through. "But your way worked too."

He turned, the quiet click of the cell door sealing her fate once again. But... something stayed. Something that wrapped around her like the glow of embers beneath a thick quilt, like the heat of a lantern after wandering through endless dark.

It bled into everything—the rough blanket, the worn cot, even the cold stone walls seemed to lose their bite.

Elara's eyes rose, seeking him once more, only to find the space empty.

He hadn't looked back. Not once.

But even as it felt like he'd left something behind—he'd also taken a piece of her with him. Something she'd unknowingly given—something he hadn't asked for, but had claimed all the same.

CHAPTER 25

Elara's steps were slow, dragging, her mind miles away while her body moved on its own. The path stretched in front of her—dark, endless, with a light barely visible at the very end. Hazy, yet... it pulled. Far and faint, but calling all the same. And then, another light bloomed, nearer this time, brighter, like a star flaring into existence.

She stilled. This was wrong. This *place* was wrong. She should be in her cell, bound by stone and iron, not here, wherever *here* was.

Yet the lights... they *sang* to her, each note wrapping around her, pulling her deeper. The far light whispered, a soft, lilting melody that thrummed through her veins, while the nearer one tightened in her chest like a rope yanked taut.

Both were calling, but the closer one... it *demanded*.

Elara turned—not by choice, but by force deeper than will. The path bent beneath her feet, drawing her toward the glowing heart. It pulsed in time with her own, faster, closer—until she passed through its shimmering veil.

The light didn't just surround her—it poured into her. Her skin prickled as if touched by static, the hair on her arms lifting. Elara squinted as she surveyed the barren landscape stretching endlessly before her. There was not a tree in sight, not a shadow to speak of. Only the sun, an indifferent eye overhead, searing the terrain into a bleached bone of a world.

And the air—it was still, stagnant, like it hadn't moved in centuries.

Could I be dead? The thought brushed her mind as her steps stirred dust, motes glittering before settling back into obscurity. Everything felt too real to dismiss. The ache from casting still throbbed behind her eyes, her clothes stiff against her skin, sour with dried soup.

And yet—something was off. As if she stood on an edge, not just between sleep and waking, but between realms.

She traced the air, catching the swirls of dust on her fingers that drifted languidly on the wind. Then she felt it.

A pull.

It started softly, a barely-there whisper at the back of her mind, but it grew, steady, like the tide drawn irresistibly toward the moon. Her breath hitched as it tugged at her chest, something *inevitable* lurking just beyond her reach.

And even if she wanted to, she couldn't resist it.

Elara kept walking and almost as if they'd been waiting, a circle of stones emerged from the haze. They rose from the desolation like jagged, broken teeth, their silhouettes dark against the bleak landscape.

They resembled the stones in the Pit, but these were different. Their edges were worn and uneven, covered in moss that had withered to a brittle shell, as if even nature had forsaken this place.

She drew a breath and stepped closer, letting the circle of stones close around her. When her fingers brushed the nearest stone, a sharp shiver raced up her spine. The surface buzzed faintly beneath her touch —old power, worn but alive, humming through the ground. She closed her eyes and listened.

"It's you."

Elara's stomach dropped in a rush of surprise as she spun around, locking eyes with the Hunter.

His heavy-lidded gaze took in the world like a man not yet convinced it was real. Sleep softened his dark eyes, curls tousled as if he'd crushed them into submission during the night. He wore simple trousers and a linen tunic, the laces at the neck undone, revealing the hard planes of muscle beneath.

"What—why are you here?"

The sound of her voice seemed to drag him from whatever daze he was in. He blinked, his frown deepening as his eyes swept over the barren, ghostly landscape. "I don't know. I... think I'm dreaming."

Elara's pulse quickened. *Yes*—this had to be a dream. The weightlessness, the way everything blurred and shifted at the corners.

She was dreaming. It had to be.

The Hunter's gaze narrowed as he studied her face. "Why did you summon me?"

"I didn't..." Her voice faltered, unsure. She hadn't called him, but something had drawn *her* here. That pull—could it have been the stones? Her gaze flicked back to him, his face still unreadable, though something shifted in his eyes—hesitation, maybe.

"Where are we?"

He squinted. "I've been here before..." He crouched low, hands sinking into the soil. Slowly, he let the dirt sift through his fingers, the fine grains catching the light, swirling like ash caught in a breeze. "We're in Arwn's Void."

"Arwn's Void?" Elara echoed. "I've never heard of it before."

"You wouldn't have," he murmured, "They wiped it from every map after Osin took control. Didn't want anyone finding it again." He gave a curt nod to the ground. "Look closer. The soil's not like anywhere else. It's alive, in a way. It remembers. What's left of the Great War... *Draoth* still bleeding through the land."

Elara's gaze traced the shimmering particles she hadn't noticed before. The dust seemed to glimmer in the fading light, as though tiny fragments of stars had fallen to the ground, glowing faintly beneath his fingers. "*Draoth*?"

The Hunter stood, wiping the dirt from his hands. "It's the *Tírrísh* word for ether."

Elara hummed softly, her gaze drifting. This land was dead—and yet ether, ancient ether, still endured, surviving where nothing else could. Her chest tightened. This place was survival stripped to its bones, clinging on despite everything.

Survival, at any cost.

Recognition stirred in her chest. Like the land, she carried something buried deep, dormant but not gone. Waiting.

Waiting for rain. For ignition. For a shift—any sign that might make sense of the path before her.

The Hunter stepped closer, stirring the dust around them. "Strange that I'd see you here, of all places," he said under his breath, almost as though he was speaking to the air, not her.

Elara brushed her fingers against the stain on her tunic. "Don't give yourself too much credit. You're just another torment *my* mind cooked up—haunting me in real life wasn't enough, apparently. Now I can't even get a break when I close my eyes."

His head snapped toward her, brow creasing in confusion. Slowly, perplexity sharpened into recognition. His eyes widened, color draining from his face as though a dark realization had just slammed into him. Like he'd uncovered a piece of a nightmare.

Elara's heart stuttered, and before she could stop herself, she took a step back.

"What? What is it—"

~

ELARA SHOT UPRIGHT, heart slamming against her ribs.

A dim, muted glow bathed the Pit, the scattered orbs casting just enough light to deepen the shadows. That faint, dull glow signaled the end of the day, just before the night shift began.

She blinked, disoriented.

Curse it. She'd slept through the entire day.

Muscles stiff and aching, she stretched, wincing at the throb in her neck. Across the cell, Reynnar lay sprawled on the floor just beyond the bars. His broad shoulders rose and fell in steady breaths, his face softened by sleep, yet there was a coiled tension in his posture, as if he could wake at the slightest sound. Her heart clenched at the sight—he had stayed close, kept watch.

She pulled the blanket tighter, but it did nothing to stop the shiver crawling over her skin. That dream—gods, what *was* it? It wasn't just a dream. It had weight, substance, as if she could still taste the air. It felt like a warning.

Elara pressed her palms to her eyes, the pressure steadying her. She'd dreamed of the Hunter before... but this was different. It felt as though he'd been there. Not just in her mind, but truly present, as if a piece of his soul had reached across whatever lay between them.

She shook her head, stifling a laugh. Impossible. Dreams didn't work like that. She was exhausted from casting—gods, she still hadn't wrapped her head around that.

And yet... he'd carried her to the cot. Warmed her cell. That was the strangest part. Why would he do that? It made no sense.

Of course her mind had seized on it and twisted it into something more. That was all it was—a dream, nothing more than an overtired brain misfiring.

And yet...

Elara shoved the blanket aside and slipped from the bed, cool air prickling her skin. She moved to the edge of the cell where the passing orbs cast just enough light. Kneeling, she dragged a finger through the dirt, sketching the stones from her dream—slow, careful, the shapes still fresh in her mind. Then, beside them, she drew the stones from the Faerie tunnel. The ones Saria had warned her never to speak of.

Her pulse quickened as she stared down. Nearly identical. The dream-stones were fractured, cracked, one split clean in half—but they were the same.

"Tá Aelfhenge tarraingthe agat[12]."

Elara blinked and looked up to find Reynnar watching her, one brow lazily raised. He dragged a hand over his face, his gaze drifting between her and the marks on the ground.

"Do you know what this is?"

He hummed, low and thoughtful, then crouched by the bars and tapped a finger against the drawing. *"Aelfhenge,"* he repeated.

Elara pinched the bridge of her nose, her thoughts racing, sifting through the endless vault of knowledge she'd buried herself in over the years. The archives, the dusty tomes, the brittle pages she'd pored over— *Aelfhenge*. The word drifted through her mind, brushing against something familiar, something just out of reach.

One book stood out in her mind more clearly than the others—a worn, leather-bound volume titled Whispers of the Veil. Within its pages, she recalled a particular passage about the Stone of Liria, a legendary Fae artifact believed to be infused with the essence of celestial bodies. The text described how, under the light of a full moon, the stone would emit a soft glow, its power reaching its zenith when the alignment of celestial bodies was precise. During these rare moments, the Fae could channel divine energies through the very bones of the earth, harnessing a force both ancient and formidable.

Could they be related somehow?

But the *Aelfhenge* didn't necessarily have anything to do with the Fae. She didn't know enough yet. She needed to find out more.

Elara glanced back up at Reynnar, biting back a sigh of frustration. For what felt like the hundredth time, she wished they spoke the same language.

"*Aelfhenge*," she repeated, and Reynnar nodded.

"Elara." She tapped her chest, and his grin spread wide, like he knew exactly what she was doing.

"Reynnar." He pointed to himself, then gestured at her. "Yoo-man" *Human.*

She couldn't help but smile. "Yes, human."

"And you're a Faerie," she said, pointing at him, her tone almost teasing. But the moment the word left her mouth, his expression darkened, the easy smile vanishing.

"*Ní hea,*[13]" his voice was low, almost a growl. "*Sidhe.*[13]"

Elara leaned in, just a bit closer, her brow arching as she studied him. "*Sidhe?*"

She rolled the unfamiliar word on her tongue, never having come across it in all the texts she'd devoured. But when she said it, Reynnar nodded, his eyes gleaming with something unspoken, like the word held a meaning far deeper than she could grasp.

"*Is ea,*[14]" Reynnar whispered, touching his chest with a gravity that rippled through the space between them. "*Sidhe.*[14]"

The air felt thick with the truth of that single word.

"Oi!"

Elara practically jumped out of her skin, her heart slamming into her ribs. She and Reynnar sprang apart so fast it was like they'd been burned. Too slow, though—far too slow.

"What did I say about talking to the other prisoners?" Malak's voice was a low, menacing growl. "You deaf or just stupid?"

Elara's stomach flipped. "I—I wasn't. It's the first time—I won't do it again. We don't even understand each other."

The world shrank to the pounding in her chest, each beat so hard she swore it would crack her ribs. If Malak took Reynnar—she couldn't survive without him. Would they punish him? Kill him? And all because of *her*. The thought hit like a punch to the gut, stealing her breath, leaving her mind spinning. She couldn't think, couldn't focus as Malak's gaze slid to Reynnar, then back to her, his lip curling.

"You're lucky I'm not in the mood to gut someone tonight. But if I catch you whispering to that *thing* again, I'll make sure you regret it."

"I won't," Elara said quickly, nodding like her life depended on it. "I won't."

"Good," he spat, canceling the wards with a sneer. "Now get your arse moving. You're wanted."

CHAPTER 26

Elara's skin burned, every inch of her feeling like it was under siege. Who knew you could be *attacked* by an entire army of beauty potions?

Malak had barely shoved her into the readying chamber before the attendants descended with their bottles and brushes. Something was worked into her hair until it shone; lotions tightened her skin until it felt stretched over bone. And the body oils—she refused to dwell on those. Not a single inch was spared. She was scrubbed, coated, polished to a humiliating sheen.

Now, standing beside Osin as he held court, Elara fought the urge to scratch the maddening itch beneath her left breast.

The Great Hall stretched out before her, swathed in a splendor that must have out-valued anything the Sanct had ever laid eyes on through all its years. Elara, her arm looped through Osin's, could hardly believe the decadence—every corner gilded, every surface sparkling as if determined to outshine the next.

As they moved through the crowd, Osin was the picture of regal grace, greeting each lord and lady with a smile that was both a welcome and a display of his unwavering authority. His laughter rang out—rich, haughty—as he accepted compliments and gifts, each more extravagant than the last.

Elara did not speak. She didn't dare. Osin's command had been clear: do not speak, scarcely breathe. She was a symbol at his side, ornamental and silent.

So she played her part—smiles measured, nods demure, gaze lowered in practiced deference. She had learned this performance long ago. But beneath it, anger coiled low and tight. Quiet. Smoldering. How many could be fed with the gold dripping from these chandeliers? How many homes warmed with the cost of a single night's indulgence?

Her smile faltered for a heartbeat, her fingers tightening in the fabric of her gown.

"Cheer up, pet. This is a celebration, not a funeral," Osin's voice flowed over her like silk, smooth and effortless, yet with an edge so calculated, that for a moment, Elara wondered if he could hear the thoughts screaming in her head. Her pulse spiked, panic flooding her veins. She sucked in a breath, the air too tight in her chest as her mind raced, searching for any sign of intrusion—any breach into her mind. But there was nothing. Just her own spiraling thoughts. Just her.

She forced a slow breath and settled the serene mask back into place, though her hands trembled.

Osin lifted his goblet and took an unhurried sip of dark red wine, staining his teeth as he swallowed. Tonight, even his usual excess had been elevated. Sapphire silk rippled over his frame like liquid light; phoenix-shaped cufflinks glittered with gemstones; silver thread stitched his high collar so finely it gleamed like moonlight. Even his boots shone to an absurd polish—wealth and power he was all too eager to parade.

And at his side, the sunlit blade rested in its sheath, incongruous against the opulence, its presence a quiet, unspoken threat.

Osin led her through the throng of guests, his hand firm on her elbow, guiding her with an air of authority that parted the crowd without a word. The lords and ladies of Latheria didn't even try to hide their stares, their gazes crawling over her, full of lust, disdain, and judgment all at once. These were the same people who nodded along with every word Osin spoke, whispering their approval while his reign of terror bled the land dry. They smiled, toasted their victories, and pretended not to see the blood staining their hands.

As they moved through the crowd, Elara's attention caught on a young man leaning casually against a pillar, his dark, tousled hair falling effortlessly over his brow, the faintest hint of a smirk playing on his lips. He wore a green velvet jacket with a cravat loosely tied at his throat—careless, yet somehow intentional.

He was already watching her, dark eyes gleaming with amusement, like he was in on a secret she wasn't. His gaze held hers for a beat longer than it should have before he gave her a slow, deliberate nod.

She looked away, heat creeping up her neck, forcing her focus anywhere but on the way his gaze lingered. Thankfully—or perhaps not—she didn't wait long for a distraction.

Osin pulled her forward and stopped before an older man. Ashen hair, thinning and slicked back in a futile attempt to mask his age, only sharpened the hard lines of his face. A goblet rested loose in his hand, untouched, as his fingers tapped idly against the glass in a slow, measured rhythm.

"Chancellor Vellon," Osin said smoothly, offering a smile, "allow me to formally present our Hallowed."

The old man dipped his head, the movement barely more than a formality, his pale, hawk-like eyes settling on her.

Elara did not flinch beneath his gaze. Up close, she recognized him. He was a member of the High Council—the very one who had hidden behind the table.

"Lord Sovereign, you honor us with such a distinguished guest," Vellon murmured, his tone thick with practiced civility. "Tell me, my dear, does the evening meet the expectations of one so... exalted?"

The word "exalted" slid from his lips, laden with such thinly veiled disdain that Elara's fingers twitched, her instinct to roll her eyes barely restrained. *Exalted, indeed.* As if the gown Osin had chosen for her didn't already make her feel like a mockery. White, blindingly so, with edges dripping in gold, draping her in all the wrong ways. It was so sheer, so absurdly delicate, that she might as well have been standing there in nothing at all.

When she'd first entered the hall, her arm entwined with Osin's, every gaze had snapped to her. Her gown shimmered beneath the chandeliers, its folds catching the light and scattering faint gold across the room like fleeting blessings. Was that his aim—to parade her like a porcelain doll, drenched in perfume thick enough to smother anyone who drew too near?

Each step felt like floating, the hem barely whispering over marble, yet she had never felt more trapped—bound to an image made for others, not herself. Admired, displayed, and utterly unseen.

And yet, beneath the layers of silk and perfume, Elara's thoughts drifted to forests and rivers, to mud beneath her feet and rain in her hair.

Osin's grip on her arm tightened ever so slightly.

"It's lovely," she managed, forcing a smile. "A truly... grand affair."

Vellon's smile broadened. He inclined his head once more, a gesture indulgent, and almost patronizing. "I imagine such a grand spectacle must be quite the stimulation for you, Hallowed. After all, it must be some time since you have witnessed anything so fine. A welcome change, no doubt, from your present circumstances." His gaze lingered upon her for a heartbeat longer, the faint smile still playing at his lips, before he turned his attention back to Osin.

Elara's pulse raced, heat creeping through her despite every effort to stay composed. *Bastard. Evil, smug bastard.* He knew—knew exactly what they were doing to her, what her "present circumstances" really meant. And he didn't care. He was a chancellor, for gods' sake, wasn't there supposed to be some shred of decency in that? Some sense of moral justice?

Her fingers twitched at her sides, itching to lash out, to tear that arrogant expression from his face, but she clenched them into the fabric of her gown, willing herself to remain still. *Breathe.* She forced a tight, brittle smile.

After what felt like hours, Osin finally ended his conversation with the Chancellor, whose endless droning about titles and achievements had long since turned to white noise for Elara. So, when Osin led her back through the crowd, she almost welcomed it—even with his hand on her back as a constant pressure.

They moved toward the high table, the towering stone edifice looming over the hall. From this vantage point, Elara finally took in the full scope of the room—and the sheer number of armored guards stationed everywhere. At least a dozen stood near the dais alone, their hands resting on their swords, while another twenty or so lined the perimeter. Even more—maybe ten—were positioned at strategic intervals around the columns, half-hidden in the shadows, yet their presence was unmistakable.

It was excessive. Even for Osin, who was never one to take chances. But this felt like overkill. Her eyes flitted across the room, catching the hushed exchanges between nobles, their heads bent close, military leaders murmuring in tight circles, courtiers fidgeting with their fans, and high-ranking Druids watching everything with unnerving calm.

Elara couldn't shake the feeling settling like a stone in her stomach. *Yes,* this was a gathering of power—nobles, generals, Druids, all in one place. Of course, security would be tight. But this? This felt like more than just protection; it felt like preparation.

Elara's skin tingled, a prickling awareness creeping through her like a brush of fingers across her neck. Slowly, almost unwillingly, she turned, her eyes sweeping across the hall, her gaze drawn to him as if pulled by some invisible thread.

There, at the edge of the hall, standing just within the shadows, was the Hunter.

The sight of him stole the air from her lungs, and for a heartbeat, the murmur of the crowd faded to a distant hum. It was only then—when she focused—that she felt it: a whisper-thin pulse, a ghost of a beat that wasn't hers but somehow mirrored her own.

He stood tall, unflinchingly so, but there was something dangerous in the way his gaze lingered on her. He wasn't hiding behind a mask this time. Just him, in gleaming armor that seemed to swallow the light, all hard edges, and lethal grace. But his eyes—they were the same. Dark, unrelenting, like he was dissecting her every breath. And she couldn't look away.

"Why did you summon me?"

Elara shivered. She couldn't help it—her eyes drifted over the hard lines of his face, searching for... something. Anything. A flicker of recognition, maybe. Or warmth that she knew wouldn't be there.

What did he feel when he looked at her? Hatred? Duty? Something else?

She swallowed, the tension pulling tighter. He hadn't always been this—this hunter in the king's service. No, he had once been a lordling, a man of status, his family one of the most powerful in the realm. Until the day his brother had tried to kill her. Until the day they'd lost it all. Stripped of their titles, their land, their legacy. What had happened to them after that? What had happened to *him*? She'd never let herself wonder before.

Elara ripped her gaze away, her cheeks burning as shame knotted in her stomach. *What is wrong with me?* So he hadn't left her to freeze on the cold cell floor—*big deal*. That didn't make him a good person. It didn't mean he deserved anything more from her than animosity. And now, here she was, her mind spiraling with thoughts about him, clinging to the smallest scraps of kindness like they meant something. Like they mattered.

But he wasn't kind. And the dream...

That's all it was, she reminded herself, *not a real interaction between them.*

Gods, she *was* losing it.

"Look pretty now," Osin murmured, his voice a velvet whisper that snapped her out of her reverie. "All eyes will be on you." Without so much as a glance in her direction, he turned to face the court, lifting his crystal glass with an ease that commanded the room. At once, a hush fell over the assembled guests.

"Lords and Ladies of this esteemed realm, welcome." He let the silence stretch, allowing the weight of his words to settle before continuing. "It is always a pleasure to see so many gathered in the name of peace and prosperity. A testament, truly, to the strength of our unity. Tonight, marks the start of Luminalia, and I ask you to reflect on the greatness we've built together—on the stability we so generously maintain. And as your sovereign, it is both my duty and my *privilege* to ensure that our legacy endures, unshaken and unchallenged."

His gaze shifted to Elara, a calculating gleam in his eyes. "The Hallowed stands among you as proof of that legacy—a divine assurance from the gods that our path is righteous, our future secure. In the days leading to the winter solstice, we will revel in this fortune, strengthening the bonds between us. This time, with our Hallowed in attendance—a living symbol of the gods' favor."

He lifted his glass again, and the entire hall followed, crystal chiming. "Let tonight serve as a reminder," he said, "of the order we've built, the future we protect. A future that we—*together*—will ensure forever."

A cheer erupted, loud and deafening, a roar of approval that rattled the very air. Elara stood there, frozen, as the crowd drank, their loyalty on full display.

Luminalia? Already? Time had become a strange, malleable thing, stretching and compressing until she could no longer keep its measure. She could hardly remember what it was like to care.

The night blurred together as Elara trailed Osin like a dog on a leash. He moved through the crowd with a king's ease, trading whispers laced with honey and venom, lifting goblets of golden wine, his laughter ringing hollow in her ears. Servers wove past with trays of roasted meats glistening under the chandeliers, pastries layered with promise, fruits shining like jewels. Her mouth watered—an instinct she couldn't silence.

But not a bite for her. The Hallowed, it seemed, was above hunger and thirst. She drifted on, a silent ghost in a pretty dress.

Her stomach was screaming when Osin decided he was done.

"Rolfe," Osin snapped and a guard appeared at his side before the sound had even faded. "Escort the Hallowed back to her quarters. I daresay the court has had its fill of her presence for one evening."

They certainly had. Elara had felt eyes on her all night—just not *his*. The Hunter had vanished after the welcome speech, swallowed by the crowd, his absence louder than all the stares that tracked her every step.

"Of course, my lord." Rolfe's bow wavered, his words thick. Elara's gaze narrowed as she caught the flush creeping up his neck, the unsteady shift of his feet. He was drunk.

Great.

"Good lad," Osin said with a hollow smile, clapping Rolfe on the back. But his attention had already drifted, his gaze locking onto a young woman across the hall. The gleam in his eyes turned Elara's stomach.

She watched as he crossed the room and slid a hand possessively around the girl's waist. She turned to him, her smile blooming wide— *too wide.* Elara caught the subtle hitch in her shoulders, the brief tension beneath the polish. A performance. One Elara knew all too well.

The girl laughed at something Osin murmured, head tipping back, her facade flawless. Then, for the briefest moment, her eyes flicked to Elara. Quick. Controlled.

Cold splashed through her all the same.

It was *her*. The girl from her memory. Those same cruel green eyes.

A throat cleared behind her, pulling her gaze. *Rolfe.*

"Are you quite ready?"

Elara blinked, startled by the softness in his tone. It had been so long since anyone had spoken to her with kindness at Mordenhall that it pushed her to ask,

"What is the name of that woman?" she said carefully. "The one with the Lord Sovereign?"

Rolfe glanced over her shoulder. "Oh, that's Lady Calista Thorne."

Calista. The name stirred nothing in her mind.

Elara's shoulders sagged.

"She's been angling for Osin for the past six months, and it looks like she's finally managed to catch his eye."

Elara paused again. He wasn't just being polite—he was offering her information, unprompted. Why? Maybe he had a taste for gossip. Her eyes flicked to the weapons strapped to his belt—sleek, efficient, and oddly familiar. They were much like the ones Dario used. Could he, too, be from the west?

"How fortunate for her," she said, her tone deliberately light, though her mind whirled with possibilities.

Rolfe snorted derisively, then seemed to remember who stood beside him. He straightened at once, cleared his throat, and muttered, "Let's get you back."

They walked in silence, the weighty doors of the Great Hall creaking shut behind them. Gradually, the distant murmur of voices faded as they wound their way through the dim corridors that led toward the Pit. Elara bit down gently on her lower lip, her thoughts racing. She combed through every scrap of knowledge Dario had ever shared about the steel craft of Bravell.

She could almost hear his voice recounting the details. Their weapons weren't like the grand swords favored by other provinces— Bravellians were known for their ingenuity, crafting weapons with dual purposes. Their blades were light but lethal, often serrated, or hooked to maximize damage.

The *crixis*, a short, curved blade with a secondary grip at its base, was perfect for close combat, allowing its wielder to twist and disarm with one fluid motion. Then there were the *vorr spikes*, slender spears with barbed edges that hooked into flesh, tearing muscle when pulled free.

Weapons designed not just to kill but to break.

To make sure the enemy never got back up.

Elara's gaze flicked to Rolfe's arsenal, noting the unmistakable gleam of a *crixis* hanging at his side, the spikes strapped across his back. He wasn't just any guard. He was Bravellian—a survivor, a fighter forged in a kingdom that had been left in ruins but refused to die.

A spark ignited in her chest, her pulse thrumming with new purpose.

She could use this. *He* could be useful.

CHAPTER 27

"Your blade... it's not like the ones the other guards carry."

Elara kept her expression neutral, watching as Rolfe hesitated just long enough to make her wonder if she'd overstepped. But then he pushed open the heavy door to the Pit, casting a glance back at her.

"A Bravellian forge doesn't craft for looks," he said with a faint smirk. "We make what lasts, not what pleases the eye."

Elara let out a slow breath, relieved. He wasn't bothered by the question. *Good.* She decided to push her luck a little further. "It's not just anyone who could handle a weapon like that... must take a certain kind of skill."

Rolfe's face flushed at the comment, his gaze darting away as he stumbled slightly on the spiraling stairs. "It's served me well enough."

Elara watched him descend, a flicker of guilt stirring over what she was about to do. *Almost.* A small smile tugged at her lips as she timed her steps, deliberately catching the hem of her gown beneath her heel. The fabric snagged, and with a soft, calculated yelp, she pitched forward, hands flying out as she stumbled.

Rolfe's arms shot out, catching her before she fell.

"Are you all right, miss?" His concern sounded genuine as he steadied her and helped her upright. Wine lingered on his breath, mixed with the clean salt of sweat and the solid warmth of his body. Elara leaned in just a fraction, letting the closeness linger.

"Fine," she murmured, looking up at him from beneath her lashes. "Though I think I might've twisted my ankle."

"Shit" He eased her down onto a nearby step, already crouching to inspect her. "Let me take a look."

Elara hid her smile. *Gods, this was almost too easy.*

His brow knit together. "It looks fine to me," he murmured, eyes flicking over her skin, "but I'm no healer." When he looked up, the haze of wine seemed to clear slightly from his hazel eyes. "We should get you checked out, just to be safe."

Elara gave a small nod, keeping her expression soft, innocent, letting him take her weight as he lifted her to her feet, her arm sliding around his shoulders for support.

"Is this all right?"

Guilt flickered in Elara's chest. He was young, earnest—perhaps the only genuine kindness she'd found in this wretched place. She pushed the thought aside. She couldn't afford it. *Focus.*

She dipped her head and let him guide her down the remaining steps and into the narrow corridor leading deeper into the Pit.

A cold sweat prickled her skin. The silence here felt wrong—too heavy. Her gaze slid to the guards lining the passage, expecting their usual rigid stares. Instead, one swayed on his feet, gripping his spear like a lifeline. Another lay slumped on the stone, his helmet rolling away with a soft clatter.

Elara's eyes widened as they passed another, his steps unsteady, mouth slack, and it finally clicked. *Drunk.* Every last one of them. Her pulse spiked. *How?* How could the warden allow such negligence? Was this normal? Did they all just lose themselves like this every time there was a grand event? The entire castle, drunk and stumbling, armor half-falling off. It was absurd—*dangerous.* Sure, it worked to her advantage, but still... the sheer recklessness of it.

She swallowed her disbelief, forcing herself to stay focused. If ever there was a moment, this was it—the opportunity she had long been waiting for to gather more information. She couldn't afford to waste it. Manipulating Rolfe was a necessary evil, and she repeated that to herself, again and again, until the words began to feel like truth. Until the knot in her chest began to loosen.

Five times, she told herself—*this is survival.* Five times, until she believed it.

It didn't help that with every step closer to the heart of the tunnels, Elara felt Rolfe grow tense, his body stiffening beneath her touch.

"Have you never been down here before?"

Rolfe froze, glancing around before scratching the back of his neck. "I—haven't, no. I was quite surprised when the Lord Sovereign tasked me with bringing you here. I've heard of the place, of course, but..."

"It's horrible, isn't it?" she finished for him, her tone cooler now.

His grip tightened briefly at her waist before he let go. "It is."

They continued on in silence once more until reaching the entrance to the labyrinth of tunnels. Rolfe's brow furrowed as his gaze darted uneasily between the dark, winding paths. "Which of these leads to the infirmary? They *do* have an infirmary, don't they?"

"They do," Elara replied, watching as the strain in his posture gradually eased. She inclined her head toward the rightmost tunnel. "It's down there."

Rolfe exhaled, a flicker of relief crossing his face as he adjusted his grip and guided her on. His arm stayed steady beneath hers while the torchlight dimmed behind them, swallowed by the dark ahead.

"How much further?" Rolfe's voice wavered, his concern clear as Elara leaned harder against him. She could feel his gaze flick to her every few seconds, his worry palpable, just as she had hoped.

"Do you need to rest?" he offered, his kindness almost unbearable.

She winced dramatically, casting him a tired look. "I think I might."

He nodded without hesitation, and gently helped her settle against the tunnel wall—right next to the large, jagged rock she'd noted on her first trip through this tunnel.

Elara sank to her knees with a slight groan, feigning a weakness that brought Rolfe to her side at once.

"I don't think I can manage the rest of the way." Her fingers brushed against the rock beside her, wrapping around it carefully, feeling the weight of it in her palm. "Do you think you could fetch someone to help me?"

Rolfe hesitated, biting the inside of his cheek as his gaze shifted from her to the dark tunnel ahead. "I'm not sure it's a good idea to leave you alone. Maybe... if you don't mind, I could carry you—"

Elara didn't let him finish. She swung her arm in one swift motion, the rock cracking against the back of his head. Sharp. Cruel. He never saw it coming.

His body jolted, shock flashing across his face before his knees buckled. He crumpled at her feet, unconscious before he hit the stone.

Elara squeezed her eyes shut, fighting the tears that surged before she could stop them.

Curse it all.

"I'm sorry, I'm so fucking sorry," she whispered, her voice trembling as she carefully lowered him onto his back. Her eyes darted to the spot where she'd hit him, her heart stalling at the sight of blood—just a small amount, enough to stain the skin beneath his hair. Her hands shook as she searched for a pulse. There it was—steady. He wasn't dead, just unconscious. Relief flooded her as she slumped back against the wall.

Tears welled in her eyes again, blurring everything, but she swiped them away with the back of her hand—rough, fast—then pinched her arm hard, the pain cutting through the swirl of emotions.

Get up. Move.

Elara pushed herself up on unsteady legs, her whole body trembling.

She had to decide, and fast. *Find Godfrey and drag the truth out of him, or dig deeper into the stones?* There was something about them— she'd felt it the moment she first saw them, a pull she couldn't shake. And her dreams had only confirmed it. They meant something.

Something important.

Her gaze flicked between the path behind her and the shadowed corridor where she knew the stones were kept. She swallowed hard, her pulse quickening. Maybe, she could manage both.

The stones first. *Then Godfrey.*

Elara clutched her gown and sprinted down the dim corridor, fabric bunched in her fists. Torches flickered along the walls, their shadows lurching and warping the space around her. At the end of the hall, a heavy door stood ajar, a sliver of light spilling through like a beacon. She shoved it open, breath ragged, chest heaving—

And stopped dead.

Every single Sidhe stood at attention. Silent. Watchful. Their faces pale in the low light.

They hovered at the bars of their cells, their otherworldly eyes fixed on her, tracking her every move with an intensity that made the hair on the back of her neck stand on end.

Their expressions were unreadable, faces as smooth as marble, yet there was something beneath it—an understanding, as if they knew— knew *exactly* what had transpired between her and Rolfe. Elara's throat tightened, her mouth suddenly dry as her eyes darted from one figure to the next. Their features too beautiful to belong to this wretched place.

No one spoke. No one moved.

They were waiting.

Elara instinctively reached for the nearest cell, her fingers just shy of the iron bars when a female lunged forward. Her skin was unnaturally pale, like the very walls had drained the life from her, and her silver hair hung in tangled mats down her back. Dark circles bruised the skin beneath her eyes.

"*Tá fáinne ag teastáil uait,*[15]" she hissed, her trembling hand rising to point at the glowing wards etched into the stone—wards Elara had missed in her haste.

Heat flooded Elara's cheeks. *Stupid.* Of course she couldn't just open the cells. She needed a ring—the right ring. Something powerful enough to break the wards. But even if she could manage that... then what? Where could she take them? Osin had eyes everywhere. She could barely keep herself out of danger, let alone protect a group of Sidhe.

Her throat tightened. She needed help, someone who knew how to handle this. She needed Godfrey. *One thing at a time.*

Elara barely breathed the words. "I'm going to help you." Her gaze locked with the female's, the vow settling between them. "I'm going to get you out of here."

She knew their pain, shared their yearning for freedom—freedom that sang with the warmth of sunlight, that danced with the rustle of leaves, that murmured in the ripple of streams. They were kindred spirits, bound by chains not of their making, and she vowed then, with the fierce certainty of one who had known cages, that she would tear down theirs.

They deserved the world beyond these walls.

They deserved better than *this*.

Without waiting for a reply, Elara spun on her heel and dashed from the chamber, the distant echo of the Sidhe's shout trailing her like a ghost. She didn't stop, couldn't—the urgency was a wildfire in her veins, propelling her forward.

Minutes later, she skidded to a halt before the ancient stones.

The air around her crackled, thick with the weight of untamed power, sending a cascade of goosebumps across her skin.

Elara drew a deep breath, steadying her racing heart as she approached the stones with the methodical focus honed through years of study among Verdara's scribes. She cataloged each detail with care, noting the strange markings carved deep into their surface—patterns she didn't recognize, spiraling inward like the rings of a tree but warped. Unnatural.

Some were so worn they looked as if they'd been scoured by centuries of wind, while others glowed faintly, like embers buried deep beneath the stone's surface. There were four in total, standing at equal distances, all arranged in a near-perfect circle, each one standing at least twice her height.

She wished she had parchment, ink—*anything*—to record them properly, but her mind would have to serve as her scroll. She mentally sectioned the stones off, one by one, committing each peculiar detail to memory, each symbol, each unnatural pulse, just in case she never got the chance to see them again.

After she'd observed everything she could from a distance, Elara hesitated. Her dream... could it have been a warning or a premonition? She couldn't be certain. All she knew was the feeling of dread coiling in her gut was not just fear—it was a prelude.

Gathering every shred of courage, she drew in a deep breath that did little to calm her fraying nerves, and stepped forward into the circle.

The shift was immediate. The air around her dropped, cold enough that her breath came out in visible puffs. A shiver ran through her, and she instinctively wrapped her arms around herself. The stones felt different from the inside—more *aware*. She could see the markings up close now, strange glyphs that seemed to shift under her gaze like they were breathing. Elara recorded them quickly in her mind. But these markings were unlike anything she'd ever studied. They meant something—she could feel it, like an itch at the back of her mind.

The longer she gazed upon the stones, the stronger their call grew, looping like a siren's song in her veins, whispering through the very marrow of the earth.

Elara's heart stuttered, fear slicing through the allure—but she couldn't resist. Her hand moved as if claimed by another will, stretching forward until her palm pressed flat against the stone.

White-hot light knifed through her skull, burying itself behind her eyes, splitting thought from thought. She tore her hands away, clutching her face as if that might stop what was already inside her. It didn't. The pain only mounted.

The ground vanished. The room, the Pit—everything folded in on itself until only the storm remained. Wind roared through her, alive and ravenous, stretching her thin, tearing at her from the inside. She wasn't falling—not quite. She was suspended, weightless, no longer flesh and bone but something fragile.

A thread, slowly unraveling.

Then—a hush.

Gradually, the world crept back in. The cold air slipped into her lungs, carrying the scent of pine needles crushed beneath fresh snow, the whisper of cold mountain streams untouched by time. It tasted clean— so clean it almost hurt, as if her chest had never truly known what it was to breathe until now.

Elara blinked, lowering her hands from her face and what greeted her... it snatched away the breath she'd barely reclaimed.

Ethereal.

That was the only word her mind could grasp, but even that felt small compared to the boundless wonder stretching before her.

It wasn't just breathtaking—it was unreal.

Perched on a mountain's edge, Elara stared out at a landscape that looked like it had been shaped by the hands of gods. It unfolded before her like a sacred scroll, ancient and untouched, written in the language of wind and sky.

Islands of rock and earth floated above the clouds, suspended in the air as if the very sky held them up. They weren't just hanging there—they were alive, tethered by twisted roots that spiraled down, like strings of some celestial harp, pulling them back to the earth below.

Each isle was its own world, a living, breathing ecosystem. Waterfalls poured upward, their streams vanishing into the clouds, while gardens heavy with mist held flowers that glowed from within, as if they held starlight in their petals.

These weren't just mountains—they were ancient titans, towering and timeless, their crowns wrapped in lush forests that clung to their sides like sacred offerings. Fog clung to their slopes, swirling and twisting in the wind like restless spirits.

Above, the sky stretched endlessly, painted in twilight hues—mauve and soft gold, streaked with the pink of a sun that never fully set. Impossibly tall spires of rock, softened by the distance, pierced the sky around her, each crowned with temples whose golden spires glinted like beacons under the pale light of twin moons.

It was a place poised in perfect balance, where the ground seemed a mere afterthought to the sprawling bridges that linked peak to peak, their stone pathways lined with fluttering banners. A kingdom of the air where the only law was the whispering wind.

Elara knew, without knowing how, that this place was not just foreign but *fundamentally* different—alive in a way that the human world could never be.

The air here felt strange, lighter somehow, yet charged with something she couldn't quite place. It buzzed against her skin, delicate, like the whisper of wings brushing past.

It was a sound, Elara realized—a soft hum, gentle but ever-present, threaded with faint laughter. She turned, searching for where it came from, heart racing. But no one was there. She was alone, yet not.

She took a hesitant step forward, eyes on the fragile-looking bridge that stretched from her mountain to the next. But the second her foot met the ground, the world twisted beneath her. That blinding white light surged up again, devouring everything—her vision, her bearings, her very sense of self. She flailed, helpless, the weightlessness disorienting as she spun through the vortex.

Terror gripped her, a scream dying in her throat as the Void yawned beneath her, that dark patch growing closer, faster—

Cold stone crashed into her like a battering ram, the force ripping the air from her lungs in a brutal whoosh.

Elara's eyes flew open as she gasped for air, her chest tight and aching. No—something pressed against her sternum, rhythmic and steady, forcing breath back into her lungs.

"She's back."

Saria's face swam into view, hovering over her. Her brow was pinched, eyes, wide and searching, darting over Elara's face, her movements quick, almost frantic as one hand pressed against her chest, the other hovering by her neck, fingers trembling just slightly as they checked her pulse.

The Pit.

She was back in the Pit, lying within the circle of stones.

All at once, the pain hit her—a brutal wave crashing back into her body. It radiated from where her hand had touched the stone, shooting up her arm, spreading like lighting down her spine, through every nerve. Elara tried to scream, to move—but body wouldn't obey, wouldn't even tremble beneath the agony. *Broken.* The word echoed in her mind. She was broken.

"Fucking hell, child," Saria said, her breath shaky before she started casting enchantments into the air. One after another, they floated above Elara, shimmering briefly before sinking into her skin. Each spell sent a flicker through her, a faint pulse deep inside, like embers catching the barest breath of air, fighting to reignite a dying flame.

Dying...

A cold sweat broke out along Elara's brow.

Three times now—*three* times she had nearly died, each encounter leaving something behind. Not visions, but *memories*. First, the encounter with the river spirit; next, when Osin's shadows had nearly snuffed her life out; and now—the stones.

Elara's chest constricted, pain lancing through her ribs as if her heart were being squeezed in a fist. Her gaze snapped to the stones, the pulse of their strange energy still lingering in the air.

Had they dragged her away, ripped her from the flow of time and tossed her into some forgotten realm? Or was it death murmuring secrets from the Void, whispering to her in the language of the lost?

CHAPTER 28

Elara spent five days in the infirmary. Five endless days, smothered by the constant presence of guards at the door and the swarm of healers fussing over every flicker of discomfort. There was always something new to swallow, something meant to soothe or mend, though the constant barrage of it all felt more exhausting than her injuries.

Saria, in particular, was relentless. Always at her worktable, grinding herbs and murmuring incantations under her breath, breaking apart old spells, and weaving them into something new in an effort to speed Elara's recovery. Her fingers moved with an almost frantic precision, crafting tonics meant to either stitch Elara back together or plunge her into that dreamless dark where even her thoughts couldn't reach her. And sometimes, Elara wished she could stay there, in that quiet emptiness, far from the ache of consciousness and the reality of everything waiting beyond the infirmary walls.

But even through that dreamless abyss, Elara had felt something *else*. A presence—soothing, steady, a balm against the overwhelming pain. The potions blurred her memory, but she could still recall it—soft hands, featherlight on her face, and a voice, warm and low, calling her back from the dark.

"You died," Saria had whispered that first night, her voice barely

cutting through the fog of potions and pain. *"Halfway to the Other-world before I dragged you back."*

If that brief brush with oblivion had indeed been death, then truly, Elara grieved her return to the living.

Since coming back, everything felt off. It wasn't just the pain—though that constant throb beneath her skin had become something she could almost ignore. No, it was worse than that—like she wasn't supposed to be here anymore. Like she'd crossed a line, left something behind on the other side, and now being dragged back felt more like a punishment than salvation.

Osin had come to see her while she lay unconscious—Elara learned that much after the fact. Two grand feasts had passed without her, and he was livid. Not the usual simmering annoyance but true, seething rage. He couldn't stomach that she had outwitted Rolfe, slipped past his guards, and reached the stones. There had been punishments for it, harsh ones. She'd heard the healers whispering when they thought her too far gone to notice—whole units reshuffled, men stripped of their ranks, others dragged out and humiliated in front of the court. And Rolfe... well, whatever happened to him, the healers weren't saying aloud, but she could guess. Osin didn't need blood to make an example of someone—he preferred the kind of punishment that left a man broken from the inside out.

Elara couldn't shake the guilt. Rolfe had been kind to her, kinder than most would have been in his position, and he didn't deserve what had come to him. No one had died—that much she knew. But she didn't want to think about what Rolfe might've endured because of her. It wasn't fair. *None of it was.* But the shame gnawed at her anyway, a deep ache she felt in the pit of her stomach.

"Lift your arm."

Elara tried, but it barely made it halfway before the tremors started. The limb felt like it didn't belong to her anymore.

"Good, now your leg."

Her jaw clenched as she forced her leg up from the cot, the muscles screaming in protest. Saria frowned, her fingers pressing into the flesh of her thigh, moving in slow, methodical circles.

"Can you feel that?"

Elara nodded, but the sensation was faint, like her leg was wrapped in thick cotton. "Barely," she admitted, frustrated. She'd already told Saria she was broken, but the healer was persistent, carefully testing every nerve and muscle, as if she could coax them back to life with sheer will.

There was a brief glint of something in Saria's eyes—concern, perhaps—but her voice remained steady. "We'll keep at it. You're making progress."

Progress. If this was progress, Elara wasn't sure she wanted to imagine what *stuck* felt like.

"Don't give me that look. I've never had anyone come back after touching the stones. Ever. That you're even sitting up after five days is a miracle." Her hand drifted to her hair, fingers tugging at the coronet braid that circled her head like a crown, silver strands already coming loose. Her gaze softened, though, just for a moment, as a small, weary smile pulled at the corner of her mouth. "Then again," she added, with a resigned shake of her head, "you're *you*."

Saria's eyes seemed to glaze over, like her mind had wandered far from the room, her gaze lingering too long on the thin, silver scars lacing Elara's wrists. Her lips pressed into a tight line.

Elara frowned, the silence stretching. "What?"

The single word seemed to pull Saria from whatever distant place she'd gone. She blinked once before shaking her head. "Nothing," she muttered, her tone clipped as she turned away toward the cluttered worktable in the corner. The sharp scent of crushed herbs and burnt sage filled the room, mingling with the steady rasp of her mortar and pestle as she ground dried roots with far more force than needed.

Then, Saria's gaze flicked, quick as a breath, toward the two guards standing at the door. With a soft exhale, she looked back down at her hands, busy but tense. "You're expected at the party tonight," she said, her tone casual, like she hadn't just thrown a boulder into Elara's lap.

Elara snorted. "And how, exactly, am I supposed to manage that?"

"I'm working on something," she said, not looking up from her task. "It'll help you get through the night, but it won't last. You'll need to take another dose every hour to stay on your feet." She added a pinch of crushed petals to the bowl, the scent of lavender mixing with something medicinal. "It's not a long-term fix, just a patch to get you through. By the next gathering, I'm hoping you won't need it."

Elara sank back onto the cot, the coarse fabric scratching at her skin as she closed her eyes. "How much time do I have?"

Saria hesitated enough to make Elara's pulse quicken before the healer finally spoke. "Two hours."

Two hours.

Her stomach twisted. She didn't know if she had the strength to pretend anymore.

Shifting on the cot, her body protested with every small movement as she began the routine Saria had drilled into her since the feeling had crept back into her legs. Simple stretches at first—lifting one leg, then the other, flexing her toes, rolling her ankles. She lay flat, muscles trembling with the effort, but at least it was *something*.

She was supposed to focus on working sensation back into her limbs, on each deliberate movement and breath. Bend, flex, release. But her mind wouldn't stay quiet. Five days since the fiasco with the stones, and all she could do was replay it over and over. She couldn't stop picking it apart—what had happened, what she *still* didn't understand.

Elara clenched her jaw, pulling her leg up again, holding it until her muscles spasmed. The stones had done more than just tear through her body—they had opened her eyes. Made her *see*. Something she'd been blind to for far too long, something that now felt so glaringly, painfully obvious.

She was missing memories.

Not just the usual gaps where people forget things but whole pieces of herself were missing. Like someone had reached inside and torn them out.

Saria had said no one ever came back from touching the stones. Not a single soul. And for the life of her, Elara couldn't figure out what their purpose was if all they did was kill anyone foolish enough to approach. She didn't have the answers. Not yet. But she would.

And Elara had a pretty good idea of just how to get them.

～

THE STONEBREW SLID down her throat thick and slow, like molasses left too long over a flame. It wasn't the worst tonic Elara had ever endured—there was a freshness to it, like crushed mint mingled with damp earth after a storm—cooling, almost pleasant, and not enough to make her gag. But it was her fourth dose of the night, and she was already creeping dangerously close to the limit Saria had set.

As the tonic settled in her stomach, she could feel it working, moving through her veins like steel, tightening her muscles, reinforcing the tendons. The tremor in her legs settled, the ache dulling to a low thrum beneath her skin.

It was enough to keep her standing, enough to fake the appearance of health.

Saria had made it clear—if she didn't take all six doses while she pushed her limits, she'd pay for it. Her muscles would seize up or fail entirely, leaving her locked in place for hours, maybe days. All the progress she'd made would be for nothing.

Six vials for six hours. Healer's orders. And even that was pushing it.

Elara rolled her eyes. Osin didn't give a damn about *"healer's orders"*.

The Lord Sovereign's rich laughter drifted through the royal gardens like honeyed wine, wrapping around the air with that slick, sensual undertone that only came when he was several drinks deep. The sound snaked through the night, curling around the rustle of leaves, slipping under the soft light of the enchanted lanterns hanging from the trees. Their dim glow bathed the garden in an almost otherworldly haze, turning the night into something soft, dreamlike—too perfect to trust.

A warm breeze stirred through the gardens, twisting through Elara's thick curls and bringing with it the heavy scent of jasmine and the sweetness of stardust roses. The party was a sight meant to dazzle—an intricate maze of silver-leafed trees, their branches shimmering like molten metal under the moonlight. But the air was too warm, unnaturally so for mid-autumn. Elara could feel the ether woven into the atmosphere, sticky and cloying, clinging to her skin like a layer of sweat. It coated everything—the food, the drinks, even the flowers. A faint, deadly undertone, like candies dipped in poison.

She'd been sure, when Osin had led her into the gardens, that he'd force her to parade around at his side like last time. But tonight he had something else in mind. He'd stationed her among the statues, making her stand there like a piece of stone while the rest of the party carried on around her. Not quite part of it, yet not entirely separate. Just another ornament for the elites to admire and forget.

She knew the feeling well enough.

Her gaze swept over the guests that were scattered across the clearing, limbs tangled in impossible configurations as they played some ridiculous game. The game was simple—players spun a crystal dial that hovered in the air, its glassy surface shimmering with runes that shifted with every spin. When it stopped, the runes would glow, marking a place on the enchanted grid beneath their feet. The tiles moved and shifted beneath them, charmed to keep everyone just a little off-balance. The more they drank, the more chaotic it became, laughter spilling out as bodies twisted, arms and legs crisscrossing in a drunken tangle of silk and gold.

Everyone was already halfway to oblivion, the wine flowing freely, but there was an edge to it. Their eyes shone a fraction too bright, their laughter cracked and wild, teetering toward madness—like their drinks were laced with a bit of something else.

Laughter echoed off the marble statues that loomed over the garden, silent watchers carved in the likeness of gods long forgotten, their stony faces indifferent to the revelry below. Elara stood rigid beside the towering figure of Aine, her hands outstretched, as if she held eternity in them. Her own hands, though far less steady, reached out to the nearest nightbloom, her fingertips grazing the cool, velvety petals. She clung to that small sensation, grasping for any distraction from the incessant ache screaming through her legs.

But even without looking up, she could feel him—Osin's gaze burning into her. She looked up to find amusement glinting in his eyes, his lips curled into a lazy, predatory smile. Everyone else was lost in the game, limbs tangled and slipping as they laughed, but not him. Osin had hardly looked away from her all night. He watched every twitch of her muscles, every slight falter. He enjoyed it—her struggle.

From across the gardens, Elara could sense the anger simmering beneath his smug exterior—a tightly coiled beast barely restrained. She knew he was furious over what she'd done. But she'd expected something worse from him, something harsher than this quiet glee he seemed to revel in.

Unease curled low in her stomach.

Elara tore her gaze away, tugging uncomfortably at the too-tight bodice, the cheap, thin fabric clinging to her skin. Layers of flimsy lace and low-cut satin, dyed in garish shades of crimson, left little to the imagination. If, at the last party, Osin had wanted her to resemble a goddess, this time, after her insult, he'd made sure she looked like a harlot. A mockery wrapped in gaudy material, designed to humiliate.

And it worked.

Their gazes crawled over her like the cheap fabric she was forced into, clinging tight. Lust. Obsession. It radiated from them, lingering on every inch of bare skin, on every scandalous curve Osin had chosen to display. The whispers weren't even subtle, low murmurs filled with heat, with a desire that made her stomach churn. Her skin prickled under their attention, but... she couldn't bring herself to care. Not tonight.

Let them look. Let them think whatever they wanted. It didn't matter.

Because her mind was locked on one thing—*finding Lady Calista Thorne.*

Elara had thought of the young woman endlessly during her days in the infirmary. The look Calista had given her at the last party—the faint glimmer of recognition—paired with those fragmented memories...

They had known each other. Elara was certain of it.

Maybe Lady Thorne could fill in those missing pieces, the gaps torn from her past. Maybe even more than that. It was reckless. Elara was grasping at the thinnest of threads, but at this point, it was all she had left to hold on to. And cling she had—four vials of Stonebrew downed, waiting for the night to spiral—for Osin to drink himself deep enough into his cups that he wouldn't notice her slip away. He was nearly there. His glances had grown fewer, lazier, drifting off as the wine took hold. At the moment, he was stretched out on the grass, telling the story of his pilgrimage.

A swarm of admirers—men and women alike—gathered around Osin, utterly enraptured by his every word. Their eyes were glowing with admiration—or lust, by the looks of it. It seemed as though they were but a breath away from flinging themselves at his feet, and Osin, ever the opportunist, basked in the attention, soaking it in as if it were his natural due.

"The climb," he said, "was treacherous, as you'd expect. The air so thin, I could scarcely breathe. But I pressed on, knowing the fate of the realm depended on me. On my strength, my will." His audience gasped, wide-eyed and enthralled, as if they hadn't heard the tale a hundred times before. Hands reached out, fingers brushing his arms, his chest. "When I finally reached the summit, Aine appeared to me. Radiant, divine, her voice thunderous. I knelt before her, pleading for the return of ether to our land. And she listened. She listened to *me*."

One of the women, eyes bright with awe, gasped. "How could she not?" she said breathlessly. "A man of your strength, your devotion..."

Osin grinned, soaking in the adoration. "Indeed," he purred, "how could she not?"

Elara rolled her eyes, unable to hold it back anymore. She endured his tale for a while longer, watching him sink further into his drink, half hoping he might let slip some new detail. But it was the same tired story she'd already read in *Osin's Sacred Journey*, repeated word for word, as if he had rehearsed his own legend. And after all she had come to learn, she found herself doubting whether *any* of it had ever been true.

Her gaze flicked to the banquet tables, and her stomach twisted. She'd never seen so much food in one place, enough to feed the guests three times over, maybe more. Her tongue flicked across her lips instinctively. Silver platters gleamed under the soft glow of lanterns, each one piled high with figs dripping in honey, roasted pheasant with perfectly crisped skin, and sugared pears that shimmered like they were plucked from a dream. She tore her gaze from the food, forcing herself to focus on the courtiers instead. Their chatter filled the air, a constant hum that blended with the soft strains of music. The courtiers drifted between tables, plucking bites from the decadent spread, sipping wine from crystal goblets. Elara's eyes scanned the crowd, searching for Calista, but a floating platter of sparkling wine slid into her line of sight, nudging her to take a glass.

She shot a quick glance over her shoulder at Osin. He hadn't noticed. Good. "No, thank you," she murmured, edging away from the floating platter, moving closer to the nearest table. At the edges of the feast, desserts sat in neat, tempting rows—rich cakes dusted with powdered sugar, pastries oozing with spiced cream, delicate bowls filled with candied flowers that shimmered in the light like tiny jewels.

Everything was lush, indulgent—a feast meant to overwhelm the senses, to pull you in, and never let go. Elara's fingers hovered just above a candied flower, its soft petals practically begging to be touched, the faint scent of honey and vanilla curling up toward her.

"I wouldn't eat that if I were you."

The voice, low and smooth as silk, stopped her at once. Elara glanced up and met a pair of striking hazel eyes. The young man before her was effortlessly handsome, with sharp features framed by dark hair that fell artfully out of place, as though nature itself intended it to rest just so. His heavy-lidded gaze, sultry and aloof, held a flicker of amusement. He was dressed in a cravat of deep indigo, tied with the kind of precision that made him look like he belonged at court, yet there was something unruly about him. Rings glinted on his long, slender fingers, each one more ornate than the last, and his posture was all casual arrogance, as if he knew exactly how he looked.

It was him. The same man from the first party. The one whose eyes had raked over her like he was just waiting for the chance to take a bite.

The hunger in his gaze hadn't changed—if anything, it had sharpened. His smile held something dangerous, the kind that made her heart stutter and her instincts flare.

"Unless, of course, you wish to share their fate," he said, nodding toward the crowd through the gardens, still entangled in their drunken game.

So, she had been right—they'd all taken something *extra*.

"Thanks for the warning."

He dipped his head slightly, that smirk never leaving his lips. "Anything for the *Hallowed*."

Elara huffed, the title grating as it always did. But there was something in the way he said it—light, teasing, as though he, too, did not take it seriously.

"Tristan." He extended his hand, palm up, and Elara simply stared at it, bewildered. No one from Ulrith greeted her with such familiarity—

hell, most didn't greet her at all. She was used to the reverent bows, the stiff nods, the distance. But a handshake? That was *beyond* strange.

Her gaze dropped to his wrist, catching the unmistakable sunburst etched into his skin. Beneath it, intricate lines traced his veins, symbols that spoke of lineage and privilege—glyphs that told a story of wealth, power, and old blood. Someone born into the heart of Arinthel, raised under its golden towers and the shadow of the throne.

He was no outsider; he belonged here in a way few did.

Still, his hand lingered, his hazel eyes gleaming with challenge, as if daring her to take it.

"Elara," she finally said, slipping her hand into his, her voice steady even as her heart gave a slight stutter.

Tristan's brow arched, his lips curving into something far too smug for her liking. "Is that so?"

A reluctant smile tugged at her lips, much to her annoyance. He was undeniably flirtatious, and worse, it was working. She couldn't afford to be distracted right now. Tearing her gaze from his, she quickly glanced over her shoulder, scanning the crowd in hopes of spotting Calista. But there was no sign of her.

Perhaps she isn't coming tonight after all...

"Anyone catching your eye tonight?" Tristan asked casually as he circled the table, coming to stand beside her. Elara barely glanced at him before he added, "That old bastard with the blonde wig over there? He's been undressing you with his eyes for the better part of an hour."

A snort escaped her before she could stop it. The man *was* ancient, and the wig he wore was perhaps the most obvious one she had ever seen.

"And how, exactly, would you know that?" she asked, side-eyeing him.

Tristan leaned in slightly, his voice lowering to a murmur that only she could hear. "Because I've been doing the same, and I like to know who I'm up against."

Elara's gaze snapped to Tristan, her eyes wide. "What—"

But before she could finish, a sudden clap echoed across the party, slicing the hum of conversation. Silence fell instantly.

Osin stood in the center of the gardens, a smirk playing on his lips, his posture casual, almost too relaxed. He spread his arms wide. "Ladies and gentlemen, thank you for your patience. At last, the moment you've all been waiting for has arrived."

The crowd erupted into cheers, anticipation thick in the air. Elara's heart pounded in her chest, her mind racing. Tristan shifted closer, the heat of his body brushing hers, but she barely registered it.

"Tonight," Osin continued, "we honor those of you who have proven your loyalty, your... resourcefulness. You see, a little birdie told me there were rebels hiding among us, traitors intent on disrupting our peace." His eyes gleamed, sweeping over the crowd. "But thanks to you, my dear guests, we found them. Those who sought to sow discord in our land have been captured."

A murmur of satisfaction rippled through the gathered elites, and Elara's blood ran cold. Her thoughts spun in a frenzy. Dominic had spoken of spies, of Keepers within the Pit... *Had they been betrayed?*

"So, to celebrate such initiative," Osin drawled, "we are going to play a little game. One that rewards not just speed, but cunning and luck." His eyes gleamed with twisted amusement as he surveyed the eager faces before him. "Each of you had a hand in catching these rebels —whether through whispers, discreet actions, or more direct means. And as we know, to the victor go the spoils."

Osin's grin only widened. "And what better reward for your efforts, than a chance to win something truly priceless?" His gaze landed on Elara. "The first to reach the center of the grid will win. And the prize, of course, is *her*."

CHAPTER 29

The crowd roared, the sound swelling like a wave crashing over her, but Elara's world was caving in.

She was the prize.

A shiver danced down her spine, cold sweat beading at her neck as Osin's words slithered back to her, his smile a serpent's grin splitting the dark.

"For those willing to pay a premium... more intimate interactions could be arranged."

Her stomach flipped, bile rising fast. She was going to be sick.

Eyes—so many eyes—fixed on her, hungry, devouring, crawling over her skin like parasites. The cheers grew louder, more savage, but it all blurred, like she was underwater, like she was drowning.

Osin raised his hands, and the crowd fell silent. "Now, now, let's not get ahead of ourselves," he purred, "there's plenty of the Hallowed to go around." As he lowered his hands, shadows pooled at his fingertips, thick and oily, creeping across the dirt like spilled blood. Elara's heart pounded, fear rising like the acid in her throat as they lunged.

Her body moved before she had time to think—an urgent, desperate attempt to sidestep, to run. But her legs gave out beneath her, and she hit the ground with a bone-rattling thud. The crowd's cruel laughter rang out, but all she could focus on was the sickening sound of glass shattering against stone.

Goosebumps prickled along her arms. *The tonics.*

A dampness spread slowly, cold and sticky against her side. Elara's hand brushed her gown, and her fingers met the broken glass, its remains leaking through the fabric. The ground seemed to tilt beneath her, the faces in the crowd smearing into a whirl of sneers and gloating eyes. She didn't have time to mourn, no time to panic over the loss—they were gone, and Osin's shadows were upon her.

They snaked around her ankles and wrists—tightening, squeezing, seeping into her veins. It was a freezing fire that numbed her limbs, stole her breath, clouded her mind. Her fingertips turned blue, nerves screaming. Fight. *She had to fight.* But the shadows moved too fast, dragging her across the grid, feet barely grazing the ground before she was lifted into the air.

Tears pricked her eyes, freezing upon her cheeks as they fell. Through the haze, she glimpsed Osin standing below, at the center of it all, like a spider in his web.

This was her punishment. For defying him. For outsmarting his men. For daring to step out of the neat little box he'd shoved her into. He'd been waiting for this—a chance to remind her what she was. A pawn to be sold to the highest bidder, as though she were mere chattel, as though she were *nothing.*

Rage flared, a brief spark in the darkness. She summoned it, *clung* to it.

"Now, we all know *Spindlebind* is a simple game," Osin said, his voice dripping with false charm, carrying effortlessly over the crowd. The players gathered on the grid below her, their eager faces lit by the glowing runes. Osin gestured toward the shimmering crystal dial hovering in the air. With a languid flick of his fingers, it spun, the runes blurring in a whirl of light. "When it stops, the runes will, of course, instruct you where to place your hands and feet." The dial spun faster. "But tonight," he continued, his tone laced with a chilling sweetness, "we've added a few... enhancements."

Osin turned toward the four Legionnaires stepping forward, their faces hard as stone. At the slightest tilt of his head, they spread out, moving to the edges of the grid, arms lifting in unison, fingers splayed as they called the elements to life. Flames roared up from the tiles as air howled, whipping through the grid. The ground beneath them trembled, the earth groaning as it cracked and shifted, while torrents of water surged from every corner, crashing together in a wild, swirling current.

"The tiles beneath you will shift as you move, and these obstacles? Let's just say they're designed to... inspire a bit more urgency." His smile was all teeth. "First to reach the middle and touch the Hallowed wins." He flicked his hand, dropping Elara into the center of the grid. "May the strongest claim their prize."

She hit the stone floor with a bone-jarring crack, pain lancing up her spine as her knees slammed hard into the cold surface. The shock rattled her teeth, and her lungs seized. Her legs—*gods*, they felt shattered. Agony flared through her, a searing, white-hot wave that left her vision blurry. Trembling, she pushed herself up, her palms scraping against the rough tiles, but the ground beneath her wasn't still—it shifted, sliding like a snake, the runes etched into the stone beginning to glow.

Then the tremors hit. The footsteps.

Like a dam breaking, they charged the board, bodies colliding as they funneled through, the elements pulling back just enough to let them pass. Earth groaned and cracked, water surged in torrents, fire hissed and sparked, wind screamed in fury—alive, furious, wild—only to snap back into place the moment they crossed, a storm of madness swirling around them. A living, breathing barrier. Unpredictable. Deadly. The only thing standing between the players and their prize—*her*.

Osin twisted the dial, and it roared to life, the runes flaring so brightly they blurred into a blinding swirl of light. The players' heads snapped up, eyes locked onto the dial's frantic spin. Anticipation crackled, the kind you could feel prickling your skin, ready to snap at any moment.

Then, with a sharp, jarring snap, the dial locked into place. The runes exploded in a pulse of red, a searing flash that burned across her vision, leaving dark spots dancing in her sight.

The first: *fire*.

Chaos erupted.

The rune—a jagged, serpent-like flame—blazed to life across the grid, a scorching red, its heat palpable even from a distance. Flames shot up from the blank tiles, twisting and hissing, consuming everything in their path. The heat hit like a wave, blistering, scorching the air.

It swallowed the grid in a swirling inferno, sparks flying, blazing at their feet. The players had mere seconds to react, to jump before the heat bit into their soles, the flames licking at the edges of their boots.

The air thickened with smoke, burning Elara's lungs. She sprang onto the nearest rune, a hiss of pain escaping her as the ground groaned, shifting, the low rumble vibrating through her bones. For a heartbeat, everything held its breath. Heat pulsed up through her legs, almost unbearable, her skin prickling from the intense burn. Then, with a low, grinding rumble, the tiles beneath her lurched again, realigning themselves like pieces of a living puzzle. She swayed, struggling to stay upright.

The heat vanished.

Water.

The silvery rune flickered, a faint pulse of light, before it erupted into life.

Cool blue waves shimmered across the surface. The air thickened, pressing close, as though the sea itself had risen to claim the space. Salt filled her lungs, brisk and unmistakable—the same brine she'd tasted on the air back in Verdara.

A low, guttural rumble vibrated through the tiles underfoot. Then, without warning, the roar hit. Water. A wall of it crashing down like a tidal wave breaking free, sweeping over the board in a cold, savage rush.

The torrent crashed into Elara, yanking her from her feet, dragging her under before she had a chance to scream.

Darkness closed in as the freezing water wrapped around her, choking off her breath. Her arms flailed, legs kicking uselessly as she tumbled, chest screaming. But then her hand brushed against something solid—*a tile*. A raised platform, just barely within reach.

Elara kicked toward it, her limbs burning before she broke the surface with a ragged gasp, water streaming down her face. She scrambled, fingers slipping on the slick stone before finally gripping the edge.

With a grunt of effort, she pulled herself up onto the raised tile, collapsing onto the glowing water rune, gulping down air.

She was going to die. There was no way in hell she could handle any more of this. It had been almost an hour since the last dose of stone-brew, and she could feel it slipping, fading out of her system. Her body shook so violently it felt like she was splintering apart, every inch of her screaming for mercy.

Elara glanced up, her vision swimming as the players in the distance struggled to stay upright, their boots skidding across the slick, ever-shifting tiles. The waves showed no mercy, rising high before crashing down with punishing force, the impact sending bodies flying. The fallen were swept from the board like leaves in a torrent, pulling them toward the outer lines of the grid. Disqualified.

The water rune on the dial flickered, a faint shimmer, before vanishing. In its place, the earth rune blinked into existence for the briefest breath, only to morph into fire with a crackling burst of heat. And again it shifted—faster, each change more volatile.

Then the earth buckled. A rolling hill of stone broke open beneath her feet, throwing her off balance. She stumbled, crashing down, her fingers clawing at the nearest tile. But the earth didn't take her off the board. No, she wouldn't get that mercy. Elara dangled, her nails digging into the stone, breaking under the strain as the rune shifted again, flickering into wind—and the tiles reset.

She scrambled toward the opal swirl of wind glowing beside her, the rune pulsing with soft light, but something made her pause. Her eyes darted upward, heart lurching painfully in her chest as she spotted him —the player barreling toward her. His features were twisted into a savage grin, teeth bared.

She screamed, stumbling back as he lunged at her, his arms outstretched, his movements a wild, an erratic blend of desperation and drunken fury.

But then the wind struck.

A violent gust slammed into him like an unseen fist, lifting him off his feet and hurling him across the grid. He landed hard, rolling to a stop, just inches away from the glowing rune. Before he could scramble back up, the wind howled again, dragging him across the board, before disappearing into the swirling chaos beyond.

Elara's chest heaved, fingers clinging to her tile with what little strength she had left. A strange numbness crept through her limbs, as if the blood had slowed to a crawl, the wind tearing at her hair, pulling at her clothes.

The grid was mayhem—players scattered across the board, fighting to stay upright as the wind lashed at them, one by one getting ripped from the tiles and flung into the gardens. Elara counted. Fifty remained. Maybe less. And they were getting closer.

She scanned the disarray, searching for some way to hold her ground, something she could use, but her mind was blank, scrambling as wildly as the players around her.

Elara rolled onto another wind rune, barely catching her breath, when a woman—a tall, lean figure with hawk-like eyes and a braid snapping like a whip behind her—charged forward. Her movements were almost unnatural, dodging the wind blasts with eerie precision, slipping between the gusts as if she commanded them. She was closing in, fingers outstretched, so close Elara could feel the air shift from her reach.

But then—*crack*.

A blur of motion. Another competitor came from nowhere, his elbow slamming into the woman's ribs with brutal force. She let out a strangled gasp, her body twisting in midair before she crashed to the ground. The moment her back hit the floor, the runes beneath her flared to life—*earth*.

Vines exploded from the ground, coiling around her limbs. She barely had time to react before they tightened, but her hand shot out, grabbing the leg of the man who'd knocked her down, her vines wrapping around him too, yanking them both off the board in a tangle.

The crowd roared along the grid, but Elara couldn't hear them over the pounding of her own heartbeat. It was anarchy. Carnage. The players weren't just battling the elements anymore—they were turning on each other. Pushing, shoving, trampling anyone who slowed them down, anything to get ahead. The grid shifted beneath them, tiles spinning like mad, and five more players went down, their bodies crashing into the floor before vines shot up to grab them.

The runes shifted, water flaring to life, and a shimmering wall of it rose before Elara, distorting the insanity beyond. She leapt onto the opal-marked tile, squinting through the cascade, and her heart stopped cold.

Tristan.

He stood at the edge of the grid, eyes calculating. Unlike the others, who rushed in desperation, Tristan waited. Patient. And then, with a precision that made her breath stutter, he moved. One step, then another, fluid and graceful, as though he already knew every shift of the tiles, every trap ready to spring.

Where the others stumbled, Tristan glided—unbothered, unhurried.

It was as if the elements bowed to him. Where flames shot up in his path, the earth rose to smother them. Wind howled, but water surged forward, breaking its fury before it touched him. Around him, it was as if the elements fought themselves, struggling against each other, leaving him untouched. Solid. And with each step, he came closer to her.

Another player crashed to the ground beside him, groaning as he hit the grid. But Tristan didn't even blink. He leapt over the fallen body with that same lethal grace. And then his gaze found hers—steady, focused, full of a quiet arrogance, like he already knew exactly how this would end—like he *always had*.

Elara's breath hitched as Osin laughed, smooth as ever, breaking through the bedlam. "Ah, it seems we have a contender." His gaze shifted to Tristan, with a hint of something dark curling. "Let's see if he's worthy."

The crowd roared as Osin lifted his hand, the very air around him buzzing with power, shadows coiling at his feet. They slithered into the tumult like smoke, twisting and curling through the grid, weaving between players. One by one, they knocked aside anyone in their path, tendrils of darkness sweeping legs out from under them or coiling around their throats. But through the madness, Elara's gaze tracked them. The shadows weren't moving at random. No—they had a target.

But Tristan was already closing in, muscles taut as he fought against the relentless wall of wind trying to shove him back. His lips peeled into a snarl, jaw clenched, a guttural growl ripping from his throat as he pushed forward. The wind roared, but he roared louder. But then the tiles shifted beneath him, glowing a blinding green, and everything changed in a heartbeat.

The earth bucked beneath them, launching him into the air like a rock shot from a catapult. But Tristan, damn him, made it look effortless. He twisted midair, using the momentum like it was second nature. Every heartbeat stretched, the seconds crawling as if the gods themselves were drawing out the moment, mocking her with it.

And then he was plummeting.

Straight for her.

Elara barely had a second to brace herself, barely a breath in her lungs before Tristan slammed into her. *Hard.* The impact sent her reeling, the air punched from her chest in one brutal gasp. They tumbled, rolling across the grid, each hit against the shifting tiles, jarring her bones, rattling through her body.

Her mind spun, trying to catch up to what just happened, when she saw it—dark, curling tendrils of Osin's shadows, creeping toward them, swirling in tight coils. But they were too late.

A growl ripped from Elara's throat as she shoved at Tristan's chest. Her palms collided with the firm muscle. "Get off me."

He didn't move. *Of course* he didn't. Instead, he braced himself above her, arms planted on either side of her head, face close, that stupid grin already spreading across his lips like he didn't just knock her flat. "Not exactly the welcome I was hoping for," he murmured, hair tumbling into his eyes—messy, careless, *still* annoyingly perfect.

Her glare could've burned through steel, but all she felt was the hammering of her pulse, the rush of blood still pounding in her ears. The blaring gong cut through it all, the sound rattling through her skull as the crowd erupted in cheers. The game was over.

And Tristan had won.

CHAPTER 30

"Tristan!" Osin's voice rang out, slicing through the fading buzz of the game as he crossed the grid. His boots clicked against the stone tiles, shadows curling lazily around him.

The players scattered across the board watched as Osin approached Elara and Tristan—some with bitter glares, others barely paying attention, slipping back into their drinks, their poisons, already bored.

Osin clasped Tristan's arm and pulled him off Elara, yanking him to his feet. "I expected nothing less," he said, "from someone of your bloodline. Though I must admit, fortune seemed particularly fond of you tonight."

Tristan let out a low, rich laugh. "What can I say? The fates *do* love me."

Osin's eyes gleamed, his smile stretching just enough to show teeth. "Indeed," he murmured, gaze sliding back to Elara, pinned to the grid. "So," he drawled, that wicked glint in his eyes, "was she worth all that fuss?"

Tristan glanced at her briefly, his eyes barely skimming over her disheveled form before flicking back to Osin. "I'd prefer not to leave her looking like a drowned rat. A proper cleanup first, then we'll see what she's worth."

Osin's fingers tapped against his thigh thoughtfully. "See that she isn't... *damaged*. No marks, no blemishes. She already bears enough of those. But the other pleasures," his voice lowered, "those that don't leave a trace—by all means, indulge."

Tristan dipped his head, a playful glint still in his eyes. "You honor me, my lord."

Tristan yanked Elara up fast, her legs barely catching her weight before they gave out. She almost hit the ground again, but his arm shot out, grabbing her under the ribs before she could fall. Gasping for breath, she glared at him, grinding her teeth against the pain that throbbed through every inch of her. Her fingers, trembling with effort, sank into his arm, her nails pressing hard enough to elicit a wince from him, but he didn't let go. His amethyst ring flared to life, the air around them humming with energy as he lifted his hand to tear open a rift—when Osin's voice slid through the tension like silk over steel.

"Oh, Tristan," he purred, "the Hallowed is to remain *here*, in the safety of my castle. After all, we wouldn't want her wandering where she shouldn't, would we?"

The power in Tristan's ring flickered, the glow snuffed out as his hand dropped to his side. His jaw tightened, but only for a breath before a soft, almost careless laugh slipped out. "I am your humble servant through and through," he said smoothly, bowing just low enough to appear sincere. But as soon as Osin turned away, Tristan's gaze flicked to Elara, a sly wink following. "When it suits me," he murmured under his breath.

Elara's eyes widened, but no words came. She couldn't force them past the tightness in her throat, every ounce of her energy focused on just staying on her feet, her body trembling under the strain.

Osin didn't spare her another glance, a flick of his hand enough to summon the guards as he melted back into the party, swallowed by the swell of laughter and music.

Two of them moved in—flanking herself and Tristan, as the last dregs of Stonebrew's false warmth slipped away. She was weak, vulnerable. She tried to breathe, tried to grasp a *single* thought, a *single* thread of hope, but her mind was drowning in a sea of slow, choking fear. Her gaze darted frantically through the fading twilight, searching for a raven, for anyone—someone who could pull her from this waking nightmare.

But the world had turned away.

There was no winged savior, no outstretched hand. Just the cold, crushing weight of inevitability as the party carried on like she wasn't about to be assaulted.

She was alone.

~

THE BEDROOM WAS MASSIVE, almost overwhelming so. High, arched ceilings soared overhead as towering windows claimed an entire wall, framing the Northern Ridge in silver moonlight. But the bed. The bed was the centerpiece, sprawling across the middle of the chamber like a throne.

Elara, leaning heavily against the doorway, barely had a moment to take it all in before Tristan breezed past her, that familiar glint of trouble dancing in his eyes. Without a moment's pause, he flung himself onto the bed, his body sinking into the layers of blankets with a casual, unbothered air, as if the room—and the night—were his to claim.

"We'll be right outside," one guard muttered, his eyes trailing over Elara like he half-expected her to bolt. *As if she could.* She didn't bother giving him the satisfaction of a response, her attention locked on Tristan instead.

His grin stretched wide, all self-satisfaction, arms folded behind his head, completely at ease. The door clicked shut behind the guards, leaving the two of them alone.

"Must you look *so* murderous?" he drawled.

Elara's fists clenched, her fingers itching to grab something—anything—heavy enough to throw at him. He might've won the game, but she wasn't about to make it easy for him. Not a chance.

"Relax," Tristan chuckled, propping himself up on one elbow and patting the bed. "There's plenty of space for both of us, if you're feeling tempted."

Elara's lip curled in disgust. "Touch me, and I'll break your nose."

Tristan's grin only widened, eyes gleaming with that insufferable, cheeky confidence that made her blood boil. "You're adorable when you're angry, you know that? You've got this lovely habit of looking like you want to stab me. Which, honestly, is the most fun I've had in weeks."

"Keep talking, and I'll make good on it."

Tristan's brows shot up, but instead of backing down, he looked thoroughly amused—no, worse. He looked *turned on*. Ugh.

"Spirited and dangerous—just my type."

"You're foul."

He sat up, his expression still annoyingly casual, though there was a hint of something darker in his eyes. "And you, darling, are forbidden fruit."

Elara's eyes narrowed, but then the atmosphere shifted, a ripple tearing through the room with a force that nearly knocked her off her feet. The crack of it ricocheted, splitting the air, and before she could steady herself, a rift appeared, dark and swirling in the corner.

"Ah, but it seems we won't be playing after all," Tristan said, his voice dripping with mock disappointment. "Ivan—*always the killjoy*—has other plans for you."

Elara's mouth fell open as the Hunter stepped through the rift, no armor, no mask, nothing but a dark cloak draped over his shoulders. The dim light caught his form, highlighting the broad span of his shoulders against the Void that cloaked around him like a mantle of night. He pushed a hand through his curly hair, brushing it back from his eyes as they scanned the room. Dark and intense, his gaze finally settled on her, stealing her breath.

She looked between the two men. "What the hell is going on?"

Tristan slid off the bed with that easy grace, walking over to the Hunter as if this was all perfectly normal. They clasped hands, murmuring to each other in low tones too quiet for her to catch.

Finally, they turned to her.

"My friend here has some business with you," Tristan said, his voice light. "Osin announced a tournament to win a night with the Hallowed, and, well, it was the perfect chance to get you alone. Though Ivan couldn't exactly compete, being all *disgraced,* and whatnot, so I did him a favor."

The Hunter crossed his arms, face unreadable except for the faint trace of wry humor tugging at his lips. "Disgraced is one way to put it. I prefer 'selectively avoiding unnecessary theatrics.'"

But Elara barely registered the words. Just noise. *The perfect setup to get her alone.* Tristan had played his part, winning the game to hand her over to the Hunter so he could try again—try to finish placing the seal on her. He must've figured out why it hadn't worked the first time.

Elara took a slow breath, steadying her mind, clearing the chaos in her thoughts. In seconds, she found the Hunter's pulse—a steady, rhythmic beat under her skin. She latched onto it with lethal focus, and a slow, wicked smile crept across her face as his control slipped. The barest wince tugged at his features, his jaw tightening.

But she saw it. And she savored every second.

Tristan glanced between them, sensing the shift. "Unhand my friend."

"And why would I do *that*?" she said, a trickle of blood dripping from her nose.

"Because" Tristan took a step toward her, voice as smooth as ever, "we're trying to help you."

Elara let out a sharp laugh. "You must think I'm an idiot."

"No, we think you're smart enough to know a good offer when you see one."

Her eyes narrowed. "Which one is it, help or an offer?"

Tristan gave a casual shrug. "Why can't it be both?"

Elara braced herself against the wall, tension buzzing through her body, her mind spinning as she weighed her options. The Hunter's pulse beat fast and uneven under her hold, and the flicker of pain in his eyes was enough to tell her she still had the upper hand—at least for now. Slowly, she let him go, more curious than anything to see what he'd say. The moment she released him, the strain melted from his face.

"Lovely," Tristan said, clapping his hands together, his grin spreading like wildfire across his face. He glanced at the Hunter, who stood like a statue, his eyes never leaving Elara, like he was waiting for the slightest twitch, ready to strike if she so much as blinked wrong. "Now, can I trust you'll be on your best behavior?"

"Fuck off," Elara snapped, wiping the blood from her nose.

"Right." Tristan turned to the Hunter, raising an eyebrow. "Maybe I should stick around?"

The Hunter's eyes shifted to Tristan, hard as ice. "I can handle her."

Elara's jaw tightened, teeth grinding in frustration. Tristan, of course, didn't notice—or didn't care. He spun on his heel, walking toward her with that same swagger that made her want to strangle him. She barely had time to react when he pulled something out of his pocket. Four vials. *Stonebrew.*

Her eyes widened in shock.

"I nicked these from your healer. Wasn't easy. You can thank me later," he said, thrusting the vials into her hands with a wink. Elara blinked, stunned for a moment, before gripping the vials tight to her chest. Relief swept through her, so fierce it nearly brought her to her knees. Strength. She'd have it again. She wouldn't be helpless for whatever was about to unfold. The thought alone was like air in her lungs after drowning, her exhale trembling as if the weight of her fear had finally cracked open, releasing her.

But before she could even form a response, Tristan was already heading for the rift. And, like the insufferable fool he was, he fell backward into the abyss, arms outstretched, leaving her speechless.

Elara stood there for a moment in utter disbelief before shaking her head. "Is he always this irritating?"

Ivan's lips twitched into a faint smile. "*Always.*"

She popped open two vials and downed them without a second thought. The change was instant. Her legs stiffened, her muscles locking into place, the shaking in her body finally stilling. She drew in a deep breath, painless this time, the relief like cool water flooding her veins. Yet, even as the tension melted from her body, she felt his gaze on her— tracing every movement like the burn of a brand pressed against her skin.

She despised it.

She straightened her spine, slipping the remaining vials into her corset. "Are you going to tell me why I'm here, or just keep gawking?"

The Hunter's gaze didn't waver. "I need to evaluate your bind."

"You already did that."

"I did," he agreed, his arms crossing over his chest, "but I wasn't able to... accomplish what I'd intended that day."

Her gaze narrowed. "*Which was?*"

He didn't respond right away, his jaw tight, like he was wrestling with the words before they finally came. "At the binding ritual... something shifted between us. But even before that..."

Elara's heart skipped, her pulse a quickening rhythm. She knew what he was talking about. That moment in the Hartling Forest—when she'd fought him, when the air between them had cracked and split with a force she still felt in her bones. That shockwave, like a cord pulled too tight, snapping between them. She hadn't forgotten the way his power had crashed into hers, like it had been lying dormant, just beneath the surface, waiting for hers to touch it, ignite it.

She hadn't let herself think about that day—hadn't dared. Because to think about it meant admitting the truth, acknowledging that strange, dangerous pull that had flared to life after the fact.

Elara's lips pressed into a thin line. "And now you're here to, what, undo it?"

He tilted his head slightly, considering her words. "I'm here to understand what it means."

'Understand it'. *Sure,* maybe only to then unravel it, to strip away the small, precious thread of power she held over him.

She rolled her eyes. "Right. Like I'm going to fall for that. From where I'm standing, I've got all the control. I can hurt you whenever I want. In fact..." Her lips twisted into a cruel smile as she squeezed the seal inside her.

The Hunter flinched, his face tightening, a vicious curse slipping through his teeth. "It would benefit us both."

Her brows shot up, eyes flashing with contempt. "How do you figure that?"

"I wouldn't be standing here if it didn't."

A bitter, cold laugh ripped from her throat. "Of course. The great Hunter, only ever doing anything when it suits him." Elara bared her teeth. "I'm not going with you. Drag me if you want, throw me over your shoulder again. I know you love playing the brute. But I'll make sure every second of it is hell for you. I'm not giving up an inch of control. Not to you."

"What do you want?"

Elara went very still. "What?"

The Hunter's gaze didn't waver. "What would it take? To get you to come with me?"

"There's nothing—"

"Just try me."

Her heart skipped a beat, the words dying on her tongue. She narrowed her eyes, studying him, searching for the trap she knew had to be there. "How do I know you'll hold up your end of the deal? You promise me now, but the moment we finish whatever hellish thing you've got planned, you'll just back out?"

His nostrils flared. "I'll swear a blood oath. Here and now. If that's what it takes to get you to come, I'll do it."

She blinked, utterly floored. She couldn't hide the surprise flickering through her as she stared at him. Still unreadable, still cold as ever—but his words... desperate.

Interesting.

A little crack she could use if she played this right.

"I want Reynnar freed," she said, testing the waters.

His shoulders tensed, the muscles rippling beneath his shirt as he crossed his arms again, his gaze hard as steel. "That's not happening." Elara opened her mouth to argue, but he lifted a hand, silencing her before she could get a word out. "I don't control the fate of the captives."

Her lips pressed into a thin line. "Fine. But at least move the *Sidhe* into bigger cells—like Reynnar's. My tunnel's nearly empty. Put them in with me. And don't pack them in like livestock."

At least for now. Until she figured out how to get them out.

If the Hunter was surprised by her use of the word *Sidhe*, he didn't let it show. His expression remained unreadable, though his eyes narrowed slightly, weighing her words. For a long moment, he just studied her, silent, and then, with a sharp inhale, he gave a curt nod.

Elara pushed her luck. "I want to see Godfrey. And I want information." She kept it vague, leaving the request wide open so she could ask for whatever she needed later.

The Hunter's shoulders tensed, a muscle ticking in his jaw as he exhaled sharply through his nose. "Anything *else*?" he bit out.

Her mind buzzed, thoughts spiraling, crashing over each other, all fighting for space. If she could just find a way to get the Sidhe back to their world, to get the rebels and Godfrey out, it would be worth it. Worth closing the chink in her bind. Worth losing the small sliver of power she had. Freedom wasn't in the cards for her—she wasn't naive enough to believe otherwise—but if she could make sure they had a chance... it wouldn't be a sacrifice. It would be a bargain.

Elara shook her head. "So, how does this oath work?"

The Hunter's steps were measured, slow, each one bringing him closer until he halted just out of reach. His hand reached for the dagger at his belt. "I offer you my blood," he said, voice steady. Without hesitation, he dragged the blade across his palm, crimson welling up from the cut. "This is my oath to you, bound in blood. If I break it, this stone will crack. And with it, something inside me. I swear to move the Sidhe, give you access to Godfrey, and answer three questions of your choosing."

"Ten questions," she countered, crossing her arms.

"Three," he repeated, unbending.

Her teeth ground together. Ten questions were what she needed, but if he got her in front of Godfrey, maybe three would be enough. Godfrey had worked for Osin for years, had rebel ties. He'd helped her once, tried to get her out of Verdara. He'd help her again—she was sure of it.

"*Fine.*"

Blood dripped down, rich and red where he held his hand over his chest, letting it pool briefly before it began to lift into the air, gathering itself like molten metal. Elara watched as it shimmered, glowing faintly, the blood twisting, and hardening into a dark, smooth stone.

Elara's heart gave a small, uneven beat. His presence, heavy and full of unspoken power, pressed against her. The stone floated between them, and with a subtle twist of his wrist, a delicate cord of vines sprouted from it, weaving together in the air. He didn't touch it—he didn't need to. With a call to the wind, the bloodstone drifted toward her, hovering just above her chest before settling directly over her heart.

CHAPTER 31

The great city of Arinthel was... grimy. At least, *this* part of it was.

The city sprawled across rolling hills and valleys, its expanse interrupted by the jagged silhouettes of towers and spires that pierced the sky. In the distance, the grand domes of the upper city glinted faintly, but here, the splendor was lost beneath layers of soot and grime.

Rain drizzled steadily, dripping from the rooftops, and running in small rivulets down the alley. The Hunter and Elara walked through the narrow passage, their footsteps muffled by the slick cobblestones. The streets twisted like veins through the district, a maze of alleys and side passages that seemed designed to confound. Some alleys narrowed to the width of a doorway, while others opened unexpectedly into small courtyards cluttered with debris. It was almost as if the buildings were erected without a plan or purpose other than to fill space.

Elara barely noticed the cold rain biting at her skin, the droplets sliding down her face and soaking into her clothes. The wind tugged at her hair, plastering wet strands against her cheeks. It didn't matter. She was *out*—out of the Pit, free from that cursed castle. For the first time in ages, she could breathe. The air wasn't fresh—it was heavy with pollution and the scent of the city's underbelly—but it was better than the Pit, better than the stench of spent ether that clung to Mordenhall.

She tugged at the cloak the Hunter had tossed her—one of his spares, thick and worn, smelling faintly of clove and earth. He'd rifted them out of the castle with ease, pulling her through the strange nothingness between worlds, only to stop just outside the city.

She had asked him why, and his answer had been simple, almost bored—he was one of the few allowed access to rift into Mordenhall, a privilege granted by Osin himself. But the city was different. Arinthel was the hub of trade, politics, and diplomacy—rifting into the heart of the capital would mean bypassing the checks and balances, allowing people to circumvent the rules that kept the city running smoothly. Osin couldn't risk that. None of its residents could. The city's power structure was too fragile for that kind of ether to run rampant. It wasn't about keeping people safe—it was about keeping power in the right hands.

Elara had no clue how it all worked, but it fascinated her. She'd always thought the capital was drowning in power and wealth, that it dripped from the walls, that everyone inside was living in excess. But that had been another lie. Maybe it was only a select few. Osin's inner circle. The ones close enough to him to hoard it all while the rest of the city fought for crumbs.

The necklace the Hunter had made for her bounced lightly against her chest as they turned into another alley, his pace steady but carrying that quiet tension she'd come to expect from him. Elara stayed close, her mind half lost in the misty rain, half still spinning from everything she'd learned when he stopped—so suddenly she almost collided into him.

Before she could ask, his hand was on her shoulder, firm but gentle, guiding her back around the corner they'd just turned. Her heart skipped a beat. "What—?"

"A checkpoint. They're verifying totems."

Elara's pulse kicked. "I don't have one," she whispered.

His gaze flicked to hers. "I know." His jaw tightened as he scanned the alley ahead. "Stick close. Don't make a sound," he muttered, already moving.

They slipped through the back door of an empty warehouse, the heavy wood groaning as it swung shut behind them. The scent of rust and mold filled the air, mingling with the faint tang of old machinery.

Puddles had formed where the ground dipped, reflecting the sparse light that managed to seep through boarded-up windows.

The only sound was the soft scuff of their footsteps as they moved deeper inside, boots brushing against debris that crunched softly underfoot. The Hunter didn't say a word as he led her toward a rusted ladder bolted to the far wall. The iron rungs were slick with rain that had seeped through the cracked skylight above, each bar coated in a thin layer of grime and flecks of peeling paint. The ladder stretched upward, disappearing into the ceiling where a cracked window beckoned—a jagged hole with shards of glass jutting like teeth.

He barely hesitated before grabbing hold, his movements fluid, climbing with that effortless grace she couldn't help but envy. Elara hesitated for a beat, eyeing the ladder warily. So far, the double dose of Stonebrew had kept her steady, but she didn't want to push it. She glanced up at the Hunter, who had stopped, waiting for her. Sighing, she wiped her palms against her cloak and started climbing.

The cold metal bit into her hands, the chill sinking deep, but she matched each breath to her steps, forcing herself to climb. Her fingers tightened on the slick rungs, knuckles blanching as she pulled herself higher, the ladder creaking under every shift of weight. Elara blocked out the burn in her muscles, the dizzying thought of how far she'd fall if she slipped, how the wind whipped her hair into wild strands, stinging her face with every gust.

Her world narrowed to the rungs under her hands and the Hunter's boots just above her, so close to the roof. Just a little more.

But then her boot slipped, and she was falling.

The Hunter's hand shot out, lightning-quick, his grip closing around her wrist like iron. One arm threaded through the ladder, his other steadying her as if he had known—*felt* the shift in her balance before she had even realized it herself. Her pulse hammered in her ears, wild and frantic, but when she looked up at him, she swore—just for a breath—that he felt it too. The panic. The fear surging through her veins. His gaze flickered, something raw flashing through his eyes, the faint ring of amber glowing like embers in the dark.

Maybe it wasn't just her...

She closed her eyes, reaching out with her senses, and there it was—his heartbeat.

Steady, powerful, but faster now.

Like her near fall *had* sent a ripple of something through him as well.

The Hunter bit down on one glove, pulling it off with his teeth before glancing at her. "You get your grip back?"

Elara tightened her hold on the ladder, steadying herself. "Yeah," she breathed.

Only then did he release her, his other hand pulling off the second glove before handing them both to her. "Put these on."

She blinked, caught off guard by the gesture. His gloves—still warm from his skin. Something so personal. She snapped out of it. Hooking her arm through the ladder for balance, she took them, slipping them on. They were too big, the fingers loose and awkward, but the grip—they helped.

Then, a warmth spread through her hands, not just the heat left in the gloves, but something else. His ether. A slow, soothing fire winding its way through the leather, shrinking the gloves until they fit her perfectly.

Elara couldn't bring herself to look at him. The weight of his kindness, from *him* of all people, was almost too much to make sense of. It was confusing. Unsettling. And she hated how it made her feel vulnerable.

"Good?"

She cleared her throat, still staring at her hands. "Good," she muttered, her voice quieter than she meant it to be.

They climbed in silence, the world narrowing to the steady rhythm of their ascent, until, at last, they reached the top. The rain had eased into a fine mist, barely more than a whisper against her skin. Elara crouched down beside the Hunter at the edge of the roof, the wind biting at her cheeks as they gazed out over the dark sprawl of Arinthel. Above, the sky was a ribbon of indigo, stars obscured by drifting clouds. From somewhere distant came the sound of a bell tolling the late hour. Below, the streets were veined with flickers of torchlight—Legionnaires, *hundreds* of them, their fire weaving faint threads of gold through the shadowed city.

Elara bit her lip, the rain cool and metallic on her tongue. "Which direction?"

"Just over there," the Hunter said, pointing to a narrow passage where the edges of a market came into view. "The stalls are packed in tight, which means plenty of cover. We stay low, move fast. No one will see us in the crowd."

Elara nodded, the damp weight of his cloak pulling at her shoulders. "Then what?"

He glanced sidelong at her, his eyes not vacant as usual, but not quite revealing any clear emotion, either—perhaps a glimmer of scrutiny if she had to peg it. Raindrops clung to his lashes, trailing down the sharp planes of his face, but he seemed indifferent to the cold seeping through their clothes. "Then, Hallowed, we meet with a friend."

She let out a derisive snort. "I didn't know you had those."

It was a half-truth. She knew Tristan counted as his friend, but the idea of him engaging in anything resembling normalcy remained an oddity to her.

He went quiet, the silence stretching between them filled only by the rhythmic drumming of rain. After a long pause, his voice came again, softer this time, rougher around the edges. "I don't have many. Not ones who last."

Elara's throat tightened, something uncomfortably heavy settling inside her chest. She watched a droplet slide off his jawline, disappearing into his cloak. The vulnerability in his admission caught her off guard. "I don't either," she admitted softly, her gaze dropping to the puddles forming at their feet.

He didn't respond, didn't offer anything in return. But he stayed. Sat there in the silence with her, with the weight of what they'd both admitted hanging between them. Elara swallowed hard, her pulse fluttering like wings against her throat.

The Hunter cleared his throat, shifting his weight. His eyes flicked back to the narrow passage ahead. "We should move," he said, the familiar guardedness slipping back into his tone. Without another word, he rose, crossing to a second ladder at the far edge of the roof. He stopped at the top, his dark silhouette stark against the misty night, a quick glance cast over his shoulder before he gestured for her to go first.

Elara exhaled, rising to her feet, her limbs still heavy. But this time, the climb was easier. The gloves, worn soft from his hands, helped her grip the wet, slippery rungs with ease. It felt like only seconds before her feet hit the ground with a soft splash.

Before she could fully take in her surroundings, the Hunter landed beside her, silent as death. He jerked his head in that familiar, wordless way, motioning for her to follow.

Without a sound, they slipped into the market—a labyrinth of narrow alleys and clustered stalls. The air was dense, saturated with the mingled scents of exotic spices, sizzling meats, and the underlying tang of damp earth. Vendors hawked their wares with hoarse shouts— offering everything from dubious potions to tarnished trinkets—while eyes hidden beneath tattered hoods assessed passersby with predatory interest. Strings of faded prayer flags fluttered overhead, their once-vibrant colors now muted and frayed.

Elara kept her head down, the hood of her cloak pulled low to shadow her features. Her skin prickled with unease, a chill that had nothing to do with the cold seeping into her bones. But the Hunter moved without hesitation, his stride confident and unyielding. His cloak billowed slightly with each step, revealing glimpses of the weapons concealed beneath. She stayed close, heart pounding.

Just as the claustrophobic press of the market threatened to over-whelm her, something caught her eye—a tent set apart from the rest, tucked into a quiet recess between leaning buildings. From within, a faint glint of metal flashed, a subtle sparkle that stood out against the drab surroundings.

Elara stopped, feet rooted to the spot as curiosity flickered to life within her. Taking a cautious step forward, she reached out and pushed the tent flap aside.

Inside, the dim light revealed a simple setup. The space was small, walls lined with tattered cloth that did little to keep out the cold. A single lantern hung from the center pole, casting a warm but flickering glow that danced over the objects laid out before her.

Rings. *Elemental* rings—dozens of them scattered across a stained velvet cloth draped over a makeshift table of stacked crates. The way they were strewn about felt careless—tossed aside rather than displayed with the reverence they deserved. Elara frowned, her steps slowing as she moved closer. She reached out but hesitated, her fingertips hovering above a ring adorned with a teardrop-shaped amethyst. *They must be fakes*, she thought, a weak attempt by some charlatan to swindle the uninformed. Yet, the level of detail was astounding—the weight of the metals, the precision of the engravings, the subtle glow that seemed to emanate from within the gemstones. These were qualities not easily replicated. Still, something about the setup made her uneasy.

A soft rustling from behind drew her attention. Elara turned to find the Hunter standing at the threshold. His hood was pulled low, obscuring his features, but not enough to hide the tight clench of his jaw.

His gaze dropped to the rings scattered across the grimy wooden crate, eyes narrowing beneath the shadowed brim.

Then it crashed into her—a jolt of rage that wasn't her own.

It tore through her veins like wildfire racing through a dry forest, consuming everything in its path. The sensation stole the air from her lungs; her chest tightened, the corset of her dress suddenly suffocating.

The Hunter's eyes flicked to hers, glinting like shards of obsidian. The shape of the stone around her neck became more pronounced—a cold presence against her skin, humming faintly, and Elara saw a flicker of something in his gaze: vulnerability there and gone in an instant, like shutters slamming closed.

"Let's go," he muttered. He turned sharply, the dark fabric of his cloak swirling around him as he strode out of the tent.

Elara stood rooted for a beat longer, the phantom heat of his anger still pulsing beneath her skin, leaving a tingling trail that raised goosebumps along her arms. She pressed her lips together, frustration and curiosity warring within her. But with a sigh, she relented. There would be another time, another place for questions.

She followed him out of the market, leaving behind the dwindling calls of vendors. The transition from the bustling square to the deserted side street was abrupt—the noise faded into an eerie quiet, and the warm glow of lanterns gave way to the dim, uneven light cast by a sliver of moon peeking through the narrow gap between towering buildings.

They turned down a narrow side street. The alleyway was tight, barely wide enough for two people to walk abreast, the way ahead swallowed by darkness save for the faint glimmer of candlelight flickering through windows. As they turned the corner, shadows shifted ahead, and before Elara could react, five Legionnaires stepped from doorways and alcoves, forming a solid wall across the narrow passage.

Elara cast a sidelong glance at the Hunter. His posture remained relaxed, but she didn't miss the subtle shift of his hand toward the fold of his cloak. She felt a pulse from the shard at her neck, a faint warmth that steadied her nerves.

The leader took a step forward, the sound of steel grating against iron as he rested a gauntleted hand on the hilt of his sword. "Hunter," he muttered, dipping his head in a show of respect. "What brings you skulking around these parts?"

The hint of mockery danced in his tone, but caution flickered in his gaze—like he knew poking a sleeping beast might get him bitten. The Hunter moved ever so slightly, positioning himself just a fraction more in front of her.

"Thought you were off chasing bigger, shinier fools than the scum around here," another sneered, a cold chuckle rumbling in his chest. His gaze slid past the Hunter and locked onto Elara. The moment stretched, unbearable, as his eyes raked over her. The smug smile faltered—suspicion flickering, then snapping into realization.

"Wait. Is that *her*?"

A spike of fear shot through Elara, the lump in her throat refusing to budge. The Hunter's stance shifted again, this time completely blocking their view of her. She could feel the heat radiating off him, the coiled tension ready to spring.

"By the gods," the leader breathed, his voice dropping to a reverent whisper. "It *is* her. The Hallowed." His hand twitched toward his weapon—or perhaps reaching for her—excitement igniting in his eyes. "Let me get a taste. Just a small one. I've heard what her blood can do..."

A shiver traced down Elara's spine, her pulse pounding in her ears.

She inched closer to the Hunter, the rough fabric of his cloak brushing against her fingers.

"Touch her," he said softly, "and you'll lose more than just your hand."

Their faces darkened, any pretense of respect dissolving into something uglier. "You gonna keep her all to yourself, then?" The leader snarled, spitting on the ground near the Hunter's boots. "While we're out here scraping by? Dealing with shortages, shaking from the damned withdrawals? And you won't share a *bloody* drop?" He stepped closer, desperation edging into his rough voice. "I'm not talking about maiming her—just need a bit of her blood, that's all I—"

His hand darted forward, grimy fingers stretching toward Elara, hunger gleaming in his eyes.

It happened so fast she barely registered it. One heartbeat, his filthy nails hovered inches from her skin; the next, a metallic crack split the air as the Hunter's hand snapped to his side. A slide-shaft glaive extended— gleaming steel slicing forward with a lethal whisper. The blade met flesh. The Legionnaire's arm severed cleanly at the elbow, the limb striking the cobblestones with a nauseating thud.

Before the second guard could gasp, the glaive whirled back, slicing through flesh, and bone as if they were air. The man's head toppled from his shoulders, eyes still wide with unspoken shock as it rolled to a stop against the alley wall.

Elara stood frozen, breath caught in her throat, the world narrowing to the metallic scent of blood and the phantom whisper of the glaive retracting back into the Hunter's cloak. His hood slipped back, eyes dark and deadly, strands of raven hair falling across his forehead. Blood spattered his cloak and face, but his breathing remained steady—as if dispatching his comrades hadn't fazed him in the slightest.

The man who'd lost his arm crumpled, mouth open in a silent scream, but no sound came. Elara's heart pounded, breath caught in her throat, her mind racing to catch up. And then she felt it. The shift as the Hunter seized the wind, drawing it in and wrenching it tight, choking off the Legionnaires' scream before it could escape.

And not just him. All of them. The wind was being drained from the alley, *siphoned* from their lungs.

The remaining guards staggered, eyes wide with panic, clawing at their throats as they fought for breath that wouldn't come. Their faces flushed, veins standing out starkly against their skin as terror contorted their features.

They couldn't breathe. No one could. Except for her.

"Hunter," Elara whispered, her voice barely more than a rasp. He didn't respond. His gaze was distant, fixed on some point beyond the physical, lost in the tempest of his own making. "Hunter!" she called again, louder, the word tearing from her throat. Still nothing.

Elara reached out, her fingers trembling as they pressed against the stubble of his jaw, turning his face toward her. "*Ivan,*" she whispered, the name slipping from her lips like a confession.

The effect was immediate. His eyes snapped into focus, the inky darkness receding as clarity flooded back. He stared at her, startled as the oppressive air eased, a gust of wind rushing back into the alley.

Around them, the Legionnaires collapsed to the ground, gulping in ragged breaths, the color returning to their faces. The sounds of the alley filtered back in—the distant clatter of a falling crate, a dog's bark carrying somewhere far off.

Elara didn't move, her hand still cradling his face, their gazes locked. She could see the conflict swirling in his eyes—uncertainty, fear, something deeper she couldn't name.

He blinked, swallowing hard, and her hand fell away.

The clatter of soldiers scrambling to their feet echoed dimly, their panicked footsteps fading as they vanished down the alley. But Elara couldn't tear her gaze from him. Her heart thundered—not just her own heartbeat but his as well, two rhythms merging into one steady drum. It pulsed in her throat, and as she drew a shaky breath, she felt him do the same.

The sensation spun her world off its axis, dizzying and intimate. She pressed a hand to her chest, fingers brushing against the cool metal of the necklace resting against her skin. The shard he'd given her. That had to be it. The reason everything felt so unbearably intense.

He'd killed those men—had cut them down without a second thought, crushed the breath from their lungs. For her.

No. Her mind pushed back, rationalizing against the swirl of emotions. It wasn't for her. It was for him. For whatever mission he was on. She was just a complication he had to protect.

"They saw me," Elara whispered, stating the obvious. Her eyes drifted back to the alley, where shadows cloaked the still bodies left behind. Blood pooled around them, dark and glistening like spilled ink seeping into the cracks of the cobblestones. A chill brushed over her skin.

"I'll handle it," the Hunter said. He didn't spare a glance backward. "Come on. We're almost there."

Without another word, he started walking, his pace fast, too fast for the tension still coiled in her muscles. She had to jog to catch up. "What were they talking about?" she asked, breathless. "The shortages, withdrawals—"

The Hunter didn't answer immediately, his footsteps stopping in front of a dilapidated wooden door. He turned to her then, eyes flicking to the necklace around her neck, the faint glow of the stone resting against her skin.

"Ask me later."

Elara opened her mouth to argue, a dozen questions bubbling up. But before she could utter a single word, he raised his fist and knocked.

CHAPTER 32

The door creaked open, revealing a young woman with short blonde hair that stuck up on one side, as if she'd just woken up. Her steel-blue eyes flicked over Elara and the Hunter in one quick glance. Barefoot, her toes curled against the cracked wooden floor as she gave him a questioning look.

The Hunter crossed his arms. "I need a favor, Sybil."

The girl—*Sybil*—didn't hesitate. She moved to slam the door, but the Hunter's boot had already wedged in the gap, stopping it cold. Elara shot him a look, one brow lifting. His jaw tightened in response.

"You really do have a knack for showing up when you're least wanted," Sybil muttered, glaring at him.

"Charming as ever," the Hunter shot back, a slow smile curling his lips. "I'd hate to think you've gotten too fond of the quiet life."

Sybil's gaze flicked to Elara—curious, wary—before settling back on him. "The last time you needed a favor, I nearly lost my life, my home, *and* my sanity."

He leaned against the doorframe, completely unfazed. "And yet, here you are. Still standing. Stronger. Wiser. Really, you should be thanking me."

Sybil snorted but finally swung the door wide, allowing them in.

"I'll be sure to send you a thank-you note when I'm buried under the rubble of your next disaster."

Elara slipped past the Hunter, eyes immediately drawn to the cramped hallway cluttered with odd trinkets, dusty books stacked haphazardly to the ceiling. The place reeked of ether—old, layered ether, the kind that settled into the very walls.

Sybil shut the door with a click before her eyes slid over to Elara, sizing her up like she was something to be toyed with. "And who's the little stray you've picked up this time?"

Before he could answer, Elara straightened her spine, and forced the words out, refusing to let her nerve falter. "I'm Elara. And I wasn't aware we were handing out pet names already. Should I come up with one for you?"

Sybil's smirk deepened, her eyes flickering with amusement. "Well, aren't you a little firecracker?"

Elara's glare hardened as the Hunter's mouth twitched.

"She's tougher than she looks."

Sybil glanced between them, eyes narrowing slightly before she nodded. "Good. You'll need to be if you want to keep up with that one. His idea of help usually ends with half a city burning or a knife at someone's throat—most of the time, *mine*."

"And yet," he replied, stepping down the hallway, "you always let me in."

"Call it morbid curiosity," Sybil sighed, leading him past a maze of piled books. "I keep hoping natural selection will catch up with you."

His smile widened. "Always knew you cared."

Elara's hand darted out before she could stop herself, fingers gripping his arm—a solid band of muscle that tensed instantly under her touch. Heat flushed her cheeks as she released him just as quickly, the brief contact leaving a tingling imprint on her skin as she leaned in. "This is your *friend*?"

The Hunter's eyes closed for a beat—just as Sybil started cackling. "Is that what he told you?" She stopped and crossed her arms, facing him head-on. "Embarrassed of me, cousin?"

Cousin?

"Sib—" he started, but she waved a hand dismissively.

"Forget it," she muttered, rolling her eyes again. "I don't care either way."

Sybil turned the corner and disappeared, leaving Elara standing there, awkward and out of place. The Hunter sighed, rubbing the back of his neck before trailing after her.

Elara shifted on her feet, her skin prickling. She didn't know where to look, what to do with her hands. It felt like she was intruding, witnessing something she had no right to see. But what else was there to do?

She followed, her steps slow as she took in the narrow hallway that opened into a cramped cottage. The walls were a patchwork of peeling plaster and splintered beams, some barely holding on as if a strong gust could send the whole place collapsing. Sybil and the Hunter's voices drifted back, their bickering a constant hum in the background.

Elara still couldn't wrap her head around it—the Hunter like this. The man she'd seen in the alley, who cut soldiers down without a second thought, without hesitation... that was the man she knew. Cold. Calculated. Deadly. Not this... almost normal, interaction with a... *cousin.*

Her fingers twitched at her sides, restless. The entire dynamic left her feeling off balance, like she'd missed a step, and now she was waiting for the fall.

Sybil led them into a crowded living room that was barely that—a space swallowed by shelves crammed with jars of strange ingredients: dried herbs, twisted roots, and bones that seemed far too large to be human. Broken furniture was shoved into the corners, abandoned and forgotten. The massive wooden table in the center dominated the room, covered in scattered vials and instruments, more a makeshift lab than a living space.

"Sit," Sybil commanded, waving lazily toward the two stools at the table. Elara hesitated, her gaze flicking to the Hunter. He gave a slight nod, and she followed his lead, perching on the edge of the stool.

Sybil leaned back, crossing her arms. "So, what kind of calamity are you dumping on me this time?"

The Hunter scratched at his neck almost absently. "The kind that needs your... unique expertise."

Sybil let out a long, weary sigh. "Of course it does." She tilted her head, studying him for a moment before gesturing for more. "Elaborate."

"I need you to test us for a *Draoth Cara.*"

Elara froze. That word... she knew it. *Draoth.* He had whispered it to her once... in a dream. She blinked up at him, confusion knitting her brow. "What's a *Draoth Cara*?"

Sybil's gaze swung toward her, brows raised. "You don't know?" She looked back at the Hunter, her eyes narrowing. "You haven't told her."

The Hunter's expression darkened. He tapped his foot on the ground. "I was getting to it."

"When?" Sybil challenged. "Before or after you put her through the test?"

He sighed, dragging a hand down his face before turning to Elara. "What we've been... experiencing, it isn't normal."

Elara rolled her eyes. "Yeah, I figured. I'm well aware it's not every day someone gets a bind with three seals slapped on them."

Sybil's eyes widened, her expression one of pure disbelief. "Rhiannon's *fucking* tits, you did *what* now?"

The Hunter focused on Elara. "It's not the bind," he said, voice quiet. "But I think it's why the seal I was supposed to place on you didn't work."

Sybil's eyes gleamed, interest sparking as she glanced between them. "Oh, this just keeps getting juicier." She ignored the Hunter's glare and turned to Elara. "*Draoth Cara* is an anomaly with casters. Normally, one bonds with earth, another with fire—simple, right? But sometimes, for reasons we don't fully get, their powers connect. They start feeling each other's heartbeats, emotions, even sensations. A touch on your skin feels like it's happening to both of you." She paused, eyes cutting back to the Hunter, daring him. "Go on. Try it."

The Hunter's entire body went rigid, his eyes narrowing to slits. "That's not necessary—"

Elara pressed her finger deliberately against a piece of splintered wood she had been playing with the entire time to calm her nerves, feeling the sudden bite as it cut into her skin. Blood welled up almost instantly.

The Hunter sucked in a breath, his right hand—the same side as hers—suddenly clenching against the table.

"You *felt* that—"

The words had barely left her lips when Sybil's hand shot out and closed around her wrist, the speed stealing Elara's breath. With a sharp yank, Sybil pulled her forward, vials clinking across the table.

The Hunter was there in the next instant—too fast to follow. His hand clamped over Sybil's, the force making her grip falter.

"Release the Hallowed," he said, his voice low and cold as ice. "Now."

The air felt ready to shatter, pressure drawn so tight it might snap with a single breath. They stood frozen, breaths shallow, the room deadly still save for blood dripping from Elara's finger down her palm.

"It's just a drop."

Sybil's voice was low, almost a murmur, but her blue eyes... they darkened, shifting to black like a cloud swallowing the sky. Elara jerked her wrist, trying to pull away, but Sybil's hand didn't budge.

"Sybil!" The Hunter barked her name and his cousin's gaze shifted, locking onto him as if sensing something beyond the present, beyond them. "I see it. The hunger. The need. You've been carrying it, hiding it, but it's there, waiting. You want that drop, Hunter. *So badly.* I can feel it—the pull, the craving to make it right. Why fight it when it's right in front of you? Take it. A single drop, and all is *undone.*"

Elara's pulse spiked as she looked between them. Sybil wasn't Sybil anymore. The snarky, playful girl had vanished, replaced by something... darker. Consumed. Something that made the hairs on the back of Elara's neck rise.

"And *you,*" Sybil said, turning to Elara. "Your past will return, but not in the way you expect. What was once a memory will walk again, flesh and bone, and you will have to face it." Then Sybil smiled—a feral, twisted thing—and it seemed to snap the Hunter out of whatever spell he'd been under.

"Let go, Syb," he growled.

The girl blinked, and the darkness in her eyes faded, returning to their familiar icy blue. She looked down at their entwined hands, almost as if seeing the blood for the first time, her lips parting in confusion. Quickly, she released Elara's wrist and stepped back. Her face was unreadable. She crossed to the hearth and set a kettle over the flames with a clang, her movements quick and jerky.

"Tea, anyone?"

Is she serious?

Elara grimaced, wiped the blood on her cloak, then shoved her finger into her mouth, coppery and sharp. Her gaze snapped to the Hunter, wide with disbelief.

"Sybil."

The girl's shoulders sagged at his tone, her hands hovering over the kettle. She hesitated for a second, her back to them, before slowly turning around, her face blank.

"Have your souls searched for each other in the dreamspace?" she asked, voice flat.

The Hunter dipped his chin in a slow nod and Elara's world tilted. The strange dreams—*they had been sharing them.*

The Hunter wouldn't meet Elara's gaze as Sybil's expression tightened. "Then it's farther along than I would like if you're here to sever the connection."

"Not sever—test it."

Sybil's eyes narrowed. "What are you thinking—"

"Are you both really going to keep talking as if I'm not sitting right here?" Elara cut in, slapping a hand on the table. "And not once has anyone thought to ask if I *want* to be tested—especially after you nearly snapped my wrist not five seconds ago." She turned her glare on Sybil. "Forgive me if I'm not exactly eager for more of *that*."

The Hunter's lip twitched, barely concealing a smirk. "Excuse my cousin. She's a seer, prone to bouts of insanity."

Sybil scoffed, but Elara's attention was on the Hunter. "You brought me to a *Soothsayer*?" she said, incredulous. The very word sent a cold shiver down her spine, dragging up memories. The Soothsayers in Verdara had been relentless in their attention, drawn to her in ways that felt invasive, even predatory. If anything, they had been the most unsympathetic and detached of all the Druids, their methods bordering on the cruel. The mere thought of them made her teeth grind. She hated them —hated what they saw in her.

A harsh, mocking laugh cut through Elara's thoughts, pulling her attention back to Sybil.

"*Please*. I'm nothing like the Druids you grew up worshipping." She leaned in, eyes gleaming. "What I do... let's just say it's not exactly lawful. Druids cling to their precious order and balance, but me? I thrive in chaos."

Elara didn't flinch, didn't look away, but she pressed her trembling hands into her lap, out of sight.

"Can you do it?"

Sybil broke eye contact first, turning to the Hunter with an exaggerated roll of her eyes. "Of course I can do it." She bent down, rummaging beneath the table, and pulled out a large mirror, placing it with a heavy thud. Her eyes flicked up, keen and expectant. "I'm going to scry. But I'll need something from both of you."

The Hunter slipped off his ring, the four stones catching the dim light as he placed it in the center of the mirror. Elara hesitated. She had nothing—no possessions, nothing of value. Not since being thrown into that prison. All she had left was her blood, and she wasn't about to offer that. Her mind raced, then landed on something else. She reached up, twisting a single strand of hair around her finger before pulling it free with a sharp snap.

She handed it to Sybil.

"That'll do." Sybil said, placing it beside the ring.

The girl hovered over the mirror, her eyes narrowing in deep concentration as she waved a hand above the ring and strand of hair. The surface of the mirror rippled like water disturbed by a single drop, then slowly darkened, as if the glass had swallowed the light in the room.

Elara leaned forward, as the mirror began to shimmer, three faint glowing threads emerging like veins of light, weaving and curling around one another. They stretched between the ring and the strand of hair, coiling as if seeking each other out. Elara's heart thudded in her chest as she watched them, entranced by the way they seemed to move with purpose.

"Do you see it?" Sybil's voice trembled, her usual snark frayed with something close to fear. Her form flickered, like a candle's flame caught in a sudden gust—part of her vanishing, only to reappear a heartbeat later. "Your connection—it's unstable."

As she spoke, the threads in the mirror trembled violently, no longer smooth and fluid but jagged. The mirror itself shuddered, the glass warping as if it were trying to contain something it wasn't meant to hold. Sybil's body flickered again, losing substance, and the room swayed.

Elara gasped as a sharp pull tore at her chest, an invisible force dragging her toward the mirror—like her very soul was being wrenched free and drawn into the dark, vibrating void.

Sybil slammed her hand down on the table with a crack, and the world snapped back into focus. The room stopped spinning, the wild pull vanished, and Sybil's form stabilized. The mirror fell still, though the twisted, trembling threads remained. Her brow furrowed, her expression shifting, and she let out a quiet "Huh," as though the storm of moments before had barely grazed her.

Tension coiled tight in the Hunter's frame. "What?"

Sybil didn't respond immediately, her fingers tracing the surface of the mirror like she was reading a map. She tapped near three distinct threads, the soft glow reflecting in her eyes. "You see these?" she murmured, her voice unusually quiet, almost reverent. "These are the connections. This one here," she tapped the strand of hair, "is yours," her finger shifted to the ring, "and this one belongs to him." Her eyes flicked briefly to the Hunter. But Sybil's eyes darkened with something like confusion as she leaned closer, studying the third thread. Her lips twisted into a frown. "This one... this doesn't belong to either of you." She tilted her head. "It's someone else's. But I can't *see* who."

Elara's stomach twisted. She glanced at the Hunter, hoping for answers, but his expression was locked in that stony mask he always wore, his eyes flickering with something she couldn't name.

Sybil shook her head, her finger still tracing that third thread as if it might reveal more if she pushed hard enough. "I've never seen this before."

"Can you sever them?" Elara didn't want this—this connection, this tether. Not to the Hunter, not to *anyone*.

The Hunter shifted beside her, his gaze steady on the mirror. Elara knew that if she wanted to, she could search for his heart and would feel it pounding.

Sybil waved her hand, and the glowing threads vanished, dissolving into nothing. "It can be done," she said, her voice thoughtful. "Normally, if two casters are linked like this, they can destroy their rings—break the connection—and start the Convergence all over again. A tedious process, yes, but for those who refuse the *Draoth Cara*, it's worth it."

Elara's fingers twitched involuntarily as Sybil's gaze darkened, her lips pressing into a tight, grim line. "But you..." she shook her head. "For starters, you're not linked to any element at all. And him..." She glanced toward the Hunter, her eyes filled with something close to pity. "He's bound to four."

The Hunter's gaze finally broke from the mirror, his jaw flexing as he looked at Sybil. "And what does that mean for us?"

Sybil's gaze didn't waver. "Your *Draoth Cara*—whatever it is—doesn't follow the same rules. It's something else entirely."

Elara bit her lip, then quickly let it go, a fleeting idea creeping in—could the Hunter feel that, too? She shoved it aside and straightened.

"So break the ring. All four stones. That solves it, doesn't it?"

Sybil raised an eyebrow, her eyes gleaming with something between amusement and pity. "Sure," she said slowly. "But nothing's ever that simple. Breaking a bond with an element isn't clean. It's bloody, painful work."

"You said it's done all the time."

"I said it *can* be done," Sybil corrected, her voice cool. "Doesn't mean it's common. When it is attempted, it's agony. Could kill weaker casters. But yes, in theory, it's possible." Her gaze turned harder, more pointed. "But our Hunter here? He might not survive it."

The Hunter stood abruptly, the force of it jarring Elara from her thoughts.

"I can't break the bond with the stones," he ground out, voice low and taut, fists flexing as though fighting to stay in control. "They weren't chosen at random. The Lord Sovereign picked each one. If I destroy even one, he'll know. He'll feel it."

Elara felt a cold weight settle in her chest. "Then what *can* we do?"

Sybil sighed, crossing her arms as she leaned against the hearth. "There are rituals," she said, her tone cool. "Old ones. They can lessen the symptoms, soften the link. But nothing will sever the *Draoth Cara* entirely. Not without risk."

"What about my bind?" Elara asked, not caring that the Hunter stood right beside her. "If I break it, could that change things?"

Sybil raised an eyebrow, her tone almost bored. "If you manage to break the bind, you'd be stronger, sure. And maybe—*maybe*—you could force the link into a dormant state. It wouldn't sever it, but it could weaken the hold."

For a heartbeat, hope flickered inside Elara. But Sybil's sharp laugh cut through it, snuffing it out as quickly as it had come. Elara's her gaze shifted between Sybil and the Hunter. "What?"

Sybil's eyes gleamed, almost pitying. "Only the Lord Sovereign knows how to break that bind. It's a *Tírrísh* spell—ancient, forbidden, and wiped from every record. Unless you plan on charming him into handing it over, there's nothing you can do."

A cold sweat prickled at the back of her neck as Sybil's words sunk in. It was as if a stone had lodged itself beneath her ribs, sinking deeper with each breath, the air growing thick and stifling. The flicker of hope she'd held onto slipped through her fingers, leaving behind the hollow ache of dread that crawled into the spaces it left behind.

She swallowed, trying to push back the growing sense of helplessness. But then, like a thread being pulled free, a thought unraveled in her mind. The spell....

The Hunter had the spell.

She'd seen Osin give it to him, watched the exchange herself.

The tension thickened, almost tangible, tightening around her lungs as her gaze found him.

He was already looking at her.

For a moment, everything else fell away—the room, Sybil, the stakes —until only the two of them remained, caught in a silent exchange. A muscle jumped in his cheek, something dark flickering across his face, but he didn't look away. He didn't need to. The truth was already there.

Elara felt the corner of her mouth twitch as her fingers rose to the necklace at her throat, curling around it. She didn't need words to know what lay beneath his silence. He had the answers she wanted—and she would draw them out of him, one way or another.

CHAPTER 33

Elara had to force down the last two vials of Stonebrew just to make it to Mordenhall on her feet. The journey back had been unsettlingly quiet. But beneath the silence, under the layers of early morning thick with sleep and the hush that followed too many drinks, there was a hum, an odd, steady pull. The streets were nearly empty now—most who had been out drinking had stumbled back to wherever they belonged. Even the troublemakers had tucked themselves away. Only a few stray Legionnaires remained, forcing Elara and the Hunter to veer off course every now and then.

But that wasn't what lingered in her mind. It was him. The restraint in his stride, the way he walked beside her stiff and unreadable, as if something had been folded inward and locked away. Whatever he wasn't saying worked at her nerves despite the peace of the empty streets.

The sky was blushing with the first hues of dawn, pale ribbons of light chasing away the stars. The chill in the air cut to the bone, but deeper still, something warmer, and far more unsettling twisted in her gut.

Pity.

She hated it. Hated that she could feel such a thing for *him*, of all people. He was a mystery wrapped in steel, a fortress she had no desire to breach, yet the cracks were beginning to show.

The way he spoke of the stones on his ring... She had thought it would be something to boast about, a mark of his standing, a symbol that commanded respect. But the darkness in his voice, the tension in his shoulders—it didn't sound like an honor. It sounded like a curse.

"In this world, everyone is bound to someone, willingly or not."

At the time, she'd thought it strange, even cynical, for someone like Osin's Hunter to say such a thing. But now, after everything she had seen... she wasn't so sure anymore.

As they moved through the thick brush along the far wall of Mordenhall, Elara felt something strange. At first, she thought it was just her own exhaustion, the ache in her limbs, the tightness in her chest. But the longer they walked, the clearer it became—it wasn't just her. Every step they took, every breath the Hunter drew—she could sense the way his muscles strained beneath his skin, the way his steps faltered ever so slightly as he pushed open the hidden door, leading them into the narrow, dimly lit staff corridors of the castle. He was hurting. Not bad, not injured in the way that would leave a mark—but sore. A bone-deep exhaustion she wondered if he could feel coming off her too.

"What?" His voice snapped, rough and cold, and it startled her.

Elara quickly looked away, heat rising to her cheeks. She hadn't meant to stare. But the question was already there, pressing at her lips. She couldn't stop herself from asking. "Are you hurt?"

She glanced back at him and found him standing rigid. He didn't meet her eyes right away, his gaze flicking down the hall as if searching for something, anything, to avoid the question. Then, after a long, uncomfortable beat, his dark eyes cut back to hers.

"I trained hard the other day," he said, voice flat. "Pushed myself until I couldn't move."

Elara's lips pulled back in a tight line, her chest squeezing as his words settled into her mind like a lead weight. The heat came next, slow at first, then raging, a wildfire roaring through her veins, setting her skin alight. All this time, she'd thought it was just her body breaking down, pushing its limits. But it wasn't just her. It was *him,* too? Her mind raced, questions hammering against her skull. Had his training kept her from regaining her strength? Had it made her weaker, left her exposed in Osin's game? Worse still... had he known? Done it on purpose?

The thought crackled, igniting the fury that surged up so violently she could barely breathe.

"You drove yourself into the ground, training until you couldn't move, while I quite *literally* couldn't move," Elara snapped, her voice trembling. "And you knew—knew it would affect me. While I lay for *days* in that damned infirmary, choking on potions, barely able to breathe under the constant watch of your leering comrades, you're telling me it was your training that slowed my healing?"

The Hunter's eyes narrowed. "You *died*, Hallowed. Or did you forget?" He stepped forward, closing the distance between them, his gaze burning with fury. "You died. And I felt every *second* of it—the pain, the cold, the emptiness. You did not suffer alone. I pushed myself until my body broke, just to drown it out."

Elara's chin lifted. "And in doing so, you kept me from recovering. You made me vulnerable."

A bitter scoff escaped his lips. "You're so *fucking* selfish. I'd almost forgotten."

Forgotten. Like he'd known her. Her heart stuttered. She had been right all along. There were more memories missing. Memories with him. But that didn't douse the fire roaring inside her. If anything, it fueled it.

She shoved him hard, her palms slamming into his chest, but he didn't budge, didn't so much as flinch. "*I'm* selfish? You didn't even tell me what was happening between us! You left me stumbling in the dark!"

"I didn't know for certain."

"You had an idea!"

He shook his head, jaw clenched so tight she thought he'd crack a tooth. "You're right. I had my suspicions *after* I felt you die. And I acted. Who do you think told the healer you were hurt? Who dragged your lifeless body back?" His breath was hot, nearly brushing her face as he leaned in. "*I* did. If it weren't for me—"

"What?" Elara spat. "If it weren't for you, what? I'd finally have some gods-damned peace? Well, thanks for that."

The Hunter's eyes darkened, something dangerous flashing in them.

His lips curled, a bitter smile that didn't reach his eyes as he took a step back, fingers raking through his hair. He opened his mouth, like he was ready to lash out, but then stopped, swallowing the words.

"I never asked you to save me."

The Hunter stilled, and she *felt* it—felt the way his breath caught between his ribs, how his heart stuttered, then restarted. There was a storm brewing inside him, emotions tangled, pulling him in two directions. But it was true—she had never asked him to help her. Not after touching the stones, not all those years ago.

He drew in a sharp breath, chest rising like he was preparing for a blow. "You remember?"

Elara's stomach flipped. "Of course I remember," she whispered. Her fingers drifted, almost of their own accord, to the scar etched into her skin, brushing over its jagged line.

"Minva sölk harn."

His gaze followed, tracing the line of her scar like a caress before sliding up her throat, inch by inch, until it lingered on her lips. Elara's breath hitched, her chest lifting as she fought to steady the sudden rush in her veins. His eyes climbed higher and locked onto hers, amber flaring bright enough to swallow the dark.

"Why?" The word came out rough, barely more than a rasp. "Why save me at all? If I'd died, you'd have one less problem to deal with. No seal, no *Draoth Cara*. You could've gone back to..."

But she didn't finish. What would he go back to? No title. No family, from what she'd heard. The one relative she knew of lived in squalor and seemed to loathe him for it. What did he even *have* besides the name *Hunter*?

He stood there, barely moving, but Elara felt every ragged breath he took, as if it were her own. "You think I would have spared you back then, only to let you die now?" He shook his head. "That's not how this ends."

Her chest locked tight around the words.

"You weren't supposed to die that night. So *no*, Hallowed, death doesn't get to take you. I claimed you first."

~

THE FIRST LIGHT of dawn bled through the windows, painting the room in a soft, pale glow when they finally made it back.

Tristan's snores filled the air like the rumble of a beast. He was a mess of limbs, one arm slung over his face, the other dangling off the bed, completely at ease despite everything. The guards at the door had mysteriously vanished, though whether it was Tristan's doing or the Hunter's, Elara didn't have the strength to care.

The moment she stepped inside, her vision blurred, and her legs nearly buckled beneath her. The Stonebrew's effects were gone. The fleeting strength it had given her drained to nothing. She swayed but pushed forward, each step a struggle, until she reached the armchair by the hearth and collapsed into it.

The Hunter made to leave, but Elara stopped him.

"We're not done, Hunter."

He paused, turning just enough for her to see the side of his face. "You're running on fumes. Get some rest. You'll hear from me soon enough."

"And if I don't?"

He turned fully then. "Then, by all means, feel free to injure yourself again just to get my attention. The second I feel a paper cut, I'll know it's your doing."

Elara scowled, but he didn't wait for a reply. The door clicked softly shut behind him, and Tristan's snoring came to an abrupt halt. She glanced over, catching sight of him stretching out, long and lazy, before his gaze found hers, and a slow, wicked smile curved his lips.

"Fun night?"

Elara rolled her eyes, leaning back in the chair. "A thrill, to be sure."

Tristan snorted and swung his legs over the side of the bed, bare feet padding against the cold stone. He stretched once, crossed to the chair opposite her, and dropped into it with a quiet thud. His gaze flicked over her—tangled hair, exhaustion etched into her features, the faint tremor in her hands.

"More of a horror, maybe?"

Despite herself, Elara laughed—a breathy, unexpected burst that startled her. Gods, she was so tired it was starting to mess with her head. "How do you know the Hunter?"

Tristan leaned back in his chair, his fingers idly tracing the armrest as he considered her question. His eyes turned thoughtful. "I've known *Ivan* since we were boys. Back before..." His gaze drifted toward her scar, the words faltering. He cleared his throat, glancing away.

Elara's heart skipped. "Did you know me too?"

His eyes snapped back to hers, narrowing slightly as if the question had surprised him. "No," he said after a pause, his voice firmer. "I didn't have the pleasure. My father kept me far from court. Said it was..." He trailed off, a faint, cynical smile tugging at his lips before he shook his head. "Doesn't matter what he thought. But I did see you once. On the first Luminalia."

Her brows shot up. "What can you tell me about that day? What was I like?"

A flicker of pity crossed Tristan's face, and it made her jaw clench.

"You were like a statue," he said softly. "Quiet, detached, as if you weren't fully there. Your eyes... they were black."

Her heart stilled. "What?"

He hummed, nodding slightly. "Like twilight, dark and endless. I was rather surprised when I saw you again at the first party, to see that they'd lightened to a beautiful shade of gray."

Elara bit her lip, ignoring his attempt at flirting. Her mind raced, trying to reconcile his words with her fragmented memories. *Her eyes had been black?* The thought lodged itself in her mind, unsettling and strange, like another piece of herself she didn't recognize. She shivered, her damp clothes clinging to her skin. She shifted in her seat, scooting a little closer to the fire, and wrapped her arms around herself. "What about Lady Calista Thorne?"

Tristan threw one leg lazily over the other. "What about her?" he said, bored.

"Do you know her?"

He tapped his fingers against his knee. "Unfortunately."

"I need to speak to her."

"And you want *my* help with that?"

Elara's nails dug into her palms. "It's important."

Tristan sighed deeply. "The woman hates me."

"Why?"

A smirk tugged at his mouth. "I broke off our engagement."

Elara blinked, momentarily thrown. "Oh."

"Yeah," he drawled, "could be tricky. That, and you're not exactly someone who gets out much, are you?"

"What about during Osin's next party?"

Tristan scrunched his nose, considering. "I might be able to—"

The door crashed open and the both of them jolted, heads whipping toward the source of the noise. Elara's pulse spiked. Malak stood in the doorway, his breath ragged, face flushed, eyes darting around the room until they landed on her. The moment they did, his whole body seemed to deflate, the tension leaving him in one slow, heavy breath.

Behind him, two guards lingered by the door, heads bowed, shoulders stiff like they'd just been thoroughly chewed out. She didn't need to guess why. Malak must've found them slacking off somewhere, panic setting in the moment he realized they weren't where they were supposed to be. That wild, desperate look in his eyes when he'd burst in —he had expected her to be gone.

"Well, that's my cue," Tristan muttered, springing to his feet with a quickness that made Elara's head spin. He grabbed his coat from the bed and turned toward her. His usual teasing smile softened, and for a moment, there was something almost genuine in his eyes.

"It was truly lovely to meet you, Elara," he whispered. Then he stepped closer, pressing a chaste kiss to her cheek. "Give 'em hell, little saint."

With a wink and a flair of dramatics, Tristan strode toward the door, his voice rising louder than necessary, as though he wanted the entire castle to hear. "Hope you all had a good night. The Hallowed certainly did!"

~

ELARA'S LEGS gave out beneath her, knees hitting the rough stone as the guards hauled her along, their grip bruising. Every breath burned, pain ripping through her, only worse this time. Somewhere in the back of her mind, a voice whispered that the Hunter was feeling this too, every damn bit of it. She shoved that thought down fast—she wasn't about to let guilt creep in for *him*.

They didn't say a word, didn't even look at her as they dragged her into the cell, tossing her to the floor like she was nothing. The impact knocked the breath from her, and for a long, hazy moment she lay there, cheek pressed to the cold stone, ears ringing. Somewhere behind her, the cell door clanged shut and the wards buzzed to life. She couldn't move. Couldn't even lift her head.

Tears burned hot in her eyes as she willed her legs to work, to remember the drills Saria had pounded into her. But it was like she was right back at square one, every bit of progress erased.

"*Fuck!*" The word ripped from her.

She wanted to sob, but she dragged her palms to her eyes, pressing hard, trying to block out everything. The frustration, the pain, the helplessness. She took a slow breath, and forced herself to calm down. *I can do this.* Elara blinked away the tears, expecting—*hoping*—to see Reynnar leaning against the bars, watching her with that quiet, unshakable strength that always made her feel like she could push through anything. But when she looked, his side of the cell was empty.

Her heart stumbled, ice spreading through her veins.

Where is he?

Her teeth ground together, a low growl slipping from her lips as she dragged herself forward. Jagged stone bit into her palms and knees, but the pain only drove her harder to his cell.

Nothing. Just darkness.

Elara trembled, every nerve raw, every horrible possibility crashing over her—Reynnar broken, his body mangled and bleeding out, or worse, cold, lifeless, gone. *No.* She squeezed her eyes shut, forcing herself to banish those thoughts. *Focus. Just breathe.* She forced herself to walk through that quiet place in her mind, willed her heart to slow its frantic hammering.

Teeth clenched against the pain, she dragged herself to the cell door. "Where is Reynnar?" Her voice cracked, but the guards outside didn't even spare her a glance. She tried again, her eyes darting around, wild, pleading with anyone who might care enough to listen. "Was he moved? Did he—"

Her words died as one guard stopped and kicked dirt into her face. Grit slammed into her skin, needlesharp, clogging her mouth and nose. She choked, coughing as her hands shook, uselessly trying to clear it.

"Quit your sniveling!" he growled, kicking another cloud of dirt at her.

Elara flinched, her body jerking as she turned quickly, pressing her back against the iron bars. Her hands shook as she fumbled for the inside of her cloak, finding a patch clean enough to wipe the grime from her eyes. Her breath hitched, uneven. *It's fine. It's going to be fine. Reynnar is okay.* He had to be. There wasn't room for any other possibility.

Over and over, she repeated the words, until they became a prayer, a desperate chant to keep the fear at bay. To keep her from falling apart. But whether it was exhaustion finally claiming her or some mercy from the gods, she wasn't sure. All she knew was that her body gave in long before her mind found any peace.

When Elara woke, the cell was swallowed in darkness, the damp chill clinging to her skin. Every inch of her back throbbed in agony, her neck stiff, and twisted from sleeping upright against the iron bars. She shifted, wincing as the sharp pain shot through her shoulders, but she wiggled her toes, testing them, and exhaled heavily when they moved without pain—small mercies.

Her eyes drifted downward, catching sight of the trays on the floor. Dinner sat there, untouched and cold, right beside the leftovers from her breakfast and lunch. Stale bread, congealed soup—all of it left to rot. She had slept through it all. *An entire day, wasted.* She cursed under her breath, bracing her hands against the stone floor and trying to push herself up. Her muscles trembled violently, weak and uncooperative, her body collapsing back against the cold stone.

Saria had warned her this would happen—the price her body would pay for pushing past its limits. The game, running through the city, using what little strength she had left, had only worsened her condition. She closed her eyes, trying to remember how long it would take her body to heal. But it was hard to think, hard to focus when everything ached.

A clank of armor in the hall caught her attention, and Elara's eyes snapped open. A guard was passing by. "Hey," she called out, trying again. "Do you know where my cellmate is?"

The guard's step faltered, hesitation flickering in his eyes as he glanced around, nerves written all over him. Elara's brow furrowed, studying him—she didn't recognize him. He wasn't one of the regulars, not part of the usual rotation. New. Definitely new. He had that nervous, uncertain edge about him, like someone who wasn't sure if they were doing things right. Maybe he was Rolfe's replacement. She winced at the thought.

"Please. Is there anything you can tell me?"

The guard shifted uncomfortably, his gaze fixed anywhere but on her. He wasn't supposed to speak to her; even as fresh as he was, he knew that much. Elara's mind raced, and an idea formed, pitiful as it was. She leaned forward, lowering her voice to a whisper. "If you tell me where my cellmate is, I'll give you some of my blood."

The guard's eyes snapped to hers, wide with disbelief and something far more dangerous. "What?"" he rasped.

"For information, and your discretion," she replied. The shame of it hit her immediately. But she *was* desperate, and there was no point pretending otherwise. Her hand found a jagged rock on the floor, and she pricked her finger, wincing at the sting. She could only hope the Hunter wouldn't sense it. She held out her hand, watching as the small bead of crimson welled up on her fingertip. "Where is Reynnar?"

The guard's eyes stayed glued to her finger, transfixed. "He's... with the others," he mumbled, never pulling his gaze from the crimson bead. "They're gathering them for the next extraction."

Elara's stomach twisted. "Where?"

"The third tunnel," he finally answered, his eyes flickering up to meet hers for a brief moment. "That's where they conduct the alchemical work. Perform the trials."

A dull throb pulsed behind her eyes, the pressure mounting with each second. *Extraction? Trials?* Were they torturing the Sidhe right now? What was Osin doing to them?

Her eyes burned with tears but she forced her expression to remain neutral. She couldn't let him see how close she was to breaking. "How long until he's back?"

The guard shrugged, his eyes back on her finger. "Could be days. Usually takes about a week."

"When did the trials begin?"

"A few days back."

Elara swallowed hard, piecing the timeline together. She'd been gone for six days—Reynnar must have been taken right after her.

"Can I see him?"

The guard blinked, as if snapping out of a trance. He shook his head. "Not until the trials are done. Then he'll be sent back."

Elara nodded, her finger throbbing with each pulse. "Where's Godfrey?"

The guard frowned. "Who?"

"The Lord Sovereign's former healer."

His brows drew together, clearly irritated. "How the hell should I know?"

Elara clenched her jaw, teeth aching as she ground them together. The guard stepped closer, sweat and iron thickening the air between them. She exhaled, resolve faltering, and reached through the bars. To her surprise, her hand slipped through the wards—just far enough for her fingers to pass.

The guard wasted no time. His rough, calloused hand clamped down on her wrist as he yanked her closer, his lips closing around the tiny wound on her finger. The moment his mouth touched her skin, Elara's stomach churned violently. His breath was hot and sticky. His eyes fluttered shut, and a soft, guttural sound escaped him as he sucked on her finger like a man starved.

Elara's skin crawled, revulsion rolling through her, every muscle in her body screaming for her to yank her hand back, but she held still, forcing herself to endure it. She tried to focus on anything but the revolting sensation, and then she caught sight of his ring.

The dull quartz embedded in the tarnished band glowed, its surface awakening in soft pulses. The sight of it made something cold curl in her gut.

"That's enough," she snapped.

Elara tried to pull her hand free, but his grip tightened. For one sickening moment she thought he wouldn't let go—then, with a shuddering breath, he released her. His fingers slackened. He blinked, disoriented, as if waking from a dream, and slowly licked his lips.

"If you need help in the future... We can arrange this again."

Elara forced the bile back, her face carefully neutral. "Maybe," she bit out, her fingers curling into a fist as she drew her hand back.

The guard stumbled away, leaving Elara to collapse against the bars, her body sinking under the weight of exhaustion and shame. Her skin still crawled from the feel of his lips on her. She wiped her hand on her cloak, scrubbing at the spot as though she could erase the moment, but the disgust lingered, festering under her skin.

Her mind drifted back to the alley, to the words of the Legionnaires. *Shortages. Withdrawals.* They needed her blood. For more than just the Convergence. Why? Her thoughts spun, circling back to Fenlin, to the Script Keepers. Was that all they had wanted from her? Just her blood? Had everything been as simple—and as brutal—as that?

Elara dragged herself toward the cot, each movement sending fresh stabs of pain through her body, harsh enough to draw a cry from her lips. Her muscles trembled, too weak to pull her up. With a frustrated sigh, she grabbed the blanket instead, crumpling it onto the cold stone floor. It wasn't much, but it would have to do. Curling into herself, she tried to block out the pain, her eyes slipping shut, when something rippled across the opposite side of the cell.

Her heart lurched as she pushed herself up on trembling arms. The ripple grew, and something thin and pale floated through. Parchment? She blinked, incredulous, as it drifted toward her. With shaking hands, she snatched the note from the air and unfolded it; a pencil rolled free. Elegant, precise script stretched across the page.

"Summoning me already? You're impatient. I've got a few loose ends to tie up. Think you can refrain from acquiring more injuries until I'm finished?"

So, he had felt it. *A few loose ends?* She shuddered, the memory of him cutting down his men flashing vividly in her mind. She didn't envy anyone who met that kind of end. With a sigh, she grabbed the pencil, and scribbled her response, her fingers trembling slightly.

"Considering I don't have working legs at the moment, I'd say I'm done collecting injuries for the day." She paused, biting her lip, then

added, *"And for the record, I wasn't summoning you. I'm just clumsy, not desperate. How exactly did you manage to get through the wards in my cell?"*

Elara rolled up the note, tucked the pencil inside, and studied the ripple in the air. After a moment's hesitation, she crawled closer and pushed the parchment through. Then she waited.

A minute passed. Her curiosity got the better of her, and she poked a finger through the ripple.

A shock of ice ripped through her.

Elara cursed under her breath, but before she could dwell on it, the parchment slipped back through. She unrolled it, finding the familiar elegant handwriting again.

"I made some adjustments last time. Now I can rift directly to you. Also, are you absolutely certain you're not desperate?"

Elara narrowed her eyes at the note, only for her gaze to catch on three vials floating in front of her—Stonebrew. Pyrewarmth. Sleeping draught. Her fingers trembled as they closed around the glass. Relief hit her so hard she almost sobbed. She didn't think. Just uncorked and swallowed them all in rapid succession.

The Stonebrew worked its magic first, sliding through her veins, calming the violent tremors in her limbs. The Pyrewarmth followed, sending a rush of heat from her core, radiating to her fingertips, her toes —gods, she could actually feel them again. And the sleeping draught was a gentle tug, a sweet lull that dragged at her eyelids.

Her breath steadied, chest no longer tight, and she scribbled a hasty response on the note, *"Arrogant prick."* With a flick of her wrist, she shoved it back through the rip in reality, already feeling the pull of sleep as her body hit the cot.

Warmth. Strength. Comfort. Things she hadn't felt in... gods, how long had it been?

As she curled into the blankets, sleep already pulling her under, something like laughter echoed in her mind—a low rumble that might've been real, might've been imagined. It didn't matter.

For once, everything was quiet.

CHAPTER 34

Elara flexed her legs, rolling her ankles.

Stretch, release. Again. And again. Her muscles screamed in protest at first, stiff and uncooperative, but she kept at it, refusing to let the ache control her. A light sheen of sweat had formed on her skin by the time she heard the distant shuffle of the early morning shift change outside. Blood was finally flowing again, her limbs loosening, waking up like the rest of her body.

She hadn't expected it—the vials of Stonebrew, sitting there at the foot of her cot, almost innocent in their placement. Just waiting. She'd stared at them for longer than she cared to admit, mind spinning in a thousand directions. What did it mean? Was it an act of kindness? Did he care? Or was it just self-preservation because he was tired of suffering through her injuries? She didn't know. She couldn't *know*. And that was the problem. Her thoughts always tangled up like this, second-guessing every damn thing.

Elara wanted to believe it was something good. That it wasn't just obligation. But gods, she'd made that mistake before—thinking people cared when they hadn't. Not really. Not when it counted. She couldn't afford to make that mistake again. Couldn't bear it.

Going through the motions, Elara stretched and tested her legs until she was sure they wouldn't give out beneath her. Then a slow shuffle carried her to the door, where a sad excuse for breakfast awaited. A piece of stale bread, barely a scrap of cheese, and a cup of something that looked like broth but tasted like water. Still, she forced it down. She needed the strength, the energy to heal. Eat, sleep, stretch. That's what Saria had drilled into her head. Keep going, even when it felt pointless.

She wondered about Saria now, wondered if the healer would come check on her or if she was even allowed to. Her gaze drifted, almost unwillingly, to Reynnar's cell. Still empty. Still no sign of him. No amber eyes watching her from across the way, no scrape of his breakfast tray being pushed into her space. Her heart clenched painfully at the absence. She hadn't realized how much she'd come to rely on the small, silent moments with him—just knowing he was there.

Blood rushed through her, a dark wrongness coiling inside her. She knew—*knew*—whatever was happening to him was happening now, and it was bad. Her teeth sank into her bottom lip, biting harder until the coppery taste flooded her mouth. She had to act.

But what could she do?

Her heartbeat pounded in her chest, erratic, loud, drowning out the distant sounds of the prison. And then, like a hammer to the skull, the thought struck her.

The pill.

Her head snapped toward the loose stone in the corner.

"It would've made you convulse, scream loud enough to shake the walls. The guards would've thought you were dying. They'd have dragged you out, right to me."

Her hands shook as she crossed the cell and dug her nails into the cracks, prying the stone free. There it was, just as she'd left it—hidden, waiting. A small vial, almost innocuous, yet heavy with promise.

Madness. This was madness. She hesitated, heart pounding in her throat, a small voice in the back of her mind whispering for her to stop, to think.

With a quick breath, she popped the pill into her mouth

The Hunter had said death couldn't touch her—not by his hand, at least. And gods help her, despite every instinct screaming to fight it, she wanted to believe him.

So, when her body jerked, when the first violent spasm tore through her like a wave of fire, forcing a scream so raw it burned her throat, she didn't panic. When her limbs flailed, hitting the cold, hard floor of the cell, she didn't surrender. Even when her vision blurred, the room spinning in a whirl of shadows, and she could feel the last threads of consciousness slipping away, she held on to that thread of trust.

The distant sound of boots clanging against stone, the cell door crashing open—it barely registered. Only then did she let herself go, sinking into that quiet dark, knowing with a strange certainty that she would wake where she needed to be.

THE SCENT HIT HER FIRST. A mix of herbs and spent ether, the air still humming with the electric tang of a freshly cast spell. Elara's eyes fluttered open, her head pounding, and for a moment, the world was nothing but a blur of muted colors and muffled sounds.

She blinked again, forcing herself to focus. Slowly, the room came into view—the infirmary. Cold. Sterile. *Empty.*

She was lying on a cot, the thin, scratchy sheets twisted around her legs. Above her, a soft, glowing mist of a spell hung in the air, shimmering faintly. Her chest heaved, muscles locking as she braced for the familiar weight of ether to press down on her. But nothing.

Cautiously, she moved. Her body tensed, waiting for resistance, for the spell to pull her back—but it didn't. Her hand lifted freely. She blinked, confused. It wasn't binding her. Wasn't holding her down.

Her pulse sped up, as her gaze flicked around the room again, just to be sure, her breath held tight in her lungs. But no one appeared. She was truly alone. Her blood roared like a current as she slid off the bed, bare feet soundless against the cold stone floor while she crept toward the door.

She paused, listening. No guards. No footsteps moving through the halls.

Where the hell is everyone?

Elara slipped down the tunnel, moving fast but keeping every step measured, ears on high alert for the slightest sound of movement. Her mind was locked on one thing—find the Sidhe, find Reynnar. The guard had said they were in the third tunnel, three down from where she was now. That was all she had to go on, and she wasn't wasting time.

With each step, her confidence grew. The silence stretched on, uninterrupted, her movements quickening as she darted through the tunnel. No footsteps behind her, no guards in sight. Was it one of Osin's debauched parties? Maybe the guards were off, getting pissed, their posts abandoned. The stillness around her felt too easy, too careless.

As she passed the spot where Rolfe had fallen, her eyes flickered to the rock she'd used, still lying there, stained with the memory of what she'd done. A flush crept up her face, shame and bitterness simmering beneath her skin. *Anger*—directed at herself, at the cruel circumstances she had never wished for. She never wanted to hurt anyone. Never wanted *any* of this. But this was the hand she'd been dealt, and she had made what seemed the only reasonable choice at the time. At least, that was the justification she repeated to herself.

What she *had* to believe.

Elara burst out of the sixth tunnel, barely catching her breath before sprinting toward the third. A commotion echoed from deep within the fortress, growing louder with each step. Panic clawed at her, the dread thick in her chest. She pushed harder, her bare feet slapping against the cold stone floor, the sound sharp in the still air, her pulse a deafening roar in her ears.

When she rounded the bend deep in the tunnel, the sight before her made her stomach drop. Lines of Sidhe stretched endlessly ahead, their figures hunched and broken. Ether shimmered in the air—spells of wind and earth weaving between them like chains, keeping them in line, corralling them like sheep.

Elara dropped into a crouch, pressing herself into the shadows, her breath shallow as she watched. A single, unbroken line, at least a hundred of them, all moving in the same slow, defeated march.

The faint hum of a spell, crackled through the air, but the guards' voices were faint, far off. Too far ahead to be watching closely, trusting their ether to do the work for them.

Elara crept out, keeping her body close to the ground, every movement deliberate as she threaded her way through the shifting currents of ether. The earth pulsed beneath her feet, the ground rippling as if alive, while tendrils of wind curled through the tunnel like invisible hands, tugging at her clothes. She slipped between the threads of energy, careful not to disturb the current, her feet barely making a sound as she eased into the line of Sidhe. Every breath felt like a risk, her heart hammering in her chest.

The Sidhe in front of her shifted, a flicker of movement catching her eye. He glanced over his shoulder, his pale blue eyes locking onto hers. They were bright, almost unnervingly so, against the grim space around them. His brow furrowed, confusion flickering across his face before he leaned closer, his voice a low murmur. *"An mian leat an bás, a dhaonnaí bhig?[16]"*

"Have you seen Reynnar?" Elara whispered, her voice barely audible, hoping—praying—he'd recognize the name.

The Sidhe's brow shot up in surprise. *"Na Tuatha? Is ea.[17]"* He jerked his chin up the line. *"An tríú grúpa, thart ar dheich gcloigeann suas.[17]"*

Tuatha?

The word tugged at her memory. Where had she heard it before? She shook her head. It didn't matter. Elara leaned in, keeping her voice low. "Reynnar is up there? You're sure?"

The Sidhe gave a curt nod. *"Is ea.[18]"*

Tears blurred her vision as her chest tightened, one hand pressing against her heart. "Thank you," she whispered, her voice cracking.

The Sidhe's eyes softened. He placed his hand on his own chest, dipping his chin in a small, respectful nod. *"Caelion."*

Oh, curse it all, she'd done it *again*.

A strange, misplaced bubble of laughter almost escaped her at the absurdity of the situation. She made a mental note to remember Caelion, to tell him her true name once she helped free him. But now wasn't the time. She gave him a small nod of thanks, then slipped further up the line, weaving through the Sidhe.

More eyes turned to her, curious, wary, but none gave her away. They only watched. It was as if they recognized her—remembered the human who had touched the stones, who had run through these tunnels in sheer madness. And now, without a word, they shifted, moving subtly to let her pass.

"Eilíara."

Reynnar's voice cut through the murmur of the tunnel, rough and low, carrying over the heads of those in line.

Elara's breath hitched, and for a moment, everything stopped. Time, the world around her, her own heartbeat—it all hung suspended between that single word and the reality crashing back in. Her name. Spoken by *him*.

Slowly, her heart began to pound again, a mix of relief, and dread twisting in her chest as she pushed forward.

It wasn't until Reynnar's form finally came into view that Elara let herself breathe, slow and controlled, in and out through her nose. Her hands clenched into fists, gripping the fabric of her gown just to stop them from trembling. He had been watching her the entire time, she could feel it—the weight of his gaze pulling her closer. But when their eyes met, the relief she'd felt at seeing him drained away. His entire body had gone rigid, muscles tensing in a way that made her pulse quicken for all the wrong reasons.

Elara's brow furrowed, a question forming in her eyes and a flicker of something—fear, frustration—passed across his features. And then it hit her. He didn't want her here. Not in this line, not in the midst of this mess. Whatever was happening, he wanted her far from it. Far from *him*.

Elara lifted her chin, meeting his gaze head-on, daring him to challenge her. She wasn't about to run, wasn't going to cower, or hide. They were in this *together*, and he knew it. He'd been there for her from the start—sucking the venom from her veins that first day, keeping her grounded, feeding her when she couldn't manage on her own. Did he really believe she wouldn't do the same for him now? That she'd stand by and let him face this alone?

His eyes darkened, a flicker of something dangerous flashing there. Then, the tips of his fangs slid into view as he smiled, slow and sharp, his chin dipping in acknowledgment—acceptance.

"Move!" A guard's voice cracked through the air like a whip, and the Sidhe around her, who had slowed ever so slightly, resumed their pace.

Reynnar moved with them, but there was something different in his posture. His back was straight, shoulders pulled tight with tension. Elara's took him in—the tangled mess of his dark hair, matted with dirt, the braids once so carefully woven now frayed and half-undone. His pointed ears were nicked, fresh cuts standing out against the bruised and bloodied skin of his back and sides. Yet, despite the wounds, despite the exhaustion etched into every line of his body, he still carried himself with that quiet, unyielding strength. The warrior she had always known him to be. Even now, even after all of this, he hadn't broken. He stood tall, bruised but unbowed, and that resilience—that quiet strength, only solidified what she already knew.

He would not die here.

Not like this.

And she vowed, with every fiber of her being, that she would make sure of it.

They reached the tunnel's end, and Elara instinctively ducked her head, letting her hair fall like a veil around her face. The guards moved in, their heavy boots thudding against the stone floor, the metallic clink of weapons echoing as they swarmed around the group. She kept her movements small, shrinking into herself, hoping to go unnoticed as they herded the Sidhe forward.

The tunnel gave way to a vast chamber, its stone walls stretching high, casting shadows that swallowed the weak torchlight. The air inside was thick, carrying the scent of damp rock and the faint metallic tang of old blood. One by one, they were funneled into the space, the press of bodies tightening with every step. Fifty—maybe more—stood shoulder to shoulder, the tension in the air palpable. Then, without warning, a group of guards halted the influx, redirecting the remainder down another tunnel.

"Strip!" The command thundered from the entrance.

Elara froze, her mind reeling, disbelief rooting her in place as the Sidhe around her began to obey. She scanned the space again, taking in the details she had missed in her initial panic. The vast chamber was lined with deep stone basins, low troughs carved into the ground, water trickling through channels along the edges. This wasn't an alchemical lab, wasn't some twisted medical trial. No, this place—this place looked like a washroom. Whatever extraction had been done to them, it was already over. And now, they were being washed? As a collective group?

Rage boiled through her, hot and blinding, her body trembling under its force. She wanted to scream, to fight—but her hands moved on their own, shaking as they slipped her necklace free and shoved it into her brassiere. She peeled the worn gown from her body, fingers numb as the fabric slid from her skin, then tossed it onto the growing pile of discarded clothes.

At least they hadn't been made to strip their underthings. Not yet, anyway. A bitter mercy—but a mercy all the same.

Without warning, water blasted from the guards' outstretched hands, a vicious torrent that hit with a force that knocked the air from her lungs. Elara's hands flew up trying to shield her face, but it did little against the onslaught. The glacial water cut into her, relentless, each drop feeling like a thousand knives stabbing into her flesh.

Around her, the others staggered, their once-powerful forms shrinking under the sheet of water pouring over them. Elara looked for Reynnar, but she could barely make out any face through the deluge. But as if on a whim, the flood halted. The world around her stilled, caught in a breathless pause.

"Get yourselves cleaned up, or it's goodbye to your cozy cells and hello to the dirt nap. Move it!" growled the pockmarked guard, his voice booming through the stone halls as he tossed chunks of soap across the ground like he was feeding chickens.

Around her, the Sidhe moved with quiet resignation, reaching for the broken shards of soap. The soft sounds of scrubbing and trickling water filled the chamber, as Elara's eyes swept over the room before landing on Reynnar. He was crouched low, his dark, damp hair hanging around his face as he gathered a few fragments. When he felt her eyes on him, he looked up, meeting her gaze before walking over to her.

Without a word, he held out a small piece of soap, his expression soft, nodding gently as if to offer some silent reassurance. Then, just as calmly, he turned and handed another piece to the Sidhe female nearby. She accepted it, but her gaze shot straight to Elara, eyes narrowing with suspicion and something else—recognition. Elara remembered her too —this was the same Sidhe who had warned her about the wards.

Elara's gaze lingered on the way their hands met. There was something in the subtle brush of their fingers—more than just the shared bond of captivity. It was familiarity. A connection. The tension between them hummed like a taut string, visible in the way their eyes met and lingered before the silver-haired Sidhe murmured something in Reynnar's ear. Then, almost as if in unison, both turned their attention toward her.

"Caithfidh gurb é seo do chéile cillín, mar sin, an cailín daonna[19]." the female said, her gaze appraising Elara with a mix of curiosity and something else.

Reynnar's response was a low hum of what seemed like affirmation, his attention shifting to Elara as a smile found its way onto his face. *"A Eilíara, seo Aoife.[20]"*

"Aoife." Elara repeated and her smile broadened, a nod accompanying her approval, as if Elara's attempt at her name had passed some unspoken test.

"Ainm láidir é Eilíara, ainm ársa i ndomhan s'againne. Nach oiriúnach gur ortsa atá sé.[21]"

Her smile was so warm, that whatever wariness, whatever suspicion she had thrown Elara with that look seemed to have disappeared.

"Enough jabbering, get on with it! Or I'll come over there and wash you down myself."

The pockmarked guard's gaze, laden with vile implication, settled on Aoife, sending a shudder through Elara at the menace it carried. Aoife, however, only rolled her eyes and began scrubbing her back.

That was when Elara noticed them—the scars.

Deep, jagged lines stretching from her shoulder blades down in two brutal slashes. Elara blinked, a cold numbness spreading through her as she watched Aoife quietly wash the wounds, her movements slow, as if she had long grown used to the pain.

Those scars could only mean one thing.

Wings.

She used to have wings.

And Osin mutilated them.

Elara's heart lodged in her throat, her pulse pounding in her ears as her gaze darted around the room. Not all the Sidhe bore those marks, only a few. Her stomach twisted when she saw Caelion among them.

She blinked, once, twice, but her vision seemed to blur around the edges. Her hands trembled at her sides, curling into fists, nails digging into her palms. She tried to focus, to pull in air, but it felt like every breath caught in her throat. The low murmur of Sidhe voices grew louder, warping into a dissonant hum in her ears.

"Eilíara."

Her throat constricted, and the room seemed to tilt, narrowing in.

"Eilíara."

Broad, calloused hands cupped her face. Elara flinched, her gaze snapping up to meet a pair of amber eyes. His eyes. Warm, like the sun breaking through a storm, like safety itself.

"Déan anáil, a Eilíara.[22]*"*

She gasped, a sharp, ragged breath filling her lungs.

"Go maith. Arís.[23]*"*

Reynnar's voice wrapped around her like a shield, firm but soothing, a tether to pull her out of the spiral. So she followed it—one breath, then another, and another, until her heart slowed—until his grip on her loosened.

Her eyes darted across his face, taking in every line, every flicker of emotion, while his hands still cradled her. *How had they endured so much pain?* It was all too much. She wanted to ask him, *needed* to— wished she could say *anything* to him. But the gods, in their infinite cruelty, had stripped that from her too. They hated her—she was certain of it. Her life, from its beginning, had been nothing but a testament to their contempt, a constant reminder that she was never meant to have anything good.

Of course she wouldn't have this either.

A sudden shout sliced through the air, freezing the room in place. Elara's head jerked up, her breath catching as her eyes darted toward the source.

Malak stood rigid near the entrance, his wide eyes fixed on her. His gaze flicked from her to Reynnar and back again, the recognition dawning in slow horror.

Shit.

His face contorted, veins bulging at his neck as he shouted something at her—something venomous, a threat, but the words blurred in her mind. Elara's pulse thundered, a dizzying rush of panic surging through her. *Stupid. So stupid.* She should have stayed locked in that cell, but she had let fear blind her.

The guards surged forward, a storm of fury and steel, their boots slamming against the stone floor like a rolling thunder that reverberated in the pit of Elara's stomach. Her eyes flicked to Caelion the second he moved. It wasn't much, just a slight shift, like the surface of a pond catching a breeze—but she felt it. The quiet authority in the way he stepped in front of her, his broad frame suddenly between her and the guards. Arms at his sides, not clenched, but ready, like he could tear them apart without even trying. And they stopped.

Then, like the ripple spreading, the others followed. One by one, the Sidhe moved forward, deliberate and steady, forming a protective wall. A *barrier*. A shield between her and the advancing threat.

Elara's heart jolted when Reynnar stepped up beside Caelion, his gaze meeting hers for a fraction of a second. Just long enough to make her stomach twist. He turned, eyes hard, ready.

Her thoughts spun as she watched the guards freeze, disbelief clear in their wide eyes. Not rage—something worse. Shock. They hadn't expected this. She hadn't been in the prison long, but it didn't take a genius to see how things worked here. The Sidhe didn't push back. They moved when told, obeyed without a word, never once raising their heads. No resistance. No fight.

Until now.

Now, Caelion stood like he'd never bent to anyone. His spine straight, unshakable, and the others followed him—slowly at first, like they were remembering what it felt like to stand for something. To stand for themselves.

It was happening. The shift she'd felt creeping closer, the lines being drawn—and they were standing on hers.

Aoife shoved her way through the Sidhe, each movement pulling at the scars that twisted across her back. Her gaze swept over the guards, a sneer curling her lips.

"*An é seo an méid atá ag teastáil chun eagla a chur ort?*[24]" She eyed them up and down, disdain dripping from every word. "*Go hainnis. Casadh babaithe beaga ní ba chróga orm.*[24]"

And then, as if to punctuate her words, she spat at their feet, the sound cutting in the silence, her eyes daring them—begging them—to make a move.

Malak blinked, like he was just now waking up from the shock, and then he stepped forward, his arm jerking back, ready to strike. But it was in that heartbeat—that fleeting, suspended moment—that Reynnar moved.

No, not moved—*exploded*.

With a ferocity that seemed to tear from the depths of his soul, he lunged at the guard, a growl tearing from his throat. It was a sound that spoke of wild, untamed lands, of freedom fought for with tooth and claw, a call of the wild that echoed in the caverns of Elara's heart, stirring something fierce within her.

But Malak, with a mere flick of his wrist, sent out a gust of ether. It was a gesture so effortless, yet it unleashed an invisible force that crashed into Reynnar like a tidal wave against a cliff. Elara's heart lurched as he was flung back, his body a plaything to the whims of Malak's power, crashing to the ground.

And then, as though Reynnar's insolence had been the very signal they'd waited for, the guards converged. Like a dark tide swelling with intent to drown everything in its path, they gathered around him. Fists and boots became weapons forged from bone and sinew. Each one of them was ready—eager, even—to stamp out that flicker of rebellion before it had the chance to ignite into something more.

The scream that ripped from Elara's throat wasn't just a sound—it was primal, a desperate howl that cut through the Sidhe like an arrow and shot straight to Malak. His head snapped toward her, but she was already moving, already tearing through the wall of bodies, shoving past limbs and faces that blurred together. Her heart pounded in her ears as she forced her way into the circle of guards, fists and boots raining down on Reynnar.

She clamped onto the nearest guard's arm. A feeble attempt to stop the onslaught, to slow the storm of fists crashing into Reynnar. But it was like trying to hold back the sea with her bare hands, and she was flung back.

The ground rushed up to meet her, knocking the breath from her lungs as her body hit with a force that rattled her bones. Blood bloomed in her mouth, the rusty, pungent tang bursting as her teeth sank into her lip from the impact.

Through the haze of pain, she caught sight of Aoife and Caelion. Their movements were a dance of fury. Aoife's teeth found their mark, sinking deep into the guard's arm—flesh tearing, sinew snapping beneath the force of her bite. The guard's cry barely escaped his throat before Caelion struck, his fists a hammer against the man's body.

Elara's breaths came in quick, ragged gasps as she watched how their actions ignited the will of those around her. One after the other, they stepped forward, their movements a symphony of controlled chaos as their bodies melded into the struggle, limbs, and fury intertwining, as they threw themselves against their captors with a desperation born of too many silent grievances.

This wasn't just a fight, but an uprising. It was a clash of wills, a battle for freedom fought with every ounce of strength they possessed. Witnessing this, Elara saw not the beaten and broken individuals she had come to know in the dim light of their prison, but a united force of warriors, each fighting not just for their own survival, but for all of them.

Instinct took over before her mind even caught up. She was on her feet in a heartbeat, the stonebrew pulsing like fire through her veins, steadying her limbs. Her hand closed around the nearest thing—an abandoned guard's baton, cold and heavy in her grip. It didn't matter. In her hands, it became something more. It became the manifestation of her fury, her will, and she wielded it without hesitation.

The first guard went down with a crack to the jaw, teeth splintering, a spray of blood following. The next barely had time to register the blow before her baton smashed into his nose, the sickening crunch fueling the storm raging inside her. She wasn't gentle. She wasn't merciful. Every swing, every crack of bone beneath the baton, was a release. A pathway through the chaos.

But her eyes—they stayed locked on something beyond the blood and violence. *Malak.* He stood just out of reach, untouched by the storm swirling around her. And that—more than anything—drove her forward.

Bodies clashed and fists flew, but Elara slipped through the violence, her movements fluid, dodging blows that grazed too close, slipping past flailing arms. Her focus was razor-sharp, driven by something deeper, something raw, and all-consuming that swallowed everything else.

His back was to her, oblivious. That mistake was all she needed. Elara summoned every shred of rage, every piece of herself, and poured it into the swing of her baton. It cut through the air, connecting with a sickening thud against the side of his face, right at his ear. He grunted, his body stiffening at the impact, but she didn't stop. Couldn't. Again and again, she struck, pouring every ounce of fury, fear, and desperation into each blow. Each swing was fueled by the untamed, wild need to make him feel it—every drop of her anger.

Blood gushed from his ear, staining the side of his face, but he spun around, and his hand cracked across her face. A white-hot burst of pain shot through her, exploding in her skull. Her jaw screamed in agony, the impact radiating through her bones as her body stumbled backward.

Malak yanked the baton from her hands, his face twisted with rage. Elara had no time to brace before the first strike slammed into her ribs, the crack of bone against metal ringing in her ears. Pain exploded through her side, sending her stumbling back. But Malak didn't stop. The baton came down again, this time against her shoulder, the force of it knocking her to the ground.

She gasped, her breath stolen by the blow, and tried to push herself up, but another hit crashed against her thigh, agony shooting down her leg. The baton whipped through the air with a sickening whoosh, slamming into her side, her back, her arms—anywhere it could find purchase. Elara curled into herself, trying to protect what she could, but it was no use. A savage blow landed against her spine, forcing a scream from her lips, her body arching involuntarily from the impact. She closed her eyes, feeling the dirt that clung to her sweat-drenched skin as she shook against the earth.

Every nerve screamed, every muscle tensed, but then—it all stopped. The blows ceased, but the darkness remained. It was different now, heavier, more real, pressing in from every side like something solid. She cracked her eyes open, barely a sliver, and a harsh shard of light sliced through the shadows, cutting her vision in two.

A gasp tore from her throat, not from the pain she expected, but from the sight in front of her.

Reynnar. His body draped over hers, a shield. Every inch of him soaked up the violence meant for her, his fangs bared in a snarl. Bruises bloomed across his skin, deep purple and sickly green under the flickering light, glistening with sweat. Every hit twisted his expression, pain ravaging him, but even in the midst of it all, his eyes—*gods*, his eyes—they never left hers, cutting through everything: the pain, the chaos, the fear.

Tears burned trails down her cheeks, each one an ode to the tangled mess of sorrow, gratitude, and a deep, gnawing despair within her. In that brief, fragile moment, Elara could almost swear his heartbeat echoed against hers. But then it was ripped away as they dragged him off her.

In seconds, chains—not of iron or steel, but of writhing vines— burst forth from the ground beneath them, binding every captive in the room. With a mere gesture, Malak reclaimed dominion over the space. He could have wielded that power from the beginning, Elara realized with a jolt. They were merely toying with them, likely bored with their routine guard duties and seeking amusement by allowing the captives a glimmer of hope in a fight. Her fists clenched as she took in the smug smirks and heard the mocking cackles of the guards, even as some looked decidedly worse for wear.

"You'll bleed for that," Malak bit out. Blood smeared his sneer, dripping from his nose—broken, no doubt, by Reynnar's fist. It should've felt like a win, but any sense of triumph was strangled by the vines ensnaring her, tightening with every twitch, every breath.

Aoife's voice cut across the room. "*Bí socair nó gheobhaidh tú do bhascadh!*[25]"

Her words sounded as though she meant to guide and save. But it only fueled the panic coiling tighter inside Elara. The vines slithered like snakes, creeping higher, winding around her throat, squeezing until her breath cut off. Her vision blurred, narrowing to a tunnel, and at the end of it, a raised boot, poised like the final judge and executioner.

The last thing Elara saw before darkness claimed her wasn't the hope of rescue or a face filled with concern—it was Malak, and the boot that swung down to meet the side of her head.

CHAPTER 35

A breath stirred the shadows, warm and tender, a whisper of life against the stillness. The faintest touch followed, a brush of fingers that barely grazed Elara's skin. Her hair shifted, swept back with a touch so delicate it almost didn't feel real.

The darkness pressed close, but it wasn't threatening. It held her, soft and weightless, a quiet presence that curled through her senses. It filled the space with warmth, seeping into the cracks of her broken body. The quiet no longer seemed boundless. It did not seek to crush her under its weight. Instead, it held her.

And though she couldn't place it, couldn't fully grasp what it meant, it felt like a vow—like something was drawing near, something beyond the pain—something that would come, as if solely for her.

CHAPTER 36

The world returned to Elara in fragments. Not the sharp, piercing pain she expected, but a dull awareness, like waking from a long, dreamless sleep.

She blinked, slowly, disoriented. There should've been pain—a deep, agonizing throb that came with every breath, every twitch of her muscles. She knew she'd been beaten, should have been aching from head to toe. But there was...nothing.

Nothing but the cold. The biting chill of the floor pressed against her back, sending a numbing shiver through her body.

Her eyes fluttered open, but the light wasn't harsh, more like a distant glow seeping through her eyelids. She blinked again, sluggish, as her hands moved instinctively to her body. Her fingers traced over her clothes—clean. Unfamiliar. Her skin, scrubbed, smooth, untouched by the grime and sweat of before.

Her pulse quickened, panic flaring. Someone had *undressed* her, washed her. Changed her. While she'd been unconscious. The thought made her sick, acid rising in her throat as her breaths came faster.

She tried to move, rolling her shoulders, shifting her weight.

Everything felt... muted.

That's when it hit her—someone had given her something.

A tonic, maybe. Something to numb the pain.

Elara grimaced, pushing herself up.

"You're awake."

That voice. The low, smug drawl that made her stomach turn. Her heart kicked against her ribs as her eyes shot open, blurry shapes coming into focus. She was in the throne room, laid out like a broken offering at the base of the dais. Osin stood over her.

"You were quite the sight, lying there in the dirt," he continued, amusement lacing his voice. "Though you clean up well, I must admit. We couldn't have you meeting your fate looking so disheveled. Don't worry," Osin whispered, "I was gentle."

Elara's teeth clenched, an ache shooting through her jaw. Her gaze locked with Osin's ice-blue eyes—cold and unfeeling, like the surface of a frozen lake, dangerous in its stillness. He stood tall, dressed in pristine black, the picture of refined menace. He was every bit the monster beneath his refined veneer—a stunning, lethal creature masquerading as a gentleman.

Her pulse thrummed against the frilly lavender fabric of her gown, its surface a sea of delicate periwinkle petals and ridiculous layers of pouf and billow.

Osin's cold features softened into a polite smile, the kind that sent a chill racing down her spine. "It has come to my attention that you've engaged in some unsanctioned activities in the Pit." He raised a pale brow. "Even developed a soft spot for those . . . *things*. But what troubles me most, is that you would betray your own kind to help them."

Osin's grip was firm as he yanked Elara to her feet, her legs wobbling, the sudden movement sending a fresh wave of dizziness through her. Her eyes dropped to the ground, heart sinking when she saw them—soft satin slippers in place of her boots. A deliberate choice. So she couldn't run.

He released her, stepping back with a theatrical sigh, his expression falling into an exaggerated mask of disappointment. "It seems you've forgotten your place once again. But, fear not, I've devised the perfect reminder for you." With a casual flick of his wrist, a snap echoed through the space, and the grand iron doors flew open, unleashing a flood of Legionnaires into the room. And there, amidst the sea of uniforms, stood Dario.

Elara's eyes widened, breath caught in her throat—*no*.

"You've proven yourself untrustworthy in Verdara, and now, it seems even the Pit isn't enough to contain you. So, I pondered: What if I conscripted someone dear to you into my service? Perhaps that might encourage a more cooperative spirit." His gaze swept over her, feasting on the dread he conjured. "Judging by your reaction, it appears I was correct."

A lump rose in her throat as she met Dario's gaze. The warmth she once found in his soft brown eyes was gone—snuffed out, as if someone had stolen the light from them. His sandy-blonde hair looked dull, ashen against the cold gleam of the Legionnaire armor. An empty vessel encased in iron.

He looked away, his gaze skittering as if her stare burned.

Osin leaned in close to whisper in her ear. "Imagine the games we could play, you and I, if you simply chose to behave." His words were velvet-coated venom as his finger traced a chilling path down her throat, pausing at the fluttering of her pulse. She clamped her eyes shut. Imagined snapping his finger, twisting his arm, breaking his neck.

"You know," he continued, "it was Edgar who thought it wise to keep you away from the capital all this time." Her eyes snapped open, and his grin widened. "Though now, I'm beginning to think that was a miscalculation. Years apart have made you so difficult." He clicked his tongue. "I can't help but wonder if the priest had a part in shaping you into this disloyal little creature. And if, that had been his plan all along. Traitors," he mused, "they seem to be everywhere these days."

Rumblings through the guard pulled Osin's gaze. "Ah, yes. Ivan," he greeted with an air of delight.

The Hunter stepped out from the formation of soldiers. Though he bowed his head in deference to Osin, his eyes remained fixed on Elara.

"Forgive my lapse in manners; I should give credit where it's due." Osin placed a heavy hand on the Hunter's shoulder. "Ivan here came up with the ingenious plan to snatch the commander of the Verdaran guard right from under their noses. I thought one of the Druids might suffice, but he assured me this guard would be the one to sway you."

The words hit her like a punch to the gut, knocking the air from her lungs, stoking the fire already raging in her chest. She glared at the Hunter. *Yes*, Dario had lied. Betrayed her. The raw ache of it still fresh, but beneath the anger, there was something else. A reluctant understanding. She had done the same to Rolfe—twisted truths and bent trust to survive. It was a brutal world. Dog eat dog. She knew that better than anyone. Dario, for all his faults, had done what he had to do. And she got that. Even if it hurt. Even if the betrayal still pulsed like an open wound. The pain didn't go away, it never would, but she understood him in a way she wished she didn't have to.

Elara held her breath as Dario stepped forward and, after a moment's hesitation, sank to one knee in a gesture of fealty that twisted the knife deeper in her heart. "It is my honor to serve you, Lord Sovereign. For the realm and the ruler." His voice carried a calm resignation, but his eyes told a different story—stormy and restless beneath the surface.

The Legionnaires shouted in unison, "By Osin's command!" their voices merging into a powerful echo that filled the chamber.

"Stand, soldier," Osin said. "I have just the assignment for you."

Elara took a small step toward Dario, her fingers twitching with the need to touch him, to pull him back from whatever edge Osin was about to shove him over.

"Now, now, pet," Osin's voice chided, gesturing dismissively toward her face. "There's no need for such theatrics. Adhere to the rules, and our dear Dario won't have to suffer."

Elara's resolve faltered as she stole another glance at him—but he wasn't there. Not really. His gaze slid past her, through her, as if she didn't exist at all. As if he was already gone.

Then it hit her. Osin wasn't just trying to break *her*. He would use them all. Everyone who had ever shown her kindness. Everyone she cared about. They were his leverage.

A weapon to bend her to his will.

"My lord," the Hunter said, pausing thoughtfully. "Might I suggest another incentive for the Hallowed?"

Osin raised a brow. "Go on."

"I set out for Bravell tomorrow," the Hunter murmured, inching closer to the Lord Sovereign, "and for this venture, I find myself in need of a lure."

A hint of amusement played on Osin's lips. "Your talent for sinking to such lows never ceases to entertain." His gaze flicked to Elara. "Very well. You may use her as bait. *But,*" he added with a wave of his hand, "no marks. I'm rather fond of that face."

ELARA HUDDLED in the farthest corner of her cell, knees drawn to her chest, arms wrapped around herself as if they could form a barrier against the hell she was trapped in. Her fists clenched so tightly that her nails bit into her palms, tiny crescents of pain. *Hold it together,* whispered the last small corner of her mind that still had fight left. But the cracks were already showing, and everything was spilling through.

Where were they—Avis, Algernon?

Were they safe in Verdara, far from this nightmare? Or had Osin already plucked them from their lives, just as he had Dario? Her thoughts spiraled. Avis had said Dario ran—but *when* had Osin found him? Or had the Hunter dragged him back? Maybe even that same night. The night he'd taken her.

Gods—had Dario been in the Pit all this time?

A ragged scream escaped her clenched teeth before she could stop it. Poison—that's what she was. A curse on anyone who got too close.

They all suffered for it, bled for it, *died* for it.

Her chest heaved as she clawed at her throat, desperate to tear the ache away, to scrape off the guilt that stuck to her like tar.

"Eilíara."

Her name—spoken in that deep, familiar voice—cracked through her like a lightning strike. She turned, her curls whipping around as her eyes widened. Reynnar. He was here.

The sight of him hit her like the first breath of dawn after a long, endless night, warmth flooding her veins, chasing away the cold that had settled in her bones. He stood there, across the cell, bathed in the flickering light of a roaming orb, casting him in a soft, glowing halo. Elara's eyes swept over him, frantic, searching for any sign of injury—

anything that might say he wasn't whole. But he was... he was *okay*. Her breath caught, then released in a shaky rush, relief flooding her chest.

But then something shifted, a flicker of movement that pulled her gaze toward the tunnel. Her heart lurched as her vision cleared, revealing figures slowly taking shape in the cells across from hers. The Sidhe. *They were all here.*

A sob lodged itself in her throat. How had she not seen them before? She'd been so lost—dragged down by the crushing weight of defeat when they'd hauled her back—that she hadn't even lifted her eyes. Hadn't cared to look beyond the fog of her own grief.

The Hunter had done it. Somehow, he'd gotten them moved.

Elara blinked through the blur of tears, lifting her gaze to Reynnar. "Are you all right? Aoife, is she . . ."

She glanced outside her cell, searching for her, but his response to the name cut through the air, pulling her gaze back to him. "*Aoife,*" he uttered, "*Tá sí breá cumasach.*[26]" He then hesitated. *"Ach is eagal liom nach mairfidh a neart go deo.*[26]"

Reynnar scrubbed a harsh hand down his face before his eyes found hers again. "Tank yeh."

Elara's heart gave a small leap, the corners of her lips twitching into the faintest smile. Was he starting to pick up Latherian? The idea sent a flicker of hope she hadn't dared to feel. Maybe, just maybe, they could understand each other. Teach each other more than words, how they had ended up here—*why* they were here.

Reynnar held his hand to his chest. "*Tá mo bhuíochas ag dul duit as an mhéid atá déanta agat. Tá sé... muise, is rud faoi leith é, an cineál sin misnigh, an cineál sin crógachta a fheiceáil i nduine daonna.*[27]"

The meaning hummed through her, more feeling than sense. His voice seemed to reach into something deep, something that didn't need words. But then the moment broke when his eyes fell on her dress, drawing a snort of amusement.

"*An gúna sin ... tá tú cosúil le maisiúchán ar bharr císte.*[28]"

A twisted smile tugged at Elara's lips, a broken laugh slipping past. He was mocking her gown. It was clear in the way his eyes lingered on the absurd mess of layers she was wrapped in. Ridiculous as it was, at least it kept her warm. The thought crossed her mind to tear off a layer and offer it to him, but the risk of him being caught with it . . .

Her throat closed up.

She shouldn't be this close, shouldn't even be *speaking* to him.

It wasn't safe. *She* wasn't safe.

Elara squeezed her eyes shut. Distance. She needed distance from him. Her mere proximity was a threat to him. She should have the Hunter move her to a different cell. She would—

A jolt pulsed through her as a warmth brushed her skin and all those spinning, frantic thoughts halted. Elara's eyelids fluttered open to find Reynnar's gaze—intense, deep, filled with concern. He had breached the cold space between them, just as he did on that first day in the Pit, reaching out with a touch so surprising in its tenderness. With his thumb, he gently brushed away a tear and her heart stumbled, lagging behind her racing thoughts.

This is wrong.

She grasped his hand and pushed it back, distancing herself as she shook her head. "Being near me, caring for me—it's a curse, Reynnar. You have to stay away. If they hurt you," her voice splintered, "I couldn't *bear* it."

Reynnar went unnervingly still, as if he'd stopped breathing. Her skin prickled, the reminder of his otherworldly nature slamming into her—an aspect she'd somehow managed to overlook after everything they'd gone through. His gaze skimmed her features, delving deep, seeking truths hidden within her countenance. Then, as if breaking from a spell, he came alive, every line and angle of his face sharpening into something decidedly formidable.

"*Stad.*[29]" Reynnar shook his head. "*Ná lig dóibh do bhriseadh.*[29]" He stepped closer, the light catching the golden specks in his eyes. "*I mo thír dhúchais, agus duine i bpian, ní thréigtear iad chun soláthar dóibh féin. A muintir féin a choinníonn iad, a thugann aire dóibh.*[29]" He gestured to the surrounding cells. "*Agus más olc maith leat é, a Eilíara, sin atá ionam anois. Atá ionainn. Muide do mhuintir.*[29]"

Reynnar's hand slipped into his pocket, and when it emerged, her necklace dangled from his fingers. The bloodstone caught the dim light, glinting like a drop of fire. Elara's heart stuttered, the air leaving her lungs. She must've lost it in the chaos of the riot. And he'd found it. He'd grabbed it for her.

Without a word, he extended it through the iron bars and returned it to her. Before she could even muster a thank-you, he turned and scooped up the sorry scraps of fabric from his cot, bringing them back to lay against the bars with a soft scrape of metal. Then he stretched out, settling easily, muscles flexing in an inadvertent display of strength before he rested his head on his arms.

A wide grin broke across his face, aimed at her. How he could still smile after everything was beyond her.

"*Goitse.*[30]" He motioned toward her own cot. "*Bíodh an diabhal acu agus ag an mhéid a raibh siad ag súil leis.*[30]"

Elara wrinkled her nose. Was he suggesting she sleep next to these bars, right beside him? His gaze lifted, full of expectation. *Yes, that's exactly what he wants.* She bit her lip, conflicted. Keeping her distance was the smart choice—but the way he looked at her, with that unflinching, brazen strength, made her hesitate. He had become her backbone in this nightmare, a pillar of stubborn resilience. And she didn't want him to think she was weak. She couldn't stand the thought of faltering in his eyes.

A small smile tugged at her lips as she turned, her heart thudding in her chest like the sea crashing against the cliffs of Aewora. Every beat seemed to echo through the cold stone of her cell, matching her steps as she crossed the distance. She grabbed the thin, worn blanket and the pillow that had offered little comfort, pulling them toward the bars with a quiet sense of purpose.

She placed the pillow down, its edge brushing the cold metal, then laid herself along the line that separated her from Reynnar. The chill of the stone beneath her faded as she exhaled, her gaze drifting to meet his. And in that moment, the world outside their prison ceased to exist.

Reynnar's smile grew as he relaxed further into his makeshift bedding, an image of contented triumph. Then, in a move that caught Elara completely off guard, his voice rose in a song.

His tone was neither soft nor soothing, but powerful and rallying— a warrior's chant.

Like a beacon in the darkest night, it cut through the heavy gloom of the Pit, deep and commanding, as effortlessly as dawn scatters shadow.

Elara couldn't look away, captivated by the fervor with which he infused each note, his soul baring itself in a melody that resonated with the clash of steel and the undying spirit of a survivor. With each line, his fist struck the earth, sending a rhythm through the ground that felt like a drumbeat calling to stand, to fight, to *remember*.

The sound was magnetic, pulling the scattered spirits of the Sidhe into alignment. The stagnant air of the Pit pulsed as, one by one, the prisoners' voices joined Reynnar's, rising together in answer to his call.

CHAPTER 37

"*Súile*," Reynnar said slowly, the syllables rolling off his tongue like a spell, each sound rich with his lilting accent.

"Soo-luh," Elara echoed, trying to mimic the way his voice shaped the foreign word. His fingers—long and broad—reached through the bars, a featherlight touch that grazed the skin just beneath her eyes. Her cheeks flushed in response, heart stumbling over itself.

"Eyes," she whispered, her own fingers following the trail he had traced moments before.

"Iyees," he repeated, the syllables awkward on his tongue. His mouth curved into that familiar fanged grin, a low chuckle rumbling from his chest. It softened the sharp lines of his shadowed face—and before she knew it, a laugh slipped from her too, unbidden but easy in his presence.

She'd never heard him laugh before. It was like nothing she expected —a rich, warm sound that broke through the lifeless air of the prison, a symphony cutting through the silence. The kind of sound that made her want to wrap it up, keep it safe, hold onto it like something precious. It was the only thing that felt real, and she ached to hear it again, to bask in its warmth, if only for a moment longer.

His eyes locked onto hers, burning with a fervor she could almost feel—a tenderness she'd never been on the receiving end of. Reynnar's lips parted, the beginnings of a word forming before the all too familiar noise of the approaching guards reverberated through the cavern. But instead of the anticipated guard bearing the day's scant offering, it was the Hunter. The door to her cell swung open with a clang, announcing his presence before he leaned against the frame as if he belonged there.

"Morning," he grumbled, his voice scratchy with the grit of disuse, as though the act of speaking had just awoken along with him.

Elara pushed herself up from the floor, her eyes narrowing. The memory of his announcement to Osin—that she was to be used as *bait*, what he had done to Dario—still burned fresh in her mind. She could still taste the bitterness of it, even as the grudging reminder of what he had done for the Sidhe tried to temper it. But she wouldn't thank him. She'd kept her end of the deal. Now it was his turn to finish his.

"What, no jabbing remarks for me today? I'm almost disappointed." He crossed the threshold into her cell but then stopped as Reynnar rose from the ground, standing tall beside her.

The Hunter's jaw twitched. "Still making friends on the wrong side of the bars, I see." His gaze flicked between Reynnar and her.

"I want to see Godfrey."

"You will," he said, and as the words left his mouth, the necklace against her chest began to warm, heat spreading like a promise. "But not today," he continued, his eyes shifting toward the door, scanning the corridor beyond. "He's not here. Osin moved him to another location. He should be back within the next few weeks."

Elara's temple throbbed, the steady pulse of frustration building behind her eyes. "Why was he moved?"

"Not here."

Elara clenched her teeth, willing herself not to explode, even though the urge to rip into him was almost unbearable. She arched a brow. "What now? Come to take me away as bait on your little mission? Or are you here to apologize for what you did to Dario."

The Hunter looked infuriatingly unbothered as ever. "Leveraging your friend was a strategic move. It distracts Osin, even if just temporarily. He won't see any action. Not yet."

"Oh, how considerate of you," Elara shot back. "I'm sure Dario will be thrilled to hear his life's been turned into a *strategic* move."

His lips twitched, but he stayed silent, watching her with that unreadable expression that made her want to punch him. Or scream. Maybe both.

She pressed her lips together, biting back the questions that gnawed at her. Why hadn't he rifted into her cell after the riot? Why hadn't he sent a note? Done *something*? Not that it mattered. Not that she cared. And gods, the last thing she wanted was for him to think she thought he cared. Which, of course, he didn't.

Elara cleared her throat, forcing herself to look anywhere but at him. "Why are you here, then?"

He stepped closer, close enough that she could catch the faint scent of clove clinging to him. Her spine stiffened, and she felt Reynnar shift slightly beside her.

"I'm taking you to my home," he murmured, his voice low enough that only she could hear. "There's something you need to see. We've got a few days while Osin thinks we're off running his errand."

She blinked, momentarily stunned by the sheer audacity. "*Your* home?" A bitter laugh slipped from her lips as she shook her head. There was a time when the idea of following the Hunter anywhere would've been laughable, unthinkable. But now? Now the weight of his oath, the binding promise between them, pulsed against her chest like a silent contract. "I'm guessing this is less of an invitation and more of a 'do as I say or else' kind of deal?"

His eyes glinted. "You really do catch on quick, don't you?"

Elara shot him a glare before turning to Reynnar, her heart squeezing painfully as her eyes met his through the iron bars. Everything—every fear, every unspoken thought—seemed to hang in the air between them. "I'm okay," she murmured, though her voice wavered. "And I'm coming back." The words felt too thin, too fragile, like they could break apart before they even reached him. But gods, she needed him to feel it—to understand that she meant it, even if she wasn't sure herself.

Her hand slipped between the bars, her fingers brushing against his. Warm, steady. Grounding. She gave his hand a gentle squeeze but when she moved to pull away, Reynnar's grip tightened, his fingers curling around hers, keeping her in place.

"Seachain tú féin air siúd. Ní nochtaíonn an daonnaí sin a rún ach rud éigin géar a bheith sa lámh aige.[31]"

~

"ARE WE NEARLY THERE?" Elara's voice carried through the wind, her fingers curled into fists at her sides, not just from the cold, but from the irritation of shouting into the howling air, knowing full well she wouldn't get an answer. Not even a glance over his shoulder.

She gritted her teeth, squaring her shoulders against both the biting wind and the maddening figure ahead of her. Each step felt like a battle, but something inside her refused to back down. Stubbornness, or maybe pure spite, drove her to match his pace.

He'd rifted them into this frozen wasteland, muttering something about how his wards required anyone entering his land to walk the rest of the way. Sure, it made sense in a strategic, paranoid kind of way. But after what felt like miles of trekking through ice-covered woods, she couldn't help but wonder if this was some sort of punishment. Though she wasn't sure what she'd done to deserve it.

From the moment they'd left her cell, he'd changed. He'd been easygoing before—*teasing*, even—a concept she still couldn't fully wrap her mind around. Then, without warning, he'd drawn back into himself, shutting her out.

She wasn't sure what to make of it.

"You know, a little conversation might make this torture marginally more bearable. Unless you're trying to freeze me into submission."

Still nothing.

She huffed, her breath forming a cloud in the air. And just when she thought the cold might finally break her—numbing her fingers, her toes, and every bit of her resolve—the forest thinned, the trees pulling back to reveal something entirely unexpected.

There, rising out of the vast wilderness like some forgotten relic, sat a manor. Dark, imposing, and completely at odds with the untamed landscape, it stood there like a rose in a field of thorns. Eerie and beautiful all at once.

Elara's gaze drifted over the dark stone spires, reaching up toward the heavens, clawing at the gray sky. Thick, gnarled vines wove through the cracks in the windows—inching toward the chimneys like they were determined to reclaim every inch of the place. The tall, arched windows, caked in dust, offered no warmth, only a reflection of the frozen world outside. As they approached a wrought iron gate, rusted and twisted, groaned with every gust of wind, as if to say, *turn back now, if you have any sense.*

This was his home?

She couldn't imagine anyone calling this place home, though, considering her own situation—*a cell*—maybe she wasn't in any position to judge.

Elara shot him a sidelong glance as they passed through the iron gates, the crunch of the dirt path under her boots the only sound between them. Had this been his family home? Had he really managed to keep it after all this time?

The moment she crossed the threshold into the manor, the biting wind ceased, but the air inside offered no warmth in its place. It was stifling, thick with the scent of age and neglect. Inside, the manor felt like it had been plucked from another time—once grand and imposing, now slowly rotting.

The ceilings still soared high above, but the chandeliers hung dim, their crystals muted and blanketed in webs. Beneath her boots, the wooden floors creaked, worn and uneven. The burgundy velvet chairs, arranged in a too-perfect circle around a baroque fireplace, had long since lost their luster, their fabric faded and threadbare. Despite the suggestion of warmth, the whole place exuded a stillness—an unsettling, creeping quiet that clung to the air like a bad memory.

The Hunter cleared his throat, breaking the silence, and Elara's gaze snapped to him. He looked tense, more so than usual. "The library's this way," he muttered, nodding toward a shadowy hallway before striding ahead.

She hurried after him, boots tapping. He stopped without warning, and she nearly collided with him. He rubbed the back of his neck, stiff and uncertain.

"Are you hungry?"

"Uh, yeah," she said, her voice betraying her surprise. *Always* hungry. The nagging ache had become a constant companion ever since she'd been thrown into that cell.

His shoulders tensed, and he shifted his weight from one foot to the other. "I don't have any food."

"Oh." *Does he not eat?*

A beat of silence.

"I'll get you some. After."

"Okay, thanks," she said, unsure of what else to say.

He dipped his chin and without another word, they continued down the long, decrepit hallway. Doors lined the walls, each one leading to rooms she mentally cataloged—parlor, drawing room, something else probably equally fancy and equally dusty. Too many rooms for one person, but all of them bore the same story: a place forgotten by time, abandoned to its own decay. The kitchens, when they passed by, looked like they hadn't seen food—or a living soul—in years.

Finally, the hallway opened up into a large receiving room. At the far end stood a set of tall wooden doors. The Hunter stepped ahead, pushing them open, and the moment they swung wide, Elara's breath caught in her throat.

It was a library—yes, but not just any library. This was a cathedral, a holy place dedicated not to gods but to knowledge. Books—*so many books*—surrounded her, immense shelves of them curving around the room in a circle, rising like mountains. Between them, floor-to-ceiling windows arched gracefully into a magnificent stained-glass dome.

The light filtering through painted the floor in a kaleidoscope of colors—gold, blue, and ruby that shifted with each cloud passing overhead.

She moved slowly, reverently, her steps soft on the marble floor, afraid to disturb the hush. It was like stepping into a painting, one of those grand scenes from an old master where everything was still and perfect and awash in light. And as she walked, the colors danced across her skin, played in her hair. Elara felt something awaken inside her—a wild, keen joy mixed with an insatiable hunger to devour every page in this temple.

From where she stood, she could already tell this room was overflowing with texts she'd never been allowed to read, let alone touch. They practically hummed with possibility. Not like the carefully censored collection she'd been granted back in Verdara.

A thrill shot through her, the kind of excitement that only came from the idea of getting her hands on something she shouldn't have access to.

"You're drooling," his voice was low, laced with dry amusement.

"I'm not," she shot back, though she discreetly wiped her mouth just in case.

The Hunter arched a brow, the barest hint of a smirk pulling at his lips, his brooding mood evaporating as if it had never been there. "*Right*. If I wasn't standing here, you'd be rolling around in those stacks like a puppy."

Elara lifted her chin, giving him her best unimpressed stare. "Just because you probably use these books as doorstops doesn't mean I won't treat them with respect."

He gave her a strange look, the hint of a frown creasing his brow before he turned away, sauntering deeper into the library. He made his way to the massive desk in the center of the room, lazily clearing away a pile of scrolls with a careless wave of his hand, like they were nothing more than discarded scraps. Typical.

She drummed her fingers against her side, trying desperately to focus on something, anything, other than him. Her gaze landed on a portrait resting on the corner of his desk, drawing her in before she could stop herself.

"Your family?"

Out of the corner of her eye, she saw him stiffen—just a fraction, but it was enough to confirm what she already suspected.

In the painting, a striking woman with silver hair that fell like a waterfall stood beside a man whose deep mahogany skin contrasted sharply with his vivid eyes—one a blazing blue, the other a deep brown. Two young boys flanked them. The older one, even as a child, had the same sharp cheekbones and mismatched eyes that marked him unmistakably as a young Thane. His features were so distinct, so familiar, and Elara had to force herself to shove down the surge of memories that threatened to rise to the surface.

She glanced back at the Hunter, his gaze still fixed on the portrait, as though he was a thousand miles away.

"I didn't see Thane in the Pit."

It wasn't a question. Not really.

Without sparing her a glance, he replied, "That's because he isn't in the Pit."

Elara fiddled with the fabric of her dress, turning his words over in her mind. She hadn't actually believed Thane was there—rumors had been swirling for ages that he'd been banished. But something about that answer didn't sit right with her. If he'd been cast out, where had he gone? The question burned on her tongue, but she swallowed it, deciding to stick to something less... volatile.

"And your parents?"

The shift was immediate, like a wire pulled taut. His shoulders drew back, eyes darkening as they locked onto hers, anger rolling off him. "Let's get one thing straight." He bit out the words. "Being in my home doesn't give you the right to dig into my past. Stay out of what doesn't concern you... unless it's directly related to our work."

He hadn't flinched when she asked about Thane, hadn't even batted an eye. But his parents, it seemed, were off limits. *Huh.*

"Fine," she muttered, crossing her arms, more curious now than ever.

His nostrils flared as he exhaled sharply. "Good."

She arched a brow. "By *'work'* do you mean to say you've found a way to sever the *Draoth Cara* or are we researching different options?" Her fingers twitched, aching to reach for the nearest book, but she forced herself to stay still.

He studied her for a beat, clearly debating something, then spoke quietly. "Come here."

Her guard shot up immediately, but she forced herself to move forward. The moment she neared the desk, her breath hitched. He was holding *the* book—*the* tome Osin had handed him. The title stared back at her: *Transcendental Bonds*. Bold. Ominous. Her fingers twitched again, nerves prickling beneath her skin.

"Two and a half seals are on you," he said, voice flat and matter-of-fact. Elara's gaze snapped to his, confusion and something like alarm flaring in her chest. "I'm going to break my half. See if it helps."

Her throat tightened. "Why?"

He hesitated for a beat, glancing away before he muttered, "It might help dampen the *Draoth Cara*. Or at least make it more bearable."

She narrowed her eyes, nodding slowly. Sure, it made sense, but something in the air felt charged now, heavier than before. "Right," she said carefully, "But won't Osin notice?"

He shook his head. "Not unless he digs into it himself, which he won't. He trusts me enough not to question it."

"Okay." She reached for the book, half-expected him to pull it away, to stop her, but he didn't. Her fingers brushed the worn cover. "What does severing your half entail?"

The Hunter moved closer and Elara's heart thumped an extra beat. He didn't say anything at first, just opened the book, his fingers flipping through the brittle pages until he landed somewhere in the middle.

He dipped his head as if to say *'go on'* and Elara scooted closer, reading.

The act of severing an Echoing Seal is no less treacherous than the creation of one. Unlike the initial application of the seal, which involves carefully weaving layers of resonance to suppress ethereal power, the act of breaking such a seal is far less precise and considerably more hazardous. To understand the inherent risks, one must first comprehend the nature of the Echoing Seal itself—a construct that reflects and restrains power through harmonic resonance, tethering the energy not only to the self but to the binder's will.

An Echoing Seal functions as a constant, echoing suppression—a feedback loop of ethereal energy that mirrors and dampens the bound power's natural state. Over time, this resonance becomes deeply ingrained, almost symbiotic in nature, making its removal akin to tearing apart the very fabric of one's soul. Severing the seal, therefore, is not merely the destruction of a bond but the destabilization of an intricate system designed to regulate and control volatile energy.

The primary danger in breaking such a seal lies in the unpredictability of the power it contains. Power, once constrained, does not dissipate; rather, it accumulates, often in unpredictable ways. Upon the removal of an Echoing Seal, this repressed energy may not return to its prior, dormant state but instead may surge uncontrollably. The power, having been forcibly muted for an extended period, can manifest violently, presenting a significant risk of cognitive, emotional, and even physical destabilization. The consequences of such a release may range from the fragmentation of the wielder's consciousness to a complete dissolution of their ethereal cohesion.

Elara couldn't take it anymore. With a sharp snap, she slammed the book shut, the sound echoing through the room. "Isn't there an easier way to get us both killed?" She threw him an exaggerated glance, pretending to peer under his cloak. "Why not just pull out that shiny weapon of yours and slit our throats now? It'd save us a lot of trouble."

"Keep going."

Elara huffed, rolling her eyes, but she flipped the book open again.

Nevertheless, while fraught with danger, the severance of an Echoing Seal is not without potential success. The key to this process lies in resonance—specifically, in matching the frequency of the captive power. A practitioner seeking to sever the seal must first attune themselves to the ethereal signature of the bound power, identifying the exact moment when the resonance between the power and the seal is at its most fragile. At this point, with sufficient precision, the seal may be broken without catastrophic consequences. However, the margin for error is exceedingly narrow, and failure to act swiftly can result in the uncontrolled release of energy.

It is important to emphasize that even successful severance carries inherent risks. The power, once unbound, may not return to a manageable form. In many cases, it becomes erratic, difficult to wield, and may fundamentally alter the nature of the individual from whom it has been released. Moreover, the psychological toll of such an experience cannot be overstated. The sudden reintegration of previously suppressed energy can lead to profound disorientation, hallucinations, and a distorted sense of self.

Her laugh rang out, brittle and edged with something close to hysteria. "Was reading the rest of it supposed to make me feel better?"

"It should,"" he replied coolly, his eyes never leaving hers. "The Binding Sigil can be undone."

Undone. The word pulsed in her mind like a heartbeat. She dragged a hand through her unruly curls, trying to steady herself. "Yes," she whispered, "but not without *considerable* risk."

He raised a brow. "Since when have you shied away from a challenge?"

Elara crossed her arms. "Since 'significant risk of cognitive, emotional, and even physical destabilization' became part of the equation. And it doesn't make sense," she continued, words tumbling out in a rush. "When I was with Dom—" She caught herself, biting down on the name. "When I was with *them*—the people you took me away from —they just cut the seal off Dario."

The Hunter shook his head. "It doesn't work like that. They must have been misled." He tapped the ancient tome. "This copy of *Transcendental Bonds* is likely the last of its kind. The rest were destroyed at the beginning of the war."

Elara narrowed her eyes. "And Osin just handed it to you?"

"I told you. He trusts me."

"Funny," she muttered, "because I don't."

He met her gaze, unflinching. "You don't need to trust me. Trust the *facts*." His chin jerked toward the book. "This isn't rumor or legend. It's the original text—the truth."

She almost snorted. He spoke with such conviction as if the truth wasn't just some shapeless thing people twisted to fit their stories.

"Even if this is the last copy," Elara said slowly, "and even if what you're saying is true—what makes you think it'll work for me?"

"Because you're different," he replied, something flickering in his eyes. "And so am I."

Different. The word lingered. Heavy. Loaded. It pressed against her chest, filling the space with a thousand unspoken questions she wasn't sure how to put into words. Her gaze drifted back to him, searching his face for something—anything—that could explain what he wasn't saying.

"Why help me?"

"I told you, it will dampen the *Draoth Cara* and—"

"Maybe that's true," she cut him off, her gaze piercing. "But it's not the full truth."

He went still. Not a muscle moved, not a breath out of place. But she felt it—the way his pulse seemed to quicken beneath the surface. He kept his expression neutral, but there was something sharp beneath it, something coiled tight and dangerous. His story didn't add up. Sure, it had to annoy him that she could squeeze his pulse with a mere thought, twist his nerves whenever she wished. A glaring weakness for someone like him. But that wasn't all. It couldn't be.

"You deceived your lord," she continued, stepping closer. "You claimed he trusts you, yet here you stand, exploiting that trust to work behind his back. All to sever the thread between us—a thread I still do not fully understand." Her gaze hardened. "This is treason. The very thing you denounced when it involved Fenlin, when it concerned the Script Keepers. And now you commit it yourself. Why not bring this matter to Osin himself? You are his most loyal, are you not? Surely, he would aid you. And yet, you hide it. Why?"

The Hunter held her gaze, unblinking, but the silence that followed felt charged. "You're pushing into things you shouldn't," he said quietly, almost too calmly.

Her pulse spiked. "Tell me *why*."

"Does it matter? If it gets the job done, why should the reason behind it make a difference?"

"The *why* always matters," she hissed, stepping closer.

He breathed out slowly. "This isn't about morality, Hallowed. It's about survival."

Her lips curled into a cold smile. "Spoken like someone who's willing to justify anything to get what he wants."

"Believe it or not, I'm trying to help you." His voice dropped lower, that dangerous edge creeping back in. "And if you keep digging, you might not like what you find."

"Oh, I'm sure I won't. But you don't get to decide what I do with the truth." Her fingers brushed the necklace against her skin and her heart kicked into high gear. "I demand you tell me the truth as part of your oath."

A rush of heat flared against her chest, and she saw it—the brief flicker of resistance in his eyes as the compulsion hit. His whole body seemed to lock up, muscles taut, and he shook his head like he was trying to force it off, trying to fight it.

"You're really going to waste one of the questions on *this*?"

She gave a single nod.

He exhaled sharply, his eyes darkening. "I don't just want to break my seal. I want you free. From everyone."

The air seemed to vanish, her breath stalling in her chest. *Free*? The word slammed into her, each syllable sinking deep, dragging her down like a riptide pulling her under.

"You mean to break the Binding Sigil completely?" She shook her head, her mind reeling, disbelief warring with a wild, desperate hope. "*Why*? Why would you help me with this?"

His jaw worked, but when he spoke, it was like every word was being torn out of him. "Because I need something from you, too."

Of course. There was always a catch. Always a price. She swallowed, her throat suddenly dry. "And what is it you need from me?"

"My brother." The words scraped from him through clenched teeth. "I need your help to save my brother."

CHAPTER 38

"You want me to help you save the person who *tried to kill me*?"

"Yes."

The Hunter stood before her, shoulders rigid, muscles coiled tight. Every inch of him was braced for the inevitable conflict, but something in his stance had shifted—he wasn't resisting the compulsion anymore. The weight of the oath no longer tethered him.

Elara's heart lurched, a cutting, painful jolt. She had just wasted all three questions. *Curse me and my absolute inability to mind my own business.*

But... even after her last question, the one that didn't count, he had still answered, *"Yes."* An honest answer, freely given, despite no longer being bound by the oath. Just like all those months ago, after Fenlin's murder. Honest, even when he didn't owe her anything. He might still answer, if she framed it right—if she hit the right nerve.

"Were you going to tell me at some point, or just hope I didn't notice until it was too late?"

He didn't flinch, didn't even blink.

She let out a dull, humorless laugh. "You've lost your mind."

"You knew him."

Her body went still, cold creeping up her spine. "What?"

"You were... close. In a way."

Close? She couldn't form a response before he turned away, striding toward a large, weathered cabinet tucked between two towering bookshelves. She watched, frozen, as his fingers traced over the runes carved into the wood, dismantling the wards that layered thickly over the cabinet—wards that seemed as strong, if not stronger, than the ones that had trapped her in her cell.

With a quiet creak, the cabinet door swung open, and he pulled out a thick stack of scrolls and loose parchment, all tied together with a fraying piece of string. Dust motes danced in the low light as he held the bundle, hesitating for just a moment, his eyes flicking to hers.

"You want answers?" His voice was low, tightly controlled. "It starts with the shade. The one who named you *Tuatha.*"

Elara's fingers curled into the fabric of her dress. *Tuatha.* The word slithered through her mind, dragging up the memory. She hadn't realized the shade had called her anything. In that moment, she'd been too focused on its fangs to notice much else. But *Caelion...* he had called Reynnar the same thing.

"What does it mean?"

He shook his head, eyes hard with frustration. "I don't know. I've been searching for answers. But you have to understand—shades are mindless. Spirits of death. No thought, no will. They're perfect weapons. They don't tire, they don't bleed, and they obey Osin without question." His face hardened. "But that one... it spoke. A fragment of its soul clawed its way to the surface, just enough to break through. Enough to speak to you."

She shivered, pulling her arms tighter around herself. "What are they?" She pressed her lips together, thinking. "I spent nearly my entire childhood reading about the spirits, but I've never come across any mention of shades." Her brow furrowed. "It doesn't make sense. There should be something—a record, a trace of their existence. Spirits like that don't just appear out of nowhere. Not without someone knowing."

"You wouldn't have heard of them. They're something new. A species Osin created... twisted through his experiments."

Elara's heart plummeted, the world tilting as a cold, hollow ache settled in her chest. The answer she didn't want but had feared all along. *The extraction. The trials.* Bile surged up, burning the back of her throat as she fought to steady her breath. Her voice cracked. "He's turning the Sidhe into those...things. Why?"

"Vredia," he said simply. "It's the last stronghold Osin hasn't claimed. He's been trying to break through the Northern Ridge for years. But the ridge is enchanted—old *Draoth* from the Mothers, from Epona herself. Her love for the Sidhe... it's woven into those mountains, blocking his armies at every turn. His men get lost—or never return. So, he sends the Sidhe, mutated into those things, hoping they'll succeed where his soldiers can't."

Elara pressed her trembling hand to her mouth. "How is Osin stealing the Sidhe in the first place? I've been trying to figure it out. Is it the Aelfhenge?"

He dipped his chin. "Yes. But it's not as simple as that. After the shade spoke... after the *Draoth Cara* revealed itself, I began hunting them down. Capturing them. Tried to force answers from them." He let out a harsh breath. "It was a fool's errand. But every time, they reacted to one word—*Tuatha*. So, I dug deeper. Pored over old records, traveled to places that kept their histories hidden before the war burned it all away."

"Bravell."

He gave a low hum of agreement. "The kingdom's little more than a graveyard now. When that led nowhere, I shifted my focus to the source of the destruction. To Osin." He lifted the bundle of scrolls. "This... this is what I found. Hidden, warded under curses so thick it took me days to unravel. And even then..." He cleared his throat, his voice dropping, almost hesitant. "It belonged to you."

Elara's brow furrowed, and she moved toward him, feeling as if her body was wading through water, slow and disconnected. The rough texture of the parchment barely registered under her fingertips as she took the stack and moved to the desk. With a tug, the fraying string snapped, and the scrolls spilled across the surface, scattering in every direction.

Drawings. Detailed sketches. Diagrams layered with strange, looping symbols. Notes scribbled in the margins with a frenzied hand. At the bottom of the pile, half-hidden between loose sketches, lay a journal. The leather cover was cracked, weathered. Her fingers hovered over the cover, an instinctive hesitation pulling her back. The energy around it felt... wrong.

"What is all of this?"

The Hunter moved beside her, his gaze flicking over the chaotic mess of papers. He picked up a drawing—a series of overlapping circles, strange symbols lining the edges. "Your research on the Void."

"*My* research?"

He nodded. "Yours and Thanes."

She blinked, once, twice, as if the world around her had just shifted and left her stranded.

They had been researching the Void? She swallowed hard, her gaze flicking over the scattered documents—rituals, symbols drawn in blood. But this wasn't just abstract theory. Her eyes caught on a sketch—a map, twisted and spiraling, trying to chart the layers of the Void. Each line pulled inward, toward a central point, like a gravitational well of shifting currents. Notes beside it theorized about the Void's power to consume energy, bend time, and manipulate space. Arrows circled pathways that led to nowhere, hypotheses scribbled in frantic handwriting. This wasn't research—it was *obsession*.

Elara flipped open the journal, the old leather creaking, and froze. A name—*her* name—written in her own handwriting. She stared, fingers gripping the edges of the paper. The letters, the curve of each stroke—undeniably hers. But the memory... it wasn't there. No flicker of recognition, no trace tugging at her thoughts. Just... nothing.

Her fingers trembled as they traced the ink, the sensation unsettling, like staring at a ghost of herself. She flipped through the pages, revealing diagrams layered with complex equations and symbols spiraling into vortexes, all centered on how the Void served as a bridge between realms. The notes weren't just about the Void—they focused on the spaces between, places never meant to be reached. They had been testing it— how to control the flow, manipulate the pull between worlds, even disrupt the fabric of reality itself. It required more than just ether; it demanded an understanding of how to bend one world's pull into another without collapsing them both.

She had even outlined theories on using the Aelfhenge as a focal point. Equations charted the flux, calculating the exact moment to force a tear, positioning the rift directly at the heart of the stones.

It was methodical. Exacting. Terrifying in its brilliance.

And yet, she didn't remember writing any of it.

A cold dread crept up her spine as she found a detailed list filled with dates, notes on strange experiments—testing the Void's impact on memory. *Her memory.*

Elara's pulse quickened, the ink blurring as her heart raced.

They hadn't just been studying the Void. They had been testing their theories on her. Trying to break through it, to cross the boundaries between dimensions, to use the Void as a doorway. And she had been their key.

The keystone.

The word was scribbled, circled multiple times in what must have been Thane's handwriting. But no explanation, no context. Just that one word. Her hands shook as she stared at it. A flood of emotions rushed through her, her throat tightening. She glanced up at the Hunter. "This is why he tried to kill me."

His brow furrowed as he studied her. "I think so, yes. Hard to say for certain. The notes are vague, but from what I've pieced together..." He shifted his stance, arms crossing over his chest. "You tested a theory. You entered the Void, and when you returned, you lost your memories. Perhaps all of them. Thane might have believed sending you back was the only way to recover what you'd lost. But that part of his research is gone."

Elara blinked, trying to process the rush of information. "Gone?"

"Osin." The Hunter's voice was hard, clipped, as he flipped to the back of the journal, revealing torn pages, entire sections ripped clean from the spine. "He either destroyed the rest or hid it away. I've been trying to complete the equations, but I keep hitting dead ends."

He sank into the chair at his desk, rubbing a rough hand over his face. His shoulders sagged, weighed down by more than just exhaustion. He'd always seemed so unbreakable to Elara, but now... sitting there, he looked bled dry.

"I wasn't... I didn't think it right to tell you."

"How long have you known?"

His lips thinned. "Not long."

Her gaze lingered a second too long, and as if sensing it, he glanced up, catching her eye before pulling something from his pocket. A small piece of parchment. The edges were frayed, the paper itself weathered and fragile, as if it had been folded and unfolded a hundred times. Like he carried it with him everywhere. For years.

"I found this," he said, his voice softer than she'd ever heard it. "The night Thane tried to kill you. It was in his room."

He held it out to her, and for a moment, Elara hesitated. Almost afraid to read the truth it held. Her fingers brushed the worn edges as she gently unfolded it, heart hammering in her chest.

What the Void consumes, only death can retrieve.

"I didn't know. I didn't know what the two of you were caught up in. All I had was this note. I'd seen him, sneaking around, watching you at court." He paused, shaking his head, bitterness flashing in his eyes. "It read like the ravings of a madman. And Thane... my brother. He was always different. I thought he'd lost his mind, dragged you into it with him. I thought I was saving you both." A harsh, hollow laugh escaped him. "But instead, I damned us all."

She could barely breathe through the lump in her throat, but she forced the words out. "So, what do we do now?"

Her question seemed to bring a bit of life back into his eyes. "Back when you lived in Arinthel, there was only one seal on you. You and Thane... you were trying to figure out how to remove it. Along with the rest of your experiments. But you couldn't do it. You didn't have *Transcendental Bonds*. I think if we break the Binding Sigil now, it could trigger something—maybe help you recover your memories."

Elara nodded, her mind spinning with the possibilities. But then she hesitated, brow furrowing. "You said you needed my help... to save Thane."

He nodded again, but she could feel the weight of what he wasn't saying yet.

"What happened to him?"

The Hunter leaned forward, bracing his hands on his knees, eyes locked on hers. "After he tried to kill you..." He shook his head, as if the thought itself was too absurd to entertain. "When Osin found out what he had done—and *why*... he used the research you both had uncovered. Opened the channels, the currents, and trapped Thane inside."

CHAPTER 39

She had a room in his house.

A room he made up just for her.

The rest of the Hunter's manor seemed to be crumbling, time wearing away at every corner. But Elara's room—*this* room—was different. It was as though someone had taken great care to preserve it. The furniture, though battered and bruised, had been scrubbed clean, and the bed was made with fresh linens, not a speck of dust in sight. Elegant curtains hung from the posts of the four-poster bed, swaying ever so slightly in the breeze that slipped through the cracks of the old walls.

Her gaze drifted to the balcony, where dying ivy clung desperately to the railing, weaving in and out of the wrought iron. Elara froze when she saw a lake. She hadn't noticed it when she first arrived, hidden behind the manor's twisted architecture, but there it was now, gleaming in the distance. But what truly made her pause was the private bathing chamber tucked away in the corner of the room. Pristine, untouched, like a hidden gift.

For a moment, she just stood there, completely at a loss. It all felt like she'd stepped into an alternate reality, one that didn't match the life she knew. The entire day had felt like that, pulling her further from any sense of solid ground.

She couldn't wrap her mind around it.

Couldn't find her footing.

After discovering that she and Thane had been research partners—of all things—and that he had tried to kill her as part of a perverse attempt to restore her memories, Elara realized that something that had defined her, shaped her entire life, wasn't what she thought it was.

They had been close. Studied together, obsessed over the Void, and its potential for transport. But what had sparked that obsession? There was nothing in their notes about how it all began. No clue as to what had brought them together under the same goal.

Had they known about Osin's experiments with the Sidhe? Had that driven them? Or was it something else entirely? She didn't have the answers—not yet. And until her memories returned, she never would. But now, she knew something more. Her theory—that with each death, a memory returned—wasn't just a wild guess. It had been confirmed, backed by what she'd uncovered. And for the first time in so long, it felt good to have that kind of validation, to know she wasn't losing her mind. She hadn't imagined it. She wasn't just grasping at straws. The truth was twisted and terrible, but it was real. Like a piece of the puzzle had finally fallen into place. A small, fragile piece, but still something. It was more than she'd had before.

"I thought I was saving you both. But instead, I damned us all."

Elara rubbed her temples. The Hunter blamed *himself.* That didn't align with everything she'd built her perception of him on. She'd always assumed he resented her, that beneath his stoic demeanor was a deep well of hatred directed at her—for what had happened, for what he had lost.

She'd spent so much time believing he held *her* responsible for his pain.

Her thoughts churned, unraveling years of carefully constructed walls and assumptions. Every interaction between them, every heated word, every cold stare—she had thought it all pointed to blame. And now with one sentence, he had undone that entire narrative.

It was almost impossible to reconcile. So many memories, so many conversations that she now had to sift through and dissect with fresh eyes.

Elara wandered further into the room, aimless. The pounding in her head insisted she close her eyes, begged her to rest, but the weight of the day refused to let her. She and the Hunter had spent hours poring over her old research, sifting through dusty notes on *The Sundering*—the ritual to break the Binding Sigil. He had sat beside her mostly in silence, only speaking when she asked him a question, offering concise, measured answers. But none of it had clicked. Not in the way she needed it to.

In her mind, the Void had always been just space between spaces—a shortcut, a pathway people once used to travel. But if she had learned something in the capital—if she had *seen* something—it wouldn't have been hard to take that basic concept and push it further. To take it to a terrifying extreme.

She clutched the stack of scrolls and loose parchment in her arms, the ones she hadn't had time to sift through earlier. She'd thought maybe she could read until sleep claimed her, but now, standing in the dim light, looking at the bed... No. She couldn't.

After weeks spent in that cold, grim cell with barely a scrap of cloth to ward off the chill—this felt like too much. *Excessive*, even though—logically—she knew it wasn't.

But the others... they still had nothing.

How could she possibly lie down in something so luxurious, knowing that?

With a sigh, Elara crossed to the small desk by the window, setting the papers down with a soft thud. She sank into the chair and began sorting through the notes. Page after page of her own handwriting, lines filled with references to a book she didn't remember reading. *The Lattice of Interstellar Theory and Spatial Anomalies.*

She scanned her notes, one section catching her eye.

Entanglement theory speaks of particles that, once intertwined, mirror each other's states, regardless of distance. It challenges our conventional understanding of space, suggesting that separations are nothing more than an illusion, hinting at a deeper, intrinsic connection across the cosmos.

She paused, fingers tapping lightly against the parchment. The concept intrigued her. The idea that what seemed like vast distances could be bridged by something more... that everything might be connected, no matter how far apart. She made a mental note to ask the Hunter if he had the book in his library. It was something she'd love to dig deeper into, to understand what had driven her past self so deep into these theories. But then—her thoughts halted.

A sound outside her door.

Elara stiffened, her eyes darting to the shadow shifting beneath the doorframe. It lingered for a moment, as if the Hunter was hesitating, hovering on the other side. Earlier, when he'd led her to her room, he'd mentioned that his room was just down the hall before walking away without another word. What could he possibly want from her now?

Her pulse quickened in the sudden quiet. The shadow slipped away, leaving only dim hall light seeping beneath the door.

Curiosity drew her up. She cracked the door open—and froze. A tray of food sat neatly on the floor.

Warm, crusty bread. Butter soft enough to spread. Stew, rich with meat and herbs. Cool water, condensation slicking the pitcher. Fresh fruit, neatly arranged.

Her stomach growled—she couldn't remember the last real meal she'd had. The comfort of it felt wrong after weeks of scraps, and as she knelt to take the tray, guilt surged anew.

She was in a warm room with a soft bed and fresh, hot food. Elara stared down at the food, her stomach twisting, desperate for just one bite. *Eat*, she told herself. *You will need your strength tomorrow, for casting, for the ritual you plan to attempt.* Eating was necessary. Sleeping on a bed of pillows, though... that was not.

With a deep breath, she brought the tray over to her desk. The first bite nearly brought her to tears. The warm, salty butter spread across the bread, dipping it into the rich stew—it tasted like something out of a dream. She ate so quickly she knew she'd regret it later, her stomach already groaning at the speed. But it didn't matter. She needed this.

When the food was gone, Elara dragged a pillow and the stack of notes to the floor by the empty hearth. It wasn't cold enough for a fire, though she found herself wishing for one—for the familiar comfort of flame before sleep.

She read until her eyes burned and the words began to blur, turning page after page, note after note. She was nearly ready to give up for the night when her gaze caught on something different.

A letter.

> *Elara,*
>
> *First, thank you for sending me the book on non-linear temporal mechanics. I've already started tearing through it, and, as always, your recommendations don't disappoint. There's a section on temporal distortions that aligns perfectly with what you were theorizing last month. If time isn't linear, then why should the past be set in stone? What if we could manipulate the flow of time within a confined space, not just observe its effects, but alter them? It opens up a whole new realm of possibilities. I've been working on some new equations that I think could complement your idea. We'll need to test it, of course, but the potential is incredible.*
>
> *That said, I need to warn you—some of my notes are missing. Entire sections gone, and I can't figure out how or when it happened. Be careful. It feels like someone's been sniffing around our research, and I don't want you getting caught up in it. Burn this letter after you read it, and don't leave any of your own notes where they can be easily found.*
>
> *I'm going to try to get another letter to you through Annette, but until then, stay away from court if you can. Something's off there.*
>
> *Write me back as soon as it's safe. I have more ideas to share, and I'm dying to hear what you think about these new theories.*
>
> *Thane*

Elara's chest tightened as she set the letter down, her mind spinning. The warning about the missing notes, about something strange happening at court... Thane had known. Maybe not exactly, but he had sensed something before it all went wrong. He had an idea, and yet, she'd ignored the signs. She glanced toward the cold hearth, his words still echoing in her mind.

Burn it.

But she hadn't.

Her hands moved mechanically as she sifted through the scattered notes, uncovering more letters she hadn't burned. A cold dread settled in her bones. What if someone found them? What if these letters had ended up in Osin's hands, leading him straight to their research? What if everything that happened—*everything*—had been her fault from the beginning?

❁

THE EARLY MORNING sun filtered through the stained-glass window, casting a soft, dappled glow across the bathing chamber. Elara sat submerged in the tub, the once-steaming water now cold, her skin prickling from the chill. The massive window behind her framed the manor's sprawling gardens, a wild tangle of overgrown hedges and dying flowers, dew still clinging to the leaves.

She shivered as goosebumps rose along her skin, but there was something about the chill of the water that felt right—like it mirrored the numbness inside her, the heaviness she couldn't seem to shake.

She hadn't slept much the night before. After finding the letters, there had been no peace. She'd read through each one at least ten times, tracing Thane's words over and over, hoping they would reveal something more. Thane had written with such a casual tone, as if everything they'd been doing hadn't been dangerously illegal. They were *". . . close. In a way,"* as the Hunter had said. Close enough to work together under the nose of the Lord Sovereign, close enough to explore theories that could unravel worlds.

Her fingers drifted over the surface of the water as her mind lingered on the letters—endless musings about science and philosophy, about books that had fascinated them both, their shared distrust of the gods. But for all the words, for all the intellect in those letters, none of it explained how they had met. There was no map to their closeness, no breadcrumbs leading her back to the start.

Elara sighed, sinking lower into the bath until the water lapped gently at her chin. Her toes had turned into a series of creased valleys. She should get out before she started resembling a prune, but she couldn't summon the energy to move. She used to do this on purpose as a child—stay in the bath until her skin wrinkled, fascinated by how her body could change, even in the smallest, most temporary ways. There had been something satisfying about it, though she hadn't understood why back then. Control. The tiniest, most insignificant piece of control over her world.

Her heart twisted for that version of herself. That girl—so naive, so *desperate* for someone to love her. She'd trusted Edgar. She'd trusted the Druids, thought they were protecting her. It had taken years of living with them, seeing their true nature, to realize she had only ever been a tool to them.

Until Avis and Dario.

Her chin wobbled, and she dunked her head under the water, the sudden rush of cold and pressure muffling the world above. *They had never been her friends.* They'd lied to her, manipulated her, just like everyone else. Even if Avis tried to justify it by calling it *"protection,"* Elara knew better now.

If there was one thing the Pit had taught her, it was that real protection meant fighting for the people you cared about. You didn't stand by, watching them suffer, lie to them, suppress them, and then call it *"protection."* She hated what was being done to Dario, hated that Osin was using him to keep her in line, but forgiveness? That was something she wasn't sure she had left in her heart.

Elara surfaced with a gasp, wiped her face, and pushed upright, reaching for the linen towel. Wrapping it around herself, she shuffled to the mirror, water dripping from her hair to pool at her feet. She barely noticed. It was her eyes that stopped her in her tracks.

For a long moment, she simply stared. Tilting her head slightly, Elara hoisted herself onto the edge of the sink, the cool porcelain slippery beneath her as she leaned in closer. Her gaze searched her reflection, lingering on the thick scar at her throat before settling on her eyes again. She searched for the dull, muddy gray she had grown used to— the flat, lifeless color that had stared back at her for as long as she could remember. But instead, her eyes seemed different. Brighter. Gray, yes, but not the heavy, muted gray she knew so well. They had almost deepened into something clearer, like a storm rolling in after a long, stagnant sky.

When had that happened?

A sudden, fierce flicker caught Elara's attention. Outside the window, an orange burst ignited—searing, comet-bright. Awe and alarm jolted through her. She scrambled away from the sink and hurried across the room.

It was the Hunter.

He stood bathed in golden light, stripped to his breeches, bronze skin slick with sweat. Damp curls clung to his temples, pushed back from his brow by the heat rolling off him. Every inch of him was taut and gleaming, muscles rippling with a ruthless, untamed power that reminded her of fire—unpredictable, fierce, utterly mesmerizing.

This was nothing like the precise, controlled ether she'd seen the Druids use. His casting was wild, aggressive, with no thought of conserving strength or energy. If anything, it looked as though he were deliberately pushing himself to the brink, testing how far he could go before breaking.

He flung a leg in a wide arc, unleashing a scythe of flame that carved through the gardens. The ground beneath him scorched, grass smoldering in charred patches where his ether struck, heat rippling in the air around him. He looked angry. Desperate. And Elara couldn't help but wonder whether the evening's events had unsettled him more than he let on—or if this fierce display was simply a facet of his being. How he trained. Who he truly was.

Ivan. His name drifted through her mind like a whisper.

Suddenly, he stilled. His head whipped around, eyes locking onto hers in a way that seemed to scorch the very air between them. Gold swirled within his irises, alive with a wild glow that pulsed.

Elara's heart lurched, pounding in her chest with a force that left her breathless. His gaze swept over her, and it felt like flames trailing across her skin, awakening every nerve, setting her whole body on edge. Heat rushed through her, pooling in her stomach, her skin prickling. She couldn't move. Couldn't think as his eyes found hers again, sparking a cutting awareness in her, stirring sensations she hadn't even realized were lying dormant, waiting to burn.

But then his gaze flicked away, and the pull between them snapped like a wire cut clean. Her breath left her in a rush, her knees buckling. She watched him stride to where his tunic lay in the grass and yank it over his head, the muscles in his back shifting beneath his skin.

Without so much as a backward glance, he walked away, leaving her standing there, breathless and undone.

Anger and panic tangled together in her chest. Could he hear her thoughts? Could he hear her *now*? Her heart pounded faster, the thrum of it filling her ears. She fought to steady her breath, her hands shaking. *No, no... If he could hear my thoughts, I'd hear his too.* The logic was shaky at best, but she grabbed onto it like a lifeline. Unless... he knew something she didn't. Knew how to block her out.

Shit.

Elara jerked away from the window, knees slamming into the edge of the tub. Pain shot through her legs, and she hissed a curse, biting back the urge to kick the damn thing. *Breathe.* Her hands flew up to cover her flushed face, fingers pressing into her cheeks. She had to work with him today, and the last thing she needed was to be rattled by whatever *that* had been.

"Morning, morning!"

Elara froze. *Tristan.*

"I've brought you cake!" he hollered from her room, and she mentally cursed. Thank the gods she'd had the sense to lock the bathroom door, but still—barging in? Really? She closed her eyes, willing herself to stay calm. Maybe if she kept quiet, he'd get bored and go away.

Moving as silently as possible, Elara got dressed, pulling her dirty gown back over her damp skin. She had nothing else to wear, so it would have to do. Her fingers worked quickly, tying her hair back into a braid, yanking a strip of fabric from the hem to tie it off. She waited a few minutes, hoping he might give up and leave.

He didn't.

Elara stepped out of the bathroom and scowled at the sight before her. Tristan was lounging on her bed, one arm propped behind his head, the other casually plopping pieces of cake into his mouth. "There you are," he drawled, not even bothering to sit up. "I thought you'd drowned yourself in there."

She rolled her eyes, folding her arms across her chest. "Don't you have anything better to do than loiter in my room, eating cake?"

Another piece of cake disappeared between his lips as he shrugged lazily, crumbs dusting his shirt. "I'm a man of leisure, Elara. Eating cake is my full-time occupation. Care for one?"

Elara shook her head. "No, thanks." Her stomach churned at the thought. After everything that had just happened, the last thing she needed was to feel any queasier.

His eyes narrowed slightly. "I thought you'd be starving."

"The Hunter brought me something last night."

That got his attention. He sat up, smirking. "*Did he now*? Well, isn't that domestic of him?"

Elara rolled her eyes, not even bothering to hide her exasperation. Before she could get a word in, Tristan sprang from the bed, cakes in hand, and marched over to the small table by the window.

"Well, don't dawdle. We've got a long day ahead of us—curse-breaking and all that. Ivan's particularly grumpy in the mornings, so it's wise not to be late."

"Grumpy in the mornings and evenings, then? I bet he's loads of fun at parties." Elara couldn't help the dry edge to her voice, imagining him scowling amidst festive streamers and jubilant toasts.

But instead of the smirk she expected, Tristan grew thoughtful. "He's often misunderstood, I think. People take his silence for anger, his focus for coldness. But he's... loyal, in his own way. When it counts, he shows up."

Elara blinked, caught off guard by the sudden seriousness. She arched a brow, leaning back. "Was that a compliment? And here I thought you were good for nothing but snide comments and unsolicited advice."

His lips twitched. "I contain multitudes." His gaze flicked over her dirt-streaked gown, lingering for a second before he tilted his head. "I might have some spare clothes lying around. Want them?"

Her eyes narrowed. "Do you live here?"

He shrugged. "Sometimes."

She held his gaze, suspicion creeping in, but she squashed it, deciding to think on it later. She took him in fully. He was tall and lean, not exactly her size, but anything was better than the mess she was currently wearing. "I wouldn't owe you anything, right?"

He barked out a laugh, the sound echoing through the room. "Not everyone from Ulrith are such pricks about lending a hand. So, no, Elara, you wouldn't owe me a damn thing." His smile was surprisingly warm before he turned and left the room.

Minutes later, he returned, handing her a pair of well-tailored trousers and a soft linen shirt. He winked—because of course he did—before sauntering back to the door and pulling it shut behind him.

Elara stared at the clothes for a moment, shaking her head. *Irritating as hell*, she thought, slipping into the trousers. But then, as she adjusted the shirt, she couldn't help but admit—just a little—that maybe he wasn't entirely awful. Thoughtful, even.

Begrudgingly, she found herself hating him just a bit less.

CHAPTER 40

The library was empty when Elara finally worked up the nerve to leave her room. She'd been bracing for an encounter—Tristan sprawled somewhere with his usual smirk, the Hunter standing off to one side, brooding as always—but no one was there to meet her.

She moved farther in, boots muffled by layers of rugs. Shelves loomed on every side, chairs tucked close to tables, lamps still glowing low—but nothing. No signs of anyone. She furrowed her brow, biting her lip in thought. If ever there was a time to snoop, it was now. The stillness of the manor, the emptiness—it felt like an invitation.

With a cautious glance around, she stepped deeper into the library, weaving through the towering stacks. The faint scent of ink and worn parchment wrapped around her. She had always loved the smell of books. There was something comforting in it, something that spoke to her in a way nothing else did. Elara ran her hands along the spines, the textured bindings soft beneath her fingertips. Here, she almost felt at home. Almost. But home had never been a place—it had always been the books themselves, the quiet, scholarly sanctuaries like this one, where her mind could roam freely.

Back in Verdara, the archives had been her escape. The world outside could crumble, but the moment she'd stepped into that maze of shelves, surrounded by history, knowledge, and the crackle of old pages, she'd felt grounded. Safe. Books had always offered her what life hadn't—answers, clarity, and a place to belong.

Perhaps that love for books, that need to know more, was a tie to the girl she used to be—the one who had snuck around, risking everything to get her hands on those forbidden texts. She'd always been reckless when it came to knowledge, seeking out answers no matter the cost. Elara's heart twisted slightly. That insatiable thirst for learning, the willingness to push boundaries for the sake of discovery—it was *still* there, still very much a part of her. Maybe the girl she thought she'd left behind wasn't so far off after all.

Elara wandered through the aisles, fingers grazing the spines of books as she read their titles. *The Song of the Lost Kings, The Alchemical Mind: Bridging the Gap Between Science and Sorcery, Vibrational Theory in Spell Casting: Harmonics of the Arcane.*

It seemed the Hunter had quite the eclectic collection, but as tempting as it was to lose herself in those pages, what she really needed were books on the Sidhe and *Tírrish*. If she could study the language while she was here, maybe she could ask Reynnar about the stones—how they were used, how he had been taken from his world. Any bit of information could be vital.

She continued walking, pulling a book from the shelf here and there, quickly scanning the pages before moving on. After wandering through the winding rows, she eventually found herself at the back of the library, where the towering windows took up almost the entire back wall. For a moment, Elara stood still, her breath catching as something unusual snagged her attention.

Crystals.

They dangled from the windows, scattered across the glass like stars pinned in a night sky. Each crystal caught the morning light and shattered it into fragments, casting tiny rainbows that danced across the room. Colors splintered and spun, painting the walls, the shelves—even her skin—in soft hues of violet, amber, and emerald.

Runes, sigils, and an assortment of unknown scripts were etched on their surfaces, humming with potent ether. Some symbols she recognized from her studies, but others were unfamiliar—far older than anything she had ever seen or could name.

Each breath seemed to fill her lungs with the energy in the room, fanning the spark of curiosity that was quickly growing into something she couldn't ignore. Elara found herself stepping closer to the nearest window, where a cluster of quartz crystals dangled.

Her fingers twitched with the urge to examine them, caution flaring too late to matter. The pull was undeniable. As if in a trance, she stepped closer, her hand hovering over the smallest gem, its surface cool beneath her fingertips.

It stirred at her touch—a light, breathy sensation. The quartz hummed softly, energy spiraling from her fingers and up her arm, weightless as captured air, already slipping away even as she held it. But then without warning, the sensation shifted. The gentle breeze that had been whispering against her skin transformed into a gust, a sudden, biting wind that swept through her veins.

Elara gasped as chill stole her breath and her fingers slipped from the quartz. The gem swung wildly on its chain. She froze, bracing for the shatter—but it never came. The crystal halted midair, then drifted gently back into place. A soft chime rang out, echoing through the chamber.

A shiver rushed through her, and the skin of her palm pulsated, revealing the script: *Chun ceolghaoth*. A chill prickled the nape of her neck, goosebumps forming along her arms. As the foreign words seared and sank into her flesh, her breath caught, only to be released in a shuddering exhale when they vanished without a trace.

Sweat gathered on her forehead.

Did she just take in a blessing or a curse?

"You're early."

Elara's heart leapt into her throat, her guilty hand instinctively slipping behind her back. The Hunter was leaning casually against the bookshelf with a steaming cup in hand. His damp hair curled slightly at the ends, and he was dressed down in clean, simple trousers, and a loose tunic—an oddly relaxed sight. Not that she knew what she'd expected. It wasn't as if he'd be wandering around his own home in armor.

How long had he been watching?

A brow arched as he slowly sipped from his cup. The quiet stretched, making her pulse pound louder in her ears. Then his gaze shifted, sliding down to her clothes. He stilled, eyes narrowing. Elara felt a heavy thump in her chest, a throb that was not her own and it made her stomach flip. His gaze flicked back to hers, calm, unreadable.

"Are you ready?"

Her throat tightened, and she wasn't sure she could swallow past the knot lodged there. Was she ready? Probably not. But she had to try. She nodded, her movements stiff, uncertain, and his eyes softened, just a little—a small shift that shouldn't have made a difference, but it did.

"You might not see it yet, but you're stronger than you realize, Hallowed." His voice was low, but there was a fierce intensity in his eyes. "I don't make bets, but if I did, I'd wager on you coming out of this without a scratch. It's in your nature to survive."

Her heart flipped, and her stomach dipped all at once. It was the kindest thing she'd ever heard from him, and it was directed at her. She didn't know how to respond. Thankfully, he seemed to take her silence for what it was, tipping his chin toward the door in a silent gesture for her to follow.

When they reached the desk, Tristan was lounging in the chair, feet propped up on the table, flipping through Transcendental Bonds. He barely glanced up as they approached, but the second his eyes landed on her in his clothes, he snapped the book shut with a loud thud.

"Well, don't you look dashing," he drawled, eyes glinting as they raked over her.

Elara shot Tristan a flat look before she caught a glimpse of something tense in the Hunter's expression—a flash of annoyance, maybe? It was there and gone so quickly she almost doubted she'd seen it at all.

She made a beeline for the nearest chair, her eyes zeroing in on the tea service surrounded by pastries and neatly buttered toast. Without asking, she grabbed a cup, filled it, and drowned the tea in honey and cream. Politeness was the last thing on her mind today, not with the *"significant risk of cognitive, emotional, and even physical destabilization"* looming over her. That sort of threat tended to strip away any interest in niceties.

And also, *tea.*

She took a long, deep sip, the warmth and sweetness washing through her like a balm. She nearly groaned, eyes fluttering shut for a second longer than necessary. When she glanced up, both men were watching with something close to amusement.

"What?"

Tristan chuckled, that lazy grin spreading across his face. "The Hallowed in the wild. It's a strange sight to behold."

Mother, save her. She didn't have the energy for this.

Elara reached for the book, her fingers hesitating just before she touched the worn cover. "May I?" she asked Tristan, even though she didn't really need his permission. His eyebrows lifted slightly, clearly puzzled by her formality, but he nodded.

She still wasn't used to being able to just take a book without asking, especially one so valuable. Old habits—ones built on rules, secrecy, and constant watchfulness—died hard, she supposed. It had always felt like access to knowledge came with conditions. But here she could just... take it. She swallowed down the strange mix of hesitation and excitement, flipping open *Transcendental Bonds,* and thumbing through the pages until she found what she was looking for.

The Sundering.

According to the text, the practitioner needed to attune themselves to the frequency of the sealed power, matching the resonance of the Echoing Seal with the exact harmony of the bound energy. A single misstep could lead to a catastrophic release—power surging uncontrollably, perhaps violently, through the individual whose essence had been muted for so long.

Elara exhaled slowly, forcing the tension from her shoulders. "Let's just get this over with."

The Hunter tilted his head. "Did the Druids teach you ritualized control?" She nodded and he continued, almost—*almost*—smiling. "I thought so, considering how fast you used the *Draoth Cara's* link against me. This is good news. Much of this process is about maintaining control over your own mind. You'll need to sink deep into your consciousness and stay anchored there while I work. The calmer you stay, the easier it will be to sunder the sigil."

Her stomach tightened, but she inhaled deeply. "Okay."

The Hunter extended his hand, and for a moment Elara only stared at it, memories flooding back—how many times she'd slapped it away, shoved him back, resisted. She'd fought him at every turn. She'd even stabbed him once. Bit him, too.

And now...

She took it.

His hand was warm as he led her to an empty spot in the room. They settled to the floor across from each other, knees nearly touching. She felt what was coming settle deep in her bones.

Tristan stepped forward, vial in hand. Elara watched as he poured its contents onto the ground, ash tracing a circle around her and the Hunter—just as Avis had done in the throne room. When the circle closed, she felt the shift. She'd read enough to recognize it now: protection. The ash wasn't merely a boundary, but a weave of spells—stabilization, balance, containment. A shield meant to keep the volatile energy they were about to unleash from spiraling out of control.

Elara closed her eyes and let her mind sink inward, following the familiar path she'd walked countless times before. It led her straight to the Hunter's seal, as though it had been waiting. His heartbeat met her there—slow, steady, a rhythm she matched with her breath.

That was the key. The cadence. The vibration. Not just physical, but resonant—something he could feel, looping between the seal and the power buried deep within her. She focused on each inhale, each exhale, letting the rhythm spread through her body and outward toward him.

Elara felt Tristan settle beside her, just outside the circle of ash. His presence was grounding in its own way, but then he began chanting, that rough, guttural tongue she'd heard only from the Druids. Her concentration wavered, trying to grasp the foreign sounds even though she didn't know their meaning. There was something wrong about the way those words fell from his lips, something unsettling that made her skin crawl.

But it wasn't just the words—it was the resonance they left behind, humming through the air and settling deep in her chest. The Hunter's pulse thudded into her awareness, brushing against her own heartbeat—and then she realized it wasn't aligned at all. It was wrong. A dissonant note cutting across an otherwise steady rhythm. His seal pressed harder now, no longer distant, but insistent, as though burrowing into her.

"Good, Hallowed," the Hunter said, his voice low and smooth. She didn't hear it so much as register it, the sound rolling through her like distant thunder.

"Now—hold your breath."

Elara's focus slipped. "Hold my brea—"

A rush of ether slipped into her like a wisp of smoke, threading through her veins and sinking deep. Ether had always been an intrusion —painful, invasive, foreign. This was different. It moved slowly, almost gently, as if testing her.

The resistance she expected never came. Instead, curiosity sparked where fear should have been. His ether wound around her bones, seeped into her marrow, heat trailing in its wake like a hand brushing old scars. Her muscles tensed, a shudder rippling through her as the warmth spread, building higher and higher until it bordered on too much. She could feel it—him—moving through her with unhurried intent.

Then he lingered near her heart.

The seal on his chest flared—a faint glow—followed by a sharp sting in her own. Then it faded, vanishing as though it had never existed. Elara held her focus as he turned to the remaining seals. These were different. More stubborn. His had never fully formed after the *Draoth Cara's* interference, but Avis's and Dario's were solid, complete.

Sweat trickled down her temple. The strain set in almost at once, seconds stretching as her muscles began to protest. Her hands tingled; her legs went numb from holding still. She ignored it, forced herself to concentrate, to keep her heartbeat steady and aligned with his. Every inhale. Every exhale. Perfectly matched.

Heat flashed across her chest—then the sting. One seal. Then the other. Gone.

Relief loosened her knees, just enough to feel it. She waited for the surge—for ether, for power—but nothing came.

The Hunter went utterly still. Through their connection, she could almost sense it—his confusion rippling across the link like a flicker of static.

"There's something else here," he murmured, and with the softness of a feather brushing against her skin, his ether touched a spot deep inside her—light, so light.

A scream tore from Elara's throat, ricocheting off the walls.

Fire surged through her veins—searing, all-consuming—obliterating every thought, every sense but one.

Agony.

Heat and light slammed against the barrier, whipping through the circle, energy rebounding wildly as if searching for escape. Elara squeezed her eyes shut, fingers splayed against the ground, bracing. It felt like something was being ripped from her—not imposed from without, but erupting from her core.

Even through the chaos, she felt his strength falter. His ether frayed. A grunt escaped him, and his trembling hands slipped against her thighs. He was losing control—fighting to hold on as something inside her resisted.

The tether snapped.

The impact slammed through her, a violent recoil that shook her to the bone as he tore himself free.

Elara's eyes fluttered open, the world blurred through tears clinging to her lashes. Her cheeks were wet, hot from sobs that had torn free without her realizing.

Tristan stood beyond the barrier, his ether surging—tendrils of water crashing against it, straining to break through. Inside, though, she and the Hunter were locked within a circle of fire, crackling and fierce, close enough to scorch but never quite touching them. Contained. Controlled. Barely.

Her gaze found the Hunter. His breaths were ragged, loud in the charged air, head bowed, dark strands of hair veiling his face. But his hands—his hands were still on her, fingers pressed into her skin, burning through her like live embers. A shiver tore through her, muscles tensing.

Then he jerked back, as if burned.

For a heartbeat he went still, shoulders rigid. Slowly, he straightened and lifted his head. When his eyes met hers, Elara's breath caught.

Darkness coiled through his gaze like smoke, pulsing, swallowing the amber at its center. Panic flared—then just as quickly, the darkness slipped away, retreating into the depths and leaving his eyes clear... but haunted.

"Let the ether go," he rasped, his voice raw.

Elara blinked, the words barely cutting through the haze of fire and power coursing through her. Let it go? She didn't have access to her own ether—only *his*.

The realization hit hard. She was drawing from it, shaping the fire around them, and he—he was holding it back, keeping it from devouring them both. "How?" she whispered, as heat surged through her veins, molten fire pulsing with every heartbeat. But it wasn't just heat. It was power. Unimaginable power. She felt invincible, infinite, untouchable—and *so very dangerous.*

He reached out, his hand finding the nape of her neck. She didn't flinch as his fingers threaded into her hair, gripping tightly. His forehead pressed against hers, their breath mingling in the thick heat. "*Feel.*"

Elara's eyes slid shut in understanding. She reached not outward, but inward—through the bond, the thread that tethered them together. It blazed between them, coiled tightly, draining them both, entwining them in a way that made her feel as though they were fused into one entity.

Elara inhaled slowly, focusing on the connection, and eased away from it—piece by piece, letting go, retracting her grasp from his ether until she wasn't feeding from it anymore. Until they were separated as much as two bound souls could ever be.

A sharp breath rushed out of him, warm and unsteady, ghosting across her lips. Then a low, almost bitter laugh rumbled from his chest, hollow in the sudden quiet—so out of place it made her flinch.

"Well," he said at last, lips curving into a crooked grin that held no warmth, "I don't know what I was expecting. But it wasn't *that.*"

CHAPTER 41

The manor's grand clock tolled from the drawing room, its heavy chimes echoing through the empty halls, marking an hour far too late for Elara's patience. Fatigue crept up on her as the last scraps of conversation dwindled. Her fingers drummed impatiently against her thigh.

Took them long enough.

She glanced up from the book resting in her lap to find Tristan and the Hunter both sprawled on the settees, fast asleep. Tristan's arm hung over the side, while the Hunter, as ever, seemed perfectly composed, even in sleep, though the strain was etched into the lines of his face.

They'd spent the entire day buried in *Transcendental Bonds*, eyes red and bleary from hours of scanning endless pages, trying to understand what had gone wrong. By all accounts, the ritual had been flawless. The seals were broken. Every step executed perfectly.

And yet—something else was inside her.

Something dark. Something that had lashed out when the Hunter touched it, when his ether brushed against that hidden place. The memory sent a shiver down her spine, terror creeping back as she remembered the way it had recoiled, striking like a wounded animal.

So they kept searching—through margins and footnotes, half-forgotten sigils, obscure bindings—hunting for whatever detail they'd missed.

After hours of fruitless searching, Tristan had finally thrown his hands up in defeat, reaching for a bottle of spirits instead. *"To ease our troubled minds,"* he'd said, pouring generous glasses. Elara had taken one, swirling the amber liquid under her nose, but only pretended to sip. She needed a clear head for what she was planning.

The men, unsurprisingly, had absolutely no such reservations. Tristan had taken to the bottle with his usual reckless abandon, drinking deeply and far too quickly, while even the Hunter had indulged in more than a few heavy swigs. It wasn't long before their conversation slowed to a crawl, their words tumbling out in that hazy, unfocused way, the bottle now nearly drained between them.

Elara had been watching them from the corner of her eye all evening, biding her time. She needed them to fall asleep, to slip into that blissfully unaware state, and if Tristan's current position, sprawled across the settee and snoring like a hibernating bear, was any indication, the time had finally come.

Slowly, she rose from her chair and set the book she'd been pretending to read back on the desk. The room remained still—broken only by Tristan's soft snores and the Hunter's near-silent breathing. She slipped from the drawing room, heart hammering, and didn't let out a careful breath until she reached the hall. Then she moved down the dim corridor toward the library.

All day, while they'd sifted through the Hunter's extensive collection, she hadn't seen a single text in *Tírrish*. Not that she'd been free to look properly. His gaze had tracked her the entire time, every movement measured, and she couldn't risk drawing attention to what she was really searching for.

Because, in truth, she still didn't know where his loyalties truly lay. Sure, he wanted her help to save his brother, and he was willing to defy his lord to do it. But that didn't mean he was against everything his lord stood for. She couldn't trust that he wouldn't stop her if he caught her trying to uncover more about the Sidhe—their language, their history. After all, he had spent years hunting down those who clung to the old ways, rooting out every trace of *Tírrish* culture from Osin's new world.

That was his job.

She *had* to remember that. Each glance, each moment of blurred judgment, required correction. The *Draoth Cara* had to be influencing her—distorting trust, reshaping feeling. She couldn't let it take hold. She couldn't afford to.

And maybe he had already burned every last book in the *Tírrish* script, wiped away every trace of what had existed before the war. Maybe she was chasing something that had long since been reduced to ash. But she had to try. His collection was immense, sprawling in ways she could never have dreamed back in Verdara. If there was even the smallest fragment left, if there was any chance of finding something—it was worth digging deeper.

Elara nudged the door open, just a sliver, the soft creak barely audible. The room beyond was bathed in a muted light, tiny orbs floating lazily through the air, casting a glow across the library's towering shelves. At night, the place felt different—almost otherworldly, as though it was a place not meant to be touched, only glimpsed from the corner of your eye. A shiver crawled up her spine, prickling at her skin, and she instinctively wrapped her arms around herself, trying to shake the eerie feeling that settled over her.

Focus.

This was what she did best—research, unraveling the threads of mysteries and pulling them into something clear, something that made sense. But where to begin? Her fingers brushed the spines of the nearest books as her mind raced, trying to piece together everything she had learned so far.

The stones, aligned with a rift, were a potential gateway—*a theoretical portal*—for the Sidhe to return to *Tír na nÓg*. That much she had established. But her research, the notes she had pored over, didn't confirm how to fully activate the gate. The equation was incomplete—two parts discovered, but the third, the catalyst, was still unclear.

Elara's footsteps echoed with purpose as she strode toward the massive circular desk in the center of the room. A chaotic heap of knowledge—scrolls, books, loose pages—thrown together with little care. She dove into the mess, rifling through it with a frantic energy, her hands flipping pages, pushing aside stacks of old parchment, searching for anything that might hold a clue. There had to be *something* here.

Minutes ticked by—precious, dragging minutes—in which her search revealed nothing but more disorder. In her haste, her arm brushed against a stack of scrolls, sending them cascading to the floor with a soft rustle and thud.

Her breath hitched as she glanced toward the doorway, heart pounding. Only when she was sure no one was about to walk in did she let herself breathe again. She turned back to the desk, braced her hands on the edge, and lowered her head. A tension headache began to throb behind her eyes.

The Hunter was such a slob! How did anyone work like this?

She moved through the stacks with mounting desperation, yanking books from the shelves so quickly her hands barely registered their weight before she cast them aside. It felt like hours had passed, though it was probably only minutes—but time had a way of warping when you were certain you'd be caught at any second.

Elara's eyes fluttered closed for a moment before she opened them again—and nearly jumped out of her skin. An orb hovered just inches from her face, its soft, pulsing light throwing gentle shadows around the room, flickering like timid flames.

She blinked at it, the ridiculousness of the situation not lost on her. "I don't suppose you could help me, could you?"

The orb, unsurprisingly, gave no response. She let out a frustrated breath, shaking her head. "Gods, I'm talking to balls of light now. This is pointless. He probably has nothing on the Sidhe, anyway."

The moment the words left her lips, the orb flared. It shot off through the labyrinth of shelves with such speed and purpose that her heart lurched. She ran after it, feet barely grazing the floor, until it drew her into a secluded corner—tucked neatly away from the rest of the library.

A curved window was set into the wall, its frame lined with a built-in bookshelf that traced the arc of the glass. Beneath it, a seat was tucked into the curve, lined with deep cushions and draped in faded fabrics, as if it had once been someone's favorite spot for reading and dreaming.

Moonlight poured through, drawing silvery patterns across the floor and casting the sprawling gardens outside in a ghostly glow. The orb hovered beside the left curve of the bookshelf, its soft glow highlighting a weathered tome nestled between two larger volumes. Its light flickered gently, as though beckoning her closer.

"Thank you," Elara murmured to the orb, her voice soft as she drew the book nearer. The cover was plain, devoid of any title, or author's name. It resembled a journal more than a formal publication. A quick look at the surrounding books revealed a series of texts proudly bearing the name Yalden Hargrave, a luminary in the healing arts. Her gaze flicked back and forth between the unassuming journal and the distinguished volumes beside it, a tangle of confusion knotting in her stomach.

Elara shot a doubtful look at the orb. "This is it? The only piece on the Sidhe?"

The orb's glow brightened for a moment, as if in confirmation.

She cautiously opened the journal, and her breath caught. The pages were filled with lines of *Tirrish* script, flowing like rivers of ink across the paper, with Latherian translations hurriedly scrawled in the margins. The handwriting was messy. As if someone had been working against the clock to translate it all.

She bit back a triumphant laugh. This wasn't the comprehensive guide she had been hoping for, but it was a start. A damn good start.

Elara leaned back against the cold window, the chill of the glass biting into her skin as moonlight poured over the journal's pages. The detail was staggering. Pronunciation notes, subtle variations in dialect— this wasn't just some amateur's work. No, whoever had written this had taken their time, documenting even the smallest of details with a scholar's eye.

She paused, her fingers lightly tracing the inked lines. It had to be the Hunter. Who else would have written this? Even though the handwriting was hurried, she recognized it as his. What caught her off guard, though, was the detail in the notes. This level of passion, this almost hyper-fixated dedication, didn't match the image she had of him at all. For someone so stiff, so chained to his sense of duty, this kind of fervor seemed unexpected. But then again, how much did she really know about him?

Not much at all, she was starting to realize.

Elara's world narrowed to the journal in her lap, her fingers tracing the faded ink that wound from the brittle front cover to the tea-stained back. Every *Tirrish* word, every hurried Latherian translation pulled her deeper. One read-through wasn't enough. She flipped back to the beginning and plunged in again, devouring each line, letting the ancient language and its meaning imprint itself in her mind.

At some point, a soft gray light crept through the windows, mingling with the warm, golden glow of the orb that had kept her company through the night. She was sprawled across the window seat now, cheek cool against the glass, limbs heavy with exhaustion, her eyelids sagging.

Elara rubbed her eyes, watching the sun peak over the horizon. She needed to leave. Any minute now, Tristan and the Hunter would wake, and the absolute last thing she needed was for them to find her like this. *Later,* she promised herself. She would come back later. She clutched the journal to her chest as she peeled herself away from the window seat, but the journal slipped from her grasp and fell open in her lap. The pages fluttered softly before settling, and her gaze instinctively dropped to the open spread. She blinked, trying to clear her vision, but something caught her eye—a phrase scrawled in the margin she had somehow missed before.

Chun ceolghaoth.

Her breath stilled, a cold shiver rippling down her spine as the words sank in. It was the same phrase—the *exact* same—that had burned into her skin earlier after she'd touched the quartz. Her heart thudded, loud and erratic, almost drowning out her thoughts. She leaned in closer, eyes scanning the page for the translation.

To Wind Sing.

"Wind sing?"

Her fingers flew over the pages, flipping through the journal in a frantic search for anything that would add context. But there was nothing. She bit her lip as a dangerous idea slithered into her mind. *Could I cast the spell?* Her heart gave an excited little jolt at the possibility. This morning, she wouldn't have even considered it—but now, after the ritual...

Maybe she could try. The thought took root, growing, tempting her. What harm could one little wind spell really do?

Wetting her lips, Elara inhaled deeply, her gaze drifting back to the journal. The words *"Chun ceolghaoth."* rolled softly off her tongue. In her mind, she heard Reynnar's voice—rich, lilting—guiding her pronunciation, just as he had done countless times before.

Elara's breath slowed, deepened. She reached within herself and found the Hunter's seal waiting. It throbbed eagerly, as though it recognized she was paying attention to it again. Clearing her throat, she took another breath, deeper this time, letting her mind and body settle.

"Chun ceolghaoth."

The moment the final syllable slipped from her lips, the surrounding air exploded. A wild gust burst from her palm, spiraling out with a force that caught her completely off guard. Before she could brace herself, it slammed her backward into the bookshelf with a resounding thud, the impact knocking the breath from her lungs. Above her, the wind roared to life, a chaotic swirl of dust and scattered papers spinning like miniature tornadoes. Books tumbled from the shelves, thudding heavily onto the floor, one after another.

Elara's eyes widened, heart racing, but a grin stretched across her face, unstoppable. The room whirled in a vortex *she* had conjured, the air thick with the charge of her spell. Heat surged through her veins, her fingers still tingling with the aftershocks.

With reckless abandon, Elara stretched out her arms, feeling the ether surge in response as though it were an extension of her very soul. She laughed, the sound bright, mixing with the howl of the wind she had summoned. Spinning, she coaxed the tempest, guiding it through the room like a conductor commanding an orchestra of chaos. Books spun into the air, pages fluttering wildly, crystals clinked and chimed in disarray, and the orbs of light flickered erratically. Every nerve in her body thrummed with the thrill of it. The room bent to her will, and for a moment, she was limitless—*untouchable.*

But in her excitement, she misjudged her control. The wind grew stronger, and before she could rein it in, a heavy book flew across the room, slamming into the crystal-laden window. The sharp crack of shattering glass sliced through the roar of the storm, the sound echoing off the walls. Her heart plummeted, the joyous beat turning erratic.

Frantic, Elara tried to rein in the current, willing the wind to obey her—but it was completely out of her control. She swallowed hard, eyes darting to the jagged hole where the window used to be, the cold night air tearing through the room.

Shit. *Shit.*

She didn't know how to stop the spell.

Wind tore through the library, rattling shelves and flinging the Hunter's belongings aside. Leather-bound books littered the floor, pages fluttering helplessly; chairs lay overturned amid the wreckage.

Shame slammed into her. *What have I done?* Elara thrust her palm toward the floor, willing the gust to still—but it resisted, surging back like a wild thing refusing its cage.

A scream tore from her throat as the force of the gust ricocheted, hurling her into the air. The room spun violently, her tunic flaring up past her waist, and everything around her—books, papers, the remnants of her dignity—swirled in her wake, caught in the whirlwind like debris in a cyclone.

She was weightless, helpless, the wild current dragging her higher and higher toward the stained-glass dome. Her hands flailed, grasping desperately for anything to stop her dizzying ascent, but there was nothing but empty air. One wrong move, and she'd fall—plummet to the floor to her death.

She was such a bloody *idiot.*

A thunderous crash reverberated from below, a violent sound that sent shockwaves through Elara's already racing heart. She wrestled furiously with her tunic, the fabric whipping and slapping against her face like it had a personal vendetta. Just when she thought she'd managed to get it under control, another gust would send it flying upward, blinding her all over again. "Oh, for the gods' sake!"

Finally, her fingers clamped around the unruly fabric, yanking it back down into place. Victory, however, was fleeting. Because there, glaring up at her with an intensity that tamed the storm surrounding them, stood the Hunter.

CHAPTER 42

His curls were a wild tangle, his shirt rumpled from sleep. But his eyes—those eyes—bore into Elara with such force she could hardly breathe.

"What are you *doing*?"

His voice was hard, each word a whip crack that sliced through the air. Elara gaped at him, her grip on her tunic deathly tight as if it could somehow save her from this disaster. "Break the spell!" he barked, and she nearly flinched at the force of it, her heart jumping into her throat.

She opened her mouth to respond, but all that escaped was a strangled, panicked sound as her back collided with the dome.

"I don't know how!" she shot back, trying to regain her bearings. "Maybe you could *actually* help instead of just standing there shouting at me!"

For a long moment he held her gaze, unblinking. And then, abruptly, he looked away, rough fingers dragging down his face as he covered his mouth.

Elara squinted at him, incredulous.

The prick was *laughing* at her.

A flush of rage crept up her neck, heat blooming in her cheeks as a retort teetered on the edge of her tongue, ready to explode. But before she could release it, he was there—hovering in front of her, like he belonged to the wind.

The air around him shifted effortlessly, a steady, controlled breeze emanating from his hand, so unlike her chaotic mess. A smirk tugged at the corner of his lips, taunting her, daring her to do something about it, and gods, did she want to slap that smug look right off his face.

"Quite a predicament you've found yourself in," he drawled, his words slurring ever so slightly. The scent of spirits lingered on his breath as he hovered before her, its earthy notes mingling with the smell of ink-soaked parchment. There was a casualness to his posture, a relaxation in his shoulders that hinted at defenses momentarily lowered—at walls that, for once, might not be so impenetrable.

The cold embrace of the ceiling pressed insistently into her back, forcing her spine into a reluctant arch. They were dangerously close, his face just a whisper away from hers, and her wild hair cascaded down, forming a curtain around them both.

"Have you come all this way to mock me?"

His brow quirked, gaze lazily drifting to her hand that spewed wind like water from a broken dam. When his eyes met hers again, genuine intrigue had replaced the playful arrogance. "How are you doing this?"

Elara shot him a pointed look. "I'll tell you all about it once you help me down."

The corner of his mouth twitched. "You'll need to release your shirt."

"Not on your *life*."

The Hunter broke into a wide grin. "If I wanted to get a *second* look at your lacy bits, Hallowed, I'd simply drop a few feet and look up."

Her grip tightened, a vein pulsing at her temple. She pictured flinging him out the nearest window. The thought made her smile—and his shoulders tensed.

"That look is a bit unsettling. Care to share what's so amusing?"

A beat passed before she decided, begrudgingly, that launching him out the window wouldn't help her current situation. "Just help me down."

"Always so demanding," he muttered, watching her battle with her clothing. "Let go of your shirt. On my honor, I won't look." A hint of a smirk played at the corner of his mouth as he reached out his hand, steady against the wild gusts.

She eyed his outstretched hand warily. "You have no honor."

He blinked, tension tightening around his eyes and the hard line of his mouth. Hurt flickered there—almost as if he cared what she thought. Elara dismissed the absurd notion as his gaze hardened into flint.

"Take my hand."

Elara hesitated only a moment longer before letting go. She braced for the fabric to snap back into her face, but it didn't. Instead, the material settled snuggly, almost obediently, around her waist. She blinked, surprised, her gaze dropping to her legs where his ether coiled like tendrils of smoke, weaving around her with a touch that was barely there.

Slowly, she lifted her gaze, her heart caught between beats. His eyes were locked on hers in a way that made her mind scramble, her breath catch. She couldn't think—couldn't do anything but stare back.

Once more, he extended his hand, and once more, she took it.

The instant they touched, his eyes slid shut. His ether stirred, reaching into her, tugging at something buried deep. Subtle at first—a gentle pull—then surging like a river loosed, flooding her veins with warmth. She felt it, almost *saw* it: a shimmering thread weaving its path from her veins to his, as if recognizing another part of its whole.

With one swift pull the spell shattered, and Elara's world dropped out from beneath her.

Air whipped past, her stomach flipping wildly, but before she could even manage a scream, his arms were around her, catching her mid-fall.

Her body slammed into his chest, the impact knocking the breath from her lungs. His scent flooded her senses—cloves, parchment, and the faintest hint of whiskey. She looked up to find his brows drawn together, as though he, too, couldn't piece together how they'd ended up here.

"You're... good?"

"Fine," she muttered, trying—and failing—not to notice how solid his chest felt pressed against her. "Thank you for helping me."

He exhaled a low laugh. "I didn't have much of a choice."

They descended slowly, much slower, she realized, than how he'd soared up to her. But his words nagged at her. "Was I... did I hurt you?"

He adjusted her in his grip before answering. "It'll take more than that to hurt me. But if you're set on using this loophole you've found, you should know that every time you pull from the *Draoth Cara*, you're not just pulling from me—you're burning through your own reserves too. It's reckless, and it'll kill you if you don't learn how to control it."

Shame crept in, settling deep in her chest. She'd known, in theory, that it wasn't safe after what happened with the ritual. But the temptation, it had been too much.

"Can you teach me?" Her eyes met his, searching for something she wasn't sure he'd give. "Teach me to cast without hurting us?"

He raised a brow. "*As I said before*, I don't think I have much of a choice."

"I won't do it again. Not without your instruction."

At that, his gaze flickered with something soft, something she couldn't quite place. "All right, Hallowed. I'll teach you."

They landed and Elara tried to steady her trembling legs—willed her spine to straighten. His grip tightened briefly, but then, as if catching himself, he quickly let go, and stepped back.

Silence fell between them, awkward and heavy. He looked like he was wrestling with something, his brow furrowed in thought. Elara shifted on her feet, the tension thick enough to choke on.

"Don't worry," she said with a dry smile. "I won't tell anyone about your heroic catch."

That seemed to ease something in him. He shifted, rolling his shoulders as if shaking off the moment. "I'd appreciate that. Can't have word getting out—I've got a reputation to uphold."

"Wouldn't want anyone to know you're capable of being decent."

He gave her a mock solemn nod. "Gods forbid."

Another silence, this one not quite as thick, and Elara glanced around at the mess she'd made. "I'm sorry about your library. I'll clean it up."

Without missing a beat, he snapped his fingers. Vines erupted from the floor, methodically setting everything back in place.

Elara's eyes widened. "Okay, that's—"

"Unnecessary," he cut in smoothly, lips twitching. "But I am curious... how exactly did you manage to cast without a spell?"

Her mouth went dry. "Luck?"

He arched a brow, clearly unimpressed. "Luck," he repeated, drawing the word out as though it left a bad taste in his mouth. "So, just to clarify—pure, random chance is what caused that." He gestured to the lingering mess the vines were still sorting through.

Elara shrugged a shoulder. "Yup."

He gave her a long, incredulous look, then glanced back at the disaster. "Maybe next time, you could try your '*luck*' outside—somewhere far away from my home. Especially if the next bit of it involves more accidental fire."

"Accidental?" Elara scoffed. "*Please*. If I wanted to set something on fire, you'd be the first to know."

"Oh, I've no doubt." His smirk deepened, that arrogant glint flashing in his eyes. For a moment, neither of them spoke, the soft rustling of vines tidying up around them the only sound. Elara resisted the urge to fidget.

"Well, if you don't need my help..."

She spun on her heel and made for the door.

"I take it you didn't sleep."

She stopped mid-stride, her whole body stiffening as she turned back around. "Do you know that because we didn't meet in the dreamspace?"

His lips twitched. "That, yes. But the dark circles gave you away. We need to be using all our waking hours strategically. There's a lot that still needs to be done." His tone softened. "Get some rest. We'll need that big brain of yours if we have any chance."

A compliment. *Another one.*

Elara couldn't help the way her pulse quickened, the way her chest tightened in response. But instead of responding, she nodded, turning back toward the door. And yet, a small, ridiculous part of her almost expected him to call her back, though she had no idea why. She crushed the thought, reminding herself exactly who—what—he was. The Hunter. The *killer*.

Not someone she could afford to soften toward.

Still, the urge to glance over her shoulder itched. She ignored it, straightened her spine, and kept moving—each step a quiet rebellion against the pull that whispered for her to turn around. Just once.

~

"WE'RE APPROACHING THIS WRONG," Elara murmured, brow furrowing as she stared at the equation between them. It was a complex calculation—one she had no memory of coming up with, but the more she studied it, the more she understood her thought process all those years ago.

She tapped the scroll. "The issue isn't the energy itself. It's how the currents move inside the Void. We've been treating them as fixed paths —but they aren't. They shift. If we don't account for the turbulence within the channels, we'll never be able to track them accurately."

The Hunter's eyes narrowed. "But we've been mapping the larger currents. They're stable enough to predict with some accuracy."

"For short-term travel, yes," Elara said, her tone thoughtful, "but if we want to use the Void as a longer route for navigation, we need to account for the fluctuations. Think of it like etheric streams—never entirely predictable, always in motion, but following a pattern we can map if we can identify the variables."

His gaze flicked back to the equation, and he scratched his jaw. "So, you're saying we need a way to track the smaller fluctuations within the larger streams? Like subcurrents?"

"Exactly." Elara's eyes brightened, leaning closer to point at a series of symbols they had sketched earlier. "*Here*—this part represents the primary current, the main channel that carries the bulk of energy. But beneath that, there are these smaller flows—subcurrents, like you said. They're what's causing the unpredictability when we try to navigate longer distances."

"So, we need to calculate the probability of these subcurrents impacting the main flow," he said, more to himself than to her. "Like trying to predict the trajectory of particles in a fluid continuum... It's a matter of probabilities, not certainties."

Elara nodded. "If we can figure out how to track those subcurrents

—how they move, how they influence the main current—we could map a more accurate path through the Void. We'd know when to adjust our course, when the channel might shift, and where it will lead."

"But how do we measure the subcurrents in real time? You and Thane had only ever tracked the larger streams, and even then, the data was inconsistent."

Elara pursed her lips, her mind running through the possibilities. "We'd need a way to measure the fluctuations as we travel. It's not about fixing a single point but reacting to the shifts."

He considered this for a moment, then slowly nodded. "So, we need a way to bind ourselves to the currents, to ride the fluctuations without getting lost in them." He leaned back against his chair. "We'd need something—some kind of mechanism or spell—that could detect and interpret those shifts instantly. Something that keeps us tethered to the larger current but flexible enough to adjust as needed."

Elara's mind was already racing ahead. "We could use a modified version of the stabilizing enchantments we use for short jumps through the Void, but with an added layer that reads the subcurrents. It would act like a compass, but one that constantly updates based on the Void's shifts."

"That could work," the Hunter agreed, nodding. "It would be a matter of refining the enchantment to handle the added complexity..." He trailed off, tapping a finger against his leg before looking back at her. "Let's refine this."

Elara nodded, her fingers already curling around the quill. If she had her memories, none of this would be necessary. All this research, all these questions—they were answers she'd once had.

There is an easier way to get your memories back... a voice whispered from the back of her mind, insidious and tempting. She shoved it aside. That was a last resort. One she wasn't willing to consider. Not yet.

She sighed. "If we can—"

"For fuck's sake, if I have to listen to another word of this Void theory, I'm going to lose my gods-damned mind." Tristan's voice broke in, and Elara nearly jumped. She had completely forgotten he was there. He was slouched in the corner, looking bored out of his mind. Ever since her arrival, he hadn't left the manor. And while he'd joked that cake-eating had become his full-time occupation, Elara was starting to suspect there was more truth in that than he let on.

"You've been at this all day," he whined, eyes half-lidded as he glanced in her direction. "Time for a rest before you both drive yourselves mad."

He wasn't wrong. They *had* been at it all day. After Elara got a few hours' worth of sleep, the Hunter began guiding her through how to pull from his ether safely, how to control it without, well, killing them both. Which, unsurprisingly, had gone as disastrously as one might imagine. She winced just thinking about it. The first time, she had nearly incinerated them both with fire. This time, it had been water—a torrent so strong it flooded the circle of protection they'd drawn, nearly drowning them both.

The Hunter had called for a break after that, and Elara couldn't blame him. They'd both been soaked, exhausted, and Tristan had been watching her like she was actively trying to murder his friend. When she'd gone back to her room to dry off, she found a fresh set of clothes already waiting for her on the bed. Simple, practical, and smelling faintly of clove. She stared at them for a moment, wondering when, exactly, the Hunter had managed to sneak them in.

When she re-entered the room, Tristan's eyes flicked up, and the expression on his face was almost comical—somewhere between disbelief and amusement with a dash of annoyance thrown in for good measure. The Hunter, however, didn't even glance her way. It was like he was intentionally avoiding looking at her in his clothes, which, considering he'd lent them to her, felt... strange.

She pushed through the awkwardness, forcing herself to focus on the research spread across the table. But after a few minutes of flipping through pages and scribbling notes, she felt his eyes on her. When she finally glanced up, there was a heat behind his gaze—an intensity she didn't know how to handle. It crawled under her skin, unsettling, making her heart trip over itself.

Elara leaned back in her chair with a sigh, pulling herself back to the present. "We don't have time for a break," she muttered, though the ache in her back told her otherwise.

Tristan threw up his hands. "Right. Because rushing headfirst into another disaster is obviously a solid plan."

Elara ignored him, turning her question to the Hunter instead. "How many more days do I have here?"

He sighed, running a rough hand down his face. "Five, maybe seven tops."

She nodded, but her mind was already racing. "What does Osin think we're doing in Bravell?"

The Hunter's mouth twitched, something dark flashing in his eyes. "Chasing down a *Cailleach*."

Elara's heart stuttered. "What?"

The name sent a rush of cold through her. She'd grown up on stories of the *Cailleach*—a primordial force capable of summoning the winter, covering the world in snow with a mere sweep of her plait across the churning waters of *Tyrnolwen*. The *Cailleach* wasn't just a spirit; she was something older, a giantess who could mold the very land beneath her. She shaped hills, carved valleys, and created lakes with a power that defied understanding. Unlike the river spirits, who were wild and untamable, the *Cailleach* wore the guise of an old woman—her strength often dismissed, but it was the kind of ancient power that only time could forge. She embodied the overlooked might of the elder, a divine matriarch who shaped the world with wisdom as old as the earth.

"And you threatened to use me as *bait*?"

The Hunter shrugged. "*Cailleach's* are drawn to the scent of a challenge, like sharks to blood. And you"—he turned, his eyes locking with hers— "you're a walking provocation."

Her eyes narrowed in irritation, but before she could retort, Tristan cut in, his tone dry as ever. "Coming from Ivan, that's practically a love letter."

Elara rolled her eyes, turning back to her notes, annoyed even though the Hunter hadn't actually used her as bait. Was she supposed to come back from this looking thoroughly traumatized? How was she supposed to pull that off?

Her thoughts stalled as her gaze caught on something she hadn't noticed before in her notes. A sketch, half-hidden beneath the parchment, of two figures outlined in radiant light, their forms connected by a thin, glowing thread. Her eyes scanned the scrawled writing beside it, piecing together the theory.

Connections between people can exist beyond physical space, beyond even time.

Elara read on, intrigued. The Void, according to the notes, was a channel through which souls could travel, communicate, and remember. Memory wasn't tied to the body—it could transcend it. If someone crossed into the Void, they could bring others with them, pulling them through dimensions, or send memories through the channels, bridging the gap between time and space.

"Have you seen this?" She passed the theory to the Hunter, and he read over it, then nodded. "I think you were both trying to recover memories from before."

"Before?"

"Your life before you came here."

"I didn't have a life before I came here. Aine created me when I was eleven. I remember it—it's one of the clearest memories I have."

He leaned forward, flipping the parchment over to its backside. "You didn't think so back when you were in the capital."

Her hands trembled as she traced her fingers across the words, the letters blurring slightly beneath her touch. Words in *Tirrish*—ones she didn't recognize—scribbled in the margins, alongside a name. *Raijin.* Written over and over, at least a dozen times.

"I think you were trying to reach him."

A chill shot through Elara, ice settling in her veins. Dread. Sadness. An overwhelming sense of helplessness crashed over her as she looked up from the name, her eyes searching the Hunter's face for something—anything—more.

"That's just what I've pieced together," he added. The earlier playfulness in his gaze was gone.

Elara sat back, the realization hitting her like a tidal wave. "*Holy gods.*"

Tristan leaned forward, but the Hunter froze, eyes locked on her, waiting.

"This theory, if it holds any truth, it could explain..." She hesitated, sucking in a breath, wondering if she should even share what was swirling in her mind. But what was the point of holding it back now? "Every time I've had a brush with death, I've gotten a memory back. I thought it was *death itself*, giving me pieces of my past, but maybe it's not. Maybe it's Thane, sending them to me."

The Hunter blanched, his expression going still, as though her words had knocked the breath from him. "Which means he's still alive in there."

It was something she hadn't admitted to him before—her doubts about whether his brother could have survived in the Void all these years. But now, her heart pounded with the truth that had been staring her in the face all along. "And he's trying to reach me."

CHAPTER 43

The days blurred together in a haze of research, the soft shuffle of turning pages and the occasional scratch of quills filling the air.

Elara's thoughts no longer lingered on anything but the endless possibilities ahead—the intricacies of the Void slowly unfolding as they combed through the ancient texts. The Hunter's library had become her refuge, a place where time seemed irrelevant, measured only by the progress they made.

It began with recalculating the variance in the subcurrents' behavior. The subtle changes in ether—initially dismissed as noise—proved critical. They spent hours buried in the numbers, examining how each fluctuation influenced their link to the primary current. And gradually, a pattern emerged.

The subcurrents weren't random.

They had a rhythm, a logic.

That was the key. It had started as a theoretical exploration, one based on the idea that the Void's subcurrents operated much like weather patterns. The fluctuations in energy, those seemingly random bursts of power and instability, could be traced back to core movements, central forces that governed the flow of ether within the Void. Like weather patterns that could be predicted if one understood wind currents, pressure shifts, and temperature changes—the Void's subcurrents followed their own set of rules.

This was the crux of their theory: If they could isolate those core movements, identify the underlying patterns, then perhaps they could create something to anchor to them.

A method, or better yet, a spell.

The spell would need to act almost as a translator—taking the subtle fluctuations of the subcurrents and rendering them into something usable, something they could react to.

It wasn't enough to simply detect the shifts in the ether's flow; they needed something that could interpret those shifts instantly and adapt accordingly. A spell tethered to the larger current, but flexible enough to respond to the changes. Something dynamic, something responsive. The mechanism itself had begun to take shape in her mind. A spell tethered not to one person but shared between them—its strength drawn from their connection to the ether. It was delicate work, balancing the power they would need with the fragility of the bond itself.

Too much pressure and the spell could fracture, destabilizing the entire process. Too little, and it wouldn't hold long enough to matter. The spell would have to function like a conduit, absorbing information from the Void without disrupting the flow, feeding back what they needed to know in real-time.

But with this discovery came a cascade of new problems. Elara couldn't ignore the fact that without mastering her control, she would be a liability. She needed to learn, needed to be able to cast with precision if she was going to enter the Void with the Hunter. That left them with only one option: *practice*.

Every morning began the same. She woke to a soft knock at her door, familiar enough not to question. She'd meet him outside, where the early morning fog swirled at their feet, and the dew clung to the grass, cool against their legs as they made their way to the lake. It was always so quiet there, the mist hanging low over the water, the silence almost sacred.

The Hunter guided her with a patience that surprised her. He showed her how to pull from the threads, how to weave the elements together into a seamless knot. How to touch the ether without forcing it, to coax it between the threads of the *Draoth Cara* like a dance.

And slowly, after countless hours of meditation and concentration, she began to sense it. The pulse of ether, faint but growing stronger. She could see it in her mind's eye, the threads weaving between them, delicate and powerful, tethered at the chest.

But even with the small bits of success they were having the warmth of it faded just as quickly as it came. She hadn't been with the Hunter long, but it felt like a lifetime—like every hour stretched impossibly long without Reynnar. The constant knot of worry twisted tighter with each passing moment, gnawing at her insides, throwing her off balance when she needed to be steady. It was suffocating, the distance from him, even though she knew this was the only way. She was here for him, to help him—but *gods*, it hurt.

At first, Tristan had been there to lighten the mood, tossing in insights, and his usual sarcastic humor, making the long hours a little less unbearable. But his departure had been as swift as it was unexplained. Apparently, he had responsibilities that went beyond cake-eating, though he hadn't bothered to offer any details. Elara didn't press him. She hadn't asked the Hunter about it either—it felt like prying, and truthfully, she wasn't sure she wanted the answer.

But when he left, it unsettled something in the air. Elara hadn't realized how much his presence had maintained a delicate balance between the three of them until it was gone.

And yet, with Tristan's absence, something began to change between Elara and the Hunter. It wasn't anything dramatic—just a subtle shift that crept in unnoticed. The hours they spent together, buried in research, were filled only with the rustle of parchment and the soft clink of teacups. But somewhere in that quiet, an unspoken understanding began to form. It wasn't about friendship, not exactly, but a mutual respect—a connection that transcended the mistrust they had carried for so long.

It was in the small things—the way he would pass her a book without needing to be asked, or how they'd both lean in a little closer when they stumbled across something promising. The quiet shared frustration when yet another lead went cold.

There were fleeting moments where she glimpsed something deeper, a flicker of something genuine behind the facade he presented to the world. He would catch her eye across a table strewn with open tomes, and in those moments, she saw not just the Hunter, but the man behind the title. *Ivan.* He was a man who could lose himself in the pursuit of knowledge, who showed a reverence for discovery that matched her own. And in the quiet moments, there was a gentle connection—a recognition of the kindred spirits within one another.

Elara found herself watching him more closely. The way he tapped his fingers absently against the edge of a book when he was thinking deeply, the rare, almost imperceptible smile that would ghost across his face when something in a text amused him. She even noticed how he took his tea—strong, without a drop of honey, but always with far too much cinnamon.

And, in turn, he watched her too. She could feel it—his eyes lingering with curiosity, especially in those moments when she lit up with excitement after unraveling a particularly complex theory. He noticed the way she chewed her nails when lost in thought, how she always gravitated toward the chair by the window where the light fell just right.

Their evenings, at first filled with wary distance, now found a comfortable cadence. After hours spent researching, they'd sink into plush chairs by the fire, the warmth seeping into their bones as they cradled drinks in their hands. It was one thing to share a task, but quite another to share silence. Surprisingly, they found themselves capable of both.

One night, the fire crackling softly in front of them, the warmth of the flames mixed with the haze of alcohol, he started asking her questions.

"Tell me about Verdara," he asked. "Tell me about the ocean."

Her spine straightened instinctively, an old defense rising before she could stop it. The question rubbed her the wrong way at first—too personal, too close to memories she kept tucked away. But then, with the firelight flickering in the dark and the strange sense of familiarity that had slowly crept between them, something in her softened. Or maybe it was the alcohol. Either way, her tongue loosened.

She found herself talking, the words spilling out more easily than she expected. She told him about her responsibilities in the Sanct—about forging with the Elmweavers, stargazing with the Astromancers, and how she'd spent countless hours in the archives, cleaning up after the scribes. She described the Jade Sea, how it glowed at night, shimmering like a field of diamonds beneath the stars. But then, almost reluctantly, she admitted that she had never swum in it. That despite growing up so close to its shore, the sea had always been something untouchable. Forbidden.

When she glanced at him, his expression had changed—surprise, yes, but something else, too. Disbelief, maybe even anger, flashed in his eyes, as though the idea of her never experiencing something so fundamental struck a nerve.

In turn she asked him about the capital, its customs, its culture. She found herself curious about the world he came from, the life beyond the confines of their research and his duty to his lord. They never delved into anything too deep, both carefully sidestepping the weightier topics as if by mutual, unspoken agreement.

Their nights followed no set pattern. Sometimes they'd retreat to their rooms at the same time. Other nights, he'd linger—lost in a book or simply sitting there, his thoughts a thousand miles away. On those nights, when she had already gone to her room, Elara found herself listening for him, waiting for the soft creak of his footsteps as he finally made his way down the hall. She couldn't explain it—the way her body seemed to relax at the sound, how her eyes would drift shut just after.

In the midst of their shared quest, reality would often intrude. The Hunter would leave, some mission of his own pulling him away, though neither of them spoke about it. Elara could always feel the shift. Then came the transformation—the armor, the mask. The scholar became the soldier, and just like that, *Ivan* was gone.

When he returned, he always looked like he'd been through hell and clawed his way back. Exhaustion etched his face, the shadows beneath his eyes deepening with each passing day. Elara was caught off guard by the flicker of relief she felt whenever he walked through the doors—but she buried it, forcing her focus elsewhere.

Yet she couldn't deny the bond forming between them—one she

wasn't ready to name. Not yet. Within the library's walls, they'd carved out something separate from the rest of the world: a sanctuary the chaos outside couldn't touch, a refuge they hadn't known they needed.

Their shared work, the stolen glances, the ease that had begun to settle between them—it felt like something solid, something they could hold onto. But beneath it all, an unspoken truth lingered, hanging over them like a dark cloud.

This sanctuary was never meant to last.

Their bond ran on borrowed time—and soon, the world outside would come to claim it.

CHAPTER 44

Slowly, the thread began to loosen, delicate and glimmering, a current of energy pulsing between them. Elara matched her breath to the Hunter's, her inhales and exhales syncing with the rhythm of his chest. She focused on the thread, feeling its pull but refusing to yank, instead coaxing it, guiding it with care, unraveling the tangled edges with the gentlest touch.

Each frayed strand she found, she carefully rewove, connecting new threads, building new links where there had been breaks.

Blood trickled from her nose and sweat pricked at her brow despite the cold wind whipping against her back. Every ounce of focus, every fragment of energy, poured into the delicate balance of unraveling and rethreading. The sheer effort—controlling the flow, pulling without pulling too much—left her breathless, her skin damp with strain.

After days of practicing, something finally clicked. She could feel it now, the subtle differences woven within the link—elements pulsing with their own distinct rhythms. It had taken time, and the Hunter's connection to all four only added layers of complexity she hadn't anticipated. But today, at last, she could separate them, could feel their individual signatures.

Earth was the strongest—steady, unmoving, a deep, slow thrum.

Fire came next, a wild, crackling heat she could almost feel sparking at the edges of the thread. Water was smoother, flowing like a cool current slipping between the others, weaving in and out like a river cutting through stone. And air danced at the surface—elusive and free, always shifting, never still.

Surprisingly, once she mastered the slightest bit of control, the Hunter allowed her to practice whenever she liked throughout the day. The first time she tried it without warning him, however, he practically leapt out of his skin, muttering something about needing a bit of notice before she decided to burrow inside his chest.

He still didn't trust her casting indoors—not after the last two... *three* incidents. This morning, he had her working with the wind again, insisting she had a natural affinity for it. Elara hadn't had the heart to correct him. She wasn't about to admit that she'd stolen the spell, taken it from somewhere she definitely wasn't supposed to. And she *certainly* wasn't going to mention how she'd been rifling through his things to find it in the first place.

No, that little detail was staying firmly buried.

"Move the fallen leaves around us," he instructed.

"You haven't given me a spell."

"You don't need a spell. Ether bends to your will, not just your words. Spells are for precision. But right now—focus on the wind, feel the leaves. Move them."

It *should* have been simple. But simple, she was learning, was much harder than brute force. The precision it took to unweave the air thread, to pull just enough energy without letting it spiral out of control—it required an almost maddening level of focus. The leaves barely stirred, a pathetic twitch, yet the strain ran deep, all the way to her bones. The *Draoth Cara* beneath her skin hummed, whispering for more. Always more.

But water kept tugging at her this morning, slipping through the threads each time she tried to pull on the wind. It moved as if it had a mind of its own, weaving through the strands, and insistently brushing against her senses, almost as though demanding her attention. She'd push it back, trying to reweave it into the main thread, only for it to return, persistent and unruly.

"*Focus*," the Hunter grumbled. Mornings were always a challenge with him—Tristan had warned her about that—but Elara had figured out that if he had his tea before lessons, he was at least marginally tolerable. Today, though, he had skipped breakfast, and the bags under his eyes indicated he hadn't slept either. There was a restless energy rolling off him. He was still wound tight, still reeling from the night before— another failed attempt to tear that *thing*—whatever it was—out of her.

Parasite.

That's what she called it, though she didn't really know what it was. All she knew was that every time the Hunter got too close, it struck back, as if it had a mind of its own. And each time she opened her eyes afterward, those dark, twisting vines had crawled a little farther across his eyes.

He'd barely spoken—just vanished in that infuriating way of his, rifting out without a backward glance. She'd almost asked where he was going, but his foul mood that morning had stopped her.

Still, he hadn't forgotten. Every night, without fail, a dose of Stone-brew and a sleeping draught waited on her bedside table.

She didn't think she needed them anymore. Her muscles had mostly recovered, just as Saria promised; a few days of rest had worked wonders. She'd told him as much—reassured him she was fine, that the brews weren't necessary. But every night, they were still there. Small, unspoken gestures he never acknowledged, as if he didn't want her to dwell on them. As if he didn't want her to think he cared.

She saved the Stonebrew, hiding it away for her return to the Pit. She had no idea what awaited her there—but she intended to be ready.

The sleeping draught, though—she had to admit—it was nice. It pulled her into dreamless sleep, quiet and empty, no more spiraling thoughts. After hours spent practicing *Tírrísh* and secretly poring over his journal, it was a relief she hadn't known she needed.

Every night, like clockwork, he would disappear—off to do whatever it was he did—and she would sneak back into the library, working on her translations until her eyes burned from exhaustion. The draught was the only thing that kept her from collapsing under the weight of it all she intended to accomplish.

But if Elara were being honest with herself, she suspected the sleeping draught wasn't just for her but for him, too. He didn't want to see her in the dreamspace; he didn't want any awkward, unintentional run-ins. Dreamless sleep meant no shared dreams, no strange moments where they ended up together without meaning to.

He was keeping things distant.

Clean.

And, frankly, she understood why. It made everything less complicated because the gods knew their waking hours were already tangled enough.

Truthfully, she wasn't even sure he slept at all. Wherever he vanished to at night kept him occupied until dawn—she heard his footsteps in the halls just as first light broke, every morning without fail. He always seemed angry, though she couldn't quite tell why.

And if there was one thing Elara couldn't stand, it was people who spread their foul moods like contagion.

You're angry? *Fine*. But keep it to yourself. She wasn't anyone's emotional punching bag. There was a baseline of decency she believed the world should operate by, and today, the Hunter was failing spectacularly—short-tempered, silent, brooding.

An absolute *wet blanket*.

Which, actually, gave her an idea.

Without thinking, Elara yanked the water thread. A heartbeat later, the Hunter was drenched. He gasped, sputtering—and when she opened her eyes, she nearly doubled over. He looked like a soaked cat, wide-eyed and utterly stunned.

Laughter burst from her before she could stop it. It echoed once— and then his eyes narrowed into dangerous slits. Immediate regret hit her full force.

Elara sprang to her feet and bolted.

Because, obviously, running would save her.

The ground shifted beneath her almost instantly, waves of earth rippling under her feet. She barely managed to leap over one before the wind kicked up, pushing her back. She could hear him gaining on her, his footsteps heavy and determined. In a last-ditch effort, she tugged at his wind thread, breaking through the gale with a triumphant grin—for all of one second—before he tackled her from behind.

They hit the ground hard, the breath knocked clean out of her. Before he could pin her down, Elara scrambled, grabbing a fistful of dirt and slammed it into his face.

"What the *fuck* is wrong with you?" he snarled, wiping furiously at his eyes.

She couldn't stop it—a wild, breathless laugh burst out of her.

"Quite a bit, actually."

He let out a string of curses, one after the other, and honestly, she was almost impressed by his sheer creativity. Then, with a deep, exasperated huff, he rolled off her, and flopped onto the ground, glaring at the sky as if it had personally offended him.

Elara's breaths came in shaky bursts as she watched pale morning light filter through the clouds. For a moment, happiness flickered—warm, weightless. Then it faded, leaving a hollow ache in its wake. The smile she'd been holding unraveled, bit by bit, until it was simply gone.

The sky felt too big, too endless, and for a brief moment, it pressed down on her. Her stomach twisted, panic spreading as a lump formed in her throat, refusing to go away no matter how hard she swallowed.

Everything she had learned—everything still left to do—felt like it was piling up faster than she could manage. No matter how hard she pushed, it never felt sufficient. She wasn't learning fast enough. The parasite still lurked beneath her skin, and her control over the Draoth Cara was shaky at best. They were likely weeks—*weeks*—away from mastering the spell to guide them through the Void's currents.

Weeks when they had only hours.

The Hunter exhaled beside her, the sound heavy, almost resigned, like he'd made the decision to let her off the hook—at least for now. She could sense the anger draining out of him, leaving behind only exhaustion.

"You know, normal people don't solve their problems by throwing dirt in someone's face."

She turned her head to look at him. "Normal people don't spend their mornings grumbling like an old man and acting like they've never heard of breakfast."

He narrowed his eyes. "I was trying to teach you something, in case you missed that. You're supposed to be practicing control—not hurling soil at me like a child."

"Or maybe you're just irritated that my unpredictable methods caught you off guard," she quipped, a small smirk on her lips.

He arched a brow. "*Unpredictable*? That's the word you're going with?"

Elara turned away, hiding her smile. She shifted her weight, starting to push herself up, when something cold and gritty smacked her in the face. She gasped, inhaling a mouthful of dirt, sputtering as her gaze snapped to him. And there he was—*grinning*. Not just any grin, but a full, unapologetic, *infuriating* smile that made her stomach flip.

He stood, brushing off his trousers. "You might actually be onto something with those *unpredictable methods* of yours."

Elara glared at him, lips pressed into a thin line, but he only grinned wider. "You know," he drawled, "I've always thought you looked better with a little dirt on you."

Before she could snap back, he crouched and brushed his thumb over her nose, wiping away a speck of dirt. She stopped breathing.

"Filthy suits you."

Her glare deepened, but he only laughed, straightening.

He turned on his heel and strode toward the manor, his parting words lingering in the air like a challenge. For a moment, she just sat there, dirt clinging to her skin, sinking into her thoughts, her boots, her hair. Her mind raced, teetering between irritation and—gods, something else, something warmer, twisting tight in her chest. She shook her head, refusing to acknowledge it, biting back the laugh that threatened to spill out.

Elara scrambled to her feet, brushing dirt from her cheeks as she hurried after him, that unwelcome warmth settling deep inside her.

CHAPTER 45

The spell ricocheted, a piercing crack ripping through the library as light splintered and rebounded. Elara flinched, hands flying up—but the Hunter was there, arms locking around her as he hauled her down, shielding her with his body against the stone floor.

It should have hurt. It didn't.

All she felt was the aftershock—energy still shuddering through the room, heat and light flashing like lightning before burning out.

When the last hum of ether faded, the room fell still. His breath brushed her cheek before he pulled back, muscles taut. She didn't flinch. Didn't tense beneath him. It was almost second nature now, the proximity. She swallowed, forcing her thoughts away from it. From how little she minded his nearness. From how his presence had become something she could almost rely on.

"That wasn't supposed to happen," he muttered, his eyes darting around the room as though searching for what had gone wrong.

"No." Elara stood, pacing. "The anchor didn't hold. The link between the subcurrents and the main current was too unstable."

He sighed. "We accounted for that. I triple-checked the core parameters before we started. There shouldn't have been any volatility in the primary flow."

She shook her head. "The framework works, but the fluctuations are too volatile. The spell overreacted. The subcurrents move faster than we can compensate."

He rubbed his temples. "We calibrated the tether for rapid shifts. It should have handled that instability. If anything, the issue should have shown up in the feedback loop, not the main stream."

She stopped pacing and faced him, arms crossed. "But that's the thing—the feedback loop wasn't the problem. The tether held, but the connection wasn't flexible enough to handle the shift. The core pattern changed too fast for the translation to adapt."

The Hunter pressed his lips into a thin line. "So, we're dealing with a translation issue?"

Elara sank into the chair at the desk. "I think so. We might have to rewrite the entire response structure. If the mechanism can't adapt quickly enough, it will just keep rebounding like this, which means recalculating how much ether the spell can pull before it overloads."

"Which will take time," he muttered, his eyes drifting over the scattered notes on the table.

Time they didn't have. Only two more days until Osin expected her back in the Pit. They hadn't been talking about it—both of them pointedly ignoring the looming deadline—but Elara felt every second slipping away, ticking at the back of her mind like a countdown. If they didn't figure this out, none of it would work. No memories, no Thane, no way to send the Sidhe home. Not that the Hunter knew about that last part.

"I need to head out for something."

Elara's head snapped up, her eyes narrowing. He never left this early...

"All right," she said, suspicion threading her voice as she watched him go. Wherever he was headed, she'd find out later.

For now, with him gone, she could sneak in more practice.

As soon as he was out the door, she moved to the back of the library. The window seat was her favorite spot—his too, judging by the state of the cushions—and she reached for his journal, flipping it open to the familiar pages where she had been slowly piecing together phrases. It wasn't enough to simply read the language; she had to speak it, to feel it on her tongue if she wanted to get anywhere close to having a real conversation with Reynnar.

Her fingers skimmed over the words, searching for phrases and constructing sentences in her mind. "*Tell me about the Aelfhenge,*" she whispered in broken *Tírrish*, her tongue stumbling slightly over the foreign syllables. "*What is the Sidhe's connection to it? How were you taken from your home?*"

Her heart tightened at the thought of him—ripped from everything familiar, everything he loved. This wasn't idle curiosity or a language exercise. It was his story. His suffering. And every word she whispered felt like stepping into a wound that might never truly heal—a part of him she wasn't sure she had the right to touch.

She sighed and leaned back against the window, cold glass pressing into her spine as she whispered the words again and again, coaxing them into something that felt natural. The language was still clumsy on her tongue. She adjusted her phrasing, muttered a correction, frowned when it still sounded wrong—then tried again.

And again.

Eyes closing, she focused—

A sound—quiet, but unmistakable. The creak of the library door. Footsteps.

Her stomach dropped. She snapped her eyes open and shoved the journal back into place, fingers clumsy in her haste, nearly sending another book tumbling from the shelf. The steps drew closer, joined by the low murmur of a voice. Her pulse spiked.

Shit.

Elara jumped to her feet, wiping her damp palms on her trousers as she grabbed the nearest book from the shelf. She barely registered the title as she hurried toward the front, forcing herself to breathe.

Act natural. You weren't doing anything wrong.

Nothing at all.

Then she rounded the corner—and stopped short, breath catching. Sybil.

The girl quirked a brow at Elara just as the Hunter stepped in behind her, his expression tightening into something long-suffering, as if he were reevaluating every decision that had led him here.

"Well, look who it is," Sybil drawled, eyes narrowing as she tilted her head, a smirk tugging at her lips. "She looks like she's ready to bolt any second. Or is that just your usual effect on people?" Her gaze flicked up to the Hunter, teasing.

He didn't rise to the bait. "Sybil's here to help us with the translation issue. I thought her unconventional approaches might help us look at it from a different angle."

Elara nodded, though her focus drifted back to Sybil, who crossed her arms. "Not without what we discussed first, cousin."

The corners of the Hunter's mouth thinned. "Of course."

Without another word, he slipped into the stacks, his footsteps barely a whisper in the quiet of the library. Elara shifted on her feet, curiosity prickling at her as she watched him return moments later, a small leather-bound book in hand. It looked ancient, its edges worn and cracked, as if it had survived countless hands.

Sybil's eyes lit up as she took the book from him. "Perfect," she said, flipping through the brittle pages, her eyes scanning quickly before she snapped it shut with a thud.

Elara's fingers twitched. She was desperate to know what was in that book, but the Hunter and Sybil were already moving toward the front of the library. She hesitated, then followed, her thoughts buzzing.

At the desk, the Hunter warmed the cold pot of tea with a flick of his hand and began explaining their problem to Sybil. Elara barely listened, watching his hands instead as he poured a cup, added honey, a splash of milk, and stirred.

Without missing a beat, he handed the tea to her, eyes still on Sybil.

Elara stared down at the cup, watching soft spirals of steam curl up toward her face. Then she took a sip.

Perfect—the balance of tea and honey, just enough milk.

He'd memorized how she liked it. He'd been watching, paying attention—even to something this small.

Elara's eyes flicked up to him, her heart stumbling—but he didn't look back. His attention stayed on Sybil, on the spell, as if he hadn't noticed her breath hitch or the way that small kindness had shaken her.

Since learning to work the threads, Elara had gained control over the *Draoth Cara*. She could mute the bond, choose when to feel him, when to pull away—and he always noticed. Always knew when she shut him out.

Except now.

Now it felt reversed. He must have muted her too, his walls firmly in place. Her fingers brushed the bloodstone at her throat—his oath—but she felt nothing from him at all.

"This is dangerous," Sybil said, her eyes never leaving the map in front of them. "Even if you manage to pull this off, there's no guarantee Osin won't sense it the moment you start moving within the channels."

Elara's stomach dropped. Of all the things she had considered—*of all the risks*—she hadn't factored Osin in.

How had she missed that?

"We'll deal with that when the time comes," the Hunter said, his tone calm—almost dismissive. But the way he avoided their eyes made Elara pause. He had a plan. Or at least a piece of one he wasn't ready to share.

Sybil seemed to catch it too. Her eyes narrowed, teeth worrying her lower lip before she looked away. A moment later, she reached for a scrap of parchment and began sketching, saying nothing as her focus returned to the equations spread across the desk.

"If you're serious about this," she murmured, barely glancing up, "you'll need a filter. Something to narrow the focus and zero in on the most consistent fluctuations. Otherwise, it's going to keep latching onto those surges and destabilize."

The Hunter crossed his arms, watching her work. "A filter... but it can't be static. The Void's core currents are fluid. If we make it too rigid, it'll fail when the next shift happens."

Sybil paused, tapping the quill against the parchment. "No, not rigid. Dynamic. A spell that adapts as the Void shifts. Something that can modify itself based on the patterns it recognizes."

"That's what we were trying to do already," Elara said, finally finding her voice. "But we keep hitting the same wall. It adapts, but not fast enough."

Sybil sat back in her chair. "It's because you're asking too much of a single spell. You're trying to make it interpret the core shifts and adapt to them all at once. That's too much. You need to separate the functions

—one spell to identify the shifts, another to react. You're overloading it."

Elara's eyes widened. "If we split the tasks, we reduce the strain on the tether. The adaptation becomes more efficient."

"We need to test the theory again," the Hunter said, holding Sybil's gaze. "But this time, with two separate components. If we can get them to work in tandem without overloading—"

"Then you might finally see some results," Sybil cut in, her tone dry but not unkind, a flicker of approval in her eyes.

The Hunter exhaled slowly, frustration still lingering in his posture, but there was a flicker of something else—determination, maybe. He ran a hand through his hair, then nodded, the tension easing slightly from his shoulders as he moved to sit beside his cousin.

"All right," he muttered. "Let's see if this works."

THE SHIFT in their dynamic was immediate. Where Elara and the Hunter usually worked in near silence—turning ideas over before daring to test them—Sybil was the opposite. Loud. Impulsive. She flung out theories and tried them before they were fully formed.

Every few minutes, she was off again—scribbling equations, muttering incantations, tossing spells into the air just to see what stuck.

It was jarring at first. Elara's head ached from the noise. But Sybil's reckless pace did something unexpected: it broke the stagnation. They stopped circling the problem and started cutting through it.

Failures came faster—and so did answers. Each half-formed spell either sparked a new idea or showed them exactly what wouldn't work.

Elara and the Hunter focused on refining the first spell—the *identifier*—while Sybil stress-tested the second: the *reactor*.

The identifier was precise, tracing the core currents of the Void, pinpointing the stable fluctuations. Elara could almost feel the ether responding to her adjustments, the spell becoming more fluid, more in tune with the Void's unpredictable nature. Meanwhile, Sybil's reactor spell was wild, adaptive—just like her. It didn't wait, it shifted, responding instantly to the fluctuations the identifier picked up, adjusting to the flow.

The problem had never been their theory—it was how much they had demanded from a single spell. Trying to force one incantation to do everything: interpret, adapt, react. It had been doomed from the start. But now it felt... right. Like they were finally moving forward.

Sybil leaned back and stretched as the light in the library softened, the last of the sun slipping beneath the horizon. Elara barely noticed the hour, still riding the adrenaline of their progress. They'd made real strides—more than she'd expected.

Still, they weren't finished. A few more days to refine everything. Maybe the Hunter could convince Osin to allow it.

Just a little longer.

Elara's thoughts trailed off as Sybil set down the book the Hunter had given her earlier. She glanced up to find Sybil no longer interested in it, now flipping absently through the notes spread across the desk.

Her brow furrowed as she read the title: *Whispers of the Weft.*

A literary novel, of all things. It wasn't what she had expected. Written by Lachlan Alden, the back cover described it as "*a captivating tale of a tailor who stitches dreams into reality, weaving stories that interlace both the fabric of her creations and the destinies of those who wear them.*"

Elara blinked, utterly baffled. Of all the things the Hunter could have handed her...

"Well, I'd best be off," Sybil said, dragging herself up from the chair. Her eyes slid over to Elara, a smirk playing at her lips. "If you actually manage to pull this off..." She shook her head, a quiet scoff escaping. "I've warned you about him, haven't I?" She jerked her chin toward the Hunter. "Always ends with something burning or someone bleeding."

The Hunter rolled his eyes as he stood and stretched, his shirt riding up just enough to reveal a sliver of muscle, the faint line of a scar, and a trail of hair disappearing beneath his waistband.

Heat flared in Elara's cheeks as her gaze lingered a beat too long. She snapped it upward—straight into his knowing look, one brow arched, amusement flickering in his eyes.

Her heart stuttered, cheeks burning as she tore her gaze away, cursing herself for getting caught.

Elara didn't need to look to know Sybil had noticed. She felt it—the prickle along her spine. When she finally glanced over, Sybil's smile was pure mischief, but her eyes held something sharper, more calculating, that made Elara's stomach tighten.

She leaned in, voice low. "You're wasting your time with all this. There's a faster way. A cleaner way."

Elara's pulse thundered in her ears. She didn't dare move as Sybil's breath ghosted over her ear. "*What the Void consumes, only death can retrieve.*"

Her eyes widened, but the seer was already pulling away. "Open a rift for me, won't you, Iv?"

It wasn't until the door clicked shut behind them that Elara realized she'd stopped breathing.

CHAPTER 46

Elara's room smelled of pine and cold earth, the scents carried in through the open balcony doors as winter crept in on the night breeze. The chill brushed her skin, but it no longer bothered her. Weeks in the Pit had taught her body to adapt.

She lay sprawled on the floor as moonlight spilled through half-drawn curtains, illuminating the room in silver. Her gaze flicked to the untouched sleeping draught beside her, the glass vial catching the pale light and casting ripples of reflection across the floor. She hadn't even considered drinking it. Despite the exhaustion weighing down her limbs, her mind buzzed with too much energy, too many thoughts refusing to quiet.

Instead of sleeping, she'd spent the last hour reaching for that invisible thread between her and the Hunter, tugging at it gently, feeling that faint, familiar pull in response. She could sense him moving through the house—his presence a steady beat she'd grown accustomed to.

A soft creak of floorboards drifted to her ears, followed by wind whispering through the curtains. She inhaled, cool air filling her lungs, her awareness split between the thread and the quiet hum of night.

Then—from the grounds below—she felt him call the wind. The air shifted, trembled, and a rift opened. When he slipped through, the thread dulled, thinning to little more than a faint hum at the back of her mind.

She sighed, curling into herself, knees pulled tight to her chest. Sleep wouldn't come tonight—she knew that. She didn't even *want* it. Hours dragged on as her mind kept circling back to what Sybil had said.

"There's a faster way. A cleaner way."

The words rang in her mind, over and over, creeping into every quiet space until she couldn't escape it. What if Sybil was right? What if she'd been wasting her time all week? Who knew how far they could have come by now, the strides they might have taken if she had some of her memories back...

Elara pressed her forehead against her knees, her thoughts drifting to Thane, trapped somewhere in the Void, reaching for her through that endless veil. The image of him there, lost, sending scraps of memories like scattered pieces of a puzzle—it twisted something deep in her gut.

And the Sidhe.

What horrors had they endured this week while she had been away?

But the Hunter would never go along with it. She knew he wouldn't even consider the idea. The bitterness he carried—the resentment he still felt toward Thane for trying to send her through the veil in the first place, still tainted his voice whenever his brother's name came up.

So, instead, she had thrown herself into the work, into their research. But the anxiety that had been gnawing at her had only grown. It drove her. Made her restless, made her push harder—*too hard*, if she was honest. She thought of the *parasite* still festering inside her, the one they were trying to understand, the hours spent practicing with the *Draoth Cara*, pushing herself beyond every boundary, past every limit. The obsession that had driven her these past days was beginning to feel familiar. That drive, that compulsion—it was part of her, had always been part of her, lying dormant. But now, with so much on the line, she felt consumed by it.

A faster way.

It was reckless, stupid even, but it *had* worked before.

Summoning a spirit.

Offering it whatever it craved until it momentarily took her own soul beyond.

Ever since the Hunter had mentioned the *Cailleach*, the idea had been lodged in her mind, no matter how many times she told herself it was madness. But if they needed answers quickly, wasn't this the best way to get them? She had called on the spirit of the Cillareen so many times it had practically become second nature. But here, she wasn't sure if she could do it. This place, this lake—it wasn't hers. It didn't know her, didn't call to her the way her river had.

Still, that itch in her bones wouldn't stop whispering: *just try.*

Elara's pulse quickened, exhaustion fading as something ignited inside her. The Hunter would be livid—she had no doubt about that. After what she'd put him through last time, she had no illusions about his reaction.

Elara pressed her lips together, her mind running through the possibilities. But if this was to help his brother, would he really be *that* opposed? She couldn't be sure. But now—while he was gone, doing whatever it was he disappeared to do every night—now was her chance. If she acted quickly, she might get it done before he even realized, before he had a chance to stop her.

She shoved herself off the floor, snagged a thin blanket, and slipped from her room. The manor lay dark and silent as she crossed it, pushing through the front door into the brisk night.

Fog skimmed the dew-damp grass, curling around her ankles as she headed for the lake. Her breath came in short, uneven bursts—but she refused to dwell on what she was about to do.

She *couldn't.*

If she gave herself even a moment to think, to second-guess, she'd turn back.

The lake shimmered under the faint light of the moon, its surface still and glassy. Elara lingered at the shore, cold air prickling her bare legs as her heart thundered. She whispered the ancient song, her voice unsteady at first, but the words still held their power—threading through the air, drifting across the water to mingle with the mist above its surface.

Without giving herself time to hesitate, she shrugged off the blanket and stepped forward. The cold bit into her the moment she touched the water, the shock of it jolting through her body. She sucked in a breath, watching it fog in the freezing air, but forced herself to keep moving. One step. Then another. Each one sinking her deeper, the icy water crawling up her legs, her body trembling uncontrollably—but she didn't stop—kept going until the lake consumed her.

The night air, the ancient song, even her fear—they were all lost to the black water.

The cold cinched tight as she swam deeper, each stroke heavier than the last, her muscles dulled by the frigid water. Her chest burned as the pressure mounted, but she held on. Waited. Willed the spirit to her.

Darkness closed in, the lake's stillness smothering.

Please, she begged, *please.*

But then—there. A ripple. Subtle at first, then stronger, a shift in the current. Her heart stilled, suspended between hope and fear, as the pull of the water yanked her forward. The river spirit. It had heard her. It had come.

Massive and ancient, its long, sinuous body twisted through the depths. Shimmering scales reflected the moonlight, rippling and shifting like liquid silver.

The spirit coiled around her, its presence hungry, weightless yet overwhelming. Elara released the last of her breath, bubbles rising like fleeting promises to the surface as the water rushed in, stealing the air from her lungs. Her back arched, fighting the burn tearing through her chest, her ribs straining under the pressure.

Her eyes fluttered as numbness crept in.

But then—

A shadow moved above. Something plummeting into the water, fast and powerful. But Elara's soul was already caught between two worlds, toes dangling just over the veil.

And then, a whisper through the stillness.

"Eiliara."

A hand reached, stretched out in the dark, soft as a breath of wind, brushing against her skin. A voice drifted through an open window, wrapping around her, threading through the strands of grass tangled in her hair, curling beneath her bare feet.

"A Eiliara. Oscail do shúile, a Eiliara.[32]*"*

Gentle, impossibly soft hands touched her, guiding her closer.

"A leanbh liom Aerú. Oscail do shúile.[33]"

And then the memory shifted, blurring at the edges, and Elara was being pulled—dragged down a winding corridor. The rough, steady grip of a calloused hand wrapped around hers. She looked up, breath catching as Thane yanked her into a hidden alcove. He pressed a finger to his lips then pointed beyond the tapestry that hid them. Her gaze followed, settling on a painting of a dagger, gleaming as if forged from sunlight, surrounded by oiche blossoms.

Thane's voice was low, barely more than a breath against her ear. "You're the key, Elara. And the Wound of Light... it's the door."

She clung to Thane's hand, pulling him closer as his form began to fade. Panic surged, her grip tightening—but it wasn't enough.

Another presence stirred—cold and wrong. A shadow crept in, twisting around her, curdling in her gut until she wanted to scream. The sound lodged in her throat, choking her as it dragged her away.

CHAPTER 47

The cold night air hit her like a slap when they broke through the surface—icy and burning all at once as it filled her lungs.

Elara's ribs strained, pulling tight as if they might split apart, each inhale scraping through her like shards of glass. She didn't need to open her eyes; she knew the feel of his arms.

The Hunter's chest was hard against her back, his breath ragged at her cheek—his grip iron.

The moment they reached the bank, he released her. Elara collapsed onto the wet grass, shuddering, teeth chattering until her jaw ached. She was too cold, too weak to do anything but lie there. The only warmth came from the fire of his gaze, boring into her as he knelt beside her, chest still heaving. She didn't dare look at him—not yet. Not when the fury radiating from him was so palpable she could almost taste it.

"Do you have any idea what you almost did? How reckless—how stupid—"

"I had to," she rasped, forcing herself to sit up. "We needed the memory—"

"And your solution was to *drown* yourself?"

He finally turned to face her.

"I didn't have a choice. We're running out of time—"

"You always have a choice," he snapped, grabbing her chin, and forcing her to look at him. His eyes were wild, blazing with such anger it made her flinch. "And you chose to throw yourself into that damn lake like you had nothing left to lose."

Elara wrenched her face from his grasp, glaring through the tears. "You think I want to die? That I wanted *this*? I'm doing this for you—for Thane. Because someone has to."

"And I'm trying to keep you alive, but you're making it impossible."

She lifted her chin despite the ache in her chest. "I'm not trying to *kill myself*."

"Aren't you?" He crouched down, his face inches from hers. "And for *what*? A memory? A fragment of something that might not even help?"

"We need it. If we're ever going to reach him, we need every advantage we can get."

"You think I don't know that?" His voice dropped to a deadly whisper. "You think I haven't considered every possible way to get him back?" His face hardened, jaw clenching so tightly she could hear the crack of his teeth. "You're a fool," he muttered, standing abruptly, his body towering over her. "You're reckless, selfish—and a fool."

Elara staggered to her feet, her knees trembling but her voice steady. "I don't care what you think of me. I don't care what happens to me."

"Well, I do!" he snarled, a hint of desperation bleeding through the fury.

She stopped breathing.

The Hunter looked away, his hands curling into fists, knuckles white, but he didn't move. For a moment, she thought he might walk away, put distance between himself and what he'd just admitted, but then his voice came out cold, controlled. "You didn't think. You never think, not when it matters. You can't help *anyone* if you're dead. You can't bring Thane back if you're gone."

She winced, an ache curling tight in her chest. "I—I *know*. But I have to try. Time's running out, and the spell… it's nowhere near ready. We need at least another week to fine-tune it." She shook her head. "I couldn't just sit here—"

"No, Hallowed," he cut her off. "I won't *just* sit here and watch you destroy yourself. I told you before—that's not how this ends."

His words hit her harder than she expected, tightening her throat, forcing her to swallow the sudden knot of emotion. He stepped closer. "Next time," he said, "you tell me. You don't go off alone, and you sure as hell don't risk your life without knowing exactly what it'll cost."

"I know the cost."

"Do you?" he asked, his tone biting, but his eyes... they told another story.

Desperate. Defeated. Pleading, even.

She didn't know what to do with it. That look. That break in the armor she'd never thought she'd see. It made her want to step closer and pull away all at once.

He tore his gaze away, his expression hardening, becoming distant. Silence stretched between them, thick and bitter, pressing in on her until it felt like she couldn't breathe.

"Why do you serve him?" The words slipped out, fragile, nearly swallowed by the night. But she needed to know. She couldn't reconcile the man in front of her with the image she had built—ruthless, cold, and yet now he'd just admitted he cared for her.

He needs you for his brother, her mind whispered, but that explanation felt too simple. There was more to it; she could feel it. A tightness throbbed in her chest, winding tighter and tighter until she forced herself to breathe again, and it eased ever so slightly. But it wasn't her pain—she realized that now. It was his. The ache, the anger, the frustration—she had been feeling him all along.

"Why the sudden interest?" His tone was frigid, *mocking*, and it sent a chill through her. But his eyes were searching her face, hunting for something.

She refused to look away. "Because you're not what you pretend to be. You follow Osin's orders, no questions asked, but then you go and do something like this. Help me."

He snorted, a dark, humorless sound. "Help you? Don't be naive. Alive, you serve a purpose. Dead..." His mouth pressed into a hard line, the tension clear, but his voice didn't quite carry the same conviction.

"Right," she said, "just a tool, then?"

He stiffened, his expression hardening. "In war, we use every weapon at our disposal. Knowledge is power, and in my line of work, power is everything. We're all tools, Hallowed. Don't mistake your importance for something personal."

The words hit harder than they should have, and she cursed herself for it.

Stupid. What had she expected?

Gods, why had she even asked?

"Well," she muttered, her voice colder now. "Good to know my usefulness hasn't run out just yet."

She turned sharply, her feet kicking up dirt as she stalked through the yard, heading straight for the manor. She took the stairs two at a time, heat rising up her neck. Her eyes burned, but she bit down hard on her lip, digging her nails into her palms. She wouldn't cry. She refused to cry. Not for him. Not for this.

He was right. She'd been mistaking his actions for something personal, clinging to a shred of warmth when he had never once said it was more. No, that was all her—so desperate, so gods-damned lonely, that she twisted any kindness into something it wasn't. When would she learn? When would her heart stop grasping for things it wasn't meant to have?

She slammed the door behind her, the crack of wood against the frame reverberating through the room, making the silence that followed feel oppressive. Her chest felt heavy, each breath dragging as she tore the soaked tunic from her body and threw it to the floor. Water dripped from her hair, cold trails running down her spine, but she barely noticed. Her gaze swept the room and landed on the neat stack of the Hunter's clothes waiting for her on the desk. The sight of them set her teeth on edge. A wave of heat rushed through her at the thought of touching anything of his. She reached for her grimy gown instead—anything but his—

The door flew open with a crash, slamming against the wall so hard it rattled the floor beneath her feet. She screamed, heart pounding as she spun around, arms crossing over her chest.

"What the hell are you doing?"

But he didn't stop. He was already halfway across the room, eyes locked on hers, flashing with something that made her breath hitch—fear. And it wasn't for himself.

"You're being summoned."

Before Elara could process the words, his hands were on her, pulling her to his chest. The shock of it—of him—stole her breath. Her head tipped back instinctively, her eyes locking with his as his ether flared to life, warmth radiating from his fingertips and spreading over her like a thick blanket. It was everywhere, sinking into her skin, filling every inch of her.

She couldn't think—or breathe—as his gaze locked on her. She felt the shift. A rift tore open at their side, and he pulled them through, arms locked around her, his ether never wavering.

Elara's eyes fluttered shut, clinging to the feel of him—the steady heat radiating from his body, anchoring her as the Void pressed in. She was angry with him, hurt in ways she'd never admit aloud, but all she could register was that warmth.

When he finally released her, the absence struck like a jolt. She blinked, disoriented. They were back in her cell already.

Her gaze flicked to him just as he tore off his tunic and, without pause, pulled it over her head.

"Put your arms through."

It took her a second to realize she was standing there, unmoving. His tunic slid over her head—warm, dry, too large—and wrapped around her like a cocoon. That's when it hit her. *She* was dry. Skin, hair, all of it. She hadn't even felt him do it—warming her, drying her—as they rifted, so she wouldn't suffer the chill of the Pit. And now he was giving her his clothes.

He ripped off his boots next, one by one, yanking off his voice strained, "*Elara*."

Her head shot up, eyes locking with his.

There was something desperate in the way he spoke her name—like a plea woven into the cadence of the syllables, a promise etched between the lines, a vow that lingered in the air long after the sound faded.

He held out the boots and socks, waiting.

Taking them from him felt like entering a silent pact.

After sliding her feet into each boot, his presence enveloped her—

close enough to share breaths. She could feel the pulse of his blood, the rise and fall of his chest as if it were her own.

"Don't go looking for trouble. Don't do anything reckless. And keep working with the *Draoth Cara*. Distance will make it harder, but not impossible."

Elara nodded, letting her gaze settle on him, truly settle, tracing every line etched in shadow and light. She'd always thought his eyes were black—dark, impenetrable. But here, with so little space between them, she could finally see it: they were a deep, rich brown, and there, at the edge of each iris, was a faint ring of amber, so fine she could barely make it out.

She took in the rest of him—the strong cut of his jaw, the proud line of his nose, his brows and lashes as dark as midnight. His curls, untamed and thick, tumbled over his forehead, soft against the warmth of his brown skin. She'd never allowed herself this—the luxury of seeing him fully, always pulling her gaze away, deflecting whenever their eyes held too long.

But now she couldn't stop herself. Her heart throbbed, needing to commit him to memory, every small detail.

His throat bobbed as he swallowed, the faintest gesture, yet it sent a tremor through her. Then she felt it—his ether. Warming. Shrinking the boots to fit, just like he had done with his gloves. She looked up at him, bewildered, nothing about his actions screaming *"nothing personal."*

He glanced at the cell door, then back at her, something unreadable flickering across his face. "I won't leave you here," he said. "I'll find another way." He closed the distance in a single step, his hand firm at her back, heat pouring from him, driving away the last of the cold.

"Stay. Alive. Promise me."

All she could manage was a nod.

"*Say it,*" he demanded.

Her throat tightened around the words. "I promise."

Even as the unmistakable sound of boots echoed down the tunnel, drawing nearer with every heart-pounding second, he remained still. His gaze was a tempest—searching her face for something indefinable. Maybe it was a flicker of resolve, a glimmer of understanding, or the barest hint of defiance that he sought.

Then, as if he had found what he was looking for, he stepped back, the warmth of his presence vanishing as he disappeared through the rift.

Her hand trembled as she pressed her fingers to her lips, the touch doing little to still the significance of the words she had just spoken.

She had promised him.

Stay alive.

But as the cold crept back in, she couldn't help but wonder how much longer she could keep it.

CHAPTER 48

Cold bit into Elara's knees, her freshly scrubbed skin raw against the polished floor of the throne room. Every shift sent fresh pain up her legs, muscles trembling—but she didn't move. Not with twenty guards standing watch, eyes fixed on her like she was a cornered animal, waiting to bolt.

What is taking so long?

She kept her gaze forward, but Osin's onyx throne lingered in her periphery, its smooth black surface catching the flicker of torchlight.

Empty. Cold.

A jagged monument to the power crushing them all.

She shut her eyes, but the image clung—like everything else in this cursed room. When she'd first entered, her gaze had swept past the throne, searching the ranks of guards for Dario.

He wasn't there.

Only a sea of hard, unfamiliar faces.

After bathing and dressing her in a gown far too perfect for what was coming, they told her to wait. So, she had waited. And waited. Each second dragging, pressing down on her until it felt unbearable.

She was meant to return shattered—a broken thing stripped of pride, barely surviving days on the run: fleeing a Cailleach across the wilds of Latheria, a week in the Hunter's grasp.

But how, in the gods' names, was she supposed to act?

Like you've been hunted. Like your spirit's been trampled to dust.

A flicker of unease crawled up her spine, a warning hiss from some primal part of her. If Osin saw through the deception it would unravel everything they'd worked for, everything they'd set in motion.

One slip, and it would be over before it even began

Her entire body stiffened, every nerve drawn tight as the grand iron doors groaned open, the sound dragging through the chamber. She couldn't see who entered, not from where she knelt, but the footsteps— slow, measured—echoed behind her, each one a hammer to her nerves. She fought the instinct to turn. Forced herself to breath.

Then, from the corner of her eye, Osin appeared. His pale hair was slicked back with meticulous care, not a strand out of place. Immaculate robes draped his narrow frame, his expression cool, indifferent—as if the moment bored him.

Another figure stood beside him, wrapped in the deep crimson of the Soothsayers, the fabric flowing like fresh blood across the polished floor. Elara's breath caught as the figure turned, and her control slipped for a heartbeat.

Branwen.

"Hallowed," Osin said, looking down his nose at her. "Lovely as ever to see you. I believe you're already acquainted with this young man?" He gestured toward Branwen, a cruel gleam in his pale eyes. "He's expressed interest in replacing poor Godfrey, after that... unpleasantness."

The rage hit her like a flame to oil, burning through her veins.

"But I don't expect we'll have the same issues with Branwen here." Osin smiled, serpentine. "He's quite eager to serve, aren't you, acolyte?"

Branwen nodded stiffly, his dark hair falling over his eyes, "Yes, my lord."

Osin turned to her then. "I expect your best behavior tonight, none of your usual tricks." He took a step closer, forcing Elara to lift her chin. "I can count on you, can't I? To be a good girl?"

Her teeth clenched, bile rising in her throat. She held his gaze a beat too long, defiance burning in her chest, before looking away.

"There's my girl," Osin purred, yanking her upright as shadows coiled tight and held her fast. With a snap of his fingers, the shadows lifted her, just enough that her toes skimmed the ground. "We're going to have another rite today. Now, I know it hasn't been three months, but I thought, why wait? You're here, after all. Might as well make the most of it."

Elara's heart slammed against her ribs, each beat a heavy thud that roared in her ears. But her body wasn't her own anymore, just a lifeless weight as Osin dragged her through the twisting corridors.

The Grand Hall came into view—long, gleaming tables stretched endlessly, laden with glistening meats, overflowing fruits, and rich pastries that shimmered under the warm glow of chandeliers.

But it wasn't the feast that stole her breath.

It was the faces around the tables—they were the real spectacle.

The High Lords sat with their families, draped in silk and fur. Opulence clung to them—crowns gleaming, jewels heavy at their throats—but none of it softened the viperous glint in their eyes. Every gaze fixed on her, watching, waiting.

Whatever drove that attention had nothing to do with the feast before them.

"A little treat for my most loyal," Osin announced to the crowd as they moved further into the room.

A chorus of murmurs rippled, heads dipping in demure gratitude. But one head caught her attention—chocolate brown waves that fell just so, lifting from a bow as his gaze landed squarely on hers.

Tristan.

He sat there like he belonged. And, she supposed, he did. She had always known he held a rank, a status high enough to be on a first-name basis with the king, to win a night with the '*Hallowed*' if he wanted. But what really struck her was who he was sitting beside: Chancellor Vellon. The resemblance was impossible to ignore now—the angular jawline, the haughty set of their mouths. How hadn't she pieced it together before?

Vellon was his *father*.

To Tristan's left sat another surprise—Lady Calista Thorne. She spoke with effortless poise, as if this were nothing more than idle gossip over tea. She barely glanced at Elara, her gaze sliding past her like she was part of the décor.

Tristan was different. His eyes burned into hers as if trying to say something—then, just as quickly, he looked away. His expression smoothed as he turned to acknowledge whoever had spoken to him.

Osin glided to the head of the table and settled into his seat, folding his hands over the polished surface. "Go on, Branwen."

Shadows seized Elara, dragging her down and forcing her to her knees beside the table—placed just far enough back for everyone to see. Shame burned hot beneath her skin.

Beside her, Branwen's expression tightened as he watched her pinned to the floor. His hand twitched, lifting as if he might act—then stilled, fingers curling back.

Elara flicked a glance at Osin from beneath her lashes.

His perfect smile faltered, just enough for the corner of his mouth to twitch.

"Do your duty, acolyte, or I will find someone else who can."

Branwen's throat bobbed as he lifted his trembling hand. A gust of wind tore through the room, snapping against her wrists like fractured ice. Elara squeezed her eyes shut, biting hard into her cheek—then felt warmth spill over her hands, blood pooling beneath her.

She blinked her eyes open, vision swimming, and looked up at the faces looming above. They watched like vultures over fresh prey, eyes gleaming with a twisted fascination she knew too well.

But not Tristan. Not Calista. They leaned close, heads bowed, murmuring.

Hope stirred in Elara's chest. Tristan had promised to speak to Calista about her—was that what he was doing now?

OSIN LIFTED HIS GOBLET, swirling the dark wine before taking a slow sip, his gaze never leaving hers. When he lowered it, crimson stained his teeth, a smile twisting at his mouth.

Branwen carried on in silence, siphoning ether from her blood into waiting vials. The drain left her weak, strength bleeding away by the second. Through the haze, she clung to the low murmur at the table—the High Lords dining and debating as if nothing were amiss.

As if she weren't kneeling there, bleeding at their feet.

Snippets of conversation drifted toward her—*ether shortages in the western provinces... Yes, more soldiers have gone missing in the north... Trade routes disrupted, patrols stretched thin... The king's latest military campaign, the push to secure the borderlands, their forces already spread too far.*

It was all politics and war, the cold calculus of power. The kind of talk that decided the fate of realms. This was how kingdoms rose and fell —not in grand battles, but in quiet rooms like this, where decisions were made over feasts and wine, where the game was played with lives, and no one at the table ever got their hands dirty.

Movement snapped her focus back to Osin. He rose, robes whispering once before the room went still. Without a word, he crossed to Branwen and lifted a filled vial. The air held as he moved down the table, tipping a single drop of her blood into each goblet, the dark swirl vanishing into the wine.

She wanted to look away, to shut her eyes against the sickening sight, but she couldn't. A cold inevitability washed over her as each lord raised their glass.

"Drink," Osin crooned, "and let the rewards of your loyalty flow through your veins."

At his command, they obeyed, lifting their goblets in unison. Elara's stomach twisted as she watched her blood vanish down their throats without hesitation, treated like a rare vintage—something familiar, savored, undeserving of a second thought.

Why?

The question tore through her, relentless. Her whole life, she'd been told her blood was meant only for the Convergence—to bridge a caster to an element. But now she saw the cracks in that lie, the pieces that didn't add up. The shortages. The withdrawals.

Osin's eyes locked onto hers from across the room, his smile faltering the moment their gazes collided. The anger simmering just beneath her skin must have been written all over her face, a challenge she didn't bother to hide. His expression hardened, and that cold, familiar menace settled over his face. It was the kind of look that usually sent her gaze darting away, spine curling under his unspoken threat. But not this time.

He stood. The blue of his eyes vanished into an endless void, leaving behind something inhuman—something *deadly*.

Elara's pulse thundered in her ears, a frantic drum signaling danger, every instinct screaming at her to break the connection, lower her gaze and cloak herself in the mask of subservience she had worn too many times before.

But with every agonized breath that rasped in her throat, she vowed silently, fiercely; *she would not grant him a show of weakness.*

No, let him choke on his wicked feast, let him find her spirit indigestible, a morsel too stubborn to swallow down. Let her mettle be the bone that lodged itself in her throat, her resilience the flavor that soured upon his tongue.

A faint twitch in his eye was all the warning she received.

His shadows erupted, coiling through the air, a blur of black that sent a ripple of screams across the room.

Chairs scraped against stone as people scrambled back—but Elara didn't flinch. She lifted her chin, teeth clenched, refusing to give Osin the satisfaction of fear.

Then the grip closed around her wrists. Cold. Crushing. Shadows coiled tighter, forcing her veins open as blood spilled down her arms.

Pain detonated—sharp, absolute—like ice ripping through her marrow, spreading with every heartbeat. The world swam, darkness creeping in as something heavier than pain, colder than fear, crashed over her.

Death.

It pressed close, whispering of stillness. The room blurred into distant noise—rustling, shouts—until only Osin remained. His head tilted, curiosity flickering.

Elara sagged as black swallowed her sight.

Her breath hitched as all-consuming night stretched out in every direction, but this time, the chill crawling over her skin wasn't enough to fool her. She knew she was dreaming.

To her left, a faint glow flickered—sickly, wrong, like light that had forgotten what warmth was supposed to feel like. It whispered to her, just as it had before. Every step she took felt like an act of treachery against her own sense of reason, a submission to a force far beyond her will. Even so, she kept going.

In the distance, there was another light, smaller, weaker.

But the Hunter's light *burned*.

The veil between their minds felt paper-thin now, and the air shifted.

A rush of icy cold swept over her skin, stealing her breath, freezing it in her throat as she came to an abrupt stop. She reached out, but the connection slipped through her fingers.

And then she felt him.

Elara turned, but there was no one there. Just that familiar, steady presence. The beat of his heart unmistakable.

His voice came, echoing softly, wrapping around her like smoke.

"Where are you?"

"The Grand Hall," she whispered into the darkness.

She closed her eyes, feeling him draw closer.

"I can barely feel your heart," he murmured, concern threading his voice—and only then did exhaustion crash over her, dragging her deeper into the dark.

"Where are you?"

The question was barely a thread in the air, dissolving the moment it left her. But even as it unraveled, she felt the pull—like that thread was tugging back, drawing closer, tightening around her.

"I'm already here," he said, so close now that his words seemed to brush against her skin. "Open your eyes."

CHAPTER 49

Elara's eyes flew open, the world around her a blur of shifting shadows and flickering light.

Her pulse thudded dully in her ears. She blinked again, and Tristan's face swam into view. His expression was tight with focus, brow furrowed as he worked over her.

A cool, soothing pressure brushed her wrists, like mist skimming still water. Elara's gaze dropped—Tristan's hands hovered there, a glow tracing her skin. His ether pulsed through her in a steady rhythm, knitting flesh as if it had never been torn.

Tristan.

He was risking everything by healing her, and she wanted to scream for him to stop—to run—but no sound came.

Then muffled voices cut through the haze.

The Hunter.

"They've breached the northern border," he said, voice clipped and cold. "Faster than we anticipated. Two outposts already wiped out. If we don't reinforce the ridge, the whole stretch from the river to the foothills will be theirs before the next full moon."

The air in the chamber seemed to grow heavier, a ripple of unease passing through the council like a chill wind. A few leaned in close to the Lord Sovereign, speaking in hushed tones, their words lost to the room but the stress clear in their furrowed brows. One by one, they turned and filed out, guards following closely behind, hands resting on their weapons.

Elara's head throbbed as she struggled to focus on what Osin was saying, but then, as if he could sense her attention, Osin's gaze shifted, landing on her.

His expression tightened. "Tristan, my boy. What are you doing?"

Tristan froze, hands suspended, then straightened and stepped back.

"One night with the Hallowed was all it took for you to warm to her?" Osin's lips pressed together as he glanced at her healed wrists.

Tristan bowed low. "Of course not, my lord. But it would be imprudent to allow her to die. A waste."

Osin raised an eyebrow, letting the silence stretch uncomfortably. Then, with a single nod, he spoke. "*Quite.* I applaud your due diligence." The praise slid from his lips, smooth and polished, though his eyes held only cold calculation. "Malak," his voice cracked through the air like a whip. "Return the Hallowed to her cell."

Elara barely had a moment to steady herself before Malak strode forward and hauled her to her feet. Her legs wobbled under the sudden force, but she managed to stay upright. She shot a glance at the Hunter, but his back remained turned, his head lowered, engrossed in conversation with the remaining High Lords.

She closed her eyes, willing the world around her to fade, and reached through the *Draoth Cara*, searching for that thread between them. The pull was faint at first, but then she felt it—the frantic rhythm of his heart, beating against his ribs. She latched onto it, feeling the pulse in her own veins, and squeezed, just enough for him to notice. A silent thank you.

He had come for her, helped her. *Again.*

Malak's grip tightened as he dragged her toward the door. Her body jerked forward, feet stumbling to keep up, but then—shockingly— there was tightness in her own heart, a gentle, answering pressure, a *squeeze.*

She froze as the realization sank in. He had been able to do it all along—reach through the *Draoth Cara*, hold her heart in his grasp. He could have broken her with a flicker of thought, could have punished her a hundred times over.

He could have. Should have. But he hadn't.

Not once.

Her chest felt heavy, the ache spreading like a burn.

Why? Why hadn't he?

Malak yanked her into the corridor, but her thoughts were far from the cold pull of his hands. She lingered in that hidden space—where their hearts collided, tethered by a bond neither of them had chosen.

The softest mercy, or perhaps the cruelest grace.

It blurred until Elara couldn't tell if the warmth unfurling inside her chest was healing something broken or feeding the fracture.

She wasn't sure which scared her more.

The Sidhe were already on their feet when Elara and Malak reached the tunnel, their eyes locked on her as she made her way down the damp, narrow corridor. Malak's hand pressed against her back, urging her forward with the occasional shove, but she barely noticed, her focus elsewhere—on the others.

As she passed each cell, her voice was a low whisper, barely audible over the steady drip of water from the ceiling. *"Bí réidh,"* she said, her words slipping through the iron bars.

"Bí réidh."

Be ready.

Because she was going to get them out. And now, she knew how.

Her cell loomed ahead, cold iron waiting, but this time, Malak didn't need to force her inside. She walked in without resistance, the familiar clang of the bars shutting echoing behind her. Malak's footsteps faded into the distance as she scanned the darkness, searching for him.

Her gaze settled on Reynnar's familiar form, standing tall behind the bars. His broad shoulders were tense, his muscled arms crossed over his chest. And yet, despite his intimidating presence, there was something in the way his gaze softened when it landed on her. She quickly looked him over, searching for any new bruises, any fresh wounds—but there were none.

"*Slán sábháilte fós, an ea?*[34]"

His voice was low, teasing, but there was an edge to it.

Elara's lips twitched, but she didn't smile. "*Is amhlaidh duit.*[35]"

Reynnar froze for a heartbeat, then slowly, a grin spread across his face, fangs gleaming. That flash of pride, of approval, made her stomach flip.

The weeks in the Pit had stretched endlessly, but one small reprieve had kept Elara grounded—listening to Reynnar speak *Tírrish*. The way the words rolled off his tongue, the patient rhythm of his teaching, gave her something solid to hold onto. She had practiced whenever she could, fumbling through phrases, and piecing the language together bit by bit. Then she found the Hunter's journal, its scrawled phrases and unfamiliar script pulling her into long nights of tracing, memorizing, and drilling the language into her mind. Her speech was still broken, rough around the edges, but she pushed herself relentlessly, because this wasn't just about communication anymore. It was a connection—a way to show Reynnar that she was fighting for the Sidhe, that she saw them. Every fractured sentence was a declaration, a promise: she wasn't like the ones who had taken everything from them.

And when Reynnar smiled at her like that it was worth every lost hour of sleep.

"*Not bad. Maybe by the time we get out of here, you'll be fluent. Or at least enough to insult me properly.*"

Elara shook her head, only catching half of what he said, but she was almost certain he was teasing her. She stepped closer to the bars that separated them, leaning forward as her fingers curled around the cold iron.

"*I need to ask you about the Aelfhenge.*"

Reynnar's grin faltered, the playfulness in his eyes dimming. He moved closer, his broad form almost shadowing her through the bars.

"*The gate,*" he said, his voice low.

"*What can you tell me about it?*"

He leaned in, close enough that the bars between them barely seemed to exist. He dipped his head down, his breath warm as it brushed against her ear.

"There are three sets of stones," he began, the cadence of his voice turning rigid, like he was reciting from some long-buried memory. *"One for each of the goddesses—Áine, Rhiannon, Epona. Each is tied to the forces they command: Time, Death, and Life. Their means of traveling through the realms after the Great Divide."*

Elara's heart raced, her mind scrambling to keep up.

Reynnar seemed to notice her struggle, his words tapering off as he studied her face. He waited, that familiar flicker of patience she'd come to know well, until she nodded for him to continue.

"Their stones were positioned based on their domains, calculated to align with the lay lines of the earth, the places where reality thinned, where the boundaries of our world and theirs touched." His voice dropped lower. *"Their stones aren't random. They form a perfect geometric alignment, spread across this earth, and mine. The positions correspond to each other, like coordinates in a vast grid. A perfect trinity. Triangulated—always equidistant. One set here, one in Tír na nÓg, the last... somewhere else. Always three points, always in balance. They exist in every world, layered on top of each other like threads in a weave."*

"Time. Death. Life," Elara repeated under her breath.

He nodded. *"Each stone is a marker in both space and time—fixed, yet bound to the ebb and flow of the goddesses' powers. You see, they didn't just travel through the realms. They are the realms. Time, death, life... they governed those forces, held them in balance. The stones are mere conduits, arranged according to their dominions. Rhiannon's sit at the points closest to where the sun dies each night. Epona's stones blossom where the earth's veins run deepest, where the land gives life to all things. And Áine... Anie's are aligned with the stars, tracing time itself like a thread across the sky."*

"A map etched across worlds."

He hummed in agreement. *"Only... ours have been silent for centuries. Sealed. Until your king figured out how to open them up again."*

Elara's pulse thudded in her temples. *"Have you seen him with a dagger? One that looks like..."* The words faltered as she struggled to describe it. *"Like... light. Sunlight?"*

A muscled feathered down his neck. *"Yes. A relic from another age. Epona's, if I had to bet. Only something a goddess forged could rip through the realms that easily."*

Elara's mind reeled. The dagger belonged to Epona? Her breath hitched as Dominic's voice, from all those weeks ago, flooded back. *"They say Aine appeared because of him, but that's a stretch. More likely, he stumbled on something powerful, something that could make a goddess take notice."*

Holy gods.

Osin held the power of a goddess in his hands—a relic so powerful it had forced Anie's hand, granting him ether. Granting him *her*. But something still didn't add up. Aine would've demanded the blade in exchange for such a gift, wouldn't she? So how could Osin still have it? She shook her head, horror building as the pieces shifted and began to fit. He must have used the dagger to open the gate, wielding it like a compass. It had to be how he navigated the Void's currents and found his way to *Tír na nÓg*.

And through that opening, he'd stolen the Sidhe, one by one.

But Thane had said the blade *was* the door—and she was the key.

She couldn't make sense of the memory he'd shared with her, but the dread simmering in her gut sank deeper. Even if she and the Hunter finalized the indicator and reactor spells, even if they perfected everything, it might not be enough.

Her fingers dug into the iron bars, her knuckles bleaching. Maybe they could find Thane—maybe that part would work—but the Sidhe? Her chest constricted, her breaths growing tighter. They wouldn't reach *Tír na nÓg*.

Not with Osin still holding that blade.

CHAPTER 50

It began slowly, like sinking into dark water.

The world reeled, its shapes wavering as though seen through smoke and glass. Elara's back came to rest against wood, smooth and cold beneath her skin.

Then the shadows gave way.

The Grand Hall loomed above her, its height swallowed by darkness. The table beneath her gleamed with a sickly sheen, its polished length stretching on as though it had no end. The air was thick with the scent of wine, tainted by something metallic—blood-close—too faint to name, but enough to curdle her breath.

Her muscles strained, yet she remained immobile, every limb locked as though weights pinned her in place. Panic sparked beneath her skin, but she couldn't even wrench her hands free as the hold around her wrists and ankles constricted.

Cold slid over her skin. Laughter followed—soft at first, distant and wrong—then swelling, filling the hall.

And then she saw him.

Osin sat at the head of the table, his pale face caught in the flicker of candlelight. Beside him, the High Council watched, eyes bright in the gloom, smiles stretched unnaturally wide.

Her heart thundered, a wild, frantic beat as they reached for her—fingers brushing her skin with a softness that felt wrong. Almost tender. But then it shifted. The hands warped, turning sharp, and in the next breath, claws.

Pain exploded, a white-hot blaze that tore through her. A scream ripped from her throat, as her body arched against the onslaught, writhing as flesh and muscle gave way under their hands. Heat spilled over her skin—thick, wet, and her thoughts splintered, grasping for reason, for relief, but there was no escape. Just the ripping, the breaking.

Nothing else.

Blood slicked their lips and fingers, dripping down their chins, and pooling on the dark wood of the table, seeping into the cracks. Osin's smile widened as he watched her body convulse, as the pain twisted her screams into broken sobs.

Then—through the agony, through the sound of her shrieks—she heard him.

The Hunter. Calling her name.

She couldn't see him. Couldn't turn. Couldn't reach. But the desperation in his voice wrapped around her like a lifeline, hauling her toward something beyond the pain.

Elara, it's a dream.

It's just a dream.

She could almost hear him say it, feel the words against her brow. But all she could do was scream, her body shaking beneath the hands of the council.

The dream shattered like glass. Elara gasped awake in her cell, cold stone solid beneath her, real. Her heart thundered, breath tearing in and out of her lungs. The shadows were gone. The laughter, too. But the fear clung, her skin still buzzing with phantom pain.

And then she realized she wasn't alone.

The Hunter held her, arms locked tight around her body. His warmth bled into her, ether chasing the chill from her bones. His hands trembled as he whispered her name—again and again—just as he had in the dream. One broad, calloused palm moved in slow, steady passes along her back. Without thinking, she leaned into him, pressing closer.

She looked up, but he was already moving—already tearing open a rift as the air bent and folded around them. Thought and breath vanished, leaving only the certainty of his arms locked tight as the world shifted.

A heartbeat later, they stood in her room at his manor. The familiar shadows closed in, but he didn't release her. Neither did she. She clung to him as though letting go might shatter something fragile inside her, face pressed to his chest, fingers fisting in his shirt. For a moment, nothing else existed but the feel of him.

Slowly, her heart steadied. She became aware of his hand warm at the nape of her neck, fingers threading gently through her hair, his chin resting against her temple.

Elara closed her eyes and slipped into the *Draoth Cara* as easily as breathing. She didn't need to reach for it anymore—just a shift of focus, and it was there. His heartbeat answered her immediately, strong and fast, hammering at her awareness. She brushed it—barely—and he hissed out a breath that ghosted across her neck, stirring her hair as his arms drew her in, bands of steel around her.

Nothing personal, he had said.

Yet, the warmth of him, the closeness, it felt deeply personal. It felt like something perilously close to longing.

Elara drew back, just enough to catch his gaze—dark, but that sliver of amber was there again, pulsing like it always did when the mask he wore slipped, when he allowed her to see him, even for a moment. She brushed against his heart again, feeling him tense, and this time, his eyes slammed shut.

"Elara," he breathed her name, and it was both a warning and a plea. *Elara.*

When had he grown comfortable saying her name? She had always been *the Hallowed* to him—a title that kept the wall intact, a distance they had both upheld. Even when others used her name, he had held to that formality, as if it alone could preserve the line between them.

But now, the way he said it, like it wasn't just a name but something delicate and meaningful, made her heart ache.

Tears pricked at her eyes before she could stop them.

He must have felt it, because he opened his, and just *looked* at her. Stared at her through the dimness of the room, the quiet between them growing thicker with every breath. His gaze didn't waver, didn't soften. Just held her there, like he was waiting for something he hadn't figured out yet.

His breath ghosted over her lips, warm and close, and it took every ounce of restraint not to close her eyes at the feeling, not to lean in.

He could kiss me. The thought hit her suddenly. *He could kiss me right now, and I would let him.*

She wet her lips, and his gaze flicked down to her mouth, his pulse pounding so wildly inside her chest that she thought her heart might explode. Her whole body attuned to it, to him. But then, in an instant, he was gone. His arms fell away as if they had never been there, and before she could process it, he was across the room.

The loss hit her harder than she expected.

"I... can't," he said, the words rough and strained, like he was forcing them out against his will. His chest heaved and he stepped further away, widening the distance between them. "I—"

Elara didn't want to hear it. Not again.

She lifted her hand, cutting him off before the words could come—the ones that would only twist the knife deeper. The sting of the last ones still lingered. She couldn't take it right now—not his cruelty, not whatever harsh truth he thought she needed to hear. Not when the ache in her chest was already threatening to consume her.

He turned to leave, hand already on the door, but the knot in her chest snapped.

"Wait."

His back went rigid. Slowly, he turned, his gaze searching her face.

The words caught in her throat—truths she wasn't ready to name, even to herself. She swallowed and met his eyes. She needed his help. There was no sense denying it now. Not when everything depended on it. If she was going to get the Sidhe out, if she had any hope of finding the Wound of Light, she couldn't do it alone. And pretending otherwise would only lead her in circles.

Still, she didn't have to tell him *everything*. She didn't have to admit it was about returning the Sidhe to *Tír na nÓg*. That part could remain hidden. For now.

"When I called upon the river spirit," she began, choosing each word carefully, gauging his reaction, "it showed me a memory."

He went still, dark eyes flashing. "What did you see?"

"Thane," she said, her voice steadier than she felt as she stepped closer. "He showed me a painting. A blade surrounded by oíche blossoms."

His brow furrowed, confusion flickering across his face.

"The blossoms," she continued softly. "They only bloom under the full moon. My frie—" She stopped herself. "Avis. She cultivated an entire orchard of them in Verdara. Even in the forest beyond. The Elmweavers use them in potions and poultices. For restoration. For strengthening whatever's weak or damaged."

Her voice wavered, a tremor she couldn't suppress. Avis had given her those blossoms before, along with lion's mane—a mixture meant to restore, to focus the mind, to heal what was broken. Elara choked back the swell of emotion. Avis had known. She must have known about the memories Elara had lost and had tried to help her. Quietly, subtly. Without drawing attention, without putting herself at risk.

"What is it?" The Hunter's voice was soft as he watched the tears stream down her face.

"Nothing. It doesn't matter," she muttered, swiping them away with the back of her hand. "What matters is what Thane said." Her throat bobbed. "He said 'The Wound of Light is the door, and that I was the key.' The dagger in the painting... it's Osin's."

"I know the one."

Elara's brow creased. "The way Thane said it... it felt like he was telling me it's the only way to reach him."

It could have been what he was saying, she justified in her mind. But something twisted in her chest, the lie sitting there like a stone. When had she started caring about lying to him? When had his trust begun to matter to her?

"What are you suggesting?" His tone was cautious, eyes watching her carefully.

Elara ran her tongue over her lips. "We keep working on the spells, but I think we should start looking into the blade. Do you know anything about it?"

He shook his head. "I've never heard of any 'Wound of Light,' but Osin's blade—now that I know is powerful. I always assumed he was harnessing the power of the sun through crystals, using it to build up ether in the blade."

Her eyebrows shot up. "*Wait*—is that why you have all those crystals hanging in the windows?"

His lips curved into a smirk. "An experiment. I've been working with stones that haven't gone through the Convergence, trying to use them as conduits for ether. The sun charges them, and with the right spell, they work. But only once, and, as you remember, they can be unpredictable."

Elara's face flushed. "So you knew all along that's how I managed it?"

He tilted his head slightly, his expression flat. "Was that ever in doubt?"

She let out a small laugh, despite herself.

"I'll look into the blade."

Elara went still. "I need something else from you."

His lips curled into that small, infuriatingly slow smile, the one that tugged at just one corner, the one she was starting to recognize right before it appeared. "Of course you do."

She didn't let herself hesitate. "I want you to teach me how to rift."

The smile faded, his expression shifting into something more serious. He didn't argue, didn't scoff, or make some quip. He just looked at her for a long moment, and she could almost see the realization setting in—how real everything was becoming, how the stakes had quietly risen, how it was more than just talk and experiments now.

"I need to be able to travel on my own."

Finally, he nodded.

"What do you know about void fractures and how they affect temporal stability?"

Elara raised a brow, trying not to roll her eyes. "I'm guessing you're about to enlighten me."

He grinned. "Let's see if you can keep up."

❧

ELARA and the Hunter practiced rifting in her room as the hours slipped away, night fading into the soft gray of dawn. They worked in near silence, the earlier tension dissolving into a shared, wordless focus.

Each attempt demanded more than she had yet mastered. Rifting wasn't brute force—it was balance. Will and instinct. The Void was always there, stretched thin between worlds, waiting. You had to feel for the fractures—the places where the veil weakened—and then, gently but decisively, part it. It came down to control. Knowing exactly when to push—and when to pull back.

When she tried to open a rift back into her cell, she felt it—a brief pull, the seams of the world loosening beneath her touch. It wasn't much. Just a spark, a hairline tear between realms before it snapped shut.

But it had worked.

For the first time, she had touched the Void and bent it, if only for a heartbeat. Afterward, the Hunter slipped her back into her cell, vanishing through a fissure in the stone as swiftly as he'd arrived.

She had surprised him. Apparently, opening a rift with only hours of practice wasn't something most could manage.

Now, as the moment replayed in her mind, she couldn't stop the surge of pride warming her chest.

She couldn't try again here—not with guards loitering outside, not with iron bars hemming her in. Still, as she sat across from Reynnar, trying to eat dinner, her mind stayed locked on rifting. The precision of it. The strain. The way it demanded exactness.

The bread crumbled under her touch. She grimaced at her plate. After a week at the Hunter's, the meal was nearly inedible, every bite tasting of damp stone.

Reynnar fared little better, despite forcing the food down. They'd spent the day combing through what they knew of the Aelfhenge, the dagger, the night he was taken—the one near his village, dormant for centuries until it called them from their homes.

His voice had dropped as he explained, as though he still couldn't quite believe it himself—how they were pulled from their homes before they could even grasp what was happening, time stuttering, then snapping forward. And then he was gone. Taken.

Elara turned the description over in her mind. It was uncomfortably familiar. Too close to the trance the Druids used on Summons Day—your body obedient, your thoughts dulled, awareness reduced to a hazy echo. It had taken her years to learn how to push back, to anchor her mind and resist, even a little.

The Hunter had said she could still reach for the Draoth Cara from a distance. Not impossible—just difficult. He'd been right. After nearly an hour of meditation, she'd managed to sense it: a faint thread grazing the edge of her awareness. She could tug, coax the connection into place, but it was fragile—barely there. In an emergency, she doubted it would hold.

It frustrated her, but she kept practicing. Slow or not, faint as smoke, the effort itself mattered. Focusing on that fragile thread—however briefly she could hold it—gave her something solid to cling to. A task. A rhythm. Proof that she wasn't entirely helpless.

"You're thinking too hard, Eiliara. I can practically see the smoke coming out of your ears."

Elara's gaze snapped up from where she had been staring at the floor, her eyes narrowing, but her lips betrayed her with the slightest twitch. Now that she could understand him more clearly, she'd come to realize just how much of a smartass he could be. It was something she'd suspected for a while, but actually hearing it in the words, in his tone...

"You're one to talk. I've seen you—"

Before the noise registered, she saw it—the way his body tensed, muscles coiling, alert. That split-second of warning was all she had before Malak appeared at her cell, leaning casually against the frame with that twisted, cruel smile that made her skin crawl.

Her pulse quickened as he pushed through the wards, the creak of her cell door echoing through the corridor.

"Let's go."

Elara felt Reynnar rise behind her, felt his presence at her back like a wall of tension. She swallowed hard but didn't move.

Malak's laugh was a low, dark rumble that sent a chill down her spine.

"Some highborn pricks paid for a night with you. Guess you're worth something after all."

CHAPTER 51

Malak led her back to the same room—the one where she'd been taken before, when Tristan had won her for the night. A part of her, larger than she cared to admit, had hoped he'd be there again, that lazy smile making everything feel a little less dire.

But instead, Lady Calista Thorne sat by the fire, regal in a high-backed armchair. The flames cast a warm glow over her red hair, molten copper in the firelight, while her emerald gaze cut to Malak with such cool, haughty indifference that Elara flinched on instinct.

"Leave us, guard," Calista ordered, her tone crisp, like she was flicking dirt off her shoe.

Elara caught the way Malak tensed—his shoulders locking, his jaw grinding as if he were biting back a snarl. It was becoming clear he didn't take well to being dismissed by women—even highborn ones, it seemed.

"Aye, my lady," he muttered through clenched teeth. Then, with a curt nod, he turned and stalked out, the door slamming behind him.

The room fell into an uncomfortable silence, the crackling of the fire the only sound that remained.

"Sit."

The command came crisp, and Elara hesitated only a moment before stepping forward. She could feel every inch of herself—her dirty clothes, her hair an untamed mess—starkly out of place next to Lady Calista's polished perfection. It was hard not to feel small under that kind of scrutiny, but she forced herself to keep her chin up as she sank into the armchair.

Calista's gaze raked over her, the barest twitch of her mouth betraying her distaste before she looked away.

"Tristan tells me you wished to speak with me."

Elara's throat tightened. "Yes, I—" She faltered, the words catching. *Where do I even begin?* She cleared her throat. "I knew you once. Long ago."

Calista's eyes flashed. "You did."

Elara exhaled slowly, her shoulders sagging as the tension ebbed from her body. "Can you tell me about it?"

"So you *don't* remember?"

Elara picked at the broken edge of her nail. "I have fragments. A memory of us together. We were talking about Lord Artan's daughter."

Calista snorted. "Of all things, *that's* what you remember."

Elara's gaze narrowed, her heart stumbling over itself. It felt like an insult, though she couldn't quite put her finger on why.

Calista leaned back in her chair, her gaze never leaving Elara, studying her with a detached kind of curiosity, like she was trying to decide how much of her time this conversation was worth. The firelight flickered, casting shadows across her face, but there was nothing warm about her expression.

"You want to know about the past," she finally said, her voice smooth, though there was an edge beneath it. "I was the eldest daughter in a family that only cared about one thing—*status*. Everything was about appearances, alliances, and who could get closest to the Lord Sovereign. I was groomed from the moment I could walk—taught to speak softly, act obediently, and make myself pleasing to powerful men.

I had a younger sister. She was allowed to be free—spirited, wild. Not that it saved her in the end. But my parents made it clear that my sole purpose was to catch Osin's attention, that my worth was tied to his gaze, his favor. And I believed them. It wasn't about love or affection. It was about being indispensable. About power."

Her eyes flickered, something darker flashing behind them. "I was obedient. Played the part they wanted. I thought if I did everything right, maybe I'd earn a place by his side. Maybe I'd be more than just the pawn they'd shaped me to be." Her mouth thinned into a line. "But that's the thing with power. It has no loyalty. It takes, consumes, and when it's through with you, you're left searching for who you were before it claimed you."

Calista leaned forward. "Don't expect to like what you learn about our past, Hallowed. I stopped caring about pleasing anyone a long time ago."

Elara stayed silent, bracing herself for what came next.

"Yes, we knew each other." Calista's mouth curved, not quite a smile. "And I hated you. You were different. Didn't care about the court gossip, barely bothered with your hair. It made you stand out, made you a target. And for us girls, you were an easy mark. We were all jealous, you know? Jealous of your value to Osin. Jealous of how you didn't seem to care about anything we thought was important." She shook her head. "You didn't play by the rules. Didn't need to. And for all of us who had spent our lives bending and twisting just to survive, just to be seen—you were a threat."

Elara swallowed, her throat tightening.

"I got close to you because I wanted to mess with you—just like everyone else. We thought you were this privileged, untouchable girl." Calista's eyes darkened, a flicker of something—regret, maybe—crossing her face before she continued. "Lord Artan's daughter, *Malinda*, hated you more than most. She couldn't stand that you had the attention of the Dantan brothers. She'd been in love with the eldest for years, and you..." Calista shrugged. "You didn't even care. That's what made it worse."

"But the more time I spent around you, the more I saw the cracks. Your life wasn't what we thought it was. It wasn't shiny and luxurious. It was cold, distant, and filled with the same kind of loneliness we all pretended not to feel."

Calista leaned back, her gaze unwavering. "I know what it's like to be manipulated by the men in your life. Groomed to believe it was your place to serve, to please. To be told over and over again that you were only as valuable as the favor you earned or the silence you kept." Her lips curved. "But do you know what's worse than being shaped by their lies? Believing you deserve it."

She shook her head. "I stopped hating you after a while—stopped pretending you were anything less than exactly what you are—someone who never fit into the mold they tried to force you into. But by then, it was too late."

Elara cleared her throat, her heart thudding in her chest. It was a lot —a flood of information she didn't know how to process. She bit her lip, hesitating before speaking. "The memory I have," she started slowly, "is of you telling me about the Hunter tripping Malinda."

Calista laughed, but it wasn't warm. Nothing about her was. "Malinda," she said with a shake of her head, "she cut the ribbons off your cloak just to see you flustered at court. It was all so childish. But that's what we were—*children*, vying for scraps of attention. We didn't understand that it wasn't your fault. You didn't choose any of it. We just hated you for being in the middle of it."

"But Ivan..." Calista's mouth twitched at the memory. "He didn't like that. After court that day, he waited for Malinda, made sure she went face-first into the mud, ruining that ridiculous new dress of hers. He wasn't one for forgiveness. Even back then, he was intense."

Elara's ears buzzed, her heartbeat pounding wildly in her chest. "So the Hunter and I... we knew each other?"

Calista tilted her head, her green eyes sharp. "Yes. You knew each other. He was... protective of you. It was obvious to anyone watching. At first, I thought it was out of some twisted sense of duty. You being the Hallowed, his family tied to the sovereign. It made sense, in a way. He was following orders, nothing more."

Calista's fingers traced idly along the armrest of her chair. "But then I caught you both one evening, together."

Elara's heart stuttered, her brow furrowing. Why hadn't he told her *any of this*?

Calista smirked. "He was reading to you. A novel. The kind your teachers never let you near. You were supposed to stick to philosophy, religion, science. But Ivan, he knew you wanted it. Figured it out somehow. I later learned from you how it started—he would climb into an alcove, a rounded window along the path you walked every day from your lessons to prepare for dinner. He'd sit there and read aloud, knowing you'd pass by, and one day you stopped. You didn't know it was for you, not at first. You'd just sit in the grass outside the window, listening."

Elara's throat tightened, her heart pounding harder.

"When you told me, you thought he was practicing reading aloud, working through some stutter or nervous habit." Calista's mouth twitched. "You were so naive. I finally had to tell you to stop being such a coward and confront him. And when you did, you were so red you looked like you'd been cooked alive. But you had that book in your hands."

"And after that, you started trading books. His were always novels, something you weren't allowed to touch, and yours... well, those boring philosophical texts you loved so much. But even after you figured him out, I still found you two there—him in that alcove, reading to the empty air. And you, sitting outside, listening. It was pathetic, but sweet."

Elara was stunned. Dumbfounded.

They had been close—not like she and Thane, but close enough that Calista's words twisted something sharp in her chest. Friends, perhaps. Maybe more.

How could he have kept that from her? What was the point of hiding it? He'd had chances—too many to count—and he'd said nothing.

She shook her head, forcing the thoughts aside. She'd deal with him later. Confront him when she could make sense of what it meant.

Still... it was strange.

She leaned forward, teeth catching her lower lip as the next question pressed at her. She hesitated. Was it safe? Could Calista be trusted with it?

"Just ask me."

Elara flinched, her thoughts crashing to a halt. "What?"

Calista smirked, a knowing look in her eyes as she leaned back in her chair. "I can see the question written all over your face. You were always like that as a child—searching for more, never satisfied. Tristan said you could be trusted, so ask."

Tristan said I *could be trusted?* Elara tried to process that, a flicker of something warm and confusing twisting in her chest. She exhaled slowly.

"I need Osin's dagger."

Calista went still, the air in the room seeming to freeze with her. Slowly, too slowly, her lips curled into a cruel smile. "And what exactly do you plan to do with that dagger, Hallowed?"

It was a fair question, but Elara didn't know how to answer without veering too far in either direction—too vague, and Calista would close off; too open, and it could get her into trouble. But something inside her stirred, a truth she hadn't quite let herself touch before now. She went out on a limb.

"I'm going to kill him."

She'd known it, deep down, for longer than she was sure she even realized. Freeing the Sidhe, getting Thane out of the Void—those had been the plans she'd spoken aloud. But in the quiet spaces of her thoughts, in the darker corners of her mind, she'd seen herself sliding that blade straight into Osin's heart.

Calista's smile didn't falter. In fact, it grew wider. "I was hoping you'd say that."

Elara's pulse quickened. "Can it be done?"

Calista tilted her head. "I don't know. Maybe. What I *do* know is that the only time he ever parts with it is when he's in his chambers. He enchants it, hides it—"

"In a painting."

Calista's eyes narrowed, her posture stiffening. "Correct."

Elara shifted slightly, clarifying, "I've seen it. I have a memory."

The shift in Calista's expression was immediate. Her face darkened, something fierce and dangerous flickering in her eyes. The sudden rage in her made Elara freeze, her mind scrambling to make sense of the change.

"Many girls do," Calista said, her voice low and venomous. "Some, fortunately or unfortunately, do not."

Elara blinked, the meaning of her words sinking in, and her heart stuttered.

Was she saying...

I had a younger sister. She was allowed to be free—spirited, wild. Not that it saved her in the end.

Had. Past tense. Elara's thoughts churned, the sinking realization pressing down on her like a stone. This wasn't just about Calista's ambition or the hunger for power she'd assumed was driving her. No, this felt darker. Deeper. Rolfe had mentioned Calista angling for Osin's attention for months now, playing the game of politics, positioning herself like she wanted to be queen. But what if that wasn't it anymore? What if her goal had changed?

"Do you know the spell to get it out of the painting?"

Calista pressed her lips together. "No. He takes that memory from us. Leaves pieces for some, nothing for others. He…" Her voice faltered, and then she stopped, like she physically couldn't bring herself to go on.

"I'm going to kill him, Calista. He doesn't get to walk away from this. Everything he's taken from you, from me, from *everyone*—I'll carve it back out of him."

The words left her lips like a vow, her rage bleeding into the air around her. Anger, hurt, every ache of helplessness—everything that had broken her over and over again—it all merged into a fire so fierce she felt it would tear her apart if she didn't let it free.

Calista's eyes gleamed, and slowly, she nodded. "I'll help you," she said, "But only on one condition."

Elara held her breath, heart pounding. She could see it in her eyes, knew the answer before she even spoke.

"I get the final blow."

CHAPTER 52

"The winter solstice is less than a week away. It's the perfect moment. He'll drug the guests—he always does. Fills the air with enough poison to leave half the room stumbling and senseless by night's end." Calista crossed her arms, giving Elara a pointed look. "And him? He'll be just as lost in it as the rest. Drunk. Drugged. *Vulnerable.* That's when we move. It's the best chance we'll get."

Elara nodded slowly, her mind already spinning with possibilities. It *would* be the perfect moment. Osin expected her presence—there'd be no need for an elaborate escape from her cell. "And the dagger?" she asked, her thoughts churning, mapping the steps, the timing. "How do we know he won't keep it on him?"

Calista leaned forward, her green eyes glinting like emeralds in the firelight. "I'll take him to his chambers near the end of the night. Get him drunk. Comfortable. I'll make sure he leaves the dagger behind."

Elara's stomach twisted at the thought. "I don't want you to do that—"

"One more time," Calista interrupted, her voice sharp but quiet, like she had already made peace with it. "*One* more time, and it's done."

There was no hesitation, no softness—just a steel resolve that dared

Elara to argue. She wouldn't. But still, deep down, she told herself it wouldn't come to that. Maybe she could find another way.

Calista's eyes swept the room before settling back on her. "When they ask, tell them I slipped away in the night, after you'd fallen asleep."

Elara blinked, her brow knitting, but before she could respond, Calista turned away. She didn't look back, didn't offer so much as a goodbye. A faint hum of power rippled through the air as she opened up a rift and stepped through.

It wasn't the violent tear Elara herself managed after hours of effort. It was graceful, effortless. A sting of envy shot through her. But beneath it, something else stirred. An idea.

A dangerous, simmering spark.

She sank to the floor, legs folding beneath her, and closed her eyes. Breath by breath, she slowed herself—steady in, steady out—until the world receded. This couldn't be hurried. The Draoth Cara answered only to patience, to stillness, to a quiet surrender rather than force.

Her breathing deepened. Her pulse eased. Beneath it all, she felt it— the faintest hum, a whisper in the back of her mind. She sharpened her focus, drawing it closer without pressing. The thrum stirred in her veins, soft at first, then stronger, unfurling through her like a slow, winding current.

It took time—too much time. Half an hour, maybe more, before the hum coalesced into a beat, a steady rhythm she could follow. Her fingers twitched as the connection tightened.

"*Focus on the seams,*" she could almost hear the Hunter say. "*Like a fracture in glass—apply pressure at just the right point, and the rift will form cleanly.*"

Elara steadied her breath, picturing the rift as a gentle parting of layers. She reached out, searching for the faint tension—a fragile thread waiting to be caught.

Carefully, she pulled.

A jolt rippled through her as the seam between realms buckled. The air shuddered, bending and twisting before tearing open with a sigh. The rift spread wide, its edges trembling.

"Holy gods," Elara breathed, the words barely audible over the pounding of her heart. She'd done it. Despite the distance, despite everything, she'd torn the rift open. Her chest heaved, a chaotic mix of pride, exhilaration, and something she couldn't quite name—something raw and terrifying. *I could go anywhere.*

Anywhere.

She stood, pulling the *Draoth Cara* closer, wrapping it around herself like armor, and stepped into the Void.

The world fell away, leaving nothing but weightlessness and silence. The absence of sound was disorienting, a stillness so absolute it made her head spin. Almost instantly, the pull began—a subtle but persistent tug in the marrow of her bones, drawing her toward her destination.

The *Draoth Cara* thrummed beneath her skin, a guide through the uncharted dark. She focused on that hum, tuning herself to its rhythm, letting it become her compass.

And then—there. A faint glimmer, so faint she almost missed it. A sliver of light, slicing through the darkness like a thread of spun silk.

Her chest constricted; blood dripped from her nose, but she pressed on, each step guided by instinct and calculation. The rift lay close, yet the currents shifted, tugging at her, threatening to throw her off course.

She adjusted, felt the *Draoth Cara* steady her, and stepped through.

The silence broke. The Void's oppressive stillness gave way to warmth—

real warmth.

Her boots hit solid ground with a dull thud, the scent of aged wood and crackling fire curling around her. She blinked, adjusting to the faint glow of the Hunter's hearth.

Her breaths came fast, fingers twitching at her sides.

She'd done it.

The rush crashed over her, pulse thundering, veins buzzing with something far beyond excitement. Validation. The theory, the practice —all of it had led here. She had commanded the Void, bent it to her will, and emerged exactly where she meant to be.

It was exhilarating. Almost overwhelming.

It didn't matter that it wasn't her ether guiding her, that she'd leaned on the *Draoth Cara* to navigate. The achievement felt no less hers. When the final sigil was broken—when the *parasite* was gone—

maybe she wouldn't need the link at all. The idea burned in the back of her mind, a tiny, defiant flame.

Elara moved silently through the entryway, the familiar pull of the thread guiding her effortlessly down the corridor, a sensation so natural now it brought a flicker of smug satisfaction.

When she pushed open the library door, she wasn't surprised to find him there, hunched over the desk with one hand tangled in his hair, rubbing his temple. A small part of her wanted to laugh—finally, she had the upper hand.

With a mischievous grin, she gave the thread a playful tug, her mental grip on his heart tightening just enough to send a flicker of sensation through him. He startled upright, nearly leaping from his chair, his wide, flashing eyes darting around the room until they landed on her.

His gaze softened, his mouth falling open as he stared, completely thrown. Her grin only widened, and slowly, as though he couldn't quite believe it, his lips curved into a smile of his own.

"You did it."

Elara rolled her eyes, doing her best to sound unimpressed. "Was that ever in doubt?"

He let out a breathless laugh, shaking his head as he stood. "If anyone could figure out how to rift in a day, it'd be you."

Heat crept up her neck, settling in her cheeks at his compliment, but it wasn't just that—it was what she needed to say next.

"I met with Calista tonight."

His smile vanished, wiped clean as if she'd struck him. He froze mid-step, searching her face. "You did?"

Elara hummed, the sound softer than she intended. "She bought me for the night. That's how I managed to get here."

He nodded slowly, but she saw it—the walls he always built around himself creeping higher with every measured breath.

"And what did she want with you?"

"I asked Tristan to relay a message for me—to tell her I wanted to speak with her." Elara watched his brow twitch, a subtle reaction that told her this was news to him. "I had a memory, something I needed confirmation on."

He folded his arms across his chest, his expression still carefully guarded. "And? Did you get what you were after?"

"I did."

Silence stretched between them, charged. Tension rolled off him, taut as a drawn wire, and she sensed how close he was to bolting. Elara steadied herself before continuing.

"She told me about us."

There it was—the lurch in his chest, just as she'd expected. She'd braced herself for it, but somehow, it still struck harder than she could have prepared for.

"Told me how you used to read to me. How we shared books." Her heart throbbed, a cutting ache. "Why didn't you tell me?"

He bit the inside of his lip—she could feel the sting. His eyes stayed locked on hers, his expression hard. A fortress, impenetrable. But Elara didn't need to see his emotions to feel them. He couldn't hide that from her anymore.

"I didn't see the point."

The words hit like a blow she wasn't ready for. That *hurt*.

"And why the hell not?"

"What good would it have done?"

His tone was even—too even. Each word carried what he refused to say. The detachment, the casual dismissal of something that mattered to her, struck a spark in her chest. Heat flared, fierce and sudden, her pulse roaring in her ears.

"How can you be so damn callous? I remember nothing from my past. *Nothing*. And this whole time—this entire time—we've been trying to piece it back together. Trying to break the Binding Sigil so I can help you reach Thane. And you—" Her words caught, choking on the knot in her throat. "You knew. You had something—a piece I could've used, that I needed—and you kept it from me. How could you—"

"Our memories wouldn't have helped us. Not with what we're trying to do. If anything, it would've complicated things."

Elara's fists clenched at her sides. "How the hell do you figure that?"

He ran a hand through his hair. "What we..." He exhaled, almost in defeat, his voice lower now. "I told you, it wouldn't have done any good."

"And that was for *you* to decide, was it?" Fury crackled through her like lightning. "Like everyone else in my life, thinking they know best, deciding for me, keeping things from me—that was *your* call, too? You couldn't give me the basic decency of a *choice*? Couldn't trust me with that?"

He shifted, like he was going to step toward her, but then stopped, locking his expression again.

Elara shook her head, incredulous. "I thought you understood— thought you, of all people, would get it. We've both had our choices taken from us, and this... this tiny thing, and you couldn't even give me that?"

His jaw clenched. "No, I couldn't."

Something inside her broke. She stepped forward without thinking, her hand moving on instinct. The slap cracked through the room, pain flaring across her palm. His head turned with the blow—but he didn't react. He didn't so much as blink.

"Stop being such a *coward*!"

Elara turned to leave, already searching for the seam between worlds, ready to rift away. But in three swift strides, he was on her, his hand gripping her arm and yanking her back until she collided with him. His fingers were at her throat before she could regain her balance, pulling her closer. She let out a strangled cry—surprised, breathless—just as he kissed her.

It was hard, bruising, all the tension between them erupting in that single moment.

He pulled back just enough, his breath hot against her lips, his voice low and rough.

"You insufferable, *maddening* woman."

Her stomach dropped, her heart flipping wildly, and she barely managed a squeak before his lips crashed back onto hers, cutting off any sound.

It wasn't just a kiss—it was an *invasion*. A kiss that plundered, as if her fury was something he craved, something he wanted to drag from her throat and consume.

Her breaths came in short, frantic bursts through her nose, her chest heaving as her heart thundered like it might break free. The world blurred around her, narrowing to the demanding press of his mouth against hers. When he shifted, capturing her bottom lip between his own, she exhaled sharply. Her hands curled into his shirt on instinct, and before she could stop herself, she kissed him back.

A low sound rumbled from him, somewhere between a growl and a sigh, as his hand slid up the back of her neck. His fingers threaded into her hair, cradling her head as though letting go was impossible. Her stomach twisted, heat and a strange fluttering spreading through her. The thought flickered in her mind that this was a terrible idea, that she should stop—but gods, she didn't want to.

His hand slipped from her neck, fingers trailing lightly down her arm, barely brushing her skin before wrapping around her. Her lips parted, and his tongue slid against hers.

A low groan escaped him, the sound rippling through her.

She met his kiss with equal force, curling her tongue around his, following him deeper, tasting him—cinnamon and black tea, fire and smoke—a mix of heat and spice.

Her nails grazed his scalp as he pulled back. "Is this what you want, Elara? Hmm? Should I just take this?"

She could only whimper in response, rising onto her toes to meet him halfway. He didn't hesitate, his hands gripping her waist as he lifted her. Her legs wrapped instinctively around his hips, and his lips stayed locked on hers as he carried her out of the library and into the drawing room. It was as if he couldn't bear to break the connection, not even for a second.

His fingers knotted in her hair, tipping her head back, baring the line of her throat. Then his mouth was there—lips and teeth skimming the sensitive curve of her neck.

Elara's breath hitched as he followed the path with heated, open-mouthed kisses. He sank onto the settee, drawing her down with him, her body settling astride his lap. His hands closed on her hips, firm, pulling her in until there was no space left between them. The sound that tore from her—a soft, broken moan—was met by his, low and guttural, vibrating against her chest.

She felt him, hard against her stomach, and exhaled into his mouth, her eyes flying open at the sensation. She hadn't expected it, and the suddenness sent a rush of nerves coursing through her. But there was something else, too—something like pride, or maybe power. She pulled back just enough to meet his gaze.

His eyes were dark, his lips swollen and red, cheeks flushed. He looked at her like no one ever had before—like she was something to be cherished, protected, *devoured*—and the intensity of it sent a dip through her stomach, her breath catching in her throat. He was watching her, waiting, his hand fisted tightly in her shirt, holding her there but giving her space to decide what came next.

It felt unreal—like her mind couldn't fully catch up that this was the Hunter beneath her. *Ivan.* The man who had always been untouchable, unshakable. And now here he was, his hands on her, trembling where they gripped her, his breathing ragged, utterly at her mercy.

His hands drifted down her arms, heat radiating from him, pulsing with the ether that always seemed to simmer just beneath his skin. They were rough, calloused from years of battle, from war, from everything that had shaped him into the man before her. He traced soft arcs with the pads of his fingers over her palms, gliding up to her fingertips before sliding back down to intertwine their hands.

Her heart clenched at the tender gesture, but all she could think about was *"nothing personal,"* how he had kept those memories from her—the ones of them together. There was a reason he hadn't told her, something that twisted her insides the longer she dwelled on it.

He wasn't trying to hurt her; she knew him well enough to believe that. But still, he had kept it from her—maybe not to manipulate, but to protect himself.

The urge to ask again, to demand an explanation now that they had crossed this line, burned on her tongue. But then his hand was on her face, his thumb ghosting over her mouth, and the question died on her lips.

"Can I touch you?" His voice was barely a whisper, and when he breathed in, his stomach pressed against hers, fluttering and tight. She licked her lips, eyes drifting up to meet his, dark and hooded.

"Yes."

That made him smile, just a little, a soft curve of his lips. Those rough, calloused fingertips trailed down her jaw, over her neck, ghosting along the line of her shirt until they reached her breast. He moved with the curve of her body. "Here?" His voice was so low it sent a shiver through her.

"Yes."

When he cupped her, she gasped, and he shifted at the sound, hips pressing closer. Whatever restraint he'd been holding fractured, and in one smooth motion his hand slid beneath her shirt, fingers slipping under the lace until skin met skin. His touch was warm, rough enough to make her breath catch, her eyes fluttering shut under the rush of it.

He let out a slow breath as her fingers traced his face, mapping lines and features she'd memorized from a distance for far too long. His skin was warm beneath her touch, and when she finally dared to skim her thumb over his lips, his breath came hot against her fingertips. His hand drifted lower, sliding over her stomach as he drew her index finger into his mouth. Her stomach flipped, her back arching—

and then the world tipped when his fingers slipped beneath the waistband of her pants, grazing the soft skin at her lower belly.

Her body jolted, and his eyes snapped to hers as he released her finger from his mouth.

"Here?"

She swallowed and nodded. His hand dipped lower, the warmth of his fingers brushing her, stealing her breath.

He traced her slowly, pressing just enough to spark sensation through her body. When he found the place that made her hips jerk against him, she gasped, her breathing turning quick and uneven.

"Gods, yes," she said—though it was so much more than okay. Too much to name.

His finger circled slowly, pleasure rolling through her in steady waves. Her hands fisted in his shirt, fingers digging into his shoulders as her hips moved on their own, chasing more with every pass of his hand.

His hips jerked back once—but by the time he pressed a finger, then two, inside her, he'd found a rhythm against her leg, grinding into her with a need that matched her own. Elara's hand slid to the back of his neck, tugging, wordless, pleading for a kiss.

He didn't move.

She saw it in his eyes—he wanted to watch her. Every breath, every shudder. He wasn't willing to miss a second of it.

Heat licked up her spine, spreading fast beneath her skin, and before she could stop herself she was moving—fucking his hand in a way that would make her blush later. His breath turned heavy, pupils blown wide, his face flushed.

She was so close—that tight, coiled pull in her belly, ready to snap—when he slowed—hovering just shy of pushing her over.

Slow, deliberate strokes drew a whimper from her, her fingers twisting into his shirt. He kept her there, on the edge, drawing her up and pulling back until she was nearly sobbing with need, blood roaring through her veins.

He leaned forward, placing his forehead against hers.

"Fuck, you're so beautiful, Elara. Look at you."

His lips brushed over the sweat beading on her skin, trailing his mouth down to her neck, his tongue flicking over her pulse before sucking gently. She knew he could taste her sweat, feel the wild beat of her heart beneath his lips, the tremble of her body as she moaned his name.

Ivan.

Not the Hunter. *Ivan.*

His hips moved faster, his fingers keeping pace, and she splintered in his hands—arching toward him, pleading. Her nails dug into his arms as his thumb circled, relentless, his fingers curving inside her, finding that spot again and again.

A gasp tore from her, lungs burning, and then her hips jerked up into him as her release crashed through her—violent, all-consuming.

Fire and lightning raced through her, every nerve alight. Pressure and heat fused into a single, blinding rush until the world dissolved. The weight of him, the rasp of his breath at her neck, the salt of sweat on her lips—everything blurred into sensation, into him, his hands gripping her, his fingers still moving as she came apart.

Then everything went black, her vision tunneling, the only sound the rush of blood in her ears and the ragged breaths they both fought for. The room, the world, the war—none of it existed. There was only him. Only the way his touch had undone her.

The return was abrupt, like being torn from a dream—one sharp jolt back into reality, as though she'd been floating and then fallen, straight back into him.

Her body buzzed, tingling everywhere he'd touched, her thoughts slow and unsteady as she gulped air through the aftershocks. He was breathing just as hard, his chest rising and falling with hers, breath warm and damp against the curve of her neck where his face was buried in her hair. Weakly, she wrapped her arms around him, muscles trembling with the effort.

After a moment, he withdrew his fingers slowly, dragging a lingering line across her stomach that sent one last shiver through her. His hand disappeared, then returned to settle at her hip.

There was so much she needed to say, but all she could do was breathe, her body still twitching as she came back to herself.

And then it struck her—she hadn't touched him.

Heat rushed to her cheeks. With Dario it had been fast and quiet, hidden in the dark. Gentle, yes—patient, because it had been her first time—but there had been no exploration. She hadn't even thought to reach for him.

Now, she could feel Ivan still hard between them, and something stirred at the thought of touching him, of returning what he'd given her.

She bit her lip, fighting the smile that threatened to break free as her hand moved toward him.

He caught her wrist.

"You don't... You should sleep."

Her brow furrowed, confused.

"You look exhausted," he continued, his hand still wrapped around her wrist, though his grip softened. "It's well past midnight. You should rest. I'll wake you before dawn and take you back myself."

His jaw twitched, as though he hated the thought of returning her to that place. But he wasn't wrong—her limbs felt heavy, liquid, and the moment he mentioned sleep, it tugged at her, her body finally registering how spent she was.

Still, her gaze flicked down to his pants, still straining between them, and her pulse kicked hard at the sight.

"I want you, Elara," he said quietly, his voice rough with restraint. His hand rose to her cheek, thumb brushing her skin in a touch that was painfully gentle, though his eyes betrayed him—burning, restless. "But right now... right now, I'm not thinking about what I want. I'm thinking about you."

His words were tender, and something warm, and heavy settled inside her.

"Okay," she whispered, and he gently helped her off him, pulling her into his chest until they were lying side by side, her body fitting perfectly against his. Elara pressed her face into the curve of his neck, breathing him in—smoke and clove, warm and heady, intoxicating like it was a drug she couldn't get enough of.

His fingers threaded through her hair, stroking slowly. The tension in her body eased, bit by bit, his warmth wrapping around her like a blanket. Elara's thoughts spun as she breathed him in. Ivan. The Hunter. The boy who had once been her friend, the boy she couldn't remember but somehow felt in her bones. The fates must have laughed themselves sick when they wove their threads together.

Childhood friends torn apart, tossed onto opposite sides of a war that neither of them chose. And yet, here they were. Something larger than either of them pulling them back into each other's orbit. It didn't make sense, but maybe it wasn't supposed to. Maybe it wasn't chance or coincidence or anything so small. Maybe they weren't meant to question it. Maybe the fates had stitched their lives together for a reason.

Sleep came for her quicker than she could have imagined. Perhaps it was the weight of him beside her, his hand in her hair, or the lingering haze of the pleasure he'd pulled from her body. Either way, it was deep and dreamless, pulling her under completely.

CHAPTER 53

The first whisper of dawn brushed against Elara as a faint tickle on her nose, gently rousing her from sleep. Her body felt stiff, like she hadn't moved all night, and the scent of parchment and something warm and spicy, filled her lungs with each deep breath she took.

It was the insistent tickle, though—a feather-like touch—that nudged her toward wakefulness.

With a groggy motion, she reached to scratch her nose, her mind still adrift. But her hand wouldn't budge. Confusion mingled with the last remnants of sleep as she gave a weak tug again, opening her eyes wide and bleary.

What—

Her heart gave a slow, startled thud as she looked down. Ivan held her wrist snugly beneath his arm, his grip firm even in sleep, keeping her against him. His hair was the culprit, the soft strands brushing her nose as she realized she was still burrowed in the crook of his neck.

Oh, gods. Oh, *no.*

But before the panic had time to truly set in, the heavy library doors slammed open, hitting the wall with a resounding crack. Tristan strode in like a hurricane.

"Morning, lovebirds. Forget something?"

Elara barely had time to process the words before Ivan stirred, froze for half a second, then shot up so fast he nearly knocked her off the settee.

"Fuck!" He scrambled to steady her, wide-eyed.

"Yeah, *fuck's* about right," Tristan said, but his usual teasing tone was absent, his smirk nowhere to be found.

Ivan pushed himself off the sofa, pulling Elara up with him, already turning to open a rift. But Tristan stepped in, cutting him off.

"Let me take her," he said smoothly. "Osin knows Calista and I have... started talking again. I could tell him she twisted my arm into spicing things up with Miss Holier-than-thou here."

Elara snorted before she could stop herself. As if anyone would need convincing of *that*.

Tristan caught it immediately, flashing her a devilish smile that said he knew *exactly* where her thoughts had gone.

Ivan ignored the exchange. "Does he know she's missing?"

"Not yet," he replied, his easy expression tightening ever so slightly. "I was up early this morning—came to see you, Elara. Found you weren't where you were supposed to be. You two are so damn lucky I decided not to sleep in."

Ivan didn't laugh. He turned to Elara, his expression hard, though his touch was gentle as he cupped the back of her neck, his fingers slipping through her hair. "I'll come for you tonight. Practice rifting. Practice threading from a distance. Tug on the bond when you're alone, and I'll come for you."

There was no room for argument in his voice, no hesitation. Elara nodded, the promise in his words settling deep inside her. He leaned in, pressing a soft kiss to her forehead, his breath warm against her skin.

"Go," Ivan said, his voice strained, already pulling away as the word left his mouth.

A rift tore open before them, faster than she could track. Tristan grabbed her arm, and suddenly, they were *running* through the swirling chaos. But there—at the edge of her vision—was the light. A sliver of gold, growing larger and brighter with each second, cutting through the darkness. The light expanded, shimmering like sunlight on water, stretching into the shape of a doorway.

They burst through it, stumbling into the bedroom with a rush of air that left Elara's head spinning.

Tristan moved first, fast and silent, crossing the room in a few strides to press his ear against the door. He glanced over his shoulder, "Guards are still there," he said, "All sounds quiet. For now."

Her chest loosened as Tristan walked toward her, his usual air of arrogance stripped away. For the first time in the weeks she had known him, he looked unsure of himself—uncomfortable, even.

"I came here this morning because there's something you need to hear. Something I need to say." He paused, taking a deep breath. "I haven't always seen things clearly. I didn't want to. It was easier to accept the world as it was handed to me—the version where people like you were expendable."

Elara blinked, surprised. Of all the things he could've said, this wasn't what she'd expected.

"I was ignorant," he continued, "I was so comfortable in my privilege, so blind to the truth of what was happening to you, to the Sidhe. And I'll carry that ignorance with me for the rest of my life." His voice cracked—just a fraction—but she caught it. *Felt it.*

"I'm so sorry, Elara. For all of it. For not seeing past the lies I was told. For doing nothing when I should have. I don't expect forgiveness, and I know an apology can't undo the harm I've done. But I need you to know this: I see you now. I see your fight, your pain, and the injustice you've endured." He took a step closer, his eyes holding hers with a sincerity that knocked the breath out of her. "And I want to help—to do better. To be better. In whatever way you'll allow me."

"I—thank you, Tristan," she replied softly, and she meant it.

She wasn't used to hearing apologies, especially not directed at her. And while Tristan hadn't been the one to hurt her directly, his apology landed heavily on her. Because for the first time, someone had acknowledged it. Acknowledged her. That maybe she wasn't imagining it, wasn't crazy for believing the world was as broken as she knew it to be. That maybe her suffering wasn't a reflection of her weakness or fragility, but of something far more insidious.

She hated that it made her feel validated, in some strange, twisted way. As though her struggles weren't just burdens to bear in silence, weren't just dismissed as overreactions or failures to adapt. It shouldn't have mattered this much—what he said. But it did.

He gave her shoulder a gentle squeeze. "I'll see you tonight."

Before she could summon a response, he was already disappearing into the Void as though he had never been there at all.

"*There was a boy looking for you,*" Reynnar said, his voice tight as he wiped the blood pooling above her eye with a damp cloth.

"*A boy?*"

Elara frowned, glancing up at him.

Malak dragged her back to her cell with his usual rough efficiency, barking for her to move without so much as a glance in her direction. He seemed irritated—like her growing silence, her refusal to fight, had stolen the pleasure he once took in watching her struggle.

So when she didn't resist this morning—didn't give him even a single protest—he made up for it. He shoved her down the winding steps into the Pit.

Her head struck stone. Her knees cracked hard against the uneven ground, pain flaring sharp and bright.

When she looked up at him, she smiled.

A bloody, wicked grin.

Because she knew the day would come when she would kill his master.

And if Malak stood in her way, she would kill him too.

Soon, his entire world would crumble, and she would be the one to watch it burn.

When they reached her cell, Reynnar was already on his feet. As if he'd been waiting—attuned to her footsteps, listening for the moment she'd emerge from the tunnel. His gaze swept over her, cataloging every bruise and scrape before Malak had even turned away.

"I'm okay," she'd murmured—though the lie had sounded thin, even to her own ears.

She remembered the tension coiled in Reynnar's frame, the anger simmering just beneath the surface. Without a word, he'd motioned her closer, his hand slipping through the bars. He tore a narrow strip from the hem of her tunic—cleaner than anything else he had—and dipped it into the murky water pooled in the corner.

Then, with a gentleness she hadn't expected, he wiped the blood from her face. That was when he mentioned, almost casually, that she'd had a visitor.

Reynnar nodded, his expression unreadable. *"Soft face, looked like he was drowning in his armor."*

Her stomach turned. Dario.

"What did he want?"

Reynnar shrugged. *"Didn't say much. Barely looked at me. But he came back four times, asking after you. Kept pacing, wouldn't sit still. Then someone told him you'd been bought for the night. He went so pale, I thought he might lose his guts all over his boots."*

A pang lanced through her chest, and she glanced out of her cell, half expecting to see him standing there.

"Is he your lover?" Reynnar's voice was measured, but there was a strange undertone to it.

Elara turned back quickly, caught off guard by the question. *"Once,"* she said, though the word felt strange on her tongue. It was the truth, but it wasn't enough to explain everything.

Reynnar didn't speak for a long moment, his gaze searching hers. Finally, he nodded. *"Then he'll be back."*

FOR THREE DAYS, Elara straddled two worlds—her cell and Ivan's manor—the passage of time blurring in the constant push and pull of their efforts.

Her days were spent with Reynnar—wrestling with *Tirrish*, weaving the thread of the *Draoth Cara* from a distance. Each practice drew her closer to the language's patterns, her tongue stumbling less over unfamiliar sounds.

The link with Ivan grew stronger each time she reached for it. The gap between effort and execution narrowed, bringing a fragile sense of control—and pulling her toward something she didn't yet understand. Something that felt as automatic as reflex, and just as dangerous.

Her nights, though, were spent with Ivan and Tristan, pouring over dusty tomes, hunting for any mention of the Wound of Light. Whatever the Hunter's reasoning, there hadn't been another moment alone between them. Whether deliberate or not, Tristan acted as a buffer—a presence that Elara couldn't decide if she was grateful for or frustrated by.

Her evenings blurred into a race against time, a frantic pursuit of forgotten knowledge and the perfection of the indicator and reactor spells. They were close—so close that, for the first time, a spark of confidence flared in her chest. It felt like she was standing on the edge of something monumental.

Maybe, just maybe, they could pull this off.

But the winter solstice was creeping closer with every breath—and with it, her plans with Calista. Elara hadn't breathed a word of them to Ivan or Tristan. From the way they spoke, Calista hadn't either. Keeping them in the dark was a gamble, but she couldn't risk even a single misstep.

Alone in her cell, she had nothing but time—time to run the plan over and over, dissecting every detail, accounting for every possible failure. She'd calculated the margins so precisely she could recite them in her sleep. It would work. It had to.

She would free the Sidhe. Save Thane. Kill Osin. Fulfill every promise, every vow. Help as many as she could.

But then... what about her?

The thought crept in uninvited. She hadn't let herself think about it before—hadn't dared. It was almost laughable. Here she was, plotting the liberation of an entire people, orchestrating the downfall of a regime, and yet she couldn't even begin to picture her own life beyond it.

What did freedom even mean for her? What came after the dust settled?

The thought refused to leave, clinging stubbornly. She hadn't planned for herself, hadn't even considered where she fit into the future she was fighting so hard to create. And she wasn't ready to ask herself why.

CHAPTER 54

The morning of the winter solstice began like any other, the faint rustle of movement tugging Elara from sleep. Her eyes fluttered open, and through the haze of drowsiness she spotted Reynnar on the other side of the bars. He was already awake, his broad back caught in a thin spill of light filtering into the Pit.

He stretched, arms lifting overhead, muscle shifting beneath his skin. His dark hair hung loose, brushing his shoulders as he rolled them. A soft crack broke the quiet when he tilted his head, then he sank into a deeper stretch.

By now, it had become almost comical—watching him repeat the same ritual each morning. It reminded her of the elder Druids at the Sanct, rising with the sun, bodies weaving beneath the early light as they coaxed warmth back into stiff limbs.

But Reynnar's routine was nothing like that. There was nothing gentle or meditative about it—it was calculated, every movement controlled, like he was gearing up for combat.

His stretches flowed into motion, seamless as he dropped into push-ups, then planks, muscle rippling with the effort. Most mornings he made her join him, insisting she keep her body active. It had irritated her at first—the idea of exercising while trapped in a cell—but soon enough she'd begun to enjoy it. To crave the movement.

Since she'd been spending her nights at Ivan's, Reynnar no longer dragged her up with him. Still, she woke just to watch.

It was hard not to.

There was strength in the way he carried himself, a grace that masked the power in every motion. He was beautiful in a way that made him impossible not to notice, no matter how hard she tried.

Elara squeezed her eyes shut and curled tighter on her cot, trying to push past the ache in her body and the fog of exhaustion weighing her down. Her limbs felt heavy, her thoughts slow, as though she were moving through molasses. She'd barely managed an hour of sleep—if that.

The night had stretched on with her, Ivan, and Tristan working until they were bleary-eyed and swaying on their feet. But they'd done it —they'd finally perfected the indicator and reactor spells. It had taken every ounce of their energy, and just when she thought they might collapse from sheer exhaustion, they'd cracked the final piece.

The rush of relief had been like a jolt of lightning, energy surging through them just long enough to test the spells—a brief dive into the Void. To know they worked.

She had been the one to say it, her voice hoarse from lack of sleep. *"Tonight,"* she'd told them, *"after the solstice, we'll search for Thane."* She'd said it with conviction, and she'd meant it. They were so close now.

Get the blade. Kill Osin. Free the Sidhe.

And then find Thane.

Elara willed her heart to slow, forcing herself to take steady, measured breaths in a futile attempt to coax her body back to sleep. She needed those extra hours. Slowly, her muscles began to relax, her body sinking back into the stiff cot, her mind drifting somewhere between the haze of dreams and reality.

But then, a sound cut through the quiet.

Footsteps.

Heavy boots on stone, closing fast.

Elara was awake and moving in the same instant, tension snapping through her as the noise surged down the tunnel. *Her* tunnel.

Across the cell, Reynnar spoke in low, urgent tones to the Sidhe nearby. Elara edged closer, trying to catch his words over the advancing march—Legionnaires, pouring in like a flood.

"What's happening?" Elara shouted over the clatter. No one looked at her—eyes fixed ahead, faces empty.

Cold crept over her skin, tight across her chest, crawling up her spine. Then the soldiers split off, groups of five peeling toward each cell. Locks snapped open. The Sidhe were dragged out.

"Stop!" Elara cried, her voice rough as she rattled the bars. She watched them shove and kick, forcing the Sidhe into tight lines. Her heart thundered as horror clawed through her, leaving her helpless to do anything but watch.

And then five of them peeled off toward Reynnar's cell.

Her stomach plummeted, her body reacting before her mind could catch up. She bolted to the right of her cell, peering through the bars.

Reynnar stood motionless, his expression carved from stone.

Accepting.

No.

That wasn't him.

That wasn't what he had taught her.

They didn't bow to despair, didn't surrender to pain or hopelessness. They fought. They endured. No matter how impossible it seemed. He'd drilled it into her time and again: *You resist. Always resist.*

"Reynnar!"

Her voice broke as they stormed into his cell. The crackle of *Draoth* filled the air, a sickening hum as they forced him to the ground.

"*Fight back!*" she cried, as the first blow landed—a brutal punch to his gut that made him double over. Another followed, a boot to his ribs, then another, until the assault became a blur of fists, boots, and raw *Draoth* battering him from every side. But Reynnar didn't cry out. He didn't flinch. He just took it—every hit, every strike—as if he had already resigned himself to this fate.

"Stop, please, stop!" Elara sobbed, her vision blurred with tears as she slammed her fists against the bars.

"Show them only your rage!"

The same words he had spoken to her when she first arrived in the Pit—broken and defeated, ready to give up. He had pieced her back together, brick by brick, showing her what true strength looked like. What it meant to be brave.

Reynnar's eyes met hers, and something inside her shattered. Her heart cracked open, bleeding into the hollow of her chest. The defeat in his gaze—the quiet resignation—was enough to choke her.

He'd given up—accepted his death—known this was coming, had made peace with it long before she could have imagined, and he hadn't told her.

"No!" she gasped, barely able to breathe, barely able to speak past the sobs tearing through her as they dragged his limp body out of the cell.

Elara crumpled against the iron bars, breath hitching. Her fingers clung to the metal, nails scraping over rusted edges until they split, the sting barely registering. Nothing did—not the blood streaking her hands, not the ache in her chest that felt sharp enough to break her ribs. All she could feel was the despair, the crushing emptiness that made it hard to breathe.

This wasn't how it was supposed to go. This wasn't the plan.

She had failed him. Failed everyone.

She wrapped her arms around herself and rocked, trying to hold herself together. The guilt was unbearable, suffocating. Pressing her forehead to the bars, she gasped for air.

A sound snapped Elara from her spiral, and she shot to her feet, head swimming.

Malak stood there, his face twisted into a smug, satisfied grin.

"Your little pet get his arse kicked, eh? I told you to stay clear of him, didn't I? But no, you had to be clever, had to go learning his bloody tongue like a fool." He tsked, shaking his head slowly, mock pity dripping from every movement. "What did you think was gonna happen?"

Elara's blood boiled, rage coursing through her so fast she couldn't think, couldn't breathe. She reared her head back and spat in his face. "I'm going to kill you," she seethed, her voice steady, cold, *lethal*. "I'm going to gouge your eyes from your skull, rip my nails down your worthless face, and tear out your gods-damned throat."

Malak didn't react—didn't even wipe the spit from his cheek as he stepped into her cell. His fist connected before she could brace, the blow so brutal her world went black before the pain could follow.

Just cold, numbing darkness—always more familiar, more forgiving than the light.

CHAPTER 55

Elara gritted her teeth, struggling to keep her temper in check as a flurry of attendants scrubbed her skin until it burned, their rough hands working at the dirt under her nails with tiny metal picks.

The room was stiflingly warm, the cloying scent of oils thick in the air as they massaged them into her scalp. The sweet, floral smell made her stomach churn. One of them even had the audacity to try brushing her teeth, but Elara snapped her jaws at the girl's hand, earning a startled yelp.

She'd woken to the sharp scent of salts under her nose, the thick steam of the bathing chamber clouding the air as she blinked blearily at the familiar face hovering above her.

"Saria," she had whispered, her voice a rasp, thick with pain. The healer had only hushed her, gentle hands smoothing salve over the fresh bruise darkening her jaw. Osin, no doubt, had insisted. His Hallowed couldn't appear like a prisoner at the solstice.

"Where are the Sidhe? Have you seen—"

Saria's eyes had flicked to the door before she shushed her again, this time more urgently. "Later, Hallowed. We will speak later."

Saria worked with a healer's precision, her hands deft and steady as she applied salves and pressed a tonic into Elara's trembling hands—one for pain, one for strength. She gulped them down without hesitation, the bitterness burning her throat. Only to promptly vomit them back up.

Saria, unshaken, handed her another dose, her patience unwavering as she waited for Elara to steady herself enough to keep it down. Even with the salves, the tonics, and Saria's care, Elara's body refused to stop shaking. It wasn't the pain—it was the thoughts she couldn't quiet.

Reynnar. The Sidhe. What was likely happening to them now.

She forced herself to breathe. Slow, measured breaths. Forced herself to calm, to focus. Because even if Reynnar had resigned himself to his fate, Elara had not.

Saria had lingered for a moment, her eyes soft but filled with a kind of sorrow Elara didn't have the strength to acknowledge, before leaving her to the vulturous hands of the attendants.

They dressed her in a gown of white silk, silver thread woven through the fabric like strands of moonlight. Icy blue accents shimmered at the hems, catching the light as it flowed around her feet in heavy, endless waves.

Her eyes were painted in lines of white and silver, a frosted look that made them glow, but the rest of her face was left bare, as if they wanted her to look cold, distant—like marble. They pulled her hair back tightly, strands twisted into an elaborate crown with diamonds and pearls woven through, sparkling with every slight movement.

She could hardly breathe, let alone move.

The more they fussed, layering her in this finery, the more restless she became, her skin itching. She needed to get rid of the dress. Somehow, she would have to lose it before the night was over. If she had any hope of carrying out her plan, of moving with any speed or stealth, she couldn't be dragging this monstrosity of a gown behind her.

They'd tried to take her necklace—the red stone too garish, too bold for their carefully curated vision—but Elara's glare had been enough to stop them. They'd dropped it like it burned them. Now, as five attendants hovered around her, guiding her out of the bathing chamber, their hands fussing over the endless sweep of fabric trailing behind her, the necklace pressed warm against her chest. It hummed faintly, a quiet reassurance, the only comfort she'd have tonight.

The corridors had been transformed, draped in shimmering garlands of silver, blue, and white—crystal icicles dangling from the arches, catching the light in tiny flickers. Frost had been charmed to creep up the walls, giving the illusion that the entire place was locked in eternal winter. It should have been beautiful, mesmerizing even—but it felt vile.

The muffled sound of music and the distant murmur of laughter carried through the halls. Each step brought her closer to the Grand Hall, its doors already open, spilling golden light out into the corridor. The hall beyond was a world of opulence—glowing chandeliers, tables piled high with decadent food, and guests draped in silks and furs that shimmered.

Elara reached for the *Draoth Cara*, her focus narrowing as she pulled on the thread and it throbbed beneath her skin. Her connection to Ivan was becoming effortless, even if he wasn't near. She was getting *stronger*.

A sliver of tension fell away. She drew one quiet breath and stepped into the hall.

Every eye turned her way, but Elara kept her expression blank, even as the scene before her nearly stole the breath from her lungs. To the left of the hall, an enchanted winter forest stretched out, hauntingly beautiful—a landscape of snow-laden trees, branches weighed down with shimmering frost. The forest seemed endless, with spaces between the trees glittering with ice crystals, tiny frost sprites darting through the frozen canopy.

The hall was laced with the scent of cold pine and winter roses, crisp and sweet, mingling with the warm amber spice curling from enchanted braziers scattered throughout. A thin layer of snow crunched beneath Elara's shoes as she stepped further in, music thrumming under her skin —a steady, hypnotic beat of drums pulsing through the floor.

She paused, sweeping the heavy folds of her gown to the side as a guest, too far gone on wine and spells, stumbled dangerously close. Crystal goblets tilted, spilling dark crimson liquid onto the pristine white ground in splattered streaks. Their masks—grotesque creations of twisted angels, beasts with too many eyes, demons crowned in iron— concealed flushed cheeks and the frenzied glint in their eyes. They rushed past her, eager to disappear into the maze of trees, like moths drawn to madness.

She felt it too—the seductive hum in the air, the sugary haze of the drug Calista had warned her about. It coiled around her senses, invisible hands beckoning her to let go, to drown in the revelry, to surrender to the heady promise of oblivion.

Elara shook her head.

Just a little longer, she told herself. Calista would be here soon, and then—

A sudden bump jarred her, sending a rush of air into her lungs, heavy with whatever poison laced it. Her head swam instantly, a dizzy warmth flooding her skin. The man who'd jostled her was still there, blinking at her as though he almost recognized her, a look of vague concentration on his face—then he dissolved into a fit of laughter. And his mirth, wild and bubbling, was contagious, pulling at her mouth until a giggle escaped from her chest before she could stop it. It spiraled out, uncontrollable, and she clamped a hand over her lips.

Get a grip, she told herself, but it was no use. The harder she tried to rein it in, the more it took over, drawing curious glances and amused smirks from those around her.

Elara threw her head back, her entire body shaking with laughter, even as something deep inside her tightened. Her pulse spiked as a distant scream pierced the haze of the party. Fear, maybe. Or excitement. She couldn't tell anymore, couldn't separate one from the other. The lines between everything were blurring, bending.

Then her gaze lifted, and she froze.

Osin stood above it all on the balcony, wine dangling from his fingers as if he were bored. But his eyes—they were locked on her. Watching. Reveling in the chaos below, in her. Her gaze darted around him, scanning the figures clustered at his back. The High Council stood there, a portrait of power and privilege, and among them, their families. Her eyes caught on Tristan's dark head, bent in polite conversation with the High Lords. He seemed at ease, schmoozing in the way only he could. Elara's focus snapped back to Osin just in time to see him raise his glass to her, a mockery of a toast, before taking a slow, deliberate sip.

The look in his eyes—a taunting, knowing gleam—made something icy trickle down her spine. There was a reason for it, a reason she should know, but she couldn't remember.

Her gaze drifted, unmoored, as a hand grabbed her, pulling her into the whirl of a dance. A circle of hands—grasping, twining, laughing—swept her along, their maniacal giggles filling the air like a twisted lullaby. Elara stumbled, her feet no longer her own, unable to resist as they led her deeper into the maze of trees.

Her heart pounded wildly, her mind spinning as fast as her body. The world tilted and twisted, and then—release.

The hands let go, and she spun and spun—until the ground rushed up to meet her. The snow beneath her was cold and wet, but she didn't care. She didn't feel it. Her limbs were weightless, the world a blur of silver. She doubled over, giggles spilling out in breathless bursts as she curled into herself, everything around her still whirling.

Snowflakes tickled her nose, her lips parted, and the taste of winter danced on her tongue. She couldn't remember what she was laughing at—or if there had ever been a reason.

Everything felt so distant, so dreamlike—so utterly intoxicating.

Elara blinked her eyes open, and through the spinning fog, her gaze settled on something—or rather, someone. A woman. She stood out like a drop of blood, her burgundy dress vivid against the wintry backdrop.

The laughter died in her throat. Breathless, she stared, studying the woman. There was something familiar about her...

Before she could make sense of it, the woman yanked her up from the snow. The sudden movement sent the world spinning again, the trees blurring into dark streaks. Elara couldn't help herself—she snickered, the sound spilling from her lips like a song she couldn't stop singing.

The woman dragged her beneath the low-hanging boughs of a towering spruce, its thick branches dripping with snow and creating a secluded nook.

Then, without warning, the woman pushed her head back, fingers digging into her jaw and forcing her mouth open. Elara gasped as she poured something into her throat—a thick, syrupy liquid that coated her tongue. It tasted like rotting fruit, and burned as it slid down. She choked, her body convulsing as the liquid forced its way deeper.

It was as if a switch had been flipped; the world snapping into focus. The swirling lights, the laughter, the haze—all of it peeled away. Her heart raced as she blinked, clarity flooding her senses.

Shit.

Elara spun around, nearly stumbling as she met Calista's icy glare.

"Is this really all it takes to get you on your back?" Her scowl deepened as she tucked the vial of antidote into her bodice.

Heat flared through Elara, crawling up her neck. "Sorry if I'm not exactly well-versed in handling being drugged against my will."

The words slipped out before she could stop herself, and she instantly regretted them. Calista's face twitched—just barely—but it was enough. A pang of guilt stabbed through her.

"I didn't mean—"

"Drop it." Calista's tone was clipped, her voice cold. "Just stick with the plan, and it'll all be over. Tonight."

She could only nod, her throat tight as she watched Calista turn away, disappearing into the snowy evergreens.

Elara let out a breath, shame still coiled tightly within her as she pressed her back against the rough bark of a tree. The coarse texture scraped her skin, but she didn't care. It was as good a place as any to hide, to catch her breath, and pull herself together before facing the madness to come.

Elara peeked around the trunk, her breath catching as a group of masked revelers staggered past. Her gaze then drifted upward, locking onto the shadowed balcony where Osin loomed. Any moment now, Calista would arrive, and she would need to—

A hand clamped over her mouth, cutting off the scream tearing up her throat. She was yanked backward, her body colliding with a solid chest. She clawed at the arm around her, her nails scraping skin as her body twisted and jerked.

"Shhh, El, it's me."

Elara froze, terror giving way to a rush of emotion.

The hand fell away from her mouth, and when she turned, there he was. That shock of sandy hair, those honey-brown eyes she'd once memorized—the face she had trusted completely, recklessly. But something was wrong. The warmth in his gaze had dulled, his face gaunt, with hard lines cutting through where laughter used to live.

Elara shook her head, struggling to process the sight of him. "Dario, I—"

But something in him just... broke.

"I'm sorry. *Gods*, El, I'm so damn sorry." His voice cracked, the words spilling out like he couldn't hold them back. "For all of it. For what I've done—what I failed to do. You weren't supposed to end up here. You were supposed to stay safe in Verdara. It was my job to protect you, and I... I—"

"Why didn't you tell me?" she demanded, her voice hard. But she didn't pull away from him. She couldn't. No matter how much it hurt, no matter how much everything inside her screamed to move, to put distance between them, her body refused to listen.

"I should have... I know that now." He dragged a shaky hand through his hair, his gaze darting to the floor. "I thought—" He let out a harsh breath. "When Edgar brought me in to watch over you, I didn't question it. I was following orders. I didn't understand what the spell meant. Didn't know what I was stepping into. The first time I saw you, you were unconscious. Edgar had me place the seal on you. Told me it was for protection—an extra layer of security, that's all." A bitter laugh slipped from him. "I'd never worked with Druids before. I didn't realize how... wrong it was. Not at first."

His hands curled into fists at his sides, knuckles whitening with the strain. His face paled, voice breaking with something close to anger—or maybe shame. "I asked him why. *Why me?* Edgar said it was because I was good. Because I was *trustworthy*. I thought I was doing the right thing. Thought I was helping you in the middle of something I didn't understand. He said that if you knew—if you found out—it would only make things worse. That it would put you at risk."

"Did you use it against me?" she bit out. "When you touched me, when we were together—did you weaken me?"

His face fell, and something inside her shattered. Her jaw clenched so tightly she felt it pop.

"Only a few times. In the beginning. But never after that." His gaze searched hers, desperate. "Once I understood what it meant... I couldn't. I refused."

He stepped closer, and she backed away, her heart splintering all over again. She had already known—but hearing it from his lips made it different. Made it real.

"Elara, please. We don't have time. Hate me all you want, for the rest of your life—I deserve it. But right now, I'm getting you out. The Script Keepers... they're closing in on the capital. Hundreds of them, and they're here for you."

A muscle feathered down his neck as he exhaled. "I've been working with them since Mabon. I've traveled across the realm, gathering what rebels I could. Prince Dominic and his men—they're all with us. It took longer than I wanted. Every day I knew you were trapped here, and I—" He swallowed hard. "Then the Hunter found me. Said I was wanted for treason. Told me Osin was feeling generous, and instead of the gallows, he'd let me conscript into the Legion, pay my debt that way."

He took a step closer to her, his eyes pleading. "It was my chance to get close to you. To put one more ally on the inside." He shook his head. "I don't have time to explain everything. But trust me... you're not alone in this."

Elara's heart thundered, her mind reeling. If Dario had truly been accused of treason, Osin wouldn't have spared him—wouldn't have let him draw another breath, let alone welcome him into his ranks. No. It had been a lie. A calculated deception from Ivan. He'd never told Osin about Dario's rebellion.

Why? Why protect him?

She dragged her fingers through her hair, her nails scraping against her scalp as if the motion could pry the answers free. The question was too convoluted, too layered to unravel now. She exhaled sharply, steadying herself.

"I can't leave with you."

Dario's brow furrowed. "Don't be stubborn. You stay here, and you're dead."

"I'm not leaving," she said, "Not until the Sidhe are free."

"The Sidhe?" His voice was incredulous. "The *Fae*? Elara, no one can save them."

"*I can.*"

A vein at his temple throbbed. He looked ready to argue—but then a flicker of light glinted off his armor.

His whole body went still.

Shit.

Elara bolted from the cover of the spruce, her eyes darting to the balcony. Osin was still there, lounging amidst a circle of sycophants, laughter curling through the air. Calista stood apart, her posture stiff as she slipped something—a small mirror—back into her bodice.

Their eyes locked.

Elara's stomach twisted, her mind racing.

What?

Calista's eye widened—intense, almost frantic.

This wasn't the plan. Calista wasn't supposed to signal until she was ready to leave with Osin. But something was off.

A bead of sweat slid down Elara's neck as she held Calista's stare, the realization crashing over her.

The dagger. Osin wasn't carrying it.

That was the signal. Go. Now. *Without her.*

"El." Dario's voice was tight. His eyes scanned her face. "What's going on?"

His words barely registered, drowned out by the pounding of her heartbeat and the shallow, frantic pull of her breaths. She reached for the *Draoth Cara*, gripping the thread and tugging hard. She had to rift to the east wing—to Osin's chambers. Calista had mapped out the basics for her. She remembered it was close to his study. The same study Ivan had dragged her to on that first day.

Her hands tingled, a faint numbness creeping into her fingertips as panic began to set in. She could do this alone. She had to.

Breathe. Just breathe.

Elara lifted her gaze to Dario. "I'll leave with you. But only after I take care of what I need to. Only then." A lie—but she was getting good at those lately.

Dario's face went pale. "What did Osin do to you? What spell did he put you under?"

Elara sighed, her patience razor-thin. "Listen to me, Dario Voland,

and listen well, or I swear I'll knock you flat." He blinked, startled. "I am not under any spell. I am not brainwashed. In fact, I'm clearer now than I've been in years—no thanks to you."

She grabbed his chin, forcing him to meet her gaze.

"You owe me this."

The fight drained out of him instantly. He closed his eyes. "Fine. Okay."

Elara squeezed his chin gently. "I'll find you—after."

Another lie. She didn't let herself feel it, didn't allow a second thought. Instead, she pulled on the *Draoth Cara*, tugging the thread until a rift shimmered into existence.

Dario's eyes widened, shock flashing across his face. He reached for her, but his figure blurred as she stepped through, the rift closing behind her.

CHAPTER 56

Dark currents twisted around Elara, alive and restless, yet for once she didn't panic. She held still, letting the cold press in, seep into the cracks inside her. It was unsettling how the emptiness moved, how it coiled through her ribs as though it belonged there.

Hollow. Eerie.

Like standing on the edge of death.

She centered herself, focus narrowing to intent—to exactly where she needed to be. Slowly, a sliver of gold tore open before her, a rift just wide enough to reveal the corridor outside Osin's study. Her pulse hammered as she scanned the hall.

Empty. Thank the gods.

Every guard must have been at the party, likely drugged or drunk. But she couldn't assume anything—not after seeing how Osin had tightened security at the start of the festival.

Elara slipped free of the Void, landing in the corridor and breaking into a sprint. She followed Calista's instructions, veering left at the turn—

The servant's passage wasn't empty.

She cursed and pushed herself to run faster.

The workers froze at the sight of her, but none dared to stop her.

Maybe they don't recognize me? she thought, though even as the idea crossed her mind, she knew better. After the way Osin had paraded her around these past months, there was no chance they didn't know who she was. She didn't dwell on it. Her legs carried her forward, past shadowed doorways and dimly lit rooms that blurred into nothing as she ran.

Ahead, she spotted a set of private quarters, one door slightly ajar. Warm light spilled into the dim corridor, glinting off polished wood. Skidding to a halt, she bit her lip, glanced around, and slipped inside.

The room was sparse, barely furnished, but her gaze went straight to the dresser. She nearly sighed in relief at the sight of trousers. She pulled them on, cinched a belt tight, then grabbed a tunic—yanking off her gown and replacing it, tucking the fabric into the waistband with hurried hands.

Her gaze swept the floor, landing on a pair of boots that looked close to her size. She ripped off her silk slippers and shoved the boots on, not bothering to tie them properly.

Leaving her discarded things behind, she bolted back into the corridor. Paintings blurred past as she sprinted through the gallery, her sights locked on a small door at the far end. She yanked it open and launched herself up the narrow staircase, taking two steps at a time.

Her lungs burned by the time she reached the top, but she didn't stop. Exiting the stairs, she ran down a short corridor, her heart pounding as she approached the heavy tapestry marking the entrance to Osin's private hall.

A strange, shivering familiarity crept over her, tingling at the base of her spine as she stared at the tapestry. She knew this. Had seen it before. How, she couldn't say—but every instinct screamed that she did.

Three women stood within the weave, their forms draped in flowing robes, hands lifted toward the heavens. The goddesses. The Three.

Her fingers drifted upward, grazing the worn threads, tracing the shapes woven into the fabric. Her hand paused over each one: Aine, arms stretched to the stars; Epona, gently cradling the moon; Rhiannon, wrapped in shadows.

She took a breath and pushed the tapestry aside.

The door to Osin's chambers was plain, unremarkable—a strange choice for someone who lived for grandeur. Elara pressed it open, and the instant she stepped inside, it hit her. A hum in the air—low, *ancient*. She froze, a prickling heat spreading across her collarbone. Something raw, something old and primal, stirred deep inside her, curling in her core like a waking beast.

She could feel it. The blade.

It was *singing*.

Elara moved through the chambers, drawn by the pull of that song. The room stretched before her, stone rising high on either side, broken only by narrow window slits that admitted the faintest light. Near the back hung two heavy black banners, each bearing Ulrith's totem. She moved silently, past the main hall and toward a narrow archway that led to Osin's private quarters. The bedroom was darker still, with thick velvet curtains drawn tight across the windows, blocking out any trace of light. The bed was massive, its black iron frame looming in the center of the room, draped in deep red silk that pooled onto the floor. To the right, a hearth burned low, casting long shadows against the dark wood paneling that lined the walls. A heavy, ornate mirror leaned against one wall, its edges sharp and angular, reflecting the faint glow of the fire.

And still, that hum—growing louder with every step.

Elara's steps slowed as she drifted further into the room, then stopped, eyes locked on the painting she had only ever glimpsed through the veil of death. Her pulse thrummed, the song in her veins rising to a fever pitch. She took in every detail: the field of oíche blossoms, petals vivid and soft, reds and pinks scattered like droplets of blood. And at the center of it all, nestled among the flowers, lay the Wound of Light.

Slowly, she walked closer, the song thrumming louder. Her hand hovered over the painted blade, her fingers just a breath away from the surface. She could feel it—like a heartbeat, waiting for her touch. The instant her fingertips brushed the edge of the painted dagger, it was as if a burst of fire struck her, searing through her blood and hollowing her lungs with a rush of energy so fierce it stole her breath.

Mother above.

Elara shook herself, forcing the feeling away, re-centering her focus. She needed to be quick. She had a plan—one that had taken root ever since Thane's memory surfaced, circling her thoughts relentlessly. The oíche blossoms. It hadn't been a coincidence that Avis had taken her to the gardens, coaxing the blooms open with her spell, spreading their roots through the Sanct.

Avis had been showing her what needed to be done. Elara knew it as surely as she knew her own heartbeat.

How Avis had known about the painting in the first place...

Elara's heart clenched. She inhaled deeply, the air shuddering through her. When she finally spoke, her voice came harsh, jagged, scraping like iron dragged over stone.

"*Druvakh.*"

The word ripped through the air, quaking with power. She pulled hard on the *Draoth Cara*, forcing it to obey. Energy surged through her, slamming into the command. She pushed everything into it—her will, her desperation, her *fury*.

For a moment, nothing. Just the crackling stillness, her breath in the air.

Then—a tremor.

The painting's surface rippled, as if disturbed by a single drop of water.

Slowly, impossibly, the dagger emerged. Unearthly steel caught the light, gleaming as though untouched by time. It hovered there, suspended, defying the laws of nature.

Elara's breath caught as she stared.

A relic of the gods.

She reached out, her hand trembling as her fingers wrapped around the pommel. The moment her skin made contact, the world stilled—a pregnant pause in the storm raging through her mind. The power hummed up her arm, electric, alive, searing into her grip like it knew her, like it had been waiting for her. And then, white-hot light tore through her skull, blinding and brutal, but she gritted her teeth, holding firm, pulling on the *Draoth Cara* to steady herself, to wrest control over the blade.

Holy gods. Holy fucking gods.

The power coursing through her veins was staggering.

Immeasurable.

Elara's grip tightened on the dagger, knuckles paling against the hilt. A faint pulse stirred at the edge of her awareness, a shadow brushing the corners of her mind.

Damn it. The surge of power had caught Ivan's attention. His presence tugged at the thread—a subtle, probing pull, almost a question.

She answered with a measured tug of her own, a silent reassurance meant to hold him at bay. Just enough to buy herself the time she needed to finish this.

At least, she hoped it would.

Elara's hands trembled as she turned from the painting, the dagger slicing through the air before the thought even fully formed. A rift tore open, effortless, like an extension of her will. The Void stretched before her—vast, consuming—but this time... it yielded.

She stepped forward, and the currents didn't lash out or pull her under. Instead, they shifted, softened, parting around her like shadows recoiling from the touch of light.

If the Void was death, Rhiannon's domain, then Epona's light seemed to counterbalance it—two forces in tenuous harmony, holding each other in check.

A slow, measured breath escaped her, the tension easing from her shoulders. Her mind shifted to the Pit—the third tunnel where the Sidhe were most likely taken, the damp stone walls, the oppressive cold. *Gods, let them still be there.* Panic threatened to claw its way to the surface, but she forced it down, tamping it into submission. She inhaled deeply, drawing on the *Draoth Cara* with everything she had, anchoring herself in the memory of the place.

But... nothing.

A chill coiled in her chest, creeping down her spine. *Breathe,* she told herself, fighting the rising dread. *You just did this. Do it again.*

She reached out into the shadows, fingers trailing through the empty, cold space, feeling blindly for the seam she was certain was there.

But something reached back.

Numbing and infinite, it slipped over her fingers like ice, twisting around her hand and locking tight.

She had no time to scream, no breath to even try, before it seized her, dragging her forward through a doorway that ripped itself open from nothing.

CHAPTER 57

Elara was sinking.

Plunging into a churning sea of mist and shadow, dragged down an endless spiral. The world reeled as she fell, breath torn from her lungs as the cold closed in. She reached out, fingers cutting through nothing, legs kicking as she tried to find an seam, a current, *anything* to orient herself.

And then—something caught her—a grip colder than Death, locking onto body and snapping her spiral to a shuddering stop.

"What treasure do you bring to these depths, earth's daughter?"

The voice rippled through the darkness, speaking in *Tirrish*, each syllable ancient and laced with power. Her gaze darted, but there was no one—only herself, suspended in the abyss.

Elara clutched the Wound of Light tighter to her chest, the erratic thrum of her heartbeat slamming against the cold steel.

"Rhiannon?"

A low, rumbling laugh moved through the darkness, reverberating around her like the growl of an ancient beast.

"No, child. Rhiannon has been silenced longer than rivers have carved their paths, longer than mountains have held their vigil, longer than stars have whispered their secrets to the night."

Silenced.

The word scraped along her spine, every hair standing on end.

"Who...who are you, then?"

"I am not one, but a collective."

Elara swallowed hard, forcing herself to speak. *"Please. Release me. I —I need to help someone. A friend. I need to—"*

And then she felt it. A rethreading. Subtle at first, but growing, like the tide turning. Something immense stirred, the air thickening with its presence, pressing in from all sides until she could scarcely draw breath.

"There are those who wish to speak with you. Do you acquiesce?"

Her heart wrenched painfully, caught in the agonizing space between hope and dread. Could it be Thane? Her throat constricted. She had to leave—had to find her way to Reynnar. But what if it *was* Thane? What if he could help her?

"I do."

In the heartbeat between her last breath and the next, Elara was gone—ripped from that weightless Void and thrown into the Pit.

Not the Pit as she knew it, but something hazed, refracted.

A memory. But not hers.

The sensation was unnerving, like slipping into someone else's skin. The air felt heavier here, weighted with emotions that didn't belong to her—desperation, pain, a fierce, burning sorrow. The energy was distinctly male, threading through her mind like smoke, like a whispered command. *See.*

She followed the pull, unable to resist, her steps carrying her down the third tunnel until it opened into a wide room. Elara slowed, her throat going dry.

Godfrey.

He was shackled, a heavy chain stretched across the room and secured to a thick rope, allowing just enough slack for him to pace. His steps dragged, the restraint scraping softly against the stone floor.

He stood at one of the cluttered desks, movements slow and weary. Bruises darkened his arms and face; fresh cuts marked his skin, bleeding sluggishly. Around him, tables were strewn with alchemical tools— bubbling beakers, glass vials, bundles of strange herbs, half-burned candles flickering in the damp air.

The entire room felt wrong, saturated with something malevolent.

Elara froze, horror rooting her in place, as a Sidhe male emerged into view. He knelt on the ground, his arms stretched taut, chains biting into the wall behind him. His head lifted and her breath hitched. His piercing eyes seemed to cut through the haze of memory, fixing on her as if he knew she was there.

The male energy surged within her, a silent hum crackling in her veins, and she understood with a startling clarity. *The memory was his.*

Powerlessly, she watched as Godfrey began a ritualistic draining, the scene hauntingly familiar. Just as he had once violated her.

The Sidhe's features contorted in agony, his body racked by searing torment as Godfrey ruthlessly siphoned his lifeblood, channeling it into luminescent symbols carved cruelly into his skin. His guttural scream tore through the illusion, through the Void, slicing clean through Elara's heart. She watched, paralyzed, as what she could only assume was his spirit—a shimmering wisp of life—separated from him.

A frantic, crushing panic clawed its way up her throat, tightening her breath. Her heart thundered. She could do nothing but watch as the male sagged, his skin turning sallow. And still, Godfrey worked— methodical, unhurried. With each whispered incantation, the male's very essence twisted and funneled into a glass beaker, swirling within it like a caged storm.

A life, a *soul*, reduced to nothing more than an ingredient.

Each droplet pulsed faintly, a dim light that flickered and faded as it merged with the potion, thickening, hardening. Finally, the crystalline substance took shape, its sharp facets catching the sparse light in the room, gleaming with a sinister glow as Godfrey set it into an iron ring.

A cold unlike anything she'd known crept up Elara's spine, seeping into her bones like ice through fractured glass. The room blurred at the edges of her vision, narrowing to the ring.

Ether. *Draoth.* It wasn't hers. It had never been hers.

Her breath hitched, chest feeling as if it had cracked wide open, the ridged pieces slicing through her insides.

The Convergence Ceremony was a farce.

It had *always* been them—the Sidhe.

Their heartbeats, their very essence, drained to feed the wellspring of mortal power.

Her stomach churned violently, a hot, sour burn rising in her throat. She doubled over, gasping. Every strand of ether she'd ever felt—the shimmering threads, the gentle hum—now seemed to scream, a mournful cry that echoed through her.

Blind rage and bitter self-loathing followed, burning its way to the surface as tears stung her eyes.

Everyone she knew—Ivan, Tristan, Edgar, Algernon, Saria—*gods*, even herself—had drawn on the Sidhe's souls to conjure ether.

Her stomach twisted, acid surging up as she turned and vomited, the contents of her stomach disappearing instantly into the Void's dark, empty silence.

Had they known? Had they all known and simply... not cared? Was access to *Draoth* worth the death of thousands of Sidhe, worth tearing their souls from their bodies and binding them into iron rings?

They were trapped.

Holy gods, the Sidhe were trapped—forced to give up every last sliver of their power, their very essence, until they dwindled to nothing. Until...

Her ears rang, a shrill, relentless pitch that drowned out everything else.

Her blood.

It was fuel. Fuel to recharge the rings, to prolong the Sidhe's torment, forcing them back, again and again, into another brutal, endless cycle.

Her stomach turned violently and she retched again. The sound that escaped her was torn, a noise she barely recognized.

Reynnar.

She had to get back to him. To all of them. She had to stop this.

"Please. Let me go. Please, I need to find my friend."

But the Void only shifted around her, the currents bending and twisting until a new memory took shape. Through the shadows a delicate figure emerged—a child, radiant and no older than seven. Silver strands, reminiscent of moonlit tides, cascaded down her back, kissed by the starlight's gleam. She twirled, lost in her own dance. Every delicate spin she took caused her gossamer gown to ripple and gleam like the flutter of butterflies taking flight in the summer's breeze.

The scene expanded, revealing a vast ballroom, its boundaries seemingly as endless as the sky itself. High ceilings billowed like clouds, shimmering with an iridescence that mirrored the early morning horizon. Gliding effortlessly across the room were figures with eyes deep and limitless as the blue yonder, hair flowing weightlessly, like wisps of cirrus clouds. On some of their backs, gossamer wings, delicate as spider silk, caught the ambient light, scattering prismatic patterns across the walls.

Laughter carried across the room. As she took it all in, she realized that the laws of nature seemed optional here; the beings occasionally lifting off the floor in graceful arcs, their steps more akin to floating than actual dancing.

A shiver of awe prickled her skin—the enchanting realm before her could only be *Tír na nÓg.*

Her eyes darted, trying to capture the details, each sight vying for her attention, overwhelming her senses. Among the revelry, a boy, slightly older yet sharing the same features of the moon-haired girl, stepped forward. His bow, laden with mischief, drew every gaze, and as he took the girl's hand, leading her in a mesmerizing waltz, time itself seemed to pause.

The collective muttered softly, resounding in her heart: *Brother.*

"Why are you showing me this?"

Her voice barely made a sound, more a breath to herself than a question to the Void.

Then, the boy looked up from his sister, his gaze shifting, locking directly onto her. His eyes were a piercing shade of silver, flecked with shadows like fractured starlight. A shiver ran through her, a deep, haunting note striking something within her.

Raijin.

The name rose in her mind unbidden, filling her with a strange, undeniable certainty. It was him—the person she'd been searching for before she lost her memories.

But then, as if the Void was impatient to tell another tale, the scene morphed again.

A moonlit forest came into view.

The same young girl appeared, her wide eyes shimmering with fear as she darted through the twisted trunks.

The trees groaned, their skeletal limbs bending low as if to snatch her, while the earth beneath pulsed, vines twisting and snapping at her heels. Each ragged breath the girl drew seemed to resonate in Elara's chest, the girl's desperation bleeding into her veins.

Elara's fingers tightened around the Wound of Light, her pulse a steady roar in her ears as she watched the girl unleash a fierce burst of *Draoth*, folding herself seamlessly into the trunk of a nearby tree.

But her haven was short-lived.

A woman with auburn hair trailing down her back, and a lean, fragile-looking young man moved toward the young girl.

Aine and Osin.

Elara's throat tightened, her nails digging into her palms as she watched the pair drag the young girl from within the tree, slice open her wrists and drink from her blood.

Aine's fingers, wreathed in shadow, sent tendrils of darkness snaking around the girl, pulling her spirit into submission. Slowly—heartbreakingly—the girl's radiant, moonlit hair darkened, the light fading as it absorbed the creeping shadows, fading to the hue of a starless night.

Elara's pulse slowed, each thud dragging longer, stretching thinner.

The shadows shifted, casting the girl's face in a harsh, unholy glow. Those delicate cheekbones, that familiar curve of her lips, even the way the girl's hair coiled around her face...

Her breath caught, jagged shards slicing her throat.

It was her.

The girl was her.

The revelation wound around her heart like iron chains, each link tightening until she couldn't breathe. Denial warred with acceptance, their conflict a tangled knot as she replayed the visions.

The ballroom filled with Sidhe of the air, laughter spilling into every corner, a lightness she could almost feel...

That place had been her *home*.

And the boy, the one with the glint of mischief in his eyes, inviting her to spin with him across the floor—that boy was her *brother*.

A family she never knew. Snatched from her grasp before she'd even known to reach for them.

Every moment she had spent feeling like an outcast, imagining herself as a lone star born from the Mother's whim was a *lie*.

She was Sidhe. Not some forsaken fragment of stardust. She had roots; she had blood ties. Belonged to a family violently ripped apart. The ache that had shadowed her for as long as she could remember wasn't the sting of abandonment—it was grief, a love torn from her and left to bleed.

And now, watching her small, lifeless form being carried away, a howl built in her chest. Every shiver of *Draoth*, every whisper that had seemed to call her name—it all slotted into place.

The *Draoth* that thrummed in her veins, the innate understanding she had of its cadences, its textures, its *smells*—it wasn't an oddity.

It was her birthright.

The Binding Sigil. The *parasite*.

They weren't just chains—they were leeches, digging in deep, siphoning her strength, her will, her very sense of self.

It wasn't just about control—it was concealment.

Slowly, the memory faded, dissolving like smoke. *Her* memory, a voice murmured in her mind, even as she doubled over, her body racked with silent, shuddering sobs.

"*There is one more,*" the collective whispered, their voices brushing against her frayed edges like a dark caress.

The shadows shifted, reshaping themselves, and then he appeared—Thane.

Younger, just fifteen, exactly as he'd been the night he'd tried to kill her.

But this wasn't a memory.

He stood there, solid and clear, as if he'd never left.

"Elara." His lips curved into a bittersweet smile. "I always believed you'd come. That you'd find the way."

Her chest cracked open, an ache so deep it felt like she was bleeding from within. "Thane," she choked out, "how do I get you out of here?"

His gaze softened, sorrow etched into every line of his face. "You can't. I've been spirit-bound for too long."

"I'm so sorry," she whispered, the words brittle.

He shook his head. "This burden isn't yours to carry."

She shivered, wrapping her arms around herself, as if she could hold the pieces of her breaking heart together. "Why are you here? Why haven't you crossed over?"

The warmth faded from his face, shadows pooling in his gaze. "I can't. None of us can. We're stuck."

"Stuck?"

"Aine—she holds the Void in her grip, keeps Rhiannon in her thrall. Without Rhiannon, none of us can pass. We're trapped here."

Trapped.

Souls trapped in the Void, *and* in the iron rings.

"What can I do?"

"Tell my brother to renounce his covenant."

Her brow knitted, a thread of confusion winding through her despair.

Thane stepped forward, his eyes urgent. "His oath with Death. Tell him to break it to—"

Ice shot through Elara, splintering along her spine.

Her body jerked backward, her arm stretching helplessly, fingers splayed toward Thane even as she was yanked away. She tried to scream, but the sound was stolen, swallowed by shadows as she was wrenched her from that darkened vision. Her soul lurched, a brutal, sickening pull, hurling her into blinding light.

She slammed against cold stone, the impact reverberating through her spine, every nerve jolting awake. Yet her fingers clung to the Wound of Light, locked in a death grip around it. She didn't need her eyes to know who stood before her.

She could feel their presence.

"What a dangerous little thief you've turned out to be," Osin murmured.

Elara's eyes fluttered open, her vision blurred and swimming before it focused—and her heart clenched, a searing, visceral ache.

Calista knelt before Osin, her spine straight, even as Osin's hand gripped her hair like a vice, jerking her head back. Yet even with her neck bared, her chin tilted upward, Calista's gaze held his, burning, unbroken, like she'd spit fire if she could.

Osin's gaze drifted to the blade in Elara's hand, his lips curling ever so slightly. "I do so despise when my belongings go wandering," he said, his eyes sliding back to her. "And you, I fear, have gone quite astray."

Her nostrils flared, a reflexive response she couldn't control.

"Oh? You disagree?" His voice was a soft, dangerous caress. "Or have you perhaps forgotten the words of the divine?"

He is your guardian, and you, his guiding light.

Aine's voice slithered through her mind, coiling around her like a serpent. It tightened, squeezed, until her head swam. How easily she'd believed them—clinging to the idea that she was chosen, that her purpose was tied to something noble, something the gods had deemed meaningful, that her suffering had meant *something*.

Osin's gaze held that quiet, terrible patience, shadows curling around him. Waiting. Expecting her submission.

She'd die before she let him take one more piece of her.

In that moment, she was more than herself; she was the embodiment of every silent fury, of every suppressed scream, of every ounce of strength mustered in the face of insurmountable odds.

"I belong to *no one*."

He only laughed.

"Now we both know *that* isn't true."

A torrent of Legionnaires poured through the gaping mouth of the cave. The thunderous roar echoed down the twisting stone steps, reverberating into the heart of the Pit. Their helms obscured their faces, but the gleam of their eyes beneath was enough—a harsh, wrathful promise of violence.

At the forefront of the throng, Ivan emerged. He was a figure carved from obsidian, a wraith given form, the faint torchlight glinting off the edges of his pauldrons and the deadly curve of his glaive.

He stopped just behind Osin, his presence a cold, oppressive weight that seemed to drain the air from the chamber.

She kept her hands at her sides, resisting the pull to reach for the *Draoth Cara*—she would never touch it again. The mere thought made her sick. Her gaze locked with his, and she bit down on her lip until the metallic taste of blood touched her tongue.

The amber ring in his eyes flared—that *same* molten gold, that *same* searing fire she'd stared at from across her cell for weeks—a piercing arrow straight through her heart.

The *Draoth Cara*, the bond—it wasn't with Ivan.

It was with the *Draoth* he possessed.

The realization twisted inside her, a knife turning ever so slowly.

Reynnar's Draoth.

<h1 style="text-align:center">CHAPTER 58</h1>

Elara forced herself upright, her legs unsteady but her grip on the Wound of Light ironclad. Power throbbed from it, pulsing in time with the fury stirring in her chest, simmering hotter with every breath she drew.

The third thread—the faint, fragile glow she glimpsed in her dreams, always lingering at the edges, a light she'd never dared to reach for. It had been Reynnar all along, barely clinging to life, flickering weakly in the depths of Ivan's subconscious.

Her hands curled into fists at her sides, nails digging into her palms as a tremor rippled through her frame.

The world narrowed to a haze of red. Her breaths came fast and shallow, each one a bellows stoking the inferno raging inside her.

Ivan.

The name drummed through her mind, tender and vicious, a caress that left behind scars. But no. He wasn't Ivan. He was *the Hunter.*

She had clung to the notion that Ivan was a distinct part of him, something she could extract and redeem. But that had been a foolish delusion—the naive fantasy of a lonely girl. There was no shared path, no common thread weaving them together. They were creations of opposing forces, drawn together only to destroy one another, bound by a pull that could lead only to ruin.

Disgust twisted in her, a molten, ugly thing. He knew—had always known; every dark truth, every heinous act, and worse, he was complicit.

To think she had dreamt of him as an ally.

Osin's steps were languid, each one deliberate, like a predator savoring every inch of ground he claimed. He dragged Calista across the floor, her body limp at his side.

Elara's instinct to flinch didn't escape him. He paused, his gaze locking onto hers, the faint glimmer of something that almost looked like delight flickering in his eyes.

"How endearing," he purred, "two childhood friends, paths crossing once more under such fascinating circumstances." He tilted his head. "I imagine there's a charming tale there—perhaps one you'll regale me with, in due course. But for now..."

Osin extended his hand, palm open. "The blade. Before I tire of this little game."

A flicker of unease prickled at the edges of the *Draoth Cara*, a ghostly thread of Ivan's emotions brushing against her thoughts. Her jaw tightened as she forced the connection away with a fierce shove and slammed the door of her mind shut, erecting towering, impenetrable walls.

Across the space, Ivan's posture flinched. *Good.*

It was empowering. *Liberating.* At her side, the Wound of Light seemed to thrum in response, a faint vibration coursing through the hilt.

Osin's eye narrowed, the veneer of patience thinning. "Come now, Hallowed. Let's not make this more complicated than it needs to be."

Calista's eyes met hers, wide and burning. *Don't you dare,* they seemed to scream.

Elara's mind spun, her fingers clenching around the blade. Give it up, and risk the Sidhe. Defy him, and risk Calista.

A line of cold sweat slid down her spine. Her grip tightened on the dagger until the leather bit into her palm. She couldn't fight him—not like this. She refused to touch the *Draoth Cara*, and though Epona's dagger pulsed in her hand, brimming with ancient power, she didn't know how to wield it. Her heart thundered, each beat slamming against her ribs like a drumbeat growing louder and faster.

No.

The drumbeat wasn't her heart—it was coming from somewhere above them.

Dust shivered loose from the ceiling. The impact reverberated through stone and floor, straight into her bones.

Boots. Dozens at first, then more.

A deadly rhythm rolling down into the Pit.

Osin's sigh cut through the noise, soft and oddly wistful. "They came for you. Isn't that... touching? Traitors. Thieves. They think they can take what's mine."

He paused, his tone shifting to something almost regretful. "This, I suppose, is my failure—a small misjudgment. In trying to cast you as a symbol of the divine, the Mother's blessed child, a living testament to her grace, I've inadvertently sparked a dangerous glimmer of hope."

Ivan shifted, his body tense and coiled like a spring. She felt his gaze but kept her eyes forward, refusing to meet it. Even so, it skimmed old scars, resurrecting pain and pleasure alike.

His gaze wasn't just on her face—it was everywhere, reading, deciphering, understanding, accusing. A reflection of the dance they had always played.

A dance of truths and lies.

Of hope and despair.

Shouts echoed from the top of the Pit, mingling with the clash of bodies and the scream of metal against metal. The Legionnaires around Osin moved closer, forming an unbreakable wall.

But Osin's gaze stayed locked on her.

A low chuckle escaped his lips, chilling in its softness. "They believe, I imagine, that you possess some sliver of power to aid their pitiful cause. Shall we show them how very mistaken they are?"

Before she could brace, shadows exploded from his outstretched hand, tearing from every corner of the Pit, a writhing, snarling mass surging straight for her.

Elara didn't think—she moved, wrenching the blade up.

Light detonated up her arm. The Wound of Light's power bursting free like a dam blown wide.

No careful threading. No measured pull from the *Draoth Cara*.

Just force.

The light ripped through her, then outward—an erupting wave that slammed into the shadows and tore them apart, scattering what remained like ash.

Osin rolled his eyes. "A party trick."

In one swift motion, he hurled Calista to the ground and slammed his foot into the floor. Shadows erupted beneath Elara, twisting up like a nest of snakes. They caught her—wrists, legs—coiling tight, dragging her down. She strained against their grip as Ivan's presence slammed into her mind, pressing hard. She shoved back harder. Refused him. Refused to use what he wanted.

Reynnar's gods-damned soul.

Elara's scream tore through the air as her fingers finally went slack. The blade slipped free, clattering against the stone beside her.

"Time and time again, I offer you the chance to prove your loyalty. To show your worth." Osin sighed softly. "For that is your role, Hallowed. To *submit*. To *obey*. To *serve me*. It is, after all, in your very nature."

"Lies!"

He cocked his neck. "Did the Void fill your head with tales, whisper promises of greatness? Tell you that you're something special, some precious *keystone*?"

Elara's teeth ground together, but he laughed. "*That* is the lie, Hallowed. You are nothing more than a stain, an abomination against humanity and against the one true goddess, Aine. Just like the rest of the Sidhe." He took another step closer, his voice dropping to a near whisper. "Though I'll grant you this—you all serve a purpose. A purpose I have been entrusted to see fulfilled. To heal, to consecrate, to give back what your kind stole before the Great Divide."

"Why go through the charade, then?" Elara spat, struggling against his shadows. "If I'm such an abomination, why the song and dance?"

His mouth twitched. "At first it was necessity. You see, the people needed a symbol, someone to embody this great '*gift*.' A shining example of the blessings bestowed upon them—until, of course, it wasn't so benevolent, wasn't quite so *free*. And when it all began to crumble, when reality bled through the illusion, they needed someone to blame. Someone expendable. Convenient."

He took a step closer, the faintest hint of mockery glinting in his eyes. "But not me. Oh, no. I remained their salvation, their hope. The one to kneel before. The one to beg for mercy, mercy I might graciously grant—if they proved deserving."

Elara's stomach churned. "You're sick."

"No, Hallowed. I am *inevitable*."

He pressed his shadows tighter, squeezing around her ribs, climbing up her throat.

Elara's vision blurred as she fought it, forced her gaze to focus, catching sight of Calista in the distance and Ivan's hand slipping something small and glinting into hers.

She tore her eyes away, a sudden, searing pain rippling through her chest, dragging an agonized whimper out of her. The shadows burrowed deeper, winding tighter, coiling like vipers around that dark, festering core—the *parasite*. Osin's mouth twitched, his eyes narrowing into icy slits at her as the sounds of battle drew closer.

And then—a flash.

A blinding cascade of ice erupted, shards exploding outward, snapping and splintering like the howl of a winter storm.

It surged from Calista's outstretched hand, freezing the air itself into a crystalline wall that encased Osin.

Calista's eyes burned with cold fury. She snarled through gritted teeth, her body trembling with the chaotic, untamed energy.

One of Ivan's volatile spells, Elara realized.

Osin's eyes widened as a sheen of frost climbed, scaling him in layers of glittering ice. His shadows loosened, and Elara gasped, air rushing into her lungs so fast it nearly knocked her off balance.

A shout rang out, cutting through as several Legionnaires broke from their defensive line, fire sparking in their palms, hurling flames at the ice and it splintered and hissed under the heat.

Elara's gaze snapped downward, locking on the Wound of Light.

It lay just beyond her, its golden surface catching the fractured light from the flames. Her fingers twitched, the tips brushing the cold, frost-streaked stone as she stretched further, her body trembling with the effort. *Please.* Her thoughts screamed louder than the clamor around her. *Please.*

Osin's snarl tore through the air as he broke free, a violent surge of darkness erupting around him.

He moved—a blur of wrath and power barreling toward her, but in that split-second—between the ice fracturing and his shadows reforming—Elara's fingers brushed the blade, barely a touch.

It was enough.

A jolt of power snapped through her hand, shooting up her arm, a shockwave that ignited everything inside her. She screamed, the sound tearing from her throat, ripped free by the force of her terror.

Light erupted from her in a blinding shield. Jagged and wild, it channeled her fear into power—a field of erratic, pulsating light clashing violently against the tempest of darkness. It was not just a barrier; it was her scream given form, her terror given light—a vortex of frantic energy spun from the sheer force of her will to survive, to resist.

Osin stalked her shield, his glacial blue eyes burned into hers, rage twisting his features. Black seeped from his pupils, devouring the pale frost until his gaze became endless, hollow darkness.

Shadows slammed into the barrier, hammering it like fists. Again. And again. The light wavered under the force, shuddering with each blow. He didn't stop. His lips curled into a snarl. Another surge. The barrier cracked, faint lines spidering across its surface.

"Fine," he bit out. "The hard way, then."

In a heartbeat, his shadows shot out, darting behind him—straight toward Calista.

Elara's gaze collided with fierce emerald eyes, wide with defiance, anguish—a thousand unspoken things crammed into a single, agonizing second.

And then gone.

The light died as Osin's shadows coiled around her, snapping her neck in a single, brutal twist.

A hollow ache split Elara's chest, driving the air from her lungs. Then came the heat—white-hot rage—flooding her veins.

She moved on instinct.

A snarl tore from her throat as she shattered the barrier and lunged —only for shadows to snap shut around her wrist.

Osin laughed, a low, mocking sound. "Still so reckless. For all your supposed cleverness, you truly are a fool." His power tightened, and Elara cried out as her wrist cracked.

"You never learn, do you? No matter how many times I take your memories away, you keep making the same mistakes."

Elara's grip on the blade trembled, and it pulsed in her hand, cold steel pressing into her palm as she strained forward, willing it to reach his throat, to *end this.*

Her memories—they hadn't just slipped away, lost to some careless experiment. He'd taken them. Found her in the Void. Ripped them from her. The realization was ice in her veins, fury and helplessness twisting inside her. Her breath hitched as hot tears burned at the corners of her eyes, threatening to spill. She forced them back.

"Now," he murmured, his voice soft, almost coaxing, "hand over the blade, and perhaps... I'll permit you to keep your new memories. A fair bargain, wouldn't you say?"

She blinked, his words sinking in, her pulse stuttering.

Why does he keep asking?

The dagger hovered inches from his face, her arm locked in his shadows—why not just take it?

Quick as a flash her gaze darted to Ivan's, the answer right there in his eyes.

Because he couldn't.

He needed her to give it willingly.

But why?

Osin's lip twitched, the darkness around her coiling tighter, snaking up her throat—and *flinched.*

A deafening crack shook the Pit, a sound like the sky splitting apart. The massive iron doors at the far end exploded inward, shards of metal and splinters of wood raining down.

Rebels poured through the breach, their war cries echoing off the cavern walls, a tide of fury.

At their head was Dominic. His eyes blazed with unrestrained rage, his sword dripping crimson, each step carrying the promise of vengeance. Without hesitation, he raised his hands, fingers curling into claws, and the earth beneath them roared to life.

The ground fractured, groaned, then erupted in a towering wave of churning rock and soil. The sheer force of it split the Pit's floor wide open, serrated cracks racing outward, sending Legionnaires sprawling as the surge of earth barreled straight for the king.

Osin whirled, a rush of shadows spiraling outward from his hands. They solidified midair, forming a thick, roiling barricade that collided with the oncoming wall of earth. The impact was catastrophic—shadows and stone clashing in an eruption of dust and raw power.

The shockwave blasted through the Pit, sending debris raining down, and the binds on her wrist loosened.

The Wound of Light gleamed in Elara's hand as she swung down with all the strength she could muster, cutting clean through the writhing tendrils, severing them in a burst of sizzling power.

A scream ripped from Osin's throat—cracked, guttural, a sound so strange, so *human*, that she almost froze, almost took that precious heartbeat to watch the pain contort his face. But she forced herself to turn, her heart hammering as she sprinted across the cracked floor of the Pit, veering right toward the tunnels.

CHAPTER 59

Don't look back.

Elara's lungs burned with every breath as she pushed herself faster. She ignored the ache in her chest, the maddening pull begging her to stop. Just one glance. One look to see if Ivan was still alive.

But she didn't. She couldn't.

She kept running.

Her legs shook, muscles screaming as she tore down the narrow, winding tunnel that seemed to stretch endlessly before her. The stale air was heavy, oppressive, every breath tasting of iron and earth and *death*. She pushed herself faster.

Her heartbeat pounded in her ears, drowning out the world—the distant clash of battle, the faint cries she couldn't place. Each frantic step hammered down the panic rising in her throat, the guilt that churned in her gut. *Too much time. You've wasted too much time.*

She passed one empty cell after another, her eyes desperately scanning for any sign of life. For Reynnar.

Please, gods. The prayer was a rasp in her mind, fragmented and broken. *Just... please.*

Her mind stilled, her feet halting abruptly as she reached a cell that wasn't empty. One figure stood inside, barely illuminated by the flickering torchlight.

"Aoife."

The Sidhe whipped around at her name, her eyes cutting through the gloom like a beacon.

Elara swung the Wound of Light, slicing through the wards on the cell and the shimmering barriers dissolved, vanishing like morning mist under the sun.

Before Elara could catch her breath, Aoife yanked the door open, grabbed her wrist, and pulled her forward.

"Where are the others?"

Elara couldn't bring herself to say his name, couldn't force it past the knot in her throat.

"Further down," Aoife panted, her eyes flicking back anxiously. *"They—they've been quiet for some time now."*

It felt like something inside her shattered, the pieces grinding together as she gasped. Her knees wobbled, but Aoife's grip kept her moving.

"Don't lose hope," she whispered fiercely. *"Not yet."*

Movement flickered up ahead, a shifting shadow in the dim light, and Elara yanked Aoife into an empty cell, her back slamming against the stone. Aoife crouched near the bars, the flickering light from the corridor dancing across her narrow features. She glanced back.

"Three guards," she whispered, her eyes dropping to the blade in Elara's hand. *"Can you fight?"*

Elara's grip tightened around the hilt. *"In a manner of speaking."*

Aoife raised an eyebrow. *"And what manner would that be, exactly?"*

"I can't claim any real expertise. But when I focus, the blade responds—light erupts from it. It feels like an extension of my will, somehow, though I can't explain it."

It was like what Ivan taught her with the *Draoth Cara*, but without precision, and no threads to control. Just... raw force.

Aoife's gaze held steady, assessing her, measuring. After a heartbeat, she gave a slight nod. *"Stay close behind me. Only use it if you must."*

Elara nodded, but a hollow weight pressed against her. All those hours with the *Draoth Cara*, all those lessons meant to prepare her, now surfaced like an ugly scar. Guilt simmered, hot and edged, shame twisting at the thought of the stolen *Draoth*—the four souls bound to Ivan she had drawn from.

Reynnar's.

Her teeth sank into her lip as she shoved the thoughts aside, but the heaviness lingered. She buried it as they slipped out of the cell.

They pressed to the wall, slipping into cracks and shadow as they crept closer to the guards. Three men stood laughing, passing a flask between them, carrying the easy confidence of those certain they wouldn't be caught. They likely assumed the solstice revelries above were still in full swing.

Down here, deep in the Pit, the walls devoured sound, betraying nothing of the battle raging at the prison's entrance.

Aoife's bare steps made no sound as she glided toward the guards, a harbinger of death slipping through the darkness. Elara shivered as she glimpsed her face—pure, murderous intent etched in every line, her fangs bared and gleaming.

The faint shuffle of boots faltered as one guard's head snapped up, his gaze catching the faintest flicker of movement out of the corner of his eye. But it was too late.

Aoife pounced.

Her claws pierced the soft flesh of the man's throat, cutting off his scream as blood gurgled past his lips. Her other hand shot out, raking across his chest like knifes. Before his body hit the ground, she was already on the second guard.

Her fangs sank into his ear, ripping it clean off in a spray of blood that spattered across the stone walls, streaking her silver hair like war paint as the man's scream echoed through the air.

The third guard's hand darted for his weapon, his body trembling as he fumbled for the hilt. Elara didn't give him the chance. She lunged and drove her dagger into his back, more force than precision. The blade bit deep, tearing through leather and flesh.

The guard choked out a strangled gasp, his body convulsing as he staggered back, arm swinging wildly to strike Elara, but Aoife was there, fangs latching onto his throat. A wet, gurgling sound escaped him—a half-formed scream—before she tore through his flesh, leaving him to collapse in a lifeless heap at her feet.

Elara could only gawk, rooted to the spot as Aoife spat—the shredded remnants of flesh landing with a wet splat. Her crimson-streaked face twisted into something savage, almost gleeful. And then, to Elara's utter shock, she laughed.

"Weak men taste like shit."

The second guard lifted his head, blood streaming from his ear. His eyes were glassy and wide, unfocused—like someone drunk on pain. But Elara felt the faint, sickening pull of Draoth from his ring, the thin tendrils of power he clawed for in a desperate bid to save himself.

Without a thought, she drove he Wound of Light into his chest.

His eyes flew open, shock etched into his face as blood spilled over her hands, dark and thick. For a beat, he was frozen, pinned in place, before his head lolled back.

Elara ripped the ring from his finger and dropped it to the ground. Her boot came down hard, shattering the jasper stone with a resounding crack. A thin wisp rose from the fragments, fading into the air.

Aoife stepped forward, crouching to strip the rings from the other two guards. She set them at Elara's feet, and Elara crushed each stone under her heel, shards scattering as faint wisps drifted upward, barely visible in the dim light.

Elara swallowed, unease twisting in her stomach. *Please*, she thought, *let them have bodies to return to.* She took a steadying breath, her gaze falling back to the men—and it hit her. She'd just killed some-one. Killed. The word echoed in her mind. Her hands trembled, the blade nearly slipping from her grip. Her gaze dropped to her right hand, smeared with blood. Her vision blurred, black spots creeping at the edges.

"Eilíara."

She blinked, her gaze snapping up to meet Aoife's piercing stare. *"Let's go."*

Elara forced her feet to move, falling into stride beside her. Each step felt heavy, the metallic scent of blood clinging thick in her lungs.

"They were monsters," Aoife said, her gaze unwavering. *"They do not deserve your gentle heart."*

"I know." Elara swallowed and nodded, though her voice wavered. She told herself she did—she had to. But the truth felt tangled inside her, and she couldn't stop shaking.

They moved in sync, their quick, quiet footsteps reverberating off the stone walls as they slipped down the narrow passage. The air grew colder until they reached a dim, hauntingly familiar lab. Shadows flickered across the stone, illuminated by the weak, dying light of a fire barely clinging to life.

"Rey!" Aoife's voice broke as she rushed to the figure slumped against the wall, his wrists shackled.

Elara's gaze locked onto him, catching the faint, uneven rise and fall of his chest, his skin deathly pale against the tangled raven-black hair matted to his face.

Her chest tightened, a sob rising in her throat, but she swallowed it down and sprinted forward, dropped to her knees beside him, and struck the shackles with her dagger in a swift, fierce slash. They fell away, and she grabbed him before he collapsed.

He's alive. He's alive. He's alive.

A choked gasp escaped her as she clung to him, her fingers digging into his back, feeling the solid warmth of him. Aoife stood nearby, watching, unmoving, as Reynnar's arms slowly wrapped around her.

"You gave up," she managed through the broken words, though anger bled into her voice. She didn't even know why—why she felt this tangled knot of relief, fury, and heartbreak all at once, an overwhelming, impossible storm inside her.

He pulled back slightly, his gaze unfocused, weary eyes flickering over her face. *His eyes.* That deep amber, so achingly beautiful. Looking into them felt like staring at a truth she'd missed, a puzzle she should have solved long ago. A surge of rage and devastation twisted within her, each emotion crashing into the next.

How had she not seen it? How could she have been so blind?

"Eiliara."

She watched the fog in his eyes retreat, clearing inch by inch. A single tear slipped down her cheek as she nodded, her trembling fingers brushing her face in their age-old code—a gesture etched into her very soul.

Reynnar's lip twitched upward. *"There she is."*

The sound of his voice—deep and teasing—broke something in Elara, a pang that rippled through her heart.

"Rey," Aoife's voice cut in, urgent. *"Can you stand?"*

He nodded, his jaw tight, and Elara slipped an arm around his waist. His legs shook with each shift of weight, a grimace carving into his features. Aoife stepped closer, her slender fingers grabbing Reynnar's chin to tilt his face toward her. Rapid *Tírrísh* spilled from her lips, too quick for Elara to follow. He grunted, giving a curt nod, and then they were moving, breaking into a staggered run.

The air grew colder, stinging Elara's cheeks as they raced down the narrow, twisting passage. The shouting reached her first—faint echoes down the stone corridor—then grew louder. Voices. *Sidhe* voices. Clanging against the bars with a fevered pulse.

Then, as they rounded the corner, she froze, her breath stolen.

Hundreds of them. Freed from their cells, spilling into the corridor. *How—?*

It clicked. The rings she and Aoife had destroyed—the three wisps of *Draoth* returned to their rightful owners. Two fire, one air. She could almost feel their power coursing through the stone, shattering wards, breaking locks, clearing paths. They had reclaimed their strength, using it to tear down their cages and free their people.

Tears stung her eyes as she moved with them, her blade flashing as it cut through ward after ward. She moved from cell to cell without pause, her breaths ragged, the weight of the Wound of Light growing heavier with every swing.

Somewhere down the corridor, Reynnar's voice rang out, barking orders, corralling them toward the sixth tunnel, toward the *Aelfhenge.*

Dozens of Sidhe poured from the cells, a rushing tide darting through the darkened passageways, their footsteps pounding a thunderous tempo against the stone. Elara pressed forward, working alongside the three Sidhe, moving in near-perfect tandem as they wrenched open cell after cell. Finally, the last lock shattered, and the heavy metal door swung open with a groan.

Her chest heaved and her limbs trembled with exhaustion as the last of the Sidhe fled into the corridor. But Elara didn't stop. She turned, forcing herself to keep pace with the others, Reynnar and Aoife close behind. Her legs burned but the stream of bodies pushing forward, the rush of movement, kept her going. As they neared the last stretch of the tunnel, distant shouts filtered in, growing clearer with each step. Elara cursed under her breath.

Reynnar drew up beside her, his breath uneven. "*How many?*"

"*Too many,*" she muttered, glancing at him. A vein throbbed in his temple, his expression strained, and she could see the way he pushed through, barely concealing the pain radiating from his injured leg.

At the tunnel's end, the noise erupted, shouts and clashing weapons echoing through the Pit, ricocheting off the walls. They were fighting their way deeper in. *Shit.*

The group burst out of the tunnel, turning hard to the left toward the sixth, but Elara faltered mid-step, her gaze snagging on a figure amidst the storm of bodies.

Avis.

She stood on the front lines, her silhouette carved against the frenzy of fire and iron. Her arms moved in fluid arcs, wielding the earth with a power that seemed almost effortless. Rocks shot upward like shields, deflecting incoming strikes, and then hurtled down like battering rams, smashing through lines of Legionnaires. The ground shifted and buckled beneath her command sending Legionnaires scrambling.

Mother above.

Avis was wielding *Draoth*.

Elara's heart stuttered, her mind scrambling to make sense of what she was seeing. *Avis is a remnant.* She had to be. She had never converged with an element—*a Sidhe.* She had failed the convergence. She had...lied.

Elara's eyes darted through the chaos, picking out faces in the fray—Dario, Yoni, Bryn, Dominic... even Saria. All of them were here, fighting for her. Her heart twisted, her body trembling as the realization sank in. Avis had always been a spy. And Saria.

Keepers, hidden right under Osin's nose, just as Dominic had hinted.

All this time...

"*Eilíara!*" Reynnar's shout pierced her daze, snapping her back to the present.

She blinked, chest heaving, then bolted after him into the sixth tunnel.

They sprinted past rows of empty cells, the desolate corridors a blur. Past the massive vaulted chamber she would never forget. The sight of it seared into her memory—the endless lines of caged Sidhe, their hollowed faces, the air thick with their despair.

And then there it was. The *Aelfhenge.*

The ancient stones stood notched and weathered, towering in the center of the chamber. The room swarmed with Sidhe, their forms a restless sea of movement. Voices rose in frantic, feverish murmurs, the words tumbling over one another in a rush, leaving her mind spinning.

As Elara approached the stones, her steps slowed, drawn forward by the eerie stillness that seemed to compress the air within the circle.

"*Don't touch the Aelfhenge!*" she called out, her voice slicing through the din. She turned back to the Sidhe, meeting their wary stares head-on. "*It belongs to Rhiannon.*"

Death.

She knew it in her very marrow. One touch had been enough to cross that boundary.

The Wound of Light throbbed at her side, heat radiating through her palm. From somewhere deeper in the tunnels, the clang of swords and the cries of battle grew louder, closing in.

Elara gritted her teeth, tension flaring through her as she stepped into the circle of stones. The air dropped, her breath fanning out in white puffs, but she closed her eyes and drew in a slow, steady breath.

Every scar, every shadowed memory, every drop of blood—this was her armor. She sank into that deep, silent place within herself, untouched by fear or hesitation, where feeling dissolved and left only purpose and unyielding will. The surrounding noise faded, replaced by the steady thud of her heartbeat, the warmth pulsing through her veins, and the electric rush prickling beneath her skin.

She exhaled, channeling every ounce of rage, every shard of strength into a single, fluid motion. Her blade sliced through the air, trailing a glimmering arc of light, the faint whisper of her tunic the only sound that followed.

Time stilled.

Slowly, the thread of light faded, and a rift formed, widening before her. Elara let out a shaky breath, her chest tight with the thrill and fear of what lay beyond. Behind her, movement stirred—the soft rustle of Reynnar and Aoife shifting just outside the circle of stones—but she kept her gaze locked on the dark, swirling expanse of the Void.

"I'll be right back," she murmured, glancing over her shoulder and catching their watchful eyes before turning back to the rift. Once again, the Void was still, Epona's blade tempering the dark expanse. She looked down at the blade in her hand. *The Wound of Light is the door, and you are the key*. Elara squared her shoulders and extended the blade, angling its tip through the subtle currents around her. The moment it touched, she felt a tremor—a *ripple*.

The currents split apart, fracturing into dozens of shimmering threads, light scattering like rays through glass. *Tír na nÓg*, she thought, her heart pounding as she focused on the name. *I want to open the gate to Tír na nÓg.*

Elara lifted the Wound of Light, the blade catching the faint glow of the currents as she traced it carefully through them, focusing on the memory—the kingdom of air she'd glimpsed weeks ago. She pictured the grand ballroom, its walls shimmering like spun silk, saw herself as a young girl, twirling with her brother.

Her throat tightened.

She bit hard into her cheek, forcing the emotion down, shoving it aside. Now was not the time to dwell on a life stolen from her—or a boy whose soul might be lost somewhere within this endless expanse.

Elara pressed the blade's tip into the fractured current, feeling the thrum of energy vibrate up her arm. The metal pulsed, alive with power —but then, her chest clenched, a searing, crushing grip that stole her breath. She gasped, her hand flying to her heart. Something dark coiled there, deep inside, twisting tighter with every spark of energy from the blade.

The parasite.

She clenched her teeth, trying to press forward, to force the rift open despite the agony stabbing through her ribs. But the pain became blinding, unrelenting, dragging her vision into a haze and tearing a cry from her lips.

Elara yanked the blade from the current, her fingers clawing at her neck as she struggled for air.

No. *No.*

She tightened her grip on the hilt, refusing to fail, even as cold sweat slicked her skin. Determined, she raised the blade again, but the moment it touched the currents, the darkness surged. It devoured the energy from the Wound of Light, consuming it like a ravenous beast.

Fuck.

Elara staggered backward, her hands trembling violently at her sides. She couldn't do it. *Gods, she had promised*, and she couldn't do it.

Stumbling out of the Void, her the faces waiting for her came into view, each one filled with silent, desperate hope. She couldn't bring herself to meet their eyes, except for one.

"*I was so sure,*" she said to Reynnar, her voice barely more than a whisper. He reached out, his fingers steady as they wrapped around hers, firm and calm against the tremor in her own.

"*Let us help you,*" Aoife said, stepping to her other side.

Elara's gaze shifted, narrowing as it fixed on the three Sidhe behind Aoife. They stood like statues carved from moonlight—fierce, otherworldly.

The two females were opposites: one with hair as dark as midnight cascading down her back, her skin pale and almost luminous in the dim light; the other with fiery, untamed hair the color of autumn leaves, her brown skin ashen, robbed of its warmth by long, lightless days of captivity. The male stood slightly behind them, tall and broad, his silver-streaked hair falling loose around a face etched with years of scars.

Their hands rested at their sides, but tension coiled in their stances—a readiness, as if they were waiting for the slightest signal to unleash the power humming beneath their skin.

Elara glanced back at Reynnar and Aoife, unease prickling in her stomach, a quiet sense of foreboding settling over her. But she nodded, resolute, and the five of them stepped forward, vanishing into the Void.

The air shifted, cool and still, the subtle currents of the Void brushing gently against her skin. The quiet was unnerving, the calm pressing in like a held breath. She raised the Wound of Light high, and sliced the blade's tip through the air, parting the swirling streams with a fierce, precise strike.

A faint glow rippled outward, fragments of the Void illuminated in soft glimmers of light. The fracture widened in response, but with it came a familiar tightening in her chest—an invisible claw sinking deep.

Elara trembled, her strength funneling into the darkness within her. She grit her teeth, swallowing back her cry as the blade wavered, slipping just enough to nick her palm. Her muscles screamed, trembling violently as she pushed the blade forward, every ounce of her will, every shred of her spirit, thrown into the desperate act of forcing the gate to open. Her vision blurred, black spots creeping at the edges. *Too much.* Her heart thundered, a wild, unsteady rhythm that threatened to stop altogether. She was loosing too much.

And then—warmth. A grounding pressure curled around her wrist, pulling her back from the edge. Startled, her gaze darted down to find the woman with midnight hair gripping her tightly. Her hold anchoring Elara as a surge of *Draoth* coursed through her veins. It was cool, rushing like a sweeping tide, filling every inch of her. The ache in her chest ebbed, the leeching sensation retreating under the force flowing into her.

Elara angled the blade deeper into the fracture, pushing forward as the currents gave way. It felt as though the sun coiled inside her, stars flaring and collapsing within her bones, filling her as the blade shook in her hand.

The other two Sidhe stepped up and poured their *Draoth* into the current—a torrent of fire that surged through her, driving the storm inside her to a breaking point. She stood at the heart of a maelstrom, pure energy coursing beneath her skin, sparking along her veins.

Then it hit her, a blow to the chest that left her breathless. The floodgates opened, and she saw it all—their fears, their fleeting hopes, and the grim certainty in their minds.

They were going to die.

They were sacrificing themselves for their people.

Her lips quivered as she fought to contain the tidal wave of emotion rising inside her, fingers curling into fists until her knuckles ached. And still, the Sidhe poured everything into her, draining themselves of every last shred of power.

They were trusting her—with their people, their sacrifice. Trusting her to carry it all across the rift. It was a faith so absolute, so fierce, it felt like her soul might fracture under it.

A deep well of sadness threatened to drown her—grief for all that had been taken from them, the torment they'd endured. But that sorrow shifted inside her, curling into something *blistering*. The *Draoth* coursing through her flared, heat singeing her fingertips before she realized she was pulling on the thread of fire within her, releasing her ire in a physical surge.

What Osin had taken from them—from her. It was heinous, unimaginable. Ripping families apart, stealing children from their beds, draining the Sidhe of their *Draoth* to cement his reign over the realm.

It was a massacre—a slow annihilation of her people. *Her people.*

The fire crept insidiously, charring her hands before coiling around her wrists, creeping upward like ivy. Her body shook, muscles taut and trembling, straining as if on the verge of snapping. Every part of her braced against the mounting pressure.

She drove the Wound of Light deeper, inch by inch, feeling the resistance give way—a slow crack splintering open in the dark.

The parasite inside her twisted, coiling and thrashing, fighting back against the power of the Sidhe and the blade.

Come on, come on.

With each drive of the blade, memories surged through her—moments of blood and grit, triumph wrested from despair, dreams shattered and painstakingly rebuilt, vows whispered in the dead of night, and defiant cries hurled against the dark. Each scar, every tear, every breathless laugh—every broken moment—braided together, feeding the fire at her core.

The world may have seen her as broken, but it was time they realized —broken things can be sharp, *deadly.*

Elara screamed, driving the Wound of Light into the fracture. And then, as if the fates conspired in her favor, the dagger tore through the fabric of reality, unleashing a cataclysmic force that bridged the two worlds.

CHAPTER 60

Reality splintered with a deafening roar, sending tremors rippling through the Void. The currents becoming wild, screaming around Elara as she pulled the Wound of Light from the rift.

The hands that had steadied her slipped away, the last traces of *Draoth* fading from her veins, leaving her feeling suddenly, achingly empty.

Nothing moved.

The silence was uncanny, weighty, broken only by the hum of the rift hanging in the air before them, alive with a volatile, uncontained energy.

Elara looked up, eyes wide as she glimpsed what lay beyond—a world of colors that defied reason, hues that seemed to shimmer and shift with each passing second. Shades of green, blue, and gold bled into one another, creating landscapes that looked like moving glass, like someone had taken the idea of wonder and spun it into existence.

Her pupils dilated, her heart stuttering between beats. A hint of a smile touched her lips as she glanced back—

—and the air tore from her lungs in a painful rush.

The three Sidhe lay still on the cold expanse of the Void, their forms already dissolving, fading into the darkness.

A strangled sound tore from her as she stumbled forward, hands outstretched. Nothing met her grasp but air.

Elara looked up to find anguish etched across Reynnar's face. Aoife stood beside him, tears streaking her cheeks, gaze fixed on the fallen Sidhe, shoulders trembling with quiet sobs.

Reynnar turned to Aoife, his voice hoarse, barely more than a whisper. "*Go.*"

Aoife gave a trembling nod, quickly wiping her eyes before turning and sprinting out of the Void. Moments later, a flood of Sidhe poured in, brushing past her like fleeting bursts of life against the Void's unrelenting chill. They surged toward the rift, toward the freedom won by the final breaths of the three who had sacrificed everything.

"*Eiliara.*"

She met Reynnar's gaze. Slowly, he reached forward, brushing a stray lock of hair from her face. "*Come with me.*" Her lids slid closed, tension coiling along her neck. Gods, she wanted to. Every fiber of her being screamed that it was the right choice, the only choice.

But she opened her eyes and shook her head, a faint tremor running through her. "*I can't.*"

His brow creased, a flicker of hurt and confusion crossing his face.

Elara swallowed and glanced down at the blade in her hand—the weapon forged by a goddess, the one thing Osin couldn't take from her. "*I promised someone,*" she murmured, "*I promised I would kill the king.*"

She had to do it—for Calista, for herself, for every soul Osin had torn apart and stolen. There was no future, no safety, until he was gone. The weight of the blade in her hand was her only certainty, its edge promising vengeance—the finality she needed to end him.

Reynnar caught her eye, reading something in her expression that didn't need words. A quiet resolve settled over him as he nodded. "*I'm going with you.*"

The words struck like ice, a wave of panic rising in her chest. "*No. Leave. You need to get out of this place. To be free of it. You've given enough.*"

Tears blurred her vision, slipping down her cheeks as the three Sidhe behind him dissolved, fading into the Void. "*You've all given too much already. Go.*"

But he shook his head, his jaw tight, his eyes unyielding. "*No.*"

She shoved him, tried to push him toward the gate, into the throng of Sidhe racing for freedom. "*Yes,*" she hissed, but he didn't budge.

Gods damn him.

Reynnar's hand wrapped around hers. "*I would sooner carve my own heart out than leave you to face this alone.*"

"*I won't be alone,*" she said, thinking of the others—Avis, Dario, Dominic. She had allies.

But his grip on her hand didn't loosen. "*No. You won't.*"

Aoife ran up to them, her face flushed. "*This is the last of them.*"

A group of about twenty Sidhe shuffled into the Void, glancing back before sprinting toward the rift. Aoife reached out and grabbed Reynnar's hand, trying to pull him along. Her brows furrowed when he didn't move. Instead, he drew her close, his hand cradling the back of her head as he murmured something against her hair. Her eyes fluttered shut, a single tear slipping down her cheek, followed by another. After a moment, she nodded, her face tight. She released him and turned to Elara, pulling her into an embrace.

"*Thank you,*" she whispered, her voice soft against Elara's hair, before pressing a kiss to her cheek. She glanced back at Reynnar. One last look, then stepped into the rift and vanished.

Elara's voice wavered as she turned to him. "*Please, go. Aoife—she needs you. She loves—*"

Reynnar raised a brow. "*My sister is needed in Tír na nÓg.*" His mouth twitched. "*She knows the stakes, and if she had a problem with it, she'd have told me—with her fists if necessary.*"

Elara blinked, processing his words. *His sister.*

She exhaled slowly, her chest tight, fighting the urge to beg him one last time to leave. But she knew Reynnar—once he'd made up his mind, there was no changing it. So she took his hand, gripping tightly, and together, they ran.

THE GROUND LURCHED BENEATH THEM, a deep, ugly shudder that rattled Elara's teeth and sent a thin rain of dust whispering down from the ceiling. Every impact ahead echoed through the tunnel like a warning she didn't want to hear, the stone carrying the violence straight into her chest. The fight had already pushed halfway the *Aelfhenge*, faster than it should have, faster than she'd let herself think about while they ran.

Her breath burned. Her legs burned. Fear crept in anyway, curling tight and cold beneath her ribs, no matter how hard she tried to outrun it.

Reynnar's hand tightened around hers before he pulled her back so suddenly she stumbled, boots scraping stone as they skidded to a halt.

"*What's the plan?*"

The plan. Right. The plan.

Her mind raced, her breaths quick and uneven. "*I need to get to the king. Close enough to drive this through his heart.*" Elara lifted the blade. "*He's strong. It won't be easy.*"

Reynnar released her hand, a hint of a grin breaking through the tension on his face. "*Then we make it easy. I'll cut through his guards, clear you a path. And if the bastard tries to run, I'll be right there, shoving him back into place.*" He tapped his fist against his chest with a quick, decisive nod. "*You just focus on getting that blade where it needs to go.*"

Elara nodded, even though there wasn't a trace of confidence anywhere in her. This wasn't a plan—it was barely even an idea, and they both knew it. But Reynnar gave her one of those steady, assessing looks.

"*You've got this, Eilíara,*" he said, "*I've watched you do the impossible before. You'll do it again.*"

Elara took a steadying breath, gritting her teeth as her hand tightened around the blade.

Reynnar's grin widened, a flash of fangs glinting. "*Stay close to me.*"

They sprinted down the tunnel, feet pounding against stone, the clash and roar of battle growing louder. The air buzzed with crackling *Draoth*, scorching her lungs with each breath. As they rounded a corner, a burst of fire erupted in front of them, colliding with a wave of earth that shot up from the ground, sending rocks and embers flying in every direction.

Reynnar yanked her aside just in time, both of them ducking as a blazing shard of stone whizzed past her head.

They exchanged a brief glance, their breaths uneven, then plunged forward, weaving through the fray. The battle churned around them—bodies pressing in from all sides, bursts of fire, water, and stone cutting through the darkness in blinding, erratic flashes.

Elara screamed as a figure burst from the smoke—a soldier with a wicked grin, his sword already swinging toward her. She ducked on instinct, clumsy and panicked, nearly tripping as she twisted away. Her grip slipped on the dagger's hilt, palms slick with sweat, and she barely managed a wild upward swing, the blade grazing his arm.

He snarled, shoving her back, but Reynnar lunged between them, grabbing the man and ripping him away, his hands finding the soldier's throat as his fangs tore into flesh. The soldier's gurgled howl faded quickly, his body slumping to the ground, blood pooling beneath him.

Reynnar spared her a brief, wild grin before charging into the next wave.

Her vision swam, her breaths shallow and ragged as she tried to keep up. Everywhere she looked, there was motion—a flash of silver, a spray of blood, a blur of bodies colliding and falling. A soldier spun toward her, eyes narrowed as he chanted under his breath, tendrils of earth twisting up from the ground. She swung the blade desperately, aiming low, feeling the resistance as it cut through his leg. He crumpled to the ground with a grunt, but not before a jagged rock whipped past her, tearing through her sleeve.

A fiery sting erupted along her arm as blood welled up, soaking into the shredded fabric.

Elara stumbled back, gasping, her gaze flicking to Reynnar as he cut down another opponent—muscles coiled, movements fluid and lethal. She started toward him, but a figure lunged from the side, mace swinging.

She ducked. Air roared past her head, missing by inches.

She didn't think—she surged forward, blade thrusting out in a rough, desperate strike.

The blade struck his side, but the angle was wrong—too shallow.

He staggered but stayed on his feet, already turning back toward her.

Elara stumbled away, lost her footing, and went down hard, hands scraping through dirt as the dagger suddenly felt too heavy to lift.

Then Reynnar was there.

A dark blur at her side. He seized the man and hurled him back, fangs bared. Steel flashed. One brutal sweep across the soldier's throat.

Blood sprayed her face—hot, metallic. Elara gagged, forcing herself upright as her vision swam. Sound collapsed into noise. Screams. Steel. The crack of magic.

Bodies rushed past in a wash of motion and light until the world became chaos and she could no longer tell who was friend or foe.

Another fireball exploded nearby, the heat searing her cheek, and she stumbled, catching herself just in time to see Reynnar charging forward, ripping through another soldier with a snarl. She forced her legs to move, half-running, half-stumbling after him, the ground slippery with mud and blood.

Her boots snagged on the outstretched arm of a fallen soldier, and she pitched forward, slamming into the dirt.

The sharp sting of gravel bit into her palms as she braced herself, her breath hitching. Bodies surged around her, their boots kicking up dust and debris that filled her lungs. She hacked, sputtering, until a firm hand gripped her shoulder.

"Are you all right?"

She nodded, grabbing his hand, and he pulled her to her feet just as a blast of earth tore through the ground behind them, sending a shockwave that nearly knocked them off balance. They stumbled forward, Reynnar keeping a tight hold on her as they surged through the melee. Elara gritted her teeth, every muscle screaming the blade feeling like dead weight in her hand, as they ducked under a burst of fire; the heat singeing her hair, her heart hammering as they pushed deeper.

Bodies pressed in on all sides—soldiers, Script Keepers, rebels—all blurring together in a mass of color and movement, blood splattering her as she slashed at anything that moved too close. Reynnar carved a narrow, bloody path through the fight, inching closer to the heart of the battlefield, where a dense circle of soldiers guarded a single figure.

Elara's heart clenched as they neared, dread pooling in her stomach.

Even before she saw him, she felt the chill of his presence, the dark energy emanating from the center of that human shield like a poison.

Osin stood motionless, cold and composed, surveying the slaughter with idle curiosity. Shadows coiled around him, snapping out in brutal strikes, twisting and wrapping around the necks of rebels who dared approach. The Legionnaires clustered around him, moving in perfect, unbreakable formation, yet it seemed almost unnecessary. Osin wasn't even breaking a sweat, his gaze calm, his expression bored, as if this massacre was no more than a mildly entertaining spectacle.

Elara's blood ran cold. She could see it, could feel it—he was *stronger*.

Somehow, the *Draoth* pulsing from him was denser—consuming everything it touched. The shadows darted out like vipers, striking with precision, and each time, they seemed to feed back into him, thickening the surrounding air with a power that felt smothering.

Reynnar's hand tightened on her shoulder, drawing her gaze to his. His face was ashen, his eyes tense. "*All right,*" he said, voice steady, slipping into the calm command of a seasoned warrior. "*Here's how we're doing this. We split their line. I'll draw their attention, create an opening for you to get through.*"

Elara blinked, struggling to process it. "*You'll be completely exposed—*"

He cut her off with a quick, fierce grin. "*Let them come. I've dealt with worse. Once you're through, don't look back. Keep your head low and keep moving forward. And when you see an opening—don't hesitate. Don't second-guess. Strike hard and fast.*"

She nodded, nerves twisting in her gut.

"*I'll be right behind you, covering your back,*" he added, voice a shade gentler, "*whatever happens, we bring him down together.*"

Reynnar gave her shoulder a firm, reassuring squeeze before stepping back, blade steady in his grip. He turned toward the line of Legionnaires, his eyes alight with deadly focus. "*We move on my mark.*" Elara's pulse quickened.

His chin dipped—and then he was gone, darting left. His sword flashed, opening the first soldier's throat in a single, fluid motion. Blood sprayed his face, but he was already moving, blade turning on the next target. The Legionnaires barely reacted—eyes widening, weapons half-raised—before Reynnar tore into them. One soldier charged. Reynnar cut him down at the knees and drove his blade home in the same breath.

The line buckled. Reynnar pressed through it.

Elara's pulse pounded as she slipped through the narrow gaps Reynnar carved open. A blade cut the air above her head; she ducked, boot skidding through blood as she fought to keep her footing.

Ahead, movement drew her attention. Other Script Keepers had spotted Reynnar, their grim expressions hardening as they surged into the fight, weapons glinting. Her breath caught when she saw Dario among them. His left arm hung limp, clearly dislocated, but it didn't slow him. He charged forward, wielding his blade one-handed, slicing through a Legionnaire before shoving another aside.

She sprinted toward him, her pulse hammering in her ears, but a pair of soldiers locked in vicious combat blocked her way. She pressed against the writhing wall of bodies, forcing herself through just as one of them crumpled to the ground, a spray of blood spattering her boots.

The copper tang filled her lungs.

Keep going. Just keep going.

Her gaze locked on Osin—still untouched amid the chaos. Shadows coiled and twisted around him, a living shroud that mocked the bloodshed at his feet.

Her grip tightened on the Wound of Light, its hilt warm against her palm. Her lips curled as she stepped forward, gaze narrowing.

Then a figure moved into her path.

Her breath stalled.

Ivan.

CHAPTER 61

Blood and steel and sweat—her eyes took him in before she could stop them, before sense or fear could intervene.

Ivan stood there battered and broken-looking, his armor streaked with blood that wasn't all his. A fresh cut split the skin at his temple, red slipping down the hard line of his jaw, and she hated how the sight of it made something in her chest ache instead of recoil. There was a softness to his mouth that didn't belong on a man like him—a quiet, brooding curve that twisted her stomach and made her furious with herself for seeing it. For *feeling* it. Even now. Even here. In the middle of all this ruin, she still found him beautiful.

Haunting coldness and terrible beauty all at once.

His eyes held hers and the chaos of the Pit dissolved. Without a word, he lifted his hand, summoning a dome of fire that encased them. The sounds of clashing steel, screams, and roaring *Draoth* were silenced in an instant—shrinking to him, to the blood-soaked ground between them.

The abrupt stillness made her ears ring. It was the same barrier they'd created together back when he'd first taught her to pull on the *Draoth Cara*—a shared thread, one that had once felt safe.

Elara's teeth ground together as she watched the flames, burning with a power that wasn't his to wield. Her gaze snapped back to his, her pulse a dark thrum beneath her skin.

"Did you know?" she demanded, her voice striking like a crack of thunder. The furious, hurt, broken pieces of her heart screamed, begging for justice, for truth, for something real and untainted.

His eyes shifted, a fleeting glimmer of vulnerability breaking through before vanishing. She saw the gears turning behind his expression, calculating, weighing, searching for the best response. Every secret, every veiled truth, every shadow he kept hidden—it was all there, flashing in his gaze.

"I didn't know it was him."

Elara's blood roared in her ears as she forced the words past bared teeth, "But did you know?"

His mouth moved, and her heart broke and mended, and shattered anew with that single, whispered "*Yes.*"

A guttural snarl tore from her as she lunged, blade flashing. He side-stepped, leaving her strike to cut empty air.

She wheeled on him, fury tightening her grip.

"Fight back!" she snapped, her voice breaking as she swung again. He didn't. He only raised an arm to block her.

"No."

With a scream, she charged, driving the dagger toward his chest. His hand closed around her wrist mid-strike. They ended up inches apart, her chest heaving, his face close enough for her to catch the strain in his eyes—the regret woven through it.

For a split second, something flickered. She felt it—the unmistakable thread of his presence. He brushed her mind, tentative. Her lips curled, and she wrenched her wrist free.

"Let me out."

"I can't."

She flinched, her mind spinning back to another moment—to his whispered confession in the dark. The first time they'd almost kissed.

I can't.

The same hesitation, the same restraint. He hadn't held back because he couldn't feel anything for her—but because he'd harbored this secret all along. His reluctance, his carefully drawn boundaries... they had been a shield, a twisted show of morality, all while knowing exactly what he was complicit in.

But none of that mattered. Whatever guilt he felt now, whatever shame or regret flickered in his eyes—she didn't care. He was still one of them. One of Osin's chosen, thriving off the backs of slaves.

Elara's bellow tore through the air as she channeled every ounce of her fury into the Wound of Light.

Its brilliance exploded, slamming into him and hurling him into the dome. He struck the barrier, rebounded, and hit the ground—and she was on him before he could move. Her knees pinned his sides, the blade pressed hard to his throat.

The power of the blade pulsed through her, lighting her from within—an unceasing flood she couldn't contain, didn't want to. Her hands shook, her vision blurred, but she didn't care. The anger, the betrayal—it all burned, blinding and red-hot.

Ivan looked up at her, his face sedate, not even flinching. A slow, almost admiring smile spread across his lips. He didn't struggle, didn't lift a hand in defense. If anything, he looked... content. As if he'd been waiting for this.

"You're resplendent in your rage," he murmured, his hand reaching up to tenderly graze her cheek. "A true force to be reckoned with."

The blade trembled in Elara's grip, its edge pressing just enough to nick him. A thin line of blood trickled down his throat. She could end it —one clean slice—and it would be over. Yet, something within her faltered.

Her *heart*.

Damn her heart. Her stupid, traitorous heart. She couldn't do it. She couldn't—

"Drop the barrier."

Osin's voice sliced through her spiraling thoughts, and she froze, her gaze snapping up to find him standing just outside the dome. Ivan's eyes flickered shut for a moment before he released the barrier, letting it fall.

Elara's stomach twisted as her eyes darted around, absorbing the chaos—the Legionnaires pressing forward, the rebels retreating deeper into the Pit.

They were losing.

They were losing, and she'd squandered her chance.

Her gaze locked on Reynnar. He knelt in the blood and grime, face smeared red, eyes still blazing—even in defeat, as if he'd torn through dozens of soldiers before they finally overwhelmed him.

She'd failed him.

"Get up, Hunter," Osin snarled, his voice like a lash.

Ivan shoved her off, rising slowly to his feet.

Elara's whole body trembled—rage, betrayal, and a bone-deep exhaustion twisting inside her. She could barely push herself upright, her vision swimming as she looked up at him.

Osin's lip curled into a dark smile. "Strike her."

Ivan's hand hovered at his side, trembling, as if he were battling some invisible force... some *compulsion*.

Elara's eyes widened. Then—his hand cracked across her face. Her head snapped to the side, the metallic taste of blood flooding her mouth.

Behind her, a roar echoed, Reynnar's voice filled with rage.

"Again."

Another blow, harder this time, his knuckles connecting with her jaw. The impact sent stars dancing across her vision, her head snapping to the side as she crumpled to the ground. For a moment, the cavern swayed, and she struggled to catch her breath. But then she planted her hands and pushed herself back to her feet.

Her teeth clenched as she glared up at him, blood dripping from her split lip. She spat, the crimson hitting the ground between them.

"Fight it, you bastard!" Reynnar snarled, thrashing against the shadows, constraining him. *"What, not man enough to shake off a little curse? Why don't you bend over, Hunter? Let him—"*

The words cut off with a strangled gasp as Osin's shadows tightened around Reynnar's throat. Osin gave a long-suffering sigh, rolling his eyes. "Always with the dramatics." He shifted his attention to Elara. "No, he can't resist. And, amusingly enough, we have you to thank for that, Hallowed. I do appreciate the irony."

He stepped closer, his voice dropping to a near whisper. *"Minva sölk harn,"* he said, the words guttural and venomous.

Elara stopped breathing.

"My soul for hers. The oath my Hunter swore the night his traitor brother tried to kill you. A noble sentiment."

Osin's smile widened, though his eyes remained glacial. "What the poor fool didn't realize was that I control the Void and, in turn, death. So, when he pledged his soul, he was pledging it to *me.*"

Elara's throat closed, air sticking painfully in her lungs. She glanced at Ivan and saw the devastation etched into his features—the resignation.

"I knew the Binding Sigil wouldn't hold," Osin continued, his voice almost delighted. "Knew the *Draoth Cara* wouldn't allow it to stick."

A low chuckle escaped him as Elara's wide eyes snapped to his. "Oh yes, I know all about that. It was my plan, you see—a little tool to keep the *Tuatha Dé Danann* obedient." His gaze flicked to Reynnar. "I took his *Draoth* and tied my Hunter to you, his 'mate,' as insurance. Just a whisper of death at my command."

Mate?

The word rang hollow and unfamiliar in Elara's mind. She glanced at Reynnar, but his brow was furrowed, his gaze darting between her and Osin. He didn't understand the language, couldn't follow the exchange.

"That *Draoth* was a gift," Osin sneered, "bestowed upon my shadow, my ward. An extension of death—of my will. And yet," he paused, his gaze settling on Ivan with a flicker of disappointment, "the moment he lied to me, I knew where his loyalties lay. He didn't betray his brother for me that night, Hallowed."

He scoffed. "No, he did it for *you.*"

Elara's heart stalled as Osin stepped closer to Ivan, each movement slow, deliberate. He tilted Ivan's chin up with a mocking tut. "All these years, pretending. Imagine my surprise." His gaze settled back on her with a twisted smile. "How amusing and dark the game's destiny plays."

Ivan didn't move, his chest still, as though he weren't even breathing.

Osin chuckled, shaking his head. "I kept an eye on you both. Watched you from the beginning, just as I watched you with his older brother, Hallowed. And what a wealth of knowledge that gave me."

His eyes flicked to Elara. "I learned so much—how to manipulate the Void, how to navigate the currents, even how to retrieve memories from those who've crossed over... or tear them away from the living."

She staggered back, her stomach twisting violently.

Osin rolled his eyes, his voice flat, bored. "But I tire of this. Now, I want my dagger back. And you," he smirked, "you're going to give it to me."

Elara's heart plummeted as Reynnar dropped, his body convulsing. His face twisted, veins standing out starkly as his lips turned blue.

"Stop! All right, *stop*!"

Osin's smirk deepened, satisfaction glinting in his eyes as the shadows loosened. Reynnar jerked once, then fell still, his chest heaving with a ragged breath.

She forced herself to steady, drawing a slow breath, even as fury churned beneath her skin. "I'll give you the blade," she said, her tone as cold as steel. "But only after I put it through the Hunter myself."

Ivan's head snapped toward her.

"Oh?" Osin's brow twitched, a trace of intrigue breaking through.

Elara turned to face Ivan fully, her eyes blazing. "You lied to me."

His expression didn't move an inch. "I did."

"You *used* me."

Something flickered—an almost imperceptible crack in his composure, quickly masked.

She tore her gaze from him and looked back at Osin, her jaw set. "Let me kill him," she demanded. "And it's yours."

Osin's eyes narrowed, his lips curving into something just shy of a smile. He held her in that calculated silence, a beast savoring the moment, before finally giving the slightest nod. "Do it."

Her fingers twitched. She stepped toward Ivan, blade in hand, lifting her chin to meet his gaze. He didn't flinch, didn't move an inch, just gazed down at her, amber flaring at the edges of his dark eyes.

Reynnar's stolen *Draoth* simmering beneath the surface.

She would see it returned.

In one ruthless motion, Elara ripped the ring from his finger and crushed it under her boot.

The ring shattered, fragments scattering. From the broken stone, a wisp of amber light shot out, streaking across the Pit toward Reynnar.

Ivan's lips twisted into a crooked grin. Osin's snarl sliced through the air. And then, across the room, flames exploded from Reynnar's mouth.

The Pit ignited.

CHAPTER 62

A searing wave of fire ripped through the darkness, consuming every shadow in its path.

Reynnar's eyes burned like molten embers, each strike was brutal, precise—a tempest of fire sweeping through the Legionnaires, their screams swallowed by the inferno.

Ash and smoke filled the room as he moved, a force of nature incarnate. The ground beneath him blackened with each step, heat radiating from his body in waves that warped the air. His ferocity left no room for mercy, only destruction—pure and uncontained, as if he could raze entire kingdoms with nothing but his wrath.

In the distance, the ground quaked beneath a surge of pounding footsteps. The rhythmic thunder of Osin's army racing back—summoned by the skittering shadows of their lord.

Elara's stomach flipped as Osin's eyes flicked to hers, shadows snaking toward her.

But something inside her snapped. The wall she had built so carefully buckled, splintering into shards. Heat surged through her veins—a force untamed and furious as the *Draoth Cara* flared back to life, burning as if it had always been waiting for this moment to break free.

Her breath hitched as a scorching force spiraled up her spine, coiling tighter with every heartbeat. Her hands lifted, trembling, drawn by the inferno building inside her. Heat rolled off her skin, the air warping around her.

Then she erupted.

Flames tore from her fingertips—wild, searing—devouring everything in their path. A wall of fire roared into being, its heat alive and vicious, cleaving Osin's shadows apart.

Across the chaos, Reynnar's gaze caught hers, his chest heaving. Understanding flared between them—wordless, instinctive. She felt the fire in him as if it coursed through her own veins. With Ivan, it had been a steady, measured beat, contained and controlled. But with Reynnar, it was everywhere—a heat that lived, breathed, and burned in every inch of him.

"Elara, open a rift and go!" Ivan's voice sliced through the roar of flames, his breath ragged, dark vines creeping across his eyes. "I'm still under Osin's control. The parasite." He clutched his chest, but a burst of shadows erupted between them.

They sprang apart.

Her body hit the ground hard, the cold floor scraping her skin raw as she rolled. Fingers locked around the hilt of her blade, she pushed herself up, her breaths frantic, her heart pounding like a hammer against her ribs.

The parasite.

That wrongness she'd felt for so long, like a thorn lodged beneath her heart—it was there in every glance they'd shared, every pulse of power he'd tried to teach her to control.

Not in her. It had never been in her.

It was his.

His covenant with Death.

Ivan had been trying to break her binds, to find some way to set her *Draoth* free, but he couldn't. Not while that twisted deal held him captive.

Her gaze darted to him across the Pit. Smoke and fire churned in the air, framing his retreating figure in stark, jagged shadows. He was purposely putting distance between them.

Her heart slammed against her ribs.

"Hunter!" Osin bellowed.

The word cracked through the Pit, lashing off stone. Ivan's head snapped toward the sound. His movements went rigid, limbs heavy—as if unseen strings had seized him. Slowly, his glaive rose. Step by step, he advanced on Reynnar, each stride grinding into the scorched ground.

Elara's breath hitched. A cry tore from her throat.

"No!"

Her focus narrowed to Osin, her vision tunneling as she sprinted forward, muscles burning with every step. The Legion swarmed the Pit, surging back like a tide toward Reynnar and Ivan, where steel flashed in the dim light.

But Osin wasn't looking. His dark gaze was locked on Ivan, a twisted satisfaction curling his lips.

In that fleeting heartbeat, Elara lunged. Her shoulder slammed into his chest, the force sending him stumbling back, off balance. Surprise flickered in his eyes a split-second before they both hit the ground, the impact rattling through her bones as a choking cloud of dust billowed around them.

Shadows clawed out, frantic, but Elara didn't falter. She drove the blade into his chest, steel tearing through flesh, slicing bone, and burying itself deep in his heart.

Osin gasped, his features twisting as the shadows around him sputtered and dissolved. For a heartbeat, his wide eyes locked with hers.

Then he laughed—a rasping, broken sound that crawled over her skin.

"Still so naive. Death *belongs* to me. Do you know what happens to those who fight the inevitable?" He smiled, an evil, wicked grin. "Time turns them to dust."

He reached for the blade, his fingers curling around the hilt, but with a savage twist, Elara yanked it out.

Osin let out a choked groan, blood pouring from his chest in a hot, dark torrent that splashed onto the ground. His eyes dimmed, but even then, she saw it—the wound beginning to close, flesh knitting itself together.

Her lips curled back, teeth bared as a sound tore from her throat—a raw, guttural snarl laced with fury and devastation. She leaned in, her voice low. "Then I'll make my own vow—to death, to time. I vow to find a way to end you. But until then..."

She slashed a deep, jagged line across his cheek, the blade splitting the flesh into a cruel, monstrous scar. She struck again, carving another line across the other side.

"When you look at your ruined, *ugly* face, you'll remember what you did. You'll remember *me*."

Osin screamed—and hands seized her, yanking her backward. She slammed into the ground, the impact knocking the air from her lungs.

A Legionnaire loomed above her as vines burst from the earth, snapping around her legs. They coiled tight, locking her in place.

She thrashed, kicked—but the more she fought, the harder they constricted.

Then came the heat.

Familiar. Wild.

Fire swept over her skin like an old memory roaring back to life. Reynnar's fire.

Flames raced up the vines, consuming the Legionnaire in a heartbeat and leaving only ash. Not a single scorch mark touched her skin.

It was his fire—always his. Fierce and consuming, yet impossibly gentle, as if it knew her, burned for her alone.

Elara flung her hands out, a barrier snapping into place, whirling back the encroaching chaos. She looked up, pulse roaring in her ears. Reynnar was sprinting toward her, fury etched into every line of his face —but her attention snagged on Ivan.

He was on his knees, shoulders heaving, gasping as though the air had been ripped from his lungs. Her strike to Osin's heart must have shattered the command to attack Reynnar.

But something was wrong.

Blood streaked Ivan's mouth, and when he lifted his head, her stomach dropped.

Dark vines crept over his eyes, winding tighter, pulsing as if they fed on him. Shadows spilled from his hands, coiling like snakes. For a beat that stretched endlessly, she thought of the Shades—their half-life, barely tethered to the world.

Terror seized her.

Then, through the pounding in her head, the memory surfaced: *"Minva sölk harn."*

My soul for hers.

Her breath hitched. That cursed vow—binding him to Death.

The Draoth Cara must have held it at bay, keeping the debt from coming due. But now, with every other soul bound to him gone, there was only one left.

His.

Death was coming to collect.

He stayed on his knees, swaying, teetering on the brink of collapse, his breaths ragged and shallow.

But then he began to crawl—to her.

His trembling hands clawed at the ground, dragging his body forward. But his shadow—*his shadow*—moved faster.

It slid across the Pit, gliding effortlessly over the distance between them, stopping just in front of her.

Elara held her breath, her pulse hammering as she lowered the barrier just enough to let it through. The shadow rose, curling upward like a dark whisper, and brushed against her brow.

In that sliver of eternity, that fragile, heartbeat stretched pause between shadows and blazing light, Ivan's gaze found hers.

It was an electric jolt, a silent collision of souls.

Suddenly, a whirlwind of his emotions and memories crashed over her—laughter echoed briefly, the bright sound of childhood joy, snuffed out too soon and replaced by the hardened resolve of a youth forced to grow up too fast. She glimpsed the hidden corners of his soul: nights spent in solitude, waging battles against demons both external and within. His eyes, those windows to horrors witnessed and betrayals endured, revealed despair so profound it could have shattered anyone else.

Yet amidst the storm of anguish, there was warmth—a tender thread of hope and the faint flicker of unfulfilled dreams. It was there in the softening of his irises, the subtle relaxation of a brow so often furrowed with tension.

And then, piercing through it all, came a vision.

Her. Bathed in the golden light of early morning, her wild cascade of hair catching the sun's rays, each strand glowing like spun fire. Dawn kissed her skin, turning it into a canvas of gold, and in that fleeting moment, she saw herself as he had: radiant.

The world was quiet. She felt the warm tendrils of sunlight, *felt them* as he had—caressing, worshipping, each golden beam accentuating the curves and planes of her face, dancing over the soft smile gracing her lips as her gaze met his.

Through his eyes she felt the heartbeat that echoed her name; the unrestrained adoration, the deep-seated respect, and the unabashed love brimming with a quiet kind of eternity.

For a breath, she was him, living that cherished moment, feeling the ribbon of joy unfurl in his soul. She tasted the depth of his feelings for her—boundless and reverent, raw and undying.

A sacred kind of love that dared to bear itself in totality, before the altar of her soul.

And then as the vision dimmed, reality rushing back with jarring abruptness, Elara was left with that irrefutable knowledge tattooed on every fiber of her being.

A tear streaked down her face as her gaze settled back on his, and he nodded.

It wasn't just a nod—it was a vow.

A yielding to her—a silent affirmation of what he'd just laid bare.

He pushed himself up on shaky legs. And then he was moving, cutting, slicing through the swell, through the chaos, through everything that separates.

And she knew.

Without a word spoken. Without a single promise uttered, she *knew*.

He would follow her.

Wherever she would lead, he would be right behind.

Elara dropped the barrier and ran. The world funneled into a narrow tunnel of sound and motion, her blood roaring in her ears. The ground churned beneath her feet, slick with mud and darker stains. Bodies jostled her, soldiers barreled past, but she didn't stop. She sprinted, every breath a jagged knife in her lungs.

Her heart was a fierce, broken beat. Mending and shattering and tearing apart again with every step closer to him.

Reynnar's gaze snapped to hers, even as his blade tore through the Legion with brutal precision. Concern flickered across his face as his eyes darted to Ivan, but his jaw tightened, focus hardening like steel. A soldier lunged—he cut him down. Another fell, then another, blood spraying through the air. Between strikes, his eyes found hers again, a silent tether pulling him closer.

With a final swing, he carved a path and broke toward her, closing the distance.

They fell into a rhythm—a deadly choreography as he turned with her, blade flashing, fire snapping out to clear her path. Bodies fell in scorched heaps behind them.

Elara skidded to a stop—nearly colliding with Ivan.

Dark vines snaked across his face, claiming him inch by inch. He swayed, barely upright, shadows pooling beneath him like a spreading stain.

A weight pressed against her chest—her heart cracking—but she didn't look away.

She gripped Ivan's face, fingers trembling against skin already cold. She bit her lip until blood filled her mouth.

"*You want that drop, Hunter. So badly,*" Sybil had said. "*A single drop, and all is undone.*"

A single drop.

That's all it would have taken.

All he'd needed. And he'd never seized it. Never even asked. He had chosen silence. Sacrifice. Death—rather than becoming someone who would take from her.

So, she kissed him.

The warmth of her blood spilled between them, searing against his lifeless skin.

His chest jolted.

His eyes flew open. Pupils blown wide. Ivan hadn't been breathing, but suddenly, he was *gasping*. His arms were around her, pulling her close, his tongue slipping against hers desperately.

The kiss was consuming, grounding—*claiming*. Elara closed her eyes and inside, there was only the rhythmic beating of two hearts trying to synchronize, two souls attempting to find their shared rhythm again.

And for a timeless, breathless moment, they did.

But then he pulled back, shadows slipping away, fading into him as his eyes cleared, focus sharpening. His gaze swept over the chaos, catching on Reynnar, the flickering fires, the scattered bodies, then back to her. And when he looked at her—*really looked*—something softened. He leaned in, brushing his lips against hers, so gently, so achingly tender that it cut straight through her, drawing tears to her eyes.

When he pulled back, he rested his forehead against hers, his breath warm against her lips. "I had to do that. One last time."

Elara's brow knitted, confusion stirring as she tried to piece together his words. But then he reached down, fingers curling around her own, around the Wound of Light, and with one swift motion, he tore open a rift. "*Go.*"

Her heart lurched, an icy stillness filling her chest. "You're coming with me."

But he only looked at her, that quiet finality in his eyes. "No, Elara. I'm not."

Ivan's hands found her waist, and before she could even react, he shoved her backward.

The world fractured, the Pit falling away as she stumbled into the rift, swallowed by the Void. Darkness pressed in, vast and cold, but just ahead, she saw it—a sliver of light.

The door to *Tír na nÓg*

She'd left it wide open.

Wide-eyed, Elara twisted to look back, reaching for him, but he was already pushing Reynnar in, his expression fierce. "Take care of her."

Her heart stilled, suspended mid-beat, as her gaze locked on him. Shadows flooded the prison, thick and ravenous, coiling around Osin as he strode toward Ivan. The wound she'd carved into his chest was fully sealed, his rage radiating outward, consuming everything in its path.

He moved like a curse, a force of destruction. Soldiers fell in heaps, necks snapping with sickening finality as he tore through anyone who dared cross his path—even his own men were not spared his fury.

"Don't do this!" she screamed as the shadows reached for Ivan, coiling around him, tightening.

He didn't flinch.

Shadows surged from his hand, a tidal force driving her and Reynnar deeper into the Void. A scream ripped through her—a fractured, wild thing, clawing for something already lost.

Reynnar's arms locked around her as they were dragged down, spiraling faster, bodies tumbling like debris in a storm. She reached for Ivan, desperate—but his face was already fading, swallowed by Osin's shadows, until only his eyes remained, dimming beneath the crushing dark.

They broke through the gate, the Void spitting them out in a sudden rush of light. Together, Elara and Reynnar tumbled onto the other side, breathless and battered, into the wild, green expanse of *Tír na nÓg.*

BONUS SCENE

Elara's skin prickled as a whisper of cool air slipped through the open balcony doors, raising goosebumps across her freshly scrubbed arms. She lay curled on the floor in front of the fire, wrapped in a patchwork of blankets, half-buried beneath a mess of open books and scattered notes. Ink smudged faintly along the inside of her wrist, and the papers shifted with each pass of the breeze, but she didn't move to stop them.

Clean.

Such a deceptively simple word—and yet she'd nearly forgotten what it meant. The sensation was almost foreign now, even though she'd bathed several times since arriving here. She ran her fingers over her forearm, marveling at the smoothness where grit and grime no longer clung, where the filth of the Pit wasn't caked into her pores or wedged beneath her nails.

Gods, how quickly she'd grown used to being dirty.

How strange, how *unsettling*, that cleanliness now felt like a luxury.

But if it had been bad for her, she couldn't fathom how Reynnar and the other Sidhe were coping. She'd read somewhere that their senses were heightened, magnified far beyond a human's perception. She couldn't imagine enduring that torture, breathing in decay and desperation every waking moment. And yet, here she was—warm house, clean blankets, safe for now, while they still languished in darkness. Her chest tightened, pulse quickening, a familiar coil of panic creeping up her spine. She shut her eyes tight, slipping into the steady, measured breathwork of ritualized control.

Inhale slow, exhale slower.

She repeated the mantra silently, picturing Reynnar's steady gaze, hearing his voice gruffly urging her to calm, breathe, focus. They were okay. He was okay. She just had to master these damned spells and get them all out. *Home.*

Exhaling a long, heavy breath, Elara rolled onto her side, propping her head against her palm. Her free hand rifled restlessly through the scattered notes—scribbles that might take weeks, maybe months, to truly decipher. The surface read-through had barely scratched the depth she needed to understand what her past self had been trying to do. With a frustrated sigh, she grabbed the Hunter's journal and flipped through its worn pages. Her eyes skimmed the familiar letters, the strange dialect already beginning to weave itself into meaning—the grammar and syntax settling into place like they belonged there.

It was almost startling, how quickly she absorbed it. How easily her thoughts began shaping around new words, new rules.

She'd never thought of herself as particularly gifted—especially not with languages. But this... this came as naturally as breathing. And somehow, that shocked her more than anything else she'd faced in days.

Elara felt the Draoth Cara tighten gently within her chest, an unmistakable awareness threading itself delicately through her bones—the Hunter was pacing with agitation through the house below. It had been one of those days. Days when he withdrew entirely, as though constructing invisible walls brick by careful brick, barricading himself behind thoughts she dared not disturb. She had learned quickly that attempting to breach those barriers was futile, reckless even. Still, it was her innate curiosity, stubborn and insatiable, that sometimes whispered softly at the edge of reason, tempting her to push just a little further, to seek the answers he so zealously guarded.

Some days, his walls were flawless, a fortress meticulously maintained. Others, cracks appeared—thin fissures where weariness eroded his defenses, allowing glimpses of the man hidden beneath. Those tiny fragments she gathered carefully, storing them away like pressed petals between the pages of her mind—delicate, faded things that no one else would see as beautiful. But they meant something. They *had* to. Even if she wasn't sure what.

Tonight, she sensed an unusual heaviness—sadness, perhaps—emanating faintly through their tether, a quiet melancholy that tugged persistently at her consciousness.

Then, the Hunter left the house, the faint pulse of his presence fading beyond the manor's walls. Irritation flickered briefly as she tried to return her focus to the scattered pages, but concentration eluded her completely. With a resigned sigh, she rose, pulling a woolen throw around her shoulders, fingers brushing against the finely woven fabric as she attempted to cover the inadequately short tunic she wore. She hadn't been given a dressing gown—though Tristan probably had an entire closet full somewhere in this labyrinthine manor. She smiled softly to herself at the thought, padding barefoot down the cold stone stairs, following the thread of the Draoth Cara as it guided her closer to the Hunter.

Descending the wide staircase, Elara noted a bitter, charred smell harsh enough to make her wrinkle her nose. It led her to the kitchen and her gaze fell on the marble island at the center, where a baking tray sat discarded, holding what might once have been batter but now resembled something more closely akin to hardened tar. She couldn't help it; laughter bubbled up, imagining the Hunter scowling down at his ruined creation.

But beneath that burnt odor lingered something else—a hint of clove drifting from the kitchen's back door, left ajar like a quiet invitation. She followed it without thinking and stepped onto the cool stone patio, bathed silver in moonlight. The Hunter leaned against the rough-hewn wall, head tipped back, eyes shut tight. Thin ribbons of smoke curled from his nose and mouth, rising slowly into the chill night air. He didn't look at her, didn't move a muscle as she settled quietly beside him—though she knew he tracked every breath, every subtle shift of her weight, just as keenly as she sensed his.

Elara crossed her arms over her chest, tilting her head back against the stone as she fought to suppress the smile tugging persistently at the corners of her mouth. "I suppose," she began lightly, gaze fixed forward at nothing in particular, "I should feel grateful I wasn't forced to sample whatever tragedy it was that met its demise in your oven tonight."

His eyes opened immediately—just a narrow, wary slit—as they fixed on her, amber-black in the moonlight. She saw clearly the reluctant curve forming at his mouth before he could hide it behind a scowl.

She raised an eyebrow innocently. "Did you burn it on purpose, or was that merely your culinary technique in full bloom?"

He huffed, eyes rolling toward the night sky as he took another slow drag from the twist of clove in his hand. Smoke trailed thoughtfully from his lips as he murmured, voice dry and low, "And I suppose your baking skills are legendary?"

"Oh, absolutely," she said, pulling the blanket tighter around her shoulders against the chill. "My cakes are frequently edible."

"*Frequently?*" He echoed flatly, turning to face her, his expression carefully neutral—but his eyes held a faint, amused glint. "What an endorsement."

Elara's laughed, bright and free, startling even herself.

The Hunter's eyes widened slightly, surprise breaking through his usual careful reserve as his gaze dipped toward her mouth. Something flickered there—a quicksilver moment, barely more than a heartbeat—before his expression shuttered again, eyes darting swiftly back toward the starlit sky.

For a long moment, neither spoke, the quiet punctuated only by the occasional rustle of leaves overhead and his measured breathing. Elara stole another glance at him, taking in the sharp contours of his face outlined in moonlight, the subtle furrow between his brows. He had always seemed to wear exhaustion like armor, but tonight, beneath the shadows, it felt more vulnerable—softer.

She exhaled quietly, breaking the silence. "What was it meant to be, anyway?"

The Hunter's mouth twitched again as he regarded the smoldering clove between his fingers with exaggerated interest. "It doesn't matter now, does it?"

"Hmm." She tilted her head thoughtfully. "Let me guess. Chocolate cake?"

"Wrong," he murmured, eyes half-lidded as they flickered to hers briefly.

"Bread, perhaps?" she tried again, pursing her lips to keep from smiling fully. "That seems simple enough, even for you."

This time, his expression cracked into a smirk.

"Maybe scones? I imagine you'd make quite a dashing baker. Apron and all."

He shot her a look of mock offense. "If I'm ever seen in an apron, assume I've been cursed. Or blackmailed. Possibly both."

Elara's smile widened. "So *not* scones, then."

He exhaled a quiet laugh, barely audible but undeniably genuine. His gaze lingered on her for a heartbeat longer than usual, lighter somehow, before he looked away again, lifting the twist of clove back to his lips. She watched him, heartbeat quickening, suddenly hyper-aware of the proximity between them, the quiet intimacy of standing shoulder-to-shoulder beneath the open sky.

Her tone softened without her permission. "Why tonight?"

His jaw tightened, but his voice remained carefully neutral. "No particular reason."

"You're a terrible liar."

"And you're *annoying*." He glanced sideways at her, the words harsh, but his voice was gentle beneath the bite. "Perhaps I simply wanted to see if your unceasingly yapping tongue could be silenced by pastry."

Now it was her turn to look scandalized. She straightened a little under the blanket, chin lifting. "I was *not* yapping. I was theorizing," she said primly.

In truth, she'd gone on far longer than she'd intended before they'd retired for the night—caught up in the momentum of her thoughts, pacing the length of the library like a Druid mid-lecture. It had started with dimensional bleeding and somehow spiraled into Void fractures and recursive loops—she was fairly certain she'd even gestured with a spoon at one point.

Still. She thought better when she said things out loud. He had to know that by now.

"You were the one interrupting me with that constipated frown every time I mentioned *anything* about the dimensional bleeding." Elara narrowed her eyes at him, but he didn't bite—just let the smoke curl lazily between his fingers, looking maddeningly unbothered. She paused. "Which, by the way, is entirely relevant to our current problem—if you'd bothered to listen."

His mouth twitched. She could see him trying not to laugh.

"I did listen," he said finally, flicking ash. "Up until the moment you started arguing with yourself about whether light behaves as a particle or a wave inside a rift."

A pause.

"I assumed you'd win either way."

She blinked at him. "That's—" She hesitated, flustered. "That's not how etheric duality works."

"Obviously," he said, voice smooth. "That's why I was making scones instead."

"Aha! I *knew* it." She pointed a triumphant finger at him from beneath the blanket. "It was scones. I was right."

He rolled his eyes with all the performative exhaustion of someone who'd just been sentenced to a lifetime of losing arguments to her. Still, she caught it—the subtle shift beneath the irritation. Maybe it was the bond. Maybe it was just her. But the heat blooming in her chest moved through her like sunlight through gauze.

Not irritation.

Fondness.

Her smile faded—just slightly. He'd spent the evening fumbling around the kitchen to surprise her with something warm. Something ordinary. Something kind. And despite the smoke and the half-burned effort, the intention had landed.

Somewhere low in her ribs, warmth began to unfurl—slow and a little too tender.

He cleared his throat like he could feel it too. "Next time, I'll spare you the smoke and fire."

Elara smiled faintly. "Can I try that?" she asked, nodding toward the clove between his fingers.

The Hunter lifted a brow, skeptical, but handed it over without a word—careful not to touch her in the process.

She took a drag, exhaling steadily. It wasn't her first time. She, Avis, and Dario had snuck worse things in the Sanct, curled up in forgotten corners of the gardens. Avis's blend had been stronger, too—laced with something that made her feel like her bones were turning to warm syrup. This one was just clove.

Still, it was nice.

"Do you have any wine?" she asked after a beat, letting the smoke drift lazily from her mouth.

He snorted. "Tristan drained the last of it."

That didn't surprise her. He'd been drinking far too much of it while she and the Hunter worked—lurking in the corner like a judgmental gargoyle, interrupting only to offer distracting (if occasionally hilarious) commentary or to shoot her a look of pure horror every time she pulled too hard on the Draoth Cara and lit the library curtains on fire.

It had only happened twice.

Still, ever since he'd left a few days ago, things had been quieter. Easier. She could think without someone watching her like she was a particularly unstable spell about to explode. To be fair, she was struggling. Fire was just...difficult. Rebellious. It didn't listen the way water did, or bend like air. It fought back like it recognized something in her and was determined to drag it out by force. Elara hadn't quite figured out why yet, only that it wanted more from her than the others. She didn't know what that said about her, and she didn't like thinking about it.

Still, she missed Tristan's interruptions less than she probably should. It was nice, being alone with the Hunter.

Elara looked at him again—couldn't help it. Some masochistic tic, that flitting glance.

He was already watching her. His gaze didn't shift away like it should have. Didn't feign disinterest or politeness or anything remotely normal. It just stayed on her, like he was cataloguing her for later.

"...What?" she said, harsher than she meant.

He didn't answer at first. Just tilted his head like he was still debating whether it was worth responding. "You're not what I expected," he said at last, almost reluctantly.

Elara studied him—hunting for sarcasm and came up frustratingly empty. The worst part was—she felt the same. He wasn't what she'd expected, either. She had assumed he'd be colder. Crueler. Easier to hate. He wasn't. Which was its own problem.

"What exactly *did* you expect?"

He reached for the twist of clove again—his fingers brushing hers this time. Barely. But still enough to send heat pulsing up her arm. He leaned back against the wall, took a drag like he needed the delay.

"I thought you were loyal to them," he said eventually, smoke trailing from his mouth. "The Druids." He paused, brows lifting slightly. "But then you threw a decanter at Osin's head." He huffed out something like a laugh. "And I realized I was wrong."

She watched the smoke curl up between them.

"All those years," the Hunter said, shaking his head. "The rituals. The conditioning—how did you stay..." He hesitated. "*You*. After everything?"

Elara stilled. That was too intimate a question from someone who had spent the last month acting like he barely tolerated her. He'd said *you* like he knew who that was. Like he'd *known her*. Not the Hallowed. Not the girl in white robes. Her. And that nagging, slippery feeling in her gut—that suspicion that they'd met before, long ago—twisted tighter.

"You're so fucking selfish. I'd almost forgotten."

He'd said it in anger—probably absentmindedly. By accident. But it clued her in to a certain familiarity they might've shared, even from a distance.

Elara went cold.

Gods, why couldn't she remember?

That was the worst part. Not the captivity. Not the bloodletting or the shackles.

The not knowing.

She chewed her lip—hard. Enough to taste the sting of iron. "I don't think I was myself," she said quietly. "Not for a long time."

He didn't interrupt. Just waited. Like she was a puzzle he could outlast.

"I was desperate," she said, cheeks burning. "*Weak.* I wanted to feel something. Anything. The Mother's love, they called it." She grimaced. "I thought if I just obeyed hard enough—if I bled enough, fasted enough, prayed enough—they'd see me. But they didn't," she whispered. "Eventually, I stopped seeking them and started looking inward."

Elara hated saying it. Hated remembering that version of herself—the one who prayed until her knees bled and still felt nothing. The one who cried in silence because if the Mothers hadn't answered yet, it meant she was still doing something wrong. She looked down at her hands. The same ones that had once trembled in supplication. "I had help," she said. "A few friends. They reminded me I was still in there somewhere."

The Hunter leaned forward, intrigued despite himself. She could see the question forming already.

"Fenlin," she said, and immediately regretted it. Her throat closed around the name, even now. "He saw I was drowning and did what he could. In his own way." A small smile pulled at her lips, but it didn't reach her eyes. "There were others, too."

He already knew about Avis. Dario. The closeness, the betrayal. He didn't press. And she didn't explain. Their names still hurt too much to say out loud. An ache that never quite scabbed over. So, she let them fade—ghosts slipping back into the dark.

The Hunter watched her. Not passively. Not in that way people sometimes looked through her, like she was a broken artifact left too long in the sun. No—he *looked* at her. Unflinching. Direct. Like he was peeling her back layer by layer with nothing but his eyes. His posture hadn't changed—shoulders squared, arms loose at his sides—but tension coiled beneath the stillness, a quiet hum that raised the hairs along her neck.

His jaw tightened once. Then again. Like the words were made of stone and he had to grind them down before he could let them go.

Then, finally—

"I remember the first time they made you do the bloodletting."

Elara froze. A single breath caught, locked behind her ribs.

"You didn't cry." His eyes flicked to the moon, then back. "I don't know why I thought you would."

Her mouth opened. Closed. Opened again. Useless. There wasn't a single rational thing to say to that. Nothing that would make the moment feel less like a punch to the gut. Not that it mattered. Because he wasn't finished.

"They taught you how to make yourself small," he said, his voice low and measured, "and called it devotion. Made you believe that pain was proof of loyalty. That obedience and suffering could earn your worth. But the thing is…" He shifted, the moonlight brushing across his cheekbone like a stroke of silver paint, illuminating the hard line of his jaw, the scar just beneath it she hadn't noticed before. "You were already worthy," he said, "They just couldn't control someone who knew it."

Elara's breath stilled in her lungs as the Hunter took a slow breath. "You didn't lose yourself," he said softly, "you were *taught* to give yourself away. One piece at a time. In the name of grace. In the name of sacrifice."

He shook his head. "That's not weakness. That's *survival*."

The Hunter passed her the twist of clove and Elara took it. Grateful for the distraction. For the weight of it in her hand, for the fire in her lungs as she dragged it in, and the thin, shaking thread of smoke she let go with her next breath.

"I watched you kneel through every rite, bleed and break and get back up like it didn't cost you something every time. The ones who shatter don't stand like that."

Elara should've looked away. Should've said something, *anything* to cut through the ache crawling up her throat. But she couldn't. She exhaled, the smoke curling between them, soft and slow. His eyes dropped to her mouth.

"You survived in a way most people wouldn't. That doesn't make you weak. It makes you… terrifying."

The Hunter didn't look away when he said it. Didn't smirk or soften or explain. Just left it there, like it wasn't meant to wound or warn. Like it was a truth he thought she deserved to hear.

Elara blinked.

The words still hadn't settled. They hung in the air like ash after a fire, drifting slow, weightless—but still heavy somehow. Still choking. She handed the clove back, what little remained of it. He took it without comment, dropped it to the ground, and crushed it under his boot. She stared at the smudge of ash for a beat too long, then cleared her throat.

"Well. That was... unnecessarily poetic for someone who once threatened to *tie me up against my will.*"

The Hunter arched a brow, just barely.

"Don't think I've forgotten," she added, crossing her arms. "It was *rude.*"

His mouth twitched—fractional, fleeting—but it was there. Which was probably why her heart decided to kick her in the ribs for no reason whatsoever.

"I'm heading in," he said, already turning.

She followed him through the kitchen, the air still tinged with the ghost of scorched dough, then up the narrow stairs and down the hall, past the creaking floorboard she always forgot to avoid. Outside her door, she stopped. So did he.

"We're going to crack the spell," she blurted, for no real reason. It wasn't a promise. It wasn't even confidence. Just—something lighter to hold after everything else. Hope, maybe. Or delusion. Same difference, really. "*Tomorrow.* I can feel it."

He nodded once. Quiet. Steady.

"Goodnight, Hallowed."

Elara barely kept from rolling her eyes at the title. "Goodnight, *Hunter,*" she replied, just as dry. That earned a smile. Small. Crooked. *Real.* She stopped breathing like an idiot, and by the time her lungs remembered their job, he'd already slipped inside his room and shut the door.

She stood there for a moment too long, the image of that smile burned behind her eyes, seared into her bones. She carried it to bed like a curse.

And didn't sleep a damn minute.

TÍRRÍSH TRANSLATIONS

1. "Your terror." "it's sweeter... how strange."
2. "I can feel your heart beating again."
3. "Your king's shadow is a slow death for us all. Keep it in your blood too long, and you'll find yourself short of a limb... or worse yet."
4. "Hold on to that light closely. This place has a way of stealing everything from you."
5. "Up, Thank you."
6. "Your fear is their life force. Show them only your rage."
7. "You did well, Thank you."
8. "It's nice to meet you Eilíara."
9. "I'll eat, but only because you're cute when you're bossy."
10. "Curious about these?" "In a fight, they're meant to sink into flesh—right here." "Where the blood flows fastest. Quick, efficient—more useful than a blade in close combat." "But they've got other uses too." "Ones that aren't for fighting... or at least, not in the way you'd think."
11. "Get back, Eilíara."
12. "You've drawn an Aelfhenge."
13. "No. Sidhe."
14. "Yes, Sidhe."
15. "Stop! You need a ring."
16. "Do you have a death wish, little human?"
17. "The Tuatha? Yeah.""Third group, about ten people up."
18. "Yeah."
19. "So, this must be your cellmate, the human girl."
20. "Eilíara this is Aoife."

21. "Eilíara is a strong name, an old name in our world. How fitting you should bear it."
22. "Breathe, Eilíara."
23. "Good. Again."
24. "Is this all it takes to scare you?" "Pathetic. I've seen babes with more backbone."
25. "Be still or they will crush you!"
26. "Aoife, she's more than capable." "But I fear her strength may not suffice indefinitely."
27. "I owe you my thanks for what you've done. It's... well, it's something else, seeing that kind of heart, that kind of bravery, coming from a human."
28. "That dress... you look like a cake topper."
29. "No. Do not let them break you. Back in my homeland, when someone's in pain, they aren't left to fend for themselves. They're held, cared for—by their people. And like it or not, Eilíara, that's what I am to you now. What we are. We're your kin."
30. "Come." "They can fuck right off with their expectations."
31. "Watch your back with him. That human doesn't show his cards unless he's holding something sharp."
32. " Eilíara. Open your eyes, Eilíara."
33. "My child of Aerú. Open your eyes."
34. "Still in one piece, huh?"
35. "Same goes for you."

Acknowledgments

There are no words that can fully express my gratitude to the many people who have made this book possible, but I will try.

To my husband, Michael – my rock, my greatest supporter, and the one who believed in me even when I doubted myself. Your unwavering love and encouragement, especially in those moments when I felt like giving up, carried me through. You've been with me at every step of this journey, and this book exists because you never let me fall.

To my brilliant editor, Ashley – your guidance has been a light on this path. Thank you for not only refining my words but for teaching me so much about the craft of storytelling. Your insights and patience have transformed me as a writer, and for that, I am eternally grateful.

To my alpha reader, Gloria – you were my second set of eyes when I needed them most. Your thoughtful feedback, sharp eye for detail, and deep knowledge of Irish culture and heritage brought invaluable authenticity to this book. I am eternally grateful for the time and expertise you shared.

To my parents – your unwavering belief in my creative spirit from the very beginning shaped me into who I am today. Thank you for your constant encouragement and for always seeing the potential in my dreams, even when they seemed distant.

And to my children – your love, laughter, and endless enthusiasm kept me going through the ups and downs of this journey. You reminded me why I started, and your belief that I could finish has meant more than you'll ever know.

This book is as much yours as it is mine.

About the Author

J.M. Grosvalet is an author based in the Washington, D.C. area. When she isn't lost in her stories, she can usually be found in her garden tending herbs and wildflowers, a mug of tea cooling beside her and paint smudges on her hands. She has a soft spot for rainy days, old books, and anything that smells like lavender.

At home, she shares life with her husband and best friend, their three wild boys who keep her laughing (and a little grey-haired), two loyal dogs, and a very opinionated cat.

Her stories are woven with myth, magic, and melancholy, exploring the strength it takes to hold onto hope and the beauty found in even the darkest places.